Dorothy Koomson penned her first, unpublished novel when she was thirteen – and has been making up stories ever since. Her six books – including *My Best Friend's Girl*, a Richard & Judy Summer Read of 2006 – have spent over twenty-five weeks on the *Sunday Times* Bestseller List. Her novels have been translated into twenty-eight languages across the world.

Find out more interesting facts about her at www.dorothykoomson.co.uk

Praise for *My Best Friend's Girl*:

'Both funny and moving, this will have you reaching for the tissues . . . A heartbreaking tale' *Closer*

'I enjoyed it immensely and I did have to dab away a little tear as early as page two' Richard Madeley

'An enjoyable, easy read that might even make you shed the odd tear' *Star*

'When a novel breezes along as lightly as this, you simply cannot put it down' *What's On in London*

'Funny and touching' *Image*

Praise for Dorothy Koomson's books:

'A totally enjoyable story full of believable characters and situations' *New Woman*

'Enjoy being moved by this story and give in to its irresistible charm and wit' *Woman*

'A touching and engaging story' *Good Housekeeping*

'From beginning to end, this emotional rollercoaster of a book confounds expectations and bombards the reader from all sides' *Good Reading Magazine*

'A funny, quirky read' *Compan*

'A poignant page-turner' *Clo*

'A dramatic, heart-tugging tale

Also by Dorothy Koomson

My Best Friend's Girl
Marshmallows for Breakfast
Goodnight, Beautiful
The Ice Cream Girls

DOROTHY KOOMSON OMNIBUS

The Chocolate Run

The Cupid Effect

sphere

SPHERE

This omnibus edition first published in Great Britain in 2010 by Sphere

Typeset in Bembo by M Rules
Printed and bound in Great Britain by
Clays Ltd, St Ives plc

Sphere
An imprint of
Little, Brown Book Group
100 Victoria Embankment
London EC4Y 0DY

An Hachette UK Company
www.hachette.co.uk

www.littlebrown.co.uk

THE
CHOCOLATE
RUN

For
my two water babies

big kisses to:

Mum, Dad, Sam, Kathleen and David, your partners and your beautiful families. Thank you for your love, support and excitement – I couldn't ask for more from a better group of people.

All my lovely friends. You've supported me in so many unique ways that I'll take the time to thank you individually.

Cocoa expert Téa Twise for the quotes.

Everyone who is reading this book – hope you enjoy the ride.

'there's only one thing better than illicit sex – illicit chocolate'

chapter one

give us a break

You're floating on a sea of chocolate.

Soft, warm, sweet, sensual chocolate . . . soothing, calming, velvety chocolate. It's lapping over your tired, naked body. Covering it. Caressing it. Taking away all your aches and troubles. Everything, the world, reality, people, washed away by the fluttering of chocolate against your skin. Peacefully, mil—

'I'll, er, be off then.'

That doesn't sound like part of my chocolate nirvana. I cracked open a sleep-deprived eye, checked my surroundings.

Oh. I wasn't drifting on a creamy, cocoa-based ocean after all. I was hunched up on my sofa with my knees pulled up to my chest, my forehead resting on my knees, and my off-white towelling dressing gown pulled around my naked body. I didn't need a mirror to know my face was saggy from lack of rest; my black-brown eyes were ringed with crusts of sleep; and my usually neat, cheek-length black hair stood up in so many peaks and spikes it resembled a Gothic wrought iron sculpture. Nope, couldn't get further from my heaven if I tried. Especially when there's a man stood in my living room yammering on about leaving.

Moving like a woman approaching the gallows, I lifted my head and turned to face him.

Greg was dressed: midnight-blue, wide-rib jumper under a knee-length coat. Navy blue jeans. Black record bag slung across his body. Dressed. Fully dressed. *Why am I surprised? If he's leaving, he'd hardly be stood in his underpants, would he?*

He looked back at me, obviously waiting for me to speak. To respond to his statement of intent to leave.

I played for time by lowering my legs, careful not to flash anything under my dressing gown. I started to fiddle with a spike of my black hair, winding it around my index finger as I tried to make eye contact without looking at him.

How am I supposed to act? It's been so long since I've done this, I've forgotten how it goes. Am I meant to be casual? Blasé? Keen? Serene? Desperate?

Then there's the speaking thing. What am I supposed to say? 'So long and thanks for all the sex?' or 'Go away and never darken my bedroom again?'

And what about breakfast? I'm pretty sure you're meant to offer it. But that's, what, another hour or so. Surely he would-n't want to prolong this by staying for breakfast. Or would he? But if he leaves now, what do we do on Monday? How do we behave – *be* – if we leave things up in the air?

There were so many questions that needed answering you'd think someone would've written an instruction manual on this, wouldn't yer? *The Little Guide to Big Mistakes* or some-thing. They'd be raking it in.

Maybe I should go for a compromise. Not breakfast, not door . . . Cab! I'll offer him a cab. That way, he'll hang around long enough for one of us to blurt out, 'It never happened, OK?' Then we'd agree to never mention it again. Ever. And then he'd do the decent thing and go away.

I cleared my throat, forced myself to make eye contact. The lock of hair was twisted so tightly around my index finger the tip throbbed. 'Do you want me to call you a cab?' I asked, sounding pleasant and calm. Nobody would guess I was having

4

trouble breathing, would continue to have trouble breathing until he'd gone.

'No, I'll just be going. Get out of your way,' he replied and didn't move.

'Are you sure?' I persisted.

He nodded and still didn't move, showed no sign of knowing how to move.

'Really, it's no trouble,' I said. 'You stand there, I point at you and go, "You're a cab." Dead easy. I do it all the time.'

He simply stared at me.

I stared at him.

Breakfast it is then.

chapter two

messy

Greg opened the lower cupboard of the unit nearest the kitchen door, pulled out the white chopping board. Next, he opened the drawer above that cupboard and rummaged through it, searching for the right knife.

I stood watching him. He moved with such ease in my red and white kitchen I was mildly surprised he didn't live here. That it was my kitchen, not his.

He unhooked my red apron from behind the kitchen door, slipped it over his head, tied it around his middle, then hoiked up his jumper sleeves. Hang on, *is* this my kitchen? Did I really own an apron? One that said . . . *Dream Stuffing*? The irony wasn't lost on me as Greg grinned above the words on his chest and rubbed his hands expectantly.

I opened the fridge and my eye fell immediately upon the giant bar of chocolate sitting on the top shelf. What I'd do for a couple of squares right now. I'd just discovered I couldn't work under pressure without it. That when the going got tough, I needed chocolate. But, nobody could ever know I sometimes ate chocolate for breakfast. I fished an onion and the last tomato from the vegetable crisper and tossed them to him. We were going to have an omelette for breakfast. You know, breakfast, this travesty of a meal I'd been manipulated into. (Yes, it was me who'd uttered the damn joke but he could've done what I've heard most men do in these situations and leave me choking on the dust thrown up by his legging it into the sunset.)

Greg caught the onion one-handed then caught the tomato with the other hand, but instead of getting down to work, he grabbed the chopping knife and a wooden spoon. 'Watch this,' he said and, one by one, tossed them in the air.

Absently, I tightened my dressing gown tie, cutting off most of the circulation to my legs, then flattened a few of the black spikes by dragging a hand through my hair. I watched the onion, tomato, wooden spoon and knife dance through the air while Greg juggled. The knife crossed the onion on its way up, the spoon crossed the tomato on its way down. The knife went up again, as did the onion. My eyes followed the smooth lines the items carved in the atmosphere. I was mesmerised. By its contradictory grace; by the natural elegance of the juggler. Chucking things about shouldn't be so beautiful, exquisite. I'd always wanted to juggle, to make things float and dance but I didn't have the co-ordination for it. Greg was perfect. Cocky git.

Tosser.

That'd been my first thought of Gregory Walterson when we met. *Absolute tosser.*

He'd been sat in a pub with his best friend, Matt, at the time. Matt had been seeing Jen, my best friend, for a few weeks and they were treating Greg and me to a meal so we could all get to know each other. Jen was desperate for me to like Matt and thought meeting Matt's best mate – who, by all accounts, was usually Velcroed to his side – would assist the liking process, hence the meal.

I'd had to work on a Saturday and entered the pub at almost a run, flustered and pissed off at being late.

7

'Ambs, this is Greg, Matt's best mate,' Jen said, grinning insanely as her gaze flitted between the pair of us. 'Greg, this is my best friend, Amber. Don't call her Ambs, ever, she hates that. Thinks it's too personal, especially when you don't know her. Only I'm allowed to call her Ambs. But Greg doesn't mind being called Greg or Gregory. He's easy-going about his name.'

While Jen babbled on, I took a gander at this Gregory who didn't mind being called Greg, and internally flinched – it was like being slapped in the face. Matt was attractive, but Greg . . . Greg had been created by someone who didn't know when to stop; someone who when presented with top-quality ingredients, chose to endow one man with them rather than dishing them out fairly amongst the rest of the male populace. Greg's eyes, for example, were like Minstrels, were like shiny discs of hard, dark chocolate. His hair was so black it was blue-black and hung like long curls of liquorice around his face. His slightly olive skin was lovingly moulded onto his strong bone structure. And his lips . . . his lips were as succulent as pink Jelly Babies.

Greg's Minstrel eyes held my brown-black eyes a fraction longer than necessary before his Jelly Baby mouth parted into a smile and he said, 'Hi.' Long and slow and overtly sexual.

Tosser, I'd thought, before I smiled a tight-lipped, sarcastic hello in return. *Absolute tosser*. No matter how tasty he looked, no matter how much I wanted to lick his eyes and his lips and his hair, it was abundantly clear: Greg was gorgeous. Greg knew it. Greg used it at every given opportunity. But, I had to be nice. Jen was madly in love with Matt even though they'd only met three weeks earlier ('Ambs, I think he's The One, I really do'), so this man was going to be in my life for a while. I had to get on with him.

We started off seeing each other occasionally with Matt and Jen, then he rather disconcertingly started to make an effort (emailing, calling me at work, asking me to meet him for lunch because we worked near each other in town) meaning I had to – make an effort that is.

I went along to lunch the first time because I was open-minded enough to know he'd spend the hour talking about himself and checking his reflection in any shiny surface, thus confirming beyond a shadow of a doubt what a tosser he was. Unfortunately, I left lunch grudgingly impressed because he had the kind of wit, knowledge and intelligence I'd only encountered a few times in my life, plus he didn't once check himself out in the butter knife.

We regularly went out alone after that. And, three years later, Gregory 'Tosser' Walterson had become my second-best mate. He was number two on all my phone speed dials; the second person I called when anything big happened; the person I spent most time with after Jen. We talked and emailed every day. He was Greg, after all. My mate. Still a tosser, but now my mate who happened to be a tosser. Nothing more. Honestly, nothing more, until last night.

'Huh? Huh? Whaddaya think?' he asked, turning to show me his juggling properly. Before I could reply, he miscalculated a catch and everything was thrown off balance and suddenly the blade end of the knife was hurtling towards his hand. He jerked his hand away with a fraction of a second to spare and the knife fell to the floor, closely followed by the rest of his tools. The spoon clattered away across the kitchen, the onion rolling behind it. But the tomato, which had been over-ripe and spoiling for a fight anyway, exploded with a damp splodge, juice and flesh and seeds oozing out on the red and white lino tiles.

Greg grimaced at the splattered tomato, then glanced up at me. 'Oops,' he said.

'"Oops"?' I replied. 'What do you mean "Oops"?'

He shrugged. 'Oops.'

'Cloth, water.' I pointed at the sink. 'Get cleaning.'

'Sorry, mate, you've seen my bedroom, you know I don't clean.'

He then picked up the onion, went back to the cupboard, took out a clean knife, returned to the chopping board, and sliced the top off the onion. He even started whistling as he stripped the onion of its outer layer.

'"I don't clean", indeed,' I said above his out-of-tune whistling. 'You're lucky I don't batter you with a teaspoon, yer cheeky *get.*'

Greg laughed. A laugh so warm and easy that I'd long suspected it came from somewhere deep in his heart. Hearing it was like having sunshine poured directly into your ears, feeling it radiate throughout your body. His laugh often made me laugh. Right then, I could only rustle up a small smile.

A few seconds later, I bobbed down with a damp J-cloth to clean up the tomato explosion.

This is so weird, I thought. *It's like every other morning he's spent here. Anyone looking in at us, at how he's chopping and I'm cleaning, wouldn't guess we'd . . .*

I lifted the lid on the bin but paused before dropping in the tomato-soiled cloth – it'd gone suspiciously quiet at Greg's end of the kitchen. And 'quiet' meant he'd broken something and was trying to hide the evidence. My 'Director' mug had gone that way, as had the scary cat mugs my mum bought me. (That was a bonus seeing as I'd tried a few times to 'accidentally' end their existence and they seemed to be protected by some kind of force field.) I glanced around to check what he was up to.

My stomach lurched to find him watching me. Openly, blatantly staring at me.

His Minstrel eyes, which had been intensely fixed on me,

10

jerked into huge circles of fear. Recovering his composure, he struggled with a small, shy smile, lowered his eyes, then spun back to continue chopping.

I turned back to the bin with my heart galloping in my chest and my whole body aflame. I flung the tomato and cloth into the bin, let the lid fall into place.

It was only a look, a glance, a mere expression, I told myself. *It didn't mean anything. Yeah, and you can walk on water.*

RRRIINGGG!

Like an unwelcome alarm clock the phone shattered my late Saturday morning peace.

I was showered, pyjamaed, and curled up under my duvet on my sofa. I'd attempted to go back to bed after Greg left, but had been poleaxed by the state of my bedroom. The rumpled bedclothes, the condom wrappers on the floor, the wicker bin with used condoms in it, clothes I'd been wearing last night flung to the four corners. Worst of all, it reeked of it. Us. What we'd done. Even after I'd opened the large sash window and let in the frosty February air, the smell was there. As though it'd seeped into the paintwork and carpet and ceiling cornicing and wasn't ever going to leave.

So, I'd done the decent thing and ignored it, knowing that if I ignored it long and hard enough, it'd magically tidy itself. I'd trooped off to the shower, returned to find it wasn't tidied, and promptly upped the level and severity of blanking (it really was going to work). I'd been drifting off with a film on the TV when the phone rang. I picked up the receiver and mumbled a hello.

'Hi, Ambs.'

Jen.

JEN!

My eyes flew open and I sat bolt upright on the sofa. *What the hell am I going to tell her? Am I going to tell her?* I told Jen everything but this was different. This was, in a word, stupid. In two words: bloody stupid. In fourteen words: this was so bloody stupid, I still couldn't believe it and I'd been there.

'Hello, lovely,' I said, now more panicked than sleepy. There was always the possibility that I'd blurt it out. She'd ask some innocuous question and I'd get a bout of confessional Tourette's and scream out the awful truth.

'Oh, sorry, did I wake you?' Jen paused, obviously to check the time. 'Your Saturday mornings are precious, aren't they?' She only remembered my Saturday mornings were precious after she'd got me on the phone.

Matt, her boyfriend, aka Greg's best friend, played football on Saturday mornings with Greg and some other lads down at Woodhouse Moor, the park near where Greg and Matt lived. Even though Jen lived all the way over the other side of town in Allerton and he spent a lot of time there, Matt still drove across Leeds to play with the boys, as it were. As soon as Matt pulled off in his car, Jen would be on the phone to me. We'd chat until Matt came back, then I'd dive back under the covers for a couple more hours of shut-eye. That's if Greg didn't call to give me a blow-by-blow account of the football game or his latest conquest. Or, as was most likely, both.

'It's all right,' I said, stretching my body in a deep arc, trying to unkink my back. 'I've been up for ages.'

'*Really?*' Jen's voice perked up. 'Why?'

'Erm, couldn't sleep.'

'Ah. How was last night?' she asked.

She knows. Greg, who hadn't talked to me about what had happened, had already told them and she's ringing to see how long I hold out on her. The big-mouthed get. First he stayed for breakfast, then he was looking at me, now he was spreading rumours. True rumours. To our friends. But rumours is rumours. 'Erm, what was last night?' I replied cautiously.

'Duh! Greg went to the film with you, didn't he?'

12

'Oh, yeah. Yeah. Sorry.'

'How was it?'

'Fine. He was fine.'

'Double duh! I mean the film.'

'Oh, sorry, yeah. It was all right. Greg liked it, but then Greg likes *Carry On* movies, so there you go. I thought it was mediocre.'

'Oh well, never mind. What did you do afterwards?'

'Erm . . . had dinner then he stayed over.' *In my bed. While we had sex. All night.*

'That's where he was! Matt called him to say he wasn't going to footie this morning and Greg wasn't home and his mobile was off. We thought he must've pulled and stayed in Sheffield.'

'Why isn't Matt at footie?' I asked, seizing this opportunity to change the subject – the less she talked about Greg, the less chance there was of me confessing.

Jen lowered her voice. 'He's going to kill me but I have to tell you. Matt asked me what I wanted for my birthday and I said, "You to move in here" and he said yes. We're going to move in together.'

I screamed. 'OHMIGOD!' I yelled into the receiver. 'I can't believe it's finally happened! FINALLY! And I can't believe it's taken you six million years to tell me! So? So? Details.'

Jen lowered her voice some more: 'Can't. Tell you Monday night, when it's all official. Don't tell anyone. Especially not Greg if you see him.'

'Why would I see Greg?' I said defensively. I wasn't being at all suspicious, was I?

'You might go to lunch or something?' Jen said carefully, as though trying to talk me down from chucking myself off a building. 'You do go to lunch with Greg quite often, don't you?'

'Oh. Right.'

'Are you all right, sweetie? You seem a bit . . .'

'Out of it? It's the whole lack of sleep thing. Not as young as I used to be, you know.'

'OK. Well, you try and sleep now. Matt's here, we're going shopping. So, I'll see you Monday, all right? Six-thirtyish at The Conservatory.'

'Yup, see ya there. Bye.'

If I hadn't been so comfy where I was, I would've done a lap of honour around my living room once I'd hung up. In my current condition, I settled for punching the air with my arms and legs, going, 'Yesss! Yessss! Yeeesss!'

She'd finally got it. A big commitment from Matt. A real, tangible declaration that he thought of their relationship as something permanent. This was big stuff for Matt – this man was sometimes reticent about breathing because of the effort involved. I never, ever thought he'd commit.

The last time Jen and I had dissected this very subject – and it had to be admitted we dissected it a lot – Jen had said, 'I want to get to the point where I can tell Matt anything and everything, like I tell you everything.'

That thought made me tug the duvet over my head. In less than twenty-four hours I'd done two unbelievable things: slept with Greg; held out on Jen.

All I had to do was donate all my savings to the Conservative Party and everyone would know the invasion of the Body Snatchers had begun.

14

chapter three

the big bang

Silence. Everything was silence.

Pure, perfect silence. The kind of silence that is invariably followed by trouble. The kind of silence, I'd imagine, that came before the Big Bang that created our universe. (Or, if you believe in creation theories, the kind of silence that came while God scratched His head and wondered if He should make the oceans blue or a nice peachy colour.) Our office had that silence. Everyone held their breath. Everyone was waiting for the Big Bang.

The five of us in the office were expecting it, but when it happened, when the explosion came, four of us jumped. I, being closest to the epicentre of the blow-up, jumped the least – I was immediately caught in the blast and couldn't physically move, even if I wanted to.

'WHAT DO YOU MEAN, YOU HAVEN'T WATCHED THE FILMS? WHAT, NONE OF THEM?' the Big Bang screamed.

This was Renée. My boss, *The* Boss. She was lovely. Honest. I've always liked Renée, have always had a deep respect for her. Even when, at times like this, she was shouting at me.

I'd just told her I hadn't done my 'homework' over the

15

weekend and because I hadn't done my homework, the meeting she had scheduled for that afternoon wasn't going to go the way she expected. I'd let her down and rather than sit there slowly imploding while giving me the full-on, pursed-lipped, teeth-gnashing silent treatment, she'd chosen to explode.

On paper, on my CV, I'd worked for West Yorkshire International Film Festival (WYIFF) for nearly eleven years.

Since I was a little girl I'd been obsessed with films and television; I wasn't allowed to play out much as a child, or party at all as a teenager, so I experienced life through the world on my TV; saw the wonders of life, love and everything through the box in the corner. That fascination with the moving image never left me.

During the first year of college we had to do a four-month work placement in a profession that we were interested in working in. I asked to work at a Hollywood film studio – I got the WYIFF.

I spent most of March to June as WYIFF's unpaid skivvy, researching and photocopying for the brochure, and I loved it. Most people whinged about not being paid; about being given menial tasks; about people treating them like fourth-class citizens. Not me. So what if I had to make the tea and do photocopying and run errands? I got to sit in an office with a group of people who knew an incredible amount about films and one of whom had snogged a rather famous American film director. And another of whom had been a very famous actress during her teens. After the placement was over, I kept 'dropping by' the office – in the same manner you 'dropped by' the places you knew someone you fancied frequented – helping out.

That following September, during the two weeks of the actual Festival, I was there again. I stood at venues, proudly wearing a WYIFF T-shirt, taking people to their seats, ripping tickets, handing out brochures that had my name in it. My name. That was it for me. I signed myself over. Pledged my soul to the god of WYIFF. Had basically walked into my idea of job heaven and didn't want to leave. So, I didn't. Every Easter, every summer, every Festival, every chance when I wasn't earning money to pay my rent or eat for the following five years, I was there, lurking around the office, offering to help. Eventually, they took pity on me and paid me to compile their brochure. Even more eventually after that they offered me a full-time position as Festival Assistant. After a proper, full-time year I became Senior Festival Assistant. And a year after that, I became Deputy Festival Director. That was four years ago.

In real terms that meant diddly-squat because there were now only three full-time members of WYIFF – Renée, the Festival Director; Martha, the Festival Administrator and me.

Me. The person who had a pile of vids stacked in her living room that she was meant to watch and report back to Renée on before her meeting with the film production company, that afternoon. From our little office, the huge, star-studded event in mid-September that showcased West Yorkshire as an area of outstanding artistic interest was executed. We organised it, came up with the themes, invited people, arranged the programme. Also, big film premieres that were held up here were organised by us – including sending out invites to getting press interest and organising the stay of any actors.

On top of that, we sometimes undertook consultancy work. If we saw a production company had potential or if we had time, we'd give people advice on getting funding, editing their work, casting and scripts. That was what Renée would be doing that afternoon, if not for me.

But, but, Saturday was a write-off once I'd put on my pyjamas. I couldn't face watching what could potentially be a shite film, and the title – *Welcome to Vomit Central* – didn't exactly inspire confidence in the product. Sunday, in between *T4*, *EastEnders* and running around town putting the finishing touches to Jen's birthday present, there wasn't enough time.

I gazed up at Renée with what I hoped were big sorrowful eyes; pleading, beseeching if you will, for sympathy. Renée looked back at me with murder glinting in the windows to her soul.

She usually looked like a teen-actress-turned-producer-turned-important-name-in-Northern-England's-film-industry. She was head to toe sophistication: sleek black hair, carefully kohled and mascaraed eyes, expensively cleansed, toned and moisturised olive skin, neutrally coloured lips. Her clothes were always designer, and crease- and bobble-free, obviously. Her shoes always matched her bags. When she wore it, her nail varnish matched her lipstick.

'I AM GOING TO LOOK TOTALLY STUPID IN THAT MEETING!' Renée ranted. 'I CAN'T BELIEVE YOU'VE DONE THIS TO ME.' Like her body, her fingers were long and thin. Her fingers always reminded me of Cadbury's Chocolate Fingers, very little knuckle to spoil the length and shape of them. And wouldn't you know it, those fingers made a very loud noise as they pounded on the desk, emphasising her words – probably the biscuit centre.

'I REALLY [*bang*] CAN'T [*bang*] BELIEVE [*bang*] YOU'VE [*bang*] DONE THIS [*bang*].'

I didn't need to glance around the room to know that Martha, the administrator, was staring hard at her computer screen, and the two work experience girls were digging escape tunnels under their desks. This was the usual drill when Renée lost it. Which, it had to be said, she was doing quite a lot lately. Usually, Renée was on the highly strung side of normal – it didn't take too much to launch her into a full-on head spin. Recently, though, even 'Good morning' could go either way:

a 'Hello' back or a rant demanding to know what was so good about it.

I knew this. Which was clearly why I said, 'At least I didn't sleep with your husband.' This was classic Amber. When a situation begins getting serious, be it seriously bad or seriously good, I'm obliged to lighten it with some attempt at humour. *Obliged*, mind you. I can't just turn it on and off. (That was where the whole 'you're a cab' thing had come from.) Many a near war situation has been averted by me trying to make people laugh, or at least titter. I can't help myself. I think it evolved from a deep-seated belief that someone's less likely to batter you as long as you're trying to make them laugh.

Except what I said was in no way funny. Mere moments after my quip Renée's sensibilities nosedived over the edge of reason.

'*What. Did. You. Say*,' she hissed, too shocked to shout or bang on my desk.

'It's only a meeting, not the second coming,' I said, then winced. There really was no need to keep antagonising a woman whose head was 198 degrees into a 360-degree head spin but I couldn't seem to stop.

Renée's flawless skin filled up to her hairline with blood-red anger. I wasn't aware humans could go that shade of red without passing out.

'HOW CAN YOU SAY SUCH A THING? WHO DO YOU THINK YOU ARE?' she bellowed.

'Oh, admit it, Renée, you know you wanna cancel the meeting anyway.' We were in a 'humour' loop – the more incensed she became, the more I was trying to make her laugh, which led to more rage. Round and round.

'I DON'T KNOW WHY I EMPLOYED YOU!' Renée screamed.

'Because the trained hamster turned you down?'

'HOW DARE YOU. FOR TEN YEARS I'VE

19

WATCHED YOU HANG ABOUT THE OFFICE, DOING NOTHING BUT EAT CHOCOLATE. WELL I'VE HAD ENOUGH OF IT. YOU ARE USELESS.' With that, she grabbed her mobile and coat, and exited stage left. She shut the glass door with such force we all expected it to shatter in her wake.

Everything was silent and motionless after the slam of the door.

Renée had never gone for me like that before. She'd never gone for anyone like that before. *Ever.* Yeah, she shouted; yeah, she threw things, but in eleven years I'd never thought she was going to raise her hand to someone. And for one moment there I'd thought she was going to slap me.

Martha gave the two work experience girls one of her 'looks' until they realised they needed the loo – really rather desperately – and left. They too shut the glass door, which had a film reel and **WYIFF** frosted on it, behind them, but quietly.

Martha and I got up in unison then walked the length of our high-ceilinged office, which was filled with desks and filing cabinets and shelves of videos, to the windows. The expanse of windows took up almost a whole wall and had window sills wide enough for people to rest their bums on. Which is what Martha and I did. Out of all the offices in the West Yorkshire Council building, we had the best one. It had high white walls, the carpet wasn't the regulation beige but royal blue. We even had framed film posters on the walls. When you worked there full-time you got to pick a poster. Renée had *The Big Blue*, Martha had *Pretty Woman*, and I had *Terminator 2*. Over the years other posters had come and gone, but the swimmer, the hooker and the cyborg had clung to the walls through thick, thin and Renée explosion.

'She's getting worse,' Martha said, twisting slightly to see the panorama of Leeds we got from this height. Martha was far more human than Renée. She was my height with shoulder-length, mousy-brown hair, mousy-brown eyes, pale white skin – she even got the occasional spot. I liked Martha, but in a different way to how I liked Renée. Renée had employed me – eventually – and I'd helped employ Martha. Also, Renée had never invited herself to my place for dinner within a month of us working together like Martha had done. I was also pretty sure Renée wasn't constantly rifling through my drawers looking for perfume, lipstick, tampons or other things most women should carry with them, like Martha was.

'I know,' I replied to Martha's observation that Renée had got worse, then instantly felt bad. Renée was, all in all, a good boss. 'I wonder why?'

'Because she's a mad French woman,' Martha replied and yanked her black cardigan across her chest to emphasise how mad Renée was. Renée had shouted at Martha on Friday for not returning her stapler. And, despite Renée going out to buy us cake 'because you're both worth it', despite a weekend's hiatus, Martha hadn't forgiven or forgotten. She wasn't the F&F sort. At some point, very soon, Martha would be paying her back in kind.

'No, Renée's all right. I wonder what's troubling her,' I said. Even after that performance I was fiercely loyal to Renée.

Martha shrugged. 'I'm sure we'll find out soon enough. I might go on a chocolate run, it feels like a bit of a Flake morning.' She paused, thought about her chocolate choice. 'Actually, sod it, I'm going to do a Renée, buy some cake and coffee and, hell, some caviar and champagne and put it through as expenses.'

'She never did that!' I said, turning to Martha.

'Too right,' Martha said. 'She does it all the time.'

'Clever, that,' I said, not meaning Renée's expenses violation. This was Martha's revenge: letting me know Renée's little secret so I'd do it and when Renée sees it, she won't be able to say a word, and it'll burn in her soul.

21

Martha's face split into a wide grin as she realised she was rumbled. 'All right, that was a bit obvious. But I'm going to get the bitch back. I'll just have to be a bit more sneaky about it.'

Instead of replying, I stared out at Leeds. The rise and fall of the buildings, the colours and shades stretching on and on. A patchwork of lives. A stitch here or there to keep them connected. Some lives overlapping, others only touching through other pieces of the patchwork.

My eyes flickered over the panorama, but I knew if I stood in a particular spot, dislocated my neck and pushed my eyes out of their sockets, I could see Greg's office from here. He worked ten minutes down Wellington Street in the *Yorkshire Chronicle* building, as Features Director on the *Sunday Chronicle*'s glossy supplement, *SC*.

'You all right, love?' Martha asked.

I returned my gaze to her, realising we'd been sat in silence for a while. 'I'm fine. A bit concerned about Renée, that's all.'

Martha nodded in understanding. 'You had sex, didn't you?' she said.

I rearranged my face so as to not look:

a) guilty
b) shocked that she'd guessed
c) like I'd had sex.

'Sorry?' I replied.

'You had sex, that's why you're acting crazy.'

'Acting crazy how?'

'How? What you said to Renée is how. Anyway, it's written all over your face. You've been celibate for yonks and now you look like you've had a good seeing to. You're actually glowing.'

I laughed. Martha was so fishing, but it'd caught her the big one.

'You did, didn't you?' Martha encouraged. 'You had sex.'

'Might have,' I replied.

Martha's face lit up. She leapt off the window sill, her cardigan showing off her white blouse as it flew open. She bounced eagerly in front of me. 'So, tell me more. Did he pass the Forty-Eight-Hour Test?'

She was referring to my theory that no one-night stand is a one-night stand until forty-eight hours after the act and he hasn't called. Some people, like Jen, have suggested that men work on a different timetable, that I should give them seventy-two hours. Sorry, but any bloke who can wait three days after sharing something so intimate with you, well, he's not interested. Because no man will wait more than forty-eight hours to call a girl – not if he really likes her.

Greg didn't pass. Course he didn't pass, but the long, yearning way he'd been studying me across the kitchen flitted across my mind as I said, 'No.'

'So you're worried you'll never see him again?' Martha asked.

'Oh no, I'll definitely see him again. I'll be seeing him tonight, actually, with some friends at a birthday do.'

'What's the problem, then?'

'Who said there's a problem?'

'Well you're not exactly dancing on table tops, are you?'

'I guess not.'

'And anyway, Amber, with you, there's always a problem.'

'Oi!'

Martha rolled her eyes. 'Well, there is, isn't there? It's not your fault, you just think too much.'

'Look, it's just . . . I don't know, it's complicated.'

'Complicated as in he's your friend's bloke?'

'No.'

'He's married/attached/gay/serial-killer material?'

'None of the above.'

'So what's the complication?'

23

If I hadn't told Jen I could hardly tell Martha, could I? Besides, Martha knew Greg. A bit too well. Once you got to know Greg you found out he wasn't a nice person. Fundamentally good? Yes. Kind-hearted? Absolutely. But nice? No. Martha knew that. She – and for that matter Renée – thought he was the spawn of Satan. If I told her she'd be ordering up an exorcism faster than I could blink. One time she'd picked up my phone and Greg had said, 'Oi, bird, I'm gonna put you over my knee and spank your bottom for being late,' thinking he was talking to me. She'd immediately offered to get a few of her fella's rugby mates to batter him. Even when I'd said he was joking she'd reassured me she wasn't. Martha and Renée were both gagging for an excuse to give him a good kicking and this would be it.

I shrugged my reply to Martha's enquiry about the complication.

'See, I rest my case,' Martha said, 'you think too much.'

She could be right – Greg was always accusing me of that too, but if I'd thought enough on Friday night, I wouldn't be in this mess, would I?

Friday night.

Friday night wasn't the culmination of years of flirting and longing and waiting for me. I don't know about Greg, but I'd never thought of him in that way. Ever. Nobody would believe me now, of course.

After I'd thought 'tosser' about him, I'd made it clear I wasn't the bonus or booby prize he got for letting my best mate date his best mate in peace. I constantly ribbed him and refused to flirt with him. At all. He tried, because he couldn't help himself, and in response I'd roll my eyes or tut. Even the lightest double entendre was met with irritable derision. When I started going out with someone, Sean, a few months after I met Greg, he got the message: I wasn't interested. We could get on with being friends. Friday night, then, was just another night for me.

I'd met Greg at the bus station at about seven o'clock. He'd been to Sheffield for the day doing a special report for the magazine. I spotted him the second I turned the corner from New York Street to the bus station. He had his bag across his body, his knee-length black coat was buttoned up, the neck of his blue jumper peeking out of the top. His hands were buried in his pockets, the tip of his nose was red from the cold and his exhalations curled up and away as white wisps. He'd obviously been waiting a while but didn't seem to mind.

If Greg being free on a Friday night hadn't told me how the evening was going to end, maybe what happened next should have: he put a tender, almost protective, hand on my waist and gently pulled me towards him as he leant in to kiss my cheek. His kiss lasted a fraction of a second longer than necessary, as though he was trying to hang onto the moment. Then he buried his face in my cheek-length black hair and his grip around me tightened as he inhaled deeply.

'Are . . . are you *sniffing* my hair?' I'd asked. Someone had once jokingly said I smelt and I'd been paranoid about it ever since. Jokes were always jokes until your boss was taking you out for a quiet chat about personal hygiene – I wasn't going down like that.

Greg laughed. 'Just checking if you need to get your roots re-straightened. If I can't tell you, who can?'

I'd smacked him good-naturedly on the back, shaken my head at him, then led the way to the private cinema in West Yorkshire Playhouse.

After a free film screening for work (my work, not his), we had a few drinks and dinner, then found ourselves on the pavement outside the restaurant. 'Do you fancy coming back to mine for a bit?' Greg asked.

I actually fancied going home. Didn't want to walk up to his

25

house in Hyde Park (and he always made us walk there), then sit about making small talk with his other, non-Matt flatmate. I wanted my pyjamas, to watch some telly and then to bed. I couldn't say that, obviously, so made a big show of looking at my watch, discovered I wasn't wearing it and snatched my wrist out of sight before he could spot what I was doing. 'To be honest,' I said, 'it's late, I should be heading back. I'll get the bus.'

Greg glanced away, his disappointment shimmering in the frosty air around us. *Oh*, I thought, *he's got something big he wants to talk about. That's why he's free on a Friday night. That's why he wants to keep the evening going.*

He wasn't exactly known for being Mr Open. If it wasn't to do with sex or work or football, you had to drag things out of him. He'd probably been working up all week to telling me whatever this was.

'Or,' I said, 'you can come back to my place. Stay over if you want.'

'Really?'

'Yeah, course. You practically live in my spare room anyway. In the morning, though, don't w— BUS!' And we pelted off down to the bus stop.

About an hour later we were still sat on the floor of my living room, music playing in the background while we talked, about the general stuff we always talked about. He hadn't so much as uttered anything vaguely secret-like. I'd found out about the people he'd been interviewing in Sheffield earlier that day; that his mother had bought a new set of saucepans; that his brother who lived in Australia might be coming back for next Christmas; that he was just behind Matt in their goal-scoring league at football. My pyjamas and duvet were calling and I was hearing general things from Gregory. We lapsed into silence. I started picking at the label on my beer bottle, Greg stared into his coffee for a while then started gnawing at the edge of his thumbnail. I slapped his hand— as instructed to by him – he jumped, silently replied with an apologetic half-smile and instead ran his hand through his hair.

His hair. His bluey-black, neck-length hair. Women apparently loved floppy hair – the amount of scripts or books I read where the hero had floppy hair was astounding – but I found it wrong. It was like Orange Dairy Milk. I love Dairy Milk. I like oranges. But together, fundamentally wrong. The same applied to men with long hair. I like long hair. I like men. Together, bone-shudderingly wrong.

As I thought this, Greg started laughing. For one hideous moment I wondered if he'd read my mind and thought I had follicle envy.

'What you laughing at?' I asked.

He shook his head. 'Nothing,' he replied, the silent laugh shaking his shoulders and smirks escaping from the corners of his closed mouth.

I pushed him. 'Whaatt?'

Greg giggled into his coffee a moment longer, then tore his eyes away from the creamy liquid and faced me full on as he said, 'Do you really want to know?'

'Yes.'

' All right.' He paused, took a deep breath, held my gaze. 'I was thinking, "Wouldn't it be funny if I kissed Amber?"'

'What's funny about that?' I replied. 'You kiss me all the time . . . Oh . . . do I *smell*? Is that it? Does kissing me make you gag and that's funny because I don't realise?' I put down my half-drunk beer, lifted my arm, sniffed. A touch of Hugo Woman and a soupçon of Dermalogica Body Hydrating lotion, but other than that, nothing.

Greg's eyes bulged in his head like I'd missed something obvious; as if he couldn't believe I was that thick. Almost in slow motion, he put down his coffee, leant forwards and pushed his lips on mine, his fingers stroked my face as his tongue parted my lips then entered my mouth. It'd been millennia since juicy lips had pressed against mine and I'd forgotten kissing was like this. Soft, warm, tender.

He eventually pulled away, sat back. Silence. Silence as Greg stared at me and I stared at my former friend. My former friend who had terror streaking his face. 'Are you cross with me now?' he eventually asked in a low voice.

Was I cross with him? No, I was stunned. More stunned than any other emotion. I slowly moved my head from side to side.

'Shall I go?' Greg asked.

I shook my head again, faster this time. No. No. He didn't get to jeopardise three years of friendship and then walk away.

A grin spread across his face. 'Can I do it again then?'

I leant forwards and kissed him. I had to try it out again. I was stunned, but galloping up behind stunned was lust. And soon, this thing called lust was overtaking every emotion, every thought. His arms pulled me closer as I kissed him, then his hand was inside my top, caressing my skin. It was as though he had insider knowledge of my body; had detailed cooking instructions:

1. Break down Amber's defences into this many pieces
2. Place her on the living room floor
3. Turn the temperature up to almost boiling point
4. Stir and stroke gently until she's dissolved into a giant pool of desire
5. Devour at your pleasure.

Greg pushed me back onto the floor, eased up my top and covered my stomach in soft little kisses. He undid my jeans, kissing every bit of exposed skin and, as he reached the last button, he stopped, his face a dreamy picture of lust and satisfaction.

'Are you sure you want to do this?' His voice was throaty with desire.

What sort of a question is that? I asked silently as our eyes met. *Of course I'm not sure!*

Let's put aside the sex with a friend issue, for a moment. This was a big step. I'd gone eighteen months without sex. And, after eighteen months, you've got to be careful about who you go with: leap into bed at haste; fake your own death, change your identity and move countries to get away from him at leisure.

On the other hand, eighteen months without sex was eighteen months without being caressed, sweet-talked and lusted after. After all those months and months of healthy eating, after more than a year of the sexual equivalent of lettuce and salad and cottage cheese, if you're offered the most gorgeous tart on a plate, the one with the freshest, gooiest jam, the fluffiest cream, the crumbliest pastry, what do you say? 'No thanks, I'm on a diet'?

I got up, bundled my jumper and his jumper under one arm, held out the other hand to him.

I'd never been good at diets.

chapter four

movie loving

It was February.

Cloudy-skied, dark by six o'clock, air loaded with moisture. A short blast of wind blew right at me, whipping up my bobbed black hair and throwing open my long black winter coat. *It's far too cold for going out for Jen's birthday dressed like this*, I decided as I ran my hand through my hair to flatten it again and pulled shut my coat.

I was wearing the equivalent to twenty-four carat gold. Amid a need to not let the side down when we went out for a posh dinner, I'd gone shopping for a new dress. It'd stood out, a red and pink shimmer in the blacks, blues and greys in the shop. I'd picked it up and tried it on before I checked the price tag. Once it was on, I turned the price tag over. Even though my heart skipped a beat, I had to have it. It could have been made for me: it emphasised my cleavage, skimmed over my waist, hugged my hips, gently flared out to my ankles. It fit all over. I had to have it. My bottle had almost gone at the till and my hand had started to shake as I signed under the three-figure sum — that's three figures *before* the decimal point. (Spending like that went right against the grain. I was earning a decent wage but, at heart, I was a sale rail girl — it was always the first area I headed for in a shop.)

I'd also re-employed my red wedge-heeled shoes with straps that criss-crossed up to my knees which always left me hobbling for a couple of days after wear. Tights weren't an option with those shoes and the minute I left the building my bare legs became a mass of painful little goose bumps.

I should know better. I did know better. I was a thirty-year-old Southerner, I felt even the slightest drop in temperature in every part of my body. I thought I'd moved to Siberia when I first came to college in Leeds twelve years ago. My first winter here I'd called my parents and asked them to post me every jumper I'd left at home; begged them to lend me some money so I could buy two duvets and more knitwear; and wore gloves almost permanently. It was still a wonder that I'd decided to settle up here. Or that I dared leave anywhere centrally heated without thermals and at least three layers.

Holding my coat close to my shivery body, I picked my way across town towards The Conservatory. Lights from streetlamps and cars shimmered up from the slick streets like the soporific globules in lava lamps; looking at them took me back to Friday night.

In the movies, when two people get together they make slow, soft-focused, backlit love to a smooth, saxophone soundtrack. They lie entwined afterwards, with strategically placed sheets covering their bits, talking in hushed tones.

Not Greg and me. When we got to the bedroom on Friday night we leapt on each other like hungry lions thrown an antelope's carcass, almost tearing the clothes off each other. Then doing it in an intense, scary, filthy way. Every time we did it, it was animalistic, greedy. Not the stuff of romantic movies at all.

Talk-wise, we didn't. After each time – of which there were eventually five – we lay beside each other breathing heavily, not intentionally touching. Not aching to cuddle up in the safety of each other's arms and murmur about how we'd been waiting for months for this to happen. We lay on the bed, not speaking. I didn't talk because the only thing I could think to say was, 'Never tell anyone I did this. Never tell anyone I was this stupid.'

He wasn't simply a shagabout, you see, he was an-out-and-out, dyed-in-indelible-ink, should-probably-carry-his-birth-certificate-to-prove-he-knew-who-his-dad-was bastard. The man was a walking, talking screwing over women machine, which was why Martha and Renée hated him. They'd heard one too many a tale that began, 'We were sat in the pub and this woman came up to Greg . . .' and ended, 'So she chucked a drink in his face/ran out the pub in tears/warned me that he'd never change.' (I didn't volunteer the information about Greg's exploits, they dragged it out of me when I'd received thank you flowers from him for the third week on the trot.) Over the years, as I'd become his friend I became his conquest confidante, his sidekick, too. I'd become the woman who spotted he was chatting up the wrong person and was likely to get a kicking as a result of it, so led him away from danger. The woman who pretended to be his girlfriend to stop someone he'd screwed over thinking she still had a chance. And, naturally, the woman he called when he needed bailing out of things like police stations.

One May morning two years ago I'd been called to a police station in Harehills to go vouch for Greg and, rather bizarrely, bring him some clothes. I'd been in the police station reception a few minutes when I was shown into an interrogation room and sat at a table, with two officers sat opposite me.

'Miss Salpone,' the male officer began.

I didn't hear him, I was fixated on the tape recorder on the desk beside me. Had been since they led me in. They hadn't turned it on and a quick glance at my wrists confirmed they hadn't slapped on handcuffs, but my heart was galloping in my chest. I kept trying to moisten my mouth but couldn't get saliva to stay in there more than two seconds. I didn't even flinch at the 'i' and 's' being left in my official title. In fact I, *Miss* Amber Salpone, was one step away from confessing to being the gunman on the grassy knoll the day Kennedy was assassinated.

'Miss Salpone,' the policeman repeated, to secure my attention, 'how well do you know Mr Walterson?'

'Erm, quite well. Um, pretty well,' I'd replied, trying to stop myself counting the hairs coming out of his nostrils, for it'd lead to a tension-relieving comment from my good self. 'I've known him about a year.'

'Any romantic involvement?' the other officer asked so casually her voice could've been arrested on suspicion of withholding evidence, but I didn't notice.

'Erm, no. I've got a boyfriend, Sean. Sean O'Hare,' I replied, having a sudden need to tell them everything. I was crap under heavy interrogation. Who was I trying to kid? I was crap under light questioning. 'And Gre— I mean Mr Walterson, is single,' I added. *Very single*.

Suddenly the whole atmosphere in the room shifted and relaxed. Everything – the officers, the furniture, even the dust – seemed to exhale. Again, I was too shaken to notice. I was busy wondering if I should give them Sean's address so they could check he existed.

'Mr Walterson is being held on suspicion of breaking and entering, and indecent exposure,' the male police officer explained briskly.

WHAT?! 'Greg Walterson?' I said. '*My* Greg Walterson?'

The policeman nodded. 'He was found naked on the porch roof of a local house—'

'Let me guess,' I cut in, suddenly seeing everything clearly. Clothes. House. Greg. It could only mean one thing: 'There was a woman inside whose husband had arrived home and she

33

claims never to have clapped eyes on Greg, I mean Mr Walterson, before in her life.'

'This has happened before?' the policewoman asked.

I sighed and shook my head. 'No, I just always expected it to. Not the breaking and entering. Greg couldn't break into anything.'

'Well, that's for the court to decide,' the policeman stated.

He's done it again, I thought. *He's dragged me into another of his sordid exploits. Except now, it's court. They're talking about court.*

'Greg, I mean Mr Walterson, he's a prat, but not a criminal.' I launched myself into a plea. I couldn't face court. Walking into a police station had been bad enough. Going into an interrogation room was hideous. Court would finish me off. 'Please don't charge him. *Please*. He won't do it again, I promise. And, well, he wants to work in America and any kind of criminal record would put paid to that. I can swear on my life that he's of good character. *Please*. It won't happen again, I promise. I'll make sure of it. And even though he's a journalist, he's always going on about what a good job the police do, especially in the current climate.' That was pushing it a bit. OK, it was an outright lie, but court! '*Please* don't let his stupidity ruin the rest of his life. *Please*.'

An hour later I was stood on the pavement outside the police station. Greg was beside me, wearing the clothes – a WYIFF sweatshirt and a pair of jogging bottoms – I'd brought with me. 'How long did the cab say it'd be?' I asked him. He'd had to borrow my phone to call a cab because his mobile, wallet, keys, oh, and clothes were in the house of the woman who'd never seen him before in her life.

'Not long . . . Oh, Amber, you look so tired,' he said. 'Did you fly back from Cannes this morning?'

'Yup. Flew back, walked in the door, got call from a desperate wannabe criminal needing someone to vouch for him.'

'Sorry.'

'Hmm,' I replied. Course he was sorry. He was *always* sorry. But not sorry enough to not do it again.

'Thanks for coming, Amber,' Greg said. 'You didn't have to . . . That policewoman told me how you pleaded my case. She said you were a good mate, not that I didn't already know that. I only told you about wanting to work in America once and you remembered. That's so special. Thank you.'

'What are friends for,' I replied.

'Hey, at least one good thing came out of all of this,' he commented.

'What's that, then?' I asked, waiting to hear how he'd put a new philosophical spin on 'a friend in need'.

Instead of offering me cod philosophy he wafted a piece of paper under my nose. 'That policewoman gave me her mobile number. We're going to go out.'

'You what?' I said, turning to him.

'She was dead sexy, don't you think? So, we're going to get to know each other a little better. A lot better, in fact.'

'You're actually going to see her?' I asked, knowing the answer. Knowing that no matter how apologetic he was three minutes ago, he was going to do this.

Greg nodded, smiling at the scrap of paper in his hand as though it was his passport to Shangri-La. 'Too right.'

I too looked at the small white rectangle in his hand. Then I looked at Greg. Back to the paper. On the back of the paper the future was being shown in glorious Technicolor. There was me, back in that interrogation room, this time in handcuffs with said policewoman threatening to throw away the key because Greg had ill-treated her and it was my fault they'd let him loose on society again. I watched the image play out a few times, then snatched the paper from his hand before he could react, screwed it up between my palms, tossed it into the gutter. The paper glanced off the edge of the grate, then toppled in. Out of sight, out of reach.

35

'That's what I think of that idea,' I said.

'What the . . . *Amber*!' Greg whimpered in open-mouthed shock, staring at the gutter. 'What are you doing?!'

'What am I doing?' I said, my voice getting louder with each word. 'What am *I* doing?! Did you even notice she was wearing a WEDDING ring!'

Greg paused, thought about it, shook his head.

'NO,' I shouted as I stormed off to the taxi, which had pulled up in front of us, 'YOU WOULDN'T, WOULD YOU?'

And this was the man I'd slept with. A man to whom I was probably another entry on his 'Must "Do" Before I'm Forty' list. But I'd done it anyway.

That was the real issue. I knew what Greg was like and I'd done it anyway. It frightened me that I could be like that. That I could sleep with him in the first place, and when I did that I could leave his body covered in bites and scratches, and deep nail impressions. We'd only stopped because we ran out of condoms. He didn't have any more, and I didn't have any at all. I could have carried on all night if he hadn't frantically searched through his clothes, then looked at me with anguish in his eyes as we realised that was it. No more sex. No more intense, filthy sex.

I'd rolled away from him as he'd climbed back into bed, closed my eyes, forced myself to sleep in case I decided to do it anyway and worry about the consequences later.

It was as if I'd worn a mask and done those things, as if I'd become Nectar, as Greg branded me (yes, Amber Nectar, he was quick like that, Greg) because I was usually too sensible for such behaviours. I was Good Amber. The steady one.

When we were growing up, it was always Eric, my brother, who got into trouble for not concentrating in class; for not doing his homework; for sneaking out of the house at night.

36

Me? I worked hard, got good marks, went to my first party when I got to university.

In college, it was always Jen who was up in front of tutors for not doing coursework, for not turning up to class; Jen who needed to take the morning-after pill; who I'd bought more than one pregnancy test for. Me? I'd had one-night stands, but I was sensible about them. I had boyfriends, but I was sensible about them too. I went to class; I had safe sex; I'd never needed to wee on any type of stick.

I stopped outside The Conservatory, where I was meeting the others, my body resting against the iron railings. My feet were whining about the shoes: 'Like walking on razor blades' was the message they sent my brain in the international language of pain. I lifted one foot and rested it flat against the railings behind me to alleviate the torture.

The thing that scared me most about Friday was how much I'd enjoyed it. How much I'd wanted to do it again and again.

Something had been unleashed in me. Something wild, unpredictable, unknown. I was acting crazy, according to Martha. I'd spent £stupid on a dress after actually going – *alone* – into one of those shops where they frisk you on the way in to check you're not wearing anything that cost less than a tenner.

I switched feet, rested my left foot against the railings behind me to give it momentary relief.

I was different. How, I couldn't put my finger on, or hold in my head long enough to examine. It went beyond antagonising Renée and decimating my bank account . . . It was . . . I launched myself off the railings, pushed a cold hand through my hair to flatten the locks the wind had whipped up.

I wasn't going to do this. I wasn't going to overanalyse things, I was going to enjoy myself.

chapter five

mr toffee man

Warmth, sweet-smelling smoke and sounds of a good time surrounded me, drew me in, as I opened the door of The Conservatory, a cellar bar in the middle of town. It had an area with large overstuffed dark leather seats and bookcases filled with real books that made it look like an old-fashioned conservatory.

I clocked my friends straight away, sitting in the conservatory area, each lounging in a leather armchair, with one empty chair for me. I took a deep breath, reminded myself that nothing was allowed to spoil Jen's birthday, and strode over.

' All right, the party can begin, Amber's here,' I said, wrenching a smile across my tight little face. My face seemed to have shrunk, having been rinsed so many times in guilt in the past few minutes. (Think of all the money people could save on face lifts – all they had to do was shag a tart and lie to their best mate about it.)

I went to Jen, who was wearing a silky blue dress with a scoop neck that changed blues with the light (£8.99 from a shop near Leeds Market – we were the bargain hunt queens, Jen and I), her wavy blonde hair was piled up on top of her head, a few tendrils framing her face. I pressed a kiss onto Jen's warm cheek, enveloped her in a bear hug. Her delicate flower scent cut through the cigarette smoke and filled my senses. Inside, I smiled because that scent was so unmistakeably Jen. 'Happy birthday, darling,' I said, handing her the bag of pressies. I'd got her thirty little things – a lipstick, an eyeshadow, a mobile phone cover, a blue purse, etc. – one for every year she'd graced the earth. 'Have you had a nice day?'

My best friend was a primary school teacher and it was half-term, so she'd had the whole day off to enjoy becoming thirty. Jen glanced lovingly at Matt. 'It's been fantastic.'

'Hope you've been treating my friend in the manner she rightly deserves,' I said to Matt, who'd taken the day off to spend with her.

'Naturally,' he replied and reached for a smile. Reached for, but gave up when it only managed to pull at the corners of his mouth. When it came to me, smiling was rarely in Matt's repertoire of expressions. The longer he knew me, the less he smiled at me because there was less he liked about me to smile at. This was obviously an ordeal for him considering we often saw each other two or three times a week. Had done since he and Jen had gotten together three years ago. We had old issues, Matt and I, so old it wasn't necessary to ponder them now, not when I had far bigger things to worry about. Namely, the person sat to Matt's left.

My heart beating in triple time, my tongue cowering on the roof of my mouth, I turned in Greg's direction.

Our eyes collided, and a long look of thinly veiled terror passed between us. *Speak*, my brain commanded. *Say hello.*

I opened my mouth and, 'Awright, Gweggy boy, 'ow's tricks?' came out. *Oh, sweet Lord, I'm being Cockney Gell.*

'Great,' Greg said, stiffly. 'How you doing?'

'Awright,' I said, unable to shake my Cockney accent. I was from South London, not East London, this accent had no business installing itself in my mouth.

'Glad to hear it,' he replied.

Please could you try to act a bit more shifty? I thought at him. *I think there's one person in Leeds who hasn't seen by your face that we had sex . . . Says the woman who's being Cockney Gell.*

I slipped off my coat and . . . nothing. Not even a flicker of interest from anyone. So much for all those numbers on the till receipt. *Stop it,* I chastised myself. *This is Jen's birthday, her thunder, and you're trying to misappropriate it.* I slid shamefully into the chair opposite Greg while Matt and Jen went to the bar. First round of drinks was always on them in here, that was the tradition because that's how they met. In this bar, at the bar.

As soon as they were out of earshot Greg virtually flung himself across the wooden table. 'You haven't told Jen, then,' he stated with some urgency.

'Yes, Greg, it's nice to see you too. I'm fine, thanks for asking, and my weekend was fantastic as well, thanks for asking,' I replied. All right, so we'd . . . but did that give him any cause to be rude? To forget that we were, first and foremost, friends?

'What?' Greg replied, frowning at me.

Evidently it did. 'No, I haven't told Jen. Why, have you told Matt?'

Greg's complexion coloured up. Not a lot, just enough. Enough for me to know he'd blabbed. He'd probably said he'd finally opened the nut that wouldn't be cracked; sowed his seed in the field that wouldn't be ploughed; and other euphemisms that'd embarrass even the dodgiest estate agent.

'I didn't exactly tell Matt . . . Look, we need to talk.'

I was about to say, 'We so don't,' but my mouth, which was hotwired to my memories of Friday night, said, 'OK, talk.'

'Not now. Later. When we're all leaving, I'll say I'll see you home and we can t— Oh, that's easy. All you have to do is get a scart lead, hook it up to your hi-fi and TV. Simple. Surround sound.'

Whaatt?! I thought, as Matt plonked four pints on the table. 'Here we go,' he said. 'But wait for the other half, she's got the aperitifs.'

Jen returned from the bar with four tequila shots, four pieces of lime and a salt shaker on a black plastic tray. A movie line raced across my head as I stared at the tequila: *Nobody gets out of here alive.*

'We've got a bit of an announcement,' Jen said.

We'd moved on to Jumbo's, a posh Chinese restaurant tucked away in Vicar Lane. It had round tables with peach-coloured tablecloths and at the centre of each table sat soya sauce in white jugs and slices of ginger in shallow white dishes. Beside each place setting, on peach-coloured napkins, rested porcelain chopsticks with blue Chinese writing on the base. Our starters of prawn toast, spring rolls and dim sum had arrived by this point.

I'd already stuffed two whole pieces of prawn toast into my mouth to stop myself speaking. To stop myself blurting out something that would tell them I'd had sex with Greg. That I'd been a bad girl. A slut. A veritable whore.

As Jen spoke I realised what else had been niggling at my mind. Matt. He'd been fiddling with his heavy cotton napkin and chopsticks since we'd sat down. He hadn't unfolded the peach napkin – he'd been worrying one of the corners, or picking up a chopstick, tapping it lightly on the table like he was playing the drums. These weren't the actions of a man who was happy with the announcement.

Matthew Shepherd had never struck me as the nervous type, but his angular features – visible cheekbones, thin lips and straight nose – were all more pinched than usual. Tense. Admittedly this was a big step. Leaving the comfort of the house he had shared in Hyde Park with Greg and another bloke, Rocky, since he was nineteen, to move in with his girlfriend in grown-up Allerton was terrifying. Knowing that your second childhood was coming to an end would scare you. It'd terrify me. But they'd been together three years, they were solid. Rock solid.

I watched Matt rub at the napkin corner, his green eyes not resting on anyone or anything for long. He was toffee. I'd known that the second I clapped eyes on him.

When we were little, my brother and I would play the Sweet Game. One of us would think of a person and the other one would say what kind of chocolate that person was. Like: 'If Mum was a chocolate, what would she be?'

'A Wagon Wheel, short and round.'

In the following twenty years, Eric, my brother, had grown up. I had grown into the game. As I discovered the illicit pleasures of confectionery, my chocolate assignments became more detailed. You could tell so much about a person by your initial encounter, your initial 'taste' of them. Talk to me for three minutes and I'll be able to tell you what chocolate you'd be.

Which was why Matt was toffee. He was in no way chocolate and all the sensuous delights it brought. Inside him, at the very core of his being, was a lump of toffee. Something that had no depth. Under each layer was nothing but more toffee. Try as you might you'd find nothing but hard, unchanging, unadventurous toffee. All right, it was made with the best ingredients – hand-spun butter; thick, gloopy cream from an organically raised cow; top-quality, sun-grown sugarcane sugar – but it was still toffee. It was still unchanging. I liked toffee, I liked Matt, but there was only so much of it you could take.

I did like Matt, though. And, if I listened to myself, I would hear 'methinks the lady doth protest too much', but he was just so one-dimensional. Even now I'd never worked out why Matt and Greg had been friends for so long. Greg was Mr Adventure, Matt was Mr *Dull*.

They'd been mates since Matt's family had moved from Doncaster to Sheffield when they were nine. They'd then gone to all the same schools and applied to college in Leeds together. How they met, neither of them could tell.

'Men don't find meeting stories important,' Matt had once said.

'Unless you were knocking off his sister or his bird at the time. Then you generally remember the fight you had,' Greg added.

I hadn't known them long at that point. I still thought of Greg as a tosser who got away with far too much because of his beauty. And Matt, well, I thought, *He's toffee, but I'll have to get on with him because Jen's mad keen on him.*

'Come on, don't keep us in suspenders, what's the score?' Greg said into the long pause that followed Jen's statement.

Jen gazed at Matt and grinned. Matt winked at her then paled a fraction more, while fid, fid, fiddling with his chopstick.

'We're moving in together,' Jen said, her face flushed with happiness, her blue eyes sparkling.

'Fantastic!' I whooped. 'When did you decide? I want to know everything.' I would, of course, be receiving Oscar nominations for that performance of 'Woman Stunned By News'.

'It's my birthday present.'

'Great present, Matt. Makes everything I bought seem pretty insignificant by comparison. Oh well, I'll have to get you a creative moving-in pressie.'

'We wanted a cappuccino-maker, I've seen a couple in Habitat,' Matt said.

'You can forget that! You'll get some paper cups with "congratulations" on them and like them, m'laddie,' I joked.

Something was missing. Someone's voice, opinion, congratulations weren't there. 'What do you think, mate?' Matt asked Greg.

We all turned to Greg. Greg's hand had frozen between taking a piece of prawn toast off his plate and putting it into his mouth, his eyes were anchored on Matt.

'Mate?' Matt repeated.

'Sorry,' Greg said, lowering his piece of prawn toast, 'that was a shock . . . um, a good shock. No, it's cool. I'm really pleased for you, both of you.'

In stark contrast to my good self, Greg was an appalling actor – he'd be sacked from a 'Man In The Crowd' job.

'When are you, um, going to do the deed?' Greg asked, his voice flat.

'This weekend. I'm working in Paris for ten days starting the following week. I've told Rocky and he's cool. He's even let me off the last month's rent.'

'Cool. We'll have to find a new flatmate,' Greg said. Again, monotone.

'Get a girl,' Matt said. 'Even if she's not single, she's bound to have single mates. It'll be a gold mine of shagging.' He accompanied this advice with a brief hitch of his left eyebrow.

My stomach flipped. Greg's eyes darted to me, I redirected my gaze to my plate. *Why don't you get on the table and say, 'Actually I shagged Amber over the weekend'?* I thought. These were tense times, but even I'd stopped being Cockney Gell.

Nobody spoke. Each of us stared at our plates or the starters in the middle of the table as silence zigzagged about us until it'd woven a shroud of noiselessness around our table. We sat in our sound-free cocoon, shielded from the restaurant's buzz of other diners, food being served, dishes being removed.

If the silence continued, I'd be obliged to say something stupid to lighten it, I realised. Except, the only thing stupid that came to mind involved me, Greg and my bed. 'Let's get some champagne,' I piped up. 'Celebrate Jen, the youngest of

44

our quartet, becoming a semi-pensioner too, and this new stage of your relationship.'

Jen grinned; Matt paled. Tight. Not only was he toffee, he was tight toffee. He never knowingly reached into his pocket first. This was most clearly shown in his birthday present to Jen. What's the cheapest present you could give your partner? Move in with them. That way, you actually get a refund on that pressie when all your bills are halved. But I didn't think that, all right?

'Greg and I will pay for it, won't we?' I added.

'Yeah, course,' he said quickly. 'Course we will.' Greg cast me an expression of pure gratitude. He'd obviously pay anything to erase his reaction to their news.

One meal, one bottle of champagne, several bottles of Tiger beer later, we paid the bill, and got ready to leave.

For the first time since Matt and Jen had got together that meal with the four of us had been tense. The whole evening had been fraught and tense. Me and Greg. Greg and Jen and Matt. Only Matt and I had no new issue with each other, although he would if he knew Jen had confided their news to me before he'd told Greg.

Despite the champagne, despite all of us dragging out our funniest stories, which made us all cringingly keen to laugh loudly and brightly, just to prove we were having Fun (with a capital F), Jen's thirtieth birthday wasn't perfect. All the way through dinner Matt and Greg communicated silently across the table, having some kind of visual row. Jen didn't seem to notice. She was odd like that: things that were obvious to most people passed her by. I thought she would've guessed about me and Greg but she didn't even bat an eyelid.

Matt and Jen's cab arrived first and they left. Once we watched them leave, Greg lowered his head and banged it against the table.

'Stupid,' *bang*, 'stupid,' *bang*, 'stupid,' *bang*.

'It wasn't that bad,' I said sympathetically.

Greg stopped banging his head, scowled at me.

' All right, it was that bad. It was horrendous, actually.'

'I can't believe I reacted like that,' he said, pushing his hair off his face.

'It was the shock factor, we all react differently to shock.'

'It's just . . . If I could . . .' He seemed momentarily bereft, as though he'd lost something very important. 'Oh, never mind. Let's go wait outside for our taxi.' Greg faced me full on. 'We can talk then, if you still want to.'

Act casual, I thought as I shrugged. 'OK, I'm easy. At least that's what it says in the men's loos.'

The sharp night air hit me like a slap in the kisser. The temperature had dropped since we'd been inside. I tugged my coat around myself, wrapped my arms over it to keep warm . . . and to stop myself throwing Greg over the nearest car and mounting him. *Whoa! Guess who shouldn't have had that last Tiger beer?*

'What did you want to talk about?' I asked casually, watching him from under the strands of my fringe.

'What do you think?' Greg replied. *Don't you get it?* his face added silently.

I said nothing, just stared at him. He stepped closer, put his hands on either side of my face and kissed me. It was a different kiss from the first time on Friday. Passionate, ardent, exciting. Now familiar, too. My internal organs deliquesced with every kiss.

'I've wanted to do that all night,' he exhaled, resting his forehead on my forehead.

'Except when you were freaking out over Matt and Jen.'

'No, you'll find I wanted to do it then, it just got a bit marginalised. When you walked in wearing that dress . . .' Greg kissed me again. He slipped his hand inside my coat and around my waist, pressed my body to his as his kisses became harder, more urgent. He ran his fingers through my hair and lip-kissed my mouth. Then he was kissing my cheeks, my neck, my chin, my eyelids, my forehead, as though he wanted to devour me. All of me. He wanted to consume me with kisses.

I closed my eyes, this was divine. Like eating my favourite chocolate, feeling it disintegrate in my mouth, languishing over my taste buds, sliding inside . . .

'But you didn't call.' Divine or not, he didn't pass the Forty-Eight-Hour Test.

Greg carried on nuzzling my neck. 'I wasn't sure you wanted me to,' he murmured through kisses. 'You were so cool the morning after, I thought you wanted to forget it.'

Cool? Since when did 'You're a cab' classify as cool? 'And you didn't want to forget it?' I asked.

Greg abruptly stopped with the kissing, his roaming hand halted its progress over my curves and he found my eyes with his eyes. 'Why, did *you*?'

'I know your MO,' I said.

'What?' he said, taking a step back and robbing me of his body heat.

'I know your modus operandi; I know how you operate.'

'I know what MO means, thank you, I don't understand what you mean.'

'I mean, I know how you work. I've seen the carnage you leave behind when you charm a girl, make sure you're all she thinks about, shag her then lead her a merry dance for a few weeks until you find someone else.'

Greg's face was a blank canvas, his eyes like glass as he stared at me.

'I've become another notch on the very whittled Greg Walterson bedpost and that's fine. I simply don't want it to become something that will ruin our friendship or in any way jeopardise Matt and Jen's relationship.' Impressive, I could talk my way out of a shag quicker than anyone I knew.

'You want to forget it,' he stated, his voice as lifeless as it had been earlier in the evening.

'Taxi? Taxi for, erm, Hyde Park and Horsforth? Greg and Amber?'

I turned to the man who was leaning out of a white car with a taxi sign on top of it. 'That's us,' I said, then headed for the back door.

Greg stood staring into the space where I'd been, then slowly went around the front of the car, passed the front door, got in the back. I'd hoped he'd get into the front – we could ignore each other more effectively then.

The taxi driver headed north east out of the city, past tall buildings I'd seen age over time. Age and decay and be torn down and then be rebuilt. It was a gorgeous city. Especially at night. You couldn't see the grime at night. It was all bright lights, half-lit shapes, faceless people, hidden architecture. Like a kaleidoscope. Twist here, twist there, always the same elements, but never the same pattern.

As we got nearer to Greg's place, which was the first stop on the way from town, I turned towards him. We'd gone the past few miles in silence. Not the companionable silence of Friday night, nor the uncomfortable silence of earlier on. This was the sulky silence of a man called on his behaviour at the point in the game when women were usually under his spell. No woman challenged Greg on his reputation once she'd slept with him. She accepted his past – then tried to change him.

But, in all fairness, he wasn't sulking alone. I was miffed because I kept wondering if he shouldn't have tried a teensy bit harder. I'd known men who were willing to walk through fire to get a flash of cleavage and this man hadn't even trotted out some tired cliché-cum-lie about me being special to get my kit off. I was sulking because he obviously wasn't that desperate to sleep with me again.

'Erm,' I cleared my throat, but he still showed me the back

of his head. 'What did you say to Matt about us? So I don't let something slip.'

Greg grudgingly acknowledged me: sneered down his slightly crooked nose as he carefully raised a scornful eyebrow. 'I told him I'd met someone I really liked but not to say anything to anyone because . . .' he gave a small, silent laugh, then returned his gaze to the window, 'because I wasn't sure how she felt. Yet.'

chapter six

day off

Not going into work today.

Not dragging myself from this bed, leaving this flat and going into that office.

After yesterday, Renée could do with a reminder as to why she employed me. A day answering the phone and dealing with Martha should do that.

Renée had done the decent thing yesterday and cancelled the meeting, then returned an hour after her blow-up and dropped a king-size bag of Maltesers on my desk. She was extra nice to me and even answered her phone without sighing first, which were her ways of saying sorry. She'd never say the words, but with Renée, actions often spoke louder than words. In fact, actions replaced words.

She'd apologised in her own way, but today would serve as a practical reminder of how much I contributed to the office. How non-useless I was. *What is wrong with you?* I chastised myself. *Has a demon possessed your brain? Since Saturday morning you have about five evil thoughts for every normal one.*

I tugged the soft, squashy duvet over my head, hiding from the light intruding through the windows. I hadn't pulled the blue curtains across last night and now the light was combining with the tequila, beer and champagne to swell every blood vessel in my head while shrinking my skull. I needed to neck a gallon of water then go back to sleep within ten minutes, or I'd feel wretched all day.

'Does it feel as though someone's used your head for a football?' Greg asked in a pained voice.

I didn't mean to, honest to goodness I didn't. It just happened. (I used to think 'it just happened' was a phrase uttered by those who'd got caught out and couldn't think of a proper excuse, but, seriously, it just happened.) After that near-compliment in the cab and thinking the longer we left it, the harder it'd be to get back on track as friends, I'd said to him, 'Look, come back to mine and let's talk. Properly.'

Greg had half-shrugged, half-nodded, a kind of non-verbal 'whatever', so I'd told the taxi driver to head straight for Horsforth . . .

I'd let us into my flat and Greg had acted like a first time guest, lurking in my corridor, waiting for me to turn on lights and flick on the radio. He even followed me to the kitchen but stood in the doorway like some kind of double vampire – unable to enter a room without express permission.

'Coffee?' I asked.

'Thanks,' he mumbled from his place leaning against the door frame.

I made him coffee – white, no sugar – and, when I turned to give it to him, found he was right behind me. I jumped a little because I hadn't heard him approach, then offered the fat blue cup across the short distance. He took it, set it down on the white worktop.

'What did you want to talk about?' he asked. He brushed my nose-length fringe away from my face, then rested his fingers on my cheek. He often did that, claiming he wanted to see my eyes while I was talking to him. Rather than swatting his hand away as I usually did, I took his fingers away from my cheek, then lowered his hand for him. His eyes seemed to register the lust that had bolted through me.

'Well, we . . .' I began.

Greg dipped his head and kissed my neck.

I gasped as my body contracted with desire. 'We shouldn't really . . .'

He pushed down my dress and bra straps and kissed my shoulder.

'Really, be doing this.'

He pushed away my hair from the other side, planted his juicy lips on that side of my neck. My body contracted again.

'We should be talking . . .'

He pushed down the dress and bra straps of that side and planted his lips on that shoulder. 'Talking about how, er, how, this will affect . . .'

Greg ran his tongue along my collarbone and my knees became mush.

'Affect, erm, affect Matt and Jen's relationship.'

Greg's tongue stopped. He stopped. With a sigh he straightened up. 'To be honest, Amber, I don't care how this will affect Matt and Jen's relationship. I don't care about Matt and Jen's relationship, full stop. I care about you.'

'Really?' I said.

Astonishment flashed across his face. 'Yeah, course. Why do you sound so surprised?'

I managed to stop 'Because you're a tart' leaving my mouth and shrugged instead.

'In the past three years you've become my best girl friend. You've listened to me, given me advice, taken care of me through some difficult times, even though I've done hardly anything for you in return. So, yes, I care about you.

'Friday night, I was planning on telling you how I felt, then leaving you to decide what to do next. But when I was sat

52

there, I couldn't think of what to say. I've talked to you for over three years but I was struggling to find the right words, so I kissed you instead. And that led to . . . you know. When I woke up the next morning and you were gone, I panicked. I thought I'd screwed it up with you.'

'And that's not the alcohol talking?' I asked. *The alcohol and the desire to get your leg over tonight.*

'Yes, it's a bit to do with being pissed, but it's also to do with never having chased a woman for eleven months before. I usually give up after two months. Three months if she's really special.'

'You've been after me for eleven months? Yeah, right,' I scoffed.

Greg leant back a little, rocking gently on the heels of his brown suede shoes, folded his arms across his chest, amusement danced in his eyes. 'You know, from anyone else, I'd think they were being coy, from you, I know you're being serious.'

'Oi, gitface, that sounds like an insult.'

'There are only so many "I'm bored, can I come over?" text messages you can send a girl before she either thinks you fancy her or you're stalking her.'

'I thought you were being friendly,' I replied. 'We are friends.'

'OK. What about the millions of times I've turned up at work to take you to lunch? Or invited myself over for dinner? Didn't you say on Friday that I practically live here?'

'I just thought . . .' My voice faded. All right, when you knew, it was obvious. If a friend had been telling me about his behaviour, I would've said, 'He fancies you!' but it's different when it's you. Different when it's me and Greg.

'I practically had to send you an email to tell you I was going to kiss you.'

'I don't think like that,' I offered lamely.

53

'I know, and that's one of the many reasons why I like you.'
He moved closer. 'Amber, just to let you know, I'm going to
kiss you. Right . . . about . . . now.'

In the morning light, I was compelled to cover myself up. I
felt . . . naked. I was naked. But this was different naked. Sex
was *naked* naked. Morning after was emotionally naked, bare
and exposed.

Greg knew me, but now he knew more of me. He knew
how I moved during sex; he knew what noises I made when
I came; how my face contorted. He knew a lot more of me,
and I wasn't sure I liked that.

'I take it you're not going to work, either,' Greg said.

'Either?' I replied.

'I booked today off, I knew it'd be a write-off day.'

'That was clever.' That meant he was staying. Possibly all
day. It wasn't that I wanted him to go, I simply wasn't sure I
wanted him to stay, either. 'I'll have to wait until ten to call in.'

'And after that?' Greg's peering through the gloom under
the duvet tainted everything with expectation.

'After that, what?'

'Do you want me to leave?'

'Why, do you want to leave?'

'I could lie here naked with you all day.'

I'll take that as a no, then.

It was too close under the duvet: stale sweat and alcohol
fumes made the air rancid and sickly. I pushed away the duvet
to let fresher air in but immediately cringed away from the
light. Greg spooned up against me, his body curved around
mine like a second skin and plump, Jelly Baby lips planted
a kiss on my shoulder. 'Of course, I could intersperse those
naked lying about moments with bouts of intense rogering,'
Greg added.

I said nothing. That wasn't the kind of thing you said stuff to unless you were well versed in the ritual of the flirt, which I wasn't.

'Do you know the best cure for a hangover?' he ventured after a few minutes of non-flirty silence.

'Don't tell me, I know this one ... could it possibly be intense bouts of rogering?'

'Correct!' Greg said.

His hand idly stroked my stomach. Greg. My friend. His hand was stroking my stomach. *And, oh, oh, he's caressing me. The stroke's turning into a caress. He's pressing closer to me. He wants to have sex.*

'Are you OK?' Greg asked, obviously sensing my body tense. 'Do you want me to stop?'

'Why would I want you to stop?' I asked innocently.

'Sure?'

'Mmm-hmm,' I squeaked.

'I'll get a condom.' He climbed out of bed, disappeared to his clothes, which were still in the kitchen.

If I told him that in the wooden 'jewellery' box on my bedside table were twelve condoms that I bought on Sunday, he'd think I'd expected this to happen again. And I hadn't. Not really. I simply wanted to be prepared. Friday night I didn't have any condoms and the ones we'd used were Greg's.

What are you doing? I asked myself sternly. *Why are you going to have sex with Greg?* Again.

I really and truly had never thought of him in that way. If I had, I wouldn't have let him see me with sleep in my eye, dribble on my face or uncombed hair as I had done since the first time he'd stayed over at my place. I didn't think of him that way until he kissed me. And even then, it wasn't because it was him who'd kissed me but because it was a man who'd kissed me and I'd been so celibate for so long that at that point I'd probably have leapt on any man if he'd made a move. I wasn't sure if I felt that way about

55

Greg now. I could be so indifferent to his maleness one minute, then gagging to rip his clothes off and use his body the next.

Take last night for example. In my kitchen (*in my kitchen!*) he wasn't only going to kiss me, as it turned out. He was also going to lift my dress, tug down my knickers, lift me up to rest on the edge of the worktop so I was the right height. And I was going to respond by undoing his belt and trousers, ferociously kissing him back. We'd done it in a scary, frantic manner that was reminiscent of Michael Douglas and Glenn Close in *Fatal Attraction*.

We'd stood there for a long time afterwards, holding each other, kissing, brushing hair out of each other's eyes, giggling at how we'd been hardly talking not fifteen minutes earlier and then we were ravishing each other. After the smirking and giggling, we'd stripped off and done it again on the kitchen floor. Madness. Couldn't work out how I felt completely. I wasn't into this. I liked the physical bit, but didn't like the waking up afterwards and finding I was lying next to Greg part. Why? Because I didn't fancy him? I must do to sleep with him. Or was it because he's good at it? This was complicated. Confusing. Chaotic. All the things I'd become expert at avoiding in my life.

I worked hard to confine my neurosis to my work, to my viewing habits, to my inner mind. I'd heard this line on a TV programme that said the secret to creating a good relationship was 'all about hiding the crazy'. And, for the most part, I was good at that, skilled at hiding the crazy. Not letting on how neurotic and insecure and dramatic I could be. Now I was slap bang in the middle of a place called Neurosis Central that made Leeds City Centre seem like a ghost town. There were so many different threads of emotion running through me and I couldn't find one to follow from start to finish. Couldn't seem to decipher how I felt completely.

I slapped my hand against my forehead, trying to knock sense into it. *Stop this. Stop it now.*

Greg reappeared at that moment, paused in the doorway, staring at me. Not because I was the sexiest thing he'd ever seen, but because I was trying to bash my head in. I stopped, lowered my hand as unsuspiciously as possible. Smiled at him in an innocent manner. My eyes ran over the length of his body: pale gold skin, practically hairless chest, his slight paunch, a crop of dark hair that started just below his abdomen, the most amazing male member. *Look at him.* Should I turn him away because I want to be internally neurotic? Hell, not even I'm that sensible.

'What do you think about Matt and Jen moving in together?' Greg asked a couple of hours later. I'd been out on a milk and paper run earlier. He in turn had to go out on a breakfast run because he'd needed a bacon sandwich and all I could offer towards it was the tomato ketchup.

'I'm pleased, of course,' I said, turning a page in the paper and a channel on the telly. 'It's what they want. Marriage won't be far behind.'

'You think?' Greg replied.

The slight squeak in his voice stopped me flipping pages of the paper and made me concentrate on him. He was a human island in a sea of newspapers on my floor. 'Why do you say that?'

Greg pushed his hand through his hair. 'I've known Matt since forever, and the only thing he's committed to for longer than three years is getting taller and even that stopped when he hit nineteen.'

'You reckon Matt's commitmentphobic?'

Greg nodded.

'Hello there, Mr Pot, I really hope you're not calling Mr Kettle black.'

'I know I give the impression of being – 'ow you say? – a Casanova [no, actually, he gave me the impression of being a whore, but that's between you, me and the garden post], but,' he went serious, 'I've had a long-term relationship. One that lasted nearly six years.'

NEWSFLASH! How come that had slipped through the net of things I knew about him? He was meant to be my best friend and now he was telling me this. That was like Jen suddenly telling me she'd been married before she came to college. Had to question him about it at some point.

'Matt's not had a settled relationship anywhere near that long.'

'Maybe Jen's The One.' I thought about what I'd just said then laughed gaily. 'What am I saying? Of course she's The One. Because if he hurts her, *I'll be separating him and those kneecaps of his.*'

Greg laughed. Realised I wasn't joking and stopped. 'The whole thing seems so sudden. She hardly knows the man.'

'Three years is sudden? What's really going on, Greg?'

'Nothing, I guess. I suppose I'm having trouble adjusting to the idea of Matt not being there. I've lived with him nigh on twelve years.'

'It'll be reet,' I said.

It must be hard for him, giving up his relationship with Matt. It was easier for me – Jen and I had stopped living together when she finished college. Her course was four years, so I'd temped and lived with her until she graduated. Then she'd moved in with a boyfriend for what turned out to be six months and, in that time, I moved back to London for nine months and lived with my parents. By the time I came back to Leeds Jen had bought her flat in Allerton, and a few months later I found my flat in Horsforth. With all of this, I had none of the separation anxiety Greg was going through. It was probably a good thing for me – I'd see more of Jen because she wouldn't be spending time she could spend with me, with him. She'd have Matt at home. The same went for Greg and Matt. I explained that to him.

'I suppose,' he conceded. 'And anyway, I might've met someone myself.'

You just couldn't leave it, could you? I thought. *You had to go and spoil it by bringing up the sex thing, didn't you?* I focused on the paper in front of me. The harder I concentrated, the faster the newsprint crawled across the sheet, desperate not to be read.

'Have I?' Greg asked.

'Have you what?' I started playing with the soft, rubbery buttons on the remote control. At least they weren't dancing in front of my eyes.

He snatched the remote out of my hand and flicked off the TV, then grabbed the newspaper from in front of me and slung it aside. When he'd finished ridding me of distractions, he sat cross-legged in front of me. 'Have I met someone? As in someone I could start dating and then, hopefully, at some point call my girlfriend?'

I went to speak but he added, 'And don't you dare say, "I don't know, have you?"'

I closed my mouth.

'Amber, I know you've got half the men in Leeds after you b—'

'Are you taking the piss?' I cut in.

Greg frowned. 'About what?' he asked, mystified.

He was serious. He genuinely thought I was pursued by scores of men. Or he was the best actor on earth (and as we all discovered last night, that wasn't the case).

'Nothing,' I said. 'Carry on.'

'We're going to have to be grown-up about this. We're going to have to decide if this is going somewhere now because we're not casual acquaintances, we see each other all

59

the time with Matt and Jen. We need to sort it out. What's going on with us?'

Well I didn't bloody know, did I?

I'd made the decision to be single and celibate eighteen months ago and had stuck to my decision so far. Did I really need this man, this Greg, to keep dragging me away from the path of righteousness? To keep luring me into bed (or kitchen floor) with the kind of sex I'd only imagined was possible? To keep weaving threads of confusion through my emotions?

'I see,' he was saying to my elongated silence. 'And, in the words of the *Fast Show*, I'll get my coat. Save you any further embarrassment.'

'I like you. A lot,' I blurted out, desperate to stop him leaving, 'but . . .'

'You think I'm a slag and that I'll give you the runaround the second you start to trust me.'

Nicely put, even if you do say so yourself. 'Something like that.'

'Amber, since I realised how deeply I felt about you I've not been with anyone else.'

I raised an incredulous, disbelieving eyebrow. Had he forgotten who he was talking to? Had he forgotten that I'd once stared down a psycho woman and her equally psycho boyfriend in a pub because he'd started to flirt with her rather than get a round in as he'd been sent to do?

'She didn't count because she was insane, she thought I was going to marry her after two days and I learnt my lesson in a big way. That's it.'

I hitched up my other, incredulous and disbelieving eyebrow.

'I tried to make a go of it with her,' he protested, 'because I thought I just wanted a relationship, but I didn't, I wanted a relationship with you. But that really is it.'

Had I another eyebrow, I would have hitched it up too. I settled for sticking my tongue in my cheek at him.

'OK, but she didn't count. She'd been coming on to me for ages and I felt obliged. It was a mercy shag.'

'Exactly!' I said. 'How many other mercy shags are there going to be, Greg?'

'None, if I'm with you.'

'I believe you. I believe you mean that and that you wouldn't intentionally cheat on me, but what if someone comes on to you? What if we have a row? What if you get drunk? There are too many what ifs when it comes to you and sex. I don't want to deal with that.'

Greg sagged in shame as he squinted at the ground. Silence, not too dissimilar to the shroud we'd eaten in the previous night, slipped its folds around us. Eventually he reached into his back pocket and pulled out a small book. 'What if I gave you sole custody of this?'

He *never* had a proper little black book.

'You get to keep it until we split up. If we make it to, say, six months, you get to burn it.'

Greg placed the leather-bound book on my lap, then sat back watching me with his bright, keen eyes, waiting for my reaction to his placing his whole sexual past, present and future in my hands.

My first instinct was to flick through it, see if I recognised any of the names. My second instinct was to flick through it, gauge how many names there were in it, see how many women had trodden the path I had. My third instinct was to ask: 'Am I in there?'

Greg shook his head. 'Even before I fell for you, you were too special for that book.'

'In other words you knew I wouldn't shag you so you didn't waste your time putting me in there.'

Greg flopped his arms up and down. 'I've just given you

my former sex life and you're bitching about if you're in there.'

Fair point. I turned the small black rectangle over in my hands, caressed the soft leather. It was warm and bent slightly from the curve of his bum, the pages well worn from overuse. 'I can't believe you own a little black book,' I said.

'I don't any more, you do.'

'I don't know if I want this responsibility.'

'It's the only way I can think to prove to you that I'm serious about this. I don't want any of the people in that book, I want you.'

'What about the numbers in your mobile?'

In an instant the colour leached out of Greg's skin. There was clearly a pecking order of people he'd shagged or wanted to shag. If he liked her, she went into his black book; if he reeeaally liked her, she went into his mobile.

I held out the book to him. 'Let's forget it. We can still be friends.'

I was trembling slightly as I handed him back his sexual freedom. And, what was this? What was stirring itself in my chest? A swirl of emotions I couldn't quite pin down. Probably mostly jealousy and sadness. Jealousy, pretty self-explanatory. Sadness, because if he took the book back, our friendship would be based on me knowing that he didn't care enough for me to give up shagging around; and him knowing that I was too petty to let him keep a few other women's numbers.

'OK,' Greg said, but didn't move to take the book from me. 'I'll write down all the relevant numbers from my mobile on a piece of paper, slip the paper into the black book and get them back if we split up.' (The faith he had in me was astounding. If we split up, did he honestly think I'd give him back his sex life? I'd burn it. No messing.)

Not exactly, 'I'll delete them all', but it wasn't, 'Oh, forget it', either. So, the ball was back in my court. I had to decide if we were going to give it a go or not.

I couldn't think under these conditions. I didn't have any distracting TV noise, no chocolate in my hand . . . the last time I tried to work under pressure without these tools I ended up offering to call Greg a cab. 'Don't move. I'll be right back. Just don't move or leave, sit right there,' I said to Greg.

He nodded as I unfolded my legs from under me, stood up and then exited the room. In the kitchen I went straight for the fridge, tugged open the door, pulled out the giant bar of chocolate Renée had bought me from Copenhagen a few weeks earlier. It was the good-quality stuff I'd been saving for when company came round – not the everyday chocolate I usually ate. I pulled open the thick, waxy yellow wrapper, did the same with the thick gold foil inside. I lifted the bar to my nose, inhaled deeply. The bitter smell of cocoa, tempered with sugar and milk powder and emulsifier, filled my senses. *Oh, yes, that's better.* I took another two deep hits. Then I pushed the pieces between my fingers until a jagged, diagonal piece snapped off. I slipped it between my lips and bit down. *Oh, oh, oh, yes.* My whole body relaxed as the taste filled my mouth. Now, I could think. Really think.

Greg.

Greg and me. And possibly giving it a go.

It wasn't a simple case of me not being interested. I was, a little. Only a little, though. Certainly not enough for me to risk everything. But, if I told him no now, he'd take it literally. I wouldn't see Greg again, not in that sense. I'd become like Kristin Scott Thomas in *Four Weddings and a Funeral*, hanging around someone who went off with other women while I played the dutiful mate.

I crammed another piece of chocolate in my already full mouth.

63

Did I want that? Did I want Greg moaning another woman's name as if it was the most delicious thing ever to enter his mouth?

The thought dawned slowly but clearly: no. Not at all.

Much as I might not want him right now, much as I might not want him at all, I didn't want him going near anyone else. *Also, it's not every day you get the biggest tart in Yorkshire offering you him. Exclusivity. That'd be like a chocolate manufacturer making chocolate, only for me. Amber Nectar Chocolate. Just for me . . . OK, stop right there or you'll implode with excitement. Get back to the matter in hand.*

Greg. Exclusivity. I ate another few pieces of chocolate to be on the safe side.

I returned to the living room. Greg had done as I'd instructed: he hadn't moved. Not a millimetre. That was a good sign, wasn't it? He was already doing exactly as I told him. Get him to comply with the little things, and complicity with the big things – like not shagging anyone else – was sure to follow, no? I returned to my place on the sofa and crossed my legs under me again. 'Go on then, put your numbers where your mouth is.'

Ten minutes later, Greg was left with fifteen (fifteen out of ninety-five) numbers on his mobile – I took great pleasure in watching him wince as he deleted each one – and I had three sheets of women's names and numbers to slip into the book and destroy at my earliest convenience. 'So . . .?' Greg asked.

'So, let's take it really, really, *really* slowly, OK?'

A grin spread across his face, catching light in his Minstrel-coloured eyes.

'And we mustn't tell the other two until we're sure we're going to be together for a while. I went out with one of Jen's boyfriend's friends once and when it ended it was a total nightmare. It nearly split up Jen and her man, not to mention the trouble it caused between Jen and me. I don't want us messing up what they've got. So, let's agree, we say nothing about us for six months. At least six months.'

'Six months,' Greg agreed, and crawled across the floor towards me. As he did so, fingers of terror curled around my heart.

chapter seven

champagne buddy

'OK, total honesty. What do you really think about me and Matt moving in together?' Jen said, settling back on my sofa with a huge glass of wine. She could, it was half-term so she didn't have to get up early in the morning for work.

Greg had left when the evening episode of *Neighbours* started. I could tell he was angling for an invitation to stay by the way he kept going on about how knackered he was. I'd told him it was Tuesday night, which was Jen night, so I'd handed him his jacket and bag and said I'd see him at the weekend.

Seven years ago I hit upon the idea to start over in London and lived with my mum and stepdad for nine months while I got myself together. It was perfect . . . for reminding me that I needed at least 200 miles between me and my family, so I returned to Leeds for good. Since then, Jen and I made sure we met up at least once a week on Tuesday nights for dinner. On alternate weeks we'd go to each other's flat – one of us would cook dinner and the visitor would provide the wine and dessert. Often we'd stay over if we were up late talking.

However, this Tuesday, I'd ordered a curry. I hadn't been

shopping over the weekend – another result of having sex – (I'd forgotten how much was involved in sex. It wasn't simply a meeting of two bodies, it was not having time or energy to buy food. Not having the inclination to do your work. And a hell of a lot of tidying up) so my cupboards were Old Mother Hubbard bare. We'd eaten so now it was down to the heavy talk. 'To be totally honest, Jenna,' I said gravely, then checked she wanted the truth by adding: 'Total honesty, right?'

She nodded, bit her lip, her eyes cloaked in apprehension and terror: we had this habit of asking for total honesty of each other and then being struck with fear because we knew we'd get it.

'I never thought he'd do it. I never thought he'd make such a bold move, it's so unlike him. I know, I know, I've spent two years telling you I thought he would but that's because it was what you wanted to hear. Deep down, I thought he'd never do it. But he did, so that's great. Fantastic, even.'

Jen tossed her wavy blonde hair, exposing her beautiful face. I didn't think she was beautiful simply because she was my best friend, but because she was. Her skin was naturally blemish-free, her slightly prominent cheekbones only needed a hint of blusher. And her eyes were such an unusual shade of blue you could never be sure what colour they really were. Sometimes they were pale blue, sometimes sapphire blue, sometimes topaz blue, and other days, like today, they were summer sky blue. If anything let her down, though, it was the shape of her eyes. They, no matter how well she shaped her eyebrows, seemed slightly too big. They were oval and not pinched enough at the ends to make them perfect, like the rest of her face. I often wanted to lend her my eyes – mine were the shape of bay leaves with finely tapered edges and huge, black-brown pupils – because she'd be 'finished', 100 per cent perfect with them.

Jen sipped her wine. 'Neither did I,' she replied and pulled her legs up under her on the sofa. 'I never thought Matt would settle down because he's like you.'

'*Excuse me?!*' I replied. If someone was going to fling the ultimate insult at me, that was it. Me, like Matt. Me, like that proverbial lump of toffee?

'You and Matt are so alike it's scary. Whenever the future's mentioned you both get cagey. You'll either clam up or make a joke out of it, anything to avoid thinking or talking seriously about settling down. It used to infuriate me because I never knew where I stood when it came to getting a house or booking a holiday, but then I was glad you were like that when I met Matt. I realised he wasn't going to run away because even though you made no plans for the future you stuck around.'

'You know what, I'll let you off because you're my best mate, any other person would get kicked out for that.'

'Oh, you want examples?' Jen said. 'Sean.'

'We do not talk about Sean,' I reminded.

'I have never known a man adore a woman like he did you,' Jen continued as though she hadn't heard the warning note in my voice. 'He was sooooo in love with you, the way he gazed at yo—'

'We are *not* having this conversation,' I cut in.

Jen observed me long and cool, trying to calculate if she could say what else was on her mind. She opened her mouth.

'And if you do try to have this conversation you can piss off home.'

She shrugged, sat back on the sofa. 'I reckon it's because your family's as deformed as mine,' Jen said.

'Listen, teacher features, just because you sort out five-year-olds' problems, don't think you can analyse me. I'm the one with the psychology degree, remember?'

'Doesn't mean I don't know a thing or two about it. Or, for that matter, Ambs, that I don't know you.'

Jen and I met in the first year of college. I was in Room 29, she was in Room 30 in our halls of residence.

I remember the exact moment I saw her walking from her room to the kitchen on our floor: she was tall, wearing a stone-washed denim skirt and sensible black polo neck. Her hair, pinned back with an Alice band, cascaded down her back, stopping at her waist. She had a perfectly oval face with cheek-bones that threatened to make an appearance the older she got. She walked with the kind of straight-backed poise they taught in finishing school. Everything about her screamed sophistica-tion, which immediately intimidated me. I'd been wearing baggy jeans with a long-sleeved T-shirt and had a nineteen-year-old's slouch, my plaits were pulled back into a ponytail with a towelling scrunchy. I was everything that Jen wasn't.

I'd watched her return to her room from the kitchen and decided she wasn't like any chocolate or sweet I'd ever encoun-tered. She was one of those new chocolate bars that you spotted as you walked into a shop. Its wrapping was so effort-lessly classy it made everything around it seem gaudy and cheap. This chocolate was unique. It was a real white choco-late. Not the creamy colour most white chocolate is, but snow white. It had lots of cream and milk and white sugar, but minimal cocoa. It was soft around the edges, very quick and easy to melt so you had to be careful how you handled it. And because of that, because of the element of risk involved, most people would ignore it, going instead for what they knew. Grabbing their Mars, Twix or Dairy Milk because, when it came down to it, most people tended to stick to what was familiar.

I couldn't, though. I couldn't ignore this unusual, sophisti-cated chocolate – find myself a Mars to befriend – because she was my neighbour. I had to get to know her. I bit the bullet and knocked on her door when her parents left.

'Hi, I'm Amber, your next-door neighbour,' I'd said to her.

'I'm Jen,' she said, and grinned. That grin dissolved my worries about her. You could fake a lot of things but not the warmth that came from that smile.

Once you bit into Jen by talking to her, by going beyond her looks, you found out how lovely she was. How her nose wrinkled up when she laughed. How her eyes sparkled when she was about to ask you something deeply personal. How silly she could be. Under that white chocolate bubbled real champagne. Fun, refreshing champagne, an experience you wanted to last and last.

We spent most of our time together after that. She was training to be a primary school teacher with English as her main degree and I was studying Psychology with Press and Publicity as my professional training subject. It was Christmas, though, that cemented our friendship.

At Christmas, when everyone was getting excited about going home, seeing friends, spending time with their families, I started to get mini panic attacks. I sat staring into space, gnawing on my thumbnails, my heart almost visible, it was beating that hard in my chest. My parents had separated when I was ten and I was trying to work out which parent would get the 27 to 30 December visit. Which one would be giving me a long, frosty silence down the phone as I explained I wasn't going to be spending the big day with them. Christmas was so fraught I often tried to ignore it. Then I discovered Jen was going through Christmas Anxiety too.

Jen's mum was an ex-model, but her mother, with her fading beauty, was a bitter woman. And her bitterness fermented into a vindictiveness aimed primarily at her daughter.

When Jen was eight, her mother told her the man she thought of as her father wasn't her father. When Jen was ten, her mother decided he was her biological father. As it turned out it didn't matter because he left when Jen was eleven, never to be heard from again. Her mother then had a succession of boyfriends, none of whom liked Jen. Not Jen the person, Jen the reminder that her mother wasn't footloose and fancy-free. The only one of her mum's lovers she did get on with was the man her mother met six months before Jen left for uni. Her mother was still with him and Jen liked him a lot, possibly because he showed her and her mother a lot of respect.

The point is, Jen and I bonded because we knew we were different from our peers. Everyone around us didn't seem to tread on eggshells around their families; we didn't run home at every opportunity. So, Jenna Leigh Hartman from Reading and Amber Salpone from London clung to each other, two dysfunctional lifebuoys in a sea of normality.

'You do like Matt, don't you?' Jen asked.

She was now lying on the patch of thick red carpet where, hours earlier, Greg's body had been stretched out while he read the papers. Jen rested the wine glass on her flat stomach, her eyes closed, her knees pulled up so the flats of her feet rested on the ground. Her hair was like a golden glow that fanned out around her head. Jen could make a casual pose seem so effortless. Yes, a casual pose was always meant to be effortless, but I had trouble with it. Say I was doing the same thing: I'd invariably get an itch in my lower back but wouldn't want to sit up to scratch it, so I'd jiggle and shift about on the floor, like a snake trying to move through shagpile. Then I'd spill some wine so I'd leap up and trip over takeaway cartons on my way to get a cloth. Or I'd be lying on the sofa under my duvet, watching telly, but couldn't relax because I was fidgeting about searching for the remote. Jen, on the other hand, could be yoga-still in anything she did.

'Mmm-hmm,' I replied, concurring that I did like Matt without actually saying yes.' (I loved the mmm-hmm, it was so generic that you could lie without technically lying.)

I was reclining on the sofa, resting my wine glass on my stomach but holding onto it while desperately seeking the TV remote.

Me and Matt. It wasn't a simple case of us not liking each other. Matt had problems smiling at me or, sometimes, even speaking to me because he thought Jen and I were too close. I knew her before him. I was a part of Jen's life that he could never be a part of and that bugged him; stopped him sleeping sometimes. If we started to laugh about stuff we did in the past, a cloud would pass across his face and he'd slide into a sulk. He gave her a hard time if she told me something before him. And heaven forbid she be on the phone to me for more than ten minutes while he was there. Matt and I loved the same person and he wanted to guarantee she loved him more than she did me.

'I do worry that you and he don't get on as well as you and Greg,' Jen continued.

You really don't want me to get on with him as well as I do with Greg, I thought. 'We're different people,' I explained.

'You and Greg are different people!' she screeched. 'He's a complete whore and you're practically a nun, but you and him get on. He's always round here or meeting you for lunch. Greg sees you more than I do sometimes.'

The mention of his name, talking about him, made stardust dance around my stomach like moonlight danced on water. 'I'll see more of Matt now that you're going to live together. Jeez, you're going to live with Matt. You're going to become a cohabitee. Again.'

'Funny, isn't it? You've never lived with a bloke, whereas Matt will be my third one.'

'I have lived with a bloke,' I protested.

72

'Who?'

'Eric. And you don't get more blokey than him.'

'Brothers do not count. You could have lived wi—'

'Book your cab home before you finish that sentence, OK, Jenna,' I cut in.

She scrunched up her lips and pulled a face at the ceiling. 'Do you think it'll last with me and Matt?' she asked. 'I lived with Karl and Tommy and I thought it'd last. I really did, but it didn't.' She swivelled her head to survey me. 'Do you think I'm doing the right thing?'

Why did everyone think I had the answers to everything today? First Greg was asking what was going on between us, then Jen was asking if she was doing the right thing. I wouldn't be surprised if Indiana Jones showed up any moment asking if I knew where he'd left the Holy Grail.

'You moved in too soon with Karl and Tommy. They were nice blokes,' I added quickly, 'but everything was rushed. Maybe it's good that Matt's been so reticent about settling down, because now you both know you're ready. He does love you.' It aggrieved me to admit this sometimes, but whenever Matt wasn't off in Paris being International Marketing Director for his company, Jen was the centre of his world. I'd have loved it if he was a neglectful bastard and then I could have licence to dislike him as much as he hated me. 'I could never say that so certainly about Tommy or Karl.'

'But you're still number one, you know,' Jen said. 'You're still the one I tell everything to.'

'Mmm-hmm,' I replied. I told Jen everything too. Except this one thing. It was only a small thing. Anyway, it probably wouldn't last with me and Greg. *In fact, I give it two months. Three at the most.*

'hmmm, a man or chocolate – put it this way, you'll never be sat around waiting for a bar of chocolate to ring you'

chapter eight

her!

'*Who* are you?' Renée's voice said sharply across the office.

Martha didn't flinch, didn't even seem to notice. I did. I glanced away from my computer screen at my boss.

Renée's professionally shaped eyebrows were hunched together; her red mouth was taut with indignation. '*What?*' she barked into the phone.

Long pause as the other person spoke.

'Why should I remember you? Did you save my life or something?'

Martha smirked, but she would. It was always me who panicked when Renée got like that on the phone because she was invariably talking to someone we should be aiming to be nice to.

'You write for who?'

See? I shoved my chair back, almost dislocating a couple of vertebrae in the process, and ran the distance to Renée's desk. Three-quarters of the way there, I flung myself across the desk, narrowly missing the pencil holder and her precious stapler, and jabbed my finger on the 'secrecy' button on her phone.

'Give me the phone,' I said, with my hand outstretched. Time was when I could fling myself onto the desk and get the phone out of Renée's grip before she could react, but over the

77

last year she'd got very adept at snatching it out of reach while I was mid-air.

Renée clutched the receiver to her chest like it was her first-born. 'No.'

'Renée,' I cooed, 'give Amber the phone.'

She shook her head. She hadn't shouted since she went overboard on Monday. As I predicted, my day off gave her something to think about. So this journalist who had innocently picked up the phone to find out about our Festival was, in fact, dealing with a woman who had four days of anger simmering away, ready to boil over.

'Give me the phone and I'll let you slag off the new London Film Festival brochure all afternoon.'

Renée's eyes flickered as she saw what was on offer: an afternoon of nit picking, sneering and downright bitchiness that I wouldn't temper. There'd be no 'Come on, Renée, be fair,' while she went on and on. It was tempting . . .

'I'll buy you chocolate and then make you coffee,' I added.

Tempting, but not tempting enough, she still clung to the phone.

'And,' I said, playing my trump card, 'you can critique their website.'

Words Renée longed to hear. I'd always stopped her having a go at their website because ours wasn't much better. In fact, ours was in desperate need of resuscitation and I'd decreed we could only slag off the things that we did better than LFF. Renée's hand shot out as she handed over the phone.

I hit the 'secrecy' button. 'Hi, sorry about that, the Festival Director had to take another call, how can I help? I'm Amber, the Deputy Festival Director.'

'Hi, Amber.'

Oh. Good. Grief. Her. *HER!*

I'd know that affected, nasal voice anywhere. I should've let Renée abuse her. I gave up my trump card for her. HER!

78

Her, the journalist from hell. The nutter journalist from hell who'd tried to get me sacked.

Last year, in an almost identical incident, Renée's phone had rung and Renée under sufferance had answered it. She'd been speechless when some woman had started prattling on about Renée's past.

Renée had been the Bridget Bardot of her day, thankfully without the fascistic leanings, and had become famous when she was thirteen by playing Lolita in a French arthouse film. She'd been an international overnight sensation, nominated for awards, starred in a number of films, blah, blah, blah, beautiful career ahead of her . . . But, Renée being Renée (and intrinsically contrary), had gotten bored of the limelight and gave it all up at twenty-one to learn about movie production. She moved from Paris to London and worked for a few film companies. She met her husband, a screenwriter, and they moved to Leeds, where he was from. She'd then got a job as Contributing Festival Assistant at WYIFF and within two years was running the whole shebang. This woman on the other end of the phone had, it seemed, called only to remind her of that.

I'd heard the silence after Renée's 'Allo, WYIFF?', glanced up in time to see Renée's face tighten, the sign she was about to start screaming. I'd thrown myself across her desk – unfortunately not missing the stapler that time – and wrestled the phone out of her hand before she invoked her tongue.

'We'd like to interview,' the woman on the end of the phone continued, and named a fairly well-known star who we'd got to attend the UK premiere of her new film in Leeds, 'which I'm sure she'd love to do because we're a glossy and the Yorkshire market is so limited. And we'd like to do a piece on how you went from being such a well-known teen star to running a festival in Leeds of all places.'

'Probably not a good idea to upset the Festival Director by saying such things,' I calmly told the caller. 'This is Amber Salpone, the Deputy Festival Director. Let's be honest, we don't have to give you access to her and because you're calling us, I'm sure you've discovered her agent is a nightmare. But if we can get it in writing that you'll give the Festival and The Mates Of The Festival a plug with contact details and you'll mention that,' I reeled off a list of stars, 'have previously attended the Festival, then I'll put you on the interview list.'

'Have they all really been to the Festival?' she replied, rather insultingly impressed.

'Yup, we're not some hick town outfit,' I laughed. I eyed up Renée, who seemed to be chewing on a wasp. 'I'll let you know about interviewing Renée.'

She, Mimi, came and, knowing she hadn't been up norf before, I met her at the station. She'd given me the once over and found me wanting. I wasn't wearing the right clothes, I wasn't carrying the right kind of bag and I was a Southerner who'd *chosen* to live in the North. 'How can you bear it?' she'd asked me as I walked her to the hotel I'd booked her into.

Her voice – nasal, imperious, affected – was even more annoying in real life. Her blonde bob had been styled by expensive fingers, her comely figure was clothed by well-named people. We had nothing in common, but I'd been nice to vile people before in the name of work so I'd smiled at her and said, 'The longer you live here, the more you love it,' and prayed that the God of Yorkshire didn't strike me down for being so disloyal.

Later that Friday night, at the after-screening party, when The Celeb had gone to bed, Mimi held court from her bar stool in the hotel surrounded by male crew from the film and male journalists, pontificating on how 'dinky' Leeds was: 'It's got a Harvey Nics, hasn't it? It's like a mini London.'

Had their tongues not been hanging out, those Yorkshire

men would've run her out of town. Among those male journalists was Greg. And, guess who disappeared upstairs with her? *You two deserve each other*, I thought as I crawled off home.

I'd been knocked out by the event, had needed to work late for weeks beforehand co-ordinating things. Sunday afternoon, when it was finally over, I'd come home after seeing The Celeb off at the airport. She, in stark contrast to Mimi, was down-to-earth with a wonderfully dry sense of humour. I'd enjoyed meeting her most out of all the stuff over the weekend and she'd promised to come back for the Festival if she could. I'd collapsed onto the sofa still wearing my coat, staring unseeingly at the television. An hour must have passed before I could get my faculties together enough to contemplate taking my coat off and getting something to eat. I'd just about raised my head from the sofa armrest when my phone had bleeped in my pocket. I'd tiredly pulled out the silver mobile, expecting to see a message from The Celeb who'd said she'd text me when she got back to London.

Instead, I got:

Help. At Hol Inn. Rm 513. She's talkin about movin 2 Leeds. Help. G.

I'd almost ignored it. I'd been saving him for over two years and I'd decided right then not to do him another good turn, ever. I deleted the message, tossed the mobile onto the sofa beside me.

'*How can you stand it up here?*' Mimi's condescending tone said in my head. *She won't move here*, I reassured myself. *Course she wouldn't. Nooo. Even if she did, Greg won't go out with her.* But what if she was different? What if she was The One? He might start dating her. I'd have to go out with him and her. *They might get married.* Ten minutes later I was on the train to Leeds.

After my third knock on 513 Mimi bad-temperedly threw

the door open, and I internally recoiled. Only a towel – a not very big one at that – was covering her comely figure. *Doesn't this hotel provide dressing gowns? Or bigger towels?* I asked myself.

'Oh. Amber. Hi?' she said, unable to hide her disappointment.

I opened my mouth a couple of times, startled by the sight of her. How overtly sexual the whole scene was. Everything smelt and felt of sex. I hadn't had sex in almost a year and now it was assaulting me from every angle. Also, I was doing a fish impression because not once during the forty-minute journey down there had I thought of what I was going to say. This wasn't like the time in the pub when I'd stared down some psycho woman and her equally psycho boyfriend who wanted to kill Greg. Or any of the other times when I'd gone up to him, slid my arm around his waist to lead him away from a kicking. This needed a story, plausibility. *Words*.

'Are you . . . *OK*?' she asked. Again with the condescending tone. Again with the begging to be battered. *Would I get away with it?* I wondered. *'She condescended to me, m'lud.'* You never know, it could work.

'Er, yeah. I, erm, uh, was, um, wondering, have you seen Greg? Greg Walterson. You were talking to him in the bar on Friday night. I thought you'd gone back to London but when I heard you'd decided to stay on a couple of days I thought you might have seen him?' There was enough confusion and desperation in my performance to make it sound real.

'You couldn't have called?' she said. Every word, every syllable went through me. Set my teeth on edge; hacked at my nerves. *She irritated me with her voice, m'lud*.

'I was in the hotel anyway . . . Look, have you seen him? I'm really worried.'

'What's it to you?' she asked.

'He's my, erm, friend,' I said.

82

Her eyes ran down me in scorn. Then reversed up the other way with a smidgen more of that scorn. *And then there were the looks, m'lud.* 'Your *friend*?'

'My *boy*friend,' I hissed.

Greg chose that moment to step out into the part of the room where I could see him, thus destroying what small vestige of innocence I had left in me. He'd pulled on the smart black trousers he'd been wearing on Friday night but hadn't done them up, his shirt was open, exposing his chest. In all the times, in all the rescues, I'd never seen him so soon after the act of sex. I don't know what my core had thought he was doing in a hotel room with a beautiful woman for the entire weekend, but it was suddenly very shaken. I was stunned to silence as I stared at him.

'Amber,' he stated, his voice a swirl of apprehension and bewilderment.

'Gregory,' I replied.

Our eyes remained fixed on each other. Another wave of exhaustion almost submerged me. I was so tired, and why wasn't I at home asleep? Because Greg was a fucking idiot. Literally. When it came to fucking, he was an idiot. Anger and adrenalin surged through me. 'This is where you've been?' I said loudly. 'I've been worried out of my mind and you've been here.'

'He didn't tell me he had a girlfriend,' Mimi protested.

'I'll bet he didn't,' I snarled at her. She pressed herself back against the door in response.

Greg stood rooted to the spot, silent.

'Why am I always finding you where you shouldn't be? With people you shouldn't be with? I've had enough of this, Gregory,' I ranted. And I had. This was the final straw. 'Do you hear me? I've had enough ... You're welcome to him!' I screeched at Mimi before I turned and stormed off towards the lift.

Greg, who saw his salvation, his one last chance to escape the hotel a single man, marching away, came to life. 'Amber! Stop! Wait!' he called after me.

I stomped down the long corridor, rage thudding in my temples and chest. I really had had enough. A few seconds later Greg came running out of the hotel room, jacket in one hand, hopping as he tried to pull on his shoes.

'Amber! Stop! I'm sorry!' he called after me. 'I'm really sorry!'

I got to the lift and started pounding on the lift call button. The lift hadn't arrived when Greg reached me. 'I'm sorry,' he said.

'This is the last time,' I snarled at him. 'The very last time.'

'I'm sorry,' he implored. He was taken aback by my anger now that he knew it was 100 per cent real. He took my arms in his hands in a calming gesture. I shoved him off so violently he stumbled backwards.

'I'm really, really sorry,' he said from where he'd stumbled to, now horrified by my rage. This was a side to me he hadn't seen. Few people had seen it. *I* didn't often see it, but now it'd been set free it was going to be hard to rein it in again. I didn't want to stop at shoving him. I had an almost over-whelming urge to punch him. Smack him right between his stupid eyes. Then kick him between the legs, hurt the thing that was always getting us into these situations. 'You're lucky I don't cut your balls off!' I shouted at him. Greg's hand immediately went to protect his crotch, scared that I was angry enough to do it.

The lift pinged its arrival at our floor, the metal doors slid open and I stormed into it. As I turned to face the doors, I found we had an audience. Not only was Mimi leaning out of her hotel door, quite a few other hotel guests were hanging out of doorways too, taking in the floorshow Greg and I were putting on. *Great, can't come back here ever again.*

Greg, not knowing when to leave well enough alone, reached out to touch me. I slapped his hand away.

'Don't touch me!' I shouted. 'Don't ever touch me!' And the lift doors closed on us.

I stomped out of the hotel into the street with Greg, who hadn't quite finished getting dressed, trailing behind me. 'You're really angry, aren't you?' he said after I stopped on the pavement, trying to decide if I should get a bus, taxi or train home.

'What gave it away, the shouting or the shoving?' I snapped.

'I'm sorry. I couldn't think of who else to ask for help. She was seriously talking about leaving her job and London. She thought I'd get her a job at the *Chronicle* and that she could stay at my place while she found somewhere to live. She was talking in absolutes and such detail, I panicked.'

'Don't you think it would've been better to find out her mental state before you shagged her?'

'She seemed normal.'

'I'm sure she is. Greg, sex is important to women. If you do it with someone then they usually think it means something to you, that it's the start of something. She seemed nice enough. Now she's sat there wondering what went wrong and probably hating herself. And I've taken part in that. You've made me an accomplice in screwing over another woman.'

'I'm sorry.'

'You keep saying that, but then you keep doing it.' My anger was dwindling now I wasn't in front of a half-dressed woman with a comely figure and expensive haircut who couldn't help patronising me by simply opening her mouth. Besides, what's that saying? 'Who is more stupid? The man who jumps off the cliff or the person who follows him?' Who was more stupid in all this, the man who got laid or the celibate woman who came rushing in to rescue him? 'I hope the sex was good enough to warrant all that, Gregory.'

'It was pretty average, actually,' he said.

I tutted. 'You're unbelievable.'

'Sorry,' he said.

He came back to my place and to worm his way back into my affections cooked me dinner, bought a bottle of wine, washed up afterwards and kept flashing his big browns at me.

I would've carried on feeling wretched for how we treated Mimi if she hadn't written Renée a nine-page letter slagging me off, saying I was unprofessional, I'd treated her with contempt from the moment she stepped off the train, that I'd physically threatened her and she'd been receiving dodgy phone calls she was sure were from me. She also said if Renée wanted to avoid a scandal when she took me to court, she should sack me. Renée couldn't stop laughing when she got the letter and kept screaming, 'And listen to this . . .' (With hindsight I should've been offended that Renée didn't think me capable of such behaviour but back then I was just grateful she didn't sack me. The letter was also the final nail in Greg's bastard coffin as far as Renée and Martha were concerned – it was the worst thing he'd ever done and they'd never forgive him after this. Nope, they hadn't heard the police station story.)

And that was her, Mimi, on the phone now. 'How are you?' Mimi asked, acting as though we were friends.

'Fine,' I replied. 'I, erm, didn't catch your name.' An easy way to let someone know that all thought of them left your mind when they left your company is to pretend you don't know who they are.

'It's Mimi Verner.'

'Right. Who do you write for again?' Just in case she thought she was important enough in my life for me to remember who she writes for.

'*Viva.*'

'Oh, erm, yes. What can I do for you?'

'Well, I heard that,' she mentioned the name of a B-list celeb Renée was good friends with who would be opening the Festival in September, 'is coming to the Festival and I wanted to interview her. We worked so well together last time, I was hoping we could work together again.'

We talked the logistics over and, eventually, she decided not to come since the celeb's movie wouldn't be new enough for the magazine. 'Oh, do you see much of, erm, Greg?' she asked when it was clear I was about to say goodbye.

Sudden, spiteful anger surged through me. Like it did that night. Only this time, it was entangled with jealousy. That bitch had him before me (although, to be fair, most women have had him before me) and I didn't like it. Let's not forget, either, that she'd tried to get me sacked.

'Greg Walterson? The journalist?'

'Yes.'

'Yes, I see him quite a lot.'

'Through work?' she asked, not even bothering to hide the desperation in her voice.

'Yes, through work. And personally – we recently got married. Bye, then.'

I hung up and hopped off Renée's desk to find the pair of them staring at me with open mouths. I never lied like that unless it was in the name of work. And even then, I'd talk around the subject, not out-and-out lie.

'She pissed me off,' I explained.

They both gasped: nobody pissed me off to the point where I admitted it. Ever. I might internalise my anger, scowl about it or go for a long walk to ease my rage, but I never said I was pissed off. 'She said Leeds was a mini London!' I hissed.

'The bitch!' Martha snarled.

'The bastard!' Renée added. 'You should've said you and Greg had a baby.'

'Actually, no,' Martha said, 'you should've let her shag Greg again. That would've been punishment enough.'

Their laughter ricocheted off all the walls in the office, bruising my sensitive skin as it went through me. I returned to my desk, staring unseeingly at what I'd been writing on the computer screen.

I hope this isn't a sign. I hope this isn't Fate telling me something. Because goodness knows, Greg hasn't called me in three days.

chapter nine

crazy lady

I let myself into the flat, tossed my bunch of keys – house and office – with its big fish key fob onto the floor by the living room door, then stopped, went back, picked them up and slotted them into the door keyhole and locked it.

Then I did what I knew I shouldn't: I checked the answerphone. It answered me with a silent, still red light. I knew it wouldn't be flashing. Everyone with my home number called me at work during the day, meaning the red light wouldn't be flashing, but still, my chest sank. My whole body gave in to abject disappointment. He wasn't going to call me. Not now, not ever.

I went to the bedroom to change into my pyjamas for the Friday night ritual. Friday nights were made for lying on the sofa with my duvet, junk food and telly. Except last Friday night hadn't gone down like that at all, had it? And because of that, this Friday night was going to be long. The Long Night of Amber Salpone.

I tugged my purple, slash-neck top over my head. *This is why I'm single*, I reminded myself as I unhooked my black bra and slung it onto the laundry pile.

The real reason. Not the reason I trotted out when other women were talking about all the good men being taken, married, gay or complete bastards. The reason I was single and celibate, the reason I wasn't sure if I wanted to go out with Greg, the reason I wasn't sure if I wanted to go out with anyone was because I was insane at the start of relationships.

While other women got excited, giggly and full of hope for the future, I became a floor-pacing psychopath who's one step away from trying to get into my man's brain with a hacksaw. I lost all sense of reality when a man entered my life. I was literally stood at the precipice of an abyss of madness, a hair's breadth from pitching forwards into it.

During the first few weeks with a new man I started to obsess about every little thing connected with him. I'd be on the verge of calling him every two minutes 'just to say hi'; if he was a stockbroker, say, I'd start reading the financial newspapers even though I rarely read my bank statements. I would even try to find out all I could about him on the Internet.

It didn't end there. Oh, no, no, no. If he lived in Lady Wood, which is on the other side of Leeds to where I live, I'd get an A–Z out, work out the quickest routes, see which other streets were around him, check out house prices; I'd see signs that we were fated to be together in every little thing – 'Wow, the time on my bus ticket says 18:00 and I met him on the 1st August 2000, so we're destined to be together for ever.' That was on top of the time I spent wondering where he was, what he was doing, what he was thinking . . . I'd know I was doing it, would tell myself off for doing it, would remind myself women had died to get us the vote and I was being this pathetic, but couldn't find a way to stop myself.

I'd sometimes almost be physically sick because I was so unsure of where I stood. Wondering if I'd been traded in for someone else. It wasn't the being traded in, it was the not knowing if I'd been traded in. Not knowing that while I went happily about my daily business, he was lying beside some other woman and making plans for their future together. Twisted as it sounded, I'd rather know if someone was being unfaithful. Probably my biggest fear was being duped, someone getting me to trust them and then betraying me.

I'd survived one affair and, even though I was older and wiser now, I didn't want those emotions back.

I felt like that normally.

When it'd been three full days without so much as a text from Greg, I was on the verge of throwing up every three minutes. Especially after that call from Mad Mimi. *Did you truly expect anything better from him?* I asked myself. *Did you honestly expect texts and calls and emails reiterating how much he wanted to be with you?*

It niggled me to realise that yes, I did. I thought I was different. He'd seemed so genuine on Tuesday. *Convincing* . . . Spoken like every other woman who's watched some conman head off into the sunset with her life savings, best friend and dignity.

I dragged my duvet to the living room, dumped it on the sofa. Takeaway. Time to order a takeaway. Thai? Indian? Pizza? Chinese? Food. I had to eat. Something. Anything. My stomach twisted in on itself as I paced the living room floor.

Was he eating? Greg. Was he eating? Working? Sleeping? Fucking? What was he doing? I laid the palms of my hands on my stomach, trying to press away the churning. Trying to get rid of the insanity.

Sean, my last boyfriend, the one before I became single and celibate, was surprisingly tolerant of my insanity. He didn't know the half of it – I hid the crazy very well from him – he was just good about the bits I couldn't hide from him under my normal façade of cool, elegant indifference.' (Yes, all right, brain, it wasn't that funny.)

I'd met him when Renée and I went to talk to a computer company about sponsoring the Festival. The Festival was mainly funded by West Yorkshire Council, which is why we were located in West Yorkshire Council offices, but we had to get other cash to help it along. Renée, despite appearances to the contrary, was excellent at charming people into parting with their cash. She knew all the right things to say: what to promise; what to hint at promising.

I'd arranged this meeting and she'd come with me. As we sat down at the long oval meeting table, I had a surreptitious gander around the table and my eyes met Sean's. And stayed there. He wasn't take-your-breath-away gorgeous, but he had sparkle. When I glanced his way I saw sparkles. There are times when you see someone or something and you know you're going to have them. It's not lust; not 'I've got to have it or I'll die'; it simply is. This feeling, it only happens a couple of times in your life, I'm sure, but you and that person, or those shoes or that car click. It was meant for you. There was no justifying it, or trying to afford it. It was made for you. Which is why I saw sparkles when I looked at Sean. He was meant for me.

His butter-blond hair was cut very short, his dark hazel eyes stared at me under long eyelashes, his lips parted into a knee-weakening smile. We'd openly stared at each other, smiling as though we shared a private joke all the way through the meeting. I kicked myself later when I left without getting his full name. Or managing to project my phone number into his head. He was meant for me, after all. Two days later, when Jen, Matt and I went clubbing I'd bumped into someone. And there he was – Mr Sparkle from the meeting. For the first time ever I abandoned my friends and spent the rest of the night chatting with and snogging Sean. We'd agreed Fate had meant us to be together and, after a cab had dropped us off at our respective homes, we talked on the phone until the sun came up.

He didn't play games, either. He bloody called me. He

called me when he said he would, he called me when he hadn't said he would. We went out, we stayed in, we had great sex. It wasn't until the three-month mark that he found out why he shouldn't cross me. He was off, dismissive, with me twice on the phone and I shut down. Stopped taking his calls, didn't return his emails, ignored his texts. That's what I was like. When someone cooled off for no particular reason or even if they cooled off for a particular reason, I headed for the door at high speed. I ran out before they could. Sean, bless him, left me a long message saying he cared about me and didn't want to finish with me. And that he was sorry he'd been off that time, he'd just got scared that we were getting too serious too soon. And he wouldn't let me go without fighting for me, so I could ignore him, but if I still had any feelings for him it'd be easier all round to let him apologise face to face. Like I say, he was good. Had it been me, I would've blackened his name to anyone who'd listen, then plotted revenge.

I sat on the sofa with a cushion on my lap, my silver mobile nestling in the folds of the cushion. I twisted the corner of the blue cushion and stared at the phone, willing it to ring. Normal behaviour for me in the first three months of a relationship. But, rather unusually, I could feel bile rise from my stomach to my throat. *What the hell is Greg doing? Why give me that performance the other day and then completely blank me?*

Yes, he'd given me his black book and his mobile numbers, but that didn't stop women calling him. Inviting him over. Starting phone sex . . .

'STOP!' I screamed out loud. 'Stop it, stop it, stop it, stop it.' I picked up the video remote and pressed a button to rewind the video to watch the bits I'd missed, but nothing happened. I glanced down, I was trying to rewind the video with my mobile. My mobile felt nothing like the video remote. I hurled the stupid thing across the room. It glanced off the edge of the armchair and landed on Scooby Doo. (I admit it, I own cuddly toys. My name is Amber Salpone and I own cuddly toys. But they're hot-water bottle covers. And they are Scooby and Bagpuss. And I only have them because I get cold. A lot.) 'Don't you dare move,' I snarled at it. 'And heaven forbid you ring.' I started patting around my sofa for the proper remote control without taking my eyes off the screen.

Nothing. It was off on another of its jaunts. I moved the cushion off my lap to start scrabbling around for the remote.

After Sean, I'd decided to avoid relationships, to be single and celibate because I didn't need to do this any more. I didn't need to spend time obsessing about one particular person. I'd broken once when a photographer during the Festival last September made a pass at me in our press room at the hotel. He'd been all right and we had two illicit snogs in the press room. He'd asked me out to dinner after the Festival but I'd turned him down. I couldn't face this. The anxiety, the floor-pacing, the sickness, the fear – it was hard on my carpets.

Once I'd made my decision, I'd actually felt a weight lift from my shoulders, a mist dissipate from my eyes, a sea drain away from my brain. OK, I didn't feel the extremes of emotion, the rawness of human interaction that I got when I was with someone, but that was no bad thing. I was liberated. Free from being a slave to wanting a relationship. Or wondering if whenever I went out I might meet someone. The shackles of caring about finding someone were loosened from my wrists, ankles, neck and heart and I felt a million times lighter. Right up until this moment in time.

Greg had done all the chasing. He'd seduced me. He'd convinced me to give it a go with him. Now he was blanking me.

Before he'd left on Tuesday we'd made vague arrangements to meet up over the weekend. 'I'll call you about it,' were his last words as we kissed goodbye. And he hadn't. I could ring him, but why say it if he's not going to do it?

Lying on the sofa, I slipped my hand right down past the cushions, into the covered frame, hunting for the errant remote. Nothing. I started to withdraw my hand but couldn't. Perfect. Absolutely perfect. I tugged harder, feeling the pull in my wrist but not my hand release. I got up, hunched over my arm so I could get more traction behind it as I pulled. I pulled again. Nada. Nothing. My hand wouldn't budge. It was probably swelling up as I tried to free it.

That's it, I'll be stuck here for the rest of my life. My mobile's halfway across the room, I can't ring for help. My neighbours have gone away, so I can't yell for help. I'm going to die of thirst. And, aaahhhh!, there's the loo. I shouldn't have thought that, now I need to go. Desperately. What the hell a—

RING-RING! My home phone. I tugged my hand.

The phone rang again, I tugged at my hand again. Harder this time. So hard my hand came out and I toppled back off the sofa and landed on the floor as the phone rang a third time. Lying on my back, I reached out and picked up the phone, put it to my ear.

' All right, so I gave in first,' Greg whispered.

Between deep, winded breaths, I said, 'What do you mean?'

'I've been waiting for you to call,' he whispered.

'Oh,' I replied.

'So . . .' he said, still in hushed tones.

'So . . . What?'

'Why didn't you call me?'

'You said you'd call when you left on Tuesday.'

'Yes, but as far as I know you were pressurised into everything. I was hoping you'd call so I'd know you were into this,' he said, still whispering.

'Where are you?' I asked, wondering why he was whispering.

'At home, helping Matt to pack.'

'So why are you whispering?'

'I don't want Matt to hear. He's been on at me to call my mystery woman because I've been in such a filthy mood since I last saw her, and I didn't want him to guess it was you.'

'As long as you're not whispering because you've got some woman sleeping in your bed.'

The line crackled with his silence. 'Is that why you haven't called me? Because you think I've been up to my old tricks?' he eventually asked.

The way he said it made it seem unreasonable to think that. 'How many women have you flirted with in the past three days?' I asked, neatly evading the question. 'And that includes people who've come on to you first and you've responded to.'

Greg paused. Then paused some more. Then paused some more after that. 'Define flirted with.'

' All right, I know you're an incurable flirt. How many women in the past few days have you given the impression to that you'd at least snog them, if not sleep with them?'

Another pause.

My heart sank.

'Old habits die hard, Amber,' he said, 'but now we're together, I won't act on any of those habits.'

'OK,' I replied, half-heartedly. This was going to be a nightmare. I, paranoid, obsessively jealous, I, had hooked up with a man who'd single-handedly kept Durex in business for the past five years. Maybe I should end it now before he shags someone else and I'm forced to have him killed.

'I'm serious,' he was saying, 'I'm serious about us. I want to do this. Do you?'

Sure, make out I've got the problem when you're the one incapable of concentrating on one person. 'Mm-hm,' I replied.

I could hear him grin down the phone. 'All right! All-right!' he almost screeched, then he lowered his voice. 'I'll see you tomorrow? I'll pick you up at eleven o'clock in the van, then after we've helped Matt to move we can go off and do our own thing. OK?'

'OK,' I replied.

'Cool, talk to you tomorrow, sweetie. Bye.'

Two things occurred to me as I put down the phone:

1. I liked the easy way Greg called me sweetie. 'Sweet'tee.' It slipped tenderly from his tongue into my ears.
2. When the hell had I said I'd help Matt move?

'Oh, put that box . . .' Jen stood in the middle of her wide hall-way and spun around, uming and ahhhing. Meanwhile, my arms were headed southward.

'Ohhh . . . I don't know,' Jen conceded. 'Matt? Matt!'

'What?' Matt called from the recesses of the bedroom.

'Where do you want to put this box?' she shouted.

'Um . . .' he called back.

I held a big red plastic box of issues of a tabloid paper that Matt had accumulated over the years. He'd kept the issues published on his birthday since he was twelve, plus special occasions like the Millennium, Euros '96 and 2000, and the World Cups. And, I'm sure he thought he was being very clever, he'd hidden his porn mags inside most of the copies. Ironic? Possibly. Sleazy? Definitely. I'd discovered his 'plan' earlier when one of the newspapers had toppled out of the box. I'd gingerly slipped the thing back into its hiding place, scared of where it'd been – and what had been on it. If Matt wanted to read porn, fine. If Matt wanted to 'use' porn, his choice. But to be so sneaky about it . . . well, as I said, sleazy. Especially when Jen had an open mind about such things. Even if he thought she'd freak, all he had to do was chuck out the old lot and buy new ones. Probably a bit too complicated for Matt, though. *Now, that wasn't very nice, was it, Amber?*

I pushed my mind elsewhere, trying to ignore the pain this deceptively heavy box was inflicting on me.

What an odd foursome we are, I thought. We were meant to be close in our quartet, but Greg was skulking around, acting as if the world was over because his best mate was moving out. No matter what I said, or how pleased he acted, he was one step away from committing hara-kiri.

Matt didn't know his girlfriend well enough to know she wouldn't mind if he read porn so he sneaked it into her house.

Jen still hadn't told Matt that the last man she'd lived with, Tommy, had been calling her and asking to see her again and, whilst she hadn't exactly said yes, she hadn't exactly said no. She wouldn't ever cheat on Matt, she just enjoyed the extra attention.

And, of course, I'd kept the biggest thing since Sean from Jen.

'Coming through,' Greg called, butting me lightly with the boxes he had in his arms.

''Aven't decided on the cuttings yet, mate, so your stuff will 'ave ta wait,' I said over my shoulder, affecting a Sarf London removal man's voice.

'Piss poor,' Greg said, mimicking my accent but not quite getting there with his Yorkshire accent. 'Would it be a crime to put 'em down in 't 'all?'

'Soz, mate, laydee says she don't *wont* 'er new floorboards scratched.'

'Sod this,' Greg said. 'OI, MEATHEAD. COME SORT OUT YOUR STUFF OR ME AND NECTAR ARE WALKING.'

As if by magic, the movee appeared. Greg knew him so well – the thought of having to unload the transit van himself had stopped him arranging his shoes in order of purchase or something equally anal but important to him. Matt flushed a shade of crimson when he saw what I was holding and almost broke his leg running to relieve me of it.

'Cheers, m'dear,' I said, 'that was giving me arm-ache. Something I'm sure you'd know all about with that box.' Matt pinked up even more. I stretched my fingers, trying to get the circulation going again.

'I think Amber's trying to tell you something,' Jen said, smudging Matt's cheek with a kiss. 'Mr Shirker.'

'DOES ANYONE CARE THAT MY ARMS ARE DROPPING OFF HERE?' Greg bellowed so unexpectedly I jumped.

'Oh for goodness sake,' I said, spun to him and relieved him of the box on top – then almost dropped it under the sudden weight. Didn't realise Greg was so strong. His biceps, exposed in his grey marl T-shirt, rippled under his browned, freckled skin, the dark brown hairs on his sculptured forearms glinted slightly in the unexpected sun of this February day. I glanced up from his arms to his face. Locks of his black hair were plastered to his damp forehead. *Boy, he's attractive*, I thought.

I always knew that, but this wasn't the same. My body, blood and hormones had suddenly clicked with his. I'd seen him for three years and thought he was gorgeous; I'd had sex with him and it'd been out of this world. But it was only at this moment that I started to fancy him. Independently of what was going on between us. It was simple, plain, pure attraction. I wanted this man. Badly.

His eyes watched me watch him and he asked, 'What's wrong?' with his eyes and face.

My lips slipped into a slight smile. Nothing was wrong. Everything was different, that's all.

The box weighing down my arms, I turned back to Matt and Jen – they were snogging the faces off each other, Matt's porn box between.

'Get a hotel room – or move in together, but do it quick because my arms are killing me,' I joked.

I sneaked an 'Aren't they cute?' look at Greg. He'd gone. He'd wantonly dumped the box of videos on the newly floor-boarded hallway and was halfway up the path to the van, rubbing the back of his head with the flat of his hand.

One 'move' later, we all flopped onto the large leather sofa, except for Greg, who was incapable of flopping. If the words 'tense' could be personified, it would be him. Every part of him was rigid – even his liquorice hair was clenched. So, while we all virtually lay on the sofa, he sat forwards in the armchair, poised to jump up and run out at a microsecond's notice.

Jen eventually hoisted herself out of the sofa, left the room, then returned with a bottle of champagne, and four champagne flutes. She handed a glass to each of us, then gave Matt the bottle to open.

'So,' Jen said, flopping down between Matt and me once our glasses were filled, 'let's make a toast.' We raised our glasses. 'To new beginnings for me and Matt . . . and to you two finding special someones too.'

'Cheers,' we all said and took a sip – except Greg who just held his glass up.

'Yup, let's hope you two meet special someones too,' Matt said, with a sly peek at Greg that was so unsubtle their upstairs neighbour probably saw it.

'All right, Matt, that's it!' Jen said. 'Why, whenever I say something about either of those two meeting someone special, do you look at Greg? You were doing it on Monday, too.'

'What?' Matt replied.

My heart left my chest and lodged itself in my throat.

'I'm not stupid, Matthew, I've noticed the looks you give Greg. Something's going on. And *I*, no,' Jen linked arms with me, '*we* want to know what it is.'

I know what it is, my tongue tried to say. I clamped my teeth together to stop it confessing everything.

Matt, meanwhile, had gone into rabbit-caught-in-headlights mode and stared at Greg. Greg, the only one unbothered by Jen's demand, shrugged casually. 'I've met someone.'

'No!!' Jen shrieked. 'When? Where? How?'

'Yes!!' Greg shrieked back, mocking Jen by matching her tone. 'About a week ago! Leeds! Through work!'

'And . . .' Jen hurried.

Greg shrugged. 'It's going well.'

Jen cuffed Matt around the ear. 'I can't believe you didn't tell me.'

'He made me promise,' Matt pleaded.

Jen's face showed her displeasure at being left out of the loop. The urge to throw myself on her mercy surfaced again.

'So, what's she like?' Jen asked.

Greg shrugged again. 'Like a woman.'

'Come on, Walterson! More. I want details. What's she like?'

'OK. Details,' Greg said as his face split into a smile that could only have been conjured up by the devil himself. He was going to tell the truth. He was going to tell the truth and get me into the biggest trouble I've been in since I was twelve and broke Eric's Action Man on purpose. Had we been in a film, I'd be leaping across the room in slow motion screaming: 'NOOOOOO!!!' right about now.

'She's average-looking . . .' *EXCUSE ME?! You are so going to get a kicking*, I telepathically said to him. 'You know, hair, two eyes, nose, mouth. And she's got the most *amazing* body, all curves and smooth skin . . .' *All right, you made that sound lascivious enough to rescind that kicking.* 'Um . . . She's all the usual stuff, clever, funny, thoughtful, friendly, etc., etc. I don't know. I can't put it into words without diminishing what I feel. She's whole. But not. Hypnotic.'

That was me he was talking about. Me. Amber Salpone. *Hypnotic*. I fingered the word in my head. *Hypnotic*. I liked that. Liked the feel, the touch, the essence of what he was saying.

I swallowed the lump in my throat. Found I couldn't and swallowed harder to get rid of it, dipped my head to secretly blink dry my teared-up eyes. How pathetic was I? All he'd said was . . . I blinked harder.

'What makes her different from all the other girls you've screwed, then screwed over?' Jen asked, destroying the reverential atmosphere.

Hurt flashed across Greg's face. 'I don't know, she's different. I adore everything about her,' he said. 'She's everything I ever wanted in a girlfriend and everything I didn't know I needed in a girlfriend, too.'

'You've only known her a week,' Jen scoffed.

'I only got together with her a week ago. Our paths have crossed before, but it was only last week that I finally got her interested.'

Jen turned to me. 'Did you know about this?'

'Not, erm, until recently. Very, very recently.' Not a lie, just not the complete truth.

'I'm literally the last to know,' Jen said. She crossed her arms, sat back, stuck out her bottom lip.

'He didn't tell me he felt like that,' I protested.

'Me neither,' Matt said.

'You obviously have a way of bringing out the poet in him,' I said.

'Hmmm, maybe. But I can't believe he feels like that after a week.'

'Thing is –' Matt started.

'Can everyone stop talking about me like I'm not here, and stop acting like I'm incapable of feeling anything other than lust,' Greg snapped. 'I feel a lot for her but it's only been

102

a week. I want to keep it low-key, but rest assured I'll keep you all posted on any developments.' Greg put his champagne glass on the floor beside his foot. He hadn't taken a sip, nor put the glass near his mouth – he wasn't even going to pretend to celebrate. 'H'OK.' He leapt out of the leather armchair. 'I've got plans, so I'm off. Amber, can I give you a lift?'

'Nah, Amber's staying for dinner,' Jen said.

This was news to me. 'Sorry?' I turned to Jen. She flushed. Matt, knackered as he was, was suddenly on his feet, moving around the living room, straightening his stuff on the mantelpiece, doing something. Anything.

'One of our friends is single,' Jen said, 'and, erm, he's really, really nice, so we thought we'd invite him over for dinner tonight to meet you.'

She made it sound like this was no 'biggie'. Like I should simply slot myself into her plans to pair me off. It would be her plan too: Matt was the epitome of the selfish gene, he didn't give a flying toffee if I was single or attached. It didn't affect his life, so he didn't think about it.

Whereas Jen . . . During my celibacy she'd been doing all she could to pair me off with the ugliest blokes on earth. Anyone who says looks don't matter is lying. Looks are important – if they weren't we wouldn't spend so much time dressing up and slathering on make-up and fixing our hair – we all just happen to find different things attractive. Physical beauty that could lead to anything romantic for me was inextricably linked to someone's personality. To their ability to capture and communicate with my mind, imagination and sense of humour. To conjure up a spark of recognition. There was this thing I read once that said love is recognising ourselves in someone else and delighting in that recognition. And that was what was galling about the people Jen set me up with – she'd known me for about twelve years and she still thought I could even think

103

about kissing someone who started a joke, 'There was this Englishman, Irishman and black man . . .' Without exception they were all lacking in anything I could work with. I'd tried, honestly I had, then I gave up all pretence of caring what any of them thought or said. Any blind date disguised as a dinner party she'd arranged resulted in me getting openly drunk rather than talking, and staggering off home before dessert. After I left during the main meal last time, she had, for the most part, stopped doing it.

Having said that, on those occasions when she did stitch me up, she'd at least warned me we were having dinner. I wasn't sat in sweat-dried clothes with frizzed-up hair and aching muscles.

A mist descended upon my body, seeping into my aching muscles, swelling the veins in my brain and speeding up my heart.

Who the hell is she to decide who I should date?

This was it. She was going to get the full length of my tongue this time. I'd reached the end of my tether when it came to Jen and blind dates. Shouting wasn't part of the Amber Salpone repertoire of response to anger: the only person I'd ever shouted at was Greg and that was generally after a rescue that had enraged me to the point of me wanting to lash out at him. But I'd never shouted at Jen. I'd come close to it a couple of times, of course, but not actually done it. I'd seen, over the years, that when someone shouted at Jen it produced a steely determination that flashed first in her eyes, then resulted in her screwing said person over weeks, sometimes months, down the line. Sarcasm and snapping, I'd found, yielded the best results. However, this time, sod sarcasm and snapping – she was getting the full extension of my lungs.

I opened my mouth to scream that I was Greg's 'hypnotic' woman; to yell, 'I'm worth much more than the idiots you feel obliged to set me up with.'

'Didn't you say you were meeting people in town?' Greg interjected.

'Oh?' Jen was surprised.

'Yes, Jen, I have a life,' I went to say.

'Yeah, come on, Nectar,' Greg cut in. 'I'll drive you home so you can get tarted up. And if you don't take forever, I'll drop you off afterwards.'

Greg took my hand then pulled me out of the chair, bundled me out of the living room and then out of the flat. I realised two miles down the road I hadn't said a word after 'Sorry?' Greg had not only saved Jen from a mouthful, he'd virtually raised my hand and waved it at them.

chapter ten

the honesty clause

'Do you mind if we stop at mine on the way back?' Greg asked as we hit Headingley, on the way to my place. Traffic seemed to have appeared from nowhere, we'd been bumper to bumper with a green Mini for about, oooh, forever. The silence in the van's cabin and my nefarious mood brought on by the blind date hadn't helped the appearance of time crawling by.

'Course, why would you be any different to every other person trying to run my life?' I snapped.

My new lover took a deep, deep breath, then exhaled at length. 'We could spend the evening there now Matt's gone,' he continued, clearly not about to be drawn into a row he hadn't started. 'Rocky's away with his girlfriend. We've the house to ourselves.'

OK, *it's not Greg's fault my best mate has issues with me being single. It's not Greg's fault I haven't got around to telling Jen where to shove her blind dates*, I reminded myself. 'All right, but let's not stay over – I know how toxic your bedroom is.'

'I tidied up a bit,' he said, 'just in case.'

Greg had lived with Matt and Rocky since they'd moved out of halls in the second year of college about ten years ago. After they graduated, Rocky's parents had bought the house for him. This meant Rocky and Greg and Matt could do it up as they saw fit. Greg had painted his bedroom white, put pictures of scantily clad women on the walls, moved a double bed in and basically used the floor to file his books, clothes, magazines, papers, shoes, videos, DVDs, CDs, etc. I'd been in there a few times and while he'd picked a path across the carnage littering the floor, I'd stood in one spot, too scared to move in case I caught something. Greg had once explained that he kept his room in a state because it kept women away – at no point would he be tempted to invite one back. His room was his palace, his castle, his sanctuary, and he avoided letting any woman in there to sleep over or even to have sex because that would mean she had a bit more of him. She could get up and run her finger along his dusty shelves, see which books he had, which books were most battered, most thumbed. She could open drawers, see where he kept his pants, where he kept his T-shirts, how he rolled up his socks. Greg's room was a no-woman zone and he'd done his best to keep it that way. That's why I'd said not to stay over, I was giving him a way of rejecting me without rejecting me.

'Do you fancy a takeaway?' Greg said as he undid the deadlock on his blue front door. 'Or I'll cook something.' He slid his key into the Yale lock.

'I don't mind,' I replied.

'Why don't you put your bag and coat in my room while I get us some beers.' Greg tossed the van keys onto the little wooden table beside the door and wandered towards the kitchen without offering me so much as a cuddle. He wasn't going to be drawn into a row and he obviously wasn't going to snog me, either.

I climbed the steep, narrow stairs, each one covered in a hideous red and blue Paisley carpet that Rocky's mum had chosen, but the lads had been too lame to argue with her about. At the top I took a right to Greg's room. He'd got the biggest room when they'd tossed for it. I assumed they meant tossed a coin, but seeing as there were three of them and two sides to a coin . . . well, I didn't like to think it through too deeply.

In the past few years Rocky had converted the attic into his bedroom and the bathroom was moved up from the basement to his old bedroom. The basement then became the boys' playroom with a snooker table, dartboard, cards table and small fridge with nothing but beer in it. Anyone else would've rented out the room – Rocky, Matt and Greg wanted a playroom. They lived such masculine lives I still maintained it a modern miracle that any of them had girlfriends.

I opened the door of Greg's room, stood in the doorway, dropped my black rucksack, then stopped in the middle of slipping off my jacket. Slowly, my mouth fell open. Greg *had* tidied up. The floor was clear, all the pictures of airbrushed women had been taken down, each surface had been polished. The bed was made with pure white bedlinen and he'd sprinkled red and pink rose petals on top. Around the room, draped on the bookcases, along the mantelpiece and around the window sill were fairy lights.

The whole thing was dressed up like something from a movie. It put me in mind of that moment in a romantic comedy when the hero wins the heart of every woman in the audience by doing something like converting his meagre accommodation into a fairy grotto or selling his prized possession so he can be with the heroine for ever and ever. I'd never fallen for such acts in films. *What man would waste his time doing all that,* I used to think, *when he knows he's going to get laid anyway?* This one, obviously.

'Do you like it?' Greg whispered, coming up behind me and enveloping me in his arms. The tug in my body, the physical manifestation of fancying him, surged through me again. He drew slow circles on my abdomen and each stroke made my body tug harder.

I nodded, unable to speak because the lump had returned to my throat. If he kept this up I could grow to feel more than 'fancy' about him. A lot more. And that would mean . . .

Are you sure you want to do this? I asked myself. This is another step along that road to the unknown. *Are you sure you want to start down there?*

In our fairy-lit room we lay entwined, laughing, giggling, chatting quietly like two people in a movie – all we lacked was a strategically placed sheet. I was calm and warm and satisfied. He was like a fleece blanket in which I'd been wrapped up. My usually frantic brain was at rest. I wasn't thinking about shopping, or cleaning, or work, or joining a gym, or visiting my family . . . I was in the here and now.

Greg stroked my cheek so softly it was how I'd imagined a butterfly's wing would feel, a whisper of a touch. 'Are you asleep?' he asked.

'Not quite,' I murmured back.

'Do you want to talk?'

'We are talking,' I said, my eyes closed.

'I mean talk about stuff.'

'Like what?' I mumbled, allowing sleep to seep into my senses.

'You, um, know everything about my past, but I know virtually nothing about yours. Like how many people you've slept with.'

'More than ten, less than twenty-two,' I mumbled, my stock answer.

'Or why your last relationship ended.'

'Mmmmm . . .'

'So . . . why did your last relationship end?' Greg prompted.

'Hmmm,' I said, trying to concentrate. 'Ummm, *Jackie Brown.*'

'What?' Greg said, knocking silk rose petals onto the floor as he sat up.

I exhaled in frustration. *Now* I was awake. 'All right, you tell me who my last relationship was with, and I'll tell you why it ended.'

'Um . . . I remember a few months after Jen and Matt got together you weren't around as much because you had a boyfriend. And I know he didn't particularly like me because we were friends. But I never knew who he was.'

Didn't particularly like you? I thought. *That's like saying the Grand Canyon is a pin-prick in the desert.* Sean *hated* Greg. Not 'didn't like' or 'resented' – full-blooded, eye-narrowing, muscle-clenching hatred. I didn't know it was possible to hate a person that much if you haven't met them (apart from me and Tom Cruise, but that's different). But Sean was living proof. He refused to meet Greg, not even so he could put a face to his hatred ('Why would I want to meet that tosser?' was his usual refrain) and became moody every time I met with Greg – even if Jen and Matt were going to be there. 'I can tell he fancies you from the way he leaves messages on your answerphone,' Sean constantly complained. Never mind I'd told him a million times I didn't fancy Greg back.

Greg didn't help matters. One time he'd walked in on me getting changed at Jen's flat and got a flash of bare back, maybe a bit of bum and thigh, nothing more. Greg, in his infinite humour, rang my answerphone and sang 'The Thong Song' (I didn't wear thongs, but there weren't any songs that said, 'Let me see those sensible black pants') into it. I'd innocently played the message when Sean was there and felt the temperature in the room plummet. Sean's soft features had hardened as he gritted his teeth, a muscle pulsating in his neck. Some bloke wanting to see your girlfriend's pants wasn't funny, especially when you hated the bloke doing the asking. I dived for the delete button and erased all evidence of Greg being interested in my underwear. 'If he touches you, I'll kill him,' Sean said in that scary tone gangsters in *The*

Godfather employ right before they sanction the murdering of someone's kin.

'But you were my friend, you were supposed to show an interest,' I said to Greg in the here and now.

'I was interested but I sort of fancied you, so didn't want to know about you and another bloke, I couldn't handle it.'

'Why do you want to know now?'

'You're my girlfriend, I can handle it,' he replied. Then added quietly: 'Mostly.'

'Do we have to talk about this now?' I said.

'Yes. Tell me why it ended and I'll drop it.'

I sighed. 'I told you. *Jackie Brown*.'

'Is she a real person?'

'No. The film. That piece of filth nonsense by Quentin Tarantino called *Jackie Brown*,' I hissed. I paused, waiting for the heavens to come crashing in. 'Wow! I said something by Tarantino was rubbish and the world didn't end.'

Greg's face fell. 'But, *Pulp Fiction*—'

'Had a horrific rape scene that didn't need to be in it,' I cut in before I got a thesis on how amazingly postmodern it was. I'd heard all arguments on that film from people inside and outside the industry and not one of them had managed to convince me that it or Tarantino was a genius. Just because something was postmodern didn't stop it from being crap. 'Everyone seems to think if you're young and into film, you have to like Tarantino. Well, Sean – my boyfriend you didn't want to know about because you sort of fancied me – thought that Tarantino was God and that *Jackie Brown* was something akin to the Holy Grail.

'And that's fair enough. Everyone is entitled to their own opinion, even if it's wrong. Except I told Sean what I thought so, the day he brought that film to my flat, I flipped. I said not to put it near my video, and he flipped in return. By the time he'd finished having a go at me, I was the Antichrist, I was crap

111

in bed and I'd always be alone. And that's why my relationship ended, because of *Jackie Brown*.'

'Did you talk much about getting back together?'

'After that day, we never spoke again.'

'What, not at all?'

'Not at all.'

'Do you think he used *Jackie Brown* as an excuse to chuck you?'

'To be honest, I try not to think about it, what with it being such a bloody stupid reason to break up and all.'

'So, if he wanted you back, what would you say?'

'We split up eighteen months ago, if he wanted me back, he'd have said something by now.'

'No, but just say he did?'

'He w—'

'I want to know.'

I was reaching for the sarky answer, the one I'd normally give to Greg, my mate, when I caught his expression as reflections of the fairy lights twinkled in his eyes. He was worried. It hit me as hard as a lorry, he was genuinely scared. Maybe he didn't think he'd be able to compete with someone from my past. Maybe he feared the idea of Sean being The One That Got Away. Whatever it was, he was scared. It wasn't an emotion I'd ever associated with him when it came to women, but he was. He was, and I couldn't add to that by being sarky. Besides, he was Greg, my lover, only sadistic bastards messed with their lover's emotions.

'I'd say, "Go back to *Jackie Brown*, boy."'

Greg physically relaxed. 'Come here,' he whispered, pulling me close and pressing his lips against my forehead. He then kissed me on the lips before snuggling back against the pillows and closing his eyes. That was all he needed to hear – that I wasn't hankering after something from the past.

I listened to his breathing as it slowed and slowed the closer he got to sleep. His hold around me loosened slightly as he finally succumbed to slumber.

I wasn't sleepy any more. I was wide awake. The fairy lights were still on. *How can I slip out of his arms without waking him and turn them off before I go to sleep? Sleep? Like I can sleep now,* I thought. *I wish Greg hadn't dragged all that stuff out of me. Why did he have to bring up Sean? When things were so perfect, he had to bring up Sean. It'd meant I had to, well, not lie, lie. Just be economical with the truth.*

Greg wouldn't be able to handle the truth. It was for his sake that I omitted a few details about Sean and me. They were salient details, but I did it for him. To protect him.

All right, so the lady doth protest too much. But it really was for the greater good.

'when you buy
chocolate you're
buying yourself a new
best friend'

chapter eleven

the thing about cannes

'I'm not going and that's final.'

'You are!'

I could hear Martha and Renée from the far end of the corridor. In fact, the second I stepped out of the lift, I heard Martha's Yorkshire accent 'explaining' that she wasn't open to the idea Renée had put to her, and Renée's Yorkshire-tinged French accent trying to 'persuade' her into it. I spun on my heels to get back in the lift.

Unfortunately, the lift doors closed in my face.

My heart plummeted and settled around my ankles as I approached the office. I didn't need a calendar to work out what time of the year it was. It'd started. The annual row that was who was going to Cannes.

'It's not in my job description. I am the administrator,' Martha shouted like a teenager telling her parents she'd go out with whoever she liked. 'I keep an eye on the accounts, I run the office, I tell you which films you can afford, I tell you how much you can spend on the brochure. Nowhere does it say I have to go to Cannes.'

See?

I slowed my walk.

'It says in your contract that you have to do whatever extra duties we decide,' Renée replied in the manner of a parent telling her daughter as long as she lived under her roof she'd do as she was told.

I paused beside the office next to ours so neither of them could see me. God knows what the people in the other two offices on this floor thought of the constant screaming that emanated from our office.

I hated rows. Even from a voyeuristic angle. *Particularly* from a voyeuristic angle. Arguments took me right back to being a girl. To what rowing meant. I couldn't stand to listen to raised voices, unnecessary insults, words being scalded as they were issued. Waiting, just waiting for that one insult too far; that word that would send someone over the edge . . .

Renée loved arguing. I was convinced she had employed Martha because Martha had 'bring it on' written all over her and I wouldn't give her the rows she wanted. If Renée went off on one, I'd say nothing 'til she finished. I'd say nothing when she finished. My basic plan of action was waiting for Renée's temper to blow itself out, which it inevitably did.

Martha, on the other hand . . . Martha had an aggressive streak a mile wide. She'd worked with WYIFF for about twenty-one months and not one of those months had gone by without her and Renée having some kind of throw-down moment, where one of them would literally throw down the gauntlet and a big fight would follow. When they started, it'd be my job to stop them. Calm them down, play best mate to both of them, reassure them they were both right, agree the other was a bitch who really did deserve to have her hair ripped out from the roots, dispense tea and biscuits. Those were the big rows, every week they had some kind of spat. Even during Martha's three-month probationary period she'd rowed with Renée, which was incredible to me. You've just started a new job, you could get fired at a week's notice, so what do you do? Tell your boss to piss off at every given opportunity, of course. Still, she'd got the job so it worked for her.

I leant against the wall, started to gnaw on the edge of my thumbnail.

To be fair, though, this wasn't just their argument – it'd gone on for all the eleven years I'd been involved with the Festival.

The Cannes Film Festival (Cannes, to those of us in the industry) seemed so glamorous when you first started working at the Festival that you never understood why nobody wanted to go. You got up close to all those actors, writers and directors. You sometimes got to be in the same picture as Denzil Washington or Susan Sarandon. That's what working in the movie industry was all about, no? When you actually went . . . Put it this way, the first year I attended, I'd arrived with sunglasses and summer clothes packed, a script and a novel to read, plus a guidebook to see some sights when I wasn't working . . .

I soon discovered it wasn't all press conferences, premiere screenings and walking around on the Riviera *being* important. It was nine days of no-sleep, arse-kissing, abuse-receiving (*West who? Film Festival*) hell. You had to go to as many screenings as possible and a lot of the ones we'd be likely to show were late-night screenings. You had to schmooze people who hadn't heard of West Yorkshire, let alone thought about attending your Festival.

Plus, you had to phone in a report to the office so they could update the Festival newsletter, which was printed three times during Cannes instead of once a fortnight. That was pre-Internet. Now we had our website, you had to phone in the report whenever anything even vaguely interesting happened so the website could be updated daily, or sometimes hourly (who said the Net made life easy?).

The first year I went I hardly saw my hotel room; I was

competing with the London Film Festival (which people *had* heard of) and I could hardly form sentences while I gave the news reports on the phone.

I'd cried all the way home from the airport because exhaustion seemed to fill every sense, every muscle. Even my blood vessels seemed compressed by weariness. Worse, I knew I wouldn't be able to sleep because I was so tired and that thought distressed me to tears. The taxi driver asked me what was wrong, expecting to hear I'd been chucked by my boyfriend, and I'd sobbed, 'I'm really tired.' He'd given me a look as if to say, 'Is that it?' and I'd forlornly nodded in reply.

We'd unofficially been taking it in turns to go since I became full-time and, since I'd gone last year, unofficially it was Renée's turn – which was obviously why she was officially trying to foist it onto Martha.

I could see Martha's point: it wasn't in her job description. And it wasn't in her life description, either. She liked her existence with her boyfriend and her run-ins with Renée and telling us off if we spent too much. She put in extra time and effort during the Festival, but she was on her home turf. She knew what she was doing and had a support network around her (I also had a sixth sense for when she was about to punch someone for giving her attitude and stepped in). Martha hadn't become an administrator so she could go around kissing arse.

When Martha had come in for her interview she'd been wearing a smart white blouse and a black skirt suit. Her shoulder-length brown hair had been combed with a side parting and she carried a briefcase. I knew instantly that she was fruit and nut chocolate. Something reliable, an old favourite you liked having around. She'd always be on your favourite list of confectionery, you'd always think of her if you were having a party or needed someone to talk to. She was unpretentious, like the chocolate, and sweet, like the raisins, in a fruit and nut. But Martha had an excess of nuts, the hard bits you weren't expecting to encounter when you were chillin'. The nut you could break your tooth on if you pushed it. You found that out very quickly because with Martha what you saw was what you got.

Martha liked her life as it was and no group of international stars was going to change that.

Having said that, the way Renée was at the moment we could end up with an international incident on our hands if *she* went. I could see it now: someone from the London Film Festival gets to Julia Roberts first and Renée pulls out a huge *Fatal Attraction*-type knife and starts hacking indiscriminately.

The only alternative was that I go. Which was not going to happen.

'I can hear you two all the way down the corridor,' I said, entering the office at a brisk, no-nonsense pace that belied the panic inside. I always stepped in when they kicked off, but it terrified me. 'What's going on?'

'I'm not going to Cannes, that's what's going on,' Martha said and folded her arms. The matter was closed.

'I've been to Cannes more than anyone else and I'm fed up of it,' Renée replied and crossed her arms. The matter was definitely closed.

I glanced from one to the other. 'I'll put the kettle on,' I said, dumping my bag and coat on my desk.

I'm not going, I thought, as I filled the kettle. Ordinarily, yeah, I'd go. I'd done it before. The year before last I'd gone because we had a Festival Assistant as well as Martha and nobody would stop screaming about how they weren't going. I'd sat there and listened and listened and listened until I couldn't take it any more. I'd been the year before that already, but I'd stood up and said, 'I'll go. I'm not doing anything, I'll go.' I'd gone. And had another cry on the way home from the airport. It'd been the same taxi driver. He'd given me a look that said, 'Tired?' and I'd nodded forlornly again.

121

Sean, who I was going out with at the time, had been majorly pissed off since he knew it wasn't my turn. 'You let them take advantage of you,' he'd grumbled before sulking the evening away. He'd obviously been overjoyed when, on the morning I got back, I trailed across town to get Greg out of the police station.

Like I said, normally, I'd go. But this year, I had Greg and I didn't want to leave him. Not for a whole week. By the time Cannes arrived it, us, would've been three months and I didn't want to leave him.

It wouldn't simply be a case of missing him – which I would – I, well, I didn't want to give him the chance to find someone else. Going to Cannes for nine days equalled nearly eleven days of Greg being surrounded by sexy, confident, 'get what I want' women. That was eleven days of not spending the night with me, or calling me 'til the wee small hours. By the end of it, I'd have an ulcer the size of Nebraska and only tufts of hair on my head from where I'd have ripped it out in frustration. Basically, it was not going to happen.

'OK,' I said, coming back to the office and setting down a tea for Martha; a coffee for Renée.

'Someone's got to go to Cannes,' I said, pulling up a chair between Martha and Renée's desk at the middle point. Martha was staring fixedly out of the window, her arms folded tightly across her chest. Renée was also staring out of the window, her arms crossed just as tightly.

'Renée, I know you've been most out of us because you went even before you were Festival Director. So, yes, you've got six-odd years on the rest of us.'

I could hear Martha's teeth starting to grind together. That nut was limbering up to break a couple of my teeth.

'But, Martha, I know it's not in your job description and I know you hate all that negotiating and networking stuff. But someone's got to go.'

122

This is the point where I usually say, 'So, I'll go.' I swivelled to Renée. My heart started to pummel itself against my ribcage; if I didn't pitch this right that iMac was going out of the window and I'd be following it. 'So, what if you take your husband, Renée?'

'We haven't got the budget for it,' Martha said.

Cheeky cow. If you're not careful, I'll fabricate a sponsorship meeting and leave you to it.

'What I mean is, why don't you take your husband and make it a holiday? He's a scriptwriter, he's written stuff for the newsletter and the website so you could share the screenings and events you go to. It might even help him get funding for his next script. I'm sure we can stretch to you having a double room for nine days. And then, afterwards, you can go off and see some family in Paris or something. So, really, you can have three weeks off work. Three weeks. Off work. In France. The country of your birth . . .'

No computers were being hurled, yet.

'And we can have a double room?' Renée said eventually.

Martha, fruit and nut administrator extraordinaire, went to protest. I could see it in the way she moved her face. I raised an eyebrow at her that said, '*We go over budget or you go to Cannes. Your choice.*'

'Yes, you can have a double room,' Martha conceded.

'And you'll make Josh go to screenings?' Renée asked. Like she didn't rule Josh with a rod of iron anyway.

'Yup,' I said. 'I'll talk to Josh. I'll write him a full brief, OK?'

Renée left the air in the office straining under expectation. We were both holding our breath as we waited for her decision. She was totally doing it on purpose. She knew a lot about dramatic tension and she wasn't going to agree or disagree without making us suffer. 'OK, I'll go,' Renée finally agreed.

Martha physically relaxed and I almost let out a sob of relief. If Renée hadn't agreed, there would've been full-scale war in the office, because I certainly wasn't going. I hadn't realised until this second that my priorities had changed. I'd found something important. Not just Greg, but me. Me and my new-found star status.

I often felt my life ran like a movie. With some of the things that happened – police station, hotel rooms, film stars calling me up at work and at home – my life was exactly like a movie. But, in the cinematic rendition of my life, I was one of the co-stars. My life was annexed onto other people's stories so, even though it was my life story, other people had far more important roles and therefore got higher billing. First, it was my parents and their spectacular marriage. Then it was my brother and his unbelievable behaviour. Then it was Jen.

It'd stayed Jen for the entire time I'd known her. She was the movie star type: blonde, fair of face, slender. The kind of woman who starred in movies and got equal billing alongside the likes of Jennifer Aniston and Cameron Diaz. Whereas I, well, I didn't. She had the types of dramas that the central character of the movie did. I didn't. I was too sensible for that.

I didn't feel inferior to Jen. I had allure, charm. I was attractive, sexy, if it came down to it, but . . . Put it this way: I could walk into a bar, sit down to wait for Jen and within a few minutes I'd be approached by a man because I'm an attractive woman. This man would buy me a drink, chat me up, try to relieve me of my phone number, but the second Jen walked in he'd lose interest. His eyes would double in size as she came over, sat down. He'd drool and pant and practi-cally trample me to death to get to her. Jen never made much of it. Would usually tell these men to get lost with a smile on her face. But, when she was around, I became invisible. It's hard not to feel like a co-star, even if it is your own life story, when you've got Leeds's equivalent of Jennifer Aniston at your side.

With Greg, all that changed. I was suddenly a star.

He made me feel like there was nobody else on the screen. In the world.

He was always asking and questioning, as though prodding at the entrance to my heart, trying to get in, the way you would to a clam that wouldn't open. It wasn't enough to ask me what I thought about things, he wanted to know why I thought that. Where that thought came from, why it'd been formulated. Did I always think that? He also wanted to know about who I was, how I felt, what my dreams were. Like the other day. We were in the bath and he was slowly caressing my back with the soaped-up sponge. (He was always wanting to bathe with me. Most evenings he'd run a bath before bed and press-gang me into it. I did ask him if I smelt and this was his way of telling me so without telling me. He'd said witheringly, 'You would think that. No, dear, it's because I like bathing with you.')

'Tell me your dreams,' he said.

'I don't have any,' I replied.

'Don't give me that, for someone who thinks as much as you do, you must have dreams.'

I wondered if I should confess to him the real truth. I was always telling people that my dream was to be director of the Festival, to run the whole show. That's what they expected to hear. In reality, my dream, my big dream, was nothing like that. Should I tell Greg? Things were different now. He was my boyfriend as well as my friend. You shared the real dreams, the real hopes and fears, with someone you were double close to. At least I suspected you did. I wasn't prone to secret sharing, not with fellafriends, not with friends. Not

125

even Jen knew this dream. 'I'll tell you, but you mustn't laugh,' I eventually said.

'Course I wouldn't.'

'My dream, if I could do anything, or be anything and money and reality weren't an option, I'd love to be a film director. I'd love to write my own script, bring it to the big screen, and direct it. I always wonder what it'd be like to sit there and see something that I've written and directed on the screen.'

Greg's reply was silence. *As I thought, mad insane dream, should never have brought it up. Said it out loud. Told anyone.*

'Please don't tell everyone, that's all I ask,' I added quickly. 'Please don't tell everyone but if you can't stop yourself, don't laugh at me too much.'

'Sorry? Oh, you mistook my silence for ridicule. No, I was wondering why, with all your contacts, you aren't doing something about it. Have you written any scripts?'

'A few, but, ah, it's one of those unrealistic things we all dream about,' I replied. I decided to change the subject before he dug too deeply and discovered how far I'd gone in realising this dream. 'What about you? What are your dreams?'

'You know my dreams.'

'Oh, yeah, you want to work in America. Why don't you go for it? They practically created that features director position for you at *SC* because they wanted to keep you. So going to America would be the next logical step.'

'Maybe, but I've got a pretty big incentive to stay here at the moment.'

'Why, do you reckon you'll be promoted soon? You never said.'

'Noooo, Ms Perceptive, the incentive is you.'

'Oh. *Oh* . . . right.'

'Lift,' he said, and gently took my hand and raised it, ran the sponge up and down my left arm, covering my brown skin with slippy, white soapsuds. Then he went for the other arm. Each stroke of the sponge soft but firm. Long and loving.

'That was one of my defining Friendship Boundary moments with you,' he said. 'When you told those coppers I wanted to work in America I realised how important you were because you remembered something I'd mentioned in passing. When we were stood in the street you looked so cute and tired that I wanted to cuddle you up. I thought, "I want to kiss her. *I want to kiss her.* But she's a friend and there are boundaries." Plus you wouldn't cheat on that bloke.'

'Sean,' I supplied.

'Hmm-huh, him.'

'You wanted to kiss me back then?' I asked incredulously. *That was two years ago.*

'Yeah, course. I'd wanted to shag you for ages because, well, I'm a bloke and you're a sexy woman. The fact you so clearly didn't fancy me was also a big turn-on. Most women would at least flirt, even if they weren't interested, but you weren't play-ing and that made me want you all the more. But that day on the street I wanted to kiss you. Only kiss you and hold you. I suddenly thought I fancied you, then I remembered that I probably didn't, it was just because you'd got me out of a sticky situation and I was grateful.'

'You're so romantic.'

'I know. Lift.'

And on top of all that attention, I got to have sex. Great sex.

You couldn't make up a life this good. Not even for a movie. With all that going for me, why would I run away to Cannes when it wasn't my turn?

I did a victory spin on my chair as I waited for my computer to boot up.

'What you so happy about?' Martha asked suspiciously.

I shrugged. 'Nothing,' I said, grinning. 'Everything.'

Renée's perfectly made-up face frowned. 'Are you on drugs?' she asked.

I shook my head. 'Nope.'

They exchanged looks of confusion.

'It's just a wonderful day.' A wonderful life.

chapter twelve

lunch crime

Jen cut a small corner off her sandwich and put it in her mouth, while I picked up my tuna melt and bit into it. The creamy filling of tuna, mayonnaise and cheese filled my mouth, a little juice trickled down the side of my mouth and I licked at it before I used my napkin to mop up the rest. Jen, meanwhile, picked up her napkin, dabbed at the corners of her crumb- and dribble-free mouth.

We were in Yates's, just around the corner from Leeds train station. We often met there for lunch before we went shopping in town. It had dark wood furniture and a gloomy atmosphere, walls adorned with flock wallpaper, and flowery carpets. A constant fug and smell of cigarette smoke hung low in the pub, but I liked it in there. It was comfortable and calming. Familiar. They also did the best tuna melts ever.

'So, how are you?' Jen said.

It'd been ages since we'd done this. I hadn't physically seen Jen since Matt moved in four weeks ago. Four weeks. Jen had cancelled the past four Tuesday nights, claiming she had mountains of work. Now that Matt had given up football she didn't call on Saturday mornings any more. If I called, there'd be no answer – not even if Matt was in Paris. I guessed it was because I'd not gone along with that blind date she set me up with. That'd been the first time I'd ever defied Jen when she set me up. I'd asked if she was pissed off with me and she'd profusely promised she wasn't.

'You should've been Clinton's defence lawyer,' I'd cut in after five minutes of listening to her deny she was angry with me. 'He could've done with someone as good at denial as you on his side.'

She'd changed the subject.

This Saturday I was looking forward to an afternoon of trailing around the shops like we used to. Shopping with Jen was such a complete activity we could probably hold night classes on it. After lunch, we'd cross the road to Bhs. Then we'd work our way up to the Bond Street Centre, dropping into Virgin to pick up CDs, DVDs or videos. I sometimes dragged her into the camera shop along there to gawp at the old 16mm film ones. Then we'd go into the Bond Street Centre, flit in and out of all the clothes shops, stop for coffee and cake. Next we'd go down to Albion Place, where the other clothes shops were. We'd then have more coffee and cake, before usually meeting Matt or, when I was going out with him, Sean for drinks and dinner. Greg had, over the past year or so, taken Sean's place.

Having said that, Jen wasn't exactly wearing our shopping uniform of jeans, trainers and top/jumper. She had on cream, close-fit trousers and a fawn polo neck in a material that bore all the hallmarks of being cashmere. Also, like loads of the celebs I'd seen in Cannes, Jen's Jackie O-shaped sunglasses held back her blonde hair (let's ignore the fact it was a cold, dull Leeds March). Checking her over, I realised Jen resembled a version of Jennifer Aniston far more than she ever had before. She also radiated that ultra-healthy glow most of the Hollywood stars I'd seen up close did. I'd often thought that healthiness was unnatural, seeing as it was usually coupled with being twig thin, but there was Jen, radiating the same healthiness: hair like silk, skin slightly flushed, eyes bright. Cohabiting obviously became her.

'I'm fine. You look amazing,' I said to her.

'I feel amazing. It's so wonderful living with Matt, I can't remember ever feeling so happy. He's the best flatmate I've ever had.'

'Awww, I'm really pleased for you,' I said, sarcasm trickling through my voice. She'd lived with me for four years and him for, what, four minutes. And it was me who'd spent those years picking up after her because it was easier than making her do it and having her sulk for a week – I couldn't see Matt picking up her dirty undies from the bathroom floor or sweeping toenail clippings off the sofa.

Jen cut off another small corner of her sandwich and popped it in her mouth. She actually 'popped' it in with her forefinger and thumb. She picked up her napkin, dabbed again at the crumb-free corners of her mouth and then lowered the napkin. She was eating a plain tuna sandwich, no butter, no mayonnaise, just lettuce, tomato and cucumber on brown bread, with an orange juice. I'd felt a right plank ordering my tuna melt and pint after that.

To cap it all, she was popping stuff in her mouth. I felt very uncouth for picking up my tuna melt, biting off a piece and chewing – like normal people. I lowered my tuna melt, slowed my chewing, surreptitiously checked my front. Thankfully, there were no bits of bread squatting on my slashed-neck sunflower-motif top or drizzles of melted cheese and mayonnaise staining it.

'Have you seen Greg recently?' Jen asked out of the blue. She was staring intently at her sandwich, meaning she was secretly watching me. She shifted in her seat and traced a line around the rim of her glass with her forefinger.

Was this a trick question? The not-looking-at-me-but-watching-me move was a classic way to catch me out. Did she

131

suspect something? I'd seen Greg almost every, all right, *every* night for the last fortnight even though we both knew we were taking it slowly.

'I saw him the other night,' I replied. That's the other night as in last night. And then, of course, there was this morning when he had to drive me into town because he kept dragging me back to bed to ravish me. 'Why?'

'He's gone right weird,' Jen said, straightening out her napkin so it was right angles to the edge of the table.

'What do you mean, weird?' He'd got less weird, actually. Less reserved, more open. Now he didn't have sexual tales to tell me, he spent more time talking about other stuff. I also hadn't realised, until we'd got together properly, how much his sleeping around and its ensuing bastard behaviour had riled me. I felt guilty because I was betraying the sisterhood by not trying to re-educate him; by rescuing him; by just listening to him.

'He doesn't come round,' Jen continued. 'The last time we saw him was when Matt moved in.'

Involuntarily, my body stiffened. The last time I saw Jen, my bestest friend in the whole world, was also the day Matt moved in but that didn't seem to bother her. In fact, there'd been no mention about being upset about missing our Tuesday nights.

'Maybe he's busy, you know, with that new girl of his,' I said.

'It's more than that. He never calls, never comes round, won't talk for long on the phone, it's like he hates us or something,' Jen whined.

'Course he doesn't.'

'Matt really misses him. I do too.'

'It'll be reet,' I said. I hadn't realised that Greg had withdrawn so much from them. Was I a distraction, his excuse for avoiding the other two? It'd make sense. He and Matt were always going out together, getting pissed, having deep manly

132

chats, but they hadn't seen each other since we got together. Not that he'd mentioned, anyway. *What if he isn't with me so much because he can't get enough of me but because he needs an escape?* I thought. Honesty prevailed upon me to admit that I spent so much time with Greg because Jen wasn't around as much. Arrogance prevailed upon me to not consider Greg was doing exactly the same.

Bleep, bleep, went a mobile phone, cutting into my thoughts. Jen and I both picked up our bags, checked our phones. I'd got the text message. 'Sorry,' I said to Jen. 'I'll just read this.' 'Peck', the message was from. (I'd come up with Peck as a nickname for Greg. He did have a hint of a young Gregory Peck about him when he stood up properly and looked serious. The fact he was always using his pecker to get himself into trouble was another factor.) I pushed buttons on my silver mobile to get the message on the screen. And up came:

I want 2 lick u all over. Peck x

I grinned as stars of lust tingled over my skin.

'Who's that from?' Jen asked, craning her neck across the table to get a look at my phone – it was probably clear from my salacious grin that this was no ordinary message.

'Oh, a friend,' I said dismissively and moved the phone so she couldn't read it. 'Do you mind if I quickly reply?' I asked, pressing 'reply'.

'It is a bit rude, we are having lunch.'

This from the woman who often spends half an hour on the phone to Matt when just the two of us are in a pub.

I cleared the message, dropped the phone into my bag.

'What was I saying? Oh yes, I miss Greg. The way he's disappeared it's, well, it's upsetting.'

I fiddled with my tuna melt as I listened to her go on about

133

Greg. *Who the hell are you?* I thought. *You're not that unusual chocolate with champagne filling. You're looking suspiciously like one of those mangy coffee creams that always gets left 'til last in the selection box.*

About five-six months ago, last September, I'd been woken at the crack of dawn on a Saturday morning by the phone. It was two weeks after the Festival had finished so I was using every moment to catch up on the sleep I'd lost in the preceding weeks. I knew as a person did even in sleep that this wasn't a normal time to be ringing. Still, I reached out, dragged the receiver under the covers and mumbled, 'Hello.'

Instead of getting a 'hello', there was a gasp on the other end of the line then, 'Oh, God, Ambs.' Jen. She followed this by bursting into tears.

I sat bolt upright in bed, my heart going a dozen to the ten. 'It's all right, sweetie,' I said gently. 'Tell me what the matter is and I'll help you make it better.'

Her sobs became shallow gulps until she stuttered, 'Pr-pr-pr-egn-n-n-nant,' into the receiver.

'I'm on my way,' I replied, throwing back the covers.

I called a taxi, all the while shoving clothes, beauty stuff and my toothbrush into a holdall. I scraped back my cheek-length hair and tied a scarf around it bandanna-style. I checked the mirror for sleep in my eye or dribble on my face. No, miraculously clean. I was in the middle of pulling on my long black coat when the taxi tooted outside.

All the way there I kept telling myself not to panic. This had happened before. In college, after college, Jen had thought she was pregnant and it'd turned out to be a false alarm. But this time something in her voice told me to brace myself for it. This was different from all those other times. Somehow, I just knew, just knew . . . *No, no, it'll be all right*, I kept telling myself.

Jen answered the door to her ground floor flat in her pyjamas. Her face was a mess of blotches, her eyes red and puffed up, undried tears still on her cheeks. I slipped an arm around her shoulders and guided her into the living room. 'Are you sure?' I asked her, furnishing her with tissues from the box on her living-room side table.

'I'm late. Really late. Nearly two months late.'

'Have you done a test?' I asked.

She shook her head. 'But I'm never this late. You know that. Never. I thought it was stress, or because I missed Matt, what with him being away so much recently, but no, I'm still late.'

'But you and Matt are careful, aren't you?' Jen couldn't take the Pill because of a history of thrombosis in her family. So she and Matt were careful. Very careful.

'It was a mistake,' she said between shakes. 'We got carried away just the once . . . He's going to kill me. He's going to dump me then he's going to kill me.'

'No he won't,' I said. But it was a struggle to sound convincing because, even as I said it, I knew he would. Matt was like that. 'Besides, he'll have to get through me first.'

Jen pressed the palms of her hands over her eyes. 'Oh, Ambs, it's all gone so horribly wrong. He won't want this baby. When he finds out he'll go mad. He'll kill me. I don't want to lose him. I love him. It wasn't meant to be like this.'

'Having a baby isn't a bad thing,' I tried to reason. 'At the end of the day, whether it's planned or not, it's a good thing. It's a new life. And life is good.'

Her head snapped up and her topaz-blue eyes flashed at me. 'You don't get it, do you!' she screeched. 'This'll be the end of us. He doesn't want children. He never has. He's always told me that. He's always said he doesn't want children.'

So he should have the snip, came to mind. *You want kids*, also came to mind. 'OK, before we start talking in absolutes, you need to do a test. Then we'll sort out if he will leave you and what you'll do. Because he doesn't have to find out about this. Whatever you do, if you want a termination, I'll be there with you. We'll go through it together.'

She nodded, but absently.

'But,' I said, putting lots of jolliness in my voice, 'I can't stand by my *wo*-man if we don't know what I'm supposed to be standing by. So, you put the kettle on and I'll go to the chemist, get you a test.'

She nodded again.

'In the meantime, I'd better go get showered and dressed.'

Jen frowned at me quizzically. I opened my coat, flashed her my blue jim-jams. She burst out laughing and it broke the tension for the moment.

The chemist looked at me rather oddly as I placed my selection of pregnancy tests in front of him. 'You don't need all of these,' he said.

'They're not for me, they're for a friend,' I said, realised how that sounded and added: 'No, really, they are.'

'What I mean is,' he said, pushing his glasses back onto the bridge of his hooked nose, not seeming to care who they were for, 'modern kits are very accurate.'

'There's nothing like a bit of back-up,' I replied.

'They're not cheap,' he added.

'When you need to be sure, you need to be sure,' I said.

He shook his head, obviously he'd had this conversation before. He scanned them in and turned to me. 'That's sixty-two pounds forty-five, please.'

WHO WITH THE WHAT NOW?! That's a week's mortgage payment; a pair of knee-high boots; two weekly shops. That's a hell of a lot of money. I reached into my purse, stared forlornly at my debit card before I handed it over.

Back at the flat, Jen, who'd gone from merely white to translucent, was a smidgen on the normal side of hysterical.

What if she is pregnant? I asked myself as she bolted to the loo to throw up. *What the hell will we do?*

When she came out of the bathroom she was still shaking. 'Tell you what,' I said, 'I'll do one as well, to check how accurate they are.'

'I don't know what I'd do without you,' Jen said.

Fourteen tests later, we sat staring at the various little windows on various white sticks. All of them laid out on the marble-coloured lino in front of us.

'They can't all be wrong,' I said, when the silence around us had stagnated and one of us had to speak.

Jen burst into tears. Loud and noisy, with fat tears that cascaded down her face, dripped off the end of her nose. How she had any liquid left in her after all her crying and weeing, I didn't know.

I almost joined her as my heart's beat slowed to normal. *Oh, thank God,* I kept thinking. *Thank God.* Over and over. Then I felt awful. Like I said to Jen, a new life is fantastic, but I was relieved she wasn't pregnant. All fourteen tests said so. The one I did said I wasn't pregnant either, but that was no newsflash.

'Did you get your dates mixed up or something?' I asked Jen.

'Must have. I could have sworn I was six weeks late.'

'You said two months.'

'Yeah, I know. It's from when you last had a period, isn't it? That's how I'm supposed to count it, isn't it?'

'No, it's how long it's been since your last period was due. Well that's how I'd do it. Because that's what late means. You know, it's meant to arrive on a certain day, so if it doesn't, then it's *late*.'

'Oh,' Jen said.

'Bearing that in mind, were you late or not?'

'I don't know. My periods often come as a surprise – I just couldn't remember the last one. But I knew I hadn't had one since that time.'

'I suppose it's a worry if you've had unprotected sex. But it's

137

not going to happen again, is it?' I said. *You're not doing this to me again.* Statistically, the next pregnancy scare was going to be positive she'd done this so many times.

'Definitely not. I can't go through this again. I'll keep a better eye on my dates.'

'And use contraception, all the time.'

'Yeah, that too. Although . . . after what you said about a new life being good, I'd all but convinced myself I was pregnant and that I could raise a baby.'

'Mmm-hmm,' I replied. When Jen said 'I' in such situations, she meant the plural 'I' as in Jen and Amber, I. And I, the singular, Amber, I, knew that she'd have spent nine months pretending it wasn't happening, then handed the baby over to me to take care of. So, yes, 'I, Jen', could raise the baby – because Amber was an extension of her and 'I, Amber' would do most of the caretaking. The irony being, of course, Jen was a primary school teacher.

'Hey, Ambs, weren't you going to visit your parents this weekend?'

'Yep.' I'd called Mum on the way to the chemist's and told her I'd come tomorrow and leave Monday morning. She hadn't been impressed, but what could I do? Jen needed me. We were like that. Always there for each other. Which was why, whilst I didn't condone what Matt felt about us, I understood it. We always came first with each other and he knew that was something he couldn't compete with.

I worried at a string of cheese as I wondered how happy Matt was right now. How much victory dancing he was doing. This wasn't my Jen. I hardly saw her, rarely spoke to her; she was different. This was exactly what Matt wanted. I bet every time Jen left the room he was running around with his arms in the air, silently cheering because she was slipping away from me.

*

Another Hollywood affectation, apart from the sunglasses in the hair, had taken hold of Jen: she kissed both my cheeks and gave me a quick squeeze before saying, 'Darling, I'll see you soon.' (If there was any Hollywood Affectationing to be going on, shouldn't it be from me? The woman who dealt with luvvie film people most of her working life? Huh? Huh?)

'Mmm–hmm,' I replied.

Our shopping afternoon was cancelled because she and Matt were going to see friends in Doncaster, 'So, have to dash, sweetie, soz.'

Why couldn't you have told me this on the phone earlier? I'd asked with my face. *Why did I need to drag my arse into town for an hour of ridiculousness?*

Because she wanted to know about Greg, a voice inside me answered.

Maybe I should have told her. Should've said, 'Greg wanted to go to Ilkley, go walking on the moors, but I'd told him no, because I was meeting you. So he might be avoiding you, but he's not avoiding me. He's not avoiding me because he's my lover. Yes, that's right, Greg is my lover.'

I stood outside Yates's watching Jen wiggle away on her new Prada shoes (I only knew because Renée had a pair exactly like that and she'd let Martha try them on, being the closest to wearing Prada Martha and I would get) and again wondered who I'd had lunch with. That woman may well have resembled my best friend, but she didn't act like her.

I crossed the road, heading towards the Bond Street Centre. Might as well do what I set out to do: buy clothes. Or, rather, think about spending money on clothes. My heart wasn't in it, though. Fantasy shopping wasn't the same when you fantasised alone. I wanted to mess about with Jen, trying on clothes we couldn't afford and eating chocolate cake. I could draft in Greg but it wasn't the same. He wasn't Jen. He'd been doing a good impression of her – of being my closest, bestest mate, recently, but when it came to the crunch, he wasn't her. I wouldn't be sleeping with her any time soon, that was for sure – I couldn't get her to shop with me, let alone shag me.

Jen was such a total girlfriend. As in, once she became a girlfriend, she became a girlfriend – totally. I became surplus to requirements until they had a row. Then, I was required. When Matt went to Paris, I was required. Now that she'd moved in with that lump of toffee, things could only get worse. She was shape-shifting; becoming Matt's idea of the perfect girlfriend. No more trainers, now it was Prada shoes. No more combats, now it was cream, slender-leg trousers. No more wacky T-shirts, now it was fawn jumpers.

I stopped outside Virgin, glanced at the open wound of their doorway where people were pouring in and out. Nope, I couldn't go in. I'd get claustrophobic on my own. Being in a crowded shop with someone else didn't feel half as bad. I carried on up the road.

Maybe this was sour grapes because, in a month, Jen had mutated into a grown-up and I'd probably have to be surgically removed from my combats and trainers. But, dammit, Jen had betrayed me. Had been lured over to the girly side by the evil temptations of looking like a grown-up and being accorded the respect it commanded.

Anyway, I reasoned, stalking up towards the Bond Street Centre, *it's more than dress.* Jen was different. She'd only nibbled at her sandwich, most of it was left untouched; she'd fidgeted and fiddled without a hint of her previous ability to be yoga-still. She'd not really listened to a word I said. She'd reminded me of her mother a bit. I'd met her a few times and she was one of those people who craved attention. Who would be restless, always fiddling with things and interrupting if you started a conversation she wasn't part of. Simply being around Jen's mum was tiring.

I passed the Bond Street Centre and headed on for Albion Place and the heart of town.

I was being unsisterly. Un-best-mately. If Jen saying I was like Matt was insulting, then me comparing her to her mother was one of those unforgivable things you could never recant. Besides, weren't you supposed to love your best friends no matter what? I was being awful. Disloyal. Which was why I'd carried on past the Bond Street Centre and was heading for Albion Place – there were more people to hide among. I could lose myself there, pretend I wasn't thinking these things about Jen.

My mobile rang, deep in my bag. I stopped. People tutted and had to move around me as my hand excavated the contents of my bag. I eventually found it. I tucked a lock of my hair behind my ear before I answered it.

'Are you alone?' Greg asked.

I looked at the Saturday shoppers milling, walking, semi-running around me. 'Not exactly.'

'Is Jen there?'

'Erm, not right now.' I wasn't going to volunteer the information that my best friend had half stood me up, that was plain humiliating.

'Did I upset you or something?' he asked.

'No, why?' I replied. I started moving again. Moving around shoppers like we were in some complex dance, circumnavigating each other without any acknowledgement.

'You didn't text me back, I thought I'd upset you.'

'Why would licking me all over upset me? No, I was in the middle of a conversation with Jen.'

'Oh, right.' He didn't sound impressed. Or convinced.

'Peck, there's nothing wrong. I'm not upset with you.'

'I thought Jen would be making out I'm the Devil incarnate because I've not seen them.'

'She did mention it. But you see them when you want. Speaking of which, she had to, erm, rush off. A mini emergency. So, we can still go to Ilkley.' Greg loved walking. I'd never met a human being who loved it as much as him. He had a car, but was often to be found walking to most places. He walked to work most mornings if he was staying at his place. He'd even suggested we start walking to work from Horsforth. 'Not going to happen,' I replied. 'Ever.' Now we'd spend the rest of the day doing it.

'Really?' he asked.

'Really.' *You walking freak.*

'Fantastic! Not that Jen's had to rush off. That's dreadful. It's great we can go to Ilkley. I'll pick you up outside the train station in fifteen minutes.'

'H'OK,' I said, turned around, headed back the way I'd come. 'Oh, bring me an extra jumper, I think I'll need it up on the moors. See you soon.' I cut the line and shoved the mobile back into my bag.

Greg was purposely avoiding Jen and Matt. And then there was the way he'd acted the day Matt moved in . . . It didn't take a genius to guess that something was going on.

chapter thirteen

icons

The perfect cup of tea is very strong, a caramel colour, usually with the tea bag left in, and very milky with half a teaspoon of white sugar. Renée placed one such cup of tea between me and my keyboard.

'Renée placing', 'perfect cup of tea'. Two clauses I never thought I'd find in the same sentence. And there she was placing a weak, milky tea in front of Martha.

'Oh, I forgot the biscuits,' Renée said, 'I'll nip out and get some.' She breezed out, black leather purse in perfectly manicured hand. I hadn't uttered a word since Renée had said, 'Who wants a cup of tea before we start this meeting?'

I'd nodded at her, as had Martha. I'd expected her to go buy them. Not that she ever went out to buy us tea. When she'd walked the length of the office, left the office then went to the kitchen round the corner, I'd given Martha a long, sideways look – to find she was giving me the exact same look. Renée never bought us tea and she'd never, in the history of WYIFF, *made* it. If someone had asked, I would have laid money on her not knowing where the little kitchen on our floor was. I would've bet my entire savings, my flat and a year's wages on her not knowing how I took my tea. But there it stood, proof that she'd listened to me call, 'Don't be skimping on the tea bags,' at Martha every time she headed for the kettle, like Martha yelling, 'None of that teabag stewing,' after me.

As soon as Renée had gone Martha spun on her blue chair and scooted over to me on it. 'Before, Renée's behaviour pissed me off, now, I'm scared. Really, really scared.'

'Me too,' I replied.

'It's like those people you see on the news who are a bit odd, then really nice, then they take to the streets with a semi-automatic weapon.'

It's always gratifying to be reminded someone has a far more dramatic imagination than you, however, in this case, I had to agree with Martha: Renée was flitting between banshee and normal so often nowadays, semi-automatic might not be far away.

'Uh-huh,' I replied.

'Anyway, forget about her, tell me, how are things going with Greg?'

I observed Martha with a cool, haughty look on my face. I hadn't told her. I hadn't told a soul. We'd been together six weeks and I hadn't told a soul. No matter how mind-blowing the sex was. Which, it had to be said, it was. I was bragging in my head all the time about how out of this world the sex was.

Not that I hadn't enjoyed sex before – Sean hadn't been a slack lover, neither had most of the others – it was simply better with Greg. I thought at first it was because Greg was, how you say, 'experienced', but, I realised after the bed-of-rose-petals night, it was because I let go with Greg. Didn't care if my hair stood on end; didn't try to flatten my stomach with a bit of muscle clenching. With Greg I could literally let it all hang out. Unlike with other men, who I had to get to know sexually, emotionally and mentally, I had a head start with this one.

We'd spent three years sat around my flat, at his house, in pubs, restaurants, on buses, trains, yak, yak, yakking. Which, of course, meant we had three years' worth of sex to cram into as short a time as possible. We'd sometimes not have dinner because we'd get caught up in each other. In Amber World, if there was something that was unlikely to happen it was me missing a meal to have sex. I wanted to tell someone all that. Wanted to. Hadn't.

How on earth Martha knew, I had no idea. I didn't keep a diary; didn't send dodgy emails from the office; didn't leave anything incriminating in my desk.

I kept my face neutral as I said, 'Greg? What do you mean?'

'Greg's the complicated one you slept with, isn't he?'

'Erm . . .'

'There's no point denying it,' Martha said. 'You said it was complicated and Greg's the only one who comes with complications that you still see. You wouldn't tell me who he is because you know how much I hate him. You've got the glow of someone having regular sex. And, most damningly, every other word that comes out of your mouth these days is "Greg".'

My eyes doubled in size as my hand flew to my mouth. 'Am I really that bad?' I said through my fingers.

'Worse. But, bless you, I haven't ever seen you so giddy.'

'I can't believe you guessed,' I said.

Martha grinned, tapped the side of her Roman nose. 'I can sniff out a good romance every time.'

'Biscuits! Wasn't sure which ones you liked so I bought a selection.' Martha and I froze. Had Renée transformed into a psycho in the time it took her to get to the shops and back? It was all 'Biscuits!' now, but on the turn of a penny it could be screaming and dismembering.

From a flimsy white carrier bag she pulled out plain and milk chocolate digestives, rich tea, custard creams, fruit short-cake, shortbread, digestives and Jaffa Cakes. Each packet of biscuits she placed on my desk, then she grabbed her tea from

145

her desk, scooted over to my desk on her chair. 'What did I miss?' she asked, her perfectly made-up brown eyes eager above her cup; her face excited and expectant. Renée could almost pass for one of the girls at that moment.

'Amber's sleeping with her best friend's boyfriend's best friend,' Martha explained to the latest member of our gang. 'You know,' dramatic pause, '*Greg*.' She said his name like it was the 'c' word. Because, I guess, Greg had become synonymous with that word over the past couple of years, not only because he shagged a lot but because he behaved so badly afterwards.

'Fantastic!' Renée replied. She put down her cup and clapped her hands in what could only be described as glee. If me skipping food for sex was unlikely, then Renée expressing glee was mythical. 'I knew there was a man involved in her transformation.'

'Transformation? What transformation?' I asked.

'You've changed. First it was that thing with that stupid journalist woman. No, no, it was the day you didn't watch those films at the weekend. You've never done anything like that and I've known you years. Then the way you lied to that journalist woman. The Cannes thing proved it, though. Usually you'd go to stop the argument, but not this time.'

Even Renée had noticed.

'Anyway, tell me . . . no, tell *us* everything.'

I glanced from the face of my colleague, to my boss, both watched me expectantly. With such a captive audience, I couldn't help myself . . .

The good humour in our office lasted about six hours. When it got to eight-thirty and we were still in a meeting trying to find the right image for this year's Festival, with no end to it in sight, we couldn't even look at each other. The meeting table had the biscuit wrappers in the middle of it, each packet in various states of consumption. The Jaffa Cakes had gone first, followed by the milk chocolate digestives. We'd only picked at the rest. The longer we sat there, though, the more appealing the dry, sugar-topped fruit shortcakes became.

Martha was resting her forehead on the table, her brown locks falling forwards over her notepads; Renée sat right back in her chair, chewing on the end of her pen; and I had my feet on the meeting table, staring at the reflection of ourselves in the blackened window.

This year, Renée had given me the honour of running the Festival: coming up with a theme for it, scheduling, deciding which celebs and film-makers to persuade to come. I'd run through a multitude of themes and eventually settled on icons. Film icons. Past, present and future. 'Where have all the icons gone?' was the official theme. That would give us enough leeway to invite different classes of celebs. Our intellectual discussions would centre around things such as how film stars had stopped being the main icons of the day. What it meant to become an icon. Could films themselves become iconic? The whole thing was shaping up to be an event worthy of something Renée had conceived – if we ever found the right bloody image for the brochure cover.

We'd thought Audrey in *Breakfast At Tiffany's*, but for posters, flyers and postcards on top of the brochure the copyright and reproduction costs would be too high, as Martha had pointed out.

Which meant holding our own photoshoot. But we wouldn't get someone as unique as Audrey. I'd thought we should go 'out there', take the mick slightly. Have a couch full of icons, from Audrey to Sidney Poitier, James Dean to Halle Berry, slobbed out, eating popcorn, watching telly.

'It's not very glamorous,' Renée had said, quashing my idea in four words. 'We *are* about glamour.' She added the other four in case I didn't glean the meaning from her first four.

Every idea one of us had, only one of us liked at any one time. Again, I swallowed a scream. I was meant to be in the pub by now with Jen, Matt and Greg – it was Matt's birthday and we were doing drinks.

'What was wrong with the fake Audrey theme?' I asked Renée. 'It's an image everyone instantly recognises.'

'If you mention that again, I will kill you,' Renée stated, not looking at me.

All righty then.

'I like the couch idea,' Martha mumbled from her face-down place on the table.

'You hated it two hours ago,' I reminded her.

'I thought we'd be going home then,' Martha said.

'It'd not be glamorous enough,' I said, parodying Renée. 'We *are* about glamour.'

Martha lifted an arm. 'See how many fingers I'm holding up?' she asked. 'That's how long in seconds I've thought about your reply.' She was showing me her middle finger.

'Don't make me angry you two, you won't like it if I get angry,' Renée threatened.

Ohhh, I thought, *I'm so scared.*

Renée was a brandy liqueur truffle, made with genu-*ine* French brandy. Classy inside and out. Smooth, pure, dark chocolate. Bitter on the outside and covered in cocoa powder. Once you bit into it, though, the brandy startled you. It was smooth, warming. It gently heated your throat, then your oesophagus, then your stomach. Once it got to know you, this brandy liqueur truffle had no kick. It might threaten it by being brandy, but in reality it was smooth and loveable. You never forgot a real brandy truffle – its unusualness was always there at the back of your mind – and you never forgot Renée, no matter how hard you tried.

Right then, though, Renée was green chocolate. Not mouldy chocolate – more like Incredible Hulk chocolate.

148

'Don't make me angry, you won't like to taste me when I'm ang—'

'Chocolate!' I blurted out.

Martha lifted her head hopefully; Renée stopped chewing on her pen.

'Go on,' Renée said.

'Well, not just chocolate. We can have a cinema screen with the old-fashioned countdown reel on it with twenty-one – you know, because this is the twenty-first Film Festival. And a woman standing there with those old-fashioned boxes for selling cigarettes that they used to carry around their necks. And then, the cinema audience can be all our movie icons. Marilyn and Bogart and Chaplin and Audrey and James Dean. But, but . . . we can then have modern icons like Halle Berry, *Terminator*, and Keanu in *The Matrix* and Will Smith in *Men in Black*. We could also do things slightly differently and get it illustrated instead of using a photo so we don't have to worry about getting good lookalikes. But the woman stood at the front, instead of selling cigarettes and ice creams she's selling chocolate. Chocolate that's got WYIFF on it.'

'No, the chocolate has got "Star Bars" on it,' Renée said.

'That's a brand name,' Martha pointed out.

'And a sponsorship possibility,' Renée said.

'And, because it's the twenty-first one, we can have the last night party as a fancy dress ball and everyone can dress up as icons,' I continued, warming to my theme.

'On the opening night, we could have women dressed up like the original cigarette girls, handing out WYIFF chocolate or Star Bars,' Renée said.

'YES!' Martha screamed, making us all jump. 'I love that idea. I adore that idea. Let's go with that idea. Please. Please!' She was on the verge of prostrating herself in front of Renée.

'Yes. Let's do it,' Renée said.

'Home?' Martha asked cautiously.

'Home,' Renée confirmed.

I left the glass fronted building and stepped into the outside world. The air wasn't warm, but wasn't cold. The sky was a darkening royal blue with very few stars – a perfect spring night for going to the pub with my mates and my secret lover. Walking quickly, I headed down along Wellington Street, then onto Boar Lane, then left up on Briggate, then up towards The Headrow. Halfway up Briggate I turned left into an alleyway, where the Black Prince's Tavern was.

Black Prince's was a long, narrow, cosy pub. Jen and I used to come here often when we were both single because we favoured comfort over pulling and a good night out involved Black Prince's. I felt so at home at Black Prince's I often had to remind myself not to kick off my shoes, undo my bra and openly pick my nose.

'You're sat in a chucked woman's seat,' Matt announced as I slipped off my coat. I'd made an effort clotheswise in proportion to how I felt about Matt – I'd put on a clean top this morning. I'd pulled my navy blue denim skirt from the laundry pile but, hey, clean blue shirt under a cleanish black cardie.

'Sorry?' I replied, already not liking where the conversation was going.

It was Matt's thirty-first birthday and I'd missed quite a lot of his drinks with it now being gone nine. I'd given him a card and even steeled myself to give him a birthday peck on the cheek. As time went on, the more it sounded as if I didn't like Matt. I did. There was simply something about him . . . it was knowing how he'd have reacted if the pregnancy scare had gone the other way. It was knowing that he had 'issues' with me and Jen being so close. It was a hundred other unspoken, unacknowledged things. But I did like him. Mostly.

'The famous Nina was sat there not five minutes ago.'

NINA?! My stomach flipped. *What the hell was she doing here?*

Nina was someone from Greg's past. An important someone. Greg met Nina a little over a year ago at a wedding, where she was with someone who went under the moniker of 'her fiancé'. The fiancé watched Greg like a hawk because Greg was a good-looking man talking to his girlfriend. Nina made no move on Greg. Greg, who was enjoying her company but also scoping the room for available talent, made no move on Nina.

As they left, she grabbed Greg's hand between her hands and shook it vigorously, pressing a note with her number and 'call me' on it into his palm. Greg did as instructed by the note – after shagging someone else at the wedding.

He called Nina and, a few days later, they met in a pub in Cookridge, miles away from where either of them lived. They talked. They snogged. They touched. They availed themselves of the pub's facilities. Ladies' room, of course.

Greg explained that lust had got the better of them: they had nowhere to go, and couldn't wait, so contorted themselves into a cubicle and did it standing up.

'You're a class act, you,' I'd said to him. He'd come round to mine afterwards because Cookridge was within walking distance of Horsforth, where I lived.

'I couldn't help it, she was so huphmnargh. She had the tightest vagina . . .'

'Shut up! Shut up!' I screamed before he launched into a detailed description, which he was wont to do. Courtesy of Greg, I knew a lot more about other women's anatomy than I did my own. I threw a towel at him. 'Get in that shower, don't want you sat around here, smelling of sex.'

Greg toddled off to do as he was told. 'And no wanking in the shower,' I called as he shut and locked the door. He laughed his easy, sunshine laugh, and I couldn't help but laugh too.

At one point I'd thought Nina was The One for Greg. He'd gone out with her for three months. Three whole months. A minor miracle in Greg's history. He'd even broken his 'no women in my bedroom' rule for her. I didn't ever meet her, neither did Matt or Jen – they only heard them having sex when she stayed over.

This was the woman whose seat I was sat in. I swung towards Greg.

'She just walked in the pub. I suppose it happens when you live in the same city as an ex,' he said quickly.

'She's not just an ex, is she, though?' Jen said. 'She's THE EX.' Jen tapped my arm. I turned to her. 'You should've seen him, Amber. Talk about weak in the presence of beauty. He was incapable. He could hardly look at her. She was gorgeous, though. If I didn't know he was seeing this mystery woman, I'd say he still had a thing about Nina. She was stunning.'

Yes, all right, I get the idea.

'She was all curves and long hair and smouldery eyes and p—'

'Weren't you getting a round in, Jen?' Greg interjected, glaring at her.

'Oh, yeah. Pint, Amber?'

I nodded. Matt got up to 'go make a big deposit in the porcelain bank'. (Matt really said things like that, because that's the kind of man he is.)

'Weak in the presence of beauty, huh?' I tried to sound jokey once we were alone. It didn't work, I sounded like I was: jealous. You always think you've felt an emotion until you truly experience it. For example, when Mimi the mad journalist had called, I thought I was jealous then, didn't I? That was a mere trickle of a sentiment compared to this. This was jealousy in all its choking, irrational glory.

'Amber, I couldn't look at her because the last time I saw her she was coming at me with a knife.'

Things ended badly with Nina and Greg. Very badly.

After being together for three-and-a-bit months, Nina thought they were in a relationship. Or at least on the crest of a relationship. She wanted to take another step forwards, for him to come meet her parents . . . In reply, Greg suggested they see other people. Greg, though, didn't meet her in a public place to finish with her, nor did he even dump her via phone, fax or text. He had to sleep with her first, didn't he? In fact, he chucked her when they were in bed. Lay with his arms around her, probably stroking her hair as he explained it wasn't working for him and they should call it a day. And he didn't want to see her again because he wouldn't want her to think they'd get back together.

Exit a hysterical Nina, enter her best friend. Literally. Nina's best friend, by all accounts a scary redhead with violent tendencies, stormed round to give him a tongue-bashing, two days later. She hadn't approved of Nina dumping her fiancé for Greg, and now Greg had emotionally battered Nina she was going to return the compliment. Greg, unable to take his tongue-bashing like a normal man, had seduced her too. Spent the afternoon having sex with her, then made it clear they weren't going to be anything more than a get-out-of-a-tongue-bashing shag. And could she possibly leave now because he was meeting some friends down the pub and had to get ready. (Yes, I know, he is a *total* bastard.) Greg, bless him, was mystified why, when he got back from the pub that night, Nina was waiting in the bushes outside his house, carving knife aloft, ready to stab him in the head. They wrestled for quite a long time – she being endowed with a mad woman's strength and him unable to hit a woman, even when she was trying to kill him – before he managed to disarm her and she came to her senses.

He'd then *driven* round to mine. A smarter person would've gone to a hospital, Greg made straight for my place. Because when you're bleeding from the head and shaken up, what you need most in the world is a Deputy Festival Director.

I'd buzzed him in then opened my door to find him leaning heavily on the banister, white and shaken. I'd helped him in and sat him on the sofa. I'd done a bit of patching up in my time and went onto automatic pilot. Using my first-aid kit, I cleaned up his face, which was covered in bright red fresh blood and the darker, coagulated stuff but looked a lot worse than it was. He hadn't flinched when I dabbed antiseptic on his cuts, didn't notice as I stuck clear plasters on his wounds. He simply talked, telling me over and over what happened. I gave him beer for the shock and sat opposite him in my living room as he repeated in a trembling voice what happened. As he spoke, I was fighting the urge to run. Run and not stop running until I was far, far away from him. To leg it so I wouldn't be drawn into this again. I didn't want to be part of another dysfunctional trio. Didn't want to be in another situation where I was wiping away blood, offering comfort, lying about cuts and bruises. But I couldn't, wouldn't, leave him. There's a 'for better or worse' clause implicit in genuine friendships and, if it was nothing else, our friendship was genuine.

After a few beers and he'd stopped talking, I'd taken him to bed with me. He was resting his good side on my chest and held me like children held teddy bears after a nightmare. 'Honestly, the things men will do to get me in bed,' I'd said. His hold around his Amber bear tightened. 'Next time, you know, if you wanna bed me, say so. Don't go trying to get decapitated. It's not attractive.' That'd made him laugh. Only a

154

small laugh, but it made his body relax. It was for times like this my situation-lightening 'humour' had been invented.

Greg, Nina and I were the only people who knew about the attack. He hadn't asked me to, but I'd kept it a secret. I knew how these things worked. When you were the person who cleaned wounds and patched up torn skin and offered comfort, your role in a dysfunctional trio was to keep shtum. We'd never talked about that night – not even the next morning when he walked around in a WYIFF T-shirt because I was soaking the blood out of the other one – until now.

'I was freaked out at her being so near to me. Being so normal when she tried to stab me,' Greg was saying as he slid his hand on my thigh. I glanced over the scar from the deepest cut, a v-shaped thing a fraction below his left cheekbone. It'd faded and been smoothed out over time. It was only there if you knew what you were looking for. 'When Jen started going on about my mystery woman I thought she was going to glass me. If on top of al—'

Greg snatched his hand away as Matt's blond head appeared from the loos and started in our direction.

'So, Amber,' Matt asked, as Jen settled the tray of beers on the table, 'did you meet Nina?'

'Nope,' I said, 'can't say I ever had that pleasure.'

'You should have heard them at it,' Jen said.

Matt cackled. 'She could scream.' He put on a girly voice: 'Oh, Gweg, oh, Gweg, oh, Gwweeeggg.'

'Greg wasn't that quiet either,' Jen added. She deepened her voice. 'Uh, Nina, uh, Nina, Nina, Nina . . .'

OK, enough with the sex talk, boys and girls.

'Is the sex as good with your mystery woman?' Matt asked.

'What's it to you, Matthew? It's not like you'll ever find out, is it?' Greg replied.

In other words, no. That'll teach me to sit there all smug about my sex life.

'Is that a no?' Jen smirked.

'Yup, Jenna, that's a no. The sex isn't as good with her . . . it's better. Every time I see her I want to make love to her. To seduce me, all she has to do is walk into a room. It's the best sex I've ever had and, as you both seem to bring up at every given moment, I've had a lot of sex. Of course, it's so good because I adore her. It's always better with someone you adore, isn't it?'

'When do we get to meet her?' Jen asked, ignoring his non-rhetorical question. I spoke Jen and, roughly translated, she was saying: 'I don't believe she exists.'

'I wouldn't inflict you lot on her. Look at the way you carry on. She'd dump me in five minutes.'

'What, you're not even going to introduce her to Amber?' Matt asked

Greg shook his head. 'Nope, because, unlike you two bastards, Amber believes she exists. Right, it's tequila time. My round.'

We spilled out of the pub when they physically prised the glasses out of our hands and stood over us, asking us to leave. In the street, I threw my arms around Matt, squished my lips against his cheek and slurred, 'Hope you had a good birthday.'

He didn't reply; wasn't used to such displays of affection from me, obviously. I then threw my arms around Jen. 'You're my best friend,' I informed her. 'I love you so much.'

'I love you sooooo much,' she slurred back. 'Come to my house next week and I'll make my boyfriend go to Paris. And then we can be best friends. All the whole weekend.'

'Okkaaayyyyy.'

'An—' Matt cut Jen's sentence short by pulling her away, put his arm protectively around her shoulders and his other arm around her waist. He eyed me in distaste. He didn't like such behaviour from us two.

I swayed so violently from how forcefully Jen had been wrenched away that I thought for a moment I was going to topple over, but then Greg's strong hands were resting on my shoulders holding me upright and still. I almost stuck my bottom lip out as Matt held Jen against him. I'd enjoyed that silliness with me best mate. 'I'd better see Amber home,' Greg stated.

I shook my head in big movements. 'Noooo. You go shag your mystery woman.' I poked him in the chest. 'You go have the fantastic sex. I go home to my vibrator. It's bri—'

One of Greg's hands clamped over my mouth as he said, 'You'll thank me in the morning.'

I noticed Matt roll his eyes slightly at Greg. Obviously meant about me. Cheeky get. The things Jen had said in pubs when she was pissed made what I was about to say seem like a nursery rhyme. I almost scowled at him, but didn't because our eyes met. For a brief moment his green eyes locked with my black-brown eyes like two pieces of Lego coming together, which weren't going to be separated any time soon.

Matt was taller than me, had bigger hands and feet than me, was a man (allegedly) but I could still take him in a fight. That was another reason why he didn't like me. Why I didn't need to scowl at him or what he did. We both knew that if we ever had a throw-down moment, there'd be a first round knockout, no messing. A muscle twitched twice in the side of his face before he broke the eyelock. See? I could take him.

'See ya, mate,' Matt said to Greg. 'Amber.' He steered Jen down the road, with her waving over her shoulder at us until they hailed a taxi, clambered in the back and disappeared into the night.

'The bus is that way,' I said, pointing towards the bus station. At least I thought it was in that general area.

'There's something we need to sort out first,' Greg said and pulled me back into the alleyway that led to the pub. He pressed me against the brick wall with his body. 'I want to make sure that you know that you are,' he said.

I paused. Screwed up my face, thought really hard. Had I missed an important bit of what he was saying? *You are. You are what?* 'What is you talking about, Peck-Peck?'

'I want you to know that you are the best sex I've ever had. I wasn't just saying it to them two. I want you every second of the day.'

'I know,' I said ostentatiously. 'I, oh yes, I, am the shag of the century. They all say that to me. All the men in the world say I am the shag of the century. I am v—'

He kissed me. Deep, long, slow. My body relaxed against his. He was really very good at this stuff. I linked my arms around his neck; he was fantastic at this. Slowly, I was aware that he was hitching up my denim skirt.

'What you doing? We can't. Not here,' I said, pulling away. I was drunk enough to kiss Matt on the cheek, but not that drunk. Suddenly he was kissing me harder. More urgently, still pulling up my skirt. This was bad. Very, very bad. And illegal . . . And, and bloody great! I'd never been this bad before. Ever. I was good Amber, after all. And this was . . . This was like being Linda Fiorentino in *The Last Seduction*; this was being so damn sexy my lover couldn't wait to get me home before trying to screw me. *Be bad*, a voice inside said. *For once in your life, be bad. Everyone else is naughty at least once in their lives.* I was suddenly unbuttoning his trousers.

'You really want to?' Greg asked.

I nodded, tugging at his trousers.

He grinned, produced a condom. *I really have to have him. To do this. How come I haven't done it before?*

Greg slipped the green condom wrapper between his lips, ready to tear it open with one hand. *Come on, come on*, I was screaming inside, but my Gregory was evangelical about safe sex. He always used condoms, even if his partner was on the

Pill. *Faster, faster*, I urged him as I stuck my hands down his pants.

Suddenly we were illuminated.

Somebody switched a light on us and a deep, authoritative voice said, 'That's quite far enough, sir.'

chapter fourteen

history lesson

This is why you need to be good.

Why I am good. Always. This is why I don't break the rules, do drugs – not even cannabis – or cheat. When you do, it ends up like this. With you being sat in the back of a police car.

The thought punched me in the head every time I blinked and opened my eyes to discover I was, in fact, sat in the back of a police car. Thankfully, they'd held off on the handcuffs. I could just see the WYIFF GATE headlines tomorrow: *ENTERTAINMENT SCREWS! ALLEY SEX SHOCKER FOR WYIFF!*

Greg would be all right, the papers were hardly going to stitch up one of their own, were they?

When the policeman had caught us attempting to break a few public decency laws, my heart had fluttered as though it was going to expire right there and then. This heart flutter had been swiftly followed by an urge to hurl. I'd only eaten biscuits in the ten hours since lunch and I'd drunk far too much. To stop myself throwing up, I buried my face in the folds of Greg's jacket.

'Would you mind coming with me,' the policeman said when neither of us moved.

Didn't know about Greg, but I minded coming with him. On every level I minded coming with him. Not only because we were going to be arrested, but also because if I moved, even a fraction, I'd throw up and I had a suspicion it'd take direct intervention from the Almighty to stop me.

Greg opened his mouth and the condom fell unceremoniously to the ground. Right then I was grateful he was so fanatical about safe sex. If he hadn't been, we'd have been much further into the law-breaking process. He rather gallantly pulled down my skirt before straightening himself out.

I moved then, folded my arms across my chest, lowered my head and followed Greg out into the main street. There was only one thing worse than being caught trying to have sex in an alley, I decided as we stepped out onto the pavement. And that was hearing a voice state calmly and politely: 'Mr Walterson.'

I glanced out the window. (Yes, I'm still in a police car.) Greg was talking to the police officer who knew his name. And how did she know his name? From the time he'd been arrested for indecent exposure and breaking and entering, of course. There were no other policewomen in Leeds. In the whole of Yorkshire, there were no other policewomen, which was why she had to catch us.

The second I realised who she was, the beer, biscuits and bile hit the back of my throat and my mouth flooded with saline. I inhaled deeply through my nose to stop myself projectile-vomiting over the officer who'd once listened to me promise that Greg was of good character.

'*It won't happen again, officer,*' I mimicked myself in my head.

She'd recognised me, of course. It'd registered in her eyes, but she said nothing except to order that I be put in the back of the car. (Yup, I'm still in a police car.) She'd then gone off a little way to talk to Greg alone while her colleague stood by the car in case I decided to bolt. Not that I could – there are no handles in the back of a police car.

I watched Greg and the officer talk. Neither of them made many hand gestures; Greg's body language was, as you'd expect, contrite. His head was lowered as he stared at the ground, hands clasped behind his back. She stood, favouring one hip, her hand resting on the favoured hip, the other hand fingering her truncheon.

She said something.

Greg nodded, looking very penitent.

She talked some more, Greg raised his eyes to look at her, held her gaze for a second, then looked away, talked, said his piece.

Eventually, after what seemed like forever, they came back to the car. The policewoman opened the door. 'You can go. You can both go,' she said. 'You're both obviously of good character.'

Bitch.

'Thanks, officer,' I said. And before I could stop myself, 'It won't happen again, I promise,' was coming out of my mouth.

'It'd better not,' she replied. 'Because for some people, it'll be third time unlucky.' She flashed me a fake smile and for one moment I thought about punching her. Right in her smug little face. I could probably take her. Probably. *Are you simply out of your mind?* I asked myself. *Or are you developing a taste for police cars and police stations?*

Greg slipped his arm around my shoulders as we walked down the road to hail a taxi.

'You slept with her, didn't you?' I said, between huge gulps of water. I slammed the Hoegaarden glass onto the table and leant on the table glaring at Greg who, having taken a seat at the dining table, was staring down at the table top. All we needed was a uniform and a solicitor and we could be in a police station. I immediately straightened up.

Greg stayed silent, knowing that anything said would be used against him.

I shook my head incredulously, stalked back across my red and white lino to the sink and refilled my glass. I was so traumatised I was drinking tap water, the fact it seemed to have a slight beige hue to it forgotten under all the pressure.

I leant back against the sink counter top, glaring at the thick, liquorice-black locks that hid his face. What self-respecting man had hair longer than his girlfriend? Longer than most women he knew? When the fashion was for men to have shaved heads, Greg had long hair. He didn't even have the decency to be balding, which would explain the need to cling to every follicle. 'After everything. Me going across town when I was knackered, reminding you she was married, destroying her number, getting grief from Sean, you *still* slept with her.'

Greg's head snapped up, his Minstrel eyes flashing with indignation. 'If I hadn't we'd both be sat in cells right now.'

I glared at him, not willing to concede this point. 'Are you going?'

'Going where?' he replied.

'Are you going to meet her?'

'What are you talking about?'

'Don't. Just don't, all right?' I warned, my South-East London accent suddenly asserting itself. 'I know you weren't stood there getting a lecture on public decency. She wants to meet you, doesn't she? I just want the truth. Are you going to meet her? The truth. That's all I want.'

Greg shook his head. 'No. I told her that you're my girlfriend.'

'Awww, course you did. Oh, sorry, dear, I'm a thick cow, aren't I? There I am, all worried about you once *again* shagging some woman to whom the binding vows of matrimony are clearly so important. I should've known all you had to say was

"I've got a girlfriend" and she'd not think it was a possibility. Actually, let's circulate that on the Internet. "Women, don't worry, if your bloke is about to cheat on you, all he has to do is say to the woman he's about to screw, I've got a girlfriend and it'll be fine." We'll win awards for that, we will. A genuine public service announcement. Come on, I'll boot up the computer, you use your journalism skills to tart up my language.'

I could've said, 'She's married, why would she care that you've got a girlfriend?' but that's not me. If I'm going to make a point, I've got to labour it into submission.

'I told her that it'd taken me a year to get you to go out with me so I didn't want to screw it up,' he said quietly.

I gulped down more water. 'And she was all right with that, was she? This married policewoman was all right with that?'

'No. Yes. I don't know. She said to call her if it doesn't work out.'

'Only she said something like, "If you change your mind, you know where I am. Call me any time," didn't she?'

Greg looked down at the table top as he nodded.

'Whore!' I whispered against the rim of the glass, teetering on that precipice of insanity, midway between getting things out of proportion and reality. Who, in all of this, was the real whore? And who was I mentally shoving in tar and sprinkling with feathers?

'What is your problem?' Greg demanded, getting to his feet. (Think it was the 'whore' comment that did it.) He sounded much more Yorkshire Boyish now – probably a defence mechanism against me suddenly becoming a London hard girl. 'It's not like you didn't know what I was like before. You of all people know what I was like.'

'You want to know what my problem is?' I said, raising my voice a notch.

'Yes,' he said at the same level.

'You really want to know what my problem is?' I cranked my voice up another notch.

'Yes!' His voice matched mine.

I slammed the Hoegaarden glass onto the dining table. Another of my points was about to submit under the weight of its labours.

'I want to go somewhere and not meet someone you've slept with. If they're not ringing me up at work, they're taking my place in the pub. If they're not taking my place in the pub, they're arresting me in the street. I can't go into half the pubs in Headingley because you've slept with some member of staff and to get you out of a jam I've made out I'm your girlfriend. We can't go into half the pubs in Hyde Park because you shagged some landlord's daughter and now he's issued a death warrant against you, me, Jen and Matt. And let's not even start on the uni bars.

'My problem is, I can't turn around without bumping into one of your conquests.'

Greg let my words stain the air, aware that he had no magic cleaner that would remove them. Nothing would erase the truth that he was, in fact, a tart. And that I was, in fact, a hypocrite because I didn't have this monumental problem with it before I started sleeping with him.

He's going to leave me, I realised as he stared down at the table in silence. *He's going to tell me to fuck off because I've raised my voice and got cross.*

'With Mimi,' Greg's other gift, apart from being good at sex, was to remember the names of every woman he'd had sex with, quite a feat, 'she made me realise that you're the most precious friend. You risked your job for me and the way you got so angry made me wonder if you weren't a little jealous. That gave me hope, made me think that I did maybe have a chance with you.'

Greg came around the table to me. 'When I met Alyson,

the policewoman, as I told you before, that was the first time I realised that I wanted something special with you. With her it was only sex and we both knew it.

'And with Nina, I tried to make a go of it with her because when I realised how I felt about you, I knew it'd cause all sorts of problems. I thought I was probably missing the security of a relationship, so I tried to make a go of it with her, but when she wanted a commitment I panicked because I knew deep down I wanted you.

'That night she attacked me, I kept thinking, I have to get to Amber, she'll make it all right. And you did. You patched me up and didn't once say, "I told you so" or, "You deserve that", even though I obviously did.

'So, to be totally honest, I don't regret those three because all of them, in their way, played a part in me and you getting together.

'With the rest of them . . .' he paused. His Yorkshire accent wasn't as strong when he said: 'There's nothing I can do. I can't change the past, I can only promise that I'm not doing it any more. And as long as we're together I won't do it. There's nothing more I can say. Except I'm sorry. And I'll hate myself if it's going to cause us problems.'

I had no comeback for that. You can't change the past. You can rewrite it for your own convenience, you can retell it so it sounds better, feels better, seems better. So that you are the hero of the piece and not a bona fide bastard. But you can't change the events. If you made a pass at someone, you made that pass at them – telling them it didn't happen won't change the fact you did it. If you shagged around, you shagged around. Pretending you're as pure as the driven snow isn't going to change that. For that matter, you can't change the future. All you can change is the here and now. That's why people are always banging on about living in the moment because that's the only thing you have control over.

But all this theorising was too much for a night that started off being a birthday celebration. 'Tonight never happened, all right?' I said to Greg, my way of saying we weren't going to row about this any more.

Relief washed over his face, relaxed his body before he laughed a sunshine laugh. 'You should've seen your face when you were sat in the back of the police car, though. Classic.'

'What police car? I've never been in a police car in my life,' I replied, my London accent had subsided now.

'Oh, yeah, sorry, never happened.'

chapter fifteen

done shagging

Who knew you could get so many different coloured sex toys?

Not me, that's for certain. Jen bought me my fluorescent pink vibrator as a joke when I'd hit the sixth month of celibacy. I wasn't naive, but it was a shock to find rows and rows of the things. Different shapes, sizes, colours. Boxed ones, ones in cellophane, ones just stood there. My eyes couldn't help but gawk at them. And the prices . . . Jen's joke had been quite expensive.

I was standing in a sex shop looking at sex toys. Why? Because Martha needed 'marry me' underwear and I preferred looking at the toys to the underwear because with my imagination, I could envisage Martha in every creation she picked up. I could see her in those crotchless knickers and peephole bra. There are some things you can go to your grave without conjuring up about the people you saw five out of seven days a week.

Renée had the day off so Martha had persuaded me to come shopping with her. Even though I was in charge, and therefore should know better, I'd leapt at the chance because I hadn't done it with Jen in yonks. I was missing girly company . . . I was missing Jen.

She had fallen off my world. It was like going to the local

shop and discovering they were out of Mars bars. And they would be for the foreseeable future. You kept going in, just in case, but always found they were out of stock. Same with me and Jen. I'd constantly ring her in the hope we'd have a deep conversation or a laugh, but it didn't happen. Any chat was forced, punctuated with, 'So how are you?', the preserve of small talk. Small talk with my closest pal, now there was something alien. Rather than confront it, though, I kept pushing it to the back of my mind, hoping it'd sort itself out. Most things did, didn't they?

'Surely "marry me" underwear would come from John Lewis or La Senza,' I said to Martha over my shoulder.

'No, that's "propose to me" underwear,' Martha said.

'And the difference is . . .'

'A wedding ceremony.'

Martha came to stand in front of me. She'd slicked her brown hair back and up into a high, dominatrix-style ponytail, heavily kohled up her eyes and put on a shiny black plastic mac to suit the occasion (those probably should've been clues we weren't going to any old shop to get her undies). Currently, she held red crotchless knickers in one hand, red bra with chain mail where the cups should be in the other.

I averted my eyes. Martha stepped into that averted line of sight. I averted my eyes to the right; she stepped there too. I caught another glimpse of the red undies. Swift as a bullet, an image of her in it, standing at the end of the bed, whip in one hand, her man on his knees, bolted through my head.

'You see,' Martha explained, 'you can buy your pretty, rose-coloured lacy bits, and sure the guy's gonna propose. But things like these little beauties,' she thrust them into my face, I flinched back, 'will make him realise that he's got a sex goddess *and* a friend *and* a good laugh *and* a woman to make love to *and* someone he can take home to his parents all in one. In

169

short, when you're wearing this kind of gear, he has to find a reason *NOT* to marry you.'

Martha's logic had some logic to it although I wasn't sure it was so simple. I'd never worn such underwear.

'I'm glad you're knocking off Greg,' Martha said, going back to her underwear.

'Could you please say that a bit louder? I don't think my best friend, who I haven't told yet, heard you that time.'

Martha laughed in a carefree, 'it doesn't matter to me if this irreparably damages your relationship with Jen for keeping this from her' way. 'You're so much more fun now,' she continued at the same volume.

'Oi!'

'Well, it's true. Before, you were so uptight. No, that's not the right word because you were a laugh before. Now, it's like you've chilled out a bit. Even when you were going out with that other bloke . . .'

'Sean,' I supplied. (Why could nobody remember his name? When I was with him, Renée – who'd met him loads of times – called him 'Your Boyfriend', like that was his name. She called Martha's man by his given name. She and Martha remembered 'Greg'. But nobody could remember 'Sean'.)

'Yeah, him, you were still so tense. Yeah, that's it. Tense. You were tense. On edge. Like you were waiting for a war to break out.'

'Are you surprised with you and Renée?'

'Me and Renée, pah! We're nothing compared to me and Tony. I gave him a black eye once. It's just the way we are.'

'Have you got your underwear yet?' I asked.

'This can't be rushed. If I don't get it right, I'll scare him, not get him to marry me. Well, not get him to ask me to marry him.'

'Why don't you just ask him?' I said.

'I'm an old-fashioned girl,' she said indignantly. 'He has to do the asking.'

'But you're not going to wait any longer?'

'There's no point. He wants to propose, he just doesn't realise it yet.'

'I see, and what if this doesn't work?'

'There is no, "what if this doesn't work",' Martha said. 'We've been together three years. Now's the time to get married. I'm no spring chicken, you know.'

Martha was coming up to twenty-six, I was thirty-one this autumn.

'I want to have children soon but I have to be married first. It's the right way to do things.'

'Says who?' I asked.

'Says me, of course. Why don't you get yourself a little something to treat Greg with?' Martha asked over her shoulder.

'Erm, no thanks. We're still in the first throes of lust.'

Martha appeared in front of me again, her eyes alight. She'd never had the chance to have this kind of chat with me. It was a miracle she knew about me and Greg at all, now she was about to get details. 'Do you do it every night?'

'Yes,' I said. All this was meant for Jen's ears but Martha was the closest to a female friend I had after Jen.

'What, *EVERY* night?'

I nodded.

'Wow, even when me and Tony got together we didn't do it *every* night. Do you even do it when you've . . . you know.'

I tried to work it out. You know, *you know* . . . 'Sorry, don't get you.'

Martha lowered her voice: 'When it's your time of the month.'

Heat flowed through me, suddenly making my head feel as

171

though it was on fire. I was stood in a sex shop, talking about personal things with a virtual stranger. I looked away, back at the sex toys, unable to speak.

'You do!' Martha whispered. 'Doesn't he mind?'

'I, erm, well, no,' I stuttered. 'It was his idea. He said if I didn't mind . . . We're not talking about this any longer.'

Martha sighed, went back to her underwear. 'You'd never have told me that before. I always knew a bit about you, but only because I asked and it was like getting blood from a stone. Now you're with Greg you're like an open book,' she said. 'Not an open book exactly, just more . . . chilled.'

'It's healthy to have boundaries.'

'You must be the healthiest person on earth then.'

'Oi!'

Martha smirked. 'Anyways, when are you going to have kids?' Martha asked, over her shoulder.

I thought about my family. Scattered across the world, so complicated I couldn't even contemplate getting married. Ideologically I didn't believe in marriage, logistically it'd be hell on earth. Other people thought they had problems with second cousins twice removed – I'd have to decide which one of my dads to invite. Did I want to add children to this mix? Nope. The madness stopped with me. My brother was different. He probably would, in fact, he definitely should have children. But then, if he screwed up, it wouldn't be such a big deal. Nobody expected 125 per cent perfection from Eric, nobody expected him to be good all the time. Nope, marriage and kids weren't for me.

'Haven't really thought about it,' I said to Martha.

'Really?!' There was horror in her voice. 'How old's Greg then?'

'Thirty-two in October, why?'

'I suppose you're both still quite young . . .' Martha said

thoughtfully 'But you shouldn't leave it too long, you know.'

'Leave what too long?'

Martha returned to her place in front of me, this time, holding lime green undies in slippery material, covered in studs. My body convulsed as I imagined her fella licking one of the studs. '*Let me out of here!*' my brain started screaming.

'Your kids will be beautiful,' Martha said dreamily. 'It has to be said, he is a beautiful man.' Martha shot me a sharp look. 'Not that I approve of him. He might make you happy but up until now he's been a total bastard.'

You don't know the half of it, I thought at her.

'Although,' she continued, 'maybe it was because he hadn't gotten the right woman. Which would explain why he's look-ing even more beautiful. I saw him in WHSmith the other day and he was looking so well. He's happy. Yeah, that's it, he's met the right woman so he's stopped all that bastard behaviour. Oh well,' she shrugged, 'I'm glad. At last the women of Yorkshire are safe.'

Martha went back to her underwear. Leaving me stood there going, *What?* 'What the hell was that all about?' I said to Martha.

'You and Greg and how beautiful your kids will be,' she said, as though she hadn't taken a detour through Manchester to get from one side of Leeds to the other.

And, hang on, what?! 'You speak like it's a foregone conclu-sion. We've only just got together. Neither of us has thought long-term.'

'Men always think long-term. From the moment he meets you he's thinking long-term. That's why he won't call after a one-night stand: he's looked into the future and seen nothing long-term so it's just a one-night thing. Obviously they'll never tell you that. And that's why a man will chuck you for no reason. A woman will go out with someone because she likes him, she'll work at it, she'll put up with the most ridiculous behaviour because she's building a relationship. Whilst men . . . they'll meet a woman, go out with her a few times then do a mental balance sheet.'

'A what?'

'All right,' Martha came back to me, this time with her hands empty. 'In a man's head, he'll have these two columns, "Costs" and "Gains".

'Under "Costs" will go things like:

"other women I can't shag any more";
"exes I'll have to stop talking to";
"time needed to spend doing things she likes";
"her bloat potential";
"her not getting on with my mates";
"parents not approving of her".

'Right? Then on the "Gains" side will go things like:

"regular sex";
"someone who'll listen to stuff I can't say to my mates";
"how good she'll make me look if she's gorgeous";
"someone to share the bills with";
"someone who'll produce good-looking children";
"not having to go on the pull any more".

'I'm serious,' Martha said, obviously clocking my less than believing face. 'He'll have this balance sheet in his head and once he's worked out all the factors, over say a five-year period, if the gains outweigh the costs, he'll give it a go. And if they stick with you after three, then six months, then he's generally thinking you've got long-term potential . . . or he's shagging you until something better comes along. Either way, he's got a long-term plan.'

'Well, I haven't,' I said, confident that my slut of a boyfriend, sorry, ex-slut of a boyfriend hadn't either.

'Yeah, but he has,' Martha insisted.

'You don't know Greg,' I replied.

'Why do you think he's looking so happy? He's looked into the future and seen your beautiful children. You mark my words, Greg's done shagging. He's thinking long-term with you, baby.'

'*I thought I was missing the security of a relationship but what I wanted was you,*' flitted into my head. Flitted in on Greg's voice. My chest tightened, such thoughts terrified me. I didn't think long-term in relationships. I didn't need to. When you don't believe in marriage or don't want to have children, you can take your time. You can leisurely find the right man, enjoy yourself along the way. You can decide to be celibate because you're insane in relationships. You can be insane in relationships because it doesn't matter. Your body isn't ticking, isn't reminding you that you need to find the right person to procreate with. You don't need to think about settling down, or planning for the future. And it terrifies you when someone reminds you that your lover might have different motivations to you and they might one day leave because you're not thinking long-term.

'Well, he's going to be sorely disappointed,' I said, sounding braver than I felt. 'Have you found your underwear yet?'

'Sure have.' She spun back to me clutching a black PVC bra and knickers with tiny silver holes all over them. She pressed the bra over the chest area of her jumper and wiggled her body. 'Sexy, huh? What do you think?' she asked.

I could see Martha lying on a bed, her Tony stood on the bed wearing that underwear and ticking off qualities on a clipboard. Suddenly, the pictures mutated to Greg wearing that underwear, holding a clipboard.

'I think I hate you,' I said to Martha, trying to chase the

175

image out of my head but only succeeding in making the imaginary Greg run faster around my head as he ticked off qualities. 'Thanks to that underwear and your talk of balance sheets, I may never have sex again.'

chapter sixteen

time bomb

A week without sex is a long time.

Obviously, it's not as long as eighteen months without sex, but it's all about relativity.

I lifted the lid on the loo and squirted some limescale remover down the white pan. Then I went back to scrubbing out the bath.

Relativity where a week without sex when you've had eight weeks of sex almost every night is far longer than eighteen months without sex. In those terms, a week felt like seven years. One year for every day. And not even I had gone seven years without sex since my first sexual experience when I was nineteen.

I stopped scrubbing the bath, stared at it. It was gleaming. It'd been gleaming for the past five sexless years: I'd discovered only eating and cleaning could stop the hell that was sexual frustration. My lover had been working long hours all week – someone was ill and they were putting out a special section with the magazine, so when he left his desk he went home. Coming over to my place was a lot further from his work and he'd only arrive at one o'clock in the morning, then would have to get up six hours later. I wasn't seeing him 'til tomorrow, Sunday, when we'd have one day. One measly day to have sex and talk and, well, have sex.

Rather shamefully, I'd gotten out of the habit of sleeping without him. It sounds icky and silly and girly and a whole host of things that I'd never thought I was, but those times when I couldn't sleep, when there was too much in my head for me to close my eyes and simply sleep, I'd snuggle into him. Rest my head upon his chest, listen to the soft, regular beat of his heart. And, I'd never tell anyone this, but he'd sometimes tell me a fairy story. Tales I hadn't read since I was young and used to go sit in the library after school so I wouldn't have to deal with my parents. Or the silence in the house before my parents. It'd started about three weeks ago. He'd noticed that I was restless, kept fidgeting about on the bed, shifting myself all over him as I tried to get comfortable and, rather than ordering me to the sofa, which was what I would have done, he'd said, 'Do you want a story?' And without realising he was probably joking, I'd replied, 'Yes, please.'

'Dragons or no dragons?'

'No dragons.'

'OK. Once upon a time, in a land, far, far away . . .' he began and told me *Rumpelstiltskin*, doing all the voices and adding his own bits.

Of course, I'd never tell anyone that. Ever. I'd watched *The Exorcist*, *The Shining*, and *Bambi* – by myself, nobody could ever know my boyfriend told me fairy tales to send me to sleep.

I sat back on my haunches, started eyeing the basin. I'd probably scrub a hole in the porcelain if I went at it again – I'd cleaned it once already today.

I got up, rubbed my knees to alleviate the ache in them. *I'll empty the kitchen cupboards*, I decided. *Clean them. That'll take up a bit of time.*

I wandered down the corridor towards my kitchen, wearing a white vest and a pair of Greg's grey jersey (clean) boxers. (Yup, not only did I need fairy stories to send me to sleep, I'd also become the sort of woman who wore her man's underwear. I'd hate myself if I wasn't me.) My black hair was scraped back off my unmade-up face. I rarely wore make-up. My mahogany skin wasn't flawless, but it was perfect enough for me to not wear make-up unless it was a special occasion, whilst my eyes were striking enough to do without mascara and eyeliner. I was lucky when it came to looks. My parents might not have gotten on – they divorced when I was ten – but they had managed to stay together long enough to create a child – me – who was able to go make-upless without looking as if her eyes had receded into her head and her skin had been used as a dartboard . . . All right, it was pure laziness. If you put on cover-up stick and foundation and powder, you had to take it off. Seeing as I could hardly be bothered to take off mascara and eyeliner and lipstick, the effort required to remove everything else was above and beyond the call of daily duty.

BUZZZZZ! of the buzzer made me do a comedy leap in the air as I clutched at my heart. I then had to grab the door frame for support. That buzzer had scared the life out of me from the day I'd moved in here seven years ago but I couldn't work out how to turn it down.

'Hello?' I said into the black intercom phone.

'I'm gonna lick you all over,' a voice crackled on the other end. Every part of me leapt to attention.

I pressed the key button on the phone then opened my front door as the downstairs door banged shut behind my caller. I then legged it into my living room and threw myself onto the sofa. I rearranged myself into a seductive position: put my legs out in front of me, sat with my back arched a fraction, had one arm resting on the back of the sofa, the other resting on my hip. I twisted slightly, to emphasise my cleavage and minimise my waist. I heard his footsteps on the top step and licked my lips, pouted . . . then realised I was still wearing my yellow rubber cleaning gloves. I tugged them off and flung them behind the sofa and returned to my pose.

Greg came in, shut the door behind him. Without stopping, he shed his jacket, dropped it in the living room doorway, then slowly unbuttoned his shirt as he crossed the room to me. With each button more of his relatively hairless, muscular but not defined chest appeared.

'Welcome to paradise,' I husked, trying to keep a straight face.

Bless him, he didn't smirk at my greeting or my vest and boxer shorts combo.

Instead, his Minstrel-coloured eyes took me in hungrily as he climbed on top of me, pushed his hand up under my vest and his mouth found mine in a voracious kiss. It'd only been a week and I missed him. How would I survive when we were parted for longer? I'd hardly see him during the two weeks of the Festival and during the run-up to it I hardly saw my flat, let alone anyone else. I'd probably implode. Now, I shall ignore how I've leapt forwards five months in time and assumed that Greg and I would be together.

I moved my head away from his heavenly kisses. 'I was promised full-on body licking, not lip kisses,' I warned. 'I could have you up under the Trades Descriptions Act.'

'Later,' he murmured.

'I want my body licks,' I continued, keeping my lips out of reach. 'I'll get placards done, organise protest marches.'

He stopped trying to kiss me, looked into my eyes, a little quizzically. He'd forgotten I was incapable of doing serious for too long. Then he shook his head despairingly. 'You're so silly,' he said and treated me to a small sunshine laugh.

180

'I try to ple—'

He used that distraction to kiss me again.

RING-RING-RING!

'Leave it,' Greg mumbled as I automatically reached out for the white phone.

RING-RING! The phone persisted.

Greg stopped kissing me, sighed. 'Go on then, I know you're dying to.'

I reached out, grabbed the phone.

'Ambs, it's me.'

'Hi, Jen,' I said.

Greg threw his head back in frustration and stared at the ceiling for a moment. He obviously envisaged an hour of waiting to get his rocks off. Then he seemed to hit upon a plan and lowered his head, very, very low and started caressing my inner thigh with his mouth. Soft butterfly kisses that made my stomach weak. I stopped myself moaning as I arched back my body.

'I'm on the train over to yours,' Jen said.

I locked, mid-arch; my eyes flew open.

'We haven't had a girly night in months,' she explained. 'Tuesday nights don't exist any more. Matt's away and I thought, why not?'

I hurriedly brushed Greg's head and lips away from my thighs. 'You're actually on the train?' I asked.

'Yup. Just pulling into Headingley.'

Headingley! That was the next station. She'd arrive in less than ten minutes.

My eyes went to Greg, who'd finally stopped nuzzling my thighs and was glaring at me.

'You're on the train?' I repeated, staring into Greg's fixed face.

'Didn't you hear me?' Jen replied tartly. 'We're leaving Headingley. I should be there in ten minutes.'

'Ten minutes,' I echoed.

181

Greg's eyebrows shot up into his unruly fringe and his eyes bulged in their sockets as he shook his head at me.

'Oh, can't wait to see you. It feels like years since we've gotten together,' Jen said. 'You don't have any plans, do you?'

Rock. Hard Place. Forming an Amber Salpone sandwich. I hadn't seen Jen in almost two months. Not if you didn't count that insane lunch and the night of Matt's birthday, which, of course, never happened.

I missed Greg after a week but I was gagging for Jen after a few weeks. And I wasn't the kind of person to dump her friends once I had a man. I was not a total girlfriend. Friends first. Friends are for ever, men are until _____ (insert as appropriate).

'No, I haven't got any plans,' I said and watched the red mist descend upon Greg's eyes. 'I'll see you in a minute.'

'Bye, sweetie,' Jen said.

'Bye.'

I hung up.

Silence.

The living room was crammed with it, stifling not only sound but movement. I was holding my breath, and the only part of Greg that moved were the pupils of his eyes as they got smaller and smaller.

'No plans,' Greg stated through gritted teeth.

'I didn't mean it like that. Matt's away and I haven't seen Jen in weeks,' I said quickly. 'Not on her own.'

'So she calls and I'm out the door.'

'Don't be like that. You know how lonely Jen gets when Matt goes to Paris, she needs a mate. Her best mate. And that's me, remember?'

'I need my girlfriend,' Greg replied. 'And that's you, remember? I haven't seen you in seven days and I won't see you for ages because I'm working late all next week.'

'We're spending all of tomorrow together,' I said.

182

'No, I've got to work. Tonight's all we've got.'

'Oh.' I glanced at the clock. The train would be pulling into Horsforth station in about three minutes.

'Let's tell her,' Greg said.

'What?'

'When she gets here, let's tell her, then I can stay.'

'We agreed six months.'

'Six months, six weeks, what's the difference?'

I opened my hands in silent prayer to God above for patience. It was fine for him to say 'tell her' but he didn't know what it'd do to Jen to find out like this. We told each other everything. I don't think Greg got that. If we told her this now, out of the blue, her eyes would water up and she'd give me a long look of pure wounding, as if I'd literally stabbed her in the back as she said something like, 'I'm really pleased for you.' That look would break my heart.

'We can't tell Jen without Matt. He'd go ape.'

Greg knelt back, stared up at the ceiling, now it was his turn to count to ninety-eight million and offer up a silent prayer for patience.

'OK.' He launched himself off the sofa onto his feet. Snatched up his shirt, yanked it on. With angry, jerky movements he did up a few of the pearlised buttons on his shirt, jerked his belt through its buckle and did it up. 'OK. Call me when she's gone and I'll come back.'

'Um, she'll probably stay over. That's what these nights involve.'

Another long silence as Greg stood, hands on hips, shirt partially open, glaring down at my red, thick-pile carpet. The moment reminded me of that day I'd rescued him from the hotel room. How startled and shaken I was then. How startled and shaken I am now. *What the hell is going on? Why is he being like this?*

'Are you ever going to put me first?' he asked.

What?! 'Jen gets so miserable when Matt goes away. She needs me.'

'*I* need you. But that doesn't seem to matter. *She* calls and I'm relegated.'

My body contracted momentarily at the venom in that one word, this was my best friend he was talking about. '*She*? This is Jen. You know, *our friend.*'

'No, you see, Jen is my girlfriend's best friend. Then she's my best friend's girlfriend. *Then* she's my friend. Two other people come before her. Namely you, then Matt.'

What Jen had been saying over lunch about Greg avoiding them floated across my mind. And then there was Greg's reaction to Jen and Matt moving in together. It could only mean one thing. 'Have you and Jen fallen out?'

'No,' Greg said quickly, his eyes avoiding me.

This was scaring me. 'You can't even look me in the eye when you say that. Why are you being like this?'

Now that it'd been pointed out to him, he turned his attention to me. His eyes and face were aflame with anger. Without meaning to I recoiled a little.

'Because Jen treats you like dirt, and it pisses me off. She stands you up to go out with Matt; sets you up on blind dates; and she's constantly making digs at you. If she was a boyfriend, you'd have chucked her by now.'

'Jen and I have always been like this. If we do take the piss out of each other, it's not serious. We understand each other. We're best mates.'

He pursed his Jelly Baby lips for a moment then, 'Whatever,' he said on the crest of a frustrated sigh. He went to the doorway, snatched up his jacket, shrugged it on. He dragged his hands through his hair in frustration. (I'll bet that's why he had long hair, for times like this. Thankfully I didn't say that – it would have been grounds for an instant chucking.) 'I'll have to drive down the long way so that Jen doesn't see me. Sometimes I wonder if this is all worth it.'

My heart stopped. Was he saying what I thought he was saying?

His eyes found mine again. 'When I was only your friend you'd move heaven and earth to be with me. Maybe I should go back to that. At least then I'd stand a chance of coming first once in a while.'

Then he was gone. Magicked out of my flat in a haze of fury. No goodbye. No kiss. I stared at the door. Waiting. Waiting . . . Nothing. He'd gone. I closed my eyes and rested my chin on my knees. He'd really gone.

Greg was angry with me. So angry he was going to finish with me. I could feel it. Anyone who'd experienced the last two minutes would've felt it: he was going to dump me. He did have a point, I did put Jen first. But she was my best friend. She was the one who'd listened in those moments when I wanted to talk about my family. She was the one who'd helped me through the major break-ups in my life. She'd always been there. She'd always be there. She was the reason I'd met Greg. She'd been there first – she got first dibs on my time.

Greg got a very close second dibs, though. He knew that, didn't he? I'd patched him up when Nina went for him with a knife. I hadn't wanted to. I'd wanted to slam the door in his face and hide until he went away, but I didn't. That was one of the hardest moments of my life. I'd gone back to being part of a violent trio for him.

And then there was the time he'd asked me to go for a HIV test with him a few months ago. We went back for the results and I'd held his hand as we sat in the waiting room. He quivered so much that holding his hand made me shake. 'It was only the once,' he kept murmuring. 'The only time I've been unsafe, it's bound to be positive.'

185

'You don't know that,' I whispered.

'Everything will fall apart if I'm positive, Amber. My whole life is over.'

'No it's not,' I replied. I put an arm around him, kissed his face. 'You'll always have me. You know I'll always be there, no matter what.' Inside, though, I was jelly. I wasn't sure how I'd deal with it. Of course I'd always love him, and always be there, but how would I deal with him falling apart? I'd probably fall apart in sympathy. He'd been clutching my hand when the doctor gave him his negative result and he'd leapt out of his chair and almost squeezed the life out of me. I'd excused myself and gone to the loo and stood over the sink willing myself not to cry. I'd been living it too. I was up for the test too, because I loved him so.

The buzzer made me jump again. Jen entered bearing wine, chocolate, videos and a host of beauty products. I wasn't in the mood nor gagging for Jen any more. I wanted Greg back. I wanted to tell him how important he was. How close a second he came to Jen. He'd get second billing in the movie of my life. He wouldn't be an 'also starring', his name would be a 'starring', too.

'You all right, sweetie?' Jen asked at one point.

'Hmm?' I replied, looking up at her.

'You seem really upset. Are you OK? Is there owt I can do?'

'I'm fine,' I replied. I pulled my duvet up over myself. Jen reached off the sofa, where she was huddled under my other duvet, and stroked her slender fingers through my black hair. *Like I'm a puppy.* The thought entered my mind fleetingly so left before it had time to settle. I didn't want to be pissed off with Jen because I was pissed off with Greg. Or, rather, Greg was pissed off with me and I was scared about what that meant.

'I'm glad we did this,' she said. 'Are you sure you're OK?'

'Yup,' I replied.

'You can talk to me, you know? Come on, tell me what's up.' Jen's eyes, the colour of blue topaz crystals, met my black-brown eyes. I wanted to tell her. It was on the tip of my tongue. Tell her everything. It was a ridiculously big thing to keep from Jen. She should know this.

'It's . . . I . . .' But if I told her everything, that I was with Greg and that he'd walked out on me, then I'd have to explain *why* he'd walked out on me, why he was pissed off: 'Greg's jealous that I put you first', and so open another can of worms I didn't know how to close. I was still wrestling with the first can of putting Jen before Greg. My eyes fell away from hers, returned to the TV. 'It's nothing, really. A work thing. It'll be reet. But thanks, though.'

'OK,' Jen replied quietly.

Teary. I was teary. It'd been two hours since my first row-like experience with a lover. Can't say I'd ever rowed with anyone before. Not properly. Maybe the odd sniping session like the night we were almost arrested; possibly the odd sarcastic comment too far. Not out and out rowing. Not that I'd said much in this row with Greg. I never rowed with Sean either. Except that one time I told Greg about, the great *Jackie Brown* Row. And, even then, when he'd been shouting I'd sat staring at him with a multitude of insults and downright evil thoughts running through my head but never voiced them. Sean had been trying to goad me into shouting back at him, but that'd been because we weren't really rowing or breaking up over *Jackie Brown*. *JB* was the symptom, not the cause. It was the thing that had finally broken the proverbial camel's back, but it wasn't what he was really mad about. That was the only time we'd come close to rowing because, as Sean was shouting at me, I'd almost said the evil things; almost said he should look at himself before he stood in my home, my castle, telling me about myself.

We'd never gone down the slamming doors, raising voices, throwing words that couldn't be taken back route. Because I wouldn't. He could say what he liked, he could scream what he liked, and I'd look at him. Which would incense him more. It was never a two-way thing. Until the day he left me.

I didn't want to do that with Greg. I didn't want to drive him away. Didn't want to be waiting for the moment I drove him away.

If Jen wasn't there, I would've been going through my mad woman in a relationship routine: pacing the floor, biting my nails, flitting between nausea and tears. The more I thought about it, the more panicked I got. I'd done it again, I'd driven someone away.

'We should've asked Greg over,' Jen said, stroking her finger through my hair again. 'He's practically a girl. I'm sure he'd have loved having a face pack.'

'Yeah, I'm sure he would,' I said.

chapter seventeen

balance

'Usually, when I row with a girlfriend, I apologise straight away so we can make up. But I'm not going to do that in this case.'

He sat across the room as he spoke and didn't seem to notice that at two in the morning I was fully dressed and wide awake. I'd actually been pacing the flat gnawing my fingers, wondering if I should call him when he'd arrived. He hadn't called all day and all night, so when he turned up it'd been a royal relief.

'This isn't some fling to me, I thought, I hoped, we were moving towards something. A relationship. I care about you.' He paused, obviously waiting for me to jump in with an, 'I care about you too.'

He got nothing. If he was going to bollock me, then I wasn't going to exhibit any emotion, particularly not affection. Being told off didn't work like that, not in my universe.

His face registered something. Possibly surprise, possibly anxiety. Hard to read his feelings. I wasn't used to this part. Nobody walked out then came back to tell me off. They generally told me off, then walked out and I rarely saw them again. Sean being the exception, for I saw him loads of times after a falling out, and we simply never talked about it. With Sean and me, any one-sided argument we had was generally forgotten the second we saw each other again. Not the case with Gregory and me, apparently.

'This is a new relationship, but it's still a relationship. You're my girlfriend, so I think I've got the right to expect you to not put other people before me.'

I went to say, 'But it was Jen,' then closed my mouth as my better judgement took over. His face suggested this was not the thing to do, interrupt – no matter how valid the defence. That *was* what being told off was like.

'All you had to do was say, "I'm on my way out" and she'd have understood. And even if she didn't, so what? You don't treat me like that. I don't care if it's Jen or Keanu fucking Reeves, if we're doing something then you don't tell anyone you're not busy. You wouldn't do it to Jen, so don't do it to me.

'If you're having trouble understanding what I'm on about, then I'll put it this way: you've come to see me during the Festival. You're so knackered you can hardly keep your eyes open and you know you've got to get up at the crack of dawn the next day to go meet some director at the airport. But, you're gagging to see me because you haven't seen me for what seems like ages. And then two minutes after you've got there, Matt calls me and says, "Mate, let's go out and get pissed, you're not up to owt, are you?" and I say, "Nah, just about to shag some bird, she can wait." What would you do? Be under-standing? I don't think so. You'd have my balls on a stick before the sentence was out of my mouth.'

True. I looked down at my hands, which hurt from being tightly clenched in my lap. It was either clenching or wring-ing.

'I've known Matt a lot longer than you've known Jen. He's closer to me than my own brother. Even then I wouldn't dump you for him.'

All right, no need to use a sledgehammer to put in a drawing pin. I get the message.

190

'Amber, look . . .' Greg slid off his seat, crawled across the carpet to me. He, with trouble, unclenched my fingers and took my hands in his. 'I don't want us to fall out. I just want you to put us first. I've not felt like this in ages. I can be totally honest with you, which is why I didn't apologise so we could have "make up" sex. I want us to be . . .' He stopped, searching for the right words. 'Solid.'

'It won't happen again,' I mumbled. It was the best I could manage. I should probably be throwing myself on his mercy, but that wasn't going to happen. As I wasn't known for arguing, I wasn't known for the mercy throwing, either. I'd found that those two things were entwined: you rowed, mercy generally expected to find you flinging yourself about its person. In this case, though, I should be gearing myself up for a bit of that flinging, seeing as I was in the wrong. No matter which way I tried to twist it, I was wrong to tell Jen I wasn't doing anything.

'I adore you,' Greg said. 'Even when we were only friends I adored you. I want to be with you all the time. Every night for the past week I've gone to sleep wishing that coming home meant coming home to you. I've woken up and wished I could be with you all the time. I don't want to be pissed off with you.'

'I don't want you to be pissed off with me either.'

'I sound awful, don't I? Like I'm trying to cut you off from your friends. If it were a genuine emergency I wouldn't mind. And I suppose I was out of order getting so stressed out. Jen is my friend and one of the reasons I adore you is because you put other people first. Fucking hell, the amount of times you've dropped everything to come look after me . . .' Greg grimaced, hung his head. 'I'm sorry.'

'Why are you apologising?'

He lifted his head, bluey-black tendrils obscured his face so he flicked them out of the way. 'For being a hypocritical git.'

'I know that. Apart from that, why are you apologising?' I said with a smile.

Greg was such a grown-up. Now he'd said his piece, he was that balanced he saw how out of order he'd been too and said so. Had I thrown myself on his mercy he would've said so. Had I done what I did and not thrown myself on his mercy he would've said so. He was like that: balanced. I was the sculpted-in-stone type. Once I thought I was in the right it took a feat of almost superhuman strength and reason to convince me otherwise. Had the roles been reversed, I would still be glaring at Greg expecting some kind of blood sacrifice to confirm how sorry he was. I wouldn't have said my piece, I would have gone through life, gnashing my teeth about it and bringing it up in my head every time Greg pissed me off. Greg was such a grown-up.

I was not.

Greg smiled at my little quip. 'I do like going out with you, you know,' I added, before the moment left me. All right, it wasn't, 'I adore you' but it was the best I could do when he was an enigma to me. A code I couldn't crack. He was inscrutable in that I was never sure of what was going on. There never seemed a clear gain for him. That sounded like Martha's balance-sheet theory, but I'd thought this before she verbalised it. I could never pinpoint the 'What's In It For Me?' factor for him. Apart from the sex, what did he really get out of it? He made me breakfast almost every morning, he made me tea in a special mug with a lid so I could drink it on the train to work, he ran me baths, he treated me like I was Cleopatra, Julia Roberts and Jennifer Aniston rolled into one. He also told me fairy stories and wanted to know everything about me.

I just had sex with him.

So I was steeling myself for him to tell me that this wasn't going to last, to say he preferred the good life as averse to the

192

girlfriend life. I suppose this wasn't exclusive to Greg. I never trusted any man not to find someone else; to stay with me if he had another option. To not find something in me that would have him heading for the hills. That was the other reason for not thinking long-term – when someone walked out, as they invariably did, it wasn't too big a shock. A disappointment, but nothing I hadn't been expecting.

'Are we OK now?' he asked. From this close I could see how bloodshot his eyes were, how tiredness was tugging at his skin, how even his hair seemed limp.

I nodded. *We were OK.* I stroked hair out of his face and gazed into his Minstrel eyes. *OK until the next time.*

'Can we continue where we left off before I fall asleep?' he asked.

'ask yourself this:
would you be the
person you are today
without chocolate?'

chapter eighteen

impostor

'Let's go to Harvey Nics first,' Jen decreed.

We'd finally, *finally* managed to meet up to go shopping. She'd called and begged me to meet her in town for a shopping fest on a Friday afternoon because she had a training seminar in the morning, so could I bunk off work after lunch and come shopping with her? Renée was in Cannes and Martha certainly wouldn't grass me up so I half-heartedly agreed.

After that night last weekend when Greg walked out, I'd been forced to confront the truth about Jen and me. We'd changed. We'd become Flakes. Two things separate. That'd been obvious when I didn't tell her about me and Greg. I had the opportunity, but didn't. I wasn't prone to sharing secrets, to confessing things in my heart, but Jen was usually the exception. She was the one, probably the only one, I could trust and even then I hadn't. I'd had to finally confront the truth that we weren't JenAndAmber any more. One word that signified the closeness of our relationship, now it was three words. Jen. And. Amber. We existed as separate entities. Jen. Amber. Sometimes the And joined us.

The other night had been an anomaly. A Twix moment – its gold and red packaging an odd patch among the yellow, gaudy vista of Flakes our lives had become.

It was like always having a Twix. Whenever you had chocolate, you had a Twix. And then, for no reason whatsoever, you decide to have something else. So you start trying new chocolates. One day you try a Mars. Then you buy a Snack. Then you get Maltesers. Then you get a Twirl. Finally, you settle on a Flake. You might not necessarily like Flake, but you know what, you've got into the habit of eating it, so whenever you pass a shop, whenever someone goes off on a chocolate run, you always get a Flake. Until that one day you say, 'Actually, I'll have a Twix,' when someone asks if you fancy a Flake. You enjoy the Twix, it stirs up good memories as it crumbles and disintegrates over your tongue, but the next day, you go back to your diet of Flake because that's what you've settled on.

That's what it was like with me and Jen. We'd had our Twix moment – our back to being close time – the other night but were back to being Flakes.

Even when she'd met Matt we'd been close, we'd been a packet of Twix. Despite what Matt intimated about me and Jen being too close, we'd grown apart. I suspected it was because I was with Greg. Which meant *I'd* become a total girlfriend. Something I swore I'd never do. I had to do whatever it took to get her back in my life.

'Harvey Nics it is,' I agreed. Yup, anything to get her back into my life. Even if it meant going into a shop where I wouldn't be getting a dress for £8.99.

Jen had lost weight.

Jen, who always looked like a Hollywood starlet anyway, had lost weight that she didn't need to lose. She had always been slender, the thinner side of a size ten. She was tallish with it, had shoulder-length hair with a slight wave, curves at the breasts, stomach and hips. Not that I purposely looked. We'd lived together for four years all together during college, and many a night after our college years we'd stayed over at each other's places, it was impossible not to see her in at least her night clothes. I knew her body – and this body had lost a lot of itself. Her stomach was practically concave: her arms were spindle-like; her breasts were swimming around her bra.

'Have you lost weight?' I asked to her.

'Yup,' Jen said happily, and spun to show me. 'It suits me, doesn't it?'

'Um, perhaps you've gone too far?' I said, my voice full of the concern I felt for her. I hadn't noticed until I spotted her body how ashen she looked. She'd lost that healthy glow she had when Matt moved in, now she was looking washed out. Almost like a faded version of Jen, as though someone had watered down her image. She wasn't meant to be this thin. And if how she'd eaten – or rather not eaten – that time we'd had lunch was any indicator, she'd got to this unnatural weight by foul means. 'Maybe you should stop now? Maybe even put on a few pounds?'

'Is somebody a little jealous because they realise they could do with losing a few stone themselves?' she said.

I froze. *Did she . . .? Did she just . . .?* If Jen didn't like something I said she'd usually tell me to piss off. Not abuse me. Not call me . . . There was a thick black line dividing 'Oi, piss off I'll starve myself if I want' abuse and 'Hey fatty bum-bum' abuse, and Jen had hurled herself bodily over that boundary. No woman called a friend fat. Even if you thought it, you didn't say it to their faces.

'What did you say?' I replied, too shocked to be anything but shocked.

'Nothing,' Jen replied brightly. 'Only joking. Matt likes me like this. [Judging by his porn collection – *Big 'n' Bouncy*; *Busty Betties*; and *Curves Galore* – she'd got the wrong end of the celery stick.] I do too. I can't stand the thought of having excess body

199

fat any more. It's immoral, you know, Amber. When there are so many people who can't afford to eat, overeating is immoral.'

Jen had deep-seated fears about food. Her mother, her unbalanced mother, would, whenever she'd been dumped by a man, go on a crash diet. It would literally involve not eating – so she'd starve Jen too. They wouldn't have evening meals and Jen would be lucky if the crash diet started midweek because she'd have paid her school lunch money upfront. If not, she'd sometimes have to go without lunch then go to a friend's house after school for tea. When she started getting pocket money Jen would spend it on things like bread and beans, but take it to school with her and bring it back because her mother would freak if she found it. That was what Jen's life was like when she was young: either have her mother date some man who resented her existence, or have her mother be single and not eat.

Jen knew what it was like to starve and had been brainwashed into fearing being fat so was always very scared of eating. Until she met me. If there was one thing that I'd never gone without in my life it was food: my mother liked to cook; I loved to cook. I loved to eat. Which was why I'd never really been worried about weight. I wasn't huge; I wasn't a rake. I was sometimes a size twelve, sometimes a size fourteen, sometimes my top half needed a sixteen, depending on where I shopped. When Jen met me, I constantly ate around her, made her eat with me, basically made eating a non-issue. She still had her moments, usually when she'd been dumped and she'd want to go on a diet, but I coached her into eating more when she'd been chucked. Why add to your pain by denying yourself the comforts of things like chocolate? Because of that, though, we'd never been women who fretted about our weight. That's why I'd been so worried when I saw her without her clothes on: she was doing to herself what her mother had done to the pair of them. Except

200

she was trying to do it to me too – she was saying I was fat. I was fat.

Like the worst kind of attack, this had been unseen and it hit deep.

But, but, I stared at my reflection in the mirror, the pounds had melted off me since I'd been seeing Greg. A daily diet of sex and eating Greg-made breakfast worked like a diet and gym combo. I only knew I'd lost weight because my clothes were looser. Some of the clothes I hadn't worn in years now fit. I wasn't to be found climbing on scales, waiting for a countdown to ideal weight. To perfection.

Maybe I should be, though. Jen's my best mate. If she thinks I need to lose weight, then maybe I've been fooling myself that I'm fine the way I am.

I continued to study my reflection. My hair had started to grow at an alarming rate – when I'd started this thing with Greg, it'd been just below my cheekbones, now it was almost touching my chin. My formerly oval face had thinned down a little – there was definition in the contours of my face, particularly around my cheeks. My neck was shapely, slender, even. My shoulders were still quite broad because I was built like that, but you could see definition too. My breasts, my stomach, my thighs, my calves . . . I was all right, wasn't I? Curvaceous, mainly because of my rather generous helping in the breast department. *I'm all right, aren't I?* Curvy, contoured, shapely, round, fat, rotund, obese.

STOP IT! a voice screamed in my head. *Stop it, stop it, stop it! You're being insane.*

'You see, I think the thing is,' Jen was saying, while I was eyeing myself up with new horror.

Have I let myself go? Do I look awful in everything? I'd bought some new gear recently. I owned three more skirts that weren't for work. I had some nicely cut jersey tops. A pair of quite smart black, flared trousers.

201

Do I look awful in them? Is Greg wishing I'd drop a few more pounds? Do Martha and Renée wonder how I dare show my face in public?

'I think Greg's in love with me,' Jen's voice said as it pierced my self-assessment.

I swung to look at her. 'What?'

'Greg. I think he's in love with me. That's why he reacted so oddly to the news about Matt moving in with me. And why he's avoiding us now.'

I couldn't stop a laugh escaping my lips. 'Yeah, that'll be it,' I scoffed. 'Greg's in love with you, his best friend's girlfriend. Of course.'

Jen stopped admiring her diminished body in the mirror and looked at me with a half-piteous, half-patronising smile on her face. She turned back to the mirror then tossed her hair model-in-front-of-mirror style. She smoothed down creases in her dress, twisting slightly to check out the bones formerly known as her hips, now they were covered in pink and purple chiffon. 'So why did he make a pass at me?'

Whoa! That was an earthquake. Probably 9.9 on the Richter Scale. Or maybe it was the Earth shifting on its axis. Or maybe it was the hells opening up and the Four Horsemen of the Apocalypse riding towards me at speed to laugh at me. 'Ha-ha!' they guffawed as they pointed their bony fingers at me. 'You thought you were the one Greg wanted.'

'Oh, I didn't tell you about that?' Jen said, clocking my face – contorted as it was in horror and shock – in the mirror.

My knees, my supposedly fat-bearing knees, buckled. I leant against the nearest mirror to stop myself keeling over. I folded my arms across my body to hide how much I was shaking. *Let's see, did my best mate tell me that the man who would become my boyfriend made a pass at her behind her boyfriend, his best friend's, back? Erm, nope. Can't say that vital bit of information was, at any point, imparted into my brain.* 'What happened?' I asked, my voice as shaky as my knees.

'Oh, it was silly really,' Jen said, taking off the dress and reaching for another slip of material masquerading as clothing. 'Eight, no, nine months ago, you know, when Matt went away to Paris for a whole month Greg came round. He said it was to return a CD and video of mine that Matt had lent him.' Jen smirked. 'Like I missed them. Anyway, he asked if he could have a beer and, about an hour later, we were sat on the floor watching TV and we were both pissed and Greg tried to kiss me. I laughed it off. He left not long after that.'

A shower of ice-cold recognition cascaded down on me. That was how Greg had seduced me. Lame excuse to come round . . . Sitting on the floor chatting . . . Kiss . . . Except Jen hadn't been stupid enough to sleep with him. And, thinking about it now, when he'd been saying all those complimentary things about me the day Matt moved in, his eyes had been fixed on Jen. Oh. My. God. He was going out with me because he wanted Jen and I was the booby prize. I was the big fat booby prize.

'Ha-ha!' the Horsemen of the Apocalypse intoned.

How could Greg do this to me? Who had he called from the police station? Who had he come to when he'd been attacked with a knife? Who risked her job to get him out of a hotel room? Who'd held his hand during the HIV test?

I would've understood if he told me about Jen. All right, I wouldn't have let him near me – I don't 'do' men my friends have done or almost done or, worse, have rejected – but I still would rather have known. I thought he told me everything. That's what I'd liked about him; that's what repelled me about him.

'Ready?' Jen asked.

I glanced at her, she was back in her Whistles combination. 'Um, yeah,' I said. 'You know me, I'm ever-ready.'

★

Greg had been here about an hour and I still hadn't brought up him trying to seduce Jen. Instead, I slammed things around the kitchen, muttering 'bastard' under my breath. I then graduated to standing in front of the worktop, chopping knife in one hand, lobbing evils at his lowered head as it read a paper at the dining table.

Loose-moralled bastard.

On one such evil-lobbing excursion, Greg looked up and caught me. He double-took at the knife, obviously having flashbacks to his near decapitation at the hands of Nina. I didn't lower the knife – I was starting to understand how she felt.

' All right, that's it!' Greg said, snapping shut the paper and getting to his feet. 'You've been off with me since I got here, slamming things around, muttering. What's wrong – and don't say nothing because we both know there is something wrong.' He'd tried to kiss me when he'd walked in earlier, but I'd shrugged him off saying I'd start dinner. We usually ate late on a Friday because his 'hello' kiss would invariably end in the bedroom. The local takeaway people often delivered food to either me or Greg wrapped up in my dressing gown, post-coital and ravenous. Not tonight, though. Tonight I was cooking without his help because I wasn't having sex with him. Not tonight. Not ever again.

I surveyed him. Him, the man I was never having sex with again. EVER. Tall, good-looking, bastard. BASTARD. I had an urge to throw the knife, right at his big pass-at-friend-making head.

'And put the knife down,' he said.

I suddenly saw the ridiculousness of the situation. Him unaware that I was aware of his crime. Me unaware how terrified he was of the implement in my hand. I laughed. From the cement-like sickness that had been lining the bottom of my stomach for hours, I laughed. It was born of cement so was heavy and stony and plummeted the second it left my mouth. Even though it was one of the scariest sounds to ever come out of my mouth, I kept making it. Laughing like cement until Greg, nervously, started to laugh, his eyes fixed on the knife. We laughed like that for quite a long time, considering how humourless the sound was.

'So, remember that time you made a pass at Jen?' I said.

The laugh choked in his throat as his face drained of all colour and his hands started to tremble. It wasn't a lie, then. Wasn't something Jen had imagined, which was the hope I'd been clinging to since leaving Harvey Nics five hours ago. It'd really happened: he'd tried it on with Jen. 'Is that what she told you?' he asked, a tremor vibrating in his voice. I'd only ever seen him this shaken once before – the night he was almost decapitated.

'Noooo, she didn't tell me that, it came to me in a dream. I'm psychic, don't you know.'

His eyes strayed to the knife. 'It was all a misunderstanding.'

'What, you misunderstood that you're not supposed to make passes at your best friend's girlfriend?'

'She called me that time Matt went away for a month,' said she wanted me to drop round her CD and video I'd borrowed. I was drunk already so I couldn't drive and had to get a bus and train and then another bus there.' He talked quickly, like a man talking for his life, which he was. 'She offered me a beer, which I needed after that journey. I stayed, watched TV and drank the beer. And then she stroked my cheek, said she was trying to get dirt off my face. I thought I'd better go then, so went to kiss her goodnight as she'd asked me to and that's when she tried to kiss me properly. I laughed it off, so did she and I left not long after that.'

I stood stock-still, replaying the story. Stories. Two stories out of one event. Two versions of the same night. Both stories were essentially the same, the returning of the CD and video.

The drinking of beer. The attempted kiss. The laughing it off. But each element of similarity had a crucial difference. Who initiated the going round? Who asked for or offered the beer? Who attempted to kiss who properly? Who was laughing it off and who was gutted because their seduction attempt didn't work?

Basically, one of them tried it on with the other and failed. One of them was lying scum who forgot about the boundaries of friendship and sex. And who, out of Jen and Greg, was the most likely to do that, eh?

'That's not how Jen tells it,' I said, the knife handle growing slippy in my sweaty palm.

'Well, it wouldn't be, would it? She's just moved in with Matt.'

'And you've just started screwing her best mate.'

'*What?!* No, I've started *going out* with her best mate, thank you. Anyway, you know that when I've done something like that I admit it.'

'Do you fancy Jen?' I asked outright. I had to know.

His eyes rested on me.

'Look.' I shrugged. 'I wouldn't mind if you did. It's understandable, she's bloody gorgeous. I haven't met a man yet who doesn't fancy her. I'd rather know now, though. Now. Not sometime down the line when, you know, we've been together a while and I walk in, find you two at it and you say, "It's something I had to do because I've always fancied her." That'd kill me. So, just tell me. I won't mind. I won't be angry.' *I'll be that unnamed feeling beyond anger. I'll be on that plane of emotion that'll make anger look like someone raising an eyebrow.* 'Honest.'

Greg's eyes continued to rest on me in an impassive, flat stare until I finished talking. 'I don't fucking fancy Jen. I never have, I never will.' His voice was low and angry. He sounded convincing, but then he would. 'Have you got that? Or do I need to repeat it? Louder, maybe? Because I can do that.'

'Why have you been so weird about them moving in together, then?'

He inhaled a couple of times, trying to calm himself. 'Come sit down and I'll tell you.'

I suppose there's nowt to lose by listening. But I mustn't get talked round into believing it wasn't him. As I moved to the dining table Greg relieved me of the knife and sat beside me.

'So . . .?' I asked.

'Do you want to get married, Amber?' he asked. Then added quickly, 'Not to me. I'm not proposing, I'm saying, theoretically, do you want to get married?'

'No,' I replied. 'I don't believe in marriage. But I suspect I might.'

'Why?'

'Because if I want to stay with someone, marriage will probably be a compromise. Most relationships don't survive a refused proposal. Will I want to? No. Will I do so? Probably.'

'And what happens when you meet the person you want to marry, because there's always someone out there who you'll *want* to marry.'

'Even if there was, which I'm not saying I agree there will be, I'd be married so I couldn't do owt about it. Anyway, what's this got to do with Matt and Jen and you avoiding them?' *Duh!* The second the words left my mouth, DUH! smacked me in the face.

'Has Matt met someone else?'

'Nope,' Greg replied without acknowledging that he'd practically given me a heart attack.

'But you think Matt doesn't want to move in with Jen, he's doing it to keep her happy?'

Greg paused. He always paused. And I hated Greg's pauses. Nothing good came from a Greg-made pause. 'Matt and Jen are Matt and Jen. I don't want to get involved in it.'

What? I asked silently, raising my hands and opening them

questioningly. 'That doesn't mean anything,' I said. 'And it certainly doesn't explain anything.'

'I . . .' Greg paused, his eyes searched the air for the right words on some ethereal script he could read from. 'Matt isn't the person Jen thinks he is. And I'm sure you know stuff about Jen that Matt doesn't know about. I think they've rushed into this. Neither of them knows what they're doing.'

'And we do?'

'Our relationship is different. We started off being friends so we've started off being honest, haven't we?'

Sean. Ex, Sean. Tall, blond, rugged. Strong features. 'Fuck me quick' smile. Can't think why he suddenly came to mind. 'Yup. Totally honest.'

'Well there you go. There are things Matt and Jen need to sort out or they'll explode right in their faces and I don't want to be around when that detonation takes place. Aren't you the one who's always following the path of least resistance? Well, I've got a licence to drive on that road too.'

True. But that doesn't change the fact that it was Greg's word against Jen's.

Jen. Best mate since first year at college; trustee of most of my secrets; newly christened cow (still bitter about the fat comment)

vs

Greg. Tart; had shagged 100 women about a year ago; kissed God knows how many; made a pass at even God probably stopped counting how many; newly established boyfriend.

Who was I meant to believe? Who did I instinctively believe?

Actually, maybe there was nobody to believe. Maybe, seeing as they were both drunk, they'd lazily gone to kiss each other's cheeks and had bumped lips. It had happened to me before. Even with female friends. There were loads of women I'd bumped lips with and I hadn't been trying to seduce any of them, not even the good looking ones.

That was it. Jen and Greg had nothing to hide. It was all innocent. It had to be. I didn't want it to be anything else. If it was, then one of them had tried to seduce the other and I couldn't . . . *wouldn't* think through that possibility. At all.

chapter nineteen

true chocolate lover

I was doing something I hadn't done since I'd stopped being single in the purest sense.

My secret lover would be horrified if he knew what I was about to do, what I used to do regularly before I started seeing him: I was going on a chocolate run.

I wasn't going to go buy chocolate; in fact, when I went on a proper, hard-core chocolate run, I never bought chocolate.

On a proper chocolate run, I went and stood in the aisles of a supermarket, picked up chocolate, read the ingredients, felt its shape, tried to sniff it through the wrapper. Basically acted like a complete lunatic. On every trip I half expected to be physically ejected from the supermarket and banned for life.

Since I'd become part of a couple, albeit a secret couple, I'd become too respectable for this. Sniffing chocolate in super-markets wasn't the sort of thing you did when you had regular sex and everything. But, now, those aisles were calling me just like six-inch ponyskin mules called a shoe fetishist – it was the siren's song you couldn't resist. I'd held off as long as possible. I'd ignored the callings, the cravings, the chocolate's song; I'd pretended that the sex was good enough to see me through. You can only pretend so much, though. I needed a chocolate run.

I wasn't a chocoholic. I didn't simply crave it or use it as an anaesthetic when things were bad; I liked chocolate. To look at, smell, feel, think about, to compare people to. The eating part was a bonus.

I went into Morrison's wearing my navy combat trousers, a plain white T-shirt and my black mac. I hid my pervy face under a cap. I picked up a wire shopping basket – a good cover for what I was doing – and headed for the confectionery aisle, my heart skipping with excitement. I almost ran the last few feet to the promised land. As I turned the corner into it, the aisle stretched before me, two pure straight lines of confectionery. I almost did a Homer Simpson, 'Hhhhnnnnhhhhh!'

I walked to the middle of the aisle. Smack bang in the middle, and stood there, looking at the chocolate. The individual, giant bars. The mini versions ganged up in their bags. The multipacks of normal bars. Hhhhhhnnnhhhhh! Chocolate, chocolate, everywhere . . . Hhhhhnnnnnhhhhhhh!

I picked up a multipack. Twix. Fingered it through the wrapper, felt the bumps and ripples through the slidy packaging. Then I turned it over, read the ingredients. First in English. Then in all the other languages they'd crowbarred onto there, cross-referencing it with the English so that I knew that 'Glucose Syrup' was:

Glucosesiroop in NL
Glukosesirup in A
and Sirop de Glucose in F.

Once I'd improved my vocabulary without actually knowing which country's language I now knew better, I looked both ways, checking I was alone down that aisle before I raised it to my face and inhaled. A mammoth inhalation. Nothing. Physically I knew I couldn't smell anything, but mentally I could. Mentally I drank it in. The sweet vanilla, the bitter cocoa, the powdered milk, the glucose syrup. Caramel. Sugar. Flavourings. Hhhhhhhnnnnhhh! My eyes slipped shut, imagining it melt. On the tongue, in a pan, on the dining table. Watching it as the surrounding temperature heated it up so it disintegrated, slipping off into little pools on the wrapper. Oozing all over the place. Lowering my head and using the very tip of my tongue to tease it up into my mouth, slowly and gently—

My eyes flew open because I sensed I was being watched. I was about to be frogmarched out of there. I cautiously checked to my left. The only other person down that aisle was a man, but he wasn't watching me, he was salivating at the chocolate as though it was going to strip for him. He was tall, solid, with a shaved head and dark brown skin.

He picked up a bar and lifted it to his nose. Took a deep breath and held it. *Is that how odd I look?* I wondered. *Probably. Now there's a sobering thought. Not sobering enough to stop me, obviously, but it's sobering.*

His lust-filled eyes slowly turned and caught me watching him. I glanced away, willing myself to become invisible. Moments like this generally preceded the words 'What you looking at?' and precipitated a hospital and/or police station visit.

'I try not to, but I can't help myself,' a voice said beside me.

I jumped a little before turning to him. 'I noticed,' I said and looked away.

'I always imagine that I can smell the ingredients,' he said.

My head snapped round to look at him. Was he taking the piss? Clearly he was strange, but was he ridiculing me too?

'Right,' I said non-committally.

'Mars smells the best,' he said.

'No, Terry's Chocolate Orange smells the best,' I shot back.

He looked at me for a moment as though wondering if *I* was ridiculing *him*. 'You're a sniffer too?' he eventually asked.

I shook my head. *Don't talk to the strange man.* 'No, not really. Occasionally. Not much.'

The chocolate sniffer grinned at me, his smile lighting up his face. 'I don't know if you're old enough to remember this, but there used to be a Terry's Chocolate Lemon too,' he said.

'I remember it vaguely. I remember there was more than one in the Terry's range and it was yellow.'

'Yep, it was withdrawn after two years, in 1981.'

'That was over twenty-five years ago, so forgive me if I only vaguely remember that. I suppose it's a bit like Snickers always being Marathon in my eyes. In about ten years only old people like me will remember it.'

'No!' he protested. 'It'll never die. In the minds of right-thinking people it'll always be Marathon. For goodness' sake, Snickers! Rhymes with knickers, you don't want to eat something that does that, do you?'

I couldn't stop myself laughing. 'No, you don't.'

'Although Marathons are a bit sweet for me.'

'No, the sweetest chocolate ever is Mars.'

'Actually, Milky Way is deceptively sweet. You don't expect it to be, but it is,' he commented.

'I haven't eaten Milky Way in yonks,' I said.

'Crunchies are sweet too, you know. All right, you knew this question was coming: what's your favourite chocolate?'

'Maltesers.'

'You didn't even think about it.'

'I've thought through the possible traumas of being sentenced to eat only one chocolate for the rest of my life and I'd pick Maltesers, no messing. What about you?'

'Erm . . .'

'You have to *think*?' I teased. 'What kind of chocolate fan are you?'

'No, no, don't write me off. Sorry. I go through phases. You know, one day it's Galaxy, the next day it's Mars. Other days I'd give my left testicle for a pack of peanut M&M's.'

'Not good enough,' I said.

'OK, OK . . .'

I put my hand up like the clock on *Countdown*. 'Dard–dada, dard–dada . . . tick, tick, tick, tick . . .'

'BOUNTY!' he shouted. 'I choose Bounty.'

'Lucky, you just got in there under the clock.'

Mr Chocolate Sniffer smiled. 'OK, another question of vital importance,' he said. 'Do you read the ingredients before or after you sniff it?'

'Before.'

'Me too. It makes the mental smelling easier, doesn't it?'

My stomach flipped. This was wrong. He was touching me without laying a finger on me. He was talking my language and that was a turn-on. This was foreplay, where the main act would be sitting in the middle of a room devouring chocolate together. He'd hold a Malteser and I'd nibble the chocolate from the outside until all that was left was the malt sphere. Then he'd slip it between my lips and I'd suck it until it melted.

I'd present him with a Cadbury's Creme Egg and bite the top off for him. And he'd dip his tongue into it and slowly lick all the sweet filling out . . . Jeez, this was wrong. Very wrong.

I chanced another look at him. He was more my type than Gregory. He was slightly older than me, thirty-eight, maybe forty. Lined, worn-in face, shaved head. His smooth dark brown skin a shade lighter than mine, his eyes a chestnut colour. He radiated a calmness that encompassed anyone within a few feet of him. And that calmness was intoxicating. I wanted more of it. I could lean forwards and press my lips onto his. Just to experience that calmness from his lips. He had that spark, the way to connect to my mind, imagination and sense of humour. I could recognise myself in this man – that was easy to feel even after a few seconds together.

I swung towards the shelves, reached out, picked up the first thing that came to hand, lifted it to read it. I couldn't even read the ingredients because my hand was trembling. Actually shaking. No man had ever had this effect on me.

'Do you fancy going for a coffee or something?' he asked.

Just like that. No waiting a year, insinuating himself into my affections; no befriending me; no lunging at me with his tongue out when he's pissed. Just a straightforward request to accompany him for a beverage. There was, of course, the possibility that he, a stranger, was often propositioning women in supermarkets, going off for coffee with them only for them to be never heard from again.

'No,' I said. No matter what his motivation, I couldn't go for a coffee with him. If Greg was doing this I'd murder him.

'I'm not a weirdo. Look, I'll give you my business card then you can call a few people and tell them who I am. Give them my details, say you'll call them every ten minutes to tell them you're OK.'

He reached into his pocket, pulled out his battered black leather wallet, flicked through it until he found what he was looking for. He pulled out a business card and handed it to me. I took the small white square card without looking at it.

'I'm, erm, seeing someone,' I explained.

'Oh,' he said, genuinely disappointed. 'But it's not serious, is it?'

'What makes you say that?'

'No wedding or engagement ring,' he said as he waggled his thick fingers with their neatly trimmed nails, and Greg's badly bitten nails came to mind.

'Not all married women wear wedding rings,' I replied.

'True, but you didn't say you'd got a husband or fiancé. And you didn't say you had a boyfriend or a partner. "I'm seeing someone" is uttered by people who aren't used to being with someone yet.'

He had a point.

'Even though you won't come for a coffee with me, am I

allowed to ask how long you've been a true chocolate lover? I hate that term chocoholic. It's such a non-word. I prefer TCL. Anyway, how long?'

'A while.'

He grinned again. 'I stopped for a bit. You know, the sniffing in public, but when I came to Leeds I started again. It helps me to feel grounded. I feel a bit lost. This isn't my home and I don't know many people. But chocolate . . . No matter where you go in the world you'll always find chocolate.'

'What do you do that takes you all over the world?' I asked.

'I'm a director,' he said.

'For which company?'

'No company. Films. I'm a film director.'

'Anything I might have heard of?' I asked, instantly knowing I was conversing with the director of *Welcome to Vomit Central*.

'Probably not,' he said. He named a couple of films and my stomach flipped. I loved those films. I'd insisted we show them at the Festival and we'd asked him to come to the Festival a couple of years ago but he was away filming.

'I saw them both.' I had an encyclopaedic memory for films and the like, but not other things. I couldn't, for example, name all of Henry VIII's wives off the top of my head but ask me to list the five top-grossing Sandra Bullock films and I'd be able to throw in international release dates as a bonus. 'One was about a wall in a small town that had, over the years, become a way of airing grievances between the religions of that town; the other was about a week in an African road. Who used that road, where they were going, where they were coming from.'

He was well known in film circles, but he was – if I wasn't misreading his eyes – flattered. 'How come you've seen my films?' he asked earnestly.

216

Now, do I tell him who I am and thereby give him licence to plague my very existence for the next few weeks – years, probably, as he tries to get me to show everything he does? 'I, erm, watch a lot of films.'

'I'm taking a break from directing and teaching a directing course. Anyway, tell me, how long have you been a fan of my work?' he asked with a big grin. I liked this man, he was wonderfully disarming – as was well-known serial killer Ted Bundy.

'Where do you teach directing?' I asked. 'And I'm ignoring that last question because I have no proof you are who you say you are so I might start complimenting the wrong man.' *I'm flirting. I'm actual flirting. This is unlike me. In general. And particularly now that I've got a boyfriend. I'll be giggling and flicking my hair next. Batting my eyelids won't be far behind. And if I do that, I'll have to go stand in the traffic and make sure the number 55 bus runs me over. In fact, I'll wear a sign around my neck saying 'PLEASE REVERSE', to make sure the eye-batting never happens again.*

'I teach down at the community college in Meanwood. It's a three-month starter course. Why, are you thinking of signing up?'

I shook my head.

'Good. I can't go out with you if you're my student.'

I giggled. *Oh Jeez, it's started. A giggle has been issued from my lips.* 'Boyfriend, remember? I have one,' I said, with the sternness of one trying to remind herself, not the person she was talking to, of her couple status. In short, I wasn't allowed to do this. This wasn't simple flirting, this was flirting with possibility. The possibility of something more. Maybe a fling, maybe a relationship. Whatever it was, it was a possibility. One I'd willingly explore – if not for the boyfriend.

'Ah, he's graduated to boyfriend status, now.' Mr CS took a step closer, our eyes still linked. I had an urge. An urge

217

to . . . 'Go on, come for a coffee. You can tell me about your boyfriend.'

An urge to . . . 'No.' If there was anything I didn't need, it was to make my life any more complicated. Good Amber knew that. But then, wasn't it Good Amber who was going to have sex in an alley and was keeping her relationship from Jen? *Stop it. Stop thinking like that.* I put down the chocolate packet I was holding. 'I'd better go. It was nice talking to you.'

'You too, gorgeous. At least give me your phone number?' he asked.

I shook my head. 'You might use it.'

'There's no might about it,' he smiled. 'You've got my numbers now, so you could call me.'

'I could.'

He shook his head. 'Even if you don't call, I have a feeling we're going to meet again.'

'Why, are you going to start stalking me?'

He laughed. 'No. We're fated to be together.'

'When they say that kind of thing in the movies it generally precedes stalking, court orders and kidnapping and/or being pushed off a building. You should know that, *Mr Film Director.*'

He laughed again. 'I guess there's no way of saying that we're written in the stars without me sounding like a psycho, is there, gorgeous?'

'Maybe that's because you're not supposed to say it. Bye.'

I didn't even take my coat or cap off before I turned on my iMac and hurried it to boot up. I logged onto the Internet, typed the name on his business card into a search engine. Hundreds of pages came up. I logged onto the first site – it gave a list of the films he'd done.

The ones I'd seen were mentioned. No photo, though. I scrolled down. Logged onto another site. No photo. I scrolled down some more. Then there was a mention of the course. I opened the site. And there he was. A picture of him beside an outline of the course. It was him. Really and truly. I'd been chatted up by a film director. He'd directed two of my favourite films. And he chatted me up. Called me gorgeous.

I looked down at the business card he'd given me, ran my thumb over the raised lettering.

How he'd smiled, the way his chestnut eyes held mine, came to mind. How I'd *giggled* came to mind too. The man directed films, taught film directing, sniffed chocolate. Where had he been during my months and months of celibacy? When I would've pounced on him like a hungry woman offered a cream bun? Oh yes, I was celibate because I was insane in relationships, but not even I would have turned away someone as suitable as him.

He was ridiculously suitable. If he and Greg were in a competition, I wouldn't have looked twice at Greg with his long hair and roam-a-cock. Whilst Mr Chocolate Sniffer . . . I couldn't see him climbing naked out of a bedroom window because some woman's husband had come home early from a business trip.

When you looked at Greg, you *knew* he was trouble. That he was capable of making a pass at his best mate's girlfriend. I'm not saying he did make a pass at Jen. But it was there. He had the potential to do it. Which is why I'd been so willing to believe it when Jen told me. Which was why I'd gone on a bona fide chocolate run. It was niggling away at me. I'd dismissed it the other day, when Greg was there in front of me. It kept coming back, though. Not in a big way, not even in a little way . . . it was simply there. Greg potentially making a pass at Jen. Reinforcing my belief that he was an enigma I'd never decipher. I'd needed to get back to something that was calming, normalising. Like Mr Chocolate Sniffer, I only went on real chocolate runs when I was feeling lost. Or insecure. Or in need of comfort.

I couldn't talk to anyone about my worries about Greg and Jen. I couldn't explain to Jen, obviously. Neither could I explain it to the next person on the list I'd call because that person was Greg. I couldn't tell the third person on the list because he, my brother, Eric, didn't know about me and Greg. The only people I could tell about my mainly formless worries were Martha and Renée. Their thoughts on him were very clear if they got a hint that he'd done me wrong, his body would be found floating face down in the River Aire less than a week later. So, despite my couple status, I'd gone out on a chocolate run to do something that was deeply soothing. Amidst it, I'd met Mr CS. Was that Fate telling me something again? He seemed the sane, sensible option. The option I'd go for if I wasn't with someone else. The option I might still go for even though I'm with someone else. I wouldn't cheat on Greg. I'd finish with him . . . because that would be easy, wouldn't it?

I looked at the card again.

I'd never wanted to call a man as much as I did right then. Ever. I wanted to talk to him. Hear all about his films. Get his opinion on my idea for a screenplay. The screenplay Greg was jealous of. Not that I was doing it, Greg simply wanted to be with me all the time. *All the time*. If I was sat at my computer trying to get down ideas, he'd sweat it out for twenty minutes, sometimes forty minutes, before he lured me away from it with sex. We often had sex in my spare room/office these days. The only way I could work was to sit with him on the sofa with a pen and paper. It'd be all right then. He'd happily watch TV or read if he could anchor me somewhere. He was like a child who needed constant attention – and my screenplay was a rival child. I could play with the other child as long as he was there too. I couldn't imagine Mr CS doing that. He'd understand about shutting myself away for hours to work on it. Even though it wasn't going to go anywhere, I still liked working on it. Imagining who'd play who. How it'd translate onto the big screen.

I looked up to the heavens, to the powers that controlled these things. 'This isn't funny!' I shouted, shaking the business card at them. 'It's not funny at all!'

'there's nothing more
satisfying than opening
a box of chocolates
knowing no one has
been there before'

chapter twenty

the weekenders

'What are we doing this weekend?' Greg asked.

Wednesday night. It was always Wednesday night that he brought up the weekend even though he spent most weekends at my place. I think he liked to fool himself that we were still taking it slowly; that we had separate lives.

This weekend, though, I had plans. And they didn't involve him. I hadn't got around to telling him that yet. I'd been putting it off and putting it off because I didn't need the grief. Like you saw a dark, cloudy sky and knew it would bring rain, I could look at my dark, brooding boyfriend and tell he'd not like my plans.

'I've got, erm, something to, erm, do,' I said, hoping he wouldn't say . . .

'Oh? What?'

I tried not to sound guilty or suspicious as I squeaked, 'Just something.'

Not that I had owt to feel guilty for. Mid-game Greg looked up from his Gameboy. (I say his Gameboy, but it was mine – he'd just adopted it. He rescued it from its place beside the TV, cleaned it up and it went everywhere with him. He fed it batteries, he played with it, bought it new games. If I didn't know better, I would've thought he wanted children.) 'What is it?' he asked.

'Nothing, really.'

'But I can't get involved in this nothing?'

'No.'

'And it's going to take all weekend?'

'Yes.'

Greg laid the Gameboy beside him on the sofa, pursed his pink Jelly Baby lips, tilted his head to one side and regarded me with cool uncertainty. 'Are you seeing someone else? Just tell me. I'd rather know than not know.'

'Yes, because between work and seeing you almost every night and going to screenings, and pretending to work on my screenplay, I've had time to start another affair. You've caught me out, it's a fair cop, guv'nor.' I put my hands up in surrender. 'I meet him on the train, we shag on the train – everyone looks at us, but we don't mind because that's the only time we get together. Then I get off at Horsforth and he carries on to Poppleton.'

Greg floundered. Became a drowning man in a sea of ignorance. I couldn't tell him, though, because he'd want to involve himself in it and I didn't want that.

Much as I liked being with Gregory, a part of me still felt overwhelmed – suffocated, almost. I'd catch myself sometimes wondering why I was serious about someone again. It wasn't my life any more, it was our life. I was no longer free to please myself. To spend Sunday in bed with telly, chocolate and the little bean bags I hurled at the screen to show my outrage. I was no longer free to *not* wait for the phone to ring if he hadn't come round. To not think twice before I spoke in case I upset him. I enjoyed being with Greg, but did he have to bleed into every area of my life? Sean didn't. He stayed where he meant to; he wasn't constantly opening doors in the hope they'd lead to my soul. Which was another reason why I went out to sniff chocolate the other day. I was on a quest to have something separate from Gregory 'Peck' Walterson, to get some breathing space, to have this pillow of a relationship shifted off my face.

Meeting Mr Chocolate Sniffer also reminded me that Greg and I had little common ground beyond our friendship. He wasn't into films; he didn't understand about chocolate; he was far too good-looking for his or my good.

Greg put his head to one side and his dark eyes held mine as though trying to read me. 'At least tell me what it is,' he said.

I said nowt. Stared back at him with a blank expression on my face.

He sharpened his look, trying to break down my defences. What he was unintentionally doing was signing up for a crash course in Amber Visagology. When it came to expressions of stone, nobody could outdo me. Eventually, his face sagged in resignation.

'Amber, I'll only work myself into a jealous frenzy if you don't tell me.'

Couldn't say I was a fan of frenzies, jealous or otherwise. And this was going to go that way if I didn't 'fess up. 'My family is coming to stay. The parents from London, the brother from Edinburgh,' I stuttered.

Picture a child holding a huge double-layer, double-chocolate ice cream. On top, strawberry sauce, wedged into that, a Flake. Now picture this child leaning forwards to take its first lick – and the ice cream toppling out of its cone cradle to land on the ground in one huge splodge. Now picture the expression that child has, right before it opens its mouth to wail. That countenance of pure incomprehension; deep injustice and ultimate pain. Greg wore that expression.

'It's our six-monthly reunion,' I said with the voice of a woman desperately scooping ice cream off the ground. 'It's always only the four of us.'

Greg's expression stayed in place, *begging* me to explain why I had kicked his perfect ice cream out of his hands.

'It's always Mum, my stepfather, my brother and . . .' I cleared guilt from my throat with a lame cough '. . . me. Not even Eric's wife comes.'

Greg's mouth twisted itself into a thin, straight line, which theoretically should've been impossible considering the juiciness of his lips; his eyes openly searched my face for clues as to why I was doing this.

Every other woman he'd been with had been gagging to introduce him to her parents. Not me. Not his Amber.

'When do they arrive?' Greg said. Each word was a struggle to sound normal; light, interested, nothing more. He was hurt, he masked it well but not that well.

'Friday. They leave Sunday night. Sometimes Eric gets the train up Monday morning.'

'Should be fun.'

'It is. Two days is all I can stand, usually.'

'Don't I know it. With my parents, I mean.' Greg smiled suddenly. A proper, charming smile. 'Come here,' he said, opening his arms to me. I shifted along the sofa to him.

We often sat like that as we watched telly or read. He'd be reclining on the sofa, his leg hanging lazily over the side, me on top of him. And he'd slip his hand down the waistband of my trousers, resting it on my abdomen. Sometimes, when he was reading and I was watching telly, he'd stroke my abdomen with his thumb, and I'd turn the page for him so he wouldn't have to move . . . We really were a disgustingly coupley couple behind closed doors.

'You still think I'm a tart, don't you?' he said.

Hey?! I tipped my head back, the top of my head resting against his chest so I could see him. 'No. Not at all.' *Not really. The thing with Jen hadn't done him any favours but I didn't think he went out looking for sex elsewhere.*

'Because I'm not like that any more, you know that, don't you?'

Ah, I see. 'Our family only gets together like this twice a year. Sometimes Eric and his wife come down for Christmas, sometimes we all go to London, but in case we don't see each other then, we always get together twice a year.'

'I thought you might be ashamed of me.'

'Never. I'm not prone to saying this kind of thing but I like being with you.' Mostly.

'Really?' Even though that wasn't exactly a resounding endorsement of my feelings, he was ecstatic. I suppose when you're with someone who rarely said that kind of thing, any positive words were snatched up and treasured.

'Of course.'

He allowed himself a small smile of satisfaction, then said, 'OK, babe, better get going,' in an 'up 'n' at 'em' tone.

'Going?' I replied. 'Going where?'

'Home.'

'*Home?*'

'Rocky was complaining the other day that he hardly sees me and he's right, I have abandoned him.'

'But—' I began.

'I wish I could stay here all the time,' he cut in, 'but I've been spending too much time here. And it's mad me paying rent there but practically living here.'

He untangled himself from me, left the living room, came back a few seconds later wearing his jacket with his bag slung across his body, pecked a kiss on my mouth and left. He left. He'd done it again. He'd bloody well walked out on me. Leaving me with acres and acres of breathing space.

My upbringing was pretty normal, pretty weird, in equal measures. I knew it wasn't ideal, but thought everyone had a life like mine. It wasn't until I got to university that the weird part became clear. When I got there I discovered that people thought of their mums as their best friends and their dads as their heroes. I thought of my parents as two people who couldn't spend more than three minutes in the same room without an argument kicking off. It was like living in a war zone. Always waiting for the next round of all-out fighting to start. That's why Jen's family trauma had attracted me to her. We were shaped in similar moulds, we understood what we'd be willing to do to keep someone in our lives. What you needed to do to make someone love you.

As I got older and both my parents settled with other people, I realised what their marriage, what the War Zone was all about. Adult stuff. It was about marrying someone you don't know very well. So, as you grew, got older, got to know this person, you found cracks in your relationship. And, soon, those cracks become craters and those craters become valleys and those valleys became expanses that were unbridgeable. By that point, you only saw negative things when that person wandered into your line of sight. Everything they did irritated you: the way they put food into their mouth nauseated you; their expression as they watched TV riled you; their voice was white noise to your ears; the way they existed in your life was a red rag to the bull of your unfulfilled dreams. Adult stuff.

I don't know who started to blame who first, but my parents couldn't communicate without one of them taking something the wrong way, without the red rag being flapped and twisted in front of that bull. And then, flamenco dancing into their lives, in a whirl of skirts and make-up and hair, came Mrs H. Even though she and my dad have been married for nearly twenty years, I call her Mrs H. Mrs H – who I'd met too many times in my life – met my dad at work. She became his confidante, the person who understood him when his wife didn't. The phone would ring, I'd answer it, someone would hang up. Then it'd ring again, my dad would answer and would be on the phone for ages, talking in hushed tones, not saying much except, 'Yes', 'No', 'Of course, of course', 'Soon'.

The first affair I knew about but didn't know about. I was only seven. Mum was a nurse, she used to work three nights a week, including one weekend night. She used to come home from work as I was leaving for school. I'd say 'Bye' and she would raise an exhausted hand before bed. She'd try to be up when I came home from school but sometimes, she was too tired. So I'd come home, wander upstairs, stick my head around their bedroom door, see if she was awake. If not, I'd go back downstairs, have a couple of biscuits and watch television until she woke up. Everything changed the summer holidays before I was going to be eight.

I came home and the house was quiet, as always, but there was something different. I felt it, it seeped into me but I didn't understand it. I dumped my bag by the door, then crossed the short walk from the corridor to the stairs and went upstairs to see if Mum was awake. She was. Their bedroom door was wide open and Mum was folding clothes into her suitcase that was lying open on the blanket-covered double bed.

I didn't, no matter how much I wanted to, ask her what she was doing. Anyway, it was obvious – she was giving clothes to charity. They were her best clothes, but my mum was generous like that.

'Don't try to stop me, don't try to stop me,' she said, not looking at me. 'I have to go. I have to go.'

I nodded at her, even though she wasn't looking at me and said, 'Yes, Mummy.' I returned downstairs to the living room, turned on the black and white television and sat watching something. I was advanced for my years, mentally. You grow up quickly when you hear your parents shouting each other's faults at each other; when you hear hand slamming into flesh. So, while part of me was thinking: *Where's Mummy going? Why would I try to stop her?* most of me instinctively knew it was because of the phone calls and the rows. I also knew she was going and she wasn't coming back. My mother was going and she wasn't coming back.

TV programme merged into TV programme and I watched them all. Every thing that came on, I watched. Some time later Mum came into the living room. Her face was drawn, dark circles etched under her eyes from where she hadn't slept. She didn't have a suitcase with her, didn't have her coat on. 'How about we have fish and chips for dinner?' she said, sitting beside me. She delved in her purse and gave me a five pound note. She didn't have to tell me, I knew what I had to do – say nothing. Not to Dad, not to anyone. I was good at that by then. Secrets were locked up inside me and nobody would ever get them out of me.

Dad left us eighteen months later and went to live with Mrs H in North London. I had to be a bridesmaid at their wedding. I still don't think about that whole experience. Eleven years old and so annoyed by the whole thing. I didn't speak for the whole day. Simply smiled when I was ordered to and stood out of the way, glowering at everyone.

Mum and Dad2 got together about two months after Dad moved out. She'd met him a couple of years before and he was duty psychiatrist in the hospital where she worked. Dad2 – his name being Leonard before he became rechristened as Dad2 – and Mum used to spend their breaks together. They drank tea in the nurses' lounge and talked about whatever two people who didn't realise they were eventually going to be together talked about.

That day I found her throwing clothes into her suitcase, it was him that she was going to as my brother, Eric – Leonard's son – told me years later. She'd already guessed about my dad and Mrs H but the day she decided to leave she'd found out through mutual friends for certain about them.

Leonard, who'd fallen in love with her by this point, had said,

'Come to me, marry me. I'll look after you.' Mum, who'd fallen in love with him but hadn't realised it yet, had been tempted for once in her life to put herself first. To think of nobody and to go be happy. I came home and ruined it. Eric never said I ruined it, I just knew I did. Mum had been on the motorway of happiness and love and I was the roadblock that jolted her back to reality. She'd had to choose and decided to stay.

Leonard, whose wife had left him a year after she had Eric and then died before she'd planned to return, was living with his sister (who took care of Eric) and moved in with us a couple of months after they got together.

Mum wore the ring he bought her on her left hand, but she refused to marry him. 'I'm only going to be married once in my life,' she said when Eric asked her why. 'That's what the vows mean.' (Eric had the kind of relationship with our parents that he could ask that sort of thing – that's why he knew so much about their story.)

Mum was horrified when two weeks after they moved in I started calling Leonard 'Dad2'.

'Do not feel you have to call him that to make me happy,' she said, one day when Leonard had taken Eric to football. She didn't understand I was calling him Dad2 not to make her happy but because she *was* happy. I'd never heard my mum sing before, which she always did when she was cooking or cleaning. She played records – Queen, the Everly Brothers, Culture Club – and even danced to them with Leonard. And, best of all, I now had a full-time sibling who I could boss around. Who I could talk to when she and Leonard were talking adult talk. He had given me a brother, why wouldn't I call him Dad? Eric eventually called my mum 'Mum' because she was the only mother he'd known.

And Greg wanted to meet them. Had walked out in a fit of pique because he didn't realise it was nothing personal.

Meeting the family wasn't on the list of activities lovers or friends took part in. Jen had met them – but that was only eighteen months ago. After twelve years of knowing her, I'd only allowed her to meet them that recently – I'd even kept them apart at my graduation ceremony. My family were my family and nobody was allowed to share them. I was hyper-protective of them, didn't want people making comments, passing judgement, deciding we weren't a real family because a wedding ceremony hadn't taken place.

Jen was OK with my need to keep my family separate from everyone else. She understood. She dragged me home with her at every opportunity as armour, a buffer between her and her mother, but she didn't ever demand that I make her part of my family weekends. Nobody had ever tried to prise them-selves into my life this much before; nobody seemed to be that bothered.

Greg was different, though. Despite how much he suffo-cated me, he let me breathe too. If that made sense. I was smothered by someone who I didn't hold back with. All right, that was overstating the case. Who I didn't hold back as much with. Whatever it was, no matter how oxymoronic my thoughts, he was different. I had to let him meet my family. If I didn't, he'd leave. Would cut his losses and walk. My whole reality skipped a beat. *He'd leave.* I couldn't let that happen, not if there was a way to stop it. All I had to do was let him meet my family.

I think I'm going to throw up.

chapter twenty-one

natural selection

'My naughty little sister is having sex.' Eric's first words as I slid into the seat beside him.

Not 'hello', not 'hi ya' as was the customary greeting. He was in Yates's, in a booth at the back of the pub. Whenever he came to visit we always met there. He'd take a half day, come down on the train and would wait in Yates's for me with his pacifier pint. I'd offered him keys to my place, but he liked it there – said it broke up the journey.

From a distance, Eric looked rock hard; like peanut brittle that'd been hardened over a long period of time, so you were always wary of it, unsure of what it'd do to you if you took it on. But he only looked like peanut brittle because of his Aryan looks: shaved, dark blond hair, navy blue eyes and sharp features. He had a lithe, six-foot two body, which when he hit Leeds was always clothed as it was then: immaculately cut suit, usually charcoal grey or black, white shirt, silver cufflinks his grandfather had left him, and loosened red tie. Eric was an occupational psychologist for a large company in Edinburgh but dressed like a businessman.

He had the look of peanut brittle, but when you got to know him, when you did taste my brother by talking to him, you found him completely different. He was more like white chocolate with coffee granules.

Yes, it sounded disgusting, white chocolate with coffee granules, but all you needed was one taste. One bite and you'd be pleasantly surprised. First there was the initial head rush. A taste sensation that hit you right behind the temples and left you hot and flustered because Eric would invariably say something outrageous. Something so outrageous you weren't sure if he meant it or not. After that initial shock you felt a connection with him. You wanted to tell him everything about yourself, everything that was in your head, all at once. And he'd be more than willing to listen. Lovely as it was, though, Eric, like the coffee granules in white chocolate, had a surprising hard edge. He never suffered fools, gladly or otherwise, so if he didn't like you, then he didn't like you. And he wouldn't speak to you. At all. With my brother, you expected a good-looking, overbearing wanker but you got a genuinely good-hearted person. I would say that, though, he's my brother.

Whatever chocolate he was, he was a very cheeky man.

'What makes you say that?' I said, taking off my denim jacket to reveal my flower motif top teamed with black combat trousers.

'Have you looked in the mirror lately? You're not just having sex, you're having good regular sex. In fact, I'd say you're falling in love.'

'You wash that filthy mouth of yours out with soap and water,' I replied.

From the centre of his face a smile sparked, spreading out across his face, catching fire in his eyes. 'It's worse than I thought – you're already in love.'

'Not funny,' I said and swished the single malt whisky Eric had bought me in the bottom of the glass. No ice, no mixer. Pure. Eric always made me drink whisky when I saw him. He never explained why, he just did. I never asked, either.

'Down in one,' Eric said, raising his whisky. We clinked glasses. I knocked mine back. 'Here's to you and Greg.'

Having cleared my mouth and begun its descent down my throat, the pale amber liquid didn't take kindly to my cough of surprise. It wasn't going to be shifted, though. It went about its way, pausing to give the back of my throat a harder kick than usual. My reaction hit the air as a series of short splutters. 'How . . .' I began through my spluttering.

'Did I know?' Eric supplied. 'Last year, when I came down, before Mum and Dad arrived, he called you. You were on the phone for, what, three minutes and you laughed the whole way through. And I thought, "Going to realise one day she's meant to be with him." Call it man's intuition. The guy obviously fancied you, he wouldn't have tried so hard to make yea laugh if he *didnae*. It stands to rights that you look so well because of him . . . Tell me all about it. I want all the details.' (Eric's voice had been bastardised from his time in Scotland. Sometimes he sounded like a Londoner, other times he sounded like an Edinburgher. Mostly he spoke with a mixture of the two.)

I told him. The best mate version. The version I didn't think of telling Martha and Renée. The version I would've told Jen if I wasn't keeping things from her.

'What does Jen say about all this?' Eric asked after hearing my tale.

I stared shamefaced into my glass as I muttered, 'I haven't told her.'

'Good.'

Eric didn't like Jen. It was unnecessary to admit this to myself. Eric was himself when he met her because he'd heard so much about her over the years. But, by the time he left for Scotland he wouldn't even look at her unless she spoke directly to him. Then, he'd tear his concentration away from that paint he was watching dry and look at her. He'd rarely, very rarely,

237

speak to her. He'd watch her until she finished talking, then shrug, nod or shake his head. Jen never asked me why Eric didn't like her – she probably didn't notice. It was like the night of her birthday when she didn't guess I'd had sex with Greg. She didn't notice some things even if they were running up and down in front of her waving a flag. I never asked Eric why he didn't like her. I did notice. I simply didn't want an honest answer, which Eric would undoubtedly give me. Sometimes, you'd rather someone lied.

'What I don't understand is why you, Martha and even Renée can see Greg and I are having a thing, but Jen and Matt, our closest friends, haven't twigged.'

Eric supped his pint. 'Remember that episode of the *New Adventures of Superman* that had that villain Tempus, who knew Superman's identity, and had H. G. Wells in it? And remember how Tempus told Lois, "What everyone can't work out is how anyone could be so galactically stupid?" because she didn't know for years that Clark was Superman?'

Strangely enough, I did. 'You think Matt and Jen are galactically stupid?'

'No. As H. G. Wells pointed out to Lois, something along the lines of, "You didn't want to see it." People are very good at not seeing things that are staring them in the face. It's a defence mechanism against things upsetting their lives. Same with Matt and Jen. Well, Jen. Matt probably doesn't notice because he's a bloke. But Jen . . . if she wanted to know that you and Greg are in love, she'd know it.'

'Nah, if Jen knew she'd tell me, she's like that.'

'Consciously she might not know, unconsciously, that's another matter.'

'Hmmm . . .' I replied. 'Us psychologists are always putting things down to unconscious thought because nobody can prove otherwise.'

Eric did The Thing With His Eyes. His head would still be

dipped because, say, he was looking into his pint, and you'd utter something he didn't agree with and, without moving his head *at all*, he'd blink, then be staring at you. In that moment of blinking he'd have redirected his gaze and would suddenly be staring at you. It was cool but unnerving. It always made me jump, as if he'd rounded on me physically. 'Has Jen fixed any more blind dates for you?'

'Not since the day Matt moved in.'

'Weren't her attempts to fix you up at one point averaging one or two a week?'

'Yes.'

'And they've stopped?'

'Yes.'

'In three months, nothing?'

'Yes.'

'I bet she's been off with you of late, too, leaving you out of things. Ignoring you. Not calling as much. Basically treating you like she did when you were going out with that other bloke?' (Even Eric, who had spoken to Sean and remembered most of my boyfriends from first year at uni, couldn't remember Sean's name.)

'You mean Sean?' I said.

'Yeah, him. Is she treating you like that?'

'I suppose.'

'She knows. Subconsciously, she knows. And, subconsciously, she's waiting for you to tell her, so she can . . .' Eric stopped. 'Anyway, we've spent way too much time talking about you, *hen*, let's talk about me.'

If The Thing With His Eyes was unnerving, Eric's ability to start a sentence, leave it half-finished but still get his point across was downright scary. And irritating. There was no point questioning him either, to try to find out if you'd understood what he'd almost said because he'd plead, 'I've forgotten what I was going to say.'

'Don't think I didn't notice you slipping that "you and Greg are in love" nonsense into the conversation. I love Greg as a friend. Nothing else.'

'Yeah, yeah. Do I get to meet him this weekend?'

Ha! I'd *be lucky to see him again, let alone you.* We hadn't spoken and hadn't seen each other since Wednesday night when he walked out. Usually we'd speak at least twice a day, but we hadn't and I hadn't got as anxious as usual. I didn't know why. Maybe because he'd done it before and he'd come back. Or maybe because I pushed it to the back of my mind with cleaning. Or maybe because this was my chance to call Mr Chocolate Sniffer. I hadn't, but it was my chance to. 'I thought we were going to talk about you,' I said.

'What's to talk about? Wife, fine. Work, could be better. Cottage, falling down.'

Eric's relationship with his wife, Arrianne, was the antithesis of my real parents' relationship. Every time I saw them, I'd meet Eric at work, we'd go back to his cottage which was an hour's drive from the centre of Edinburgh and she got a better reception than me. As though they hadn't seen each other in months, they'd practically leap into each other's arms, snog each other's faces off, talk excitedly, giggle. *Giggle.* I'd once asked Eric if they were always like that. And he'd shrugged and said: 'Yeah, course,' like it was the most natural thing on earth.

Freaks, I'd thought and asked about the rows.

'So, have you and Arrianne managed to have an argument yet?' I asked jokingly. Whenever I asked he told me they didn't argue. Ever: '*We agree about everything.*'

Eric gave me a long hard look, as though sizing me up. Seeing if I could handle what he was about to tell me.

'Do you think I'd make a good father?' he asked.

'Yeah, course. What's that got to do with . . .' Oh no. That's why he'd looked at me like that, he was trying to work out if

I could handle this information. Eric was very sensitive with me when it came to arguments or splitting up. When he and Arrianne split up years and years ago, he'd rung me to tell me and to reassure me that they were still friends, that she definitely wouldn't vanish from my life. He might as well have saved himself the trouble if they were going to split up now. Sickness speared my stomach. I didn't want Eric and Arrianne to split up. Or argue. It was freakish not to argue, but I could put up with that; I could deal with no arguing as averse to screaming rows.

Eric gulped his pint. 'All we do now is argue. First time in twelve years. Y'know, even when we split up, we *didnae* argue. It was decision we made because we both wanted to see other people. And now . . . now . . . oh, fuck it. Just fuck it.'

My heart rate increased at Eric's frustrated, despairing tone. Please no. I didn't want them to tear each other apart. I loved Arrianne. She was like the sister I'd never had. Jen and I were close, but we'd chosen each other. Arrianne had been brought into my life by a relative, like a real sibling, and I loved her. Her and Eric had met on the first day of college, in Edinburgh, and they'd been friends for years. When they finished college, they'd got together and settled just outside Edinburgh, where Arrianne's from. They'd split up once, six years ago, started seeing other people, but got back together after a year. In that year Arrianne still called me and wrote to me like she'd always done. When they got back together they'd married less than six months later.

I didn't want to see two people I loved go through the ritual my parents went through. That 'anything to hurt the other one' battle that only ended when one of the fighters was so wounded they didn't have enough left to fight with. 'But you said everything was fine,' I whined.

'It is. It will be.'

'What's the problem, Ez? Why don't you want to have kids?'

241

Eric slid down in his bit of the booth, raised his pint glass to hide his face. 'Dunno.'

'Like hell you don't. Tell me.'

Eric ignored me, started looking around the pub.

'If you don't tell me I'll mention in front of Mum that you don't want to make her a grandmother. Heaven knows she's given up on me ever getting married, let alone having children, so . . .'

' All right, I'll tell you. But you mustn't tell anyone, not Mum, not Dad, not Arri. No one.'

'I swear,' I replied.

He drank more of his light-coloured pint until all that was left was a hint of pale liquid and islands of white froth all around the glass. For a man who liked neat whisky, he surprisingly liked lager too. 'All right.' Deep breath from big brother. 'It's going to sound awful, but I don't want to be married to someone's mother. I don't want to end up superfluous to our life. I talk to men every day who find it almost impossible to go home because they feel shut out of the life their wives have with the new baby. They're knackered and get depressed and have nobody to talk to. I don't want to lose Arri to that. She's my best friend. A baby will wreck that.'

'Then of course there's the fact your mother ran off to start a new life a year after you were born and died before she could come back.'

Eric's face tightened in displeasure. 'My *mother* is on her way here as we speak, with my father,' he spat, his voice challenging me to argue.

'You know what I mean,' I suggested gently.

'No. I. Don't.' Eric refused to acknowledge his birth mother. Dad2 had tried to talk to him about her but Eric always said he didn't want to know. I knew about her, what little Dad2 would tell me, but Eric had decided she didn't exist. That encompassed his mother's side of his family. They tried to contact him over the years and sometimes he'd speak to them but he made it clear it was for Dad2's sake, not because he wanted to know them. It was such an unEric way of behaving but I didn't want to upset him by asking him about it.

I touched his arm, didn't want to alienate him. 'Ez, your relationship with Arri will change, course it will. But you'll adjust. We all adjust to circumstances good or bad. Like me and Greg. I never thought I'd go near him, or anyone like him, but here I am, seeing him. Actually, not just "seeing him", having a relationship with him.' *I think.*

Eric stared into the mid-distance as I talked. He didn't move or react.

'Look how well you take care of me. You're depriving at least one child of all that love and sensibleness and all-round irritating goodness you personify. You'd be a great father. Don't let the things that might never happen stop you from becoming the fantastic things you can be.'

We sat in silence for a while. 'I never thought of it like that,' Eric eventually replied. He looked me up and down in wonderment. 'Although, must say, you should take a bit of your own advice, *hen*. OK, my round. Then we'd better get back to yours to shower and change before Mum gets here and gives us the six-hour version of the passive smoking lecture.'

Eric slid out of the booth, headed for the bar.

I watched him flirt with the barmaid. Not a patch on Arrianne, but Eric, like Greg, found it necessary to befriend or flirt with most people he met. He might grow to dislike them, but it was his intention to get on with everyone . . .

When we first met, one summer's day when the rain was coming down in sheets outside, Eric was going to be ten in ten days; I was going to be ten in three months and ten days. Mum and Dad2 had been 'going out' for two weeks and I'd met Dad2 twice. To me he was a tallish white man with blondish hair and a permanent smile.

Eric was the same height as me, but puffy around the face, circular around the body and Dad2 had, rather cruelly, dressed him in green and white horizontal stripes so he appeared more circular than he was, with smart blue trousers and shiny black shoes.

I was wearing a red and white gingham, puffy-sleeved dress with black tights and equally shiny black shoes.

Eric Hampton, aged nine and eleven months, held out the white paper bag in his right hand instead of saying 'Hello, Amber' as instructed to by his father. 'Would you like a Cola Cube?' he asked, as though he'd practised the line for a school play.

I looked to my mother for guidance. Was I allowed to accept the proffered confection? Mum, with her hair pinned back into a bun, smiled and nodded. I took an orangey-red cube, covered in crushed sugar.

'Would you like to play Ludo?' I asked in the same school-play-rehearsed voice.

Eric looked at his dad for the same guidance I'd looked to Mum for. Dad2 smiled and nodded too, then we ran off to play. He became my weekend best friend and then my brother when they moved in.

The woman behind the bar flushed as Eric paid her a compliment. I moved my bag onto my lap, took out my mobile. *Take my own advice*, I thought. *Take my own advice*.

'*Sunday Chronicle*, hello?' the voice said as they answered the phone.

'It's me,' I said.

'Hi,' Greg replied, frost in his voice.

'What are you up to tonight?' I asked.

'This and that.'

'Oh. I was wondering if you'd like to come to my place for dinner?'

Greg said nothing.

'Well, it'll be my place for dumping stuff and getting changed. We'll go out for dinner tonight. Then we'll go shopping tomorrow, have lunch in town and back to my place for dinner. We usually all lie in on Sundays, pad around in our pyjamas, eat late breakfast, then they all leave.'

Greg still said nothing.

'You don't have to be around for all of it. Mum'll freak if you see her braless and in her pyjamas, but you're welcome to come out tonight and see if you could stand a whole weekend with my family.'

Still silence. *Isn't this what he wanted? A piece of me. A piece of my family. That mythical something very few people got? Why was I getting the silent treatment?*

'Greg?'

'Are you sure about this?'

'I wouldn't ask if I wasn't sure,' I lied. But it was only a small lie.

'Shall I come round to yours for about seven-thirty?'

'Perfect, see you later, darling.'

'See you later, gorgeous.'

As Eric put our drinks on the table I realised I'd unintentionally called him 'darling'. He was, I suppose. He was my darling. Special. He was going to go where no man had gone before.

'You didn't answer my question, am I going to meet Greg this weekend?'

'Yup.' *You are now.*

chapter twenty-two

parental guidance

Mum and I have an odd relationship. 'Reserved' is one word for it.

I'm always pleased to see her, our 'reunions' are usually a laugh, and Christmas, holidays, times we spend together are good, but I do often wonder what things would be like if Dad2 or Eric weren't there as well.

I knew Mum before them, she knew me before them; when she was perpetually unhappy and I was constantly afraid. I knew Mum when she spent more time shouting than she did sleeping. When she could ignore me for days because I hadn't finished all the food on my plate at dinner. When she tore apart my favourite book because I'd given her a look. I knew Mum when everything she did was full of resentment and bitterness.

Eric looked like peanut brittle; Mum *was* peanut brittle, except to look at her small, round body with her curly black hair you'd think she was fudge. You thought she was soft, my mum, but she was hard as nails. Most people think of their mothers as fudgy – all sugary and comforting – inside and out, not mine.

My mum had become hardened during her time with my dad, Dad1. She was difficult to get to know, to get close to. I'd never seen her cry, not once. She found it easy to be angry; easy to be independent; hard to show her joy. Anything good I did was snatched away from me, made into something she did that got me it. Like when I got a 2:1 for my degree. Dad1 had been disappointed I hadn't got a first; Mum had told me she'd been praying non-stop for twenty-four hours for me to do well. I wasn't good enough in Dad's eyes; I hadn't spent months slaving over books in Mum's eyes. And on graduation day . . . Dad, in a rare moment of unDadness, told me he was proud of me. Before those words had a chance to penetrate the shield of calm I'd constructed to get through a day of my parents being in the same three-mile radius, Mum had snapped at him, 'You should've told her that years ago, it's too late to say it now.'

So, sometimes it'd take me a while to warm up to Mum. Not only because I remembered her when she was unhappy, mainly because I remembered how resentful I was of her when she was unhappy. Guilt, I suppose. I spent so much time alone, worried that something I did or said would set my parents off, that it became difficult, if not nigh on impossible, to look at either of my parents when I spoke to them. Yes, as an adult, I understood what they were going through. Didn't stop me, though, for the first few hours of seeing them, feeling like that girl sat in the back room while they went at it in the front room: shouting, smashing and everything that went with it.

I loved my mother, I loved my real father, but it took a while for me to warm up to them.

'To whom do these belong?' Mum asked, holding a pair of grey jockeys between her fingertips. She and Dad2 had arrived a few minutes earlier and she'd gone to change out of her travelling clothes – which in Mum speak was to check how untidy my flat was – and she'd reappeared thirty seconds later with the undergarments.

Warmth and life ebbed out of my body as I stared at Greg's pants. When I'd gone into the tidying frenzy required of an imminent visit from my mother, I'd meant to collect all of Greg's bits and pieces, put them into a box and stash them under the futon in my office where Eric slept (he wouldn't go through my stuff). Meant to, completely forgot. And why did I forget? Because Greg was moving in with me on the sly.

I knew women who'd done this. Martha, for example, had started leaving bathroom things at her Tony's place, then underwear, then jumpers and pyjamas; Tony only realised she hadn't spent a night away from his flat in a month when he found a box of tampons in his bathroom. I'd thought only women were that sneaky until I started seeing Greg. He'd made it his duty to do the weekly wash now, not out of an altruistic need to make my life easier, but because half of it consisted of his clothes – he'd stopped carrying spare clothes with him a millennia ago. In the bathroom, a spare toothbrush had appeared. Not the type of spare toothbrush I used to carry in my bag when I was dating Sean. Nope, Greg's was a per-manent fixture, slotted into my toothbrush stand like it belonged there. Aftershave had appeared on the shelf in the bathroom, as had a shaving kit. He never got up early to go home and change any more. When I was going out with Sean, that was for over a year, I'd often be seen by people I knew boarding a bus to his with half my wardrobe and the contents of my bathroom shelf crammed into a holdall, no matter how long I was staying. I hadn't left so much as an earring at Sean's. Or at Greg's.

Greg had so successfully and slyly moved in with me, I'd not noticed that his stuff shouldn't be there. If I'd forgotten to hide Greg's pants, then I hadn't hidden other related para-phernalia. My body went weak. My vibrator. I'd left my fluorescent pink vibrator in the top drawer of my beside table – Greg had been chasing me around the flat with it the other day and I'd blithely chucked it in the drawer afterwards. And, oh no, on the bedside table, in the wooden box, were the condoms. *The condoms.*

As all these thoughts galloped through my brain, there was silence in my living room. Dad2 had paused in putting his glass of beer to his lips. Eric, who was stood about two foot away from me, was also staring at the pants. Even the television was holding its breath. The pores on my forehead opened and sweat started to creep out. I was thirty, for goodness' sake, surely my mother wouldn't still think I was a virgin. But then, knowing my three parents, they'd think I'd be a virgin until my wedding day and the man I married was my first boyfriend.

My mother was holding my boyfriend's pants. Could things get any worse?

BUZZZZ! The buzzer exploded into the silence and D2 and I leapt out of our skins.

Eric, the calmest man alive, said: 'I think you're about to meet the owner of those pants, Mum.'

I moved past Mum and the offending article and went into the corridor, to the buzzer. I picked up the black phone by the door, grunted into it.

'It's me,' Greg said.

Too horrified to speak, I grunted into the receiver again, pushed the button with the key symbol on it, then opened my front door ready to whisper to him, warn him, that my parents knew we were having sex and therefore not to make any comments that could be taken in an 'I'm having my wicked way with your daughter and there's nothing you can do about it' manner. My voice shrivelled and died in my throat as I clapped eyes on him.

WHAT THE HELL IS HE DOING?

As if I hadn't had enough shocks in the past three minutes, Greg was presenting me with another: he was wearing a three-piece suit. Waistcoat, jacket and trousers. All charcoal colour, teamed with white shirt, navy-blue tie. His hair was freshly washed and combed back off his face into a ponytail. (He might as well wear his suit jacket over his vest and hitch up his sleeves because ponytails on men were synonymous with 'eighties wanker' as far as I was concerned.)

My heart, which was already beating in double time, sped up to quadruple time. He was meeting my parents, not my bank manager. And even my bank manager, cool as she was, wouldn't expect him to dress like that.

'Do I look all right?' Greg whispered as he arrived at my door.

I nodded, mute. And scared. *Dear God, please don't let him start talking in a posh accent or something.*

I led the way into the living room. As we entered, Dad2 stood. Mum and Eric were already standing but, thankfully, Mum was no longer displaying Greg's underwear. All three of them looked expectantly to the door as Greg stepped into the living room behind me.

I could imagine what Greg was seeing: a five-foot-nothing woman, with black, curly-permed hair. She has a nice face and is wearing a blue pleated skirt, white blouse and a big cream cardie. To the woman's left, about half a foot taller in height, is a white man. He has glasses on that don't hide his lined, jowly face. What hair hasn't receded is white. He wears suit trousers and a white shirt, with the collar open, curls of his chest hair showing at the top. To the woman's right, taller than both of the older people, is an Aryan type in baggy blue combats and white T-shirt.

'Everyone, this is Greg . . .' My voice died. *Shite, hadn't even thought about what to call him,* 'My . . .' *What was he? My boyfriend? Yes, obviously. But I'd only called him that out loud to Mr Chocolate Sniffer. And nobody who could even vaguely be described as my boyfriend had met my parents. This was all too brand new.* 'My erm . . . boy . . . fmnd. Greg, this is my mum, Dad2 and my brother, Eric.'

250

'Pleased to meet you,' Mum said, taking Greg's proffered hand.

'The pleasure's all mine,' Greg replied, straight into flirt mode – the creep even kissed the back of her hand.

'Hello, Greg,' Dad2 said. 'Are you named after Gregory Peck by any chance?'

'Yes, sir. My mother absolutely loved *Roman Holiday*.'

SIR?!

'All right, mate,' Eric said, shaking Greg's hand warmly.

Greg visibly relaxed. 'Hi,' he said with a grin.

'Mate, thanks to you, I'm going to have to change,' Eric said. 'It's not a good way to start things, you know? Making your girlfriend's brother look bad.'

'Sorry?' Greg said.

'Look at yea. Suit. I'll have to change. Wear my suit. If I don't my *ma* will go on and on about how smart yea look. Won't yea, Mum?'

Mum gave him a look that said, *Stop being so silly*.

Greg shrugged. 'Sorry.'

'A wee tip for yea, lad. Always try to impress the brother, not the old folks. Brothers have more sway with the girl-friends.'

Mum raised an eyebrow at Eric that said, *Go to your room and change*.

'See?' Eric smirked at Greg, then headed for the office/second bedroom.

Eric's mucking about had been an attempt to put everyone at ease. The pants incident hadn't done Greg any favours so Eric made Mum relax enough to give him a couple of her world-famous looks. Mum and Dad2 went off to change, too, leaving me with Greg.

'That went all right, didn't it?' Greg whispered anxiously.

'I suppose, if you don't count the pants and the condoms.'

★

'Bye, everyone, it was great to meet you. I'll see you soon,' Greg said, picking up his jacket and tie. I stood too, ready to see him out.

Dad2 chuckled. 'Soon? Yes, lad, I guess tomorrow is soon,' Dad2 said.

'I don't know why he's going home anyway, pretending he doesn't sleep here. It's not like Mum hasn't already found his pants,' Eric smirked.

Dad2 almost spat out his beer as Eric collapsed in laughter. Mum had the beginnings of a smile teasing around her eyes (two small sherries had loosened her up). I hooked an arm through Greg's. He was the only person who hadn't had a drink because he'd driven us to the restaurant. He looked confused.

'See you tomorrow, lad,' D2 said.

'See ya tomorrow, mate,' Eric said, tossing Greg a can of beer. 'Have this when you get home.'

Greg caught it one-handed.

'Good night, Gregory,' Mum said, 'see you tomorrow.'

Greg and I started to the door and as I shut it behind us D2 called out, 'Don't bring the car tomorrow, lad, we'll pay for your taxi home. You've got to have a couple of drinks with us.'

'Aye, and none of that suit nonsense, either,' Eric added.

'Byeeeee,' Mum called.

Fresh air pulled its cool blanket of oxygen and nitrogen and all the other elements that made up the air we breathe around us as we stepped out of my building and went to his red Escort.

Greg opened his car door, threw his jacket across into the passenger seat. Immediately his arms wrapped themselves around me, pulling me tight against him. I was a whole galaxy of emotions, but the sun in my galaxy right then was relief. Greg hadn't batted an eye about my family. I hadn't caught him giving sly looks or acting like he was trying to work things out. He came, he saw, he accepted. He'd even had the common decency to be scared they'd hate him. That's all I wanted, for him to realise my family is like a box of chocolates: we all looked different, but were essentially made from the same stuff. We belonged together.

Greg was lovely. I kept forgetting that. I kept expecting him to turn into Darth Vader when he was so blatantly Han Solo. He didn't need to be constantly held at arm's length. And I didn't regret lessening the distance between us now. I'd almost driven myself crazy by worrying about it beforehand, but it'd been done and he didn't run away, and I hadn't wanted to run away either. He was special.

'So, you suit-wearing weirdo, do you think you could handle a weekend with my family? Will you come back tomorrow?'

'Do you want me to?' he asked.

'After only three hours you're like part of my family: Eric likes you; D2 thinks you're a laugh and Mum was impressed with the suit and the "yes, sir". But, apart from all that, I'll miss you.'

'Really?' He was surprised. But not as surprised as me – all the nice stuff I'd been thinking had spilled out.

I pushed my lips on his. If I kept talking I might say something stupid. Greg pulled me away after a few seconds.

'I'll have to stop you right there,' he murmured against my lips. 'After three days a simple kiss could get very messy.'

'OK, get in the car before I drag you back upstairs. And, Sunday night, no telly, no food, just sex,' I said. I leant in through the car window as he shut the door behind him. 'Did her parents adore you after about six seconds too?'

'Who?'

'The six-yearer, did her parents adore you straight away?'

Mid-breath, Greg froze. His whole body meanwhile

seemed to drain of colour and life. Ahh, there it was, 'something stupid' courtesy of Ms Amber Salpone.

Maybe if I back away from the car he won't notice that I've dredged up what is obviously a painful memory.

'Do you really want to know? About her?'

Not really. Not when you have a penchant for telling me every detail about what you've got up to in the past. Not when you don't yet know that I was highly selective about my past. 'If you want to talk about it,' I said neutrally. *Please say no, please say no.*

Greg leant across, opened the passenger door. 'You'd better sit down.'

Great.

I got in the car, shut the door, twisted in my seat, pulled my knees up and draped Greg's jacket over me, hooked it under my chin. It smelt of him. His soft but manly scent. It reminded me of going to sleep, listening to his heartbeat. Greg twisted slightly in his seat so he could look at me while he spoke. *Do not say anything sarky or 'clever'. Even if it looks like the conversation's going to get heavy, you are not allowed to become Sarky Salpone,* I warned myself.

'Kristy and I slept with each other on and off during college but in the final year we got together properly. She was my soul mate. I know it sounds weird, a bloke saying that, but that's how I felt. Anyhow, during our fourth year together we talked about going travelling. During our fifth year we talked about splitting up. During our sixth year she got pregnant.'

OK, heart, please start beating, this is no big shock. Greg's got a child. I suppose nobody who shagged around as much as he did could not be a baby father to at least one child. No, heart, I'm not kidding, please start beating. Please . . . Thank you.

'I was so excited when she told me. I got down on one knee and asked her to marry me. She said yes. Everything was so good, so perfect. There I was, about to marry my soul mate and have a baby with her . . . Kristy started doing forgetful pregnant things, leaving things lying around, leaving letters lying around. I was practically living at her flat then. I know I shouldn't have read it . . .' He stopped.

Greg, who had a key to her flat because he was practically living with her, had been there all alone. Bored, restless, wanting his pregnant fiancée to come home so he could take care of her. The letter was lying on the bedside table. He hadn't meant to read it. It's just, he saw his name on the blue sheet of paper. Like hearing your name in a crowded room, his name and the word 'baby' jumped out at him. This was odd because they'd planned to wait three months before telling anyone their joyous news.

I don't think you should tell Greg the baby isn't his, the letter read. *You never know, it might be. Just hold off until after you get married.*

'And do you know what I did?' Greg asked me.

I shook my head. I didn't want to know. Not really. I just couldn't be with a bloke who hit a pregnant woman. Or even hit a woman. My life had been through that too many times already.

'I pretended it wasn't happening. I cooked dinner as usual, sat and waited for her. I don't know how I did it, but I put it right out of my head. Kristy knew, though. It might have been out of my head but it showed on my face. When she went into the bedroom she saw she'd left the letter out and guessed. The whole story came out then. That year we'd gone through hell, she'd got close to another guy. She'd fallen in love but leaving me would be like leaving her best friend so she stayed.

'She stayed out of pity. She was convinced the baby wasn't mine because she never used contraception with this other man. We'd been talking about having a child, so she came off the Pill and we carried on using condoms until we definitely decided to start trying for a baby. So, the baby wasn't mine.

She knew that. She'd wanted his child, didn't want mine. It all came out that night. How she really felt. How she'd wanted to leave.'

Greg paused, rubbed his hands over his eyes.

'And do you know what I did?'

'You started sleeping around?'

'No. Oh, nooo, nooo, noo. I begged her. I begged her not to leave me. I lost all self-respect. I didn't care about self-respect, I cried and ranted and broke things and begged. She lost what little respect she had left for me and asked me to leave her flat.

'It didn't stop there. For months I practically stalked her. I wouldn't leave her alone, I kept ringing her, writing to her, turning up at her place. Then, one morning, I woke up and decided no more. I stopped. Left her alone. Literally just left her alone. And began my life of serial shagging.'

I bit my tongue to stop myself asking which was better, Cornflakes or Weetabix, during his time of cereal shagging. Then I had to bite my tongue harder. I did feel sympathetic. Which was why I had to ruin things by getting sarky. It was my natural defence mechanism against things getting too serious.

'I couldn't . . .' Greg began, 'I couldn't risk getting into that situation again. When you sleep around you can have that close human contact, connect with people, be intimate, but not have to risk getting as hurt as I was by Kristy. I've always needed that contact, so I got it but didn't have to feel that pain and humiliation again. Five years of it until you.'

'Did you ever see her again?' I asked in a sensible, grown-up voice.

Greg laughed humourlessly. 'Once I decided I wasn't interested, she wanted us to get back together. I was tempted. I was so tempted, but I decided no. Weeks I agonised over it. I even slept with her again. She'd had a termination. Her dream man didn't want to father her children after all. We talked and talked. And then, I said no. She moved to Dublin a few weeks later.'

'Oh,' I said. *Was it that bad a shag she had to leave the country?* I thought, then instantly hated myself.

'And to answer your original question, no, her parents didn't adore me, or even like me. It took six years and just when they were coming round to the idea of this lad who wasn't good enough for their daughter being in their lives, we split up. Your family's cool, though, very cool. You really think they like me?'

'What's not to like?' *Apart from that ridiculous hair.*

We fell silent. The car was suddenly too small and cramped for all those big confessions. All the information, all the exposure and soul-baring, should've been done somewhere bigger. And Greg, who wasn't prone to such deep revelations, probably felt naked, emotionally vulnerable. I'd know how he felt if I'd ever done it myself.

'Well, better be going back, they'll be thinking we're having sex down here – mainly because Eric will have told them that.'

'Yeah.'

'Yeah.'

'OK, good night.'

'Good night.'

'See you tomorrow.'

'See you tomorrow.'

Painful. Like we were on our first date and didn't know if we should kiss or not. To be honest, I didn't know if we should kiss or not. This revelation had altered the very fabric of our relationship.

'Are you going to kiss me?' I thought it, Greg said it. 'You don't have to. It's just . . .'

'Greg.'

257

'Yes?'

'Shut up and kiss me.'

Back upstairs, everyone had gone to bed. Mum had left a duvet on the sofa along with a couple of pillows. The side spotlights were still on, as was the TV. I sat heavily on the sofa, resting one arm on the pile of bedlinen.

Unexpectedly, sadness conquered me. Greg's story made me so sad the corners of my mouth turned down. Sadness for what he'd gone through. Sadness for his pain. Sadness because he'd been in love before.

chapter twenty-three

good girl

'Try this one on,' Mum said, giving me an armful of dresses. We'd been out shopping for a good few hours and Mum had spent most of the morning pointing out nice dresses and pretty blouses and smart skirts. Mum had nightmares about my combats and jeans and jersey tops and didn't realise I owned all the blouses I was ever going to own – none.

Even though Mum had been on a mission to reinvent me for the past few hours and even though I was surrounded by my family for the first time in six months, I couldn't stop reassessing my boyfriend.

Greg Walterson

I thought Greg Walterson was a slag because he could be. He had the tools for it: elegant looks; easy, unassuming charm; stamina. Greg was the man most men would be if they had two of the above tools, let alone all of them. At least that's what I thought. There was no excuse for the way Greg behaved – there's never an excuse for bad behaviour – but now I knew there was a *reason* for it. It didn't vindicate him, but it explained him. And I couldn't stop staring at him. When he was laughing with Eric, trying to impress Dad2 or flirting with Mum, I'd find my eyes were looking over Greg.

Wondering who he was. Wondering what else there was to find out about him and be horrified by.

But why was I so freaked, unsettled, disassembled by this reve-lation? This was good news, no? The unveiling of Greg 'Tart Face' Walterson as someone who had a heart, who had layers, who was indeed a selection box rather than a lump of milked down, solidified cocoa was cause for celebration. He'd always defied classification before. He had Minstrel eyes, sure, but he was always changing, altering. In the three years I'd known him he'd been practically every type of confectionery made. He'd started off being one of those showy, tosser chocolates that was shiny and tasty-looking, but when you ate it, it went straight to that tooth with a tiny piece of exposed nerve and caused the kind of pain you never fully recovered from. Before I'd slept with him he'd become a Twirl – something I'd buy if I couldn't get my favourite chocolate. The second choice on my list.

The unveiling of him as a possible Flake, something that crumbled and disintegrated, that fell apart under pressure, was only positive. Showed the ability to love. Showed he had a heart, one that could be broken. One that had been broken. He knew how to hurt. This meant I wouldn't be the woman he tried out his emotions on.

It'd never bothered me before when boyfriends had experi-enced that mythical thing called 'love' pre-me. Which begged the question, why did I feel so weird about it? Why did I feel any way about it? The answer, of course, was blatantly clear. Was facing me every time I caught a glimpse of myself in a reflective surface. It was one of those answers I didn't want to acknowledge.

If I acknowledged why I was so upset – upended, dis-turbed – then I would have to admit that I wasn't as pure of thought and deed as I liked to suppose. I would be admitting that I, despite appearances to the contrary, had an ego the size of Ghana's last cocoa harvest. I didn't want to think of myself like that. It was like thinking of your parents having sex – you knew it happened, but if you didn't think about it, you didn't get upset by it. I didn't want to be an ego woman who had a problem with someone loving someone before me.

While I'd been wrestling with my ego and reassessing Greg, Mum had been emptying the rails of dresses.

'I can't afford them,' I said, relieving her of the bundle, then almost keeling over under the weight. 'Not even one of them.'

'We are paying,' Mum said. 'Just go and try them on.'

I turned towards the changing rooms. 'Don't forget to come show us,' D2 called after me.

'Why don't you just call me Gerbil in front of Greg and be done with it,' I mumbled.

In the changing room I took a proper gander at the dresses. All variations on a theme – Mum trying to get me to be more girly. She was fighting thirty years of comfort dressing. Besides, I was incompatible with dresses because they're mostly made for right-way-up pears – small breasts, big hips – and I, with my big breasts and smallish hips, was an upside-down pear. Despite what Jen had said, I had lost weight. Not enough for me not to have a big chest, but my tummy was less round, almost flat in parts, and my hips more slender . . . *Stop it, stop it, stop it. Stop thinking about your weight*, I ordered myself.

I hated worrying about my weight, wondering about my inches. Since Jen had made that comment, even though I knew she was wrong, it kept coming to me. I was always thinking twice about eating anything. Had started reading the calorific value on things in the supermarket. (It drove Greg up the wall because checking the values in everything I normally bought added another half an hour to our shopping time. He'd taken to snatching things out of my hand and slinging them in the trolley, giving me the scowl of a man not to be messed with.) Maybe I am fat, I often mused as I got dressed in the morning. Maybe it was immoral how much I weighed. If my best mate, the woman I loved and trusted, thought I was fat, then maybe I should reconsider how I looked. Your friends are the ones who are meant to tell you these things. As if there wasn't enough in my life to be neurotic about, onto my list had been scrawled 'fat knacker status' and 'Greg being in love before'.

I checked through the dresses hanging on the chrome hooks in front of me until I found the least offensive and most likely to fit. It was the palest blue in soft shiny material with long sleeves and a scooped neck. I pulled it on, the folds falling gently over my curves, caressing my skin.

I looked into the mirror, twisted slightly. It didn't look too bad. I was quite presentable, in fact. It felt gorgeous on. For one moment I felt like a princess.

I stuck my head out of the curtain into the corridor to check it was clear, then dashed the short distance to the entrance to the changing room. As a bloke, D2 and Greg's jaws dropped open as I stepped into view. Tears sprang into Mum's eyes. Eric smirked.

Jeez, what's this all about? 'Is it that bad?' I asked. Were they all horrified by the curves bulging in the dress? I wrapped my arms around my waist to hide them.

'Stand up straight,' Mum ordered, pulling my arms away from my waist and adjusting the position of the dress's shoulders, blinking back her tears until they were a memory.

'You look lovely,' Dad2 said, tears in his eyes too.

'My sister's a girl,' Eric smirked once more.

Greg clutched my black leather rucksack in front of his lap as though his life depended on it. He was a slight shade of pink. I'd know that shade of pink anywhere. I pressed my lips together to hide a laugh: he had an erection. And with my mother stood not two foot away. When he saw that I'd spotted what he was doing, he blushed deeper until he glowed.

'I don't know why you want me to get this,' I said to my parents, 'it's not like I've got anywhere to wear it.' Yes, it felt nice on, but that didn't mean I'd wear it – especially when my mother had chosen it.

'Well, the next time Gregory takes you out somewhere nice,' Mum said, looking pointedly at Greg, 'you will have something nice to wear.' What she meant was: 'I may not be able to stop Gregory having his wicked way with you, but he'd better at least treat you like a lady.'

Greg, under Mum's scrutiny, blushed a deeper maroon. Any more blushing and he was going to pass out.

Eric laughed, obviously finding this highly entertaining.

'I don't know what you're laughing at, lad,' D2 said, 'we're buying you a suit next.'

Ha! I thought as I poked my tongue at Eric's scowling face.

Eric fought harder than I did.

Even though he must've known it was a losing battle from the moment Dad2 mentioned it, he still fought and fought. With our parents together on something, there were no ifs or buts. If they asked you, 'Wouldn't you like fish, it's better for you,' they weren't asking your opinion, they were stating a fact. They were telling you that you would indeed prefer fish, what with it being so good for you. And you may well have been salivating over that moist sirloin steak, cooked slowly in its own juices, smothered in mustard, but you would prefer that nice bit of poached cod. *OK*.

I was path-of-least-resistance woman. In most things, but particularly with my parents. All three of them. (Mrs H, Dad1's wife, did not count as a parent.) The path of least resistance for Eric would've been to try on the navy-blue suit with cream shirt and blue tie and be done with it. No. Eric argued. He wanted black, if anything. If not black, then brown tweed. If not that, then kooky green. On and on. We left with the blue suit, blue tie and cream shirt.

On the way back to mine Eric sulked. I did mention to him at one point that my dress had cost £60 while his suit, even though it was off the peg, had come in at £300. That's five times more fiduciary love they had expressed for him, but you didn't see me bealing on about it.

'Sod off, Gerbil,' had been his reply. He'd rooted in my bag for my mobile, took it and stomped off along the train platform to call Arrianne. If anyone would understand his outrage at being forced to own a blue suit it would be Arrianne. *Oh well*, I thought as I watched him dial, *at least it'd made him call her.*

I hadn't pushed him on it, but Eric hadn't called her since he'd arrived. He didn't own a mobile – 'They're the work of the Devil' – and when I reminded him to call her to say he'd arrived safely, he'd replied he'd do it later. And hadn't. Before our parents arrived I'd asked him if they'd rowed before he left and he'd half shrugged and started questioning me about Greg. It was a blatant diversionary tactic that had worked because I didn't want to upset him.

While the rest of us sat on the train, waiting for it to leave, Eric walked back and forth along Platform 1a as he talked. The scowl on his face relaxed with each passing minute. His face slowly came alive. His jaw unclenching, the knot of a frown on his brow smoothing itself out. I hadn't realised until now how aggravated and tired he'd looked since he got here. I wished there was something I could do to make it OK for him. I couldn't bear to see him suffer. Not emotionally or physically. What hurt him hurt me, deeply. He was like my twin. Greg shifted in the seat beside me, pressing his thigh close to mine as I watched Eric walk and talk.

A sudden feeling crawled up my neck then spread its tingling tentacles across my body. Eric wasn't talking to Arrianne. The way he was smiling – his face excited and keen – told me he wasn't talking to his wife. Things were worse than I thought: my brother was having an affair.

'How serious are you about Gregory?' Mum asked as she sliced onions for dinner. She was going to make Ghanaian stew, followed by semolina pudding. The menfolk had volunteered to go out for semolina and rice. (There were two bags of rice in the cupboard, but not enough Mum had decided. Because you never know, do you? Jesus could drop by any second with his five thousand mates, all claiming that those five loaves and two fishes weren't filling enough.) The 'volunteering' by the menfolk meant, of course, they'd ensconced themselves in the Fox & Grapes round the corner. For which Greg would be getting a couple hours' cold treatment – how dare he make me into the little woman staying at home while he went drinking; D2 would be getting a mouthful for the entire length of the M1 tomorrow; and Eric? Weeellll, Eric had a blue suit, cream shirt and blue tie.

How serious was I about Greg? Now there was a question. One I hadn't answered for myself, let alone for my mother. My *mother*. I didn't talk boyfriends with Mum. I didn't talk anything like that with her. It was icky. Anyway, we weren't like that. Eric had always talked to her and Dad2 about girlfriends and stuff. I couldn't, I wouldn't.

I had a far more different relationship with them. They weren't there for that kind of thing. I'm sure, usually, Mum would've assumed the foetal position and screamed her head off if I tried to drag her into my love life, whereas Eric did it because he did. He didn't care how they reacted. He wanted to share with them, so he did. Although he probably wouldn't be confessing to them about his affair. (I'd decided, in the tradition of so many before, to ignore what Eric was doing. I was still trying to assimilate the shocking information that my beloved brother was a bastard.)

So, why was my mother questioning me? 'We just got together,' I said.

Mum's knife froze in the middle of slicing up pinky-white chicken breasts, horror and disgust plastered across her face.

Oh.

Ah.

Mum now not only knew that I had defiled myself with the sexual act but I'd done it within a short amount of time; I'd just told my mum I was easy.

'Is that right?' she said, evenly, then started slicing again.

'I've known him for three years, though,' I said, back-pedalling for all I was worth. 'You know Jen? He's her boyfriend's best friend. We've known each other for three years.'

'Is that right.'

'Yeah,' I husked and stirred at the Ghanaian stew that was bubbling away on the stove. She'd found the pants. She'd most likely found the condoms and the vibrator, she knew I'd shagged Greg in record time, might as well complete things with our favourite positions.

'What future do you see with him?' Mum asked.

She wasn't going to let this go, was she? 'I haven't thought about it,' I replied.

'Do you think he's serious about you?'

I thought about it. Then realised I didn't want to think about it. He'd met my family. How much more serious did Mum think I was? How much more serious could anyone get in three months? 'What do you mean?' I asked.

'Do you think Gregory wants to be with you a long time?'

'I suppose.'

'Amber, why would Gregory want to stay with a woman who is . . .' She paused, struggling to find the right words. 'Free with herself?'

Free with herself?! I thought, glaring at the tomatoes breaking down to become the stew in the pot. *Why don't you say, 'A woman who is a whore,' because that's what you think I am, isn't it?*

'He will probably think you're like that with all men,' she continued.

'What, that I sleep with them?' I said in an uncharacteristic moment of free speech.

'Yes.' Mum was embarrassed but I felt my body bridle.

'Did you have this conversation with Eric when he got together with Arrianne?' I asked.

Mum was always doing this. Setting me the kind of standards that Eric wasn't expected to meet. I loved Eric, but sometimes I wanted to have what he had. The freedom to be bad. My brother was always so naughty, so awful, when we were growing up and nothing ever happened to him. But if I tried anything . . . Put it this way: when my dad, my real dad, lived in England – he moved to Ghana three years ago – I went to visit him (and Mrs H), those months I moved back to London. I'd been to the pub with the people I was temping with and got a bit drunk. Not falling-down drunk, just drunk enough to make me mega chatty. Considering it was a struggle to speak to my dad at the best of times and I only spoke to Mrs H when I absolutely had to, imagine their delight when I became Ms Chatterbox. *I* thought I'd had the best night in a while with them; they thought different. Dad wrote a long letter to Mum blaming her for me turning into a juvenile delinquent. I was twenty-four at the time.

During that same nine months, Dad2 took me to one side when I'd stayed with a friend three nights in a row and said he and Mum didn't want me behaving badly. In other words, having sex – I wasn't even having sex. I'd lived away from home for nearly five years at that point. *I was twenty-four.* I was twenty-four, but between the ages of sixteen and eighteen Eric had regularly climbed out of his bedroom window to go have sex with his twenty-nine-year-old girlfriend. All hell broke loose when they found out when he was seventeen, of course. It was the worst few days since Eric and Leonard had come to live with us, but despite the shouting and threats and long, long silences, it didn't stop Eric. He told them there was nothing they could do about it. Whereas when I was twenty-four, I couldn't drink or sleep out without it being a crime. I got pressure from all sides to be good.

'Eric is different,' Mum said.

'Why?' I asked.

'These things are different for men. No man will respect a woman if he thinks she's like that with all men. Do you think your father would have married me if he thought I was like that with all men?'

I almost dropped the wooden spoon in my hand. *What?!* Was I hearing this correctly? My mother, who was living with a man she wasn't married to, was eulogising her relationship with my father. My father, the man who ended up married to someone else after cheating on her and rowing with her and hitting her.

Besides, if a man doesn't respect you after you've slept with him, then he didn't respect you beforehand, did he? What was it going to change? Sex was important, it distinguished things from other relationships, but if he did a runner after sex, he sure as hell didn't intend to stay before sex. (Unless you were truly truly awful in bed.) Also, what about women respecting men? Was Greg's father pulling him to one side and saying, 'Son, you wanna stop all that shagging about, no woman will respect you if you carry on like that'? Nope. It was women buying into this nonsense that kept it going. If women didn't look down on women who shagged and fucked around instead of 'making lurve within the boundaries of a relationship', we wouldn't be having this conversation. All these arguments fought to get out of my mouth.

'Things are different nowadays,' I said. If ever there was a clear and firm statement of how I felt, what I thought, the principles of the creed by which I lived my life, that was it. Not.

I started quivering inside. Adrenalin whizzed through my veins, making my heart pound and my breath quiet but laboured.

This was why I was path-of-least-resistance woman; why I didn't row with people. If I did want to, I couldn't. I became physically incapable. The fight or flight response inside me was broken. I got too much adrenalin so I could neither row nor run, just speak in spasmodic, breathless tones. It'd started when I was young; when I saw what arguing got you. I learnt that if you answered back, you got a punch in the face. A kick in the stomach. Called names. That's why I was always giving way with Jen. Why I didn't row with Sean. Why I got panicky when I heard Martha and Renée rowing. It was also why I knew Greg was different: more than once I'd come close to rowing with him.

My broken fight or flight response was also why I reacted with humour in times of stress – I was trying to defuse a situation with laughter.

In the present, with Mum, the best I could do was, 'Things are different now.'

'It does not matter,' Mum said. 'Even now, Amber, I get looks and comments when people find out I'm with Leonard but our surnames are different. Leonard's sister still won't speak to us because we are not married. You don't have to go through all that. You can not have anything lasting with Gregory if you behave like this. If you don't make men respect you.'

'It's not like that with Greg,' I said.

'Listen.' Mum slammed the knife down so hard onto the worktop I jumped inside. She wouldn't ever hit me; she would never hit anyone, I knew that. I knew most people wouldn't hit you. But people can hurt you without hitting you. Which is why I was terrified of people's reactions. Even if they don't hit you, even if they don't slap or punch or kick you, they could take their love away. They could shut you out of their lives. That was why I never pushed it with Jen. Even if she was being unreasonable, I couldn't risk her abandoning me. Couldn't do anything that would result in her becoming a past tense in my life.

'I am far older than you, I know what I am talking about,' Mum said.

I concentrated on stirring the stew. I was holding my breath. Hoping Mum wouldn't carry on with this. Because if she did, despite my fear, despite the possibility she'd stop loving me, I was on the verge of telling her to leave it. That no matter how perfectly she expected me to behave, I wasn't going to finish with Greg. He was here for the foreseeable.

The key slid into the front door, halting our potential row. Moments later, the men came stumbling in, bringing with them a fuzz of alcohol, smoke and levity from the pub. Eric was carrying the rice and semolina while Greg clutched a bottle of red wine in one hand and a bottle of white wine in the other. Dad2 went over to Mum and peeked over her shoulder at what she was doing. She gave him an unimpressed sideways look. It wasn't a proper Mum look. She might have squeezed her lips together and narrowed her eyes, but she wasn't really cross with him. His absence had made it possible for her to tell me what she thought. Anyway, she loved him. She rarely stayed angry with him. They didn't row, either. I was always waiting for it but it never came. I suppose because Dad2 is like good-quality milk chocolate. Very easy to get on with. The kind of chocolate you'll stick with throughout your life: the taste is simple, comfortable, so you'll keep going back to it time after time. You may think about trying something else, but you'd always, *always* go back to the smooth-tasting, sweet treat that you knew and loved.

Dad1 is like that too. *Now*, he's like that. Before, he was like one of those Wonka bars that had crackly bits which would explode unexpectedly. You'd always be careful when dealing with it because you couldn't be sure when you'd encounter an explosive bit; when it'd blow up in your face. Now, after getting older and less angry, I suppose, Dad1 is like good-quality milk chocolate too.

'Nice time in the pub?' Mum said to Dad2.

'Don't be like that, Eden,' he said. 'We had to talk to Greg. Make sure he's treating our precious Amber properly, didn't we, Eric?'

'Yes, Dad,' Eric slurred. 'It's our duty, as the men of the family.'

I jabbed at a bit of tomato in the pot. They were doing it too. Acting as though I had to be protected from sex. Yes, it was a joke, but it came from the same place.

Greg, who seemed to sense the tension and anger emanating from me, came to me. He moved his head slightly in front of mine and our eyes locked.

He was asking silently if I was OK. I smiled a little smile at him. I smiled, but inside I was wondering if I could have anything lasting with Gregory?

Can I have anything lasting with any man if this is what I get from my family?

'true strength is being able to eat a bar of chocolate without feeling guilty'

chapter twenty-four

talk

Tense.

It'd been a fortnight since my family had visited and things had been tense between Greg and me. Very tense.

Greg had met my family. We were practically engaged in my head now. Not a good thing when you didn't believe in marriage. When I spoke to a family member, they asked about him. Asked about my man. He'd become my SO (Significant Other) and I wasn't even sure I could have anything lasting with a man.

I wasn't sure if Greg was reacting to my behaviour, my slight withdrawal from him, or if, now he'd bared his soul about Kristy, he felt closer to me, but he'd been different too. On edge. Which translated into him being mega clingy. It was a shock to discover that someone who used to be a cold, calculating bastard could mutate into someone who infected every moment with his cloying presence. Every day he sent me long, long emails about nothing even though he was going to be seeing me in a few hours. He had to know where I was every second of the day, even if I was sitting beside him and got up to go to the loo. (I almost asked him if he thought I was going to climb out of the bathroom window or something.) He'd even asked if I preferred Tom Cruise when he had long hair or short hair – I suspected he was asking me if I wanted him to cut his hair – and I replied: 'I preferred him when he'd had his head repeatedly kicked in by his ex-wife.'

'Amber, that never happened,' Greg reassured me.

'Oh,' I replied, 'well, a girl can dream.' (Yes, that had been my chance to get rid of his ridiculous hair, but he did have to ask me about the one celeb I actually hated, didn't he?)

Tense. Nervous. Strained. The pressure had been building up until today.

Today you could slice off chunks of the tension and sling it on the barbecue because, today, Greg had stretched my very last nerve as taut as it would go and was dancing up and down on it.

We'd gotten out of bed at eight o'clock – *on a SATURDAY MORNING* – to go flat-hunting. By two o'clock we'd seen, what?, six *trillion* flats and none of them were right. For example, the last one we'd been to: a one-bedroom flat in a modern, purpose-built block, second floor, all mod cons, £105 a week plus bills. It was smaller than my place but Greg was essentially living out of one bedroom at the moment, so having a kitchen/living room, bedroom and bathroom plus cupboard space for himself would be more than enough. But Greg had uttered the immortal 'I can't see myself living here' – as he'd been uttering all morning – and turned it down.

At which point, I'd lost the will to live, let alone flat-hunt. It wasn't like I needed to flat-hunt. I had a flat. I lived there very happily. I couldn't imagine myself living there when I'd seen it, but it was close to Horsforth station, close to a pub I'd been to several times as a student and I knew the area because my ex-college was up the road. Regardless of whether I could see myself living there or not, I took it. Then found I could see myself living there because I did live there.

We must've walked every inch of Headingley today and were still no closer to finding the place where Greg could see himself living. My feet were killing me, even in trainers.

Greg held the newspaper we were working from in his hands. 'There's still a couple left we can see,' he said hopefully.

I perched on the low, whitewashed wall outside the Skyrack pub on Otley Road. He perched beside me. 'It'd be easier if I was looking with someone. I could buy a place then. It'd be a joint effort.'

'You? Buy a place? You'll be wanting to get married next,' I scoffed.

Greg's expression was knocked asunder by my comment. 'Of course I want to get married. Don't you?' he said.

'Haven't we already had this conversation?' I replied testily. Didn't like house-hunting, just like I didn't like moving. I didn't begrudge this as much as I begrudged helping Matt to move because Matt had never given me a multiple orgasm – and, thankfully, never would.

Greg didn't say anything for a few seconds. 'Maybe I should go ahead and buy a place.'

He was thinking out loud. For fuck's sake! What was he vacillating about? This man, the one sat next to me, ran a department on Yorkshire's biggest Sunday paper and he was dithering about where he should live, when he had somewhere to live.

The psychologist in me knew there was something else under all this. Beneath each layer of his finding a place but not liking it, under every leaf of his indecision and now considering the option to buy, was a scared little man. Probably his fear of responsibility. If he gave up his student house that would mean, effectively, giving up his student lifestyle. Although he'd done that already and simply didn't realise it. The woman who didn't like flat-hunting in me wanted to tell him to get a bloody grip and choose somewhere.

'Why are you moving again?' I prompted.

Greg rustled the paper. 'Well . . .' he cleared his throat. 'I don't want to live with Rocky any more. I'm a grown-up. I should have my own place. It's, like, now I've got a proper girl-friend, I've looked at other parts of my life and found them wanting. I'm basically living like a superannuated student. And,' he looked at me from under his long eyelashes, 'and now I've got a girlfriend, I want to have her over whenever I want without worrying who'll find out.'

Sure, blame it on me. 'If you feel pressurised into moving, then you probably shouldn't do it. Especially if you've got a reasonable deal at the moment and you're not a hundred per cent committed to moving.'

'I am committed. It'd just be easier if someone would move with me. You know, share the responsibility of finding a place, setting up home, decorating, that kind of thing.'

'I guess, but I did it alone. It was fine. Actually, it's a lot easier doing it alone, you avoid the rows about what colour to paint everything, what walls to knock through, what flooring, etc., etc., etc.,' I replied.

'So you're not planning on sharing your space with anyone soon,' Greg stated.

I flopped my hands up and down in frustration, the psy-chologist in me had given it her best shot, now the woman who didn't like flat hunting was taking over. 'Don't know, haven't thought about it. How did this become about me? We're trying to find you a place to live.'

'And you wouldn't think of moving in with me?' Greg said.

I smirked, glanced at him, then swallowed the smirk before it evolved into a laugh. His face was set in the more mature version of the way he'd looked when he'd first kissed me all those years ago. No, not years. Three months ago. Which meant he wanted me to move in with him after three months. Nah. Course not. He couldn't be serious. My eyes met his big dark browns. *Could he?* Then I remem-bered, Greg was the original tart with a heart. Course he was serious. As serious as wearing that heart of his on his sleeve. He'd brandished his heart at bicep level when he kissed me. He'd done it again when he asked if I was sure I wanted to sleep with him. He'd done it again when he wanted me to go out with him. And now, he was doing it again with . . .

'I've scared you, haven't I?' he said.

'More, surprised,' I said. *If surprised means absolutely terrified.*

'I've only been hinting at it for days. Weeks, actually. And, of course, most of today.'

'Have you?' I asked. *This is what surprised is.*

'I forgot how perceptive you are. How many times have I said, "I want to be with you all the time"? Or, remember, "Every night for the past week I've gone to sleep wishing that coming home meant coming home to you"? Or, how about, "It's mad me paying rent at Rocky's when I'm hardly ever there"? And, you might remember this from about five minutes ago, "It'd just be easier if someone would move with me. You know, share the responsibility of finding a place, setting up home, decorating, that kind of thing". Any of these phrases sound familiar to you?'

'Yes, all right, I get the picture. But I'm not used to people, well, you, being so subtle. I expect you to say what you think.'

'I just did.'

'We've only been together three months.'

'Three months, three weeks, one day, but who's counting?'

Greg *counted* the time we were together. He wanted something it'd taken Jen three years to extract from Matt. And, all right, we were older now, but still, *three months*. Nobody knew about us; we hadn't even done the 'I love you' bit.

'You don't like me as much as I like you, do you?' Greg observed.

Why did he say that? Hadn't he been there these past three months? Wasn't he there when I fell asleep on him after he told me a story? That he told me stories anyway? Is that what Mum had been trying to tell me? That even though things are different now, if I slept with Greg he wouldn't trust me? That he'd need other, big gestures to prove he was special? 'Why do you say that?' I asked.

'Oh, I don't know, something to do with you not exactly looking thrilled about the whole idea. You don't even like the possibility, do you? Most women I've been with would be overjoyed to be asked. You look as though I've asked you to run down Briggate naked.'

'Greg, this whole thing is mad . . .' Greg's face fell and he stared dejectedly at the pavement. 'Not us, I like us,' I said quickly, 'us is fantastic. But I'm still getting my head around the idea of having a boyfriend.'

'Your boyfriend's a friend. You've known me for years. I've spent more time at your place than most couples spend together, we do almost everything together, we practically live together already but . . . We never talk about the future.'

'The future?' I echoed.

'The future. The long-term. It's been three months, but we still haven't talked about long-term contraception, like possibly you going on the Pill.'

'I can't take the Pill, it makes me wheeze.'

'You see? I don't know that.' Greg talked quickly, nervously. 'How am I supposed to know? You never tell me things like that. So, you know, I think we're still just dating, seeing how things go, not having a relationship, building something together. Like you've never asked to meet my family.'

'I have to ask?' I replied. 'You didn't ask to meet mine.'

'I wanted to. But I knew you'd get freaked out like you always do when the future's mentioned.'

'I wasn't aware that we talked about the future.' *You just said we didn't. Make up your mind.* 'Or that I freaked out.'

'OK, I'll give you an example: do you know why I always ask what we're doing at the weekend on a Wednesday?'

I shook my head.

'Once, when we were just mates, I asked you if you wanted to go to some exhibition in London with me a couple of weeks beforehand and you went all weird on me. You completely blanked me for a week then didn't come to the exhibition. It happened a few times after that until I worked out that Wednesday night was the earliest I could bring up the weekend without you freaking out.' Greg had obviously forgotten that he'd subsequently told me that he'd asked me to come to an exhibition in London with him because he'd been planning on seducing me, then turning me into his sex slave so I would satisfy his every sick pleasure. All right, the sex slave bit wasn't exactly uttered, it was simply implicit in how he'd said it. *I should probably not be retreating into humour at a time like this, I should be concentrating on what my boyfriend is trying to tell me.*

He dragged a hand through his thick black locks, frustration flashed across his features. 'I want a commitment.'

Maybe I shouldn't be concentrating on what my boyfriend is trying to tell me. Not if he is telling me things like that. Bloody hell. How did this happen? We were meant to spend the day walking around Headingley, crossing flats and houses off the list. Then we'd buy food, go home, have sex. Maybe go to the cinema later.

Instead, we were having 'The Talk'. And it wasn't fair. With any other man, bringing this up after three months would result in being drop-kicked out of his life quicker than a rugby ball in the Five Nations. You'd be lucky if you got a 'you want too much from me' conversation, it was most likely he'd just stop returning your calls, emails and texts. So why wasn't I making like a man in this situation and telling him he wanted too much from me? Why wasn't I telling him that I couldn't give him what he wanted because it wasn't in me to give? That he'd gotten more from me than any other person on earth had got and that's where it ended. Why wasn't I saying this? Because . . . Because.

Greg stared at me. I stared at Greg. Time ticked on.

'Let's go see this flat down on School View, it sounds quite nice from the description,' he eventually said, dropping his eyes to the paper. 'But then, most things do, don't they?'

He got up and headed off towards Burley Park train station. I watched his trainer-covered feet, his firm, jean-sheathed legs, his leather-jacketed back and his long hair irritatingly caressing his collar as he walked away.

There were no doors, but he'd done it anyway. He'd walked out on me.

chapter twenty-five

moving on up

'Hi, girls, sorry I'm late,' Renée called as she wandered into the office, laden with carrier bags. *Since when did we or anyone qualify as 'girls' in Renée's universe?* was my first thought. *Why is she apologising, she's the boss?* was my second thought.

Renée was laidback about time-keeping mainly because when the Festival began we rarely got to work after six in the morning and we rarely left before one in the morning. We were in the run-up to the Festival so, as it was, our hours were getting longer – I was at my desk by nine and didn't leave much before eight.

The Festival basically took over our lives as surely as it took over all the cinemas and some of the galleries in Leeds for two weeks solid. From opening on a Friday night with some premiere blockbuster to closing two Fridays later with an equally large blockbuster and a gala night ball.

Nearer the time, volunteers came in to help, which meant that next week the office, which most of the time was an agoraphobic's worst nightmare, became a claustrophobic hell, even for people who didn't mind crowds and confined spaces. Phones would be ringing non-stop, people would be running around, packages would be arriving and others being sent off, wranglings going on about who was in charge of which screening, someone crying. And that was before something went wrong.

That was also when Renée came into her element. She became the calmest, most centred person on earth. Nothing fazed her. Not even the time one of our prints got stuck in Spain – the day before it was meant to be shown at the Showcase Cinema just outside the city centre. We couldn't find another print of it anywhere in the UK and when we got the call saying we couldn't get it for another week, I, the Festival Assistant, knew this would be the final straw. The Deputy Festival Director, a hysterical man who knew more about films than the woman he'd worked with for a couple of years, started to unravel when he got the call and sat staring into space, on the verge of tears. It would've helped his case more if he'd started swearing or cursing someone's parentage, but no, he looked like he was going to cry. When Renée saw him, she said in her calmest – and therefore scariest – voice, 'If you tell me one more time that we can't get this print, I will kill you.'

He'd looked up at her with tears forming in his eyes. 'But . . .'

'I will kill you,' she insisted.

I'd stepped in. Angry, violent energy crackled around Renée and Terry looked as if he hadn't worked out what to do about stopping it.

'Well, Terry did have an idea,' I said, knowing that despite my fear at causing a fuss, at speaking up, I couldn't let Terry be dismembered. 'I've, um, got my passport with me. If you bought me a ticket to Spain, I could fly out there and bring it back. It'd be tomorrow, but I'd be back in time.'

'Why have you got your passport with you?' Renée asked archly.

'I, erm, just have?' I replied. Didn't like to say that during every Festival I carried my passport with me in case I met a gorgeous actor and he wanted to take me off to Paris or Monte Carlo or Las Vegas at the drop of a hat. It hadn't happened yet, but I was still hoping.

'And you'd go?' Renée asked.

'Yes. I've got nothing planned for the next couple of days.'

'Terry will buy you a ticket, *since it was his idea*, and then you can go. We'll pay your expenses, of course.'

I went, got the print, was a hero for all of two minutes. It was exciting and scary because I could've been locked up at either end and it was the closest thing to bad I'd done. Right after that Festival Terry went off to spend more time with his family, which consisted of a pet hamster, a new Deputy Festival Director was installed for what turned out to be a year, and I got the job of Senior Festival Assistant.

But Renée was right about her being late – it was going on for eleven-thirty. Renée's carrier bags clinked as she put them on the meeting table.

'Don't let it happen again,' I said.

Renée laughed at my little quip, but didn't bother to take off her white PVC coat as she headed for the middle filing cabinet along the wall. She went for the bottom drawer and fished out three of the twelve champagne flutes we kept in there for emergencies. (A champagne emergency was something like Halle Berry being in town and dropping by. We'd seem pretty amateurish if all we could offer her was warm wine in tea-stained mugs. All right, like the passport thing, it was a fantasy, but it was my fantasy and I loved it. Or, rather, I lived it.)

Renée clinked the glasses onto the meeting table, opened a carrier bag and took out a bottle of champagne. 'You know I've been having a few days off recently and I've had a number of meetings with the big boys?' she began, as her ultra-slender fingers unfoiled the champagne.

'Yes,' Martha and I replied.

'Well, darlings, I've got two bits of news about that.'

She uncorked the champagne with a small pop, white wisps of vapour escaped before she poured the pale liquid into the glasses.

'OK,' Renée handed a glass to each of us, then picked up hers. 'The first bit of news is that,' she beamed, 'I'm pregnant.'

My jaw hit the ground, scraping away the skin on my chin. I'd never thought of Renée as anything other than 'The Boss'. And 'She Who Must Be Obeyed'. Not a mother.

'That's amazing!' I screamed.

'Fantastic!' Martha squealed.

'That's why I've been *such* a bitch over the past few months. First of all we were trying and it didn't seem to be happening. I thought I'd never get pregnant and it was driving me crazy, which is why I was so on edge. And then when it finally happened, I couldn't tell you because of the three-month thing and in that time I did become a little crazy because of my hormones.' Renée waved her hand dismissively. 'Anyway, I'm officially apologising for the way I was, especially "the stapler thing", Martha, and the "I don't know why I employed you thing", Amber. It was my hormones and I'm sorry.

'I want you both to be godmothers,' Renée continued. 'Seeing as, apart from my husband, I've put you two through the most incarnations of hell, I think you deserve it.'

'Us? Haven't you got any real friends?' Martha said.

'Isn't this funny? Time was I would've bawled Martha out for that comment, but now,' Renée moved her bony shoulders up and down in a shrug, 'I don't care.' She grinned. 'I guess I haven't got any friends who are closer than you two. Even if I did, I'd still want you to be godmothers to my child. My children. You know, when I have more, you'll be godmothers to them all.'

'I'm so pleased for you. And honoured you want us to be

godmothers,' I said, making up for Martha's Marthaness. 'When's he or she due?'

'End of October.'

My heart skipped a beat. That was only six weeks after the Festival.

'Which brings me to my next piece of news. It's been agreed that Amber will take over while I'm away.'

I sprayed champagne through my mouth and nose. 'That's a joke, right?'

'No. I'm not going on maternity leave until after the Festival, but I might go into labour early, so you need to be prepared. You can do the job standing on your head, I told them that. They had no real doubts, they were just worried who would replace you. So Martha's going to get the joint title of Administrator and Senior Festival Assistant.'

Martha sprayed even more champagne.

'We'll then get a temp administrator, who Martha will oversee and a temp Festival Assistant. Amber, as Acting Festival Director, will oversee everyone.'

'That's really funny, Renée, I know they're going to be getting someone in to oversee things,' I laughed.

'No they're not,' Renée said. 'Don't be so modest, Amber, you're great at this. You've got so much sponsorship over the years, even when it seemed some companies weren't interested, you found a way to wheedle cash out of them. You're a great scheduler, you have a great imagination. You're fantastic. You both are.' Renée raised her glass. 'Let's make a toast, raise our glasses to my baby and your promotions. To us.'

Martha looked at me. I looked at Martha. 'To us,' we chorused. 'I'm still not going to Cannes,' Martha added before she drank her champagne.

I've been promoted. I had been promoted. I'd never thought this would happen. I'd thought it was a miracle that I'd been promoted to the inflated position of Deputy Festival Director.

(So had Mum, Dad and Dad2. They'd all been so grateful to Renée for giving me a job in the first place, then giving me an important-sounding title, I sometimes wondered if they'd paid her to do it.) I'd never had a real career plan. As I told Greg, my dreams, my ambitions were so impossible I never seriously considered realising them; I never thought about 'what next'. 'What next' would probably be a promotion to Festival Director, but that would mean Renée wouldn't be around and that wasn't something I liked to think about. For all her hysteria and beauty, I did like Renée. I loved her, in fact. Loved her like the brandy liqueur truffle she was. She was a constant in my life.

I'd once been offered a job as Senior Festival Assistant with the London Film Festival, which would've meant a pay rise; working with more people; schmoozing with a different class of celeb; and being far more high profile but I'd turned it down because I couldn't bear the look on Renée's face as I went to tell her I was leaving. Naturally, when Renée pissed me off, as she often did, I wished I'd taken the job.

Now, I'd got a promotion. And Renée wasn't going to be gone for too long. It was the perfect solution. BLOODY HELL! I'VE BEEN PROMOTED.

'Right, you two, drink up, lunch is on me today,' Renée said.

'Where are we going?' Martha asked, necking her champagne.

'Granary Wharf?' Renée replied.

'Oh yes, that's classy enough for me . . . *Now that I've been promoted!*' Martha squealed. She grabbed her bag, informed us, 'I'm off to put me face on,' then disappeared to the loo.

Renée's mobile rang and she picked it up, started talking in French.

I scuttled over to my desk, snatched up the phone to spread my good news. I dialled 2, then stopped. *Who you gonna call?*

I asked myself. Jen, my best friend? Or Greg, my boyfriend? Had I been going out with Sean, I would've called Jen, no question. She came first. I wasn't with Sean, though, I was with Greg Walterson.

And, as Mr Walterson had pointed out, I was always putting Jen first. Since three weekends ago when he'd asked me to move in with him, I'd been more aware of how he viewed my involvement in our relationship. He'd been quiet for most of that Saturday, not sulking quiet, more sad. We'd chatted and stuff, but when he thought I wasn't looking he'd stare off into space, a picture of heartbreak. He hadn't brought it up since, but it was there, always there, not being talked about.

Since then, though, I knew that while I'd been happy to muddle along as we had been, that muddling along translated into him thinking I didn't care as much for him as I did. My actions didn't speak louder than words and, if he found out about this second, he'd see it as further proof that he wasn't highly important in my life.

Jen. The way she'd been recently, she'd probably ask me if I could do the job. But, like not resigning because of the look on Renée's face, I couldn't tell Greg first because if Jen ever found out I couldn't handle the betrayal she'd feel. As things lay I was dreading the day she'd find out about me and Greg because she was going to drown in hurt and betrayal. I knew Jen, that's how she'd feel. Better not add to it with this small thing.

Unbidden, anger washed over me, almost dousing the flame of excitement I had burning inside me. This was a fantastic day: one of the best days of my life, and those two – my friend and my lover – had tainted it. I couldn't enjoy the moment; I was, instead, fretting about who to call. This was what it was like with my parents. Who did I call first? Who would be pissed off that they got to hear second my degree results; that I'd got a job; that I was settling in Leeds.

I'd known an age ago that I wasn't going to get married. Not with my family. I couldn't contemplate getting married without Dad2, the man who'd brought me up from ages ten to eighteen, the man who called me every weekend even if Mum didn't, being there. It'd hurt, really hurt, that he and Eric hadn't come to my graduation ceremony because Dad1 was there. They watched it on video, but it wasn't the same. So, even if I did believe in marriage, I'd not be able to do it because part of my family wouldn't be there.

This was what Jen and Greg were doing to me again. Thirty and still, *still* being torn apart by two people. I didn't like Matt, Matt didn't like me, but I never gave Jen a hard time about putting him first. I tried to like him. I didn't do what Jen and Greg were doing.

I pushed down the button on the phone to cut the line, then called the one person who'd be happy for me and wouldn't be offended when I called them. Eric. I called Eric and decided to tell Jen and Greg, or Greg and Jen (whichever) when I saw them in the pub later. That way, nobody would feel left out. My parents would have to be fretted over another time.

chapter twenty-six

beware the ex

I was enveloped by the evening air as I left the building. It was the perfect evening for seeing my mates down the pub.

Me, the newly promoted woman.

A little shiver of excitement went through me every time I thought about that. Promoted. Temporarily, but still. I started down the road, walking in a haze of champagne and good food. We'd had a four-hour lunch break that had involved more champagne for Martha and me. Time back in the office had sobered me up a bit, though. We'd got proofs for the brochure cover and the repro house had somehow managed to cock it up. The dates, the number and the name were wrong – WLIFF, indeed. When the designer had sent it off it'd been fine but, somehow, between leaving her computer and getting back to us it'd gone horribly wrong.

I wandered up through town. People were out enjoying the light evening and warm air. I felt a part of them. All of them. Even though I didn't know any of them personally, wasn't part of their groups or families or lives, I felt like I belonged. The air was so hazy and gentle, it seemed to bind us together. I was probably smiling at people as I passed them, which would explain why I got so many odd looks. It was either my smile or I had ice cream around my mouth. I was heading for

Black Prince's Tavern. We'd managed to avoid that particular establishment since our unfortunate adventure, but not tonight. I'd been on at Greg to get Matt and Jen to meet somewhere else, but Greg had said it was Matt's favourite pub so if he was going to convince them, he'd have to tell them what happened. (A bit of a lame excuse considering the man had talked his way into more beds in Leeds than I cared to remember, but I'd let it slide.) I smirked as I trundled down the alley towards the pub. If you thought about it, it was funny – trying to have sex with your boyfriend in public and getting caught by the police. But it was only funny now, and only to me. My humour wouldn't stretch to laughing about it with anyone else.

I pushed open the pub door and spotted Matt's short blond hair and Greg's long bluey-black hair at the same round, rickety table we always sat at. I checked the bar to see if Jen was getting a round in, but there was no sign of her among the bodies stretching over the bar, trying to get the barman's attention.

'So, the upshot is, I'm going to buy somewhere,' Greg was saying as I approached their table. 'I think.'

'You're a good lass, you,' Matt said, his green eyes sizing me up from my trainered feet and down from my bobbed black hair.

'I'm a what?' I replied, slipping off my jacket and wondering why I'd got such high praise from Matt. It's a wonder the words didn't stick in his throat.

'You're the only girl I know who could get this one to settle down,' Matt explained.

'I've *what*?!' I said. *OK. Be calm. Don't panic. Greg wouldn't have told Matt about us.* Would he?

I turned to Greg, hoping my terror wasn't plastered across my face.

'I was telling him how you came out flat-hunting with me

292

the other week and that by the time we'd looked at everything you'd put the buying somewhere idea into my head.' *Course he hadn't told Matt, Matt wasn't gagging, was he?*

'Here we go,' Jen said, settling a tray onto the table.

I turned to smile at her and the smile froze on my face. I wasn't actually looking at Jen. I was looking at some creature with Jen's voice but nothing else that was Jen-like. Not only had she lost weight and started wearing designer clothes – I was still concerned about how she could afford them with a teacher's salary and a tight toffee of a boyfriend – she'd had her hair butchered. Her sensuous, silky blonde locks that used to tumble down over her shoulders to touch the top of her back had been hacked back to just below her cheek-bones, bullied straight with a blow-dryer and shaped into a bob.

The shortened hair emphasised her weight loss. Of which there had been more since I last saw her. Her skin was now clinging onto her cheekbones for dear life, scared as it was of sliding off along with the rest of her body. Some people were naturally thin, small framed and petite and they looked good with it. Jen wasn't one of those people. She was naturally slender, not rake thin. Ill-thin. Added to the new and very ill-advised dusky pink lipstick, and heavily kohled eyes, she'd been transformed into a much older version of Jen. Almost as though she'd been aged on a computer. Shades of her mother came through in her look. Not only shades of her mother . . . her new look put me in mind of someone else. Possibly some teen's sexy mother. The kind of mother other mothers inspected with snide envy at parents' evenings because she was turning their teenage sons' heads.

'Oh, hi, Ambs, how you doing?' Jen smiled. Her face seemed far too small for that kind of smile.

'Great. How you doing?' My voice was stiff, almost rigid.

Nobody would guess I was talking to my best friend. I didn't recognise her and I couldn't speak to her normally.

Our friendship was getting more and more tenuous. Ethereal. We weren't even like two Twix, separated before consumption, any more. We were more like Dairy Milk and Caramel. Two chocolates made by the same people, but so different you couldn't put them together under any similar category. We contained approximately 50 per cent sugar, 25–30 per cent milk solids and 20–25 per cent cocoa solids, but there was something intrinsically different. We melted at different temperatures, we felt different, we tasted different, we were different. Now, nothing but our source linked us.

'I'm doing really well,' she replied and placed a half-pint in front of me.

What the hell is going on? My sensibilities screamed at me as my eyes took in the squat drinking implement. We'd agreed a long time ago that women who drank halves might as well check in their right to vote too. It smacked of those times when women couldn't get served pints in pubs, and when barmen would serve women a pint in two glasses – which had actually happened to us a couple of times when we were in college. I bad-temperedly picked up my *half* and glanced at Jen. She was drinking what looked suspiciously like a gin and tonic. *Don't blame me if you start sobbing into your glass,* I almost said. We'd also agreed any woman who drank G&T was clearly looking to spend the rest of the night crying because some guy had chucked her when she was fourteen.

Bloody hell, I thought as I sipped my mini pint. *I have no idea who this woman is.*

'Guess who I saw the other day?' Jen said about an hour later.

'Hitler,' Matt said.

'Xena Warrior Princess,' I offered.

'Halle Berry,' Greg contributed.

Jen rolled her eyes and sighed in her usual irritation. We always did that when she said that, and it always riled her. Didn't stop us, though.

'Sean,' she said. A trio of blank faces greeted her. '*Sean!*' she repeated, as if emphasising the word a bit more would make it any clearer. She tutted, sighed, rolled her eyes. 'Sean, Amber's ex, Sean.'

'Ohhhh!' the three of us said, finally getting it. Then we reacted thus:

Matt (Mr Selfish Gene) lost interest and stared into his pint.

Greg (Mr New Boyfriend) became all interest and stared into his pint.

I (hadn't seen Sean since we split up) felt my entire being leave my body as I wondered if Jen was about to land me in it with Greg by telling them why I'd really finished with Sean.

'How is he?' I said, aiming for a tone of little interest. Little interest, not total disinterest, which Greg would see as me faking it.

'Fine. Great. Looking rather sexy, actually.'

This sparked Matt's interest, this did involve him. 'Oh?' he said.

'Chill out,' Jen reassured him. 'He's not my type.'

Matt glanced across the table at Greg, who I hadn't felt move since we'd found out it wasn't Sean Connery Jen had seen. 'You all right, mate?' Matt asked.

Greg glanced up, noticed we were all looking at him, pulled a smile across his face. 'Yeah, fine.'

'Anyway,' Jen continued, 'Sean lives a few streets down from me and Matt now.' Great, not only did I have to look out for muggers and rapists in Alwoodley, I'd now have to beware the ex, too.

'Of course, he was asking after you, Amber.'

'Really,' I said.

295

'Oh, come on, girl, show a bit of enthusiasm, this man was the love of your life.' *Thanks, Jen.* 'He asked if you were seeing anyone, so I lied, said you were seeing a friend of Matt's. Didn't want him thinking you were the sad single type.'

Heat rose in me. 'I'm not the sad single type. And, anyway, I don't care if he thinks I am.'

Jen pulled a little face 'Well, he doesn't, thanks to me. Even now he's still into you. His eyes lit up when he was talking about you. Then he started saying he still couldn't understand why you backed out of marrying him.'

Matt sprayed a not very fine mist of beer across the table; Greg froze.

'You almost got married?' Matt said, swiping a sleeve across his mouth to mop up the beer he'd wasted.

I said nothing, seeing as I couldn't move. Or breathe. Or believe we were talking about this. We didn't talk about it in private, let alone in the bloody pub.

'Yeah. Didn't you know?' Jen said.

'No!' Matt said. 'Did you?' he asked Greg.

Slowly, deliberately, Greg shook his head.

'Neither of you knew?' Jen asked, incredulous.

'No, Jen, neither of them knew,' I said through clenched teeth. 'That'll be because I said to you, "Don't tell anyone."'

Jen's eyes widened and her mouth formed a silent 'O' of understanding.

'So how close did you come to doing the deed? Did you pick out rings? Or a dress?' Quite obscurely, this was from Matt.

'She had the ring, we made an appointment to see dresses, then she and Sean finished and she didn't explain why.' Quite annoyingly, this answer was from Jen.

'Must we talk about this,' I said flatly.

'Yeah!' Matt said. He was suddenly and inexplicably excited. 'It's like, suddenly, Amber has hidden depths.' *Look who's talking.* 'I knew you weren't as anti-settling down as you made out, and now I've got the proof.'

'You've spent time wondering if I'm into settling down?' I asked, surprised that I didn't leave Matt's mind the second I left his company.

'Yeah, course. Me and Peck even talk about it sometimes. We've all come close to it, except you. Except now I know you have.'

'I didn't come close to it.'

'But you said yes to him and that's as good as.'

'I did *not* say yes to him. I didn't even say I'd think about it. If you must know, he had to prise open my fingers to put the ring box into my hand because I was so shocked I couldn't move or speak. I never wore the ring. I was so freaked out that I didn't tell anyone And didn't want my blabbermouth friend telling anyone either.'

As I spoke, Greg's feelings emanated from him loud and clear. To put it mildly, he was not happy. To put it more realistically anger and jealousy instead of blood flowed through them there veins of his. He was definitely going to leave me this time.

'So, were you going for the meringue or the pavlova in wedding dresses?' Matt asked.

Jen smirked.

'You seem to know an awful lot about the wedding business, Matt, something you want to tell us?' I asked. 'Or Jen, got any more announcements? Any secrets you want to share with the group? Come on, don't be shy.'

As a person they clammed up. Matt got to his feet. 'Right, my round,' he said. He must be feeling guilty about something to be willingly reaching into his pocket.

'Not for me, mate,' Greg said, standing. 'I'm off to see a woman about a dog.'

'Your mystery lady, eh?' Jen said.

Greg half shrugged, half raised his eyebrows. 'Actually, she's not my mystery lady any more, she's my girlfriend.'

'Things must be going well,' Matt commented.

'Yup, and you know why?' Greg said. 'Because she's totally honest with me. Your relationship's nothing if it's not based on honesty. See ya.' And he left.

He'd left the three of us sat there, but I *knew* he'd walked out on me. AGAIN.

chapter twenty-seven

lady in waiting

I never thought Greg would find out about me and Sean – that's why I'd left out the small detail of Sean's proposal.

And he'd never have found out if Jen wasn't being a complete and utter stick of carob. Not even a real chocolate. That hideous substitute that nobody could ever pretend was good enough to compare to chocolate.

I'd sworn her to secrecy. She'd promised we'd never talk about it, not with anyone else, not with each other. And now look what she'd done. Only Sean, Jen and I were meant to know. I didn't go running my mouth off in front of Matt and Greg about her pregnancy scare because I understood that it was the kind of thing that you didn't share. Or drag up in the pub. Jen was an alien to me. The old Jen would never do anything like that. Ever. The new Jen felt no way about calling me fat and bringing up my secrets in the pub.

I was going to have to deal with this at some point. I was going to have to do more than say Jen was an alien, a stick of carob, someone I didn't particularly like. It wasn't going to sort itself out. I was going to have to address the issue of why our friendship had changed. Maybe even have it out with her. Ice trickled down my spine. Have it out with Jen? Shout at her? I was more confident, I'd almost stood up to my mum, but Jen? No way. I had to do something, though. Something.

However, Jen wasn't the most pressing problem in my life. Greg was.

I turned into my road. Brownberrie Walk, my road. My home. The place where Greg was waiting to chuck me.

From a few yards down the end of my road I saw him sitting on the wall outside my flat. He must've been there for at least half an hour because I'd stayed that long after him in the pub.

Greg was hitting his heels against the brickwork of the wall when I arrived in front of him. He didn't say anything, just looked up, held my gaze, then looked down again.

'I, erm, suppose you should come up,' I whispered. I cleared my throat and repeated the sentence.

I found my keys and, with trembling hands, opened the doors to my flat. I was scared. Scared of Greg. Of what he was feeling. Of how pissed off he was. If he was angry enough to leave.

He entered the flat, went straight to the sofa and sat down.

'Tea?' I asked from the corridor.

'Thanks,' he said, without tearing his eyes away from the off TV.

I filled the kettle, plugged it in.

He was angry. So angry he couldn't even turn his gaze in my direction. I was such a coward; had a yellow streak a mile wide when it came to him leaving me. To anyone leaving me. But, right now, I was dealing with only one imminent departure.

I leant forward over the counter, stared into my Gary Larson cartoon mug. In its belly nestled a tea bag. *Things could be worse, I reasoned, I could be a tea bag, minding me own business, blissfully unaware that I was about to be drowned in boiling water.*

This wasn't fair. It was on par with being told I was allergic to chocolate. That the one substance I loved more than any other would kill me the next time I slipped it into my mouth. I went cold at that thought. No Greg, no chocolate. They'd be scraping my body off the M1 about ten minutes after I made that hideous discovery.

The kettle boiled, billowing steam up at me. 'Sorry,' I said to the tea bag, then doused it in water. We were both going the same way but the tea bag was going on to a higher purpose: it was about to offer refreshment. When my relationship met its demise, there'd be nowt purposeful about it.

I put one sugar in Greg's tea. Picked up the cup, stopped, scooped in another heaped teaspoon of sugar. Good for shock.

'Here we go,' I said, and handed him the mug.

He moved his face in thank you, took the cup, but didn't otherwise acknowledge me.

'I, erm, haven't got any biccies, sorry.'

He nodded slightly.

My head was throbbing, each temple pounding out its own ache; my eyes were heavy; gravity seemed to tug at each part of me as I sobered up. My mind had been frightened into clarity but my body was struggling to catch up.

I took my place beside him on the sofa.

What was I supposed to do? Leave him to start? Or start explaining why I hadn't told him? Not as easy as it sounded because I couldn't for the life of me remember why it seemed a good idea not to tell him.

This waiting, this was what it was like when I was younger. Waiting for my parents to flip out about something. Waiting for one of them to say something slightly off-key to the other and then for the shouting and smashing and sadistic silence to start. The arguing was never as bad as the waiting for the arguing. Because at least with the fighting it was tangible, something to be afraid of. With the waiting I could imagine myself up a lot more bad scenarios than the actual row. I could never relax, either, because I knew the second I did that's when the first angry word would be lobbed into the atmosphere and it would start. Waiting was hideous.

301

Greg drank his tea.

Sip.

Sip. Pause.

Sip.

Sip. Pause.

Pause. Sip.

Sip. Sip.

Is he deliberately torturing me? Is he trying to drive me mad? Does he get off on making me wait for my punishment?

He hoisted himself off the sofa and spun to me. 'So, Amber almost got married but forgot to tell me,' he accused.

I stared up at him.

'It's understandable really. We all forget about our plans to get married, don't we?'

'It wasn't like that,' I protested in a small voice.

'Oh? What *was* it like?'

I opened my mouth, made a few hand gestures in a genuine attempt to explain, but found I was mute. No words would come out. Eventually I shrugged, defeated.

'DON'T FUCK WITH ME!' he screamed and hurled the cup. It flew across the room, its contents spilling through the air until it slammed against the wall and exploded, sending pieces across the room.

I'm eight. I'm sitting in the back room, my pencil pressing hard into the page of my exercise book as I write my twelve times table. The pencil makes black-grey grooves in the page, and my mind concentrates really hard. Really hard. So hard I can't hear something hitting the wall of the living room and smashing into a million pieces I'll have to sweep up later. I can't hear voices screaming at each other. I can't hear hand pounding flesh, cries being choked back. All I can hear is twelve times four equals . . .

I stared at Greg, wide-eyed, breath caught in my chest, muscles rigid, waiting for what came next. More smashing. Overturning furniture. A punch in the face. A kick in the stomach. Holding me down as he pummelled my features flat . . .

He stopped. Startled still by something. 'I'm not going to hurt you,' he said.

I nodded.

He stepped forwards, I flinched back.

'No, really, Amber, I'm not going to hurt you.' He looked confused, concerned, and probably loads of other things beginning with C. 'I'm pissed off, but I won't hurt you.'

I nodded.

He moved back and perched himself on the edge of the armchair. 'I wouldn't ever hurt you. Not like that. I just got so crazy. Why didn't you tell me about Sean? Were you going to marry him? Is that why you didn't tell me? Because you still love him and you want to be with him?'

I shook my head. Still staring at him, waiting for it. Waiting for him to punch me. I never thought this would happen with him. But here it was. Here we were.

'I'm sorry,' Greg was saying. 'I'm sorry. I just hate feeling like a twat. You were engaged and you didn't tell me. Not as a friend, not as my girlfriend. And then Jen starts bleating on about it like it's common knowledge. You made a commitment to spend your life with someone and you didn't tell me.'

'I didn't get engaged,' I said. I redirected my gaze to my feet. My chest moved in heavy, laboured breaths. 'When he asked me, I thought about it. I really thought about it. I loved Sean. We got on well, he was kind, generous, funny, attractive, the sex was good. And I knew that even though I don't believe in marriage, I couldn't just say no, because very few relationships survive a refused marriage proposal and I didn't want things to end just like that with him. But it kept coming back to one thing. Could I say yes to being with a man who loved *Jackie Brown*? It sounds silly, but could I be with forever a man who

303

could sit there and listen to all that racist language and then have the temerity to tell me that I shouldn't be so sensitive about it? When he'd never had to deal with it? To him it's something cool Tarantino drops into his films, not something I have a right to be offended by if I so choose.' With each word my voice became stronger. Surer. I even looked up.

'And if a man I consider spending the rest of my life with can't see that, well, then, we're not suited. It was an underlying difference that I couldn't assimilate. So there, we broke up because of *Jackie Brown*, like I said.'

'Why didn't you tell me this from the start?' Greg asked.

'I had this suspicion you'd freak if I said I'd thought about marrying someone else.' I dipped my head towards the tea-stained wall.

Greg flushed. 'Point taken. I am trying not to be Mr Jealousy but it's so hard. I keep panicking that you're going to think, "What's in it for me?" one day and leave. And that terrifies me.

'You've been so odd since I met your family, slightly distant. I keep wondering if you're just dragging it out 'til you finish with me. There were signs with Kristy, you know. She'd be off with me, distant, avoid me, sometimes we'd spend the whole night together and not talk. I've been panicking that it's happening with you. Every morning I wake up wondering if this is it, the day you tell me it's over.

'I've been smothering you, I know. But I can't stop it. The more distant you become, the more clingy I become, which I know makes you more distant. I hate myself for it . . . I've never been like this before. I never thought I could be like this. But I keep thinking that if I can let you know how much you mean to me, you won't leave me. Earlier . . . Oh, I'm sorry. I'm sorry.'

'I know,' I whispered. He probably was, but that wasn't the point, was it? I couldn't be with a man who might blow up like that. I'd be waiting for it to happen again. And I hated that kind of waiting.

'I'm such a fuck-wit sometimes. I didn't mean to scare you but that's no excuse. I'm sorry. It won't happen again. I won't do that to you ever again.'

That's what they all say. Violent men don't mean it, do they? They never start off meaning it. But it happens once, it happens twice, then they progress to smacking you around regularly for every little slight – imagined or real – and saying, 'Sorry, I didn't mean it, it won't happen again.'

'Anyway, I'd better get on with clearing up,' he said quietly. *'I'm sorry, I didn't mean it.' How many times have I heard that?*

'You know I'd never hit you or anything like that, don't you?' Greg asked in the middle of the night. We'd gone to bed a couple of hours earlier and since neither of us were up for anything physical, I'd put on my pyjamas and he'd put on his jogging bottoms.

I'd watched him clean up and, as with all his cleaning, he'd left the place spotless. He'd found all the pieces of cup and put them in the bin. He even found some carpet shampoo – *I have carpet shampoo?* I thought – and cleaned away the tea stain.

After the clean, I'd said I was tired and was going to bed. I'd been taken aback when Greg had asked if it was OK for him to stay over. 'I'll understand if you want to sleep alone.' I'd expected him to walk out as per usual.

'Whatever you want,' I'd replied.

He'd glanced down at his feet. I braced myself. *Was that the wrong answer? Is he going to smash something else? Smash me?* 'I think I'll go home then. It's probably best?' A question, not a statement of intent, a question.

I'd rubbed my hands over my face. 'If you want to stay, stay. If you want to go, go. It's up to you. I'm off to bed. Night.'

He'd stayed. And we'd lain awake in a pit of silence for what felt like forever, until his question about whether I knew he'd never hurt me.

My chest tightened in anticipation of a row, my stomach started churning. I'd been promoted today. I'd been promoted and had thought the day couldn't get any better. I was right. It couldn't, it simply got worse and worse.

'I'd never hit you or lay a finger on you in that way. I might get angry and smash things, but I'd never hurt you.'

'Then don't,' I whispered through my tight chest.

'Don't what?'

'Don't smash things. I don't like it. It scares me.'

'OK. I promise. I won't smash things. I've only done it three times in my life. When Kristy left me. Another time when I was so angry with myself I had to break something or drive my car into a wall. And earlier on. I'll never do it again.'

'OK,' I said.

'Please believe me, I won't.'

'Do you promise?' I said.

'I promise.' Greg shifted across the bed and folded his arms around me.

'What happened to you?' he asked, some time later.

'What do you mean?'

'Were you beaten as a child, in an abusive relationship or what?'

'I don't know what you're talking about,' I said abruptly. We weren't going to talk about this. Not now. Not ever.

'When I went off on one earlier you were terrified. It stopped me in my tracks. I've seen you do some brave things, like that time when you stared down the woman in that pub whose boyfriend wanted to batter me, and I've heard through Jen how scary you can be. You watch violent films, but earlier you were so scared, terrified, then you went into one of those trances you often go into. What happened to you?'

'Even Rambo would've been scared – my favourite mug didn't survive, did it?' I joked.

'You can trust me,' Greg reassured, 'with whatever it is.'

'My parents. Not Dad2, my mum and my dad. They rowed a lot. And, erm, sometimes my dad got physical. And, erm, I did a lot of clearing up. I . . . Anything like that scares me. I don't know where it'll lead. Or how it'll end . . . I . . . can't deal with . . . I get . . . Never tell anyone that, OK? Please.'

'OK.'

'No, really, please,' I said, clinging to his arm, searching his face for understanding. He had to realise how important not telling anyone was. 'I haven't told anyone. Not Jen. Not even Eric knows. So, please, don't tell a soul. Not ever.'

'I won't,' Greg said gently. He brushed my hair out of my eyes. Looked into my eyes. Looked into my soul. His face had never been so earnest and open as it was then. 'Thank you for trusting me. I promise, on my life, I won't tell a soul.'

My hero. He was the hero. In the movie of my life, Greg Walterson was the hero. My hero. He'd always be with me. How did I know? Because I'd never said that to anyone. Not Jen, not even Eric. It happened before he was born; reborn as my brother. Greg had made me break my silence. It wasn't intentional. I'd opened my mouth to tell him I knew I could trust him and I'd found myself saying that. Each word had to be dragged into existence, but it'd been done.

And he didn't think I was weird because of it. This part of my crazy, the part I'd hidden from him – the part I'd hidden from everyone – had been freed and he hadn't run away. He might walk out a bit more regularly than I liked, but he always came back. We always sorted things out.

I didn't have to keep holding back, worried that he'd find something out that would make him leave. I didn't have to

307

keep editing myself and my story. This secret, this part of my life, had weighed down heavily on me. I was always restricting myself, secreting away big parts of myself, knowing that nobody would understand why I didn't trust people. Didn't trust men not to cheat, not to hurt you physically and emotionally. I knew you had to be good, constantly, or people wouldn't love you. I didn't think about the future because the past was what I mainly remembered. What I mainly feared. Fear of the past meant I didn't think about the future. Fear of the past, which was always pressing down on my chest, infecting my mind, had finally been lightened. Shared. I'd told Greg. So simple but so complicated. Easy, but difficult. Now he knew all of me. I could tell him anything. I was free.

'I don't want all the secrets and half-truths any more, Greg. I think we should agree, no more secrets, except birthday presents and the like. I've told you my biggest secret. It's not something I want to talk about again, ever, but you know, let's move on from here with total honesty.'

In response, Greg treated me to one of his infamous pauses. One of those pauses when he was going to say something I didn't want to hear.

'No more secrets, right?' he reiterated.

'Right.'

'There's something I've got to tell you.'

Holy shit. 'Go on then.' *It was all very well asking for total honesty.*

'I've been wanting to tell you for ages but it never seemed the right time.'

But do I want total honesty with Greg? What was the worst with him?

'I was terrified of your reaction; what it'd do to us.'

Taking nude photos of me whilst I was asleep and putting them on the Net? Bestiality?

'Thing is . . .'

What was the worst with Greg? I'd never really thought about it. Maybe I should have before I made my declaration of honesty.

He paused, took a deep, deep breath. 'I, erm, well . . . I love you.'

'Oh, thank goodness,' I breathed.

'Thank goodness?'

'You sounded so serious . . . I thought you were going to say you'd had sex with a cow or something.'

Greg laughed. 'Non-sex with a cow aside, I do love you.'

'Thank you.'

'You're welcome,' he giggled. 'You're so welcome.'

'love? it's only
chocolate without
the calories'

chapter twenty-eight

coming out

We're going to tell Jen and Matt tonight. The thought cheeped around my head like fluttering bluebirds. (That showed my state of mind, bluebirds indeed.) We were going to go public tonight.

It'd been seven months and we were still together. It was only seven months, but, sometimes, even after seven months, you knew. And I knew. Even in a year with Sean I hadn't felt this. It wasn't only lust. We'd progressed from lust a long time ago. We still had sex virtually every night we saw each other, but it was more than that now. We didn't use sex as our main way to communicate, we also talked to communicate. It seemed easy, natural, now Greg knew all of me. He knew something even my brother didn't know, he'd been given a piece of me nobody else had. My dysfunctional trio had moved into a dysfunctional quartet and I didn't feel so alone. So burdened by it any more. I could talk to him about almost anything. Also, now that he knew I trusted him 100 per cent, he had a part of me only two other people knew about, he'd stopped being so clingy. He relaxed, accepted I wasn't going to leave him and even went back to occasionally eyeing up other women. Probably even flirted with a few. Obviously not when I was around, but he was back to being the Greg I knew and

313

fell in love with so it was fine . . . All right, it wasn't fine, but I preferred that to how needy he'd started to become. The lesser of two evils, as it were.

We only had to take one more step, to go public to Matt and Jen, and then everything would be perfect. So, we were going to tell them tonight. Tonight. The last night of the Festival.

The Festival had gone fantastically well so far with only a few minor hiccups. Plus, Martha and Renée had only two throw-down moments – a Festival miracle – and I'd sent Martha out to get chocolate before they came to blows. Tonight was the fancy dress gala ball, where all the best films would be awarded prizes and I got to dress up as the movie icon of my choice. I glanced at my dress hanging up behind the wardrobe door of my hotel room, still in its black dress cover.

Martha, Renée and I always had rooms in the hotel where our guests stayed and where our press office was, for the first and final nights of the Festival. The last fortnight, as always, I'd virtually lived in the press room because of my duties taking care of the directors, producers and screenwriters who came to the Festival.

We'd switched hotels this year. Usually, it was the Holiday Inn, but this year I'd wangled a special deal with the Queens Hotel, which had a huge ballroom that would be perfect for the gala night event.

The ballroom had been breathtaking when I left it last night. The stage, where film-makers would come receive their prizes from our other honoured guests, had been set up. Silver stars hung from the ceiling, while huge hangings with Andy Warhol-type prints of various film icons adorned the walls. The waiters and waitresses would be dressing up as cinema ushers with boxes around their necks instead of carrying trays.

Today, Martha, Renée and I had the afternoon off so we could get ready for tonight. I was using this afternoon to sleep and then to go get my hair professionally put up. Martha was off getting her hair done too. Her film icon of choice was Marilyn à la *The Seven Year Itch* and she was doing it properly. She wasn't only hiring the dress, she was also having her hair cut and dyed. A big sacrifice for work, but there was no telling her.

Renée, who'd gone from svelte to heavily pregnant seemingly overnight, was going as Mia Farrow in *Rosemary's Baby*. I'd tried to explain the folly of this: 'Asking for trouble' kept slipping from my lips, but she wanted to wear a cute sixties dress. 'The woman was impregnated by the Devil,' I reminded her. But she wasn't listening. I was the only one being normal.

I glanced at my dress again. I was going as Holly Golightly from *Breakfast At Tiffany's*. I'd found the perfect black dress that flowed down my body to pool around my ankles and flattered every one of my curves. It didn't have the split that Holly's had, but everything else looked the same. I also had fake diamond jewellery – necklace, earrings, bracelet and hair clip – long gloves, high-heeled black shoes and a long cigarette holder. When I'd had my hair put up I was going to look like the star of the show.

It was a tradition that Matt and Jen came to the last-night party of the Festival, and booked themselves a room in the hotel for the night. Greg, who got an invite as standard because he was a member of the press, often stayed in my room (Sean never came to the Festival, not even if I got him free tickets – he just wasn't interested) unless he pulled – in which case he usually booked a room to impress said pullee. Tonight, after the speeches and prize-giving, though, Greg and I were going to sit down Jen and Matt and explain how we felt about each other. And, then, tomorrow, I was off on holiday. *We* were off on holiday.

Holiday. Ten days. With Greg. He'd arranged it, OKed it

with Renée so I wouldn't have to oversee the dismantling of everything tomorrow, then booked us a nine-day trip of a lifetime. The ultimate chocolate run. We were doing Lille, Belgium and Switzerland. He said we'd do Mexico and Ghana another year. He hadn't told me about the holiday until two days ago, yes, 'til Wednesday, because he didn't want to risk me freaking out. Greg knew me so well. He was indeed my perfect boyfriend.

I stopped in the middle of unpacking my bag as my heart skipped a beat. I sat heavily on the bed, clutching my make-up bag. My perfect boyfriend.

I thought I knew what I wanted from a relationship until I got together with Greg. He had depths. Real depths. He wasn't one chocolate, he was a whole selection box. I knew that, but it kept surprising me.

I could sleep now. I slept BG (Before Greg), but now I slept through. I rarely woke up at 4 a.m. and lay thinking, worrying, fretting, reworking any more. It was the reworking that was destructive. Should I have married Sean, just gotten over the whole *Jackie Brown* and 'I don't believe in marriage' things? Should I be nicer to Mrs H because, after all, my dad does love her? Should I have accepted that job at the London Film Festival? On and on I went. Not with Greg. If I woke up in the night, I'd simply roll over, go back to sleep.

It wasn't simply having a boyfriend, it was Greg's Gregness. It was knowing that all the pieces of the selection box he was made him my Malteser. My favourite chocolate. Greg was my Malteser and I could be still with him. My mind could rest. I could be at peace.

I lay back on the bed, spread my arms wide out. I never knew this was what love felt like. It was almost as good as chocolate. Dare I say? Better than chocolate . . . No, that's wrong. Nothing is better than chocolate. But this, this love business was 99 per cent as good. Hell, 99.99 per cent as good.

★

'As you can see, I am with child,' Renée said.

She was giving her speech, the final one of the Festival. She was glowy and striking in her orange and white A-line sixties minidress that emphasised her bump. She'd scraped all her hair under an elfin-cut blonde wig to go for the full Rosemary look. 'Despite rumours to the contrary, this is not the Devil's child,' Renée added.

The three hundred or so people in the ballroom tittered. 'I will be stepping aside as Festival Director for the period of my maternity leave. Thankfully, I have a more than able replacement. Most of you have dealt with her, negotiated with her and sometimes been told off by her. It is, of course, our Deputy Festival Director, Amber Salpone.' I went cold. She didn't tell me she was going to announce this. Most people don't make a big deal of things like this. They go off on maternity leave and pray that their stand-in does a shite job so everyone remembers how fantastic they are. 'Come on, Amber, step forward,' Renée cajoled.

I stepped forward but with difficulty – my Holly Golightly dress had only so much give, walking wasn't exactly easy.

'This is the woman who you'll have to wine, dine and generally be nice to,' Renée said, fanning her fingers out like I was the prize on a game show.

I plastered a smile on my face. *What do I do with my hands? Where do I look? I'm not used to this. Not sure I like it. Despite all I've wished for, I don't like being the centre of this much attention.*

I looked out into the crowd, at the sea of Marilyns, Bogarts, Hollys, Chaplins, Halles, Denzils and, quite obscurely, one Princess Leia. The first person I locked eyes with was Mr Chocolate Sniffer, dressed as Will Smith in *Men in Black*. He'd become a Festival volunteer and we'd had an awkward moment when he realised who I was and why I knew his films. 'I see why you watch a lot of films,' he'd said.

He was attractive, yes, but he didn't have the same effect on

317

me he had last time. I wasn't in that lost state I had been when I last saw him so I'd been a bit more reserved this time, but that didn't stop him attempting a bit of flirting at a screening one night. He'd rested his hand on my arm as he asked me to come out for a drink with him after the screening. He'd been stood very close again and I'd marvelled at how smooth his skin was, and how engaging his chestnut eyes were. But, I wasn't panicky like last time. I only had eyes for Greg. This man was beautiful, but not Greg.

'No,' I replied.

'Go on, just one.'

I shook my head and, in response, he'd flashed me a beatific smile, went to say something, then the smile froze on his face. 'Your man, is he white with long black hair, looks like he could handle himself in a fight?' he asked in a stage whisper.

'Suppose,' I replied, slightly confused.

'Interesting. Right, so I'll remove my hand from your person and ask you out another time.'

I'd turned and found Greg shooting malevolent looks at Mr CS's retreating form. Still, it didn't stop us having a laugh, and him being pleased for me. I grinned back at him, then stepped back out of the limelight.

Renée finished her speech and then the prizes were handed out. After the speeches, for me, came the schmooze. I had to talk to a number of people and set up meetings for when Renée left; others needed their egos flattering because they hadn't won the award they thought they deserved; others still wanted to chat as the lights were lowered, music came on, people started dancing in our magical ballroom crammed with icons.

When I escaped the final schmoozee, I stood at the foot of the stage, my eyes scanning the ballroom looking for a Mafioso from *The Godfather*, Bridget Fonda from *Single White Female* and, ahem, James Bond. In other words, Greg, Jen and Matt.

The first person I spotted was Greg. He was wearing a black suit, black shirt, with black tie. He was stood alone, leaning against a pillar, staring into the mid-distance. I'd love to have taken a picture of him like that. Hair tumbling forwards over his face, his body almost propping up the pillar. He'd look brilliant in black and white. I decided to write it into my screenplay. Man stands against pillar, looking broody. And horny. Well horny.

Greg straightened up as I approached, his face brightening with a smile. I linked my arms around his neck.

'Hey, this is public contact,' Greg warned, his Minstrel eyes doing that trick where they were fixed to mine, but at the same time looked over every inch of my face.

I shrugged. 'Don't care. You're my fella and I don't care who I tella,' I said.

Greg laughed a small sunshine laugh. 'Jen and Matt have gone to get something from their room. Actually, I think they've gone to have sex . . . but, hey, you did really well. Amazingly, in fact.'

'Of course,' I replied cheekily. 'Did you expect any less of me?'

'You're pissed,' he said and planted a hand on each of my bum cheeks.

'No. Just happy.' *And pumped up from pulling off my first Festival.*

'And just beautiful,' he replied.

'Well, I didn't like to say anything,' I joked.

I got another dose of sunshine poured into my ears. I brushed his hair out of his face so I could see his chocolate eyes. 'I've been thinking about that living together thing,' I began.

Greg's expression froze. His heart raced so hard in his chest I could feel it against my chest.

Maybe I should have left things alone. I'd thought of taking this step constantly during the last few weeks. Every time I went to

319

sleep without seeing or talking to him I'd thought about how I could have him there all the time if I took the next step.

'And I was going to say that I'd like to go for it if you did, but by the look on your face, maybe I should've left it alone.'

'My face was scared you were going to flip out again.'

'I didn't flip out.'

'Oh yes you did. I've never seen a woman get so freaked in such a short space of time. Why do you think I haven't brought it up since?'

'So, what do you think? About moving in together?'

'Hmmm,' Greg said, scrunching up his lips in thought.

'I'll totally understand if you've changed your mind,' I added. Knowing I so wouldn't. *Why wouldn't he want to live with me? Why w—*

Greg lowered his head, moved his lips a fraction from mine. 'Course I want to live with you. I love you, don't I?'

I closed my eyes in a drunken haze of happiness as Greg kissed me. He was perfect at lip kisses, perfect at making this block of chocolate dissolve. I kissed him back, remembering the last time we'd done this.

It was the night before the Festival started. I'd left work after midnight and got a taxi round to his because I hadn't seen him properly in almost a month. On the doorstep I called him and said I'd sent him a little something because he'd been so understanding about not seeing me in the run-up to the Festival. He'd stomped downstairs, opened the door and given me the ego boost of a lifetime when his face transformed into a picture of pure joy. He'd pulled me into the house and I managed to kick the door shut before he was tearing at my clothes, kissing me, dragging me to the ground and then emptying out my bag to find a condom. We'd done it right there in the corridor. He hadn't orgasmed so much as exploded inside me.

'I'm guessing you're pleased to see me then?' I said as we got our breath back. He'd smiled an indulgent smile, shook his

320

head slightly as he remembered my inability to do serious for too long. 'I want you to stay with me,' he said, suddenly serious. I went to explain that I couldn't, that I had to go home and sleep before the big opening, and he'd said, 'Please. Stay.' So I had.

That was two weeks ago. Sixteen days. Sixteen years in Greg and Amber sex time. We were making up for it now, though, with heavenly kisses that were more than likely to end up with us sneaking off up to our room.

Nothing else mattered, existed, as we kissed. Nothing, except the voice that bellowed in my ear, 'WHAT THE HELL IS GOING ON?'

chapter twenty-nine

friend or lover?

Greg and I sprang apart, like two people who shouldn't be kissing who'd been caught with their faces welded together. We stood with guilt daubed across our faces, staring at Jen and Matt.

They glared back at us. Highly unamused. Stupefied? Put out?' Extremely pissed off? Yes, yes, and yes. Amused, no.

I averted my eyes as giggles started escaping from the corners of my mouth, silent laughter shaking my shoulders. To make matters worse, I felt Greg's shoulders shaking as he started laughing which, of course, made me worse. One look back at our audience did it, though. Matt's big frown and Jen's wide open eyes had the laughter booming out of my mouth. I fell against Greg as we laughed as though it was the funniest thing on earth. Which it was – after seven months of sneaking around, we're caught out three minutes before we come clean. Eventually, we pulled ourselves together, Greg slipped his arm around my waist, and I wrapped both arms around him.

'If you hadn't guessed, we're together,' Greg said.

Matt and Jen simply stared at us, their expressions unchanged. Greg looked down at me, silently asking if he was allowed to tell them everything.

I nodded.

'And we're moving in together.'

'FANTASTIC!' Matt screamed so loudly that even above the music we jumped. He came hurtling towards us. 'I always thought you two should get together!' he screeched. 'You're so well suited, and now you're settling down. That's amazing!' All a bit expressive for a Yorkshire boy lump of toffee who didn't like me, but maybe he wasn't as unchanging as I'd cast him as, after all. Maybe he was all right. It's not as if I didn't like toffee.

While Matt leapt on us, almost choking me when his bicep linked around my neck – I assumed that was unintentional – Jen didn't move. She stayed in the background, frozen still. Immobilised by horror. Everything about her – her face, her body, her eyes, particularly her eyes – were etched with horror. Then she came out of her trance and joined the group hug.

Later, the men did the manly thing and went to the bar to get drinks. I did the womanly thing and said they could put it on my room tab.

Jen, who'd come as Bridget Fonda in *Single White Female*, was wearing a clingy little black dress that showed off every diminished inch of her, stood with me by our chosen pillar. The second Matt and Greg were out of earshot, she turned on me.

'Why didn't you tell me about you and Greg?' she asked, her big blue eyes, which seemed sunken in her face, narrowed into a fierce glare. They were just blue, not one of the usual variations they used to be, just blue. I always thought Jen would be hurt when she unearthed my secret, not angry. And horrified. And fearsome.

'I meant to,' I explained. 'I really meant to, but, um, remember in college I went out with your fella Connor's best mate and I dumped him after a few weeks because he was *so boring*?'

She gave a curt nod, her dusky pink lipstick making her lips a flat line as she pressed them together.

'Remember how much trouble it caused between you and Connor and how you kept trying to get me to give his friend another chance? And it caused so much trouble between us. We almost fell out over it. I didn't want that to happen to us again. To be honest, I didn't think it'd go so well with Greg. I thought it'd be over in a few weeks so nobody need know.'

'But you're going to live with him, it must've been going well,' she hissed.

'We were going to tell you tonight, but they made that announcement and I got tied up talking to people and . . . I've never felt like this about anyone. Never. Not Sean, not anyone. He's my soul mate. Not that I ever believed in such things before. But he is. I . . . I . . . Oh, please be happy for me, Jen. *Please*.' I was begging her. Begging her because I wanted all this to stop. I wanted my Jen back. Not the one who called me fat or bought me half-pints. The one I'd spent the last twelve years with. The one I called my best friend.

Jen's face softened into a huge smile as she put her spindly arms around me. 'Course I'm happy for you, sweetie. I'm very happy for you.'

As I hugged her, I felt every bone in her. Shame washed over me – I'd let this happen. I'd let Jen slip into this by not being a proper friend, by being so caught up in being with Greg. While I was falling in love, becoming more confident, Jen was becoming a shadow of her former self. *Well*, I decided, holding her closer, *I have to get the real Jen back. And that starts with getting her weight up.*

I hit the loos at a run. A feminine run that was more a swift walk because of the confines of my dress and because I was trying to cross my legs as I walked.

I was aware that I was probably doing a wiggly-bum walk as

324

I crossed the dance floor, keeping close to the fat pillars that ringed the dance space until I reached the heavy oak doors. I stepped out onto the thick, springy carpet of the corridor, then wiggly-bum walked into the marble-floored loos. The air was heavy with pot pourri and expensive perfume. A loo attendant sat on a gold chair with a red velvet cushion. It was so posh in there it was technically a powder room; had I not been busting to go, I would've wondered if it was too posh to piss in.

I emerged from the loos altogether more composed. A couple of people stopped me to congratulate me on how great the Festival had been and on my promotion. I grinned back at them as I said thank you. I was important now. Admittedly I hadn't exactly liked the limelight earlier when I had to stand on the stage, but I was behind-the-scenes important. I was a behind-the-scenes star.

Now that Jen and Matt knew, my night was complete. Greg and I could hold hands, or, as we'd been doing, he could slip his arms around my waist, and kiss my neck, lean down to whisper 'I love you' into my ear as we talked to the other two . . . Yup, we were a disgusting couple. That had to stop. But not tonight. Tonight was the night we'd finally come out, so we were allowed to be disgusting. Matt had been unbelievably overjoyed about Greg and me getting together. He kept thinking back over the past few months and then saying things like 'So, when you were going on about the best sex ever, that was Amber?' and Greg would nod, very smugly.

I returned to the ballroom, heading back through the smoke and almost-visible pheromones as bodies writhed to 'Careless Whisper', heading towards what had become our pillar. I stayed close to the pillars that ringed the dance floor so I wouldn't be caught up in the mass of people who'd got lucky and intimate. Once upon a time I would've vilified these people, but now I could understand. I was that yucky couple.

I was one of those people who wanted to snog and grind to George Michael with someone I found—

'Amber was the one you were talking about that day at my flat?' Jen was saying, above the music.

'Yup,' Greg replied.

'So you like her?' Jen asked.

'We're moving in together, what do you think?'

'*I* think you fucked me and you've moved on to my friend because I told you it was a mistake.'

The earth lurched on its axis, taking me with it. '*I think you fucked me.*'

I stood stock still but I heard it again: '*I think you fucked me.*'

And again. '*I think you fucked me.*' Those words popped in my ears, under my skin, exploding like fireworks in my blood.

'*I think you fucked me.*' It started to kick in my chest. Kick in my stomach. Kick in my guts.

'No, Jenna, *I* told *you* it was a mistake. And we agreed never to bring it up again.'

Acid-like, champagne gushed up my throat and hit the back of my mouth.

I sensed movement to my side. My eyes swivelled towards it. Matt. He was stood near me. Matt. So smart in his black tuxedo, white shirt, black bow tie. He was holding four champagne glasses. And then he wasn't. They slipped from his fingers, twisting and falling as they headed in slow motion for the floor. They exploded, showering both our feet in champagne.

The music stopped for a fraction of a second, a fraction of silence that magnified the smashing of champagne flutes. Greg and Jen turned to the source of the sound, as did half the room, I'd imagine.

Greg and Jen. The image of them naked, covered in sweat, moving together bolted across my mind. Him moving inside her. Whispering her name, telling her he loved her.

Greg and Jen.

Jen and Greg.

I clamped my hand over my mouth to prevent champagne spewing out, spun on my fancy heels. Had to get out of there. I wanted to run. Wanted to sprint out of there but the dress bound my legs together and I could only do that stupid wiggly-bottomed walk.

I heard him calling my name. Above the music, I heard him. Heard him like he was far away and I was slightly deaf. Or should that be dumb?

I hitched up the dress to my knees. I could move faster. My legs propelling me out of the ballroom, into the corridor and towards the lift as the doors were sliding together. I threw myself through the gap and the doors clunked open again.

Greg wrenched open one of the heavy oak doors from the ballroom, came running towards the lifts. The doors had begun to slide shut but not quick enough – at the speed he was running, he'd make it. He'd make it, jump into the lift, start talking to me, start trying to explain. Trying to explain the inexplicable.

Close! I willed the lift doors. *Close! Close!*

Greg reached the lifts with only a sliver of a gap between the lift doors. It was enough, though. Enough to see the look on his face. Imploring. Pleading.

Stop, his look said. *Stop and let me explain.*

chapter thirty

secrets and lies

I couldn't get my keycard into the door slot.

I held it in my gloved hands, but they were shaking and it kept slipping. Wouldn't fit into the rectangle and let me in. *Calm, calm.* I took a deep breath. Then another. Stilled my hand and tried again. CLICK, it went as it slid into place.

I turned the door handle and rushed in.

Should I change my shoes or throw up first?

This was a big decision. Should I change my shoes or try to purge that choking ball of bile that was lodged between my throat and chest?

I had to get rid of the bile. But my shoes. My shoes. I looked down at the black heels. They weren't the sort of thing I wore. I was a trainers girl. I hated these shoes. Hideous. Stupid. Pointless. I kicked the right one off. It flew in a high arc and disappeared under the bed. Then I kicked off the left one. It too arced through the air but landed by the bathroom door. *Stupid things. Don't you know you're only meant to be worn by the star of the show? Not people like me.*

I hitched up my dress, got on my knees, grabbed my trainers from under the bed. They were battered, dirty, old. But mine. I loved them. Nobody could take them away from me.

Wear them first. Use them first. I sat on the bed and pulled them on, laced them up. That's better. That's me.

Now, pack! Get the hell out of here! my brain screamed to me like it was watching me in a horror movie, sat on the edge of its seat screaming, 'Run, you stupid bint. Run in the opposite direction!' as the rest of me went to investigate a loud howling noise on the roof with only a fake Manolo Blahnik sandal thing for protection. With only my trainers for protection. *Pack, then get the hell out of Dodge!*

I sat on the edge of the huge bed, staring at the door. Unable to move, just waiting. Waiting for the monster to show up.

The door burst open and the monster appeared in the doorway.

I stared at the monster. The monster stared at me.

Who the hell are you? I thought. He wasn't my hero.

He couldn't be. Heroes didn't do this kind of thing. Heroes didn't leave blatant clues as to why they were the villain of the piece. Every time I thought about it, more clues came up. Hints and clues that told me about this:

1. Why he'd reacted so badly to Jen and Matt moving in together.
2. His thinking they were moving too fast even though they'd been together three years.
3. His walking out when they were snogging on the day Matt moved in.
4. Staring right at Jen as he described his perfect woman – and I thought it was me. Ha!
5. His avoiding Matt and Jen – he couldn't face seeing the woman he loved with someone else.
6. His jealousy at me putting Jen first. Not because he wanted all of me, but because he wanted something of hers to love him better.

7. Him wanting to tell her after six weeks so as to make her jealous.

They was all there – all those clues – and I'd missed every last one of them. After a lifetime's worth of Sherlock Holmes, Agatha Christie and other murder mysteries, after all those years of me sat there going, 'It was him', 'It was her' (I'd even guessed it was the wife halfway through *Presumed Innocent*), I'd missed every clue. I knew nothing about nothing.

Sure, Greg was fond of me now. He liked me, he'd probably even talked himself into thinking he could love me. He'd always treat with kindness and affection the woman who rescued him but he *wanted* Jen. She was the star of his life. I was the understudy. Not even the co star, I was the understudy, the one he'd called upon when the star wasn't available. I loved him. He wanted Jen.

'I thought you'd be gone, but I'm glad you're not,' the monster said.

I didn't say anything, just stared at him.

'What did you hear?' he asked, his suit-covered chest heaving from, I presume, running up here.

BANG! BANG-BANG-BANG! at the door made me jump. I looked to the door, but Greg ignored it, carried on talking.

'What did you hear?' he asked again.

The braying continued, getting louder, more insistent. They'd be hammering through the door soon. Not even Greg could talk over the noise, so he spun on his heels, marched to it, turned the handle. Again, the door burst open, and suddenly the room was filled with raised voices, all shouting to be heard over the other. There was pushing and shoving, too. Matt, pushing and shoving Greg. But he wasn't pushing as much as he was shouting, possibly because Greg could kick his butt with both hands tied behind his back, standing on one leg, with a bad cold – indignant and angry Matt may be, but he wasn't that stupid.

Slowly, I could make out what they were saying. Matt was calling Greg every bastard under the sun and, as it turned out, there were a lot of them. Greg was saying sorry and calm down at the same time, Jen was screaming that they should both stop it.

I sat on the bed, feeling removed from the whole thing, as though I was watching this on a screen. Watching a lot of films will do that.

Greg took several steps back into the middle of the room, and, 'Let's all calm down,' he said. His voice was so calm and commanding that it had the most amazing effect: Matt instantly stopped looking like he was going to batter Greg and stalked off to the other side of the room and threw himself into one of the armchairs. Jen went to the window and jumped up to sit on the wide window sill. Greg stood his ground, arms folded across his chest. He was staring at me. I was staring into the mid-distance. I was so stressed I was on the verge of telling a 'knock, knock' joke.

I never knew Greg could do that with his voice. But then, I never knew he could roger Jen, so there you go: he was a rich box of chocolates, new varieties of which I was discovering every day.

Matt sat glowering at Greg. He opened his mouth. Shut it again. Then opened it again. He did the fish thing a few times, then eventually, 'So, all the time you were trying to put me off Jen it was because you were knocking her off?' came out.

'You were trying to put him off me?' Jen said, aghast. 'You *bastard.*'

'I wasn't knocking off Jen,' Greg said, looking at me for some reason. 'Amber, I promise you, I wasn't. It only happened the once.'

Once is enough, I meant to say, but my vocal cords were paralysed.

'ONCE IS BLOODY ENOUGH!' Matt screamed. 'YOU ABSOLUTE WANKER!'

There's no need for that kind of language, I went to say, but again, nothing came out. *Besides, if he was an absolute wanker, we wouldn't be having this drama, would we? It was because he was an absolute shagger that we were here.*

'YOU'VE BEEN AFTER JEN ALL THIS TIME. YOU WANTED HER FOR YOURSELF SO YOU TRIED TO PUT ME OFF HER.'

Greg rounded on Matt. He was suddenly so angry his whole body trembled with unspoken rage. Rather than shouting, though, he controlled his words. 'You know that's not true.' He glared at Matt. 'You *know* what I meant.'

I was glad Matt knew. Glad that Greg knew. And glad that Jen probably knew too. Because I didn't have a bloody clue what was going on. I was still back at the '*You fucked me and moved on to my friend*' stage, if I was honest.

'And what did you mean, exactly?' Jen asked indignantly.

Rather than answer Jen, Greg focused his Minstrel eyes on Matt's harassed, aggravated face until they met with Matt's emerald eyes. Greg was wrestling with whether to let it out of the bag or to leave it, to accept being tarred as an 'absolute wanker'.

A look of understanding passed between them. Even in my state I saw it. It was something big.

Matt's rage faltered, then evaporated. Completely disappeared into the ether. One minute he was murderous, then he said evenly: 'Let's talk about this later, when we've all calmed down.'

'You're right,' Jen concurred, 'let's all calm down.'

What the HELL is this? What's going on? Why the sudden conspiracy? How come nobody's angry any more?

'No, let's get everything out in the open.' Me. I said it. My voice had returned.

'Let's wait 'til we've calmed down,' Jen insisted.

'So you know what's going on between Matt and Greg then?' I asked.

'What's going on between them?' she replied.

'You didn't see that look they gave each other? They're hiding something else. Something bigger.'

Jen laughed a hollow laugh. 'No, they just don't want to lose their friendship over a couple of girls. I think we should take some time out, calm down, then talk about this.'

'You can calm down,' I said. 'I *am* calm. I am the personification of calmness. It's oozing out of every pore. See this face? Calm. And if I don't find out what's going on right now, you're all going to see exactly how calm I am up close and personal.'

'Nothing,' Matt said.

I turned to Greg. 'Greg?'

He said nothing. He didn't know who to side with. His best friend of twenty-two years, or his girlfriend of seven months. Had it been any other time, I would've taken a sick pleasure in him now knowing how hard it was to choose between two people you love. 'Remember that time you had a go about me putting Jen first? Well, this is how it feels,' I would've said.

As the situation stood, I wasn't taking any pleasure in Greg's dilemma. In fact, I was about to up the ante: 'Greg, if we're going to salvage anything from this then tell me what's going on.'

'DON'T YOU DARE!' Matt exploded. 'YOU OWE ME. YOU SCREWED MY GIRLFRIEND AND YOU OWE ME.'

Greg's line of sight went from me to Matt to me. He realised there was only one way out of this. 'Tell them,' Greg said. *Make Matt confess.*

'YOU CAN FUCK OFF!'

'Tell them.'

'NO.'

'If you don't, I will.'

'WHAT IS IT?' Me again. I'd found my voice and was shouting.

Matt took a deep breath, stared down at his shiny black shoes. Then, in a small, small voice, he said: 'I've got a wife in France.'

chapter thirty-one

truth

I fancied myself as being so tortured and so in need of a good think that I'd spend the night, hands in pockets, head down, wandering the dark streets of this sprawling metropolis, like the hero does in a movie when, for no clear reason, it's suddenly dark, rainy and even the most deserted village suddenly becomes a city and is rammed with people. All of this is done to a whiny sax soundtrack. Within ten minutes of leaving the room, I was sitting in the hotel's gardens. But I did sit there with my hands in my pockets, staring at the ground and if I strained hard enough I could hear that sax.

Everything that had gone on in the past few hours kept jumping into my head. All of it. Not one part which I could make sense of. Everything. Every time I tried to remember something, to hold it up to scrutiny, to dissect and understand and digest it, the rest of it would leap in too. All tumbled and knotted, like a demented ball of vermicelli. I needed time to untangle it.

OK, Amber, focus. Focus, focus, focus.

Matt.

I hadn't read anyone so wrong in, like, ever. I'd thought he was a lump of toffee: rich and smooth and, ultimately, unchanging. However, he was a two-faced, double-dealing, double-lifed, married man. His way of behaving, his boring exterior, hid a seething core of duplicity. His tightness, the way he paled every time he was called upon to put his hand in his pocket, came from having two lives to support.

Matt did a degree in French, which meant he spent a year living in Paris. During that year, he met Françoise; their fling helped with his French no end. (Matt didn't say this, I added it because it was probably true.) When he returned to England after his year, he and Françoise kept in touch. And when he graduated, he returned to Paris and got a job. After too much wine one night, he proposed. Two months later they got married. Only Greg knew. He was the best man, of course, and Matt being commitmentphobic – as Greg had tried to tell me once upon a time – had panicked. He swore Greg to secrecy: nobody in England must ever find out, especially not Matt's parents. He'd gotten round the parents issue by saying his parents, especially his dad, were very racist and had a particular hatred of the French. His poor parents, whose only crime as far as I could see was to spawn this creature called their son, were therefore a banned subject with Françoise. Matt had constructed two lives and rather effectively ran them concurrently. He had two mobile phones, one that Jen thought was for work, so when he got calls and started talking in French, she didn't get suspicious. He'd told Françoise that he was house-sitting for a friend so he wasn't contactable at Rocky's place any more. When he was in France, he'd call Jen from work.

'After a year of being happy together, I was offered a transfer to Leeds for six months. They were starting a company over here and needed English people. Me living in Leeds for all those years made me the ideal choice. By that point the honeymoon was over for me and Françoise, we'd not been getting on for months, so six months apart seemed the ideal solution. I came back to Leeds, got my old room back with

Greg and Rocky, and whenever I saw Françoise again things were perfect. Time apart was what we needed.

'When the six months were extended to a year, we decided to go for it. I had to go back quite a lot to Paris – this was before the days of video conferencing and emails, so my relationship with Françoise was safe.' Matt ran a hand through the spikes of his blond hair, his green eyes fixed on the carpet.

'Then they offered me a permanent position in Leeds. It was a dream come true, but Françoise didn't want to leave France. Her whole life was there. We spent so much time arguing about it. I'd lived there with her, why couldn't she come be with me? I might even have introduced her to my parents. I didn't want to miss this opportunity, so we got used to living apart. Then I met Jen.'

Oh yes, I thought, *here it comes. The nonsense that will excuse his behaviour.* 'She was different from other girls.' *Yup, that's right, Matt, you neglected to mention that you'd shagged around when you were in Leeds, didn't you? It was implied, now you've confirmed it.*

'I started to fall for Jen and at the same time, Françoise was talking about me coming back to Paris full-time, us having a baby . . . I panicked again. Stopped going to Paris as much, just spoke to her at work. I told her I wanted to concentrate on my career. If she wanted to be with me then she'd have to come here. I often said I didn't want to talk to her unless she'd at least try living here. She said no, so I spent more time here. But I couldn't finish with Françoise or Jen . . . I kept things as they were, ignoring the fact that Françoise wanted a baby, saying she had to come over here if she wanted us to try for a child, which I knew she'd never do. When Jen asked me to move in, I said yes without really thinking. That's why that thing,' he nodded towards Greg, 'freaked out when me and Jen announced it. He always liked Françoise. But that's probably because he shagged her too, ain't it, mate?'

I turned to Greg. *Course he has. There are few women he's met who he hasn't shagged.*

'No, I haven't shagged her too,' Greg spat. 'But then, I could've done, the amount of time I spent with Françoise, covering for you. You know, like the time I had to drop everything and go to Paris because she was distraught that you'd disappeared and she couldn't find you. I could've shagged her then while I was busy not telling her that you'd gone to Los Angeles with Jen. And, that time Françoise turned up out of the blue and you and Jen had gone to Prague for a week, I could've shagged her then, couldn't I? Or, I could've kept your secret and looked after her and when I saw Jen's best mate in town not mentioned that the woman beside me was *your wife.*'

I'd met her? Matt and Jen went to Prague at the end of last year. I feverishly racked my brain. I'd bumped into Greg a few times in town around then. And the day I saw him when Matt and Jen had gone away . . . It came flooding back to me. Greg had looked so jumpy that day I saw him in Albion Place, outside WHSmith. I hadn't understood why he was so shifty. He'd introduced the woman beside him really stiffly, but I was rubbish at names. I was better with faces . . .

Cold tingling flooded my body. She was slight, her face angular from being so thin. Her blonde hair was cut into a stylish bob that sat just above her cheeks. She wore chic, designer clothes, Prada shoes, dusky pink lipstick. That's who New Jen reminded me of – Françoise, Matt's wife.

'You turned Jen into your wife,' I said to Matt incredulously. 'That's why she lost weight and hacked off her lovely hair and wears that ridiculous lipstick. You wanted to spend day after day living with a version of Françoise in Leeds.'

'What are you on about?' Jen was half laughing.

'I met Françoise when she was with Greg. And Matt's turned you into her. You were right when you said he preferred you so thin your hipbones poke through your clothes and your hair so short you look fifty, because that's what she looks like.'

Jen looked to Greg; he glanced away. She swung round to Matt. 'Matt?'

Matt said nothing.

'You said I'd look better with short hair, with less weight. And all along you wanted me to look like your *wife*? YOU BASTARD!'

She ran at him, started scratching at his eyes and face, while her feet tried to kick him. He put his hands up to protect himself. Greg and I watched them struggle until Matt managed to grab her wrists, stand up and fling her onto the bed. She bounced unceremoniously beside me a couple of times, then glared up at him.

'At least I didn't shag Amber, eh, *lover*?' Matt shouted at her.

'Like you'd ever get the chance,' I said.

'You're comparing you living a double life, lying and screwing with my mind to a drunken mistake? You're unbelievable,' Jen shouted back.

'*HE'S* UNBELIEVABLE?' I suddenly screamed, turning on her. I hadn't known I was going to shout until it was coming out of my mouth. 'What about you? Matt has always been a twat. I knew that from the second I clapped eyes on him. I thought it was because he was boring, but no, it's because he's clearly the village idiot's Neanderthal brother. But you, Jen, you were meant to be my friend. And you've done nothing but put me down and treat me with contempt. Tonight was the icing on the cake.'

'You're blaming me?' she asked, aghast.

'Yes, I'm blaming you. You just couldn't leave it, could you?' I snarled. 'You saw that Greg and I were happy, and you couldn't bear it. You like to keep me in your little box. Little Single Amber who you can take out and set up on hideous blind dates, or impose upon when your relationship's rocky or your lover's gone away – to see his wife, as it turns out.'

'Greg slept with me too. I didn't force myself on him,' Jen said.

'Yeah, and why bring it up tonight when it's likely that I'll overhear? I'll tell you why, because you saw that he might possibly care about me so you couldn't wait to go rushing in there to remind him that you were the prettier one, the sexier one, the one he had first. The one he really wanted.'

'But he's no good for you,' Jen said, tears in her voice. 'He really is no good for you.'

'What you mean is, I'm not good enough for him. You couldn't stand it, you couldn't bear it that messy, plain, fat Amber could sleep with good-looking Greg and keep him. While you, sexy, feminine, thin Jen could only get a shag.'

Jen wiped at her mascaraed eyes with her fingers. 'That's not fair, Amber.'

'FAIR!?' I screamed. 'FAIR? And this is all fair, is it?' I stopped as my chest heaved, tears blossomed in my eyes. I was damned if I was going to sob in front of them. I got up, went to the wardrobe, took out my jacket.

'You disgust me. You all disgust me,' I said. 'And you make me disgust myself.' I shoved my hands into my pockets and felt it – the extra special pressie I'd bought for Greg. I'd rooted it out last night, ready to present it to him after I asked him to move in with me. I removed it from my pocket, sneered at it for a second. 'I think this belongs to you,' I said, then tossed the soft, leather-bound black book at Greg's feet.

He looked at it, then his horrified eyes flew up to my face.

Without another word, I left.

I opened the door, not particularly quietly because I knew Greg would be long gone. My heart lurched when I saw his outline sitting in a chair, half turned to the window, his feet resting on the wall. Along the window sill were a line of mini-bar bottles. *Oh yeah, sure, now he decides to stop walking out on me. Now he decides to stay and sort things out. Or maybe he's just waited for me to come back — no point walking out on someone if they're not there to witness it.*

I stood in the doorway. Should I pack and go home? Or pack and go get another room?

Another tidal wave of exhaustion crashed through me. Sleep. I needed to sleep. I hadn't done that properly in two weeks. Longer, if you counted the run-up to the Festival. I just wanted to sleep.

'I hoped you'd come back tonight,' Greg croaked. He moved and the moonlight on his face showed his puffy eyes, each one ringed with moisture.

My heart jumped. I wanted to put my arms around him, hold him. Then I remembered, he'd brought this on himself. You reap as you sow.

And I'd brought this on myself. I knew what he was like. I knew he hadn't met a woman he wouldn't have at some point tried to bed. What else did I expect? Of course he'd done the unthinkable and slept with the one person in the whole world I wouldn't, no, *couldn't* accept him sleeping with.

'Didn't come back to talk,' I said. 'I'm so tired. Just want to sleep.'

Greg nodded. Raked his hands through his hair. In his lap was the little black book and his mobile. While I'd been out walking, he'd been setting up the next week's shagging. Good for him. It's best to get back on the horse as soon as possible.

I grabbed a T-shirt and jogging bottoms from my bag, which had my clothes spewing out of it. Having only had two days to pack, I'd done so in a bit of a haphazard way. 'I'll buy you clothes in France,' Greg had said when I'd told him I didn't have time to do any washing before the holiday. I'd never thought I'd meet a man who'd say tha— *No, stop it. That's over. It's all over.*

341

I went into the bathroom and removed myself from my Holly Golightly costume: taking all the pins out of my hair, stripping my face of make-up. Piece by piece I dismantled my film star persona until there she was in the mirror. The old Amber. The pre-ball, pre-Greg Amber. Plain old Amber.

By the time I vacated the bathroom Greg was lying on the far side of the bed, almost on the edge. His clothes were neatly folded on the chair. No walking out was scheduled for tonight, then.

I climbed between the cool white sheets, careful not to get too far into the bed, and lay on the edge of my side of the bed facing away from him. An ocean of silence separated us.

'It was before you,' Greg said from his side of the bed. 'The second it was over, I regretted it.'

'You shouldn't have done it,' I replied.

'I know. But I've felt awful ever since.'

'YOU. SHOULDN'T. HAVE. DONE. IT.'

Greg started breathing heavily, tiny vibrations from his body rippled across the bed.

He was crying. I wanted to shuffle across the bed, put my arms around him, love him better. Wanted to. Couldn't. It wasn't my job any more.

'i'd try therapy
if chocolate wasn't
quicker and
sweeter'

chapter thirty-two

the runaway

A week passed in a flash, thus disproving all theories about the relativity of time and fun.

When I'd left the hotel I hadn't known where I was going. I had a week off work, a bag packed with clothes, but I couldn't face my flat. I'd asked him to move in with me, had spent so much time there in the past seven months with him I couldn't face going back there. But I had nowhere else to go. In the end I'd made a hysterical call to Eric asking what I should do. Eric, even though he was going through his own hell, said to get on a train to Edinburgh and that he'd be waiting at the other end.

I'd never spent a whole week, well, nine days, with Eric and Arrianne before. Had it been under better circumstances it would've been fun. Unless you knew it, you couldn't tell that they weren't getting on: there was no leaping into each other's arms, but they weren't being off with each other. Or shouting. Or even the dreaded being polite to each other. They were normal with each other. As normal to each other as they were to me.

Eric and Arrianne, being proper psychologists, let me sleep in for the first day. And for the first two days I was allowed to mope around, stare into space, stay on the edge of tears. Day three, I was dragged from my bed at 8 a.m., and told I had to earn my keep: bring in coal and wood – they stopped short of making me chop it up, wash up – cook, vacuum, clean. And it helped. I didn't have time to think about Greg and Jen. Jen and Matt. Matt and Françoise. Matt and Greg for all I knew. Those thoughts were saved for the still of the night. For those moments between sleep and consciousness, when I couldn't chase away my memories with a big stick. Most evenings, to help me sleep like you would a hyperactive kid, Eric would take me for a long walk into the countryside where they lived. Up hills, down vales. Arrianne came with us once, decided we wussy English folk walked too slowly and didn't come again.

On my last day, I said bye to Arrianne at the crack of dawn because I was getting the first train to Leeds and Eric drove me to the station.

'I'm going to miss having an unpaid maid around,' he said as I prepared to board the train. 'Our house has never been so clean. Not even when Mum comes to stay.'

'You don't do all that every day?'

'Course not, we do have a life. And a cleaner, but he's on holiday for a couple of weeks. You arrived at the perfect time.'

'Duped by my own brother. Is there no end to my betrayal?'

'It was good for you. Stopped you spending so much time thinking. And as we all know, you think too much as it is.' My face must've registered something because Eric added: 'That's what he used to say to you, right?'

'Before anything happened. When we were friends.'

'Friends who become lovers. Probably the most fraught kind of relationship there is. You always start off knowing far too much about each other. And a little knowledge can be a dangerous thing. Come on, Gerbil, on the train.'

As I stepped through the doorway, Eric said, 'Remember what I said.'

346

This is what my brother, my peanut-brittle-looking, but caramel-hearted brother had said:

On the last of our nightly walks we stopped on a hillside, sat side by side on the dewy (read: wet) grass. From that distance, all you could see were the lights from the houses of the villages below. And they looked like reflections of the stars above. The heavens mirrored on earth. Heavens below.

Silence closed in, wrapping us up so tight I felt stifled, suffocated. I had an urge to start saying random words to loosen its hold around us.

'I can't believe Greg slept with that slut,' Eric said out of the dark. He and Arrianne hadn't brought it up since I first told Eric what had happened. And now he *was* bringing it up, he was starting with this.

'Jen's not a slut,' I replied, almost as a reflex.

Eric shook his head sadly, sighed. 'As I suspected, you're willing to forgive Jen anything, but Greg is confined to hell.'

'Are you really that surprised? He's a man and that's what men do, anything for a shag, no matter who it's with. Or who it'll hurt.' I turned to Eric. 'Even you were having an affair.'

Eric's blue eyes narrowed and eyed me suspiciously. 'Why do you say that?'

'Oh, come on, Ez, this is me. My real dad did it, I've known other men do it. I used to think I had a radar for it. Until Greg. And I know you, the way you were when you came down to mine, it was obvious. So, how long did it go on for? How long did you cheat on Arrianne? How long did you do to the woman who is practically my sister what my dad did to my mum? Or are you still doing it?'

Eric shook his head. 'Nothing happened. I didn't even kiss her. When I came to Leeds I was thinking about going beyond just flirting but then you said that thing in the pub and I couldn't stop thinking about it . . . Besides, it'd be over with

347

Arrianne if I did. It'd never feel the same with her again. And if she ever found out she wouldn't ever forgive me or let me back. I remembered that, thankfully. It was a stupid flirtation that was over before it began . . . Anyway, we're not talking about me. We're talking about why you've condemned Greg and let Jen off the hook.'

'And I answered your question.'

'Uh-huh. Do you want to know why I dislike Jen?'

Not particularly, I thought. But if I said no, Eric would never tell me, no matter how much I begged. Even if my curiosity wasn't piqued, I had to find out now or never find out. I'd learnt that the hard way. 'Why?' I asked flatly.

'Because that time I met her in the pub, we'd been sat there ten minutes when she put her hand on my thigh.'

What? Shock petrified my body, every muscle became rigid with horror.

'She didn't stop there. She kept touching me, even though I kept shoving her hands off me. When you went to the bar, she started this stream of filth about me and her. I reminded her I was married and she said it'd be our secret.'

WHAT?!

'It wouldn't have been so bad if I thought she genuinely liked me, but she didn't. She clearly didn't. My guess is she wanted to damage my relationship with you. I knew if I'd fallen into sex with Jen you would've found out about it at some point.'

'Why? Why did she do that? She's my friend.' Standing on the outside, that sounded pathetic. But I was on the inside. Right on the inside, pathetic was all I had to offer.

'Jen has an unhealthy obsession with you. And you're unable to see what she's really like. Plus, the way she was so odd with Mum and Dad, I reckon she has a lot of parent issues to resolve . . . But what I'm trying to tell you is, Jen isn't the perfect friend you seem to think she is. Meaning you shouldn't

348

assume that Jen was the one who was seduced, the one who deserves instant understanding. And don't assume that Greg was the one who was seduced. Unless you speak to them, don't assume anything.'

I nodded absently. Not really listening. I was replaying that weekend Jen met my family. She had been tense around Mum and Dad2, but since I was always tense when I met people's parents, I hadn't thought much about it. It didn't even occur to me that she'd try something on with Eric. My brother. No wonder she never asked why he didn't like her. She knew perfectly well why. Did I know Jen at all?

'What are you going to do when you go back tomorrow? How are you going to sort things out?' Eric asked.

I took in the air. It was so fresh and pure it almost burned as it worked its way through my respiratory system. I hadn't really thought about it. Not properly. What with being worked to the bone and only thinking about what had happened, the future hadn't cropped up in my thoughts. Besides, I wasn't exactly known for planning for the future, was I? I shrugged at Eric.

'Be honest with me,' Eric said, 'did you love Greg?'

Nobody had asked me that directly. Not even Greg. And, whilst I knew how I felt, it was a different kettle of fish admitting it out loud.

'I thought he loved me,' I said, 'but all along he was with me to get to Jen.'

'Yeah,' Eric said sympathetically. 'Bummer, isn't it? Greg wore a suit to meet your mother; put up with you calling him your "boyfumnd"; drank whisky to please me and Dad even though he hates the stuff because he wanted Jen.

'And when we went to get the rice via the pub, he told Dad that his intentions towards you were entirely honourable and that he was hopelessly in love with you . . .' My head snapped round to stare at Eric. He nodded. 'Oh yes, he said

349

that. Those exact words. It was one of the funniest moments of my life because it completely freaked Dad out. But *aye*, Greg said all that to get to Jen. Oh *aye*, and I think he wanted to move in with *yea* after three months because he wanted Jen.'

I rubbed at my eyes, they were stinging. Burning, almost.

'I know he wanted to move in with you because when Dad went to the bar, Greg asked me what I thought about him asking you to live with him. He wasn't asking my opinion, he was asking my permission. Freaked me out, but like telling Dad his intentions towards you were honourable, he wanted us to accept him. He knew how important your family are and he was desperate to be accepted by us. But no, no, you're right, he did all that because he wanted Jen.' (We weren't genetically connected, but my brother and I were identical twin-like when it came to labouring a point into submission. Anyone else would've said, 'Don't be silly, course he loved you.')

I couldn't see for all the prickling of tears in my eyes.

'You were happy with Greg, weren't you?' Eric said gently. 'I've never seen you so happy. So relaxed. You were happy with him, weren't you?'

I shrugged.

'Why don't you try sorting it out with him? Find out why he did it.'

'But he shouldn't have done it,' I said.

'I know that, you know that. *He* knows that. Even the woman down the end of our road knows that, but he *cannae* change it. He *cannae* unsleep with Jen, but he can explain it.'

I wiped away a tear with the palm of my hand.

'Greg's done something stupid, but you can't stop loving him just like that. You're not that cold, you're not th—'

Couldn't hear any more. Blood was gushing into my brain, my head was swelling up, tears were slipstreaming down my face and I leant forwards over my knees, covering my face with my hands. Crying and crying and crying. Sobbing and sobbing my stupid, flaccid heart out. Because we weren't a particularly huggy family, Eric sat beside me and let me cry.

'Thank God for that,' Eric said, handing me a large neat whisky and flopping beside me on the sofa.

'Thank God?' I replied. Was still trembling from my epic cry. Hadn't cried like that in years. I'd done a bit of sobbing in my time – like when I realised it was over with Sean – but not complete breakdown as I had done on the hill.

'Arrianne and I had bets on how long it would take you to cry. I had three days, Arri had two weeks.'

'I'm glad you get such entertainment from my life.'

'Me and Arri have been pissing ourselves since you got here because how upset you are is hysterical. And, in winter, we take to the streets and laugh at homeless people.' He was a sarcastic *get*, my brother.

'What I meant was, thank God you've finally cried. I was scared that you'd got so good at running away from intense situations that you'd get through this whole thing without shedding a tear.'

'I don't usually cry,' I reminded Eric.

'That's nothing to be proud of. Crying when you're hurt releases pain, be it emotional or physical. Arrianne had two weeks because she said you spent so much of your life slotting yourself into other people's lives, that you *didnae* know how to let the world know you were hurting.

'You weathered your parents' marriage, you made Mum's life easier by calling Dad "Dad2" almost straight away. You'll do anything to avoid trouble, even if it means not telling people how hurt you are.'

'Life's too short to waste on pointless battles,' I explained.

Eric smiled. 'It's not that short. Especially when there are some things that need to be fought for. Like your relationship with Greg.'

'But he slept with her. If there was anyone in the whole world I didn't want him to sleep with, it's her. *Her!*'

Her! Perfect, gorgeous Jen, Miss Star of the Show, who I don't measure up to. And who I'll never measure up to. Who can charm anyone into doing anything. Charm anyone into sleeping with her. Even Sean used to look at those blonde locks and topaz eyes as though he'd never seen anyone so beautiful. Everyone wanted her. Loved her. 'I can see them, up here.' I pressed my fingertips against my forehead. 'I can see their bodies, their faces, hear the sounds they make. And I can't stop it.

'You shot down my theory about him using me to get to Jen, but you can't tell me that he didn't even once compare us. That he didn't once think of her while he was with me.' *Didn't often feel a stab of disappointment because he'd gazed down and discovered he wasn't making love to Jen but fucking Amber.*

'No, I can't. But he can. He can explain.'

'There's nothing to explain. He made love to his best mate's girlfriend – *my best friend* – and then lied when I almost found out.'

Eric rolled his whisky glass between his hands and stared into it. He was either trying to boil the whisky with his sight or he was in deep thought. I wanted to put my throbbing head down on the sofa armrest and sleep.

Eric sighed suddenly, long and frustrated. 'You're so perfect I'm always amazed you haven't got a halo,' he said. 'I used to call you the Sainted Amber Salpone.'

'Why are you turning on me?' I asked, sounding as fragile as I felt.

'Because growing up with you was hell. You were so good, *all the time*, that it accentuated how bad I was. Except I wasn't that bad.'

'Climbing out of your bedroom window to go have sex with a twenty-nine-year-old woman when you're sixteen isn't bad?'

'Not when put into perspective: I wasn't mugging old ladies or taking drugs. I was no worse than anyone else my age, apart from you. At what became my weekly bollocking, Dad was always holding you up as a shining example of what a child should be like.'

'So, what, fifteen years later you're bitching about it?'

'No ... well, yes. But I'd have thought that you'd have realised by now that it's all right to be bad sometimes. It's all right to be angry. It's natural. When Dad told me we were moving in with you and Mum, I went mad. I threw the biggest tantrum of all time, screamed and cried. It wasn't that I didn't love you both, I just wanted my life to stay the same. I gave Dad such a hard time about it for months – even after we'd moved in. But you ... you welcomed us with open arms, fitted in around us without any thought for how it'd ruined your life. You started calling him Dad2 to make our lives easier and you never did a thing wrong.'

Eric didn't know what happened when you weren't good. When you didn't go along with what others wanted.

'That's what I meant about you relaxing with Greg. It was the first time ever that you weren't on edge, not trying to make things right. I'd never seen you so relaxed, not even when you were with that other bloke.'

'*Sean*. His name is *Sean*,' I hissed.

'Yeah, him. When you were with Greg it was the first time you weren't slotting yourself into everyone's life. That's why you were glowing. You'd finally chilled. It wasn't just that he loved you or you loved him, you'd finally found safety. I thought, hoped, that now you'd done that, you might've stopped.'

'Stopped ... Stopped what?' I asked tiredly. Listening to

353

myself being deconstructed was exhausting. Every piece he picked apart and slung on the ground had to be dusted off and glued back onto my personality. I didn't have the energy for it.

Eric replied: 'You know what film you always remind me of?'

Stopped what? I asked silently as I shook my head.

'Well, it's not a film. More a line from a film, a line from *Heat*. Robert De Niro, I think it's Robert De Niro, maybe it's the Al Pacino character, no, no, it's Robert De Niro . . .' Eric stopped, I obviously radiated an unimpressed attitude. 'Anyway it's that line where *Robert De Niro* says something like: "Don't have anything in your life that you can't walk away from in thirty seconds flat if you spot the heat coming."'

'What are you saying?' I replied.

'I think it's pretty obvious what I'm saying.'

'I'm involved in lots of things that I can't walk away from. I've, I've bought my flat! And I've got a permanent job. And . . .' I ran out of steam. I didn't seem to have that many things I couldn't walk out on in thirty seconds if I thought about it. But did anyone? 'Anyway, if my memory serves me correctly, the one time he did get involved in something he couldn't walk away from, he got killed. He should've taken his own advice.'

'You're doing it again. Except it's don't get involved in a conversation you can't use a joke to wheedle your way out of in five seconds flat.'

'Eric, I've got ties. I couldn't walk away from my life in thirty days, let alone thirty seconds. I am capable of settling down.'

'Why did you walk away from a relationship that made you so happy in five minutes, then? If it took five minutes, what with you being such an expert at running away.'

'Me? I am not.'

'Yes you are. That's what I meant, Amber, about hoping,

now that you'd found safety, that you'd maybe stop running. But no, first sign of trouble, you take to the road. And that's what you're always doing, running away from anything that gets even slightly intense.'

'I've worked at the Festival for years and that's intense,' I replied.

'Yeah, intense, but it stops you following your heart. You work at the Festival because it's not what you really want.'

'I love my job.'

'I don't doubt it. But you want to be a director. I always knew you wanted to be a director. When we were young you used to make me and anyone else you could get to act out scenes from *Monkey* and *The Water Margin* and *The Pretenders*. It was a pain in the arse playing with you because you were always giving us these ridiculous lines to say. It was the only time, too, that you were bossy. Nobody could argue with you when you were in television mode. You want to be a director but you won't let yourself take the leap of faith that's required because you might fail; you might not be perfect at it.'

The script I'd vaguely been working on wafted across my mind.

'You've run away from everything important in your life because it's easier than getting in there and feeling it.'

'Don't know what you're talking about,' I whispered.

'Don't give me that. In your flat, the flat where you've lived for, what, seven years, you've still got packed boxes. Every time I visit I wonder if they'll be unpacked. But they're still there. Waiting for you to decide it's time to move on.'

'What's that got to do with anything?'

'Everything. It shows that you're a constant runaway, you never intend to settle, no matter how happy you are. You've done it again with Greg. You've run away from him for what? Sleeping with someone *before* you? Yes, it was Jen, and yes, he lied about it. But it was before you. You can't dump a person

355

for having sex before he went out with you. Especially when you haven't even talked to him about it.

'I can understand why you run away, though. First you saw your mum packing to run away, and then your dad essentially ran away. You *cannae* bear it when others leave you, so you get in there first. You get them before they get you. But what it usually turns into is you getting yourself before they get you. You hurting yourself by disappearing or walking away or not experiencing what can be truly wonderful about coming out the other side of a bad patch.'

I put my head on the arm of the sofa.

'Amber, for once, don't run away. Not physically, not emotionally. For once, see things through. Go into the pain, see how brilliant things can be when you make it to the other side.'

Eric made the 'call me' signal at me from the train platform.

I nodded as the train shuddered.

Then we waved at each other as the train whined to life and pulled off.

chapter thirty-three

the beginning of . . .

I opened the door to the *SC* office of the *Sunday Yorkshire Chronicle*, and for a fraction of a second thought their hard-faced receptionist, who knew me from the amount of times I'd visited Greg at work, had warned him I was there because he stood up, very slowly.

But he didn't turn to the door, instead he said in a loud voice, 'Can I have everyone's attention, please!'

The twenty or so people in the office stopped: some put down phones, others halted in their typing, others still paused conversations to look at him.

'I WANT EVERYONE TO STOP ASKING ME IF I'M OK,' he bellowed. 'THE WOMAN I LOVE HAS LEFT ME AND MY FRIENDS HATE ME. AND YES, I'M SURE MORE THAN A FEW PEOPLE IN HERE WOULD AGREE THAT I AM SCUM AND I DESERVE THIS. SO, LEAVE ME ALONE. I JUST WANT TO GET ON WITH MY WORK. THANK YOU.'

Greg looked so defeated as he flopped back onto his seat I almost turned on my heels and fled. I didn't want to do this. But fleeing, according to Eric, was what I did best. And I had to stop that. I trailed over to Greg's desk. His unshaven face looked up at me as I arrived at his desk.

'I think we should talk,' I said.

'Naturally, you heard all that,' Greg said, as he made swirls with the teaspoon in his cappuccino foam then licked the foam off the spoon and put it back into the foam to make more swirls. It hit me with a start to realise that it was a habit of mine. It was so irritating, it was a wonder anyone ever drank coffee with me. Actually, nobody did drink coffee with me more than once.

'Yup, I heard it,' I replied. 'I assume you were talking about me.'

Greg's face flashed surprise, then hurt, then his features settled on a half-smile. 'I suppose I deserve that. And, yes, I was talking about you.'

'Do you often lose it like that?'

'No. But since I lost my friends and you left me, it's hard keeping it together.'

'Still not made it up with Matt?'

'Matt has issues. And those issues mean he won't speak to me, or see me, or return my emails. What about you and Jen?'

'I'm going to see her later, when school's finished.'

'Mind if I tag along? Haven't been to a cat fight in years.'

I raised an eyebrow. 'Cat fight? Sexist *get*. What's it called when two men fight?'

'A fight, of course.'

'Not a dog fight?'

'Hmmm, since all men are dogs, you could have a point there.'

'Didn't I tell you I was always right?'

A wash of colour returned to his stubbly face, the dark circles under his eyes became grey instead of black, as he grinned.

'Anyways, I don't know why Matt's blaming you,' I said.

'He'd been cheating on his wife for three years and when he went away on "business" he was cheating on Jen. Out of all of us, he was the worst. You just kept his secrets.' *And shagged his girlfriend.*

Greg treated me to a stare almost as stony and rock-filled as one of Martha's. Didn't know he was capable of them. 'What did you want to talk about?' he asked sternly.

'What do you think?' I mumbled. This was hard. Harder than I expected. Part of me was so angry, felt so stupid and duped and second-rate, that I wanted to chuck my tea in his face. The rest of me, the part of me that Eric had got through to, was ready to do almost anything to be with him. Anything.

This was what I felt whenever he walked out. Whenever anyone got cross with me. I was scared of being that little girl finding her mother packing to run away all over again. Of being the little girl who came back from school one day to find her dad had gone. Vanished. The room that became Eric's bedroom was Dad's office and I came back to find it empty. His stuff was gone from my parents' bedroom and he never came back to the house. Never. Never explained why he left, either. He just packed and never returned. Mum had said he was living somewhere else and that in time I'd be able to go see him. I didn't want Greg to disappear like that. Or at all. But . . .

'You look well.' His voice had softened again. Maybe he could see I was scared. 'Really well.'

'I've been to see my brother. He kept dragging me out on long walks and making me drink medicinal whisky and eat healthy food.'

'I suppose he hates me now as well,' Greg said, smiling sadly.

Of course he doesn't. But I'm not going to tell you that. I inhaled deeply, tried to get the air to give me strength. The strength to do this. 'Why Jen?' I asked.

He ran a hand through his long hair, stared into his coffee. 'Remember I told you that in the time I fell for you I slept with a woman who'd been coming on to me for ages?'

'The mercy shag?' I was flabbergasted. 'That was Jen?'

Greg nodded. 'The mercy shag was Jen.'

'Is that what you wanted to tell me the night you broke my mug?'

Greg nodded, carried on playing with his cappuccino.

'So I was right, you had had sex with a cow.'

A smile rose to Greg's mouth, but didn't quite reach his eyes. I don't know why he wasn't rolling on the floor clutching his sides. It was funny and it was true. It was funny *because* it was true.

'Tell me what you wanted to tell me that night in the hotel.'

Greg shook his head, ran his hands over his face. 'That was a lifetime ago. It's too late now.'

'Tell me.'

'I don't see the point.'

'Tell me, please. I was too angry and hurt and shocked and paranoid to listen before. But I want to hear it now.'

'I . . .'

'Pretend we're in the hotel room. I've just come back from my walk and . . .' I went to the café door and stood there, looking at him. I went back to him. 'Now, you say, "I was hoping you'd come back." And I say, "I didn't come back to talk, I just want to sleep." And then we get into bed. And you say . . .'

'It was before you. The second it was over I regretted it.'

'You shouldn't have done it.'

'I know, and I've felt awful ever since it happened.'

And we're transported back to our hotel room. It's dark, moonlight streams through the windows, bathing our room in magical light. There's still a gulf of anger and shock between us. 'Why did you do it then?' I say from my side of the bed, still facing the wardrobe.

Greg turns over in bed so he's facing me. 'She made me feel special.'

'How?'

'She'd been coming on to me for ages. She and Matt had been together a year when it started. Every time we were alone she'd flirt or tell me I was gorgeous and sexy.'

'Don't all the women you sleep with tell you that?'

'Yes, and I'd always tell her not to be silly or ignore her. But, that night, when she rang me and said could I bring back her CDs and videos, I'd been doing some serious drinking. I can't remember how much I'd had to drink, but I knew I didn't want to stop. Nina had been on the phone. This time, she didn't do her usual "you're a bastard" routine, she said some evil things that I knew were true. She said I'd always be alone, that nobody who I loved would stay because I was so incapable of love.'

'Why didn't you call me? You always tell me these things.'

'I tried. I picked up the phone to call you, but then I stopped. It was so humiliating; I'd never felt so worthless. Not even after Kristy left me. And I was in love with you, I couldn't tell you those things. Even if you didn't believe them straight away, they'd still be "out there". Still be lodged somewhere in your head. As it is you only half trust me.

'When I got to Jen's I was barely keeping it together. I drank more and she was giving it the whole routine: touching me, complimenting me. I kept reminding her and myself about Matt. She was wearing this dress . . .

'It's no excuse, I know, but I felt wanted. After what Nina said, I just wanted some affection. I did realise that I shouldn't be responding to Jen so I got up to go home. At the front door she asked me to kiss her. I kissed her cheek. She kissed me properly. We broke away, and then my body took over.'

I do and don't want to hear all this. I have to hear it for my sanity's sake so I don't imagine worse things like slow-mo kissing and soft lighting and sax music . . . but I don't want to hear it because it's my boyfriend and my best friend having sex. 'You made love in her and Matt's bed?'

'It wasn't lovemaking. It wasn't even sex. It was a fuck. A quick, meaningless fuck. It could've been with anyone, but it was with Jen.'

I shift in bed to look at him.

'The second it was over I knew I'd done something terrible. This was what Nina was talking about. I was emotionally corrupt. I remember saying sorry to Jen and that it'd never happen again. She said we should talk about it in bed.'

They spent the night together?! Her slender body nestled against him, listening to his heart as she fell asleep, his hands stroking through her blonde locks. He probably told her a fairy story as well.

'She wanted us to go to bed because, I think, it would've made the whole thing seem legitimate. As if we liked each other. But I told her no, made her promise we'd never talk about it again. That we'd pretend it never happened. I went home and I smashed up my room. It was either that or drive my car into a wall.'

Jen must've felt great. You sleep with her then run.'

'It wasn't easy, especially as I knew what Matt was up to. But then, she knew what I was like. I'm a bastard. How many times has she said it over the years? She should have known that having sex with me would end up in me running away.'

'Why didn't you just tell me all this?' I ask. 'You told me Nina had a tight vagina, you've called me from police stations and hotel rooms, why couldn't you tell me this?'

'Because you wouldn't have given me a chance. We wouldn't have got together.'

'You don't know that.'

'Yes I do. You wouldn't have let me near you if you thought I'd even flirted with Jen, let alone . . .'

'Do you blame me? Would you have gone near me if I'd slept with Matt? . . . No, wait, don't answer that question, I already know the answer.'

362

'I kept waiting for you to find out. For Jen to tell you and for my whole world to come crashing down around my ears. Every time you saw Jen or spoke to her, I braced myself for you to find out. It was the biggest mistake of my life, and I regret it every day.'

I say nothing.

'Amber, I love you. I've not said that to a woman in over five years. I love you, I don't want to lose you.'

This is the part where I melt. Where I sobbingly tell him that I love him; that he won't lose me now he's explained.

The music swells, close-up on our linked fingers, cut to close-up on our teary eyes. Cut to sun rising outside: the world brightens, you know it's going to be all right. Love will win through in the end . . .

I am not in a fucking movie.

If I've learnt anything it's that I'm not in a movie.

'What makes you think you haven't already lost me?' I ask. 'What makes you think that every time I look at you I won't see you making love to my best friend? Or hear you lying when I almost found out?' It's over. I think I'm telling him it's over. I can't even check if I am because I don't know. I've never had this kind of conversation with a man. Not one I care about. Eric was right about that, I suppose. I'd never got to this point. People walk; I walk. I've never discussed it before.

'What makes you think I won't always wonder if you were comparing me to her?'

'It wasn't like that.'

'But how do I know? I keep wondering if you went with me as some kind of consolation prize. If all along you wanted her and I was just convenient.'

'I never wanted Jen.'

'You've got a funny way of showing it.'

I've always been mildly clairvoyant when it comes to the end of relationships. I can see the end, I can tell in the way someone talks, in what they say, in what they don't say. I can feel it coming so I don't bother returning half-hearted messages; don't take solace in friendly-ish

363

emails. And, once someone has made a move towards the door with a word, look or deed and I've bolted through it before they can, I don't go back. I don't do reunions and I don't do breaking up speeches. But this sounds suspiciously like one.

Greg laughs, low and husky, like Mutley. But Greg's laugh has no humour, just a sound. Moonlight catches his eyes and they glisten.

He's crying. Not laughing, crying. He knows, I think. He knows what I'm saying. Even if I don't, he knows that we're finished.

Greg covers his face with his hands and goes into free fall. I can feel him clawing at his dignity and pride, knowing they're way out of reach as he cries. He's lost everything. His best mate. His friend Jen. And, if he's to be believed, the woman he loves.

No matter what he's done, he's hurting. And I can't listen to someone I love falling apart and do nothing. I couldn't listen to someone I didn't know falling apart and do nothing. I shift across the bed, put my arms around him, stroke his hair, hush him.

Slowly the room brightened. Darkness fell away and it was daylight. The hotel room melted and we were in a café, the bed dissolved and we were sitting at a table. Greg had his head buried in my chest and his arms around me. I held him, and stroked his hair. 'Come on,' I whispered, 'I'll take you home.'

chapter thirty-four

the end

Jen had on her royal-blue rain mac. I was wearing my red mac. We'd bought them from Leeds Market a couple of years ago and they cost a tenner each. I'd forgotten Jen owned anything other than clothes with posh labels.

I wasn't allowed on school premises without special dispensation from God, signed in triplicate, so I approached Jen via the fence. It was home time and she was supervising the picking up of children. She saw the red of my jacket from the corner of her eye and turned to its source.

'Hi,' I said through the lattice wire fence. My heart was in my throat. That sickness I'd felt when I was talking to Greg? Nothing compared to how scared I was now. If this went wrong, I'd lose Jen forever. And that . . . I couldn't think about that. Not even as an abstract.

'Hello,' she replied with ice in her voice. She kept one eye on the kids tearing around the playground. 'I still don't know how I feel about everything, so just say what you've got to say and leave. I'll get back to you.'

I frowned, trying to work out what the hell she was on about. And, bingo! It came to me. 'You think I'm here to apologise,' I stated.

'Of course.'

'Why would I apologise?'

'You were really out of order. You said some really hurtful things.'

I opened my mouth to point out that she had months on me in the hurtful things stakes, but stopped. 'I didn't come to argue,' I said. 'Or to apologise.'

'What did you come for?'

'To see what we can salvage of this friendship.'

'*Friendship?*' she spat. 'If you were my friend you wouldn't have disappeared when I needed you most. If you were my friend you would've stayed, talked last week. Instead you just disappeared, you didn't answer your mobile, you didn't return my messages. Nothing. For a whole week.

'It was like that in college, too. You'd go out for a pint of milk, or to post a letter, and I wouldn't see you for hours because you dropped in to see someone, or you went to the cinema or went for a walk. Half the time I expected you to go on a chocolate run then never to see you again, like those men who go out for a packet of cigarettes and are never heard from again. And when you moved back to London, you didn't tell me you were leaving. Me, your best friend. Your landlady knew, Yorkshire Electricity knew, British Gas knew, BT knew, Abbey Storage knew, but not me. The first I hear of it is when you stop off in a taxi, drop off my stuff you've borrowed and say you'll call me when you get to London. For almost a year.'

'I had to get away,' I offered lamely. Maybe Eric had a point about the *Heat*/walk away from something in thirty seconds thing.

'I needed you this week, Amber – my whole life fell apart but once again you'd disappeared.'

'Much as I love you, Jen, not even I could counsel you about your relationship with Greg,' I replied.

Jen signalled across the playground for another teacher to

take over her hawkeye duties, then she swivelled to face me. 'There was no relationship with Greg. Greg hates me.'

'He doesn't. He may not like you very much at the moment, but he doesn't hate you.' *I know I shouldn't, but I can't help it. It's almost automatic trying to make Jen feel better.*

'What difference does it make? The point is, I had no relationship with Greg and, as it turned out, I have no relationship with Matt.'

'Tell me about you and Greg.'

Jen fired a shot of pure hatred at me with her blue eyes, but I didn't look away. I held her gaze. She didn't get out of this with scowls, no matter how evil they were. She had to tell me. I'd stand here all night if I had to but I had to hear her side of it.

' All right, me and Greg,' she conceded through gritted teeth. 'About two years ago, when Matt and I had been together a year, we all went to a club for Matt's birthday, remember? You and Matt were off on the dance floor – you were both so pissed you were actually dancing together. I went to the bar to get a round in or maybe I went to the loo . . . I don't know, can't remember, anyway, I'd almost got back to our table when I spotted Greg. He was slouched in his seat and swigging from a bottle of beer, but he was transfixed on something and he had this look on his face. This look of total happiness, affection . . . joy, even. I followed his eyes to where he was looking and it was you. You made him that happy. He wanted you. That made me so angry. Another bloke was going to fall in love with you and not me.'

'*Excuse me?!*'

'Blokes fall in love with you, and Greg, who could have any woman he wanted, was doing it.'

'Blokes don't fall in love with me, they become my friends.'

'No they don't. They all want you. It was like that thing between you and Ross in college.'

Ross was one of Jen's boyfriends who I liked even less than Matt – oh yes, that was possible. Jen seemed to have a predilection to hooking up with rotten men. Ross had a habit of undressing women with his eyes and I was one of those women. When he graduated to brushing up against me and grabbed my breasts, I told Jen. His defence was that I was always flaunting my figure in his face and it was what he thought I wanted. The old, but surprisingly effective 'she was asking for it' defence. Jen had carried on seeing him and just kept a better eye on him. In other words, made sure he and I weren't left alone together.

'That really hurt. You were meant to be my best friend and . . .'

'Hang on, when you say "that thing with you and Ross" you mean when he kept grabbing my breasts and rubbing up against me?'

'You both had different stories.'

'Jen, the man kept groping me. That's not different stories. He was a creep and I'm sorry it took you seeing him with another woman to work that out.' They split up when he left Jen for someone else – she thought they were going to get back together right up until he stuck his tongue down the throat of said someone else in front of her.

'He kept going on about what a womanly figure you had and how I should think about implants.'

'What further proof do you need? The man was a creep.'

'But he was right. Men do want women like you.'

'In which reality?'

'Gawd, Amber, blokes respect you. They respect you, then they fall in love with you. With me they either want to shag me or they're too scared to come near me. There's all this bravado, this coming on strong, but when everyone's gone, they're just scared little boys who run away.

'And when that happens a few times you start to put up

barriers, you start to behave how they expect you to. And you get this reputation as "the ice maiden", "the ice queen".

'So you start behaving in that way even more. All the while, your best friend is getting this reputation for being warm and friendly and nice. And that's all you want. To be loved. Adored. Respected.'

Jen paused, swallowed hard. 'Then Matt came along. OK, he wasn't as good-looking as Greg, but Greg was a tart, he didn't want a relationship. He didn't look twice at me. But you . . .

'That night in the club, it was happening again. Greg had fallen for you. Once again, warm, friendly Amber gets the man. Well, I decided that night, no more. If Greg was going to be with either of us, it was going to be me. Not the warm one, not the curvy one, me. I went over and started flirting.'

'Let me get this right, you didn't sleep with him because you wanted him, but so I couldn't have him? Are you mad?'

'I didn't sleep with him.'

I noticed she'd ignored the 'are you mad?' bit.

'There was nothing remotely sleep-like about it. Five minutes, against the wall in my corridor. It was all so hasty we didn't even have time for a condom.'

Jesus. Christ. JESUS CHRIST. I thought I'd heard the worst of it. I knew first-hand how fanatical Greg was about safe sex – even when he hadn't seen me for almost a month he'd practically torn off my clothes but had waited to find a condom before penetration. But not with Jen. Not with fucking Jen. And . . .

'*It was a mistake. He's going to kill me. He's going to dump me then he's going to kill me,*' Jen's voice echoed in my head. 'That was why you were so frightened about being pregnant,' I managed. 'You thought it was Greg's child.'

Jen nodded.

Her dalliance with Greg had cost me £180. She hadn't at

any point offered me cash for the pregnancy tests or for me rebooking my train tickets. She didn't say thank you for me putting her before my parents. Not that I needed or wanted a thank you. Just the truth. The truth. Was that too much to ask from my closest friend?

'Afterwards, I knew he'd forget about trying anything with you. That day I told you that Greg had made a pass at me, well, Matt had said they'd got drunk together and Greg had confessed he thought you were sexy. So I told you about the pass. I knew you'd ask him about it and he'd be reminded how I could screw up his life if he came anywhere near you.'

I had to ask again. 'Are you mad?'

'*Amber.*' Jen could raise her voice now most of the children had been picked up by their parents. 'You get filthy looks from women because of your chest. Imagine getting them because of your face. You don't know what it's like to be beautiful. Women hate me, men don't want me. I wanted, for once, to have what you had. I just wanted to have Greg look at me with all that affection.'

What Jen was saying was poignant, touching, heart-rending. *Cheeky bitch.*

Cheeky bitch who had crossed the mythical line in the sand; who had done something I couldn't forgive. She was calling me ugly. '*You don't know what it's like to be beautiful.*' I never realised that was the thing that couldn't be taken back with me and Jen. It wasn't being called ugly, *per se* – I'd much rather be called ugly than stupid – it was because of who was saying it.

When your best friend can't even *pretend* you're beautiful, why is she your best friend? What's a best friend for if not to bolster your ego? Sure, she's meant to tell you if that lipstick makes you look like a cheap whore instead of the high-class hooker style you were aiming for; or if you have broccoli in your teeth; or if that bloke's playing you for a mug. It wouldn't have been so bad if she'd slept with Greg because she genuinely felt something for him; I wouldn't have liked it, but if she'd genuinely wanted him then I'd find a way to understand.

She didn't feel the same about me. She'd called me fat, I'd let it slide. She'd set me up on blind dates, I'd let it slide. She'd lied to me. She'd manipulated me. She'd even tried it on with my beloved brother.

Now, she was saying I was ugly. And there was only so much you can let slide before you become buried under a mountain of bitchy comments and ill-treatment. Before you become a world class mug.

In my head I went through all the thoughts I had of Jen, like searching through a crowded wardrobe. Each positive thought I had I unhooked then flung down onto the floor of my mind, banishing her good name from my thought closet. There went 'caring'. Next, 'thoughtful'. 'Encouraging'; 'friendly'; 'vivacious'; 'understanding'; 'exciting' – all of them, piling up around my head, waiting to be removed.

I finished plundering my mental wardrobe, purging it of all things Jen, until I had nothing left of her. It'd all been put out for the bin men. Screw her. Screw her and her pretty life.

Jen finished her monologue of pain and confusion, of being a pretty blonde in an ugly world. 'So, you see, there is no me and Greg.'

'You really have no feelings for him?' I asked.

'Only friendship. I only want Matt. I know, I shouldn't, but I love him. I wish I hadn't done that to him.'

Never mind what she did to me. At no point had she said sorry to me. Or that she wished she hadn't done that to me. Because she'd always known that she could do whatever she wanted to me and I'd be there. She knew that my terror at being abandoned would mean I'd put up with anything from her.

'I'm sure it'll be all right, if you give him time.'

Jen's face lit up. 'You think?' she asked eagerly.

'I'm sure he will. Look, you'd better go, your after-school classes will be starting soon. I'll call you later.'

'Yeah. Neither of us has got anyone else to be with right now. We might as well be together.'

'I guess so.'

I took one last look at Jen. Her short blonde hair, her gaunt face, her wretchedly thin body. Then I walked away. It was over with Jenna Leigh Hartman. Our friendship had run its course. For us, this was the end.

chapter thirty-five

the end, part two

I wish I'd forced Greg to go home after the café.

I'd tried to take him home, but when the taxi driver pulled up outside his house he'd clung to my hand, his eyes desperate and scared, like a man clinging onto a branch as he dangled over a cliff edge, so in the end I'd taken him back to mine. Got him settled on the sofa before I started the epic journey across town to see Jen.

Jen. My heart trembled every time I thought about her. I'd actually stopped on the way to the bus stop to throw up. A couple of people gave me odd looks, schoolchildren leaving the school had gone 'Euurggh' and run away. (Pretty third-rate for kids – most of the ones I knew had a wider four-letter vocabulary than me.) But I couldn't help it. The reality at the one thing I hadn't wanted to happen, happening had made me physically sick. I'd had to rinse my mouth out with the bottle of water in my bag.

The TV was on as I pushed open my front door and the air was stained with something. I sniffed. Cleanliness. The air was stained with clean. I sniffed the air a couple more times. Lemon. Beeswax, too. Soap powder. Washing-up liquid. I glanced down, the red hallway carpet had been vacuumed. The picture frames on the corridor walls had been polished. I went into the living room, pristine too.

Sprawled on the sofa, his head resting on one hand, his eyes fixed on the TV was Gregory. He'd been sat in that exact same position when I left. Looking at him, I could almost believe that the cleaning fairies had visited my flat and whilst Greg watched telly they'd straightened up, done the dishes, vacuumed, polished surfaces, emptied bins, put a box of Greg's stuff at his feet.

Internally, I shrank back; cowered in a quiet place inside when I saw that box.

It was a big red plastic box I'd used for moving. Big as it was, it was overflowing. His clothes, his books, CDs, shoes, videos, toothbrush, aftershave, vitamins, hair products. He really had been moving in with me on the sly. At least he wasn't going to be moving out as sneakily. I shouldn't really be surprised, should I? I'd already told him it was over, he'd acted like he knew. We were on the same page on that score. But I hadn't considered that it being over meant he was out of my life.

'Over' = 'going'.

I lowered myself onto the sofa.

'How did it go?' Greg asked. Couldn't tell if he was looking at me or not because I couldn't tear my eyes away from the box.

'I, erm, I don't know,' I said, pushing my hand into my hair.

'Are you friends again?'

I swallowed hard against the lump in my throat, I couldn't speak it. It was over. Over between me and Jen. The longest non-familial relationship I'd ever had. Finished.

'I don't know,' I managed again.

'Oh,' Greg replied.

I stared at the big red box with my boyfriend's things in it. 'Why . . . I mean . . . how come . . . erm . . . you cleaned,' I struggled.

'It was partly my mess. I also packed up my stuff. You know, in case . . .' He purposely let the sentence peter out. He didn't want to say it, but wanted to talk about it. Wanted to know where he stood.

Nowhere. He stood nowhere. I thought he'd worked that out, I thought that he'd realised I was telling him it was over, even though I wasn't sure I was. Why else would he pack?

'So . . . About us . . .'

'I don't know,' I confessed. *I don't know about anything any more.* If there was one, no, two things I'd learnt in the past few hours they were:

1. I'm not in a movie
2. I know nothing about nothing.

'What does that mean?'

I rubbed my hand across my eyes. 'It means, I don't know.'

'And I'm supposed to hang around until you do know?' Greg's voice was raised. Why was he shouting? Did he think it'd make me know faster?

'You don't know, so I've got to what? Wait? Wait until you do know? Is that it?'

I stared at the wall opposite. The wall was painted white and I tried to blank my mind like that.

'I wait around until you decide otherwise? Listen, Amber, either we work this out now, or . . .'

I finally turned to him and he stopped talking. He took a deep breath as his eyes drilled into me. 'If we split up now, then we split up for good. I mean it. No calls, no friendship, no meeting up, no thirty-something angst over getting back together. Nothing. Me and you, over.'

I could hardly look at him without wanting to retch. Dramatic, but the truth. He'd slept with Jen. That was awful news. Knowing that he'd orgasmed inside her . . . I wanted to retch. He'd done something so intimate with her and not me. Or any other woman apart from Kristy, because Greg was almost evangelical about safe sex. Except that one time when . . .

How could I be so bloody stupid? The thought smacked me in the face.

The HIV test. It was because of Jen. That's what he meant about his life being over. Because if he was positive that would've meant Jen would've been positive and Matt would've been positive and Matt's wife would've been. And their construct of lies would've come tumbling down. *How could I be so bloody stupid? Around the same time two of my closest friends went through a sex-related crisis and I thought nothing of it. I didn't at any point connect the dots. I couldn't be more stupid if I became a brain donor.*

'So?' Greg demanded. 'What's it to be?'

I couldn't look at him. I hated him being near me. I returned my gaze to the wall opposite.

'Fine! Fucking fine!'

He picked up his box, tried to tuck it up under his arm, but couldn't because there was too much stuff; instead, he pushed his arm under it, picked up a black bag that had been resting behind the box. 'I DON'T KNOW WHY I EXPECTED ANYTHING ELSE FROM A CONTROLLING BITCH LIKE YOU. I DON'T KNOW WHY I EXPECTED SOMEONE WHO ALWAYS WANTS EVERYTHING TO BE ON HER TERMS OR NOT AT ALL TO CHANGE. BUT YOU KNOW WHAT?'

He bent down, 'IT'S FINE!' he screamed in my face, so close I could feel spittle on my skin; the warmth of his breath; his divine scent of vanilla and spices.

I pulled my knees up to my chest as I listened to Greg trying to escape. Slamming things, dropping stuff, swearing blue murder. Swearing Amber murder. I wrapped my arms around my legs, rested my forehead on my knees. And, suddenly, the leaving noise and its soundtrack of swearing ended. My flat was still. Calm. Empty.

He wasn't coming back. It was over.

I curled up on the sofa, put my arms around myself, safe and warm and small.

I'm going to go to sleep, I decided. *And when I wake up everything's going to be as it was. I won't have slept with Greg. I'll still love Jen. Everything will be as it was.*

chapter thirty-six

starting over

You expect your life to change, of course you do.

But mine hadn't. Not dramatically. Not like I expected. A month went by and I didn't fall apart.

Greg had done a pretty thorough job of clearing out. There was no sign of him in my house. There were holes in my CD rack, on my bookshelf, in my wardrobe, on my bathroom surfaces – meaning every time I went to the bathroom, to the living room, to get dressed I was reminded anew how much he'd moved in with me. But, when he left, he totally left. Took everything with him. He'd cleaned the smell of him off every surface. Put the sheets in to wash, vacuumed. There were no love letters or photographs of us kissing because we weren't that kind of couple.

Our letters were written on our skins when we had sex. Made love. Fucked. Whatever. Our photographs were mental, like the time he put on my bra and came wandering into the living room. The time I made him laugh when we were driving to Harrogate and his face had exploded into the biggest grin and he'd glanced sideways at me with such a look of affection I grabbed his hand and kissed the back of it. The time he'd drawn a heart on top of a bacon sandwich in tomato ketchup and I told him off because the bread looked yucky and he'd said I was a stroppy bitch in the mornings, but I'd better bloody eat that sandwich. The time we had a picnic in my living room with beer and toasted chocolate sandwiches. The time I'd been out drinking and called him from the train station to say goodnight, and he'd driven to town to pick me up. There were loads of times. Loads of mental photographs.

Jen. Jen was different. I didn't think about her. At all. Our daily phone calls had stopped months ago anyway. Our weekly meets had been cancelled. I had a wealth of memories with Jen, photographic and mental, but I didn't access them. Didn't think about Jen.

I was starting over, not breaking down. I hadn't even cried. I was doing OK. Because it was OK. Honest.

I wasn't even flinging myself into work because the month after the Festival was our quietest period. We had time to sleep, regroup, rethink. Gather ourselves together to prepare for next year. Renée, even though she was officially off work, still came in every day and would continue waddling in from Roundhay until she gave birth. Her husband worked from home and if she stayed there, she said, she'd kill him. Martha, who had decided to stay blonde – because, it had to be said, it did suit her – had secured her marriage proposal and was getting hitched in the spring so she spent a lot of time with wedding magazines or on wedding websites.

'It's like waiting for war to break out,' Martha said three weeks or so after my separation from Greg and Jen.

'I'm so glad you said it first,' Renée said. 'It's exactly like that. I tell you, it's not good for my baby, all this waiting.'

I continued to flick through a film book, searching for a write-up about a film for the Festival newsletter. I hardly paid attention to them any more. When they started rowing, I went to make tea. And stayed in the kitchenette making tea until they finished. I didn't play referee; didn't try to pour oil on their troubled waters. Part of me was embarrassed they'd seen what happened. Part of me didn't want to get involved again. Despite what Eric said, I had settled, had gotten involved in things I couldn't walk out on in thirty seconds flat, and I'd learnt my lesson.

'Amber,' Martha said.

I glanced up. The pair of them were staring at me.

'We're talking about you,' Renée finished.

'Why, what have I done?' I asked.

'We're both on edge, waiting for you to break down,' Renée explained.

'It's only natural,' Martha added. 'We won't think any less of you.'

I gave them a 'hard-luck' smile. 'I don't do breaking down. It was no big deal. It's over and I've dealt with it. You know, moved on.'

Both of them stared at me, not a look of belief between them.

I reached into my drawer, pulled out a white envelope. 'I was going to wait 'til you got back from maternity leave,' I said, 'but now seems as good a time as any.'

Colour drained first from Renée's face, then from Martha's. Synchronised paling, impressive.

'I'm . . .' I glanced away, I couldn't bear those expressions; that's why I'd stuck here for so long. Why I'd put down roots. 'I'm leaving. I've got a job, Associate Director of the Brighton and Hove Film Festival. I'll leave a month after you get back from maternity leave. I could leave earlier, but I wouldn't do that to you two.'

'You're going nowhere,' Martha said.

'Thank you, Martha, you took the words right out of my mouth.'

'I've been here twelve years, I think it's time . . .'

'Amber, you're going nowhere,' Renée said. 'Do you think

380

we've spent years grooming you to be Festival Director to have someone else benefit from it? We're not losing you to another festival.'

'And, and, and,' Martha said in a panic, 'and you can't.'

'If you were going to be a film director or something, I would understand. But another FESTIVAL? No. I won't allow it.'

'And, and, and,' Martha added, 'you can't leave me with her. It's not fair. You stop me and her rowing. And she has a go at you instead of me.'

'You're going to be godmother to my child.'

'You're going to be one of my bridesmaids, I haven't told you both that yet. But you're both going to be bridesmaids,' Martha added.

'I've accepted the job now,' I said.

Both Martha and Renée got up, came round to me. 'You're the constant in our lives,' Martha said. 'Our office doesn't work without you.' (Typical film person bastardising a film line for their own ends. And a Tom Cruise film at that.)

'But we're not in an office,' Renée said. 'We're like a family. You complete us.' (Now Renée was at it. If either of them uttered another convoluted line from *Jerry Maguire* I'd lose it.)

'Yeah, well, maybe that's why I need to leave,' I said. 'Maybe I need to do a job, not be in another family.'

'Don't make us suffer because of Greg,' Martha pleaded.

'It's got nothing to do with him,' I said. I wasn't just saying that, it really had got nothing to do with him. And, all right, it had everything to do with him. And Jen. And me. And Martha. And Renée. And needing to start over. I had to get away. From everything that led to this. If I started again, maybe I could wipe the slate clean. Forget everything.

'Cry, cut your hair, spend a lot of money, screw that director who's always calling you, but don't *leave*,' Renée said, as though 'leave' was a euphemism for 'slit your wrists'.

'You're going to Cannes next year,' Martha said. 'Because if you don't, that bitch will make me go. And I ain't going. In fact, if you leave, I'm leaving. I ain't dealing with her alone. No way. No bloody way. Life's too short.'

'I'm not coming back after my maternity leave if you go. I'm not dealing with Martha. Remember that week you had off? It was hell. She was such a cow. Wouldn't answer the phone. Wouldn't go out on chocolate runs. I'll have a new baby. I was only going to come back as Associate Festival Director anyway. Work part-time. You were going to keep the title of Festival Director. But you know what? If you go, I am not coming back.'

'You two are the worst people in the world to work with,' I whispered, staring furiously at my desk top. I wasn't meant to do this. Not here. Not now.'

'Us?' they replied.

'You're always rowing. And you never take responsibility. And you don't answer the phone.' A little sob escaped from my mouth.

'We know.'

'If I'm going to stay, there'll have to be changes.'

'Anything.'

'You have to make tea,' I said.

'Yes.'

'And you have to stop leaving me to calm the film-makers down.'

'OK.'

'And no more rowing.'

Silence.

'Sorry, Amber, not going to happen,' Martha said.

'There is a limit to what we'll do to keep you,' Renée said.

I collapsed onto my desk and started sobbing for real. I put my hands around my head, making a small private circle. My body heaved with sobs I didn't know were in me.

382

It really wasn't Greg. It was everything. It was Mum saying I couldn't have anything long-term with Greg. It was Eric saying I was always running. It was not getting my nightly story. It was not talking to Jen. It was the Festival ending with me finding out Greg had slept with Jen – when I thought he'd liked my type to be the heroine, he'd obviously wanted the Gwyneth Paltrow, always-going-to-be-the-star type. It was spending the day of my thirty-first birthday alone because I chose to. It was being tempted to speak to Jen when she rang and sang 'Happy Birthday' into my answerphone. It was returning the flowers she'd sent me. It was Martha and Renée probably being the worst workmates in the world but being great because I couldn't leave them. It was realising I'd spent three years pretending to like Matt when I'd always hated him, but I'd seen him sometimes three times a week and got on with him just to make Jen's life easier. It was knowing that Eric was right, I was path-of-least-resistance woman because it was easier than saying how I felt. It was finding out that Sainsbury's didn't do aubergine dip any more. It was *every* thing. And it was *no* thing.

Martha and Renée went into crisis mode while I cried. When there'd been tears before it'd been me running for tissues and tea and kind words. I wasn't sure they knew how to do it, but they did a great job. One produced tissues, one produced tea. Both found kind words.

'We love you, Amber. If you really, really want to leave, we'll cope. We'll love you forever. I'd love a visit to Brighton.' This was Martha.

'Before you go, I'll organise the christening. It'll be a big party, you and Martha will have to buy new frocks. And hats. A lot of my film friends will come. But we can combine the christening with your leaving do. Make it bigger than the Festival.' This was Renée.

'What are you talking about?' I said through my sobs. 'You know I'm not going anywhere.'

'Fantastic,' Martha said. 'I hate the South.'

'I'm so glad you're staying,' Renée said. 'Because now, I'm going to ring up that bastard and give him a piece of my mind. Trying to steal my staff indeed.'

'Here you go, love,' Martha said. She dropped something clattery on my desk. 'I've been keeping these in my drawer just in case. I know they're your favourites.'

I lifted my head to look at it. A packet of Maltesers.

My stomach turned. I scraped back my chair and legged it to the loo to throw up.

'what's all the fuss about chocolate? give me a packet of crisps any day'

chapter thirty-seven

wedding nerves

The invite stares at me.

I stare at the invite.

I've been sat here on my sofa, staring at it, turning it over and over in my hands since it was delivered.

'What is it?' I'd asked the courier who'd brought it to my door two hours ago.

'A wedding invite,' he replied as I put my moniker to his sheet. 'I only know because it's been in the office a few weeks but we were given specific instructions not to deliver it until tonight, love.'

I'd given him a smile, took the envelope, headed straight for the kitchen. I'd then ransacked the place looking for chocolate.

Since . . . since all that happened months ago, I'd stopped eating it. Stopped going out to sniff it. Stopped buying it. To eat chocolate was to be reminded I couldn't read people. That I knew nobody. Not even myself. The closest thing I'd found to the real thing in my kitchen was cocoa powder right at the back of a cupboard. I'd snatched it from the shelf and shovelled heaped teaspoons of it into my mouth. It'd instantly absorbed the very little saliva in my mouth and set like cement, but I couldn't stop. I carried on until it hit the spot.

Until I was calm enough to sit on the sofa and stare at the invite.

A lot has changed since . . . since. That's what it's become in my mind: since . . . since. A lot has changed in three months. Renée gave birth to a girl and called her Johanne Jayne. We hadn't had the christening yet, but she was gearing up for it. There were so many film people down to come a celeb magazine had asked to cover it. Luckily, I got the phone out of Renée's hand before she replied. (It was her home phone as well – things haven't changed that much.)

Martha found her wedding dress, and mine and Renée's bridesmaids' dresses – she was serious about us being brides-maids. She let me know last week that she was planning on conceiving on her honeymoon (heaven help Tony's sperm if it didn't comply).

And I finished my screenplay. I had so much time. Evenings stretched into nothingness. Sometimes I'd come home and lie on the sofa, stare at the Bahamas-shaped water stain on my ceiling and simply think. Hours would pass and feel like minutes. Minutes would pass and feel like hours. Everything was out of proportion. So I'd started to use that time, those hours and hours that stretched into infinity, con-structively. When it was finally finished, I'd given it to Mr Chocolate Sniffer to read. (There was an immense attraction between Mr CS and me. The more we saw of each other, the more obvious it was. And well . . . well, I was different.) He and I spent a lot of time working on it. We spent a lot of time rowing over it. He was brutally honest and I was different. I stood up to him. It didn't take much for me to passionately disagree with him. I felt deeply about my screenplay, it was my baby and nobody would insult it. Nobody would tell me this bit didn't sound right, this bit wouldn't look right. That bled into other areas of my life, too. I was different. If I still ate chocolate, if I still thought in chocolate, I'd say that I was the kind of chocolate they'd never sell because I was now such an eclectic mix.

All the things I kept right down at the bottom of my soul, the nuts, the raisins, the honeycomb, had come rising to the surface. Hard bits – I got pissed off and said so and didn't apologise and didn't fret about it. Being the boss now meant I had to be hard sometimes and not worry about it. I had sweet bits, the raisins that made me giggly and girly. I had ultra-sweet bits, the honeycomb that made me cry at the end of the most ridiculous made-for-TV movies (all someone had to do was say, 'I love you' and I'd be in bits because I knew they'd be about to kick the bucket). I had caramel bits that made people want to stick to me – I noticed now that people approached me with the same respect that they went to Renée with. Yep, I was different.

Greg was true to his word and didn't call. Didn't email. Didn't text. Didn't visit. Didn't write, either. Technology was good like that, it helped remind you how much someone was blanking you.

Jen called, emailed, wrote. But I screened calls. If I answered the phone at work and it was her, I'd say I'd call her back and not bother. There was no going back with me and Jen.

Matt. I didn't know about Matt. I didn't care, either.

I stare at the invite. A cream envelope, thick paper. Expensive.

Maybe I should rip it in half, chuck it out unread. I can't go to Matt and Jen's wedding if I don't get the invite. Or, maybe it's Greg. I read a piece in the *Sunday Chronicle* the other month that he'd gone to Dublin. Dublin, where his ex, the infamous Kristy, lived. He'd apparently looked up old friends while he was there. Whether he meant it literally or not, I wasn't sure. How would I deal with that? How would I deal with Greg getting married? It didn't hurt like it used to any more. It wasn't the first thing that came to mind in the morning, or the last thing I thought about at night. I thought about it now and again. Only four or five times a day.

I slide my fingers under the flap of the envelope, tear it open. I pull the cream card out. *OK, deep breath. Look at it.*

My heart stops. Physically stops. In that moment I'm struggling for breath, willing my heart to beat again, feeling all life drain from me. I'm actually having a heart attack. I clutch at my chest, trying to force air into my lungs.

In my hands I hold:

Eden Salpone
and
Leonard Hampton
Request the pleasure of your company at their wedding

I turn the card over.

Tomorrow.

Mum and Dad2 are getting married tomorrow. At three o'clock. At their local registry office in Lewisham. Tomorrow. TOMORROW.

I race through every conversation I've had with my parents over the past few weeks. Nothing. No mention of nuptials. No mention of 'going legal'. No mention of marrying a person you've already slept with. Hadn't Mum said that wasn't possible? Hadn't we almost rowed about that?

She hadn't exactly said, 'I told you so,' when Eric told her I'd split up with Greg – there was no way in hell I'd tell them – but she hadn't exactly said, 'I thought it was going to last,' either. In fact, she'd been, if anything, indifferent. It'd been Dad2 who'd tried to bully me into giving it another try with Greg. 'Why don't you call Greg, love?' he'd say on a nightly basis. 'Try again. You were so good together.' Mum was obviously just relieved that I wasn't going to be having pre-marital sex.

I bet Eric knew. They'd all probably plotted to keep things from me because I was still in mourning for a relationship built on lies and deception. Well I'm going to give that Eric the fu—

RING! My body lurches as the phone rings.

'WHY THE HELL DIDN'T YOU TELL ME?' Eric screams when I answer.

'WHY DIDN'T I TELL YOU? WHY DIDN'T YOU TELL ME?' I scream back.

Pause. Heavy breathing. 'So, they didn't tell you?' Eric says.

'Eric, they never bloody tell me anything. Especially not this.'

'Not even to cheer you up because you split up with Greg?'

'No.'

'They sent me and Arri two airline tickets. They're mad. Why now? Why keep it a secret?'

'Maybe . . . I don't know. I really don't know.'

'Let's call them. You call Mum, I'll call Dad on his mobile.'

'OK, talk to you afterwards.'

I hold the receiver in my hand, push the button to cut the line and RING!

I almost drop the phone, then after a bit of struggling put it to my ear. 'Have you got it?' Mum asks.

'Huh? Got what?' I say, feeling dim and numb.

'The invite,' Mum says impatiently.

'Oh, the invite to your wedding that you told me nothing about.'

'We wanted it to be a surprise.'

'Well, it was that.'

She pauses. Obviously waiting for something. 'I'm waiting for you to say it,' Mum says.

'Say what? Oh, sorry, congratulations. Despite the shock, congratulations. I'm really pleased for you.'

'Not that, Amber. You're very angry, I can tell.'

391

'Angry about what?' I ask.

'Me marrying Leonard after everything I said about you and Gregory.'

'Mummy, I'm very pleased about you marrying Dad2. I adore him. It was just a shock. I'm not angry. Why would I be angry?'

'I wouldn't change the last few years with Leonard for anything. I was happy with things the way they were, and that's what I should have remembered about you and Gregory. You were happy with Gregory. Leonard told me what Gregory had said about you. How much he respected you. I didn't know; I simply assumed he was using you.

'I was so cross with myself when you split up with him because it might have been because of something I said. I was just worried that he was in your life so quickly. I thought you were going to get hurt.

'I worry about you, Amber. I worry that you don't realise how proud of you your father and I are. We've always been proud of you, whatever you do. But we are worried you are never going to get married or have children. You have spent so much time alone and I worry about that. We don't want our marriage to put you off settling down.'

Mum pauses to take a breath and I jump in. What Mum had said was big stuff, was like her walking naked down the street. And it was also the start of a big conversation that we weren't going to have. Some people need that kind of emotional openness, but not me. Not with my mother. We were fine as we were, Mum and I. We didn't need to force some kind of emotional bond between us when we had a bond. If I'd learnt anything in the past three months it was that you are responsible for your role in a relationship. You and only you. That how you respond to people is far more important than how people treat you. If you don't like the way someone treats you, then you change it. If you carry on with it, then you're telling that person it's OK to treat you like that. Like, in my life. Mum, Dad and Dad2 always expected the best of me because I delivered. I was the good girl so they expected a good girl. Eric hadn't lost their love because he was bad, because he did what he wanted. If I took a leaf out of Eric's book, did what I wanted instead of fretting about who would hate me as a result, then I'd be happier. At a very basic level I'd have done what I wanted; at the very top level I would've found out who truly loved me, who'd stick with me. That's why I loved Eric so: he'd always wanted me to be who I was. Why I'd loved Jen; I used to think she wanted nothing from me than for me to be me. And why I'd loved Greg more than anyone. Because, out of all of them, he pushed me – sometimes unintentionally with his outrageous behaviour that made me angry – to be me. Like every person on earth seemed to see – and say – I relaxed with Greg. Relaxed enough to be me. I had a moment of stillness. I could see where I was in this world. And it didn't end when he walked out, either. All this realisation came from doing a lot of thinking. A lot of moving on. A lot of growing up.

So, I didn't need this conversation with Mum. I didn't want her to strip off for me because she felt guilty. Didn't need her to explain to me why she'd been so cold and unavailable when I knew why. Mum and I were never going to be best mates; I didn't want to be her best mate. I wanted her to be my mother. To love me and be connected to me because we were related. No deep and emotional chats were required for that.

'I wish you'd told me sooner about the wedding,' I jump in. changing the subject. 'I've got nothing to wear.'

'I seem to remember buying you a dress for a special occasion,' Mum says, smoothly taking up the subject change. I can hear the relief in her voice. She didn't want a deep and emotional session, either. Like daughter, like mother.

The heavens open and a chorus of angels sing as everything becomes clear. That's why, at thirty, Mum had pushed that dress on me and that suit on Eric. That's why they both had tears in their eyes when I came out of the changing room. They weren't getting silly in their old age – they were getting emotional because the next time they saw me in it, it'd be on their wedding day.

My parents are getting married. The crazy, fantastic fools.

'I'll get the first train down tomorrow morning. Hopefully I'll make it down in time.'

'You'd better do, my dear daughter, you're my only bridesmaid.'

'Of course I'll be there. Let me speak to Dad2, I'm sure he's talking to Eric.'

I wander across King's Cross station concourse, caught off-guard by how Christmassy it is. Decorations, carol singers, tinsel in all the shop windows. I've forgotten it's Christmas. Next week. It was all around me, but I've been insulated from it. It's something other to me. With my family, Christmas has always been a fraught time. A couple of times Jen and I spent it together, getting drunk and eating junk food, safe from the scarier elements of families at Christmas. This year, since I haven't even noticed properly it's Christmas, I haven't even thought about where I'm going to spend it. Probably alone since Mum and Dad2 will be off on honeymoon, Dad1's in Ghana, and Eric and Arrianne could probably do with time to themselves. Christmas alone, not as scary a prospect as it once would've been.

I spent the best part of two hours yesterday on the phone to Mum and Dad2, going through the arrangements, being told what was expected of me, which relatives I had to take care of.

'You'd better not have put on any weight,' Mum had said

before she hung up, 'that dress fit perfectly when I bought it.'

If anything, I've lost weight. Since . . . since, I've spent more time at my computer than eating. The dress is loose—

A movement, the movement of a familiar figure walking across the station concourse catches my eye, stops my train of thought. Tall, broad, but the hair – *black*-black, bluey-black – is cut short. Almost a skinhead. I only see the back of the figure, almost a flash of its profile. Greg.

GREG!

I go to call his name, then remember Greg is no longer part of my life. So, even if this figure with his unusual-coloured hair and purposeful stride is Greg, what am I going to say? 'Hi'?

The figure disappears in the crowd, a flash of something almost familiar in the midst of this crowd of unfamiliarity.

Maybe I'll email Greg when I get back. I'm sure he'd want to know that my loca parents got married. Only to tell him that, though. Nothing else.

I head for the Tube. I've got to stop off on the way to the house to buy some suitable shoes – Mum'll freak if I walk down the aisle in trainers.

Eric and Arri are at the registry office, greeting guests; I'm waiting for Mum to finish getting ready. I'm not allowed to see her until she's finished. The house is full of Mum's relatives, full of people I haven't seen in a blue moon, and probably won't see until the next blue moon. The air is full of happy chatter, Ghanaian dialects, delivered in loud, cheerful voices.

The doorbell goes. Before I can move to answer it, someone else has got it.

'Amber?' a familiar voice says a few seconds later.

I freeze in examining my expertly painted nails. *It can't be. It really can't be.* I slowly ease my gaze up. It is. It really is.

'Daddy?' I say as I stand.

My dad, my real dad, the loins of which I am the fruit,

stands in the doorway. Taller than me but not much, lined face with greyed black hair, wearing a blue suit with cream shirt and navy-blue tie, much like the one my parents had bought Eric.

Before I can ask why he's here, a hush falls on the house. Silence has descended because Mum has appeared at the top of the stairs.

A lump forms in my throat, tears sting my eyes. She's stunning in a cream two-piece suit with a high collar, edged in gold embroidery. Around her hair is a gold and cream head-wrap.

'You look beautiful,' Dad says. He takes the words right out of my mouth and I almost fall over. Dad *never* said that sort of thing. Ever.

'Amber, I forgot to tell you, your father is giving me away,' Mum says blithely. As though it's the most normal thing on earth for your ex-husband who – as far as your daughter knows – you haven't spoken to in ten years to give you away.

'IS IT ANY WONDER I'M SCREWED UP WITH YOU TWO FOR PARENTS?' I want to scream. 'IS IT ANY WONDER I'M AN EMOTIONAL FREAKSHOW?'

'Here Comes the Bride' plays as I lead my parents down the registry office aisle.

Maybe I won't tell Greg about this. It's Grade A weirdness. My parents, the people who hated each other, the people who made my childhood hell are both here. Arm in arm, walking towards my mum marrying my other dad, Dad2.

The look on Eric's face shows he's been kept in the dark too.

I glance around at the sixty or so people in the registry office, check what their reactions are. My heart jumps. Lurches, then starts racing in my chest. There's that man from King's Cross again, the one who, from behind, looked like

Greg. The man turns towards the bride, who is following me; his face is exposed because of his close-cropped hair. His eyes leave the bride and rest on me. Big shiny pools of Minstrel chocolate meet my eyes.

I miss a step but right myself before I go arse over tit. His eyes, like his face, are expressionless. They stop staring at me and return to my parents. I stop staring at him and stop walking, because we're here, in front of the registrar.

All through the service, I can feel Greg's eyes on the back of my head.

chapter thirty-eight

married with children

He's going to shag her.

I can tell. He's resting his bum against the back of a chair, hands in his trouser pockets, his eyes fixed to hers, but taking in all of her face. Like he used to do to me. Plus, he'd once told me he had some of his best sex at weddings. And she's bloody gorgeous. She, one of my unmarried second cousins (on Eric's side) with her long, white-blonde hair and slender figure, had literally picked herself up and flung herself at Greg the second everyone arrived at the hall. She'd probably spotted him in the registry office, seen he was alone and decided he was hers. He isn't exactly fighting her off.

Git. Git who's going to be having sex tonight. Here. I'll probably walk in on them, be r— I've drunk too much. Too much, too quickly, on an empty stomach. Things are a little fuzzy around the edges. I haven't drunk enough to stop me drinking, though. I gulp my champagne, look away from the flirting couple and cast my gaze further around the room. Eric is getting to know my dad. They are sat alone in a corner, eating their buffet food from paper plates and talking.

I still can't believe Dad1 is here. Dad2 had told me earlier that Mum and Dad1 had only been on better terms for a couple of months. She'd called him and asked him to come to

398

the wedding because she wanted a fresh start. Not for herself, not for Dad2, not for Dad1. She wanted a fresh start for me. She wanted me, Dad2 said, to know that it was all right to talk to them both. OK to spend time with one of them and not have to worry how the other would take it. To not feel responsible for either of them being happy.

'She wanted you to know that what happened to them wouldn't happen to you,' Dad2 had said. 'Not that she'd ever say that, love. You know what your mother's like. She can say a thousand things without saying a word.' I'd smiled at Dad2. It's odd that someone as closed as Mum had met probably the only man of their age group who's able to say these sorts of things. Odd, but fantastic. My life would've been so different if she hadn't got together with him after Dad1 left. 'You know, love, your mum and your father don't want you to be alone because you're scared of being hurt.' Dad2 had accompanied that last comment with a pointed look in Greg's direction.

I do the same. He's still talking to that woman and, if I'm not imagining it, she's stepped a little closer to him. They *are* going to have sex. I tear my horrified gaze away, back to Eric and Dad1.

'Go talk to him,' Arrianne whispers in my ear.

'Who, Eric?' I reply.

'No, the tall dark handsome stranger you've been staring at. And who stared at you the whole way through the ceremony and the speeches and who's doing a very poor job of ignoring you now.'

'We've nothing to talk about.'

'Sweetie, I never thanked you for talking sense into Eric about the baby thing. He was so unEric about it. I *couldnae* get through to him and I felt he was slipping away from me. But what you said turned things around. We started talking after the weekend he stayed at yours. Talking rather than rowing.'

'No thanks necessary, Arri,' I reply. 'Just name your first baby after me. Girl or boy, I'm not fussy.'

Arri laughs. She really is the sister I never had. I love her so much. I'd never have forgiven Eric if he'd driven her away. Actually, I would've forgiven him because I can forgive Eric almost anything, but I would've given him a hard time about it.

'You laugh, but I'm serious,' I say. I'm one step away from throwing my arms around her and saying how much I love her. *I really have drunk too much.*

'You told Eric not to let the things that might not happen stop him from becoming the person he could become. In your case, the worst thing has happened, Greg has slept with your best friend, you've split up. What might not happen has happened. You survived. You know you can make it through the worst. So, go talk to him. What you're scared of might not happen, and, if it does, you'll survive.'

I listen to her words. Then I listen to the meaning behind the words. But I can't. I might've moved on, but not so much I can go up to him and start a normal conversation. Or even a conversation.

'I'll think about it,' I say to Arri.

'Don't think too long, *hen*. If he shags her, I will have him killed.'

'Before you ask what the hell I'm doing here, Dad2 asked me to come.'

Greg and I have inevitably run into each other outside the loos. He had to wee sometime and I kept going until our bladders coincided. I wanted to see him up close, wanted to confirm he looked as awful as I sometimes feel.

'Did you say "Dad2"?' I ask.

'He asked me to call him that. He thought Mr Hampton was too formal and I could never call him Leonard. And he said it's a shame only one person calls him that, so would I call him that too.'

'You're best mates with my parents now, are you?'

'No. Dad2 said it was a shame about . . . about, but would I come to the wedding anyway. He begged me for days before I said yes. And I only came for him, not to s—'

'*Days?* You've known about this for days?'

'Weeks, actually. He swore me to secrecy, told me not to tell you a thing.' His face hardens. 'I said there'd be absolutely no problem with that.'

That hurt. 'Great. You of all people knew about my parents' wedding before I did. How did they get in touch, anyway?'

'Through the paper.'

'Oh.'

Silence. Everyone else is dancing, having fun, eating, drinking; we stand beside the entrance to the hall in a tight, stifling silence that chokes the living breath out of me. His body has lost weight too. He's much leaner up close, his charcoal suit – the one he wore to meet my parents – is much baggier on him.

'I heard you were going to move to Brighton,' Greg says.

'Oh? Who from?'

'Renée. She called me. Told me that if you left, she'd have someone come round and reassess the position of my kneecaps. She added that Martha would cut off my balls with a pair of pliers.'

If only he knew how serious they were.

'I didn't realise what true fear was until I'd been threatened by a French woman and her Yorkshire friend.' *Maybe he does know.*

'Seems you speak to everyone in my life but me,' I say.

Greg glances away. More silence. More choking silence.

'So, how was Dublin?'

'You read that, huh? It was great. I sorted out a lot of stuff with Kristy.'

Just as I thought.

'Although, once we'd done all our talking I spent most of my time with her husband and kids. They loved me telling them stories.'

Oh. *Oh!* I smile inside. Silence. More silence. We used to spend hours together just talking and talking, now we're struggling to fill even a mere few minutes.

'Do you see much of the other two?' I ask. I'm curious. Curious to see if they've carried on without me, to see if they've patched things up and become an odd threesome instead of the odd quartet we were all that time ago.

'I see Matt,' Greg says quietly. 'We go out for the odd pint. We're working on being friends again . . . He's done some awful things over the years and I've forgiven him so . . . we're working on it.' He scrunches up his lips for a second, shrugs slightly. 'Besides, he realised quite quickly that he had no other friends except Rocky and me, and Rocky . . . well, he was monumentally pissed off when he found out Matt's been lying to him and using him as an alibi for ten years. He's banned Matt from even calling the house, definitely won't talk to him. Rocky only let me stay because I did something awful to Matt. Matt's only other choice was me. Like I say, we're working on it.'

And Jen? Is he 'working on it' with Jen as well?

'Haven't heard about . . . you know.' He seems to struggle with her name. 'I've got no reason to see her.'

And now, more of that silence stuff. More silence as I digest what he's saying. He's trying to be mates with Matt again. I suppose he did once tell me they were closer than brothers. And I always knew that people were important to Greg. People and friendships. He could tolerate so much more than I could. Mainly because he rarely let the resentment build up. When you call people on the tiny slights when they occur, they won't lead to an accumulation of hurt that results in one big blow-up. It won't end up with you severing all ties with loved ones. Unless, of course, it comes to me.

I'm the only person on earth Greg can do that with.

'Well, you look like shite,' I say, trying to make him laugh, although why that would make him laugh is a mystery, even to me.

'Thank you very much,' Greg replies. 'You don't look so healthy yourself.'

'When this make-up comes off, I look worse,' I say, trying to keep the 'joke' going even though 'you're a cab' is better than this one.

'I don't doubt it.'

'Says the man who looks like he hasn't slept in a month.'

'Make that three months, two weeks and five days, but who's counting, eh? Mate, I'd love to stand around trading insults with you all night, but I've got something better to do.' Greg turns to walk away.

'Shouldn't that be someone better to do?'

He freezes in his tracks, spins on his heels. He glares at me with something nearing what I'd imagine pure hatred looks like. 'Fuck you, Amber.' Unnecessarily he enforces the look with three angry words. One of which shouldn't technically be angry because it's my name.

'I think you'll find you already did,' I reply calmly. 'Or have you forgotten that amongst the hundreds of women you've fucked?'

Greg narrows his eyes slightly. 'No, I remember you, you're the one who thought she was perceptive but needed a postcard sending every time I wanted to touch you.'

I can't stop a small smile wrestling with my lips, fighting to find expression. 'Why exactly are you pissed off with me?' I ask. 'You know, so that one who is only used to you talking in hints can work it out.'

'I'm not pissed off with you, it was you who started the insults.'

'It was you who started all that aggressive "before you ask what the hell I'm doing here" stuff. And, sorry, but you do look like shite.'

'So do you.'

I shrug. 'I'm not trying to pull anyone.'

'And I am?'

I spot the second cousin heading towards us. Obviously her conquest has been away too long and he's talking to an unaccompanied woman. I can't watch this. I find the mating ritual painful enough as it is, all that simpering and eyelash batting. (Admittedly, I'd once partaken of that particular activity with Mr Chocolate Sniffer – in public – but I'd already accepted myself as a hypocrite.) With Greg, it'll probably finish me off.

Greg's going to sleep with someone else. I could reach down, touch my chest and feel the pain dissecting my heart. He can shag who he likes, but he's going to actually do it. Here. At my parents' wedding. Right in my face.

'See you around,' I manage before the second cousin on a promise arrives.

'Huh? What?' Greg replies.

I duck into the loo to hide.

I stick my head out of the loo door a bit later: no sign of Greg and the second cousin whore. *Cool, I'll sneak off back to the house.* I'll see my family at the family lunch tomorrow. Thankfully, no second cousins are allowed, so there'll be no cat who got laid smiles to contend with. And no Greg.

In my bedroom, what used to be my bedroom back in my parents' house, they've taken down the bed and put its single mattress on the floor, as well as a couple of sleeping bags for Eric and Arri. Dad1 is in Eric's old room, a couple of people are staying in Mum and Dad2's room, a couple more are in the living room. Mum and Dad2 are staying in a hotel tonight.

I hardly slept last night. I'd been too worried about missing the train so ended up getting up at six, even though, like I'd done for the past three months, I'd gone to sleep at three or something. I snuggle down under the duvet on the single mattress.

I used to lie in this room and wish for this. For silence and peace. All the time I was growing up I wanted a substitute for the noise inside and out. Mum and Dad2 never argued; waiting for it, though, was just as noisy. Loud. I'd gotten used to waiting for the rows, even though they never came.

This used to be my house of horrors. I'd do anything to avoid going home. Would go sit in the library after school, would get up early to go to a friend's house before school. Now it's stilled.

I think again of my parents.

They've changed. They've changed enough to make an effort for me. They've finally found a reason to stop all that hatred. Can't see them becoming friends, but they aren't chomping to tear a strip off each other. Which is all I wanted – I'd never wanted them to get back together or to be the best of friends, just to not want to kill each other.

My life has changed so much in the past three months – actually in the past year. In the past year, I've gained some perspective and can see my parents aren't evil, just people. What they did wasn't intentional but it hurt all the same. It hurt more, though, because I clung to it. Used it as a weapon to beat off all attempts of love, to keep myself 'safe' by not taking any big risks. The biggest risk I'd taken in all my years was with Greg.

My life with my parents made me constantly run, constantly afraid of being tied down. And I know now the exact moment I stopped running. It was unconscious, but I know the exact moment.

I pull the duvet over my head.

Seeing my parents together had slotted the last piece in place. The mo—

The bedroom door is pushed open and I steel myself for Arri and Eric stumbling around, getting undressed, giggling and probably snogging . . . *Eww! I hope they don't try to have sex while I'm in the room.*

'Excuse me,' a voice whispers. 'Is this where Eric and Arrianne are meant to be sleeping?'

I know that voice. I pull away the duvet.

'Amber?' he says as I sit up.

'Greg,' I state.

'The, the . . . *bastards*,' he snarls. 'I should've known it was too good to be true. I can't believe they stitched me up.' He flops his arms around in frustration. 'Eric offered to swap my floor space in East Finchley with his and Arri's floor space here. He said the East Finchley room would take ages to get to, and that the person I was going to stay with would be one of the last to leave. He handed me the keys to the house and said they were meant to be staying in the room on the right.'

'This used to be my room.'

'He said that. He also promised, *promised* you wouldn't be staying in the house.'

'Ever get the impression someone's trying to get us to talk?' I state. 'I'm so going to give Eric and Arrianne a mouthful tomorrow.'

'Well, you'll have to have a go at your parents as well. Much as I got on with Dad2, I get the impression I was invited to talk to you.'

'You could have a point.'

'Are the other rooms free?'

'Nope, planned with military precision, every room is taken – even the sofa is booked. Although the bathroom's free. I've slept in a bath before, it's not so bad once you get used to slipping about. And that moment when you wake up and think you're in an open-topped coffin. Plus people keep waking you up when they go to the loo.'

'I'll go get my floor space in East Finchley back.'

'OK, fine, whatever, but can we really not spend one night in the same room without it turning into a drama? We did it for years before. I'm half asleep already, I'll be out like a light in another five minutes. You do whatever you want then. Except wanking. I don't want to wake up to the smell of sperm and sweat. But if you want to go to East Finchley be my guest. I'm going to sleep. Good night.'

'All right,' Greg says, 'I'll stay. If you're sure.'

'Mm-hm.'

He shuts the door until there's only a sliver of light. I hear him undressing, then slipping into the sleeping bag nearest the door and furthest from me, which suits me fine, of course. Time ticks by. I can smell him. That scent he cleaned from my house. That heady, musky smell of him. Vanilla and spice. I loved that smell. Loved it when it was on my skin. Loved it when I could bury my face in his chest and sniff him. More time ticks by. I try to slow my breathing. Concentrate on going to sleep.

'I didn't sleep with her,' Greg says after a while.

'Who?' Obviously a valid question, I mean, who hasn't he slept with?

'That woman, Salene. I didn't sleep with her.'

'Clearly.'

'All right, I didn't sleep with her, I didn't shag her, I didn't make love to her, I didn't fuck her. I didn't even kiss her. I haven't touched another woman since you. Since that night that started in my corridor.'

That's why he looks so awful – he's not shagged out.

He gives a small laugh. 'You know that night, when we were lying there in the corridor, I looked in your eyes and I

407

almost asked you to marry me. When I said, "I want you to stay with me" I'd actually gone to say, "I want you to stay with me for ever, marry me." Thankfully I stopped in time, or you would have run screaming from the house.'

He was really going to ask me to marry him? That's so . . . mad. So . . . Greg-like. He knew I didn't believe in marriage, but he was still going to ask. It was things like that that made me love him. I was bad at relationships and so was he. When one of us was clingy, the other was running in the opposite direction. We were often on the same page – but in completely different books.

'With you, I got a taste of something better than constantly shagging around. And once you've had the best, it's pretty hard to go back to something else,' he's saying. 'What about you? Are you seeing anyone?'

I pause. Pause in that way he used to before he said something he knew I didn't want to hear. It's not as calculated as it seems. It's hard knowing you're going to say something that will hurt someone you care for. 'Kind of,' I say.

'Right.' He inhales deeply. 'Who is he?'

'A film director I met. He's been helping me with a script I've written.'

'Right.' Another deep inhalation. 'Is it serious?'

'Depends what you mean by serious.'

'Have you . . .' he stops, takes another big breath, 'have you slept with him?'

I pause. 'Have we spent the night sleeping in the same bed? No. But if you're asking if we've had sex . . .' I pause again. 'Then yes. Yes, I've slept with him.'

The breath catches in Greg's chest. It sounds painful. I could've lied, but then why go so overboard about him and Jen, and him and Matt, if I was going to do the same thing. 'Right. Right. Well, I'd better get some sleep,' he says evenly. 'Night.'

'Night.'

The room is in silence save his breathing, which sounds as though someone is holding a pillow over his face while something heavy presses on his chest.

'Amber.' Greg fights his way out of his sleeping bag, sits up. 'I don't want you seeing this man any more. I know I've got no right to ask or to say anything, especially as I wasn't exactly fighting off Salene, and I slept with your best mate once upon a time ago, and it was me who didn't want to be friends, but I don't want you seeing someone else. I don't want you making love to someone else.'

'I'm not making love to him. I've just had sex with him.'

He makes that funny noise with his breathing again. 'You make that seem like a little thing but it's not. It's not. Especially when he sounds so perfect for you, he can do things with you that I can't, like work on your script. He sounds like the kind of bloke I expected you to end up with. It'll kill me if you settle down with him.

'I'm not over you. I haven't moved on. I haven't thought about moving on. I don't know how to. Move on to what? I've had girls come on to me these past few months, yes, despite how shite I look. But I couldn't, I just couldn't.

'The thought of someone else even kissing you, let alone knowing he's touched you, it's driving me crazy. It's killing me . . .

'You don't seriously think I came to the wedding because Dad2 invited me, do you? I came to be near you. Anything to be near you. I even cut my hair because I know how much it irritated you. When I was in Ireland Kristy said she hated you because it took five years and a pregnancy to make me propose to her. She'd been hinting for years about me moving in, about us getting married, whereas I'd gone to propose to you after six months and wanted us to live together after three months. When Renée told me about you moving to Brighton, the first thing I did was get on the Net and look for jobs down there.

409

'I thought you knew me. You must've known that when I said I didn't want to be friends, it was nothing to do with you being a controlling bitch, it was because I couldn't face seeing you day after day knowing the reason I couldn't touch you or hold you was because I was so fucking stup—'

'SHUT UP!' I shout suddenly. 'SHUT UP. SHUT UP. SHUT UP. IF I HEAR ONE MORE WORD FROM YOU, I WILL MAKE THAT BATH SEEM LIKE THE LUXURY OPTION.'

Greg, wisely, does as he's told.

'I had sex with him once. Only once. To prove to myself that I could do it. I didn't want the last person I slept with to be someone who'd been with Jen. It was too painful already, I had to do something to erase that. It was only once with this man and, yes, it was good sex, but even then we haven't done it again. He constantly asks me out, wants me to be his girl-friend, for us to do it again, and I've not said yes. Or even maybe. I've always said no. I only see him because I'm work-ing with him.'

'Oh,' Greg says. 'So you're not interested in going out with him?'

'Not properly, no.'

'And the sex wasn't amazing?'

'No. It was good, not amazing.'

'We always had amazing sex, didn't we?'

'Yes, Greg.'

'And you won't do it again with him?'

'No, Greg.'

'Fantastic.'

I now know the exact moment I stopped running. It was that second after Greg kissed me. The one person who brought out the worst and the best in me kissed me, did some-thing so outlandish that my subconscious decided to join him. Decided to do the unthinkable and see things through. I'd known that weekend that something was different, that I'd changed. And that was down to Greg doing something I didn't run from.

I've missed him. Not just the sex and the storytelling. The routines and the laughs. I missed Greg. So, he didn't sniff chocolate. He was too good looking. He'd shagged my best friend. But, I'd been still. On Martha's balance sheet, that stillness outweighed everything else. My perfect man wasn't perfect.

He simply gave my soul that soothing stroke I used to get from eating chocolate.

I start laughing. 'You're such a big wuss,' I say through my giggles. 'Oh, boo hoo, Amber's shagged someone else. Boo hoo.'

Greg's big sunshine laugh, the one that comes from somewhere in his heart, hits the air, making me laugh even more.

'Oh, what about you, Miss "I Wonder If He Shagged Kristy When He Was In Dublin?" and Miss "I Bet He Shags Salene"? If you'd seen your face . . . You were right jealous.'

I laugh harder. 'No, I just thought you could do better.'

Greg chuckles. 'I've always had appalling taste in women.'

'I know,' I say through my giggles. 'Ah, fucking hell, you're so funny. I love you.'

The laugh dies in Greg's throat. 'That's not even remotely funny.'

'I wasn't trying to be funny.' I pause. 'I was trying to tell you . . . I was trying to say that even though I never said it when we were together, I did love you. I want you to know that. In case you doubted it.'

'And now?'

'Now, I know I can live without you.'

'Right,' Greg says.

'But I don't want to.'

'Are you saying you want to get back with me?'

411

'I'm saying I'm over the Jen thing. And the Matt thing. And the liar, liar pants on fire thing. Basically, we're crap when we're not together. And we're absolutely disgusting when we are together but at least then we get to have amazing sex.'

Greg climbs out of his sleeping bag, crawls across the room, grabs me from under the covers and pulls me onto the sleeping bag beside us, envelops me in his arms. His face is inches from mine when he says, 'After much consideration, I've decided to let you take me back. It's best all round.'

'You're only in it for the sex,' I laugh.

'Too right,' he replies. Before he kisses me I push my fingers onto his lips.

'I need to ask you one thing before you engage those lips, buddy.'

'No, the thing with Jen didn't mean a thing. It was the worst mistake of my life and every day I wish I could take back the moment of madness that made me do it.'

'Thanks for sharing, but that wasn't what I was going to ask.'

'Oh. Sorry. Pretend I didn't bring it up. Ask away.'

'Will you move in with me, you old slapper?'

epilogue

the chocolate run

'Fancy meeting you here.'

No way. This is the voice of a person I do not want to see. Ever. Eric and Greg tried to send me out to get them chocolate while they watched the football and I'd been on the second round of abuse when Arrianne interceded on their behalf and requested I go because she had a pregnancy-induced craving for it. And now look.

I turn to my left, a chocolate bar in each hand.

'And what do you want,' I say.

She holds her shopping basket close to her, like a shield. She looks like she used to, pre-Matt Makeover. Wavy blonde hair, fleshed out face, fuller body. She looks normal again. It's been nearly nine months since I last saw her in the school playground. Of course I haven't forgotten what she looks like without and with the weight, but I'm still staring into the face of a stranger.

'To see you,' she replies.

I have to hand it to Jen, she has thick skin. She's called me almost every day for the past nine months, whether I speak to her or not. She'll ring, email, write, even though I'm still having none of it. She'd stopped short of showing up until now. After Greg moved in, I changed my numbers. No, our numbers (still getting used to that after six months).

'And Greg set me up.'

'No, Eric.'

'My brother *hates* you.' Probably a little uncalled for, but there you go.

'He has good reason. But he knows how much I love you. He said he'd get you out of the house so I can talk to you.'

Eric's the only person on earth who knows how much I miss her. Greg wouldn't dare tell me to make up with Jen. He's very careful what he says about her, full stop. When we finally stopped the round-the-clock, back-together shagging, Greg and I sat down and talked. And talked. And talked. (I'd never talked so much about my feelings in my life – it was bloody exhausting.) We'd agreed that he could see Matt whenever he wanted because he did – for reasons that still escape me – want to patch up their friendship. He could even talk to me about Matt and I'd be a grown-up and listen and ask questions in the right places, but, under no circumstances, would I be requested to see him or talk to him. In the same spirit, Greg wouldn't torture me with his jealousy whenever I met up with Mr (there's still a spark between us) Chocolate Sniffer.

When seeing Jen re-entered the equation, Greg had tried to initiate another big talk session, but I headed him off at the pass (I couldn't face all that yakking again) and told him to do what he wanted because I trusted him. Plus, I knew he'd have enough sense to flee the country if things got vaguely sexual with Jenna because he'd not live to see the sunrise following me finding out about it. ('Fair enough,' Greg had said, 'how's your little film director friend?')

Besides, I don't mind Greg seeing Jen – I get to hear about her; have a connection to her without having to do anything.

Eric, much as he doesn't like Jen, is on at me all the time to at least talk to her – he knows there's a big gaping hole in my life where she should be. That I miss her friendship. Yes, I might be missing a friendship, a closeness and depth, that didn't exist, but I didn't know. That's what Eric was always saying: 'There's unfinished business between you and Jen. If it's really over with you two, you *wouldnae* have any kind of reaction to her contacting you. You *wouldnae* have a gob on yer whenever speaking to her is mentioned.' I wonder if I have a gob on me now that I am speaking to her.

'I'm back with Matt,' she says. 'We're the only ones who'll put up with each other. He's quit his job and only works in Leeds now. He's getting divorced.'

'Greg told me.' Greg told me that Matt had begged her for ages to give him another chance, claiming that she was the one he wanted. And she had. She wasn't my friend any more so she wasn't my problem and I wasn't allowed to feel any way about it . . . Even if it was the most stupid thing to do since bungee jumping without a rope.

'We're getting married next year,' she continues. 'Did you know that?'

'Yes.'

'I was hoping, wondering, hoping you'd be my bridesmaid.'

What's the chocolate like on your planet? 'I don't think that'd be a good idea,' I say out loud.

'OK. Maybe not. Greg said that you and Renée are sharing the Festival Director's role and that you'll be starting a part-time masters degree in film direction later this year.'

'Oh, I get it, you're here to tell me I'm too fat, ugly and warm to do it.'

She closes her eyes as if in silent agony. 'I'm sorry,' she says and returns her gaze to me. 'I'm so, so, so sorry. For everything. For how I treated you, for trying to keep you and Greg apart. Even that day you came to see me I was a cow to you. I tried to blame everything I'd done on you. I don't know how I ever thought I could justify what I did. I'm so, so sorry. I didn't even

415

realise how much of an evil bitch I'd been until you cut me out of your life. I'm surprised you stuck with me so long.'

'Yeah, well,' I say, 'I probably should have told you about me and Greg earlier.' *So you could've ruined it sooner.*

'So I could've ruined it sooner?' Jen replies.

I can't help but smile.

Jen grins back at me. 'That's what you were thinking, wasn't it?' Her smile disappears. 'It's true, though. If I'm honest, part of me suspected about you and Greg. I knew something had happened between you the night of my birthday because you were both so shifty with each other, but I thought that maybe he'd made a pass at you or something. That's why I set you up on that blind date that weekend and kept on about what a git Greg was.

'I hoped you'd back off, but no, you were as close as ever. Closer even. So I lied about him making a pass at me, tried to chip away your confidence. It was the only way I could get you back in my life.' She sighs. 'I could feel you were slipping away from me. I was the centre of your life for so long. For years you cared about me and everyone else came second, but then all of a sudden I wasn't number one. I guess because you were with Greg.

'It was like that with my mum – whenever she got a new bloke she lost interest in me. I'd be lucky if I saw her most weekends. It'd always been all right with you before. Even when you were with Sean you put me first. I had all this uncondi- tional love from you that I'd never had in my life. When you and Greg started being close mates you transferred a lot of your attention and affection to him. You two were always doing things together, things I couldn't, like going to lunch, going out at night during the week. You obviously cared for him and I didn't like it. I *hated* it.

'That night in the hotel I panicked. When you said you were moving in together I knew that'd be it. We'd never get our friendship back to how it was, and you'd put him first. I couldn't let that happen. I was so jealous and angry, I just panicked. You weren't meant to hear. Not like that. Not ever. I'm sorry.'

Something that's niggled at my mind for years occurs to me. 'Did you say something to Sean about me and Greg?'

Jen bites her lip, stares at me with big sorrowful eyes. 'I, erm, might have mentioned Greg's reputation for sleeping around.'

'What else?'

Jen lowers her head. 'And, erm, that Greg had told Matt that he'd sleep with you given half the chance.' Jen adds quickly: 'It was true! Greg did say that. But it was a choice between me, you and their sixth form tutor. Sean didn't know that part.'

'You basically tried to sabotage any relationship that seemed more important to me than you, including the one I have with my brother.'

'Yes. I'm so, so sorry.'

You're unbelievable, that's what you are. I turn back to the chocolate.

'It's all such a mess,' Jen says to my silence.

'No it's not. My life's pretty sorted. So's yours by the sound of it, got the man you love, getting married next year. Greg said you were trying for a baby. You and Matt have got Greg back as a friend, so it's not a mess. Let's keep a sense of proportion.'

'Every time we see Greg all he does is talk about you – partly because you're his favourite topic of conversation, but mainly because I keep pumping him for information on you. He's my hotline to you.'

'Poor bloke, I do the same to him about you. And every time I do, I can tell he's wondering why I don't just speak to you . . .' *No, do not weaken. Remember what she did. How much she hurt you.* 'I've got to go.' I put down the chocolate. 'I don't

417

think any of them deserve these after they so wantonly set me up.'

Her face struggles not to collapse in disappointment as I head for the door.

And then, something else inside me speaks. Reminds me that I was no victim in this. When you don't speak up for yourself, how do you expect people to know how to treat you? It was not speaking up that got me into this.

If I'd had the courage to tell Jen that our friendship meant everything to me and that nobody would change that, maybe things wouldn't have gone the way they did. When I was in runner mode, I didn't tell anyone how much I cared. It'd happened with Greg too – he'd been so unsure of my feelings he'd had to demand a commitment from me. It was the same with Mum not knowing, not understanding, that things were different with Greg because she'd never been given the chance to meet other boyfriends. Once I started opening up, stopped running and started giving myself the opportunity to feel and hurt, life got better. Fuller, rounder, coloured in. I should have opened up to Jen a long time ago. Should've stopped running and talked to her before it came to this.

I turn back to her. 'Jen.'

She looks up, her topaz-blue eyes a mess of burgeoning tears.

'Do you want to meet our kids?'

'Your kids?' Her voice is wobbly, about to collapse into tears.

'Me and Greg have adopted so many fish over the past few months we'll probably have to move to a bigger place so they can have their own room.'

'I didn't know you liked fish.'

'There's a lot of things about me you don't know. And there's a lot I don't know about you.' My eyes meet her eyes. 'But we can find out.'

We can find out if there was ever anything real between us. We can find out if we had any friendship at all, or if we only stuck together out of habit – a bad habit that we might have to give up. Whatever we find out, things can't go back to how they were before, can't return to 'normal'. Everything's changed. We've changed.

'So, do you want to meet them?' I ask.

'I'd love to.'

'Come on then. It's their dinnertime soon. Bartleby and Loki eat loads, but Captain Picard's a bit funny about eating. Mark Twain's my favourite, but don't tell Greg that, he's always going on about me loving them all the same or some such hippy nonsense.'

We have to find a new normal. That won't be so bad. Not as long as we've got chocolate.

The Chocolate Run, v. & n. *Colloq.* v. 1. The act of going out to purchase chocolate. v. 2. Moving with quick steps on alternate feet while in possession of chocolate. n. 3. The life of a person who thinks in chocolate and spends her life avoiding intimacy. n. 4. The emotional gauntlet we all go through at some point in our lives, eased by the consumption of chocolate.

THE CUPID
EFFECT

For
my twelve little samurai
(you know who you are)

the luvvie bit ...

Heartfelt thanks to:
Colette Harris; Sharon Wright and David Jacobson; Marian and Gordon Ndumbe; Graeme Delap; Ginny and Paul Baillie; Sharon Percival; Maria Owen; Stella Eleftheriades; Rhian Clugston; Mark Barrowcliffe; Martin and Sachiko O'Neill; Christian Lewis; Tracy Jurd; Selina Bromley; Tasha Harrison; the Cunniffs; and lovely Janet, for inspiring this story.

Also:
Thank you to my parents, Agnes and Samuel; my sibs, Sameer, Kathleen and David; the in-laws, Habiba and David; and the little peeps, Maryam, Dawood, Maraam, Muneerah, Yusuf, Ahmad, Muhammad, Ameerah and Sara; Liah, Skye and Aysah; Luc; Jonathan and Rachel; Connor and Leah. Your love and support has kept me going.

the cupid effect: where it all started

Every time I go into a shop that sells books, I always check to see if they have any of my novels. Even now, over half a decade after my first book was published, I still feel a thrill to see my name 'in lights'; experience a glow of pride to see my words on a shelf.

I must admit I get an extra thrill whenever I see *The Cupid Effect*. I love all my books equally; it's just (to loosely paraphrase George Orwell) I love *Cupid* a fraction more equally than the others.

Cupid may not be the novel that put my writing in front of a worldwide audience, but I will always have a special affection for it, for many reasons. One reason is that I share certain similarities with the main character. I'm always at pains to point out that I am *not* my main players, but if I was forced to name a character I share most traits with, it'd be *Cupid*'s Ceri D'Altroy. She and I are both sci-fi geeks who are obsessed with the same TV show; we've both taught Psychology; and we both have a large number of long-sleeved tops in our sartorial repertoire. Probably most crucially, we both have a habit of listening to people's problems then giving advice we *really* wish said advisees *wouldn't* take.

Another reason for my big love for *Cupid* is that it makes me laugh. It has its serious moments, but there are many, many scenes and phrases that tickle me enough to make me LOL (as the kids say). I laugh mainly because I can remember what inspired that particular scene or phrase.

My love of *Cupid* is that bit deeper, though, because it is my firstborn. The novel that allowed me to drop the first two letters of 'unpublished' and brand myself a published novelist. That day in February 2003 when I walked into a London bookshop and saw my name emblazoned upon the cover of a book is a day that permanently changed my life. It represented the culmination of months of writing every second I wasn't earning money to pay my bills. It represented years of reading, writing and dreaming. It represented everything I've wanted since I was thirteen years old and wrote my first full-length story. It represented me daring to follow my heart.

Cupid is essentially a book about having the courage to follow your heart and accepting that the power to change your life is in your hands. Not necessarily quitting your safe job and trying to do something you're not sure you're qualified for, like Ceri does; it is more about seeing what you would like to alter and striving to effect that change. Even if it is just a case of changing how you view your current circumstance.

As I said, I am proud of every single one of my books, and I love seeing them on the shelves in shops, so I'm especially excited that I'll be seeing *The Cupid Effect* 'out there' again, with a brand new cover: it'll be showing me and the world where I started and how far I've come.

I hope you enjoy reading it as much as I enjoyed writing it.

Dorothy Koomson, 2009

prologue

Good Intentions

1. Thou shalt sort out thy cardiovascular system
2. Thou shalt NOT get involved in other people's lives
3. Even if they're really, really nice thou shalt remember Commandment 2
4. Thou shalt think before thy speaks
5. Thou shalt think again before thy speaks
6. Thou shalt watch less *Angel*
7. Thou shalt remember that Angel is a 250-year-old vampire who dated Buffy The Vampire Slayer, not the man you're going to be with for ever and ever.

Simple. No? Easy. No? And I've broken two of them within, oooh, four hours.

chapter one

Heart's Desire

I blame Oprah.

This is all her fault.

I mean, if it wasn't for her, I'd be waking up to 'just' another weekend, right about now. The usual: Saturday morning telly, wander round Bromley shopping centre, battle for food in the Savacentre.

Instead, I'm stood at Leeds train station with my worldly goods at my feet.

I've *really* done it this time, haven't I? I've done some stupid things in my life, most of them either involving sex or money or shoes, but this time I've truly surpassed myself. And it's all down to Oprah Winfrey.

Oh, it started innocently enough. I woke up one morning and I couldn't *get*.

I couldn't get up, get showered, get dressed, get to the station, get on a train, get to work. I couldn't get, so I pulled a sickie and I saw *Oprah*. My life went pear-shaped right after that.

Up to that point, any doubts I had about my life were formless. Just floating around at the back of my consciousness. After my sickie, though, these doubts and insecurities had a voice. An American talk show host's voice.

3

First, I was taping Oprah's show. *Every day*. Next, terms like 'heart's desire' and 'you can't change what you don't acknowledge' were never far from my lips. Then came the books. I became the Noah of self-help manuals. I was hoarding them two by two as though, instead of a flood, there was a predicted self-help drought coming and yea, verily, it was almost upon us. A few moments after that – or maybe it was months – I was headed for Leeds clutching a one-way ticket. Because that's where my heart's desire was. Supposedly. Two hundred miles away from everything I knew and loved.

I glanced down at my suitcase and holdall.

WHAT THE HELL HAVE I DONE?

I've given up everything to go back to college, that's what.

Two hundred miles away, in London, I had a life. I had my own flat. Two televisions, a sofa, a wardrobe, bookcases, video shelves, a bed made from reclaimed antique wood. Not some cheapo self-assembly job. It was actually made for me from antique wood. How many people could say that? Not many, that's how many.

And, down south, I had friends. Hoards of them. I couldn't go down the end of my street without tripping over them. Up here, I had my best mate Jessica and . . . and . . .

The breath caught in my chest, my heart started flinging itself against my rib cage. *Oh God. I'm insane. I'm actually insane.* (That revelation was on a par with finding out I was never going to marry Arnold Schwarzenegger. Except I'd cried quite a lot then.)

This was what everyone said. My family, my friends, my colleagues. They'd all reminded me how I'd struggled to pay off my student debts and buy a flat and decorate it and become respected in my career. 'And you're giving it all up to go back to living out of one room? Why exactly?'

'Because Oprah told me to,' would've been the short answer.

4

I explained, though, that I was leaving because life is too long, not too short. What if I get to ninety with my memory intact? Wouldn't I be *more* pissed off if I got to that ripe old age and realised I'd not had the courage to follow my true heart's desire and do what I really wanted with my life instead of carrying on with the day to day because it was easier not to rock the boat? Life's too long not to do it; not to be true to myself. Most people understood when I spelt it out like that. Either that, or they lost interest halfway through and agreed with me to shut me up.

But why didn't anyone stop me? If I really thought someone was going to do what I'd done on the strength of an American chat show and a few self-help tomes, I'd have gone in for a spot of kidnapping and self-help deprogramming. But that's just me, obviously.

Anyway, it's too late now, isn't it, Ceri D'Altroy? You're here now, they're expecting you on Monday, and someone else is living in your flat. Might as well get on with it. Start dealing with the now. (Dealing with the now? Dealing with the now?! I was even thinking like an Oprah guest. The pre-Oprah me would've said, 'Right Ceri, move your bloomin' arse.')

I hoisted my holdall onto my shoulder, gripped my suitcase handle with renewed purpose and vigour then headed for the taxi rank outside.

As I staggered towards the station exit, I kept my line of sight firmly lowered, with my head down, my chin-length black hair hiding my face. I often walked like this, as though I had the weight of the world, as well as half my flat, on my shoulders. I wasn't a miserable old cow, I'd actually trained myself to not look up. To not look anyone in the face or initiate eye contact. The last thing I needed at this stage of the game, when I was already fragile, was to make eye contact with a stranger. Catch someone's eye and you soon found yourself signing up for a

5

credit card, giving some freak a fake phone number or hearing about some old dear's gall bladder operation. At least, that's what happened to me. Regularly. More regularly than should've been statistically possible. Most people didn't get on a bus and get off fifteen minutes later knowing the entire life story of the woman next to them. I did. There were whole bus routes where I knew most of the passengers by their ailments, not their names.

This was my talent; my gift. Unintentionally eliciting personal info from perfect strangers. I never did have the brass front to tell these people to get lost or even ignore them. The best I could do was not make eye contact in the first place. And I'd found it perfectly feasible to go about ninety-two per cent of my daily business without looking anyone in the eye.

I wrestled my slipping holdall back onto my left shoulder, ignoring how my rucksack lacerated that soft, fleshy bit between my neck and shoulders. *I can do this. I can do this*, I repeated in my head.

I hadn't got past the entrance of Menzies when a body stepped into my path. Shite. This happened sometimes. The 'no eye contact' thing didn't work. People approached me anyway. But, I could still get out of this if I kept my head down and moved on.

'Sorry,' I mumbled, and stepped to my left without looking up.

The body stepped with me.

I stepped to the right, the body stepped to the right.

Left, the body went left. We danced on – right and left, left and right – like this for a few more seconds, then I attempted a double-bluff, left step, but actually went to the right.

But my escape plan was foiled by a fiendish body block. This person had me bang to rights. And I was going to be signing up to be a Jehovah's Witness in, oooh, three minutes.

6

With a silent sigh, I looked up.

I wasn't greeted by a magazine promising to save my soul (but let me die if I needed a blood transfusion), instead, a cardboard sign with:

Kerry Dalboy

was thrust in my face.

My eyes shot to above the sign. Jess grinned back at me so wide I could hardly see her face.

'Welcome home sweetie,' Jess cried and threw her arms around my neck. As she did so, our combined weight tipped back onto my overstuffed rucksack and before either of us could do anything, we both went tumbling to the ground.

chapter two

Student Country

In the short-stay car park across from the station, Jess stood behind me as I struggled out of my black rucksack. Her legs buckled as she took the strain. We both then huffed and puffed as we pushed the rucksack onto the back seat of the car. We'd silently agreed never to mention again what had just happened in the station. Ever.

'OK, one, two, three . . . hnnnugh!' We both heaved my suitcase into the boot. I had, of course, managed to travel across London and nigh on two hundred miles with this stuff on my own, but the grunting and straining made my efforts seem all the more heroic.

'I thought you'd be bringing more stuff,' Jess said as she squashed my holdall on top of the suitcase. She knew I couldn't pack light if my house was on fire. And I'd *never* packed a two bedroom flat into three luggage items before. Which is why I'd been up half the night packing and repacking and repacking. I'd finally fallen asleep at about three a.m., still wondering if I should take everything out and start again. I'd never had to pack for twelve months before. Not even when I was in college – it'd always been packing for a few months until I went back to London.

I haven't brought that much with me, have I? Maybe I'd been a bit too ruthless in deciding what I couldn't live without. Clothes, shoes, books, videos, my photo albums, my beloved iBook, toothbrush, beauty shelf or two. But not enough for twelve months away from home. 'I'll probably go back next weekend for more,' I said.

'Oh Ceri,' Jess said, she paused in the driver's open doorway, 'that'll cost you a fortune.'

'It won't cost *that* much, I'll get an Apex,' I said.

'You'll be knackered though.'

'Yes, Mum.'

'Oi, watch it, Cockney.'

'That's the sort of thing you'd say to your kids, isn't it? "You'll be knackered."'

'I don't know, you show a person a bit of concern and she just flings it back in your face.' Jess sounded hurt. 'Well, if you don't want my concern . . .'

'I'm surprised you ain't got fake tears to go with that fake upset.'

She laughed and started the car. 'You're all heart, you.'

'I learnt it from you, Teach.'

My life path had crossed with Jessica Breakfield's life path when I was a first year psychology and media student at college in Leeds and she was a psychology lecturer. So that should be, *Dr* Jessica Breakfield. She hated me calling her that, though. 'You use it like mothers use middle names,' she'd once said. 'It always sounds vaguely insulting or like I'm in trouble.'

She terrified me when I first met her. Jessica was the first woman doctor of psychology I met who looked and was under thirty-five. She had theories to her name, she was young and she made lectures interesting.

9

Jess remembered me as prone to hiding behind my waist-length hair and not talking very much. Probably something to do with me staring at her in wide-eyed, nineteen-year-old awe.

I'd done a comedy gulp when she was assigned as my personal tutor, but as I got to know her and began to relax around her, she began to see my face because my veil-like hair got shorter and shorter. (The shortest being the crop, and cleanly shaved at the back, which resulted in my parents not speaking to me till it grew back.)

It was at the end of college, though, when I decided to do a PhD that Jess and I became proper mates. She helped with my PhD proposal and the more time we spent together, the more we found that we had loads in common: a love of television, a worship of chocolate and an almost fanatical obsession with not getting out of our pyjamas on a Sunday unless we really, *really* needed to buy food. But these were only the tips of the icebergs floating in our sea of similarity.

Our connection went far deeper than was first visible to the naked eye. It was as if Jess and I were separated at birth – twelve years apart. She had a husband – Fred, teenage twin daughters Sharon and Colette – and grew up in Harrogate. I didn't. She was five foot ten, slenderish with waves and waves of auburn hair and a Yorkshire accent. I was five foot four-and-a-bit, nearly five foot five, actually, curvyish, with a shiny black bob and a posh Sarf London drawl. (Yes, that sounded like an oxymoron, but there I was, saying 'scowns' (scones) and 'cheeky caaa' (cheeky cow) in the same sentence. Well, I'm pretty sure I've said them in the same sentence.) We were definitely the odd couple on the outside. Had you to pick out the two partners in crime in a line-up you'd never put the two of us together. Age, height, looks, background, nothing went together. But when Jess and I were together we were one person. We thought alike, we argued alike, we were scathing on demand. Under it, though, was a deep understanding. Jess was the only person who hadn't said, 'You're mad you' when I told her what I was doing. She'd been extremely supportive. Actually, what she said was, 'Awww, honey, that's fantastic! I knew you could do it. But you can't live with me. And you can't live within walking distance of me. I'll never sleep if you do.'

I never did get on that PhD course, but I did get the most honest, caring, strangest best mate known to womankind.

Jessica parked Fred's metallic blue Mondeo outside the orange-brick house, slap bang in the middle of Stanmore Vale, Burley Park. I'd lived near here, in Burley Park, when I was a Leeds student the first time. This area was unofficially Student Country.

You had to leave your maturity, dress sense and need to keep regular hours at the various border checkpoints around here. Student Country was made up of Hyde Park, Headingley, Burley Park and Kirkstall; it was where most of the students who went to Leeds Uni, Leeds Met, All Souls and the other colleges in Leeds lived, loved and drank. It'd occurred to me more than once that you could wipe out at least seventy per cent of the student population by napalming that relatively small area of West Yorkshire.

Three streets over was the last student house I'd lived in. Now *that* was a student house. 98 Stanmore Avenue. I'd never forget that address. So much had happened to me in the year I lived in that house it was hard to believe it was only a year. I'd got pneumonia in that house. I'd met the love of my life when I lived in that house. I was dumped by the love of my life *in* that house. I had what turned out to be my last shag in Leeds in that house (and hadn't had another one for about two years after that). I got my finals results in that house. It was a very momentous house. I was hoping that 17 Stanmore Vale, the

11

house I was about to move into, would be far less dramatic. I'd grown out of student dramatics.

I'd been clutching my *Leeds A to Z* and a borrowed copy of *The Itchy Guide To Leeds* when I first knocked on 17 Stanmore Vale. It was the first time I'd been back round these parts in well over six years and I'd needed a little help in finding my way around.

Jess, who taught at Leeds Metropolitan University ('The Met' to most people), had seen the advert for a double room and thought it'd be perfect for me: I knew the area (ish) and it was living with two post-graduate students as averse to first-time-away-from-home, freedom-insane undergraduates who'd want to party all night and slob all day as I was. And it was a good twenty-minute drive from her home. So, she'd noted the details then went round taking down all the flyers she could find so I'd have a chance to look at it before anyone else did.

The front door had been opened about two seconds after my knock by a lad with messy, rust-coloured hair and a pierced eyebrow. He was casually clothed in baggy jeans and a plain white T-shirt. I say lad, he was more a bloke. But could pass for a lad because he was younger than me. (Not that I was old. He was twenty-five, twenty-six and I'd almost left my twenties. But only almost.) His light eyes sparkled as he said, 'Hi, you must be Ceri,' and grinned. His whole face relaxed into that grin and I fell instantly in like with him. I was a relatively simple creature like that. You were nice to me, I liked you. Hell, I'd been out with blokes on the strength of them being nice to me as opposed to any kind of attraction.

'And you're Jake?' I replied, grinning back.

'Yup, that's me. You're right on time. Come in. Have you just come up from London?'

Is it that obvious? I wondered. I glanced down at myself. I did indeed look like I'd just crawled away from a three-hour train journey. My jacket and jeans were travel-creased, my Walkman, crisp packets, spare jumper, notebook and reading material all bulged in my bag. 'Yeah. I'm going back straight away as well,' I said, looking back up at Jake. 'I could only get the afternoon off work. They're not too happy about me leaving so want to get every second out of me.'

'Oh, right, better get on then. This way.'

My feet bounced slightly on the ruby red carpet of the hallway. Quality carpet, and from the cushioning effect, it probably had underlay. *Clever colour choice*, I thought, as I followed Jake. Subconsciously you felt important, like VIP material, because you'd come into a place where they'd laid out the red carpet, literally. Or it could be a way to get a murdered body out of the house without the worry of blood stains on the carpet (but that was the kind of thought that plagued my mind).

Opposite the stairs lay the living room. I stepped in after Jake and my mouth fell open. It was straight out of a homes magazine: porridge-coloured carpet, cream walls and two squashy, tan leather sofas. Standing guard over the fireplace was a professionally-framed Dali print – *The Metamorphosis of Narcissus*. At the other end of the room were two huge bay windows with net curtains and everything. This was a proper sitting room, not a hashed together, student job. I'd steeled myself when I knocked on the front door for threadbare carpets, limescale plumbing and tales of a nightmare landlord.

Jake explained that he was in fact that nightmare landlord, that he owned the house, as he showed me round. 'My parents lent me the money for a deposit on this place and acted as guarantors when I first came to college here just over four years ago. I was a mature student, I mean, not that mature, but

I couldn't stand the thought of a normal student house, so I talked them into it. They also lent me the cash to do it up properly. That's why I rent out the other two rooms, it covers the mortgage and pays back my parents.'

I was only half listening to him; I was far too busy falling in love. The red carpet and living room were like passing someone attractive in the street and glancing back to get a second look. The rest of the house was like getting to know someone, dating them, sharing with them and finding out that everything about them is wonderful. Finding no reason *not* to fall in love with them.

We wandered down the narrow corridor to the kitchen and my heart fluttered. It was another large space, this time with real wood flooring. A chrome and beechwood dream, white cabinets with real wood worktops that, Jake explained, needed special oil rubbing into them – 'we take that in turns'. A breakfast bar divided the room, and around it stood four high, padded stools. The kitchen had stainless steel appliances, a blender, a real coffee machine, canisters that had 'tea', 'sugar', 'coffee' and 'biscuits' on them. (I had a sneaking suspicion that each jar was filled with what was written on the outside of it.)

'There's a little bit of a garden-patio area that we sometimes sit on, but me and Ed don't use it that much,' Jake added as he nodded to the back door. 'Do you want to see upstairs now?'

'Oh yes,' I whispered.

The soft-pile redness of the corridor went all the way up the stairs, both flights of them. The room on offer was right at the top of the house.

I trailed behind Jake as he swung open the white painted door to the attic room, my heart pounding hard in my chest, my breath short with anticipation. I fell completely head over heels as the door revealed the mysteries of the attic.

Part of the ceiling was slanted, with two skylights set in it. The cream walls made the room seem even larger. It had a double bed, a grey metal-framed desk, an oak wardrobe, and rather thoughtfully, a window had been installed in one of the walls so you could look out at the treetops and into bedrooms of the opposite houses when you lay on the bed.

I was speechless with lust as I turned to Jake and said, 'And you don't want to move in here now that it's free?'

Jake shrugged and shook his head. 'It's too far to stumble if I come home drunk or stoned or both. Bill, that's the lad who lived in this room before, would often sleep on one of the sofas downstairs cos he couldn't make it up here when he was pissed. It's a long way.'

'And what about the other lad?' I added, just as breathlessly. 'Doesn't he want a bigger room?'

'All the rooms are quite big. But Ed? Nah, he doesn't want it. He's a boy, and to him more space equals more to clean.'

'I see,' I said in a small, small voice. *If I don't get this room, if I end up in a hovel in Hyde Park with bars on the windows and doors, then I was Attila the Hun in a former life.* 'So, do you need references or something if I want to take it?'

'Um, no. I mean, there's a standard six-month contract and I'd need a month's deposit and a month's rent in advance, but no references,' Jake said. 'But you'd be interested in moving in?'

I almost nodded my head off. 'Oh yes.'

'Right. Well, there's no one else waiting to see it. It's weird, actually, no one else has rung up about it. I don't know why . . .' Jake went off into a stare. 'I put up loads of flyers and no one's called.'

'Really?' I replied, sympathetically. *It'll have absolutely nothing to do with Jess taking down the posters all round the college campus, I'm sure.* 'That *is* weird.'

15

I reached into my bag, pulled out my cheque book, rummaged around for a pen. 'So, that's £600, is it?'

'What?' Jake said. 'Oh, yeah. You can make the cheque out to Jake Halder. We can set up a standing order after that.'

I was already writing at the speed of light, just in case he changed his mind and decided to investigate the case of the disappearing flyers more closely.

'You're not a psycho, are you?' he asked as he led the way back down to the ground floor, my HSBC cheque peeking out of the top of his jeans back pocket. 'The lad who lived here before, Bill, turned out to be a bit of a nutter. Me and Ed were well pleased when he got chucked off his course and had to move. You're not one, are you?'

'I've been told I'm a bit strange sometimes, but not a nutter.'

'Cool,' Jake said. And there was me thinking *I* was easily pleased. 'Anyway, let me know when you want to move in and either Ed or I will be here. Then I'll give you your own set of keys and you can sign the contract. Do you want a cup of tea before you go?'

And that was it. I'd got myself a place to live. The only bind I could see would be trailing down to the second floor to the bathroom or to use the loo. But that bathroom had floor-to-ceiling blue and white mosaic tiles, a power shower and squashy rubber floor tiles – it was the kind of suffering I could handle.

'Hi,' I said to the stringy lad who answered the door of 17 Stanmore Vale this time around. He was about twenty-two, looked like he'd been elongated on a rack, had long blond hair and wasn't there when I'd looked around the house. And there ended the list of things I knew about him. I couldn't even remember his name. Eric or something.

He in return cast an eye over me, my luggage, the woman

16

technically old enough to be his mother behind me. Then he made no secret of his confusion: his forehead knitted together, his green eyes tried to calculate what was going on. 'You all right?' he asked, vague flirtations with a non-Yorkshire accent lilted in his voice.

'I'm Ceri D'Altroy. I'm moving into the room? Upstairs?'

'Ah, right,' he replied. 'I'm Ed.'

Ed. That was it. 'Hi, Ed. This,' I indicated to Jess with a slight nod of my head over my shoulder, 'is my best mate Jessica.'

'Hi?' Ed offered cautiously, his face blanking out completely. He made no move to let us in. He stood guarding the doorway like one of the guards outside Buckingham Palace; we were one moment away from him putting on his bearskin hat, picking up his rifle and totally ignoring us until his shift was over.

'OK Ed,' Jess said, 'are you going to let us in, or do we have to break in round the back?'

Ed, blankness aside, was polite and friendly. He made Jess and me a cuppa, even though I rarely drank proper tea. I'd been hoping he had herbal, but when I mentioned it he'd got that glazed-over expression he'd got when I introduced Jess as my best mate so 'Ordinary's fine,' I'd said, quickly.

Jess gulped hers down the second he set it down on the coffee table. While gulping, she twiddled locks of her auburn hair around her fingers. She was gagging for a cigarette. She'd abstained all the way from the station (Fred, her husband, didn't allow smoking in his car) and she didn't want to light up in what was so blatantly a smoke-free environment. It was painful to watch; I twisted in my seat so I wouldn't have to. Watch, that is.

After making the tea, Ed said he'd take my stuff up to my room.

'You don't have to, I'll do it later,' I'd said.

17

'It's no trouble,' Ed replied. 'I'm going upstairs anyway. Getting ready to go out later.'

'If you're sure . . .'

Ed shrugged his whole body. 'Course.'

'Thanks,' I said. 'I'll make you dinner one day as a thank you.'

'Yeah, she does a fantastic Pot Noodle,' Jessica chimed in.

I elbowed her, hard.

Despite his slender frame, Ed picked up the rucksack, suitcase and holdall effortlessly. We watched his progress up the stairs with admiration. He must've been muscle and bone, rather than skin and bone as he looked.

Jess hopped up on the sill of the left bay window the second he'd gone, swept back the net curtain and opened the window. One cigarette went down in frantic silence – with each puff she visibly relaxed. The second cigarette was smoked slower, she could even talk. And, 'I'm glad you've got a nice place,' she said. 'Ed seems all right. I hope you'll be happy here.' Most best-est friends in the whole world would've been reassuring, possibly offered a hug, not Jessica. She called it like she saw it, even if I was falling apart.

Those words sparked my anxieties again. 'Do you think I'm mad?' I asked urgently.

'In general, yes. In doing this, no.' Jess's eyes studied me, her cigarette burning away as she hung it out the window. 'Well it's too bloody late to have doubts now, isn't it? You've chucked it all in down south and made a commitment up here.' (Most best-est friends in the whole world would've been reassuring, possibly offered a hug, not Jessica. She called it like she saw it, even if I was falling apart.)

I nodded in understanding. She was right of course. It really was too late. Sudden, violent nausea surged through my veins. Every heartbeat made me feel sicker. Less sure of what I'd done. Sure, it was all sane and rational and 'woo-hoo, life affirming' in theory. Even on paper. In reality, I'd jacked in a life. My job was gone. My flat was rented out. My friends had thrown me a leaving do. Most people, when they had a life crisis, bleached their hair or shagged someone unsuitable. I jacked in a life and moved two hundred miles.

I chewed on my inner cheek and stared beyond Jess. It really was too late now.

'When I finish this,' Jess said, nodding at her cigarette, 'we'll go get you some food in Morrison's in town and then, if you're very good, I'll buy you a video recorder as a welcome home pressie.'

This was how Jess was supportive. Platitudes and empty reassurances in times of need weren't her thing; acts of true love – like buying me a video – were.

'Don't grin too soon D'Altroy, a video's no good without a telly.'

chapter three

Thou Shalt Not . . .

Where the hell am I?

I know I'm in a college. But, beyond that, I'm lost.

I was stood at the bottom of a winding stone staircase with wooden handrails, wondering if I should go up it or stay where I was, stuck in that first day at school nightmare where I don't know where I'm going and don't know anybody. I'd had that nightmare quite a lot over the weekend because it was my first day back at school, kind of. Except I'd be lecturing as well as learning. But still, I'd had the same dream over and over. I was wearing my hideous blue school uniform and I couldn't find out where I needed to be. When I eventually got there, all the students were older than me and laughed at me because I was wearing a school uniform. It didn't take a psychologist to work it out. I was scared. On every level of consciousness I was scared. And now the nightmare was coming true. I couldn't find where I needed to be.

I glanced around me, wondering how to get help. It probably had something to do with initiating eye contact.

All Souls University College, the institution who'd agreed to employ me for a year of teaching and researching, was only small. So small it'd been merely affiliated to Leeds

University for years and years and had only become a college of the University in the last two years. There was a distinction between being a college affiliated to the University and being an actual college of the University, and that distinction was probably something to do with money. Most things were something to do with money. All Souls was a picturesque little college in its own way, surrounded by green playing fields. Most of it was sandstone-coloured because it'd been built during the sixties and that was the colour that was *en vogue* then. It was small. There were, what, 3000 students here? Small, intimate, part of the reason I'd applied here. Not as many people, not such a big pond to be a small fish in.

So why was I being belittled and looked down upon by the architecture?

I glanced up. The ceilings were so high, they were almost sky level. I took a peek at the ground. The parquet floors were made from king-size blocks, the windows went on for ever.

Scariest and biggest of all, though, were the students. I *wasn't that big when I was a student*, I thought as I side-stepped a gaggle of undergraduates. Most of them had been born in 1981 for goodness' sake, how could they be so huge? Was there some Thatcherite plot to make the voters of the future so big and brainwashed they'd scare off anyone who didn't think like she did? (I always knew that woman planned to stay in power for ever – Dr Evil was slightly naughty compared to her.) Were those hormones pumped into meat to make cows bigger and yield more meat, finally being shown in the youf of today? Or, horror of horrors, was I actually shrinking? Was I now shorter than the five foot four-and-a-bit, I'd left the house as this morning? Was it finally happening? My nightmare. The only age-related thing I was truly, TRULY frightened of. Getting shor—

'You look lost,' a male voice said behind me.

I spun to him. He had kind eyes and a soft face. He was wearing a white, long-sleeved T-shirt and blue Levi's. Most importantly, he wasn't as giant as everyone else. He was a lecturer.

'Yes! Yes, yes, I am.' *Could you please try to sound more desperate there, Ceri, he is after all the Pope and he did just ask you if you wanted sex before marriage sanctioned by the Catholic Church.* I cleared my throat. 'I mean, a little.'

'I'm Mel,' he said, 'I'm a sociology lecturer. You're about to start work in the psychology department, aren't you? I remember you being shown around last month.'

I nodded. 'That's me.'

'What's your name?' he asked and smiled. He had good teeth: white, straight, brushed and flossed twice a day. He was probably on first name terms with his dentist.

'Ceri. Ceri D'Altroy.'

'OK Ceri, where do you want to be?'

At home, in London, watching *Trisha*, eating bananas on toast in bed. 'The place where the secretaries are.'

'The department office?' he said.

That'll be it. 'Er, yeah. Just forgot the name of it for a second.'

Mel laughed, he thought I was joking. I was so scared, so panicked, I barely remembered my own name.

'It's this way.' He started up the stairs.

The canteen was, like everything else in this college, huge. Long, with regulation parquet floors and round tables with room for eight (maybe ten people, if everyone ate with their elbows tucked in). The right wall was floor to ceiling glass, giving you an unhindered view of the various halls of residence that were dotted around the campus. All the halls of residence looked like slightly narrower and shorter versions of sixties tower blocks, they were the same colour, probably designed by the same architect. As you entered the canteen through big wooden swing doors, you headed left for the service line: a long counter with glass protecting us from the food; behind it stood women and men in white kitchen overalls and white net caps ready to dish up.

I ordered fisherman's pie with a double side order of peas and a bottle of water. I paid, stepped away from the cashier, then went into new girl free fall. I was all alone here.

The canteen instantly doubled in size. Then tripled. Then tripled again. It went on tripling in length and width until the far wall was nothing but a blip on the very distant horizon. I was suddenly the smallest girl in the world standing in the biggest room in the world.

I'd just come from the longest, most tedious briefing in the history of job briefings, there was nothing in my job description I didn't now know. The horror of it was going to live for ever in my mind. I did not need to eat by myself on top of that.

The room buzzed with chatter and eating and drinking and cutlery hitting crockery. And bonding. I couldn't see anyone sat alone. My footsteps would probably echo and echo and echo as I headed for a solitary table. Everyone would make 'look at saddo' eyes at each other about me as I took up a seat alone and ate alone. Gwen, the head of department, had sent me off to lunch on my tod, saying, 'I have lots of important things to do. I've scheduled your meetings with the three other lecturers you'll be working with for later this afternoon. Bye.' It didn't occur to her that me being new, this being my first day, I'd need someone to lunch with. Or, failing that, directions to the canteen.

Across the canteen, someone waved, and the room

23

returned to normal size. I wasn't wearing my glasses so I couldn't tell who it was from their face. They were a blue and white fuzz amongst the general colours and shapes in the canteen. Maybe they weren't waving at me at all. The room swelled again. I glanced over my shoulder, no one but the cashier behind me and she had her back to the waver. I peered forward, craning my neck and narrowing my eyes; the shape seemed familiar, as were the clothes. A white, long-sleeved top and blue jeans. Mel? He got up, beckoned, pointed to the plastic orange seat opposite him. My body sagged with relief. *Thank you, God! I will try very hard to get to church some time very soon.*

'Hi,' he said as I approached.

'Hi,' I grinned. Mel probably thought I spent my entire life in a constant state of relief and desperation.

'This is Claudine,' Mel said, indicating to the serene woman on his right. She was make-you-jealous gorgeous. Cropped, raven-black hair, Mediterranean skin, plump lips. This woman, this Claudine, had eyes that actually smouldered as she looked at you. 'Claudine, this is Ceri, she's the new person I was telling you about.'

Claudine's face broke into a friendly grin. 'Hi ya,' she said, 'how's it going?'

'Not bad, so far,' I said and reached for my fork – only to find it wasn't there. No cutlery. Great. I'd have to do the walk of shame back to the cashier. I'd feel a 24ct fool, sidling up to her, smiling, nicking a fork then running away again. Those were moments I had nightmares about. I'd already relived a million and one times flailing about with another woman on Leeds station concourse. Each reliving brought a new and deeper horror. Sophistication was all about *not* doing those sorts of things. Bet women like Claudine didn't do those things.

24

'Here,' Mel said, giving me the second fork on his tray. 'I got this for Clau, cos she always forgets her cutlery, but for the first time ever, she remembered.'

Claudine rolled her smouldery eyes. 'Just give her the damn fork Melvin. All Ceri needs to know is that it's clean, and your lips haven't been anywhere near it.'

'Thanks,' I said, taking the fork, digging into the creamy sauce, hitting the white flesh of the fish with gusto. I was hungry. The kind of hunger that came from being so nervous I couldn't eat on Sunday and I couldn't even force water down my neck this morning.

'What's your PhD on?' Claudine asked after they'd watched me wolf down a couple of mouthfuls. I was that hungry the food didn't even touch the sides.

I swallowed a full mouthful, not wanting to talk with my mouth full – I was well brought up like that. In fact, I was constantly horrified that people sat happily chewing away while telling you some convoluted tale. 'I'm not actually doing a PhD,' I said to Claudine. 'I'm not technically studying either. I'm doing a year's research in the psychology department. I've had this idea in my head for years and I'm actually following it up. I'll also be lecturing first year, a bit of second year psychology, and taking tutorials. If it works out, I might be allowed to apply for a PhD course, though.'

'I didn't realise All Souls did that,' Claudine replied.

'They don't, usually. I happened to write to them about it around the same time that woman from the psychology department left.'

Claudine turned to Mel, 'Is that Eva?'

Mel nodded.

'Yeah, I think her name was Eva. They were desperate cos she left so late in the year,' I continued. 'I've taken over most of her teaching duties, well, I will be from tomorrow.'

'I guess from your accent you're from London?' Claudine asked.

I nodded. 'Although I did my first degree up here in Leeds. I lived up here for five years altogether.'

'Do you lecture in London?' Mel asked.

I shook my head. Braced myself to tell them what I did. 'No. I'm . . . I was . . . I am, I suppose, a journalist.'

I was terrified of not sounding qualified or experienced enough for my current teaching position. Journalist to psychology lecturer did not sound experienced or qualified a leap. Even I wasn't convinced about the leap and that leaping was being done by me.

'I've got a masters in journalism, I did that in London, and I have taught and lectured in psychology,' I added quickly. 'I mean, I taught psychology A-level for a bit before I went back to London, and I did a bit of psychology lecturing in London, on the subject I'm researching. I also lectured a bit in journalism. You se—'

'Whoa, calm down,' Mel said.

'This isn't an interview,' Claudine finished.

I relaxed against the uncomfortable orange seat, an interview was exactly how this felt. How everything felt. A gigantic test. Because I couldn't help thinking there'd been some kind of mistake. I'd written to the college on spec, on the off chance that they had an opening in the psychology department for someone who wasn't very experienced but who could take seminars while doing research. And All Souls took me seriously. Suddenly they were inviting me to an interview, then another interview, then a written test. Then a test lecture followed by another interview and, WHAM-BAM! I'd got this made-up position. My sister wouldn't trust me with her goldfish when she went on holiday, and this college was entrusting some ninety or so formative minds to me. How was that going to work?

'Do you two always have lunch together?' I asked them to deflect the attention firmly away from me.

Claudine and Mel looked at each other, then returned their joint gaze to me. 'Yeah, pretty much,' they said together.

Awww, bless. I got a kick out of seeing couples in love. It gave me hope: if other people could find that sort of closeness, then so could I. It could be done, so I could do it. Besides, the bitter, twisted jealous route had got me a bad rep and wrinkles.

'That's really good that you two can work together and lunch together every day and not have it damage your relationship. How long have you been going out?'

'Sorry?' Claudine replied.

'Excuse me?' Mel asked.

'You two, how long have you been going out together?' I repeated.

Silence hacked into the good humour like a machete into plywood.

Oh, good God. I've done it again.

I was infamous for wading into situations, mouth first. I tried not to, I just couldn't help myself. A question formed in my head, it came out of my mouth a microsecond later. There was no time for the thought to drop by the 'how's that going to sound out loud?' centre of my brain, in fact, it bolted right past it, wearing a disguise so good no one recognised it.

It was my total lack of fear in asking the questions other people pussyfooted around that made me a good journalist. And a nightmare dinner party guest. I'd once asked someone across a dinner table, 'So, did you finally end your four-year celibacy with that blind date last weekend?' Everyone else was thinking it, I'd said it. Silence was the reply, then, too.

I stopped eating as the current silence lengthened. I couldn't fit any more food into my mouth anyway, what with there being a size eight trainer rammed in my gob.

27

'I live with my boyfriend, Kevin,' only thin veins of ice laced Claudine's previously warm voice. 'Have done for two years.'

Mel's tone had evened out as he said: 'I'm not seeing anyone special.'

But, but . . . I looked from her face to his face to her face . . . two seconds with them and you knew, you just knew they were together, emotionally linked, *COUPLED*, dammit. It radiated from them like heat from a flame. Their emotion, their adoration, their affection, their attraction. Felt and reciprocated.

'Oh, sorry, I was doing that thing again,' I launched myself into an apology. 'You know that perception thing?' Blank faces greeted me. 'There's this theory in psychology about perception and how people often fill in the missing information in stuff like pictures and sentences with what they expect to be there. That's what I was doing, filling in the missing information with something, anything, the first thing that came to mind. Sorry.'

They both looked at me.

NOOOOOOOO! Not The Look. Not The Silence. If you've messed up, and are trying to explain, the worst thing – other than being told you've disappointed someone – is to get The Look back. Hostility, disgust and hurt all balled up in one expression. Coupled with The Silence, it's unbearable.

I could now either shut up and let The Silence take its course, or keep talking until my voice ran dry/someone told me to shut up.

I'm not good at silences.

'Thing is, at our age, I kind of expect most people to be coupled up,' I explained. 'That's not to say that everyone should be coupled, I just expect them to be. Even though I'm

28

not. And when I see two people getting on so well, I kind of . . . That's not to mean . . . Just cos you're friendly with someone you're automatically going out together, I suppose I wasn't thinking and it j—'

'It's all right,' Mel said, or maybe it was Claudine. Who could tell the difference?

'We get that sort of thing all the time,' Claudine said.

'Yeah, most people just hint at it though,' Mel added.

'No one has actually come out and said it before,' Claudine continued.

'Not directly,' Mel finished.

See? *SEE?!* They didn't simply finish each other's sentences, they knew what the other one was thinking; they actually voiced each other's train of thought. That's not normal. That's not 'living with a boyfriend for two years'; that's not 'seeing no one special'. That's, 'I'm involved with the person I'm sitting next to'.

'Sorry, I'm a bit too direct. People tell me I'm like Cordelia, you know, from *Buffy The Vampire Slayer*? I think something, I say it, people look at me like they want to rip the tongue right out of my head. Sorry.'

I started shovelling food into my grand canyon of a mouth, then swallowed. I didn't see the need for chewing. I wanted to get away as quickly as possible.

Part of the reason I'd run away from London was so I could stop spreading my foot in mouth disease. I could reinvent myself. Be quiet, demure, sophisticated and – most importantly – not get involved.

I'd even sat on the train and formulated my own Commandments. (No offence whatsoever to God was meant. I knew I couldn't come up with a set of Commandments to rival His, but I needed something to work towards.) They went something like this:

1. Thou shalt sort out thy cardiovascular system
2. Thou shalt NOT get involved in other people's lives
3. Even if they're really, really nice thou shalt remember Commandment 2
4. Thou shalt think before thy speaks
5. Thou shalt think again before thy speaks
6. Thou shalt watch less *Angel*
7. Thou shalt remember that Angel is a 250-year-old vampire who dated Buffy The Vampire Slayer, not the man you're going to be with for ever and ever.

Simple. No? Easy. No? And I've broken two of them within, oooh, four hours. A personal best.

When my throat was definitely taking no more lodgers, I put down the fork and swallowed hard to get rid of the food lump so I could speak.

'Anyway, I'd better get going, I've got to meet another lecturer and find out what I'll be doing for them.' *In an hour and a half.*

I put my hands on either side of my tray, stood. 'I'll see you both around?' I knew I sounded desperate, but I couldn't help it, I thought I'd managed to get myself some friends then. Nothing major, just a couple of people to sit with in the canteen, extend my social circle in college to two.

'Yeah, course,' Mel said.

'When you're assigned an office, I'll come over and we can have a coffee, if you want,' Claudine said.

'Great, I'll see you soon.'

Yeah, yeah, I'll be lucky if I see either of you again.

spring term

(and it was 'term', dammit. No one is going to make me call it a semester)

chapter four

Dress Rehearsal

'I really don't know why you've asked me to come here,' Jess said, from the comfort of my bed. She was supposedly helping me to choose what to wear for my first lecture tomorrow morning, but in reality, she was under the covers watching *Coronation Street* while I paced the length of my room – of which there was quite a lot – and fretted about my first day as lecturer proper.

Me. Ceri D'Altroy, a lecturer.

The very thought made my stomach turn and twist like a wind chime in a strong breeze.

This had all been fantastic in theory. Y'know, like the heart's desire thing, I wanted to do it when it was an idea I'd scrawled down on a piece of paper under the heading 'goals'.

I'd always quite liked the idea of being an academic. That was why I'd applied for a PhD all those years ago. I wanted to carry on learning while helping with the teaching process. I liked lecturing, enjoyed the power it gave me. You stand up there, in front of people, you tell them what you know, they interject with their theories and together you helped to build a new theory, a new understanding.

I'd been seduced by that idea; of having that power all the

time. Even though over the years, Jess had told me that students had changed. 'They don't have a thirst for learning like they did when you were a student,' she said. 'They're more interested in what they need to know for the exams than in expanding their minds.' I suppose that was part of why I wanted to do this as well. I wanted to see if I could help turn back the tide. Stop students being simply fixated on the exams. When I was a student, we – rather sadly some might say – used to look forward to certain lectures when we could debate stuff. Like in Jess's lectures, the philosophy of psychology. There was so much to think and talk about we'd often overrun. Or we'd stop at the end, go get coffees, come back and debate some more. I wanted that with my students. I wanted them to be so into my lectures they didn't mind if they overran.

Of course, with this lecturing lark, it didn't hurt that I'd get to talk, too. I loved talking. Not speaking, *per se*. I loved to think out loud at someone, to formulate theories and ideas and self-invectives through communicating with other people. I loved listening and having that spark of understanding or that flame of indignation lit in my head. So, on top of continuing to research what had, over the years, become my specialist subject, this was my idea of a dream job.

I just had no idea what to wear.

'I asked you here because I needed a second opinion on what to wear tomorrow. I can't very well ask Jake or Ed, I've only lived with them for three days, they'll think I'm mad. So, you'll do.' Jess had planned to spend the evening with her husband and daughters, and had got quite far into that plan, which meant when she'd turned up at my place she'd been shrouded in her mac and Wellington boots. Underneath them she was wearing the grey fleece pyjamas I'd bought her last Christmas – they matched mine. She'd got straight into my bed and put on *Emmerdale*.

Jess's eyebrow arched up and her head creaked round to face me. 'Oh will I now, D'Altroy?'

'Yes.' Her expressive eyebrows didn't scare me. Much.

'What I meant was, I don't know why you asked me over for this. We all know what you're going to wear.'

I stopped pacing. 'Do we?'

Jess flung back the covers in a move born of frustration, got out of bed and marched across to the large oak wardrobe, threw open the wardrobe doors. 'OK, let's see what's in here, shall we.' She reached into the wardrobe's depths, pulled out an item of clothing on a hanger. 'What's this?' she said, raising the hanger so I could see it.

'My white long-sleeved top.'

Jess flung it onto the floor – the bed was too far away for her to hit it. She reached into the wardrobe again. 'And what's this?'

'My red long-sleeved top.'

'Hm-hm.'

That went on to the floor too.

'And this?'

'My white v-neck top,' I said, testily.

'But what has it got?'

'Long sleeves.'

'Right.' On to the floor.

'And what about this?'

'My grey top.'

'Does it by any chance have long sleeves?' Jess said, sarcastically. 'Oh, look, yes it does, now there's a surprise.'

She reached into the wardrobe again, pulled out another top. 'Tell me Ceri,' Jess said, turning to me, 'do you see a theme developing?'

'Maybe,' I said, petulantly.

'Far be it for me to criticise, but you'd think a person starting a new life would start off with a new wardrobe too.'

35

'Oh yeah, says Mrs "I've Been Wearing The Same Clothes Since I Was Twenty". What was that, fifteen, twenty years ago?'

Jess, surprisingly, laughed. Surprisingly because usually she'd throw something at me. 'Ah, but you see, I haven't spent however many years working on fashion magazines. You'd think some of it would've rubbed off.'

'Whatever,' I said, flopping my arms around. 'I still need help deciding.'

'I understand, no, really I do. Should I wear the round-neck long-sleeved top or the v-neck long-sleeved top? Those decisions will keep a girl up all night.'

'Do you want some chocolate cheesecake or not?' I replied.

'Ceri, it doesn't matter what you wear,' Jess said. Ever the mum, she started picking up the tops she'd dropped on the floor. 'I mean, when I was lecturing you, did you ever notice what I was wearing?'

I thought about it. I didn't remember now what she used to wear. And I can't remember at any point thinking, *Wow, she should* not *be wearing* that. 'Suppose not.'

'My rule of thumb for dressing for lectures has been,' she went back to my bed and got in, taking custody of the remote controls again, 'to wear what makes you comfortable. Cos people will notice if you're fiddling with your waistband or bra strap.'

'But do you think they'll have a problem with the fact none of my tops ever cover the waistband of my trousers and that there's always this strip of midriff showing?'

'No, sweetie, I don't think they'll be sat there going, "Who cares what Piaget said, look at that midriff on her".'

I went to my wardrobe, opened the door, took out my favourite long-sleeved top, the white one with a slightly plunging v-neck. 'I think I'll wear this one with my dark blue jeans,' I said, decisively.

'Good, you look lovely in it,' Jess replied, without looking away from *Corrie*.

'Trainers or shoes?'

'Shoes.'

'Why?'

'Because you're going to wear your trainers anyway.'

'Funny.'

Jess deigned to tear her attention away from *Corrie* and rested it on me. 'I'll tell you what you should wear, though.'

'What?' I glanced anxiously at the open wardrobe.

'Your bloody glasses, you vain madam. You won't be very authoritative if you're squinting at everyone.'

'We do not talk about them,' I hissed. 'They do not exist and we do not talk about them. Ever.'

'OK, Mrs Magoo.'

'Grrr . . .'

Jess was right about one thing, I didn't really need help in deciding what to wear, I'd hauled her over here from Horsforth because I needed company. Someone to fret at. I didn't know Jake and Ed well enough to unravel in front of them. And it didn't work down the phone, so that ruled out most of my London friends. The only person it could be was Jess. She knew that, which was why she came, I guess. She was my surrogate boyfriend in such situations. It had to be said, I wasn't usually the fret out loud type. I was the gnaw on my fingers, stare into space, sometimes scrawl out a list type.

But then, I'd never taken such a huge leap of faith before.

Whenever I'd started a new job before, it'd always had an element of sheer terror because I'd always moved upwards on the career ladder: first from junior sub-editor to sub-editor, then to senior sub-editor, then to chief sub-editor and then, finally, to contributing features editor. My career jumps had always been into a position I wasn't sure I could handle. Naturally, I'd lie awake panicking about being sacked; being 'found out'. In comparison to this, what I'd felt then was a mere smidgen of terror. A small quantity of fear that could be beaten into submission by ordering a desk tidy and sending my first email. With this lecturing lark, a desk tidy wasn't going to cut it.

What did I think I was doing?

This was just one idea on a page. I'd written down what I wanted to do on a piece of paper, as per instruction in one of my self-help/follow your dreams/Oprah books. *Write down all your dreams. If you could do anything, what would it be? Go on, write it down. Even if it's ridiculous, write it down. No one else will ever see it, so what's the harm if you put it down on a piece of paper?*

What's the harm? I'll tell you the harm. Once it's in blue and white, once it's written down, it seems possible. Not quite so ridiculous. Not quite so airy-fairy. And, once something seems even remotely possible, it starts to grow. Like a baby growing inside you, your idea – your dream – grows, takes from you, feeds off you, gathering strength, slowly but surely becoming part of you until it's ready to be born. To become something tangible in its own right. Then, without realising it, nothing else seems as exciting or important or worthy. Everything you do comes back to your dream. Comes back to whether your current life is helping to feed, nurture and strengthen your dream. Next thing you know, you're pacing the floor of your bedroom fretting about giving your first lecture. Me, lecturing. For real. Full-time. Well, seventy-five per cent of the time, but full-time in the sense of what my title was and what I was paid to do.

'If you don't stop wringing your hands you'll have no skin left on them,' Jess commented.

I glanced down, my hands were twisting and twisting themselves together as I paced the floor. I hadn't even noticed.

I went over, climbed into bed with Jess and pretended to watch *Corrie*.

'We'd better not move about too much,' Jess said. 'Ed and Jake will think we're having some kind of love tryst.'

'I should be so lucky,' I said. It'd been a while since I'd had sex.

'You would, to get me.'

'Ha-ha, ha-ha, ha-ha.'

'You would be lucky to get me. Haven't you heard how hard it was for Fred to convince me to go out with him?'

'Yeah. He said "hello", you were his.'

'You're a cheeky cow, D'Altroy,' Jess laughed.

I slid out of bed again. I couldn't settle. My insides were in flight, my mind was in flight, my body needed to be in constant motion too. I started to pace the floor of my bedroom again. I was lucky, this bedroom seemed to have been constructed for fretful pacing.

'I feel like I've made the biggest mistake of my life,' I admitted suddenly.

'Bigger than moving in with Whashisface Tosspot?' (We never spoke the name of the man I lived with for a year, because that would be asking for him to get in touch. That would be like standing in front of a mirror and saying 'Candyman' three times when you're the star of a film called *Candyman*. In other words, that was asking for the unholy to blight your life again. Or, in even fewer words: that was looking for trouble.)

'Yes, even bigger than that catastrophe.'

I met Whashisface Tosspot when I was doing my journalism masters in London. We were together for two years and I spent most of the time wondering why I was with him. I moved in with him at the end of college, when we'd both been looking for somewhere to live and he suggested we get a place together. I'm still convinced he used some kind of Jedi Mind Trick on me because I'd stood there, looking at him, thinking, '*You what?! Move in with you? We are so not on the same page, are we?*' but 'All right then' came out of my mouth.

Jess had laughed when I told her he'd asked me to move in with him. When I told her I'd said yes, she'd hung up on me. She'd previously spent the better part of a month coaching me into dumping him, and that night was the night I was supposed to do the deed. The night I was supposed to rid my life – and therefore Jess's life – of him for ever. Instead, I came away, having agreed to live with him. Having, basically, further ensconced him in our lives.

'At least when I realised he was Prince Of The Undead I got out . . .' I said to Jess.

'Eventually,' Jess cut in. 'Very, *very* eventually.'

'Yes, all right, eventually. But the point is, at the time I didn't know it was a mistake. Not really. I kind of thought I was doing the right thing. At least I convinced myself I was doing the right thing. With this . . .' My voice trailed away as terror took over again.

'With this, you're feeling lost. And that's only natural. But look at what your life was like before. Remember how unhappy you were? Almost everyone you met or talked to wanted you to sort their lives out; all those dramas you were involved with. I couldn't believe half of them and as you know, I watch all the soaps. You couldn't untangle yourself from all those lives. But you can start again here, can't you?'

Jess was right on that score. I had managed to embroil myself in the most ridiculous dramas when I was down in London. None of them were mine, though. Not one of them. When most people heard I was leaving, they'd gone into shock. Not because they'd miss me but . . . well, put it this way, when I went to resign, my boss had paled, she'd lost all her natural colouring and her whole face had become a study in horror. In fact, she'd reminded me of that hideous picture, *The Scream*, but with more hair. She'd stared at me from across her desk, her thin but muscular face contracting and convulsing as she struggled to speak. 'I thought we were friends,' she'd finally managed in a shocked whisper.

'I just can't do this job any more,' I'd replied, neatly avoiding the 'friends' issue. 'I'm sorry. It's nothing personal.'

'Couldn't you have come to me before? Talked to me? I thought we were friends.'

Just because I know that your husband has to call you 'Mummy' before he can have sex, and just because I know you had a fling with your husband's sister, doesn't actually *mean we're friends. It simply means I know too much about you. You and the rest of this office. In fact, the rest of this city,* I thought darkly. And that was how it was. Somehow, some way, I'd become the person everyone came to tell their secrets to. People would often sidle up to my desk, say, 'Ceri, can I have a word?' in a desperate manner and my heart would skip a beat. Initially, I'd thought something big and bad had happened. When I realised this was rarely the case, my heart would still skip a beat because it might well be the one time when something hideous was wrong. I'd get up from my seat, follow them to the smoking area outside the building with my heart racing in my chest. 'What's up?' I'd say.

They'd launch into some tirade that they'd been too chicken to direct at the cause of their rage. I'd listen, nod, go, 'Ah, right,' in the required places, then when they finished I'd follow them back to the office, knowing that *they* felt better for having got that off their chest but being none the wiser as to what it was all about. I was Sounding Board/Vent

Your Spleen At/Share Your Secrets With Woman and I'd been looking to shed that persona when I started following my heart's desire. I didn't want to do that any more. I had to get my own life. In fact, I had to get a life. Hence the Commandments. All right, so I'd broken a couple of them with Claudine and Mel, but that could be rectified, all I had to do was not get involved.

'I suppose,' I mumbled, in response to Jess's comment cum question about how I could start again up here.

'Ceri, you're a natural control freak so it's equally natural that doing something you've not really done before is going to unsettle you. Or freak you out.'

I started making the eeey-orr sound of a woman hyperventilating.

'But, but,' Jess added quickly, 'so many people spend their lives wishing and wondering, "What would it be like to live my dream?" You've done it. You're doing it. That takes a particular type of courage. You wouldn't believe how many people wish they had your type of strength. Or could get out of their rut and take that chance.

'But the thing about you most people would love to have is your ability to appreciate chocolate as much as me. Speaking of which, didn't you lure me over here with the promise of chocolate cheesecake?'

I stopped in my floor-pacing tracks. *Oops.* 'Now there's a funny thing about that. You'll laugh. You'll really laugh . . . Jess, put down that remote control . . .'

'You will be all right, you know,' Jess said later. She was back in her Wellingtons and mac, Fred was waiting outside in the car with the engine running. 'There's only one thing you really need to remember tomorrow and every day after that.'

'And what's that?'

42

'The students don't know that you don't know everything so, if they ask you a question you can't answer, just bullshit. That's how I got through my first year of teaching.'

She hugged me and left.

chapter five

Life Orgasm

Elephants stampeded across my stomach as I walked around before the lecture started, leaving four-page handouts on the desks. To say I was nervous was like saying Madonna is a bit of a pop star. Things hadn't got better in the time that had elapsed between Jess leaving last night and this morning. If anything, I'd got worse. I'd started to have wild nightmare-like fantasies and vivid visions about what would go wrong. Which was one of the reasons I was putting handouts on the desks before the lecture.

Most lecturers dispense handouts as the lecture progresses, but I'd already seen the potential pitfalls. Literally.

Scenario One: I pick up the pile of handouts, ready to give it to one student for them to pass on, I trip, I fall and find myself lying face down in a pool of paper.

Scenario Two: I ask the students to come up and get them, there's a stampede, someone knocks over my drink – necessary so my tongue doesn't Velcro itself to the roof of my mouth – and all my overhead projections are ruined.

Scenario Three—Anyway, there were quite a few scenarios. I'd actually forgotten how vivid my imagination was. I'd begun to think it'd been blunted over time, taken up as it was with visualising Cupid sorting it out so me and Angel could end up together. But no, when I was in need of truly nightmarish scenarios, there was a rich vein of horror just waiting to be let.

I was putting out handouts in a room that was situated at the top of a building right in the middle of the All Souls campus. This block was an octagonal with a paved over quad at its centre where students lurked and lunched. The room I was to teach in wasn't huge, not as huge as I'd expect after yesterday's foray into the land of the giants. Light streamed in from the arched-top windows, leaving pools of light around the room. The ceiling was quite low, surprising considering the windows. The floor was still parquet, scuffed slightly, obviously well-trodden ground with bits more scuffed than others.

The forty or so chairs with little desks attached to one side were set out in a kind of arc. Behind me hung a white board which I had to bring my own non-permanent markers for. Above and behind the chairs was a wall to wall two-way mirror because this room doubled as a psychology lab and next door was an observation room. Thankfully, there was a heavyweight blue curtain that could be drawn across the mirror so I wouldn't have to worry about looking at myself for two hours or there being someone else observing me lecture for two hours.

I sat on the edge of my desk. Just stopped. For a second, stopped. Took time to breathe. To breathe and think about what I was doing. What was to come.

And it happened. Total peace descended upon me. At the very core of my soul, a celestial being touched me and I felt peace. I was peace. Pure peace. Suddenly I was flooded with power and joy and happiness. All I'd yearned for when I'd accepted this job. I was complete. Whole. This was it. I was there, on the brink of it. On the brink of a life orgasm. I'd only ever felt this sense of pureness when I'd orgasmed. Right in the middle of an orgasm, you are nothing but pure emotion. Nothing else exists except that one moment of sheer, unadulterated bliss; when your body and mind give themselves up to immaculate pleasure. That's what I'd been chasing when I gave up my life in London. For that moment, sat on the desk, I felt it. How life was meant to be. How life could be if I carried on with this.

The first student arrived five minutes before the lecture was due to start. Tall, malnourished thin, long greasy hair, wearing a baggy jumper. He was the type of guy you'd expect to come in last to the lecture, but no, he came wandering in, nodded a hello at me then sat himself at the back of the class.

Next came a girl who was very money. Chatting on a chrome phone, dark brown hair cut with very expensive scissors, the kind of clothes I used to see all the time on the pages of the pricier magazines I worked for. She smiled at me, but wasn't going to finish her conversation until the lecture started. A chunky lad came next, Scouse, again with long hair, surrounded by a gaggle of good-looking women, all of them laughing at something he'd obviously just said. He grinned at me as he walked over to the far corner of the room, sat himself under the large window, and the women sat at other seats around the room.

More of them poured through the open gash of the door: a blonde with a tight perm; an older woman with short blonde hair and petite body; an older man who had 'pervert' scrawled across his scraggly beard; another older man who had 'narrow-minded Thatcher lover' written in his eyes; a woman with black plaits right down to her bum; a man who put me in mind of a Wham-era George Michael, more and more until the room was full with about forty students.

I put on a charming, welcoming smile for them all. Hoping

46

I looked confident, a natural, as if I'd been doing this for millennia.

OH SHITE! my brain screeched.

I'd lectured before, but that had been on the understanding I wouldn't see those people again. I'd be like hundreds of guest lecturers they'd encounter in their lives: transitional, flibberti-gibbety. Nothing more than the sum of notes on the page, a voice on a tape recorder, a name in a handbook. It was like a one-night stand. You tried to enjoy it while you were there, but you could be someone else, flamboyant, tarty, even dominant because you'd never see them again. It didn't matter how you behaved because it was only ever going to be for a few hours. Whereas I'd be expected to bond with this lot. I had to leave my phone number, answer their calls, reveal more and more of who I was. Form some kind of lasting relationship with them over the coming year.

I was about to be found out as the fraud I was. I didn't know jack about anything and I'd sure as anything couldn't impart it, ensure it entered other people's minds and stayed there long enough for them to write about it in essays and exams. I was going to be publicly ridiculed. Laughed and pointed at in the street. Tarred and feathered, branded a liar and cheat then sent packing through the streets of Leeds with my rucksack on my back.

OK D'Altroy, back away from that panic. Calm down. If you don't calm down you'll start getting sweat patches all over your lovely white top and then it'll be see-through. They'll all be able to see your bra . . .

OH MY GOD, WHAT THE HELL HAVE I DONE!

I should be sat in London, reading about make-up, I thought. This thought was swiftly followed by *Run away! Very fast. Just leave everything where it is and leg it.*

I smiled at each and every one of them, waiting until almost all the seats were occupied. Most of them talked with each other until a natural hush, then a silence fell upon the room.

Ms Money flipped shut her phone.

OH MY GOOD GOD.

All right, smile. Smile, goddamn you. Now open your mouth, say: 'Hi.'

Expectant faces gazed upon me as though I was about to impart the meaning of life, the universe and everything. That I was going to explain it wasn't, in fact, forty-two, but ninety-eight – and I had proof. Or maybe they thought I was going to give them next week's lottery numbers. Whatever it was, each face was so expectant my voice dried up as I croaked, 'I'm Ceri. Ceri D'Altroy. It's written on th—'

The door slammed open, and 'I'm sooooo sorry,' a voice cried out from nowhere, as a woman hurried in. 'I'm so sorry I'm late. The bus didn't turn up. I ran all the way here from the bus stop.'

She rushed off to her seat across the room, no one blinked, she obviously did this all the time. I, meanwhile, having leapt in shock, leant with one hand on the desk, the other hand clutching my chest, and breathed like *I'd* been running.

The class weren't sure whether to laugh or be scared.

I laughed. Couldn't help myself when I'd tried so hard to get the lecturer look right and it all fell apart when someone made me jump. The room erupted into uneasy laughter with me, until we all relaxed into normal laughter.

OK, this is better. I can work with laughter. Didn't they always say you should start a presentation or speech with a joke? And you don't get much funnier than old lecturer lady having a coronary cos someone comes late. 'All right,' I said, feeling my body relax a fraction, 'as I was saying, I'm Ceri. Ceri D'Altroy. I'm taking over Eva's teaching for the rest of the year. I'll be teaching you the history of psychology as well as taking tutorials and doing all the other things that Eva did and I don't know about yet.

'On the sheets in front of you, I've written out a brief run-down of the modules as I see it. Before we get into a more detailed discussion about what you should have done as told to me by Gwen and what you've *actually* done, I wanted to get something clear.'

I took a deep breath. 'I'm here to help you learn. If you don't want to do the reading or prepare stuff for tutorials, that's fine with me. I'm not your parent or God, I can't make you do it. But, what you do or don't do will be reflected in your marks. And, to be very honest, I've got my degrees so feel free to piss about, make excuses, not do your work. I'm not open to bribes so it'll only hurt you in the end. I really hope, though, that you get into the learning stuff and if not enjoy it then at least understand the History of Psychology.'

This all sounded very cool and very laid-back, I'd fancied myself as a cross between Robin Williams in *Dead Poets' Society* and Miss Jean Brodie in her prime. Experienced, but 'down with the people'; friendly, but worthy of respect. Which was clearly why I delivered my speech with sweat trickling down my back, making the white v-neck top cling to me.

Thankfully, I'd stopped short of writing it down before prattling it off – *prat* probably being the operative part of that word – because I'd be triply sad if I had to read my cool and laid-back attitude to the class. An audience of faces gazed back at me. It was still to be seen if my speech had worked, but for now, no one looked as though they were about to leave. Which, when it came down to it, was the important thing.

chapter six

Ed's World

'Someone called for you,' Ed, my new flatmate, said, with only his head stuck around my bedroom door. His long blond hair hung like grease-sodden chips around his thin face, his eyes watched me like I was an alien species.

I'd been living here a week and was still becoming acclimatised to the houseshare experience, so spent a lot of time in my bedroom, reading, working on seminar stuff or watching TV. I didn't want to get in their way, what with being new girl in the house and all.

Ed and Jake, my two flatmates, seemed nice. From what I remember of being a flatmate, though, a week wasn't enough to tell. Most flatmates were fine, friendly and fun – until you borrowed a splash of their milk and suddenly you'd been bashed over the head and buried before you could say 'carpet that doesn't show bloodstains'.

I hadn't done the housesharing thing since I left Leeds, six years earlier. I'd lived with Whashisface Tosspot for a year when I was in London, but that was different, I felt at home there. It was 'our place'. When I bought my own place and our relationship finally ended, I'd had over two years of being able to walk around naked, if I so wished, and as it turned out,

I did so wish, quite often. I was no weirdo naturalist/naturist/flasher, it was simply easier to know I could roll out of bed and answer a call of nature or put on the kettle without scrabbling about for a dressing gown. Especially since I lived on the first floor and most of my windows were obscured by trees. That'd all changed the day I went to fill the kettle wearing only a pair of black knickers and a casual glance to my left, out of the six-foot sash window, had shocked me twice over.

Shock one: The creepy man who lived downstairs had cut down all the trees that obscured the view of my windows.

Shock two: A queue of people at the bus stop below were staring open-mouthed at my floppy tits and black tanga briefs.

I'd developed a closer relationship with my dressing gown after that.

Flashing the neighbourhood not withstanding, I enjoyed living alone. I could leave the bathroom door open to hear the stereo or TV when I was in the shower; I could talk to myself out loud all the time, and I didn't have to rely on other people to pass on my messages.

At the time of Ed's appearance with my message, I was curled up in bed, watching an episode of *Angel* on video.' (This, of course, meant drawing the curtains, putting on my side lights, changing into my pyjamas, surrounding myself with junk food and beer. Watching *Angel* was like taking part in a ritual. Ed was privileged, I was usually out to callers when it started.)

'Oh? Who?' I said to Ed, having pressed the mute button on the TV remote.

'A bloke. Dan? Um . . . Derek? Drew? Yeah, Drew. Said he'd call you back later or you should call him back when you'd stopped, er,' colour rose in Ed's cheeks, 'stopped, er, creaming yourself over, er, *Angel*.'

'The git!' I replied. Was too outraged to be embarrassed

51

by my outing by my so-called mate. Ed was obviously going to find out about the man in my life at some point, he wasn't meant to be told that said man only existed in the nineteen-inch world of my telly so soon into our living relationship.

'When did he call?' I asked Ed.

Ed coloured some more, his eyes shifted about. 'Um, this afternoon. Meant to, uh, write you a note but couldn't find a pen. Then I forgot. Sorry.'

'Don't worry about it. Come in,' I shifted up to make room on the bed for him to sit, 'if you want.'

Ed pushed open the door, came in, perched himself on the very edge of the bed, only a fraction of an inch of his butt was on the bed. Ed was doing a PhD in English at The Met and he was into heavy metal. His clothes suited his hair and his heavy metal reputation: dirty blue jeans, black T-shirt with a lurid, heavy metal band picture on the front. Over the top he wore a red and black lumberjack shirt. But, under the dirt and grease, under the clothes, he was the cutest boy. Young and untouched by life. It showed in his clear green eyes, his smooth skin and the contours of his face. He just needed a wash and blow-dry all over.

Ed glanced at my TV screen, smiled when he saw what I was watching. 'Is he your boyfriend? This Drew bloke,' Ed asked, refocusing on me.

'No,' I replied. 'Just an old mate. That's a mate I've known for a long time, not a mate who's old.'

I was rewarded with one of Ed's blank stares. They were a natural miracle: his clear green eyes would glaze over, his face would become flat as he stared at you. Maybe he was computing something behind that look or maybe he was wondering if he should make a run for it. 'Do you have a boyfriend?' he asked, coming out of his stare.

'No, I'm currently between relationships and boyfriends. What about you? Are you seeing someone?'

He nodded grimly. 'No.'

I inhaled deeply.

Ed was on the verge of confessing something deeply personal to me. He was going to do to me what people had done to me on buses, trains and in cafés and pubs for years: invite me into their world. Drag me into their life; their innermost secrets.

On one level, it was flattering, I was trustworthy enough to know people's secrets. But on almost every other level it was bizarre. Perfect strangers giving me flashes of their hearts. Telling me things they didn't even tell their best mates. It was also exhausting because I couldn't just listen, walk away. I had to listen, then I had to give my opinion, advise, *get involved*. Hence my Commandments. Hence walking around without making eye contact. It was easier all round to appear miserable and moody than to start getting involved.

At this point in the night, though, I was too tired to fight it. I had to go with it. Take one giant leap into Edness. And besides, he'd earned the use of my ear, by bringing my bags upstairs on the day I'd moved in. I'd just not get involved. Listen. No involvement. I could do that.

'Complicated is it?' I prompted.

'No. Not really. It's quite uncomplicated. I love her, she doesn't know I'm alive.'

Your typical stalker scenario, then.

'She's doing a drama MA at The Met too. Her name's Robyn. You might've seen her. She's been on telly and stuff, she's so beautiful.'

Definitely your typical stalker scenario, then.

'But it's more than that. She's so funny. I've spoken to her,

53

I've spoken to her loads. She's almost a friend. She's really nice, and clever, and interesting a—'

'You really don't have to justify your feeling for her to me. You like her, that's all that matters,' I interjected before he ran out of adjectives. For an English student his vocabulary was distinctly third rate.

Ed's whole persona relaxed. 'Most people I tell think she's just wank material cos she's so beautiful.'

'I believe you like her. But, can I just say, even if she was just wank material, that's OK too. Some of my best relationships have been based solely on physical attraction. That's how these things happen sometimes. Not that your thing with, er,' *shite, what was her name, what was her name,* 'Robyn! is like that.'

Ed, who now he'd unburdened his soul obviously felt more at ease with me and in my room, rested back on his elbows, turned his head upwards and stared wistfully at the ceiling. 'She's perfect.'

I wanted to say that no one is perfect; to label someone as perfect was to set yourself up for disappointment when the one fatal flaw in their character that proves them to be imperfect makes an appearance. One look at Ed's face was enough to tell me he didn't want to hear that. Most people didn't want to hear it. They'd much rather get their expectations up, then have them dashed.

'She reminds me of this line from a song, "I feel so lucky loving her, tell me what else is magic for?".'

He was quoting Robert Palmer. Ed, heavy metal Ed, was quoting Robert Palmer. I'd underestimated his feelings for this woman. No one reached for Robert Palmer lyrics unless they were more than knee-deep in the mire of love.

Without warning, my heart started to race. Really pound, hammering and hammering against my rib cage. The sound filled my ears and made me quiver slightly. This was what Ed was feeling for this Robyn one. The emotions he felt ran deep, that was obvious. Robert Palmer had been the first clue to how he was feeling. How he looked now, the expression on his face, was the next clue.

Beyond his limited vocabulary flowed unfathomable seas of emotion. She made him smile, inside and out. He wanted to make her laugh, he often thought of something and wanted to call her to tell her about it. Sometimes he'd lie on his bed, replaying their conversations, enjoying the fact that he'd spent time with her, not knowing that hours had passed while he lay there. She made his heart beat faster by just entering the room.

And his lust. She wasn't just wank material but . . .

Every cell in my body pulsated with his passion. I was suddenly, inexplicably turned on. I hadn't felt like this in a long time. Not even when I'd last had sex, it wasn't like this. Every part of me burnt with lust. A cold shower wasn't going to cure this. How Ed got through the day with all this pumping through him I didn't know. Watching *Angel* now would be a bad idea – I'd probably end up dry-humping the TV screen.

If anything, Ed was understating his feelings. Maybe he just didn't have the right words to explain how much he felt. Well, with me he didn't need to. Sitting next to him told me how he felt.

'So, she doesn't know you're alive, what are you going to do about it?' I asked.

Ed froze for a few seconds, then his head creaked around to face me. 'Do?!' He'd screwed up his face. '*Do?!*'

'Are you going to ask her out?'

'Don't think so,' he scoffed.

'Why not?'

'Erm, possibly because she goes out with actors and businessmen, she even went out with a duke once. Those are the kind of men she goes out with – famous, important men, not people like me.'

My legs ached from sitting cross-legged. I prised my lower limbs apart, stood up a little shakily because they weren't used to being contorted like that and shook them out to get the blood circulating again. 'How do you know she doesn't go out with people like you if you've never asked her out?' I asked Ed.

'I just do,' he said with the conviction of a man who knew someone was totally out of his league.

'What if she doesn't go out with people *like* you but actually goes out *with* you.'

'She wouldn't.'

Seeing as I was in love with someone who happened to be a 250-year-old vampire that lived only in my telly, I didn't think of anyone as out of my league, so didn't see why Ed, when he knew this person, should think like that. I mean, if I knew I was going to end up with said vampire, then why shouldn't he at least ask this woman out?

'There's this expression us old folk use,' I said, staring at Ed. 'It goes something like, "Faint heart never won fair lady". Be a coward about this and you'll be dreaming about you and her until you read about her wedding in *Hello*. Besides, the worst that can happen is she'll say no.'

'No, the worst that can happen is that she laughs in my face, tells me to piss off then emails all her friends and they laugh at me too. Or she could publish my picture on the Internet with a transcript of our conversation, so the whole world will laugh at me,' Ed replied.

'Or she could say yes and turn out to be a total cow, which'll mean all this time you've loved her from afar has been wasted on some silly bint. That's the worst that can happen.'

'No, the laughing thing is definitely the worst.'

He had a point. I took my seat back in the bed, covered myself with the duvet again. 'I know how you feel.'

Ed smirked. I'm sure he thought I had no idea what love of the unrequited sort was all about. He'd be surprised. My unreturned affections hadn't been exclusively aimed at fictional TV characters.

'No, really I do,' I reassured Ed. 'I spent over nine years in love with someone and, it's a long, loooonnnnggg story, but the short of it is, I'm between relationships. And, sometimes, I mentally kick myself when I talk to him. Or he leaves messages with my new flatmate.'

'Ohhhh . . . Drew! He's Drew?'

'Yes. He's Drew.'

Drew and I had been in the same psychology classes and I'd had a major thing about him since we were assigned to work together on a project in first year. We'd become friends after that assignment, but despite us being very close friends, I'd never really known how he felt about me. On the one hand, we'd spend hours on the phone often talking about sex (some of our conversations were so pornographic they bordered on phone sex), we'd sit too close, hug for too long, stare too much. He'd often turn up at the house I shared with three other people with a six-pack of beer and a video and we'd cuddle up in my bedroom and watch it. On the other hand, nothing happened. *Ever*. Not during college, not after college. I sometimes got the feeling that he was thinking about kissing me, thinking about taking our relationship to the next level, particularly when we were lying on my bed watching something he'd taped, but it was all just think with him. He never *did* anything. I did consider kissing him, of course, but I was never sure how it'd be received. You see, if there was one thing I'd learnt about men, it was that if they liked you enough, nothing, except possibly an act of God – and even then it was a close-run thing – would stop them making a move. So, why did Drew never just lean down and cover my lips with his, even when his arms were holding me close to his chest? Because he didn't like me enough, was the short answer.

Still, even though I knew this, even though I had this short answer, I was confident that would change over time. He went out with other people, I'd see other people but none of those relationships ever lasted. Because the two of us were going to end up together, weren't we? When we were single, we'd flirt till it hurt, all preparation for us getting together, I thought.

Three years ago, he met his girlfriend, Tara. Met her, then rang me up in a tizzy saying, 'Ceri, it's happened, I've met her. I've met the woman I want to spend the rest of my life with. I've met *The One*.'

I'd always listened with interest when he'd met other women. It was the kind of interest that came from knowing it'd never last because, well, they weren't me. He and I were meant to be. It was written in the stars, in the Domesday Book, practically anywhere you looked it said 'Drew & Ceri 4 ever'. This time had been different. I could hear it in his voice. The excitement and joy and shock that he'd met his ideal woman. He was in love. After two hours, he was in love. She was, indeed, The One. And she wasn't me. Or like me in any way. (Whashisface Tosspot asked me to move in with him about six hours after I got that call from Drew. By all rights, I should've taken to my bed with a bottle of wine and a box of tissues, instead, I'd gone to meet Whashisface Tosspot. Maybe I'd suddenly realised that now my long-term plan for happiness was heading off into the sunset with someone else and I needed a back-up plan, a sunset companion of my own, Whashisface Tosspot became it. It could've been that, but personally, I favour the Jedi Mind Trick/Work Of The Devil explanation.)

I'll never forget the sudden horror that rushed through me when I heard Drew's words. It'd hit me, right then, that we weren't eventually going to end up together. That maybe, if I'd told him earlier how I felt, things would've turned out different. I didn't want that for Ed. Or for anyone. 'What if' was no way to live your life. 'Always regret the things you did do, never the things you didn't,' someone once said. They weren't wrong.

'I'll tell you Ed, nine years of unrequited love that results in nothing more than friendship hurts, quite a lot. Hate to see you waste your twenties like I did, mate. Ask her out and if she says no, at least you'll know. You can find someone else to lust, I mean, love.'

Ed was silent for a very long time, he pursed his lips slightly and his eyes clouded over, he was thinking very hard by the face on him. My eyes strayed back to the TV screen and to the gorgeous but silent David Boreanaz. I jumped guiltily when Ed rejoined me in the land of the speaking.

'You really think I should ask her out?'

'I do,' I replied. 'I would. But only because I know now that the one thing more painful than rejection is looking at yourself day after day and wondering "What if". There's this line in *Strictly Ballroom* that I remind myself of whenever I start to chicken out of stuff. It goes, "A life lived in fear is a life half-lived". And, let's be honest, who wants to live half a life when you can have a whole life? That's like eating half a chocolate bar when you're hungry enough for a whole one and you've got a whole one in your hand.'

'All right, all right, all right,' Ed mumbled, nodding slowly.

'Anyway Ed, I've got to watch *Angel* now, but feel free to stay.'

Ed smiled at me wryly. 'Is that OK?'

'Course. But no talking.'

'Are you sure you don't want to enjoy it, you know, alone.' Ed waggled his eyebrows suggestively.

I grabbed a pillow and thwacked him with it. 'Listen you cheeky *get*, you ask out actress woman then you can take the mick out of me and how I run my love life, all right?'

Ed grinned, accepted my proffered can of beer and lay back on my bed.

Bless you, but you still need a wash and blow-dry.

What if?

I asked myself that a lot. A lot. I still, for example, thought: What if I'd taken English lit A-level instead of politics A-level? Would I be the politically-minded journalist I'd become before I ran away to Leeds? Or would I be someone else? Would I have become interested in Psychology or have done an English degree? And what if I'd done an English degree, would I have met Jess? What if I'd never met Jess . . .

Thinking 'What if' always made me homesick. And after talking to Ed, I started feeling homesick. Not for London, I had nothing to be homesick about in London. My parents, my sister, my brothers, their various families, a few friends were there. I'd left them behind, but since I didn't live with any of them, I didn't miss them. In fact, I'd probably start to see them more now I didn't live within an hour's journey of them. Two hundred miles apart was probably exactly what I needed to inspire me to see my family more often. No, I was starting to feel homesick for my time in college. To see all the people I'd gone to college with. Pastsick, really.

After Ed gave up on *Angel* and went off to bed (or to play heavy metal quietly), I got my photo albums out and lay on my bed looking through them. Pictures of my room in halls, pictures of the living room in my last student house, three streets over from where I was now. In that pic, I'm stood by the stone fireplace, wearing my floor-length blue velvet, long-sleeved ball dress. Specially bought – at a bargainous £10 in Oasis – for my graduation ball.

I flicked on a few pages and there was a picture of me and Drew at the graduation ball, a few hours later. Him in his smart black tuxedo, black bow tie, his razor-cut blond hair and cheekbones making him look rather effete. I was *so* in love with him when that picture was taken. At least I thought I was in love with him. That fierce, all consuming love hadn't changed until, what, three years ago. Like I said to Ed, I spent most of my twenties in love with a man who didn't even know I was alive. We had our heads close together, in the picture, my jet black bob almost touching what was left of his blond hair, our faces glistening with sweat because we'd spent half the night dancing and we were both flashing 100 watt smiles at the camera. Drew's arm was slung casually around my shoulders. I knew exactly what I would've been feeling – quivery and giggly, thinking, 'Oh, GOD! Drew's touching me in front of a camera! It's a sign! He does love me really. Tonight could be the night.' I stroked my fingers across the plastic covering the photo, as I got another pang of pastsickness. Awww, young Drew, young Ceri. So bloody stupid. We didn't even get less stupid the older we got. Well, I didn't.

After the initial shock of Drew meeting 'The One', which resulted in me moving in with Whashisface Tosspot, I'd gone into denial. I'd hung up the phone, sat staring into space for ages until I reached a very important decision: *I'm not going to think about it. At all.* Drew, my love, my long-term plan for happiness had met his dream woman, so the best course of action was to enter denial, quietly and calmly, without any fuss, and not think about it.

Since I'd decided not to think about it, I could think about nothing else. It was always there at the back of my mind. Kicking away, dancing up and down, waving a red flag, demanding attention. When I woke up in the morning, when I got ready for work, when I sat at work, when I came home from work. When I made dinner, when I ate it, when I watched telly, when I was having sex, I thought about it. My stomach churned; dipping and rising, spinning and twisting. I found it hard to eat without feeling sick afterwards. I'd be sat at my desk, editing copy and find my right leg perched on the ball of my foot, bouncing nervously up and down. And all because I'd decided *not* to think about it.

Three months later, exhausted by the effort and nausea involved in not thinking about it, I decided to think about it. I decided to let myself off the hook, stop being such a brave little martyr and go into the pain. Go into it, embrace it, accept it. I was, at least, allowed to cry about it. I picked a weekend when Whashisface Tosspot went away to his parents' (of course, they had a huge house in the country but he was always pleading poverty). As he drove off very late Friday night, I got myself all the tools for grieving I'd previously denied myself – a couple of bottles of wine, a multipack of tissues and some appropriate CDs – and took to my bed.

Except, my mind, twisted as it was, refused to collapse. Refused to let me cry and wallow and give in to how much pain Drew's news had caused me.

As I lay under my duvet, *Can't Live If Living Is Without You* playing on loop in the background, there was no emotional retching. No physical heartbreak. No tears. No open-mouthed ugly cry. Not even when I squeezed really hard. All that came to me were all the negative things about him. About this Drew, this man who I thought I was going to spend the rest of my life with.

My brain kept dredging up examples of his caddishness any time 'but I love him' thought of rearing its pathetic head. How he'd cuddle up with me, but never made a proper move on me. How he'd go out with other people and flaunt it in my face (how many times had I heard how great his latest woman was, how sexy, how good in bed? Too many, that's how many). How he'd disappear from my life if he met someone else and only call me to ask for advice when they were going through a hard time. How he'd give me the cold shoulder for days if I snogged someone and would refuse to listen to anything about them, at all.' (When I'd admitted I'd been seeing Whashisface Tosspot for three months, Drew had blanked me for a whole month. Didn't return my calls, didn't text or email me, ended calls after a minute if I caught him in. *Nada*, for a whole month.)

It wasn't just that, though. I started remembering how most of his girlfriends hated me, would be blatantly rude to me, probably because he told them that I had a thing about him. How he didn't come to visit me when I was in hospital for a week with pneumonia – even though the hospital was only a twenty-minute bus ride away. How he'd once forgotten my birthday. Me, his best mate, he'd forgotten my birthday. How he'd got all our mates together for a do one Christmas after we'd all left college – and neglected to invite me. On and on my mind went. By the end of the weekend, I actually hated Drew. Every time I thought of him, I mentally growled. He was an emotional tease. He'd get me all whipped up, let me believe that some way along the line we'd be together. It wasn't all his fault, though, I'd been led on by all those movies and books which propagated waiting it out. Which told you that if you just hung in there long enough, he'll realise that you're the one for him and give up going out with supermodel-types who'll smash up his car windscreen because he didn't call.

(Yes, one of his girlfriends did that once and I'd gone with him to get it fixed.) No, he'll discover he wants to be with the woman he comes running to emotionally and physically when he's single.

Suddenly, I realised he'd been a bastard to me but because I thought I loved him, I hadn't wanted to see it. And this falling for 'The One' was the final act of treachery as far as I was concerned. It was all right for him to go meet his perfect woman, all right for him to fall in love, all right, even, for him to realise he wanted to spend the rest of his life with her. But why the bloody hell was I the first person he called up about it? Because he had no respect for me or the feelings he'd nurtured in me, was the short answer. (I was good at short answers, but this was the first time I'd actually paid attention to one.)

Drew, my beloved, was a bloody bastard who wasn't worthy of my love or attention.

By four o'clock Saturday afternoon I'd thrown back my duvet, leapt out of bed and called up a couple of friends to meet me in Soho for a late lunch. Three of us had sat in a café on Old Compton Street, London, drinking wine and eating cake. It'd mutated to going to a pub, going to a club, then staying at a friend's house in Fulham. We'd then gone for a pub lunch and got some more drinks in. By the time I got home, Whashisface Tosspot was back – unimpressed by how legless I was at six o'clock on a Sunday evening – and I'd re-entered my place called denial.

Except, this time, when I decided NOT TO THINK ABOUT IT, I really didn't. I wasn't nauseous and jumpy. I'd crossed the desert, the wide, barren landscape that was my feelings for Drew. I'd made it through the hardest times, the mirages of plentiful water supplies that were his jealousy at me seeing other people; I'd made it over the sand dunes of hurt that left me feeling worthless when he met someone else; and I'd survived those months of craving for the merest drop of affection to wet my lips on when he blanked me. Now, thanks to a weekend of negative thinking, of being surrounded by nothing except the cacti of his bad behaviour, I could see the other side of that desert and I was almost there.

Two months later, I finally reached the other side of the desert when someone called and asked if I'd spoken to Drew recently and I realised I hadn't needed to shove him to the back of my mind because he hadn't even entered my mind.

When you're so infatuated with someone, like I was with Drew, it's very difficult to see them for what they really are. But once I'd made that desert crossing, Drew stopped being the man who could do no wrong. He also stopped being the man who would one day wake up and find he loved me, because it was not going to happen. Once I could see him clearly, he became a good friend. A proper friend with no undercurrent of 'What if?' He became a friend because, well, I can forgive my friends most things, but I couldn't forgive the man I was supposed to love for not even liking me enough to make a pass at me. How embarrassing was that? He could cuddle me, he could flirt with me, he could talk sex with me, but he couldn't even close his eyes, think of Leeds, and kiss me full on the mouth.

Part of me clung to the notion that Drew was the one who got away, that I wouldn't feel this for anyone else – three years on, I could see that I really didn't want to. Because that wasn't love. Love is a two-way street, except with me and Drew it had been totally one way. If he'd loved me, even a little, he wouldn't have emotionally teased me.

★

I flicked through more pages in the photo album. We all looked so young.

I stopped over a picture of me that Drew had taken a few days after our final exam. I was lying on the grass in Hyde Park with sunglasses on, a huge smile on my face and sticking two fingers up at him. I looked quite good then, even if I say so myself. I was happy. I'd just finished my finals, I had a few weeks to go until the results. The world was my lobster. A group of us had gone to the park to play a game of rounders and I'd taken a break, lay on the grass not caring about getting grass marks on my short red dress (with white cycling shorts under it for decency).

As a shadow fell over me, I opened my eyes and found Drew stood over me, his camera poised. Just as he hit the button, I'd stuck my fingers up at him.

I didn't look that different in that photo, actually, not if you looked at the photos of me then. But when you looked at the photo then looked at me . . . I was older. Not particularly wrinkly (wrinkles weren't a worry of mine), just older; I suppose I'd done a lot and it showed on my face. I'd run a department on a women's magazine. I'd found out that love had to be two-way for it to mean anything. I'd discovered that I'd much rather stay in with a video than go out 'on the pull'. And then, of course, I lived with a man I'd torn out of every photo he'd managed to infiltrate. This was against everything I ever believed in, I loved to take photos, to take snapshots of every time of my life. To have it there to look back on if I ever got pastsick. With Whashisface Tosspot, I just couldn't bear to be reminded of the biggest mistake of my life. It was bad enough that I'd slept with him for two years, did I really want to look at him too? No, was the short answer to that, too.

I slammed shut the photo album. Didn't I just say to Ed that

'What if?' was no way to live a life? Erm . . . maybe I didn't say it, but I'd meant to. And, constantly dipping into my photo album was no way to live a life in Leeds, either. *Yer have to look forwards* I reminded myself.

And I will, right after I've watched a couple more episodes of Angel . . .

chapter seven

Blurting

Before I'd touched down in Leeds this time around, I'd decided to doff my cap to health and fitness. Devote some of my time and effort to what probably should come naturally. Not go crazy, not become a gym bore, not even attempt to lose weight or start chasing that mythical dream of 'firming up'. I simply fancied the idea of being able to walk up more than two flights of stairs without making the asthmatic donkey sound of someone who'd had a thirty-a-day habit since she was sixteen. It was downright embarrassing that Jess could do the stairs thing without a hint of a donkey about her when she had been a thirty-a-day person since she was *fourteen*.

The gym on the college campus, a stand-alone annexe, was adequate for my purposes – a line of treadmills greeted you as you entered, flanked on the left by a large handful of exercise bikes. On the right was the weights area, plus rowing machines; further on and then down a short flight of stairs was a swimming pool and a circuit training gym.

I'd come here, the first day at college, straight from my final meeting with the last lecturer, Sally. (Sally had been lovely. The meeting with her had been left till last because she was the woman I'd be sharing an office with. Out of all the other three lecturers I'd met, she was the only one who seemed to be able to speak in short sentences.) That night I had my body introduced to the equipment and the ways of the gym. That should be reintroduced, welcomed back into the fold of the gym.

This wasn't information I liked spread around, it was a shameful secret I'd buried and hidden from – but I'd joined a gym once before.

I was in college then too. Young, impetuous, easily brainwashed. If that wasn't bad enough, I joined then, dot, dot, dot, *went on a regular basis.* To add insult to potential injury, I went every other day, in fact. On alternate days, I did aerobics.

It'd been a membership of necessity, though. Everyone I knew had gone travelling for the summer, or returned to their home towns, or had left college. They all had a life. I did not. And, that summer, I became depressingly thinner and healthy. Depressingly, because I'd always have lodged somewhere in my memory the image of what I'd look like if I took care of my body, exercised, drank less and slept more. And, much as I'd love to be bright-eyed, clear-skinned and a size ten all the time, I'd much rather have a life, see my mates, drink alcohol, eat what I want and watch telly. It was a fair trade off, as far as I was concerned.

Now, however, I was lost all over again. Whilst Drew worked as a management consultant in Leeds, he lived in York. So on those days when he left work on time, he liked to drive straight home to spend time with his girlfriend. Also, when I finally saw Drew for the emotional tease he really was, I stopped calling him as much. Didn't need to ring him up to say 'hi' or to just listen to his voice. Didn't need to ring him to get a laugh. He was simply a good friend who I didn't speak to that often.

My only real anchor in this city was Jess. And she liked to see her daughters and husband quite often, too. With only a handful of acquaintances in Leeds, and the knowledge that it'd be a while to get some — particularly if the Mel/Claudine/lunch/mouth-foot thing was any indicator — I was forced to take refuge, once again, in the high-energy embrace of the gym.

This time, though, I was treadmilling or cycling, just to sort out my lungs. To make my cardiovascular system work properly. Nothing more. My hands, my body were going nowhere near any weights or complicated machinery. I knew my mind, all it'd take would be one well-timed movement in front of a mirror and I'd be launched back into trying to get that final year of college body again.

Just in case my body decided it was going to stay any longer than necessary in the gym, I wore the most ridiculous outfit: royal blue, daisy-covered cycling shorts and a baggy sweat top with 'Michigan State' emblazoned across it. My black socks were rolled down to just above my ankle bones and my trainers had seen better days. To stop my hair frizzing, I'd scraped my black bob under a scarf. Gorgeous was not the word for me. Truly.

I stood with my feet on either side of the treadmill's moving part as I keyed in **30 mins** to the treadmill.

I paused, stared at the LCD. A bit too ambitious for my first time here in eight years.

I pressed CLEAR, then keyed in **10 mins**. *Wimp. You're a big girl's blouse.*

All right, **20 mins** it is. *I can do twenty minutes. No problemo.*

I focused on the TV screen in front of me. *The Simpsons* was on. Without sound, though. In the background, around the gym, the constant beat of something lively and funky pulsed. It was designed to get you moving in time to it. To get you motivated and moving. The genesis of perpetual motion. I opted to walk quickly, but not in time to the music. If I wasn't careful, I'd train myself to head to the gym every time I heard that beat. I'd become a Pavlov-type animal, not salivating every time I heard footsteps because I thought food was coming, but wanting to run everywhere, simply because I caught a snatch of something high-paced in a passing car. And th—

'Hi, Ceri?' A voice cut into my thoughts.

Without breaking stride, I turned to the person who'd spoken.

AAAGGGH! Claudine. Damn.

I might've known she'd frequent these parts. Very few people got those elongated, willowy looks with clear, glowy skin if you didn't habitually visit the gym. Of course, the first night I make it here since receiving my training programme, she appears. And on the treadmill next to me. I'd spent the last few days keeping an eye out for her and Mel, then running away. Very fast. I still physically cringed at how I managed to fit the whole of my foot very neatly into my mouth. I hadn't wanted to do that again. And now look.

'Hi,' I said brightly. Too brightly. That sounded fake. Like I'd been avoiding her and now was overcompensating. Which, of course, I was.

'Are you all right?' She stood with her legs wide open, each foot resting on the platform beside the moving part of her treadmill. She'd paused in keying in information into the treadmill display. 'You looked pretty fierce just then. Is something bothering you?'

'No.' I jumped like I was doing a jumping jack, so I could

71

get off the moving treadmill and stand with my feet on either side of it. My heart sprinted in my chest, my whole body heaved in my attempt to get more oxygen. 'I'm fine.' *Breathless, but fine.*

Claudine's face became a picture of concern as she said: 'You looked like you had something on your mind, that's all. You can tell me if you want.'

'I, erm, I was actually thinking about Pavlov's dogs, brainwashing and music and if it's possible to brainwash people in the same way that Pavlov did with the dogs, but using music.'

Claudine's concern mutated to fear. With every moment her impression of me was lowering.

'*Really?*' she asked.

I nodded, aware that I sounded like a complete loon. 'Unfortunately, yes. I don't have big subjects like boyfriends to occupy my mind.'

'Right.' Claudine pulled the big red button on her treadmill display to get it working, hopped on then started walking. 'You'd better not cool down too much, unless you're about to stop.'

I hopped back onto the treadmill, started to walk again.

Beautiful as she was, Claudine was clearly proof of my gymlife relativity theory. She had trendy, up-to-date label gear that was obviously used. After about two seconds of warming up, which I was still doing, i.e. walking briskly, she started to jog. Slowly, at first, each step carefully considered, expertly dealt onto the machine. She'd obviously done this before, several times, regularly. Ergo, no life. The worst part, as she increased her pace, her slender arms pumping away, her long, svelte legs working without wobbling, was that there was no moisture in sight. Me? After five minutes of my brisk walking, my body was a tidal wave of sweat. Every ounce

(I still hadn't got around to metric-sizing my thoughts) of moisture in me was taking a day-trip to my outer epidermis. Claudine didn't even have the decency to 'glow', she simply increased her stride, running. Now that was a concept, running. On a running machine.

My feet moved quicker. Didn't want to be outdone. There was my pride at stake. My lungs, clearly left out of the pride rousing lecture, complained almost straight away. They burnt their displeasure into my chest. *Piss off!* my brain replied. *No one outdoes us.*

I monitored Claudine from the corner of my eye – each time she upped pace, I upped pace. I matched her stride for stride, step for step. Soon, we were running equally. Both of us heading for the imaginary finish line neck and neck. While she had eventually started to glow, rivers of perspiration washed down my back, making my top stick to me, oceans of the stuff cascaded down my face.

'What are you doing after your workout?' Claudine asked, over the din of the treadmills. She spoke in her normal tone of voice, she could even breathe, the bitch.

'Whuh-huhow?' I replied.

'Yeah. I'll only be doing an hour today. I was wondering if you fancied going for a drink afterwards?'

I tried to speak, my lungs refused (they'd gone on strike since that 'piss off' thing from my brain). I nodded, instead.

'How long are you working out?' she asked.

I gave up, slowed down. I'd never win against her in this race. I glanced down at the LCD display. Held up three fingers. 'Three minutes.'

'You're not doing anything else?' she asked.

I shook my head.

'You really should do weights as well . . .'

Suddenly, things got nasty. Claudine's mouth started spewing filth about more exercising. Workout, weights, swimming, muscle tone, endurance . . .

Why don't you just call me a whore and be done with it?

The beer was divine on my tongue, in my mouth, sliding down my throat. I gulped at it the second the pint glass, cloaked in condensation, touched my bottom lip. Claudine did virtually the same thing with her glass of wine.

'See, isn't that better?' I almost said. I'd talked her out of that 'workout' nonsense and had flat out refused to sit with her if she ordered a soft drink.

'Bliss in a glass,' I gasped, finally giving my drink a reprieve.

'You're not wrong,' Claudine said.

We both sighed deeply at the pleasure that could be found in the form of alcohol, then sat in silence as we contemplated how easily pacified we were. She left the air between us silent for a few seconds more before she asked: 'Were you really thinking about Pavlov in the gym earlier?'

'Um . . . yeah.'

'I see,' she said, eyeing me suspiciously. She sipped more of her drink. 'I suppose being a psychologist those things come to you all the time. Kind of like an occupational hazard?'

There was that . . . there was also the fact it was a mad, scary world inside my head. I once spent the better part of a night thinking through the intricacies and possibilities of being battered to death with a teaspoon. I'd seen a news story about being battered to death by a hammer, the teaspoon thought process followed from there. Naturally.

'I teach contemporary and cultural studies,' Claudine said.

'Oh. How long have you taught that then?' I asked.

'Since I finished at The Met. My tutor said I should think about doing a PhD because I'd done so well over the three

74

years. So I signed up for a PhD at All Souls and eventually, when they realised they couldn't get rid of me, they gave me a job. I've done it properly for two years now.'

'Do you enjoy it?'

'Yes and no, like most jobs I'd imagine. There are good times, there are bad times.'

'I know what you mean. That's why I left my job and London in the end. I found that the bad times were getting longer and longer and the good times were so few and far between that they'd virtually disappeared.'

'What made you decide to do it then?'

'No one thing. It all built up I guess. Then someone said something and I knew, kind of, what I had to do.'

'God, they must be pretty wonderful. Who was it and what did they say?'

Claudine thought I was odd anyway, and I wasn't trying to impress her, but she, like most people, wouldn't understand the whole 'Oprah told me to do it' thing. And did I really want to still be repeating that line when I was very nearly thirty? 'Oh, just a person,' I supplied. 'It's been fun though, being able to start again.' Fun and scary.

'And it's a nice place to do it at. Small, intimate. It's like a family college. I like lecturing there.'

'It seems nice,' I agreed.

Claudine sipped her drink. 'The thing with me and Mel is complicated. It's not a simple case of us being friends and you being wrong about us. It's . . . it's so complex.'

I wasn't shocked by this non sequitur in conversation – at all. If people who are about to invite me into their lives didn't do odd little things like Ed had done a few nights earlier, they just blurted at me. Stopped mid-conversation and blurted.

It'd taken time to understand what was really going on with these confessions and heartfelt blurts. When blokes would spontaneously confess that they were single and looking to settle down/meet the right woman/fall in love, I'd used to think they were secretly coming on to me. I'd excitedly tell my friends about it and would sometimes go as far as asking them out. I'd only cottoned on after several blokes ran away at the very idea of dating me, and several more spent the 'date' unloading their hearts and minds and problems on to me, instead of flirting that I understood. I had booked an honest-to-goodness night out with the possibility of a snog at the end of it; they wanted a confidante, someone who wasn't backward at coming forward with advice. Or, failing that, the phone number of that gorgeous woman they'd been after for ages.

I wasn't stupid, just a dreamer. I still hadn't completely accepted that Cupid, Venus, Eros or whoever governed the laws of love had a grievance against me. I lived in constant hope that a bloke would want to go out with me for me being me. Not a free therapist.

With women, I soon discovered their deeply personal blurts weren't on a quid pro quo level; it wasn't a precursor to a long and/or meaningful friendship. They didn't want to know about my stories, my worries, they wouldn't be there during my upsets or in my times of need; what they wanted was a non-friend to listen. Someone who couldn't judge like a friend might. They latched onto Ceri, the listener, the someone who wouldn't expect the favour returned in kind.

Sometimes it pissed me off, usually when I'd had a four-in-the-morning panic and knew that if Jess wasn't around the next day to listen, I'd be carrying the weight of that panic around for days and weeks, because when it came down to it, more than half the people in my phone book didn't want to know my problems.

But that disgruntlement was only sometimes. Most of the time I just put up with it. What else was I going to do, tell them I'm not interested?

'What do you mean?' I asked Claudine, my latest blurtee.

'We . . . well, we're very close,' Claudine said.

'I see,' I replied.

Claudine cast her dark, smouldery eyes over me – assessing if I could handle the truth. Like you could tell by the cut of my jib how sturdy my mind was. Weak chin, weak mind.

'Can you keep a secret?' Claudine asked.

If I couldn't I'd hardly say no, would I? I'd most likely not realise I couldn't keep a secret. As it happened, I could keep a secret. I could keep several million secrets. My head was like the Fort Knox of secrets, except, of course, no one tried to break into my head to steal the twenty-four carat stuff stored in there. Not yet, anyway. 'I can,' I said.

Claudine swigged some French courage. 'The thing is . . .' more courage down her neck, 'last year, that is, a few months ago, around Christmas . . .' big gulp, 'Mel and I, well, we . . .'

Made love? Wore each other's underwear to work? Spent the limit on your credit cards on ice-cream?

'Kissed.'

Right. And that's bad is it? 'Was it the first time it'd happened?'

'It was a bit more than kissing.'

My mistake, shan't interrupt again.

'Quite a lot more, actually.'

I sipped my drink.

'We were practically naked.'

I sipped more drink.

'And in his bed.'

Sip.

'And we were totally naked.'

77

Some kiss, I thought as I watched her from over the rim of my glass.

Claudine looked me in the eye as she delivered her next earth-stopping revelation. 'We didn't have sex, though. I didn't want to do that to my boyfriend and Mel didn't want to do that to his, er, wife.'

'Mel's married?' I asked. *I seem to remember him saying 'I'm not seeing anyone special.'*

Claudine twirled the stem of her wine glass between her forefinger and thumb; with the other hand she pulled wisps of her cropped hair around her face. 'They split up not long after, you know.'

You didn't have sex? 'Ah. Right.'

'Like I said, it's complicated.'

'I guess so. How about I get the next round in and you think of the least complicated way to tell me about it.'

'Get me a large wine,' Claudine called after me. 'I'll leave the car at college and get a cab home.'

The bar of the Fox & Hound, down by Horsforth train station resounded with dark broodiness. Most of it came from its dark wood interior, the lead pattening of the windows. We were sat in the larger of the two alcoves that looked out to the bar. We'd rested our exercised carcasses on highly upholstered booths beside the empty fireplace.

I stood on the foot rail and leant forwards over the bar, waiting for the barman to notice me. While I waited, I checked out the only other person at the bar. He was leant across the bar too, waiting to be noticed, but his height excused him from needing the chrome foot rail. His body, leant across the bar as it was, turned him into a sleek line, like smooth easy brush strokes on a page. If I blurred my eyes he'd be colours and smudges against the dark canvas of the bar. More aesthetically pleasing than if I did it to other people in this bar. I stopped watching him before he caught me and I found myself in one of those eye contact situations. I concentrated, instead, on getting the barman's attention. The barman was busily working through a large round. I'd probably get two rounds in at once, that would save me interrupting Claudine's story by doing anything as wanton and thoughtless as needing more alcohol.

The hairs on the back of my neck tingled suddenly as though someone had stroked ice-cold fingers across the base of my skull. My head snapped round and my eyes connected with the man who looked like brush strokes on a page. Unusually for me, my eyes didn't immediately rip themselves away, they were startled still. Startled by the way he was blatantly staring a hole into my head. He had his head slightly to one side, studying me as though I was something he'd just discovered under his microscope.

Worse, he didn't even stop, now I was facing him. He continued to stare away like it was the most natural thing in the world to watch a woman who'd caught you watching her. I offered a very small, very nervous smile; he didn't. He carried on staring for a few more seconds, then looked away, leaving an air of faint disapproval as he did so.

What the hell was that all about? I thought as my whole body burned in indignation at being so closely scrutinised. He'd probably even studied the huge flea bite that was developing on my neck.

I didn't dwell on it for too long though. I had to listen to Claudine's tale . . .

'After that night, you know, the night we got naked and physical, everything about our lives changed. Mel . . .' She paused, drank deep from her drink, then swished what was left around the bottom of the large wine glass. 'Mel says he loves me. And that he's in love with me.' She sighed, glanced at me, was probably surprised to find my face interested but impassive. I was, in the main, unshockable. Not even *Jerry Springer* had thrown me – it may have disgusted me, but not shocked. I'd heard it all before – literally.

'I don't know what to do. It's been, what, four months since it happened, but I don't know what to do. I keep thinking about it, but it's not any clearer.'

I knew what I had to ask now. It was in my script. I could do this listening, confessor thing from any level of consciousness. There was a set way to coax these stories out of people, not that by this point they needed much coaxing. They just needed me to follow my script to get them to tell me everything. And the question next on my list wasn't: 'How do you feel about him?' It was . . .

'What's your boyfriend like?'

'Kevin? Oh. Um. He's one of the best blokes you'd ever want to meet. He's great. Really great.' Claudine twirled her glass between her fingers again. Then sighed. Then sighed even deeper. 'But he's not Mel.'

'I see,' I said.

Time for a little assessment of the situation. OK. Kevin isn't Mel. Mel says he's in love with her. Mel's no longer with his wife. He isn't seeing anyone special. A fair summation of what she'd told me, no? The question on my lips now was, of course: 'So why don't you leave?' Not that I'd ask her outright.

'I don't leave because it's not that simple.' I didn't need to ask. 'You don't just walk out on a life. Not when we've been together for four years. I mean, most women struggle for some kind of commitment from their boyfriends. I didn't. It was Kevin's idea for us to move in together after two years. We bought our house, we've built a life together from scratch, we've been happy together for ages. You don't just walk out on that.'

'I see,' I said. *You wouldn't be the first, you wouldn't be the last*, I thought.

The world is chock-a-block with people – male and female – who've walked out on a marriage, family, kids, friends, jobs on a whim. On a look. Let alone a near-shag and a confession of love both offered and felt. Not that I was advocating leaving (I'd never advocate anything I haven't done myself and even then, just cos it worked for me, doesn't mean it'd work for anyone else), it simply seemed . . . it came across that Claudine was, to all intents and purposes, waiting for something.

'It's not like Mel's putting pressure on me. I get the impression he'd wait for as long as it takes.'

'What about you? How long are you prepared to wait?'

'Wait?' Claudine replied. 'Wait for what?'

'Sorry, my mistake,' I said, started gulping down my drink at the rate of knots. *That was a question I should've thought, not said.*

'No, no, tell me. Say what you meant.'

'I'm probably wrong, so don't take what I'm about to say as anything other than my opinion.' I sighed, silently. *I am a bigmouthed old slag.* 'When you were talking just then, I got the impression that you were waiting for the answer to present itself. We all do that when we're in the middle of something big, but it's as though you've pressed pause on the whole matter and are kind of waiting for someone else to press play and sort it out. Unless Mel's going to make it up with his wife, or Kevin finishes with you out of the blue, that's not going to happen. The remote control is firmly in your grip. But, like I said, that's just my opinion. My last relationship that lasted longer than three weeks was two years ago. I know very little about very little.'

Claudine swirled her wine a bit slower and stared into her glass, as though hypnotising herself.

I often did this to people after a blurt session. I often made them think about something so deeply they checked out of the conversation and became sad. Upset that there was something they could be doing but weren't. An option that was staring them in the face that they couldn't see. It was all right for me, I could come out with these theories, because it wasn't my life. I could see what to do clearly if it wasn't my life. Couldn't everyone? One step removed you had twenty-twenty vision.

However, the result of my clear-sightedness sat opposite me, swirling pale wine around her smeared glass, looking so forlorn, she probably qualified to have her picture beside the entry for 'forlorn' in *The Oxford English Picture Dictionary*.

If there was one thing I shouldn't do, it was offer my opinion. I was getting better, though. Better at not saying everything I thought, even if others had started it by telling me far too much, way too soon. There was a time when I would've said all that stuff about people leaving on a whimsy to Claudine, thereby totally alienating her. Whilst now, there was only about seventy-five per cent alienation going on – if you factored in the lunch thing.

'What would you do?' she asked me.

'Me?' I replied.

Claudine nodded vigorously. 'In my situation, what would you do to "press play"?'

'To be totally honest, Claudine, I don't know. I don't have all the facts, because I wasn't there. I don't know how Mel acted afterwards, how he's acted since. I don't know if Kevin's noticed a change in you, if you've been off with him or trying too hard. Like I said, I've not got all the facts so I don't know what I'd do.'

I'd actually forgotten what a mind terrorist I was. I came wandering in, lobbing confusion grenades left, right and centre and then when I was asked how to disarm them, I shrugged and said, 'dunno mate'. I should be locked up.

'Thanks Ceri,' Claudine said as I stumbled out of the taxi an hour or so later. 'Thanks for listening, you were a great help.'

'Any time,' I slurred.

She grabbed my cuff before I reeled away from the open door and fell into the house. 'Don't tell anyone what I told you,' she said, frantically searching my face for understanding.

'About what?' I replied.

'Me and Mel,' she said.

'I know. I was being funny.'

'Oh. Ha ha. That wasn't very funny.'

'No, I guess not. Bye.' I shut the car door before she took that the wrong way too.

chapter eight

Copying

Apparently, photocopying was an ordeal round these parts.

Either you spent hours camped out in the photocopying room situated in the furthest, darkest corner of the social sciences department, waiting your turn to watch lights flash back and forth, back and forth, back and forth, back and forth; battling with toner and collating and getting the book to lie flat enough to get a good copy. Or, you took it to the reprographics department and had them do it. Because that's what they were there for. They worried about getting good copies and stapling and other stuff like that. Our department just paid for it.

The whole reprographics department was situated just opposite the library, had swing doors and a photocopied, laminated sign outside that said: REPROGRAPHICS in block capitals. The whole demeanour of the place said, 'Don't come hither. And if you do, expect to be insulted'. Sally had warned me about them. Said to not go there if I was sensitive. But I wasn't sensitive. I could handle most things, I was a South East Londoner. You didn't survive 'Darn Sarf' if you were sensitive.

I headed down there the day after I'd been out with Claudine and did not feel well. Every step reminded me I did not feel well. In fact, how I was still standing was a mystery. How I'd got out of bed in time and got to the bus stop and managed to stay upright long enough for the 731 to arrive I'll never know. At one point last night it'd looked like I wasn't going to get to bed . . .

I'd opened the door after Claudine's cab pulled away, trying to be quiet and normal just in case the boys were asleep. Still going for the quietness, I moved to shut the door, but it sprang out of my hand and slammed.

'Shhhh!' I hissed to it, bashing my finger against my lips. 'Shhhhhh!'

'You all right there, Ceri?' a voice asked.

I leapt around to look at him. Jake. *Uh-oh. Landlord. Act normal. Don't want him to evict you.* 'Fine,' I said, trying to stand up straight. Never mind I smelt like a beer mat and swayed like a blade of grass in a gale.

'Do you want a cup of tea or something?' he asked.

I shook my head violently. 'No. Thank you. No. No thank you.'

I seem to remember him looking confused. 'OK,' Jake replied. 'Did you have a good time?'

'I went to the gym,' I said. My arms started making running movements. 'I ran on the treadmill.'

'It's midnight. Must've been a long run.'

I nodded enthusiastically. 'Twenty minutes.'

Jake frowned. 'Right.'

I pointed to the stairs. 'I'm going to bed now.'

'OK. Night.'

'Night.'

'Oh, Jake, Jake,' I called urgently, even though he hadn't moved at all.

'Yes?'

'Thank you. I really like living here.'

'I'm glad.'

'No, no, really. It's a nice room and it's so cheap and you and Ed seem like nice blokes and I don't even think you'll smack me over the head and drag me out over the carpet that doesn't show up blood stains cos I used some of your milk. Not that I have. I don't really drink milk, but I don't think either of you would. Thank you. Good night.'

I started up the stairs, then realised how mad I must've sounded. So, on the top step of the first flight of stairs, I turned around and went tearing down them, practically ran into the kitchen where Jake was filling the kettle.

'I'm not really mad,' I said, loudly.

Jake jumped so much he almost dropped the kettle. 'Sorry?' he asked.

'I'm not mad. When I first looked around you asked me if I was a weirdo and I'm not. I'm in love with Buffy The Vampire Slayer's ex-boyfriend Angel, and I'm addicted to *Star Trek* but I'm not a weirdo.'

'OK, I'll take your word for it.'

'Good night.'

I went happily skipping off to bed after that.

And woke up red-eyed, shaky and with a thirst that could not be quenched by water alone. I'd stopped off in the canteen on the way in this morning to get water and had nearly passed out at the food smells. The week-old oil that had been used to fry that morning's hash browns, clung to the air. Even the cereal smelt enough to make me want to hurl. And, on top of that, I had three sets of tutorials to do *and* see Jake later.

First things first: photocopying for the next morning's lecture.

The wire-mesh windows of the reprographics swing doors

were obscured by paper so you couldn't see in as you reached out and pushed open the right door. The room was brightly-lit, a waist-height wood counter separated the world from the department. High shelves seemed to go on and on as you approached, stacked with piles of photocopying, reams of paper, lots and lots of different colours. It was like walking into a library of paper.

'Hi, I'd like these photocopied forty times for tomorrow,' I said to the woman behind the counter. I even managed a smile with my dry, furry mouth.

The woman looked up slowly from the book she was making notes in and gave me a partially-hidden sneer that suggested that I hadn't actually asked for photocopying. I had, in fact, informed her that her biological mother and bio-logical father were close blood relatives.

Time crawled on as she looked me up and down from behind her large, plastic-framed Deirdre Barlow glasses. Once she'd appraised me, she opened her mouth, which had been so clenched it was almost caving in on itself, and sneered, 'Photocopying has to be brought in at least fifteen days in advance.'

'Fifteen days?' I said.

'Fifteen days.'

Do you see this face? It is suffering. It does not need to be told it has to wait fifteen days for something it needs tomorrow.

Sally had warned me. '*Show no weakness*,' she'd said. '*They do not understand weakness. They do not respect niceness. They chew up nice people until they are mulch, then they spit you out and stamp on you.*' I knew all this, but I still said, 'Can't I get it done sooner?' in a pathetic, 'be nice to me' voice.

She sighed with her whole body.

'I do not have time to explain everything to you. You should know all this if you're a lecturer.'

'How? By subscribing to the college's psychic newsletter? Or by simply putting my head against the reprographics sign outside and letting it seep in by osmosis,' I replied.

'You *are* a lecturer, aren't you?'

'Yes, but I'm also a new lecturer so I don't have a handle on everything yet.'

'That's not my problem, is it. *Dear.*' Her superiority had clambered up to a new level now she knew I was in a weak position, I was a novice. 'Fifteen days.'

'But I don't know what I'll need that far in advance,' I replied. 'Sometimes I only find books and articles that are necessary a couple of days in advance.'

'That's not my problem either, is it,' the woman behind the counter replied, picking up a stack of forms and tapping them on the counter to straighten them while wiggling her head in an officious manner. 'Maybe you should plan your lectures more carefully.'

Even in my state, even as hungover and unwell as I was I couldn't abide that kind of rudeness. (Particularly not from someone I could soooo take in a fight.) 'Excuse me?' I replied.

'I was under the impression that lecturers were meant to work to a set timetable. You know, *plan things.*' As she spoke she waggled her upper body in that selfsame officious manner. 'Be prepared.'

I picked up my stack of books and articles. 'Tell you what, you don't tell me how to lecture and I won't tell you how to press the little button on the photocopier machine.'

'You cannot speak to me like that,' she said. 'I will report you to your head of department.'

'Right. Well, you do that. Don't forget to read the college's psychic newsletter to find out my name, and when you've reported me to the head of department, why don't you report me to God too because He's the only person I'm really scared of.'

Had I been able to, I would've slammed the swing door behind me. But I kicked it, leaving it fump, fump, fumping open and shut behind me.

WHORE! I said in my head. *Whore-faced old bag. Who does she think she is? No one talks to me like that and gets away with it. Stupid old mare.*

I'd stamped my way to the Senior Common Room before reason pierced my anger: I'd been insulted by some officious mare in a department. And she couldn't do that if I wasn't part of the grand scheme of things.

Hey, I'm a proper lecturer now.

I slid my key into the front door and almost collapsed with happiness as the door swung open. I never thought I'd be so happy to see the inside of a place in my life. I never thought I could sleep with my eyes open, either, but I could. I'd just done it.

The nonsense I'd heard about developmental psychology this morning had almost put me to sleep for real. But I'd propped my eyes open with sheer willpower and had nodded and asked questions when people read out their work.

The worst part was, to sit there, listening to students spewing what was essentially something they'd put together on the bus . . . it made me think of all the times I'd done that and thought I'd got away with it. It hadn't occurred to me that lecturers would see through it. That they'd be sat there thinking: *Are you kidding me? Do you really want me to believe that what you were talking there was a week's worth of extracurricular reading?*

I went staggering into the living room, dropped my papers and books onto the sofa and flopped down beside them, dropped my head onto the cushion. I could stay like this for ever. And ever. And ever.

'Hi Ceri,' a male voice said. I hadn't been here long enough to work out who it was. I turned my head a little to look at him. Ed.

'Hi Ed,' I replied.

Ed threw himself down onto the other sofa, picked up the remote control and turned on the television. 'Suffering?' he asked.

'Yeah. I've had to deal with photocopying psychos. And this lecturing lark's a lot harder than it seems,' I mumbled.

'So it's nothing to do with being laroped last night?'

'Jake told you?' I said.

'Jake told me. He said you wouldn't stop talking.'

'Oh, Godddd. Did he sound scared when he told you?'

'Well, he was quite pleased that you took the time to re assure him that you weren't a weirdo. And that you didn't think either of us would whack you over the head if you borrowed our milk. Not that you drink milk.'

'Ohhhhhhhh.'

'He thought it was quite funny, actually.'

'Yeah, they all think it's funny until they ask you to move out,' I said into the cushion.

'Hi Ceri,' Jake said.

I sat bolt upright. Dragged my hands through my hair to make it lie flat. 'Jake, about last night . . .' I began.

'Forget it,' Jake said, brushing away my apology before I'd even started it. He sat beside Ed, wrestled the remote control off him and flicked the TV over.

Ed wrestled it back, flicked it back to the other side.

Jake nudged Ed, held him back with his elbow, got back the control and turned over the TV. 'We're having sausage casserole for tea,' Jake said, he'd got Ed in a head lock and was holding the remote out of reach.

'Yeah, and I made Angel Delight for dessert,' Ed choked.

'You do eat meat, don't you?' Jake said.

'I do,' I said, watching the fight progress.

'Cool. But don't have any Angel Delight, Ed's a really bad cook even when it's just whisking powder into milk.'

Ed managed to grab a pillow from the sofa and started to bash Jake with it. I lay face down on the sofa again. I had moved into the right place. I could feel it in my soul.

chapter nine

The Boss

Time moves quickly, time moves slowly.

The longer I stayed in Leeds, the more I understood Einstein's theory of relativity. Not the entire theorem, more the relative part. How things seemed.

Time sped by at weekends, time almost stopped when I was giving a lecture, from the looks on some of the students' faces and the way they stared forlornly at their watches, they felt the same. And, for some reason, every day seemed to be the day before Wednesday, or Wednesday. Wednesday was half-day at most universities and colleges so the students could pursue physical activities and play sports. Most uni competitions and matches were held on Wednesday afternoons. This meant I could pursue my favourite activities – cooking, eating, watching television without infringing upon official work or study time.

The relativity of Wednesday to every other day of the week should, then, have been joyous. It was not.

The usual drill for Wednesday pre-lunch, post-morning, was for Gwen, my boss and the head of the psychology department, to come in after giving a cognitive psychology lecture and flop down next to me, offer me a cigarette (I'd always refuse, emphasising how much tobacco smoke bothered me with a reply of 'I don't smoke') and proceed to chain-smoke her way through the entire two-hour lecture. That is, recounting it between long drags of her high-tar fags.

'I don't know why I bother, I really don't,' she said, searching her handbag for something. Cigarettes I presumed. This was my third Wednesday. She'd assumed the flop beside me position and was now searching for her props before the drama that was lecturing unfolded. I braced myself for a face and body full of the brown stuff people had to use paint stripper to get off pub walls. 'Do you know what they've done now?'

I'd been in Gwen's office a few times since I started, and discovered it was like walking in to an Ashtray Temple. Ashtrays littered the desk, her bookshelves, there were a couple on the window sill. Each was different in size and colour but her office was clearly a holy place for the things. Drawn here to worship at the fingers of the great, white smoker. Each and every ashtray had some kind of cigarette debris in it, as though she stubbed out her cigarette in whichever ashtray she happened to be passing at the time. Most disturbingly, every cigarette was fully-smoked.

I'd sat opposite her at her desk and studied the cigarettes the first time I'd been in her office. First, I'd looked at the ones in the ashtray by her computer, then at the ones in the ashtrays I could see. Every cigarette was smoked, right to the edge of the filter. No fag escaped her ownership unsmoked or half-smoked. Or even three-quarters smoked. That showed a particular type of dedication. She didn't simply want a boost of nicotine, she wanted every last drop, every last microgram. Gwen was one step away from injecting nicotine.

'Do you know what they've done now?' she repeated, her hand still digging around the bag.

Rather conversely to all laws of physics and biology, Gwen

spoke with the girliest voice. The kind of voice I used to affect when I wanted to get around someone by pretending to be pathetic and unable to think due to a lack of brain cells. She spoke with an educated squeak that became posher and squeakier the more riled she got. Her voice suited her clothes though: Laura Ashley-style skirts or dresses, pink or powder blue blouses. And, most bizarrely, always, *always* thick black tights. We'd had a rash of hot, sunny days recently, but still Gwen's sixty deniers stuck to her legs, and stuck out of her black open-toe sandals. She wore those whether it was sunny or cold or rainy, too.

Gwen found her cigarettes and pulled them out of her big, flowery cloth bag. She flipped the top of the packet open. 'I really don't know why I bother,' she repeated.

'Why, what's happened?' I said, catching on that, unlike previous Wednesdays, I had to work for the information this time. She lit her cigarette with her solid gold lighter, a present from her husband – I'd seen the inscription – and inhaled almost all of the cigarette in one suck. It was bad. It was very bad. I didn't yet understand just how bad it was, though.

'Not one of them had done the reading. Not one,' she squeaked, a notch or two higher than normal. She was very agitated. 'And then one of them had the audacity to . . .' huge draw, 'to say she didn't know what I was talking about. She didn't know what I was talking about. Can you believe it?'

My heart sank, my throat tightened and I swallowed hard. Unfortunately, yes, I could believe it. In fact, I could've prevented it.

My second lecture with the first group I'd taught as a proper lecturer, I'd relaxed into the role far more. I wasn't reading straight from the script in front of me. I could ad lib, drop in little quips. I was working up to big detours and anecdotes.

That second lecture, they'd relaxed with me, too. We'd only been in the room for a few minutes when the woman with the tight, blondish perm raised her hand slightly.

'Er, yeah?' I asked. 'Oh, do you mind saying your name before you speak? I still haven't learnt your names.'

'Um, I'm Roberta. Can I ask you something?'

'Yeah, course.'

'Do you think Gwen's mad?'

'Sorry?' I replied.

Mr Wham-era George Michael raised his hand. 'I'm Joel, I think what Roberta's trying to say is, we don't understand what she's on about half the time. And none of us are learning anything.'

'No, Joel,' Roberta said, 'I was asking if Ceri thought Gwen was mad. There is a difference, even if you're too polite to notice.'

'Right,' I said. *Oh bollocks*, I thought.

After that, the flood gates were bust open as a tidal wave of disgruntlement crashed down onto the room. Gwen was boring. Gwen was confusing. 'She scares the b'jasus out of me with the way she teaches,' one of them said.

I'd listened to the first wave of discontentment, then said: 'She speaks very highly of you, too.'

Another tidal wave of disgruntlement crashed down on us then: most of them skipped her lectures, they said. The ones who did go to her lectures were far too scared to point out how little they were learning. Or to even reply to her questions. They all lived in mortal fear of her asking them a question. They simply weren't learning anything, but were too worried about being given a failing grade to say owt to her.

I wasn't stupid. Stunned, but not stupid. The general gist of what they were saying was, 'Could you say something to her for us?, i.e., could you get her to stop being Gwen and be a little human when it comes to her teaching style?

I tried to impress upon them that they were responsible for what they learnt, no one could put it in their heads. But they were having none of it. They merely dragged out more examples of how bad a lecturer Gwen was and how it was practically my duty, as the new, young, trendy lecturer who'd started off by being nice to them, to say something to her. That'll learn me to try to be cool.

With the burden on my head, I'd meant to say something to Gwen. Really I had. I simply never found the right moment, the right time, the righ— OK, OK, I was scared. She was the head of department. My Boss. She could revoke my position with the stroke of a pen. How was I supposed to tell her, she who had years of teaching experience, compared to my fifty hours' experience, to stop it. Besides, I'd be trapped in her smoke-filled office while I tried to explain their position to her. I had meant to at least broach the subject. I'd just kept putting it off and putting it off until, well, now. Woman thy name is coward.

I looked at Gwen as she finished off her cigarette. 'I, er,' I began, not sure what I was going to say before I opened my mouth. But then, I was rarely sure what I was going to say before I opened my mouth, and it hadn't stopped me before.

Again, I was saved by Mel. He blew into the Senior Common Room, a mass of papers and folders. Papers slipping, eyes searching the room, he always moved as though someone was chasing him. 'He could cause a riot in an empty house,' that was a phrase my mum used and it was so apt for Mel. He approached the low coffee table Gwen and I were sat in front of and I had my feet on, paused – giving me a silent one-second warning to move my feet, before they were avalanched by his lecturing materials and essays. I pulled my feet away just before he dropped his load. He then reached into his back pocket and pulled out a picture postcard.

'Guess who I got a postcard from?' he stated to the room. It'd filled up a little, but not much. Not enough for him to be making such a big-voiced announcement, anyway.

'Who?' Gwen replied for the room. Her demon year group forgotten.

'Eva.'

The name sparked a couple of 'awwws' and some interest around the room. A couple of people – mugs in hands – wandered over, others looked up from what they were doing to listen.

'Listen,' Mel said, cleared his throat.

Dear Everyone – and Mel. Greetings from Barcelona. Am having the time of my life. Even better than I could have hoped for when I left. It's warm here and I'm walking around in a lot less than I would in Britain. There's so much to tell but not much space. Have met a couple of nice people and we'll be working our way across to Spain's Atlantic coast and then on to Tangiers. I can tell I'm going to be a travel bore when I get back. Miss you all but don't miss College. At all.

  Love and Peace, Eva.

  PS Mel, you waster, you'd better pass this on.

'Cheeky cow,' Mel muttered.

A few pleased sighs went around the room. Eva was the woman who'd kindly vacated her position about three days before I wrote to the college.

'Wish I was travelling,' Gwen mumbled, a petulant tone in her voice.

'Have you been travelling before?' I asked, grateful that we didn't need to talk about the demon year group any more.

Gwen lit another cigarette with her lighter, breathed it to life, shook her head. 'No. My husband and I didn't ever get around to it.' She snapped her head around to me. 'We meant to. We simply got tied up in our careers. It's just, the first ten years were devoted to getting ourselves established in our careers, and then it was too late. But we did mean to.'

I'd avoided asking Gwen much about her family because:
a) I hadn't forgotten she abandoned me at lunch on the first day
b) I wasn't allowed to by The Commandments
c) I didn't want to get into any conversation that would end up with me having to accept an invitation to dinner. (If I'd only narrowly escaped becoming a Jehovah's Witness, how much more would I be able to turn down an invitation to dinner? It wasn't in my nature to say no to people when they asked me nicely.)

There were inherent dangers in any Gwen-related dinner invitation: if the chintz her house would surely be decorated in didn't burn the retinas off my cornea, then the smoke would get me. And if her husband smoked half as much as she did, I'd end the night in an oxygen tent. Of course, there was also the small talk factor. ST had never been my forte. It was pretty unnecessary when most people came out with deeply personal stories from the off. But I didn't want that with my boss.

You needed a little mystery with the people you worked for. I remember when I'd been a secretary during the summer holidays from uni. I got to know far too much about my bosses. One boss in particular when I temped in a media agency used to take me out for drinks to whinge on about her relationship. She often told me things my fragile mind didn't ever want to hear. I suppose the bedrock of my unshockability came from that summer, with her. I'd lie for her when her partner called, I arranged her life, I even cleared out her office when she moved floors. And the stuff I unearthed in there unsettled me. Let's say, I'd never seen things like vibrators or crotchless knickers up close until I worked for her. I came to her a non-virgin innocent. I left knowing too much about sex – like how having a threesome with your partner's best friend could really mess you up emotionally.

Basically, there was no mystique between us and that's necessary in a boss-employee relationship. How could you take seriously someone shouting at you for being late when you knew she'd once cried in the street because Shelley's had sold out of white stilettos?

I did not want to cross that line with Gwen. Having said that, guilt gestated in my conscience. I wanted to go back in time and warn her about the coming student revolution. That they were not going down the *coup d'état* route – they wanted blood and beheadings. I couldn't go back though, despite all *Star Trek* had led me to believe, so I had to be nice to her in the present. 'What does your husband do?' I asked, risking the dinner invite.

'Do? He doesn't do anything. Whatever do you mean?'

'You said about your careers . . . I just wondered . . .' *Freako*, I thought.

'Career? He's a banker. One of the top executives in the City.'

'Right. Sounds interesting.' I.e. boring as tooth plaque. Although, I shouldn't malign tooth plaque – under a microscope it was probably more interesting than her husband's job.

'Vernon seems to suit it.'

'But you'd rather be travelling?'

'No, no, of course not. It's just a pipe dream that we, well,

99

I think about. Sometimes. Only sometimes. How can you not when you hear postcards like that? Of course I wouldn't rather be travelling. I love my life. I love my life.'

Chill baby, you don't have to convince me of owt. I don't care if you travel or stay in Leeds. 'I see,' I replied, absently. I'd tuned out, fuzzed my brain to Gwen, focused instead across the room on Mel and Claudine.

Claudine and Mel sat alone at the table at the left end of the SCR, while he described something on the front of the post-card to her. He'd obviously been to Barcelona, his right index finger traced something along the postcard, every two microseconds his eyes would go up to her face, keen to ensnare her in his tale. She, while clearly interested, kept her dark eyes focused on the postcard, nodding to show she was following him but studiously avoiding eye contact.

There was something going on there. Yes, she told me that last week, after the gym, but there was something more going on between them. It wasn't purely body language that gave the game away. Not with them, not with other people.

It was the way people looked at each other in unguarded moments. The way they didn't look at each other in guarded moments. I'd become a bit of an unintentional expert in non-verbal communication over the years. I'd studied people on the sly, listened to their tales and watched them afterwards. Despite what people pretended, despite what people said to my face, they couldn't stop those tell-tale signs showing through.

With Mel and Claudine it wasn't as simple as the picture she painted for me the other night. I'm sure they had 'got physical', but *how* physical was still up for debate. Not that Claudine was a liar, she wanted to believe what she told me, which was why she'd been able to look me in the eye as she said it; you can lie if you want to believe the lie enough. Maybe more had happened, maybe less had happened. The

100

point was: something had happened. And they were both struggling to deal with the consequences of it. Claudine, from the way she was behaving and talking the other night, was clearly racked with guilt over whatever it was. (I'd personally not worked out how anyone could cheat. It was far too much guilt to live with on a day-to-day basis. To look in the mirror day after day, knowing what you'd done . . . that was too much like hard work.) And, like I said to her, she was waiting for the answer to her dilemma to fall into her lap so she could decide what to do.

Then there was Mel. Sitting beside Claudine. Nice guy Mel who'd cheated on his wife with his best friend. Those weren't the actions of a nice guy. But, as I'd found over the years, nothing was as simple as we all hoped it would be. You could rarely point your finger at the average person in the street and say, 'All bad.' 'Completely evil.' It was only the people who'd gone out of their way to cause destruction and death and hurt and pain and ignorance who could be classified in such terms. Most people, your average Joanne Public, your next-door neighbour, your lecturer in the common room, had levels of behaviour, levels of badness, reasons for doing the things they did. Even if they did destroy other people's lives. Mel was one of those people.

Take the way he was with Claudine now. How he was looking at her, how he was talking to her, he cared about her deeply. If he and his wife only split up a few months ago, *after* his indiscretion with Claudine, then that would mean he couldn't be feeling rebound love for Claudine. He'd most likely loved her for years. If he'd loved her for years, then why wait until he got married to make a move on her? And *then* finish with his wife and tell Claudine how he felt. Something more was going on. It was more complicated than love. Love was great. Love was everything as far as a lot of people were concerned, but with Claudine and Mel, it was more complicated than love. They had depth of friendship; years seeing other people; a present that meant working together. For them, love was only a small element of it, a tiny piece of the Mel and Claudine jigsaw. If love was the be all and end all in their case, they'd be together, wouldn't they?

Mel and Claudine. Claudine and Mel. I really needed to hear his side of the story to get the fuller picture of their jigsaw. However, it was nothing to do with me. At all. It was j—

'Well, would you?' Gwen asked, impatiently.

I turned to her, smiled. I trawled my memory for what she'd been saying while I'd been observing Mel and Claude. I'd heard it, but not enough. And Gwen's face, lined and freckly and obscured by cigarette smoke as it was, hung on a precipice of either pleasure or upset. The guilt that had been gestating earlier was almost ready to come out, kicking and screaming the truth, the whole truth and nothing but the truth. I was very close to either telling her I'd known about the students hating her, or I'd invite her to dinner myself.

'Why not,' I replied, careful to keep my tone ambiguous so she wouldn't know I'd completely tuned out.

Gwen's face broke into an unexpected grin. I'd never seen her grin before, it suited her. She should smile more often. She should probably relax more often, too. 'Fabulous. I'll let you know,' she squeaked. 'It'll be within the next month or so. I'll have to check with Vernon, but I'm sure he'd love having you over for dinner.'

chapter ten

Tea Circles

Mel was the new Levi's type. The kind of lad who always had the latest style of Levi's, two minutes after it hit the shops. I bet he had the latest DVD machine, the toppest-of-the-range stereo. I'd heard, though, he'd supplemented his wages by giving private A-level sociology lessons.

Currently on Mel's wear list, as he stood at my front door, was the distressed blue denim with the twisted seams. Jeans and jacket. He'd teamed them with a black polo neck. He didn't look like a dork, though. I'd always been theoretically against putting same-coloured denim together, it looked like you were trying to wear a casual suit. But what did I know? I lived in combats, jeans and long-sleeved tops.

I smiled a welcome at Mel, he grinned at me. Maybe he didn't look like a dork because he stood erect, showing off all of his six foot frame. Or, possibly because of the chaotic way his brown hair curled on his head. Or maybe it was his light hazel eyes. Whatever it was, Melvin looked at ease in his gear. He always did. When he had his large blue rucksack slung casually over his shoulder and he wandered the corridors of the college, he seemed more student than lecturer, which was probably why so many of the students looked genuinely pleased to see him, why he often stopped for a quick chat and why he got invited to lots of student parties. He was Mr Popular, not only at our college, but also at The Met.

His popularity at The Met was how I'd found out so much about him. I'd mentioned to Ed and Jake a nice young sociology lecturer who'd helped me on my first day. When I said he was called Mel, they told me they knew him from playing footie at The Met. When I'd said we'd sat at lunch together, they'd sat me down and imparted every morsel of info about him they knew. There'd been more than a hint of the 'you get in there, girl' as they told me about him. 'He's single now, you know,' Jake and Ed had said at various points. *If only you knew*, I thought back at them.

Mel had never shown up at Ed and Jake's before then – over a week after I'd been for a drink with Claudine.

'Come in,' I said, stepping aside to let him into the warm hallway. The mid-March air still had a winter's bite about it and I'd begged and begged Jake to let me have the heating on. He'd relented but he and Ed took to walking about in shorts. Ed, though, still wore his red and black lumberjack shirt. I was pretty sure he'd die wearing that shirt.

'I forgot you lived here,' Mel said, taking off his jacket and loosening his scarf.

Lie. Total lie. I mean, if he'd truly forgotten, then why no surprise when I opened the door? In the hundred watt lighting of the hallway, I could see the different shades of pink that made up Mel's blush. He knew I knew he was lying so he avoided eye contact as he handed over his jacket, then took it back to stuff his scarf in the side pocket. The blue scarf spilled out like the jacket's guts were falling out. I draped it over the hook.

'Who is it?' Ed called from the depths of the living room.

We'd all settled down to watch the second instalment of *It*. (When I'd said that if I watched the film I'd end up sleeping on the floor of one of their rooms, because I didn't 'do' horror films, they'd both laughed like broken drains. 'You think I'm joking,' I said. 'Wait till you wake up and find me kipping on your floor with a teaspoon for protection.')

'Mel,' I called back.

'All right mate,' Jake called.

'All right,' Mel replied, sticking his head around the living room door. 'Room for a little one?'

'Depends if you've brought any stuff,' Ed replied, putting his forefinger and thumb close together and moving them towards his thin lips.

'Nuh, huh, no drugs, we agreed,' I said, returning to my space on the sofa furthest from the widescreen telly.

'Yeah, Ed,' Jake added, 'Ceri's old, remember.' Wouldn't mind if the cheeky *get* wasn't only a couple of years younger than me. And Mel was my age.

'Oh yeah,' Ed said.

'Whatever, just wait till I've gone to bed.'

'With your slippers and cocoa,' Mel chimed in.

'Watch it, you, I get a vote in if you're allowed to stay or not, you know.'

'While you're up, Cezza, put kettle on,' Ed said.

My bum had almost touched the seat, as well. I sighed and hoisted myself up.

'Mel can help, to earn his keep,' Jake decreed.

Funny he should say that. I got the impression Mel was going to help me anyway.

Being a Southern Softie, I'd bought a water filter – to the amusement and constant abuse of the lads. I filled the filter from the tap while Mel helped by leaning against the worktop closest to the back door and staring into the mid-distance. The water dribbled and dripped through the filter, I found clean cups, dropped three ordinary tea bags into the three white cups, dropped a strawberry, Southern Softie bag into the fourth black mug. Mel's latest contribution was to stand still in the kitchen.

'Claudine's nice, isn't she?' Mel eventually said. Very eventually. So eventually I'd thought he'd never get it off his chest. That he'd leave with his soul still burdened with whatever it was he felt so compelled to travel here to see me about. That wasn't arrogance, his lie about forgetting I lived here proved that. And, I didn't want to prompt him to tell me what he wanted to tell me. I could prompt him to reveal the wrong thing.

'Yeah, she seems nice.' I wasn't sure how much Claudine had told Mel about our impromptu night in the pub, or if she'd even mentioned that night to him. So it was best to use my new-found power of keeping shtum.

'Oh, she's lovely. I've known her, what, ten years now. We met at The Met.'

'Ah, right.'

'We were in the same halls of residence.'

'Right.'

Silence. More silence. *Come on Mel, spit it out, it might be a bus. And, to be honest, I'm getting spooked stood here in silence near the sink. You know, where water comes from and where the scary clown from the film comes up and grabs people.*

'It was funny you saying that the other day,' he said.

'About?' I stopped myself adding: "I'm that funny, I need constant reminding of my witticisms."

'About me and Clau and how long we'd been together.'

I grimaced. Even though I now knew what I knew, I still physically cringed every time I thought about how I'd done that on my first day here. 'Yeah, sorry about that.'

'It's all right,' Mel shrugged. 'It was just funny that's all.'

'Funny how?'

Mel shrugged again. 'Because you obviously guessed how I feel about her. Even though we really are just mates now.'

'And you weren't before?'

'I know I probably shouldn't tell you this, but Claudine is the love of my life, she always has been. I was, er, married for four years.' Mel watched the sink while he talked. He cleared his throat. 'My marriage fell apart over Christmas. The happy season was not happy for me, I can tell you. It turned into the worst few days of my life. But,' Mel had the grace to look ashamed, 'even before I tied the knot I was gone on Clau. I fancied her from the first year. I mean, you've seen her. She's gorgeous. And, well, last year, just before Christmas we got very drunk and . . . made love.' Mel paused, obviously waiting for judgement or shock from me.

'I see,' I said. Probably not the time to mention Claudine remembers it differently.

'It was the first – and only – time it happened. Clau was so ashamed she'd cheated on, Ke— her boyfriend and what we'd done to my wife that she wanted to pretend we'd stopped at the last minute. She and my wife used to get on really well, they were mates actually. They often went out together on their own cos they got on so well. We'd actually planned to spend Boxing Day together, the four of us. My wife and I weren't getting on anyway, but what happened with Claudine turned out to be our death knell. Clau still feels ashamed about it. I try to be normal but she can't seem to forget it.'

'It's hard to be normal if you think you've ruined someone's life. Especially if yours is still intact,' I replied. This was actually a cleverly-disguised question. I was trying to get him to reveal more about the state of his marriage before he and Claudine got physical.

'I don't know why she'd think that. She of all people knew that my marriage was far from perfect. I'm sure Fran, that's my wife, told her about it – Clau spent more time with her than I did at one point. We talked, me and my wife, but it always seemed to be about bills or what was for dinner. That's how I got to know Jake and Ed so well – I started spending almost every night out, joined a footie team. Then I spent time here with them. As it got to Christmas time, I spent all my time with Clau . . . I'm not saying the means justify the end, but for me it was always going to be that end. Me and my wife splitting up.'

'So it could've been anyone, not just Claudine?' I asked.

Mel's face narrowed into a fierce frown. 'What are you saying? I adore Claudine.'

'So you said,' I replied.

His eyes narrowed to slits, his face twisted.

Mel was the angry type. Great time to find *that* out. The Angry Type scared me. They were the type neighbours said of, months later, as bodies were unearthed from their back garden, 'I always thought they had killer eyes.' I had no intention of going that way. I opened a cupboard, the nearest one to me, and started moving things around, seeking biscuits and sugar, even though both things stood in clearly labelled jars on the worktop. I couldn't face his look of anger and betrayal and not fear for my life.

'Why did you marry your wife?' I asked, my head still in the depths of the cupboard.

'Because she was beautiful. And nice. And funny. And clever and lovely.'

'Did you love her?' I might as well get buried for a cow as a mouse. (The saying went something like that.)

Mel slammed down his cup with such force, I expected a loud smashing sound to follow it. His tea was surely slopped all over the worktop. I couldn't see, I still had my head in the cupboard.

'*What?!*' he snarled.

'You said you were gone on Claudine,' I said, moving the pepper onto the marmalade. 'You adored her when you got married. So, did you love your wife at all?'

'Course,' Mel said quickly. 'Of course I did. It wasn't just a simple case of I loved Clau and didn't love Fran.'

'Right, I see. Did you like Fran?'

Silence was Mel's reply. Not angry silence. Not even silence lightly flavoured with indignation. Just plain ol' silence. It was safe to out myself now. I withdrew my head from the cupboard. Mel was staring down into his cup of tea, making patterns on the worktop with the spilt tea. Jake would love that, Mel staining his real wood worktop with his thought-filled tea circles.

'Yeah I liked her,' he mumbled. 'Course I liked her.'

'Oh, so she was a mate, too? I mean, did she match up to all your other friends?' In other words, was she as good a friend as Claudine?

Mel's tongue started to explore his mouth, seeking renegade bits of food to dislodge and chew on. I stared at him rather openly as I waited for his answer. *Come on, tell me, did your wife match up to Claudine in the friendship stakes?*

'Erm, the lads will be gagging for these by now,' Mel said. He threaded his fingers through two cups with one hand and picked up his cup with the other hand. 'You know how much they love their tea.'

The poor cow never had a chance, did she Mel? I picked up my cup, the strawberry scent filling my senses. *She thought she was marrying someone who she was going to spend the rest of her life with; you, well you wanted something completely different. She stood a snowball's chance in hell. Poor, poor woman.*

During the second part of *It*, Mel cast me long, thought-filled looks, redrawing those tea circles with his eyes over the space I occupied in the room. He was rethinking his marriage; his 'friendship' with Claudine. The lads probably thought he was running through the *Kama Sutra* in his head with me.

Ed started to skin up the second the credits rolled on the film. I dragged myself from the sofa, and headed for bed. *Can I hold off going to the loo or brushing my teeth until morning?* I wondered as I shuffled out of the room. *No way am I going near any kind of water when that clown could appear out of the plug hole. In the morning, the lads will hear sounds of my demise if the clown does appear.*

'See ya,' I called. *Only goody two shoes brush their teeth twice a day anyway. And remember how you once held off going to the loo for six hours when you were in Egypt? If I go to bed straight away, I'll wake up in the night and not remember the clown until after I've used th—*

'Oh, Ceri, hang on.' Mel handed the joint to Jake and skipped out of the room after me. I stopped on the second step, my eyes hurt from telly-watching without my glasses, I blinked a couple of times to ease their discomfort and strain.

'Yup?' I asked Mel.

I could feel, rather than see, the lads leaning out of their seats to catch a snatch of our conversation.

'You won't tell anyone what we talked about, will you?' Mel asked in a lowered tone.

'Course not,' I replied in the same low tone.

Mel smiled at me, placed a hand on my hand. I could feel the lads' eyes widen. I took my hand away before they gave him a pack of condoms and directions to my bedroom.

'Thanks for listening,' he said.

'My pleasure,' I said. 'Good night boys.'

'Night Cezza,' they called back.

And good luck with all that thinking and rethinking you've got to do, Melvin, I know it won't be easy.

chapter eleven

Only the Lonely

Who thought that seeing this little bit of dirt track road, made up of pebbles and mud and huge great holes, would make me so happy. That I'd feel my heart leap with joy as I turned off St Michael's Lane into the road I now called home. I'd been deeply depressed for the past five hours or so. Actually, for most of the weekend.

I was returning from a weekend in London.

London, my home. Ha!

I'd decided to go back, visit my parents, visit my brothers and my sister, get some more of my belongings and remind myself that London was a trillion times more hip than Leeds. That while I was settling in Up Norf, my heart was buried deep in the south. Ha, ha, ha. (That was a humourless, bitter laugh.)

Bloody Oprah and bloody heart's desire.

It'd felt like I was entering a strange land when I got off the train at London's King's Cross. Even in a month things seemed to have changed. By the time I got to South East London, where my flat was, I felt as though I was on the moon.

Ridiculous really, since I'd grown up in London. Twenty-four of my twenty-nine years on this planet had been spent in London. But, I didn't feel like I knew anything. Everything seemed smaller, dirtier, stranger. Alien. I felt like ET walking into my flat (he wouldn't have spent so much time bealing on about going home if he'd been confronted with what I had when I'd stepped over my own threshold). The woman who'd taken over my flat for the year had made her mark on the place. Not with the decor, she hadn't painted or lain new carpet or owt, which would've been nice cos I hadn't really done that in the two years I'd lived there, either. But she'd taken down the huge framed photo of Angel/David Boreanaz that previously hung over my fireplace. My videos had been stacked up in boxes, in their place were books. *Her* books. Rows and rows of the tomes and 'intellectual' novels people put on display but few people actually read.

My books, of which there were over six hundred, had mostly been boxed up too. They had those 'intellectual' tomes amongst them, and I had actually read them. And I'd read all my Judge Dredd graphic novels too. I was widely read like that. Her tomes all looked untouched by human hands. My cushions and stuff had been moved to the spare room, which was now an office again. An office-cum-second bedroom. The metal-framed futon was now put up as a sofa instead of put down as a bed. My clothes were all folded and hidden away in suitcases under the futon. My beloved Batman bust was back in its box.

She and her boyfriend had moved into my bedroom, of course. I'd valiantly ignored thinking about the two people having sex in my bed thing, just made a mental note to buy a new bed the *second* I moved back to London. I'd felt like I'd sold my flat years ago and was visiting to see what they'd done with the place. It was my place still. Except it wasn't. My name was on the mortgage papers and on the lease, it was my

113

furniture but that was it. The shell was mine, the soul of the place now seemed to be hers.

I thought it'd always be my place. Home is where the heart is, *n'est-ce pas?* I hadn't been prepared for the shock and ill feeling I'd got when I went around. I could've made those adjustments, I could've had those brown suede cushions and cream cotton cushions on that cream throw in the living room. I could've put up those blinds. I could've had rugs, dammit. It hurt so much I had to spend the night with my parents. I'd have been cheating on my own taste if I'd slept there. Just to compound the upset, none of my London friends had been around for the night, owing to having husbands, wives and children to think about, so I'd spent the night in with my parents. Saturday night with my folks. Much as I love them, fun as they are, Saturday night sipping cherryade in front of the news was akin to hell.

As the woman who'd possessed my flat made me tea (fancy that, someone making me tea in my own flat, treating me like a guest), I'd had another wave of wondering if I was doing the right thing. Yes, I was enjoying it in Leeds. But maybe my heart's desire could be found at home in London. Originally, when I started doing the 'follow my heart's desire' thing, I'd thought of Leeds because it seemed the perfect escape route from all that nonsense I got myself embroiled in in London. I could walk away from living other people's lives. Well, looksee, I was doing the same thing in Leeds wasn't I? It was just now condensed into a smaller area and had been done in a smaller amount of time. While in London it'd taken me years to get truly embroiled in everyone's life, I'd done it in under three weeks Up Norf. Mel, Ed, Claudine, a couple of the students.

On top of my feeling like a failure because I had managed to get involved in Leeds, I was going back to London and feeling displaced, lost in the nowhere land between living in someone else's home Up Norf and not having a definite home in London. I'd made South East London my home when I finally returned to London from Leeds six years ago and I never thought I'd feel this loneliness. It was so illogical. Why did I feel like this? I could get my flat back whenever I wanted, I had loads of contacts in London I could freelance for, I could go back if I wanted. I could be a homeowner and journalist again just like that. It wasn't as though I'd *sold* everything to come to be a lodger and an employee far down on the career ladder. Just loaned it out. I felt so lost though. I'd often felt like this when I was younger – displaced and homeless – emotionally. Not really sure of where I fitted in the world.

Maybe I should just accept I'm not good with people. I may listen to them and advise them, but like I said, there were very few people who'd be there if I had a four-in-the-morning panic and wanted someone to talk to. Jess was only there when her family life would allow and I didn't even think Drew would be there should I need him. I was in constant wonder at how many people kept in touch with friends from school and college and beyond. I had friends from college, but I always felt on the outside looking in. That I wasn't one of the first people they thought of when it came to births, marriages and reunions.

I trundled up Stanmore Vale, sighing inwardly. That was the truly ironic thing about my life, really. I could connect with people quickly. People dragged me into the deepest enclaves of their lives in the blink of an eye, but I had hardly anyone I could do that with. I gave – my time, my ear, my advice – but rarely received. Ceri D'Altroy, she who was open to callers twenty-four/seven, couldn't get the time of day from most people.

Already on my list of advisees were Claudine and Mel and Ed. Although Ed was slightly different. He'd just opened up to me the once and had gone about his business, completely ignoring what I'd said. Claudine and Mel were, I could tell, long-termers. They'd keep coming back and coming back, neither of them noticing that when they were getting their advice and listening ear, while they unburdened their souls, I was dying to talk about myself. Talk about why I had very, very few close friendships. And why I couldn't keep a relationship going for toffee.

My relationship history read like a horror story. During college, I had a few boyfriends, but nothing serious. I met The Love Of My Life during the third year of college – which sent Drew into such a jealous rage he'd picked a fight with me, told me to f-off and walked out, only to reappear properly when The Love Of My Life left me for someone else. I never craved anything serious after that, partly because I was still holding out for Drew, partly because relationships or my lack of them weren't the be all and end all. Telly, junk food, reading – far more important than bemoaning the lack of a man in my life. Then I moved back to London and did my masters, where I met Whashisface Tosspot. I saw him for a year, then we moved in together. I then spent *that* year trying to escape whatever Jedi Mind Trick/Work Of The Devil he had me under. He was nothing like a boyfriend. We had sex, we sometimes went out, I didn't go out with anyone else, but still, he was nothing like a boyfriend. I had no burning passion for him. Mainly because, when I'd originally snogged him I'd been trying to make him feel better. And it'd rather spectacularly back-fired . . .

I knew N—Whashisface Tosspot, from college, he was in the next halls to me, he had friends in my halls and I'd spoken to him a few times. He seemed nice enough, not overly friendly, not overly unfriendly. Just nice enough. About two months into the course, I'd gone to a party with a group of people from my halls and he'd happened to be there. I'd been contemplating the wisdom of leaving my coat in one of the bedrooms; wondering what the likelihood was of it being used by someone to have sex on when he'd come over to talk to me. During the conversation he'd asked if I was seeing anyone and I'd said no. Out of politeness, rather than genuine interest, I'd asked him if he was seeing anyone (those were the kind of questions that led to people pouring their hearts out to me).

'Umm . . .' he'd said, then looked very uncomfortable. 'My last relationship was cut brutally short, six months ago.'

'Right,' I said, and sipped on the home-made punch in my hands. It contained vodka and cranberry I was pretty sure, but there were a few other things I couldn't quite place.

'Yeah,' he'd continued, 'my lady and I were going to get married and she left me. Smashed my heart into smithereens. Now she's cohabiting with someone else. I was completely blindsided by that. As I said, my heart was smashed into smithereens.'

I'd had a strong suspicion that the conversation was going to become a blurt session when he'd asked if I was seeing anyone, but now we were heading up that path, I was determined to take us down another route. It was Friday night, I was at a party. For once, this man who had hunted me out to blurt at me was not going to get a listening ear. I just couldn't be bothered. It was Friday night, for God's sake!

I decided to avert the blurt session with a bit of levity. 'I've forgotten what kissing's like,' I joked.

'I'll be more than happy to help you out in that matter,' he replied.

I jumped inside. Actually, physically jumped, then my body froze. That'd never happened before. No one who'd been on the verge of blurting at me had taken a flip comment like that the wrong way. Then again, none of them said 'smashed into smithereens' either.

My head moved slowly as I turned to look him over properly. I'd seen him before, of course, but I hadn't been offered the opportunity to kiss him when I'd contemplated him before, so I hadn't *looked* looked. He wasn't bad. He had receding dirty blond hair, a largish slightly hooked nose, small eyes. In his favour, he didn't have a mono-brow. He wasn't bad, but he wasn't exactly overly endowed with attractiveness, either. Nothing about him said, 'snog me'. I'd snogged men before who weren't even vaguely good-looking, but had something about them that drew me to them.

'No, you're all right,' I replied. I really hadn't drunk enough to snog someone whose best feature was not having a mono-brow. 'I'm being silly. I, er, need to go to the loo. See ya.'

Later, much later, back in halls, when the group of people I'd gone to the party with had broken out the tequila and hash, I went to make coffee. It was going to be an all night session and I wasn't drunk enough for more tequila nor sober enough to go to bed. Whashisface Tosspot came to help with the coffee making. Even though I was only making one cup for myself.

'I didn't mean to offend you earlier,' he said as he fussed around the sink and I stood beside the kettle waiting for it to boil. 'I simply find you enchantingly interesting. And attractive.'

Who talks like that? I asked myself. 'It's OK, I wasn't offended,' I replied and willed the kettle to boil faster. He fancied me, I suddenly realised. He'd more or less told me I was a bit of all right, in that odd language of his; he'd taken my comment earlier the wrong way and had been overly eager to kiss me and now, he was looking at me. I could just tell he was looking at me, acting shy and nervous – as you did around someone you fancied. I could feel something from him and at first glance it seemed to be attraction. Except, on closer inspection, it wasn't really a genuine type of attraction. The fact of the matter was, he only *thought* he fancied me. Like people start to fancy their therapists or their priests, he thought he fancied me because I'd listened to his story, all two seconds of it. He could probably sense that I'd listen to his story again, should he feel the need to open up some more. And this having someone there to listen, in his mind, translated into fancying me.

It's so obvious what his problem is, I thought, as I watched steam funnel up out of the white jug kettle. He needed someone to make him feel attractive. He'd been hurt when his (ahem!) lady left. He was probably cautious around women. Unsure of his feelings and how they'd be received. What he wanted, what he needed, was to win. Just once. To get an ego boost that would send him off into the world feeling like a man. Feeling that he could pull. What he needed was a mercy snog. A small act of charity that would get him back on the dating horse.

Besides, if I didn't snog him, there was every danger he'd start talking again – and completely ruin my night.

Instead of pouring hot water on the coffee granules, I crossed the kitchen, put my arms around his neck and kissed him before I could think twice about it. He was a bit taken aback but soon his lips were kissing me back. He wasn't that bad at it, either. We stood snogging in the kitchen for ages but when he murmured, 'Let's go to your room' things came to an abrupt halt.

Kissing was as far as my charitable acts were going to go. Besides, I'd grossly underestimated the vital roles of Messrs

Vodka and Cranberry in this merciful act and as I was sobering up, I was feeling far less charitable.

'No, I don't want to rush things,' I replied, not wanting to undo all the good work by telling him I didn't even fancy him.

As it turned out, he didn't want to rush things, either: he started coming to see me every day. He wanted us to 'date'. A lot of the time I'd open the door and wonder how to tell him that I really wasn't interested. That I'd wanted him to get up enough confidence to find himself a girlfriend, not think he was dating me. Because, with Whashisface Tosspot, dating involved two things:

1. Coming to my room and pouring his heart out about the long-term relationship that went wrong
2. Watching telly in my room.

I was more than partial to a bit of telly, as the world had probably guessed, but watching it with him was an ordeal. He had something negative to say about everything I watched: *EastEnders* (dull); *Corrie* (people with funny accents); *Brookside* (people with funnier accents); *Sliders* (odd nonsense); *Star Trek* . . . well, he realised the second he opened his mouth that it could end violently. He'd survived slagging off *Sliders*, slagging off *Star Trek* was giving me mitigating circumstances at the resulting murder trial. However, because of his negativity about my viewing habits, I'd invariably be sat watching television, my body tense, waiting for some comment he thought was highly original and highly incisive.

The more I saw of him, the more he riled me. Particularly his story of woe, which, on the scale of one to ten (ten being worthy of a made-for-Channel 4 drama) was a minus five. To him, being dumped by a woman he'd thought about maybe one day asking to marry him was the end of the world; to most blokes it was a lucky escape. He felt his heart, broken and damaged as it was, needed to be poured out at every given opportunity.

I listened because I listened to almost everyone and he had no one else to listen to him, but not even I, listener extraordinaire, could listen to him murder the British language for more than thirty minutes at a go. After half an hour I'd lean across and kiss him just to stop him talking. He'd willingly kiss me back . . .

Our relationship developed from there. I started getting used to him and his language loosened up. He found other things to talk about, so I stopped getting riled by him. Also, there was no one else on the horizon, so we started to see each other – in a very casual way. In other words: no one was allowed to know about us.

To be honest, I don't think either of us really went beyond liking each other. Actually, neither of us went beyond tolerating/liking each other. We had nothing in common, we weren't always gagging to have sex, even in the first few weeks, and I got more laughs off the evening news. We were a passion-free zone.

Despite all this, he wouldn't let go. He wouldn't accept there was nothing between us and let me go. He seemed to have a sixth sense for me deciding to do the decent thing and end things. I say this because whenever I found the right time and the right words, he'd treat me to breakfast in bed, would book a weekend away in a nice hotel, or tell me how much he liked (*liked*) me, to remind me he wasn't all bad. When he knew I'd made up my mind to move on, though, and that croissants and orange juice weren't going to cut it, he'd dust off his *pièce de résistance* – reminding me how much he'd been hurt in the past and how grateful he was that I was helping him get over that. (My instinct to help always won out over common sense.)

121

At every other time he treated me with the kind of contempt most people wouldn't put up with from someone they hated. When it came to telling people about us, he developed a mental block that stopped him actually saying the words. People thought we were friends – particularly his family (he'd never tell his family that we were together because that would mean he'd gotten over his heartbreak and he would never admit that). When we looked for flats together, we had to get a two-bedroom flat and have our own bedrooms so everyone would know we *weren't* living together. Sex was rationed out so we only did it on Friday or Saturday nights, i.e. the nights when he didn't have to get up for work. If I tried to initiate it any other day of the week, he'd always reject me, reminding me that we weren't actually seeing each other so probably not a good idea to have sex.

I did get the last laugh on that score, though: when I started to extract myself from him I went cold turkey with sex and turned down his seduction attempts. In response they became more elaborate and fervent, even started coming on 'school nights'. After a couple of months of 'er, no, I don't think so', he realised he'd have to seek his sexual favours elsewhere and so took to pleasuring himself. Unlike most other blokes, though, he pleasured himself while stood over the loo so he wouldn't have to clean up the mess afterwards. (And thus, his full name was born. Jess had always called him 'Whashisface' because to use his name would mean she'd accepted him as part of my life – and she'd never do that. When I walked into the bathroom and caught him *in flagrante dewanko*, the moniker 'Tosspot' was added.)

'He sucks the life out of you,' Jess constantly said. 'I'll never understand why someone as vibrant as you is with someone as turgid as him.' She was right, of course, but I couldn't seem to snap out of it.

I often looked back on that time and wondered why I put up with it. And then I'd have my answer: Jedi Mind Trick or some kind of power endowed him by the devil.

Theoretically, after I'd extracted myself from him, the quality of blokes should've increased. To get any lower, they would've had to start digging because Whashisface Tosspot really was rock bottom. So, the only way should've been up. Up, to lads who wanted sex on week nights, who didn't tuck their jumpers into their trousers and who could watch telly in silence for a bit. Except, it didn't work like that. The blokes I met were after a free therapist or were psychopaths. It was one or the other, nothing in between. In fact, by the time I met the last bloke I was seeing, I was convinced that I had NORMAL BLOKES NEED NOT TRY stamped across my forehead.

Maybe I should just accept I'm not good at human relationships, full stop. I was crap at getting close friends, I was crap at not getting embroiled in other people's dramas and I was crap with love.

I pushed my key into the door of 17 Stanmore Vale feeling very lonely and sorry for myself. I could talk myself into a bout of self-pity faster than anyone I knew. *Woe is me*, I'd probably be sobbing as I fell dramatically onto my bed, the back of my hand covering my forehead. *Woe is me without any friends*.

I pushed open the door, hoisted my rucksack onto my shoulder and pulled my holdall through the door. As if by magic, Jake and Ed appeared.

'Hello!' they both screamed. 'Hello!'

I jumped at the loudness of their hello, then took a step back, eyed them even more suspiciously. 'Hi?' I offered cautiously.

'Did you have a nice time?' Jake asked. They were both grinning maniacally.

'It was fine,' I said, remembering everything I'd felt like a kick in the guts. But that wasn't for them to know. I even managed to sound happy.

Jake and Ed's faces fell slightly, but then, in unison, they both grinned again. Now they were freaking me out. Should I close the door and run away? Should I try to make it upstairs before they attempt to sacrifice me to whatever god they'd taken to worshipping over the weekend?

'Let me take your bags,' Ed said, coming towards me.

'Yeah, and I'll make you a herbal tea. I filtered some water earlier. And I went to town yesterday and bought some chocolate cheesecake.'

'I got the Jaffa Cakes,' Ed said.

'Yeah, well I got the caramel digestives,' Jake replied.

'And I got the green olives and chorizo slices.'

'But who remembered the focaccia?'

They were going to fatten me up before the sacrifice. I stepped even further back, ready to run for it.

'Come in and sit down,' Jake said.

Ed wrestled my rucksack and holdall out of my grip.

Jake came to me, and led me into the living room. I sat cautiously on the sofa nearest the window. I could make it out of the window if it came down to it. One foot on the window sill, short jump down into the paved-over front garden and I'd be away down the road before either of them could even blink.

Ed raced upstairs with my stuff, Jake legged it to the kitchen and returned with a tray of biscuits, a cup of strawberry tea and a bowl of big, juicy green olives. One of the many things on my favourite foods list.

Jake and Ed sat on the other sofa, looked eagerly at me.

'All right, what have you done?' I said.

'Done?' they asked.

'What's going on, why are you being so nice? What have you done?'

They looked at each other, looked at me. 'Nowt.'

'Have you rented out my room and are now trying to soften me up before you break the news?'

'No.'

'Have you accidentally burnt my belongings?'

'No.'

'Oh no, you haven't broken one of my *Angel* tapes, have you?'

'Noooo,' they chorused.

'Didn't you say we'd die horribly slow deaths if we touched them?' Ed added.

'Yeah, well, you'd be surprised how ineffective that threat is nowadays,' I mumbled.

'We haven't been near them, we swear,' Jake said, hand on heart.

'Then what is it?'

Jake and Ed looked at each other. 'You tell her,' Ed said.

'No, you,' Jake said.

They carried on like that until Jake finally gave in and said, 'The thing is, Ceri, we really missed you.'

'Yeah,' Ed added. 'We didn't realise how much a part of our family you were until you went away.'

'And then Ed started saying that if you had a good time when you were in London you'd probably want to move back there.'

'You were the one who said she'd probably realise what a strain it was living with two lads and would decide not to work her notice and go straight back to London, Jake.'

I didn't know if I should laugh or cry. But tears crept into my eyes.

'And it were you who were almost crying at the idea that

we'd end up going back to stained teaspoons and toothpaste smudges on the taps, Edward.'

'You actually started crying.'

'Liar!'

'Is that why you bought all that food?' I asked.

They nodded in unison. 'And we got you some wine.'

'And beer.'

'Yeah, and beer.'

I started laughing, causing a tear to break free and crawl down my face. I wiped it away with the back of my thumb. 'I'm not going anywhere.'

'Sure?' Jake said.

'Really?' Ed said.

'Positive. Ceri D'Altroy is in this house for the duration.'

Both lads grinned like I'd promised to get them subscriptions to the porn channels of their choice. I had to laugh. Just when I was feeling so low I could take to my bed with an armful of *Angels* and a bottle of wine for a week, Ed and Jake had made me feel loved. Wanted. That's what I needed when I got my bouts of loneliness dressed up as depression.

How I got sometimes wasn't, I knew, depression. Not hopelessness when I couldn't get out of bed. More, teariness at being alone. Emptiness at not having a someone who had it in their job description that they had to be there for me. Pain at never quite getting it right on the relationship level. I could make friends, acquire confidences at the drop of a hat, tell other people how to fix their relationships, but when it came to intimacy with men, things fell apart. Having to accept my life would probably be a love-free zone for ever.

These were the thoughts that dogged my night times, made my heart heavy and achy. That, I suppose, had been part of what I'd been feeling as I traipsed from London to Leeds.

There, in the midst of it, were Jake and Ed. Two lads who

actually wanted me around. Who'd panicked at the thought I wouldn't be around.

'Thanks for all the effort boys,' I said, getting up. 'I missed you too.'

'Group hug!' Jake screeched, then they both charged at me, leaving us all in a laughing bundle on the soft-pile living room carpet.

chapter twelve
Party People

'Oh come on, Cezza, there'll be men there,' Jake said.

'There's men on my telly,' I replied, stuffing garlic mash potato in my mouth.

Ed and Jake were off to a party being held by some of their Met buddies and, seeing as this was my first weekend back after my visit to London, they weren't going to leave me alone. They'd put me on a kind of suicide watch since that Sunday, where one of them had to know where I was every hour of the day. I was constantly called or emailed at college. I had them knocking on my door to offer me tea or food if I sat upstairs. I had two shadows who wanted nothing but my happiness – that phrase 'be careful what you wish for' kept replaying itself in my head when I started griping that no one would miss me if I wasn't around.

They weren't going out this Saturday night without me – and Jake seriously thought blokes at a party would be enough to prise me out of my pyjamas and away from my bowl of comfort food. The choices were: garlic mash, pyjamas and a blockbuster movie on TV or traipsing through the streets, going to a party where I only knew two people and having to move from my sofa to get ready. There was no contest. I was going nowhere.

'Yeah, but these men will talk to you,' Jake persisted.

'The men on my telly talk to me. And, sometimes, I even talk back.'

'But you might get a snog off one of them,' Ed chimed in.

What do I say to that? 'I'll get a snog off one of the men on my telly?' *And* not sound like a freak?

'All right. But if I don't get a snog, you lot are in for such a hard time.'

They laughed.

'Obviously, neither of you realise how hard I can make things for two boys like you.'

They both grinned as I put down the bowl of garlic mash, threw back my duvet and stomped to the stairs.

'Wear your leather pants,' Jake called.

'How do you know I've got leather trousers?' I called back.

'You just look the type.'

'Yeah, and wear your sparkly gold top, too.' Ed added. Fashion advice from Mr 'Live In My Lumberjack Shirt', himself.

I got showered, dressed, brushed my teeth and put on make-up in record time. The lads, very wisely, wolf-whistled when I descended the stairs. I was indeed wearing my leather trousers and my sparkly gold top.

With most proper student houses you had to enter through the back door because the front door usually led into someone's bedroom. It was a way to make a four-bedroom house into a five-bedroom house. This student house, where the party was being held, was no exception.

Ed and Jake went to find their mates – aka the people with the drugs – as soon as we walked in through the back door.

They left me in the living room with the rest of the partiers. 'It'll increase your chances of a snog,' they reasoned, 'not having two men around.'

'Yeah, cos I'd even look twice at either of you,' I replied. 'No offence.'

I leant back against the wall of the living room, ignoring the way my jacket stuck to the wall.

This was a proper student house. The single red light bulb did nothing to mask the horrors that had been regurgitated on the carpet. The furniture had been pushed back to the far end of the room and showed signs of overuse. Generation after generation of student had skinned up on the arms of that browny sofa and non-matching armchair. God alone knew what those stains between the threadbare bits were, but I had my suspicions.

I leant against the wall and let my mind wander back in time. Back about twenty years, actually. I couldn't help thinking that the eighties may well have been the decade that fashion forgot – actually, that fashion taunted – but at least they knew how to put together a choon in those days. Every other song you got in the eighties you wanted to dance to or sing along to – even if you were wearing a puff ball skirt, a batwing top, bright blue eyeshadow and your perm had been back-combed and hairsprayed to stand at a ninety-degree angle. And anyway, all the people you were dancing to were just as badly dressed as you, they too found joy in frilly white shirts and lip gloss.

Harking back to another era instantly doubles your age, I thought, and started gulping beer. And being stood at a party while doing the harking tripled my age . . . but it was true. Music was music in those days: Duran Duran, Spandau Ballet, Madonna, Luther Vandross, Haircut 100, Barry White, Howard Jones, Phil Collins all so much better than the trendy nonsense served up nowadays.

Please, put a bit of Howard Jones on. Seriously. Anything but this 21st century nonsense.

Erm, Ceri, how old are you? I asked myself sternly.

Time was when I'd be elbowing my way to the centre of the room so I could be seen by everyone as I danced. I had that much faith in my body-moving abilities. Time was, though, when I wouldn't have turned up to a student party in leather trousers and heeled boots. In my student days, any person turning up to a party in leather trews would've been lynched for being the capitalist, cute-ickle-animal-hurting bastard they were. Nowadays I was more likely to get stock tips on which type of animal you got the best hide out of.

Not that I dwelt entirely in the past, but when I was a student, I had things to worry about beyond where my next joint was coming from, mainly because I didn't do drugs. (I was completely of the 'do what you want within reason' mentality but drugs were not for me. Alcohol did strange things to me; adding drugs to that equation would be asking for my parents to identify my overdosed body.) Even in sixth form I was politically-minded. I stood on the picket lines with the ambulance men; I organised a convoy of coaches to go to Brighton to march in protest against student loans. In school I boycotted any company that had holdings in South Africa.

In college, I lobbied Parliament; I joined the Students' Union and actually tried to get students involved in political stuff. It goes without saying that I actually got down on my knees and thanked God the day Thatcher resigned. I cast my eye around the room, I'd be lucky if most of this lot knew who was Prime Minister at the moment.

Right Ceri, lighten up. It's a party. I cast my eye about the room again, this time less critically. This time, looking for boys.

131

Ohhh, he was all right. Him with the shaved head, beautiful brown skin, huge eyes, flat nose, pouty lips. Hmmmm, very all right. Now, fix him with a look that says you're interested. No, *interested*, not desperate, lighten up on the eyebrows, smile a little more, hey, he's smiling back . . .

I peeled myself off the wall, smiled a little more, fixed him with my dark, mysterious eyes . . .

The lad smiled back. He nodded, 'come here'. I finished unsticking myself from the wall and a young slip of a girl skipped over to him, flung her arms around his neck and started snogging his face off.

He looked about fifteen anyway.

I guzzled beer, looked even further around the room. And this time, I caught someone's eye. He was definitely looking at me, his eyes were practically drilling into me. I'd recognise that stare anywhere – he was the man from the pub a couple of weeks ago. Across the smoke and flashing lights and music, he was leant back against the wall, can of beer in one hand, glaring at me. I knew it was me because I glanced around me, there was no one else even remotely close enough to be on the receiving end of that glare. Maybe I knew him. I peered through the smoke and moving bodies to get a closer look. But no, he didn't look familiar. I was pretty sure I didn't know him. Maybe he was a writer I'd commissioned in London who was unhappy with the final edit of his feature, so he now scowled at me in revenge.

Like the time in the pub, he made no attempt to hide his glare now that I'd spotted him: if I was caught giving evils to someone – even someone I hated – I'd at least have the good grace to look away, go back to glaring in a minute or two. This man clearly had no grace. He glared and stared and evilled like I had my back to him.

Well, two can glare at that game. I shifted slightly, blanked my face so my mouth was a flat line, my eyes flat, then returned his stare. Mine wasn't so vicious, I'd save the viciousness for later. I simply stared at him like he stared at me. Pretending the music and dancing people and haze weren't ther—

'Fancy seeing you here!'

I jumped slightly as Mel stepped between me and Staring Man. 'How you doing?' he shouted above the music.

'Fine. How you doing?' I shouted back.

Mel shrugged untidily. 'Do you want a drink?'

I raised my can. 'Got one, thanks.'

'Oh,' Mel replied. He swigged from his can of beer. He was, of course, wearing a Levi's combo, but this time he had on a white T-shirt instead of a jumper. 'Are you all right, then?' he asked. This had all the hallmarks of becoming a small talk conversation. He was embarrassed because he'd shown me a side to him very few people saw. And, while part of him yearned to get back to that intimacy, the rest of him was horrified about it. Why would any sane person tell a virtual stranger all those things, especially one who they saw in and out of work? Why indeed. I often asked myself this when someone had dragged me into their life.

'Yeah, I'm fine, Mel. How are you?'

Mel shrugged again.

'How come you're here?' I asked. 'I came with Jake and Ed.'

'What?'

'I came with Jake and Ed,' I said loudly. 'Who do you know?'

'One of my students from All Souls. She lives with The Met lot. And I know quite a few of The Met lot anyway. But my student asked me to come here.'

'Right.'

'Do you want to dance?' Mel asked, indicating to the now packed dance space in the cleared out living room.

'Honestly?' I replied.

'It's shite music, isn't it?' Mel laughed.

I nodded.

'Give me a bit of Wham any day. I only come to these parties cos it beats sitting home alone.'

There spaketh a lonely man. Mel was used to company. His marriage had just broken up. It was, I suppose, understandable that he needed someone. The noise and the distraction. The only way to stop the constant noise in your head. To stop thinking about what you did to ruin your life. Going out was so much easier than living with the pain. Than thinking the thoughts and feeling the feelings.

'I know what you mean,' I replied. The music mutated into another 'song' bastardised from a good tune, dubbed into oblivion.

'I've been doing a lot of thinking,' he said, 'since I came to your place.'

I nodded. *I thought you might.*

'It's . . . I've been doing a lot of thinking.'

'Thinking's not all it's cracked up to be, is it?' I replied.

'No. No it's not. I, er, almost called my wife.'

Oh?! 'Oh?'

'But I didn't know what I was going to say so I didn't.'

'You could try what I do: open my mouth, say whatever words find themselves in my mouth at the time. It's almost as good as having a plan.'

'If I did that, I'd probably tell her about . . . you know . . . and she'd be devastated.'

And she isn't now? 'Why did you split up? I mean, if she doesn't know about,' I waved my hand about expressively, 'why are you apart?'

Mel looked about him, checking the coast was clear before he shouted more of his love life story above the music.

'COME DANCE!' a student screeched in our faces. Young, dark-haired, not as pretty or sophisticated as Claudine.

'No,' Mel laughed. Almost like an ageing uncle telling his young niece he didn't want to dance at her older sister's wedding. (Well she wasn't going to be talking to me, was she?)

'Oh, come on!' she persisted, she grabbed his hands, pouting. 'Don't be an old git!' Did she give me a sideways glance, when she said 'old git'? Cheeky cow. I should get out there, show her what dancing's all about. Or just slap her.

Mel gave me a 'should I? Well I'm going to anyway' look. I dutifully took his beer and his carrier bag of cans from him.

The young lady dragged Mel out into the middle of the living room, elbowing aside anyone who had the audacity to get in her way. She had her man and she was going to make sure everyone knew it. She soon wrapped herself around Mel, arms around his neck, body welded to his. She was angling and positioning herself for a kiss, her head kept looking up at him from a side angle, just perfect for him to lean down and place his lips over hers. She was the student who'd invited him to the party, I'd guess. And she'd taken it as a personal come-on that he'd shown up. If I was her, I would – I'd once taken it as a declaration of love that Drew gave me 10p because I didn't have enough to buy an ice-cream; a man coming to a party that I'd invited him to would've meant he was proposing marriage and offering painless childbirth. It wouldn't occur to her – or me if I was in her position – that he'd come out to escape the silence in what would've been his marital home.

Mel openly wasn't interested. His body moved in time with the music, but his attention moved everywhere, settling nowhere. And it went nowhere near the woman who was attempting to become his second skin.

In a microsecond of silence between tunes, the atmosphere

135

charged up, someone stuck the whole room into a plug socket and flicked the switch. I felt the electricity of the moment bolt through every cell in my body. Mel froze mid-dance, as though someone had just pressed the pause remote at him. But it was just his body that froze, his face mutated itself into the very picture of horror and terror, his eyes fixed to the door that led from the back door. I looked to the door. Claudine. She was ex-Met. He was ex-Met. The party was Met. It'd stand to reason she'd be here.

Now, from Claudine's standpoint, this didn't look good. I could clearly see how this might come across: Mel, who'd been confessing love and all sorts to her, who'd been saying 'leave your boyfriend' without actually saying it, was dancing rather closely with a good-looking young student. Those last two adjectives ('good-looking' and 'young') and one noun (student) when applied to someone Mel was dancing with weren't going to help matters, either. From Claudine's point of view, these weren't the actions of a man who's madly in love with you. Or even in love with you.

Claudine wrenched a smile across her face and came into the room, followed by her friends. Not lecturers at All Souls, but most of them were her age, well-dressed and very sophisti-cated. (That was how I wanted to look, all the time. Well-dressed and sophisticated, even if I wore a bin liner. And, whilst one of them looked like she was wearing a bin liner, she still looked sophisticated. I bet her farts smelt of flowers, too.)

Mel extracted himself from the student and, smiling, went to Claudine. The student followed him, stood beside him as Mel and Claudine talked. It was quite comical really. The student slung her arm around his waist every other second and Mel kept shrugging the arm off, while talking to Claudine. No matter how much he removed the arm, the following second, it tried again to re-establish itself on Mel's body. She didn't even seem to mind the fact he was completely blanking her. Mel and Claudine talked for a bit, then Claudine gave the most bothered 'I'm unbothered' shrug and stalked across the living room with her friends. They were soon surrounded by the men. Real men. People who were nearer my age than the rest of the students' ages. *Where the hell had they come from?* I thought as I watched them salivate over Claudine and her friends. *I've been here since, like, for ever and I didn't notice one single eligible man and now they've all come out of the woodwork. That's fair, isn't it?*

Mel, followed by his student, came back to me, snatched his carrier bag from me. He raked his hand through his hair a few times, all the while glaring at Claudine. 'I'm going home,' he said. 'Do you want to come with me?'

Clearly, the best offer I was going to get all night.

chapter thirteen

Cheat

Mel made angry tea.

That's not tea that was called angry, he made tea angrily, huffing and puffing as he slammed cups onto the breakfast bar, then slam-dunked tea bags into them. Having said that, if *Like Water For Chocolate* was to be believed, all his anger and frustration would come through in the drink and I'd soon be choking on his fury by simply taking a sip of the tea. As it was, I was too scared to tell him I didn't drink proper tea unless it was an emergency.

He lived about three streets away from the party and it'd been an angry pound from there to his house. Part of me had been scared. Not that Mel was a scary man, *per se*, it'd been his nefarious mood upon leaving the party. Of course, the other night I had thought he was kill-and-bury-you-under-a-patio material. But, even in the dark of the party I could see he needed a friend. *And, yes, all right, all right, brain, I'm not meant to be doing this sort of thing any more, but you try walking away from someone who's suicidal.*

Mel wasn't overtly suicidal. Mel wasn't booze and over-dose, or take a shotgun to his chin suicidal. He was down a bottle of whisky and go pick a fight with a really large individual suicidal. He would get the living daylights beaten out of himself, to hurt physically so he wouldn't hurt emotionally. So he wouldn't have to feel what he was feeling. That's what happens in his situation: first, the only way to douse your feelings is to drink. Then you drink, and drink more. Then, the booze stops helping and the going out being surrounded by other people while totally bladdered stops helping, so the next stop is physical pain. Punching the walls, or going out to pick a fight with an obliging thug so you could get your head kicked in. I'd felt Mel's desperation, his eagerness to be hurt at the party, started to feel desperate too, so, naturally, I went with him.

'My wife is an interior designer and decorator,' Mel explained as I oohhed and awwed over his American-style fridge, his huge sixties leather chairs, the cream carpets, white walls, padded breakfast stools, fake fur rugs, light wood and chrome fittings. This is how my flat was meant to look. How it was always going to look – until I actually moved and discovered how expensive and time-consuming decorating was.

'Ah, right.'

'That's how we met,' he said, plonked a cup of tea on the glass-topped side table in the living room and threw himself into one of the leather sixties chairs. He slumped in the chair, his head hanging, his feet not quite reaching the ground, swinging his legs back and forth. Mel reminded me of my five-year-old nephew and how he sat when he felt unjustly blamed for something.

'I'd just bought this place. It was a student house the landlord had got bored of running so I got it dirt cheap. I even had money left over to get some decorators in. I found her number in the book and booked an appointment. I went to her office and . . .' Mel stared down into his tea, suddenly less angry,

139

more lost. 'And she was the most beautiful woman I'd ever seen.'

He paused. 'We flirted outrageously during that meeting and, of course, I asked her out. She didn't date clients, but she made an exception with me. About six months later, she moved in here. She started her own business in that time and our house became a bit of a show home for what she could do. Philippe Starck chairs, Bang & Olufsen speakers, Habitat rugs, chrome, light wood, Smeg fridges, etc., etc. . . . Her office was upstairs and my office was upstairs too. The rest of the house had to be kept immaculate cos of clients coming round. My room – my office – it's a tip. Always has been. Always will be.'

I sat on the sofa playing with my mug of angry tea.

'We got married about a year later. We didn't even need a wedding list cos we had everything most newlyweds ask for.'

'Did you feel that you missed out on starting a new home with someone?' I asked.

Mel's face registered surprise; looked at me as though realising for the first time I was still there. Shrugged. 'Maybe. Who knows?'

'You still haven't told me the reason you split up, if she doesn't know about you and Claudine.'

Mel perfected the stance then, looked so much like my nephew I wanted to bundle him up, saying, 'It's all right, I know you didn't mean to do it.' He sighed. Then smiled, bitterly.

'The thing with Claudine happened just before Christmas, the weekend that Fran went home to see her parents in Sheffield. Basically, we'd decided this was going to be the first Christmas that we spent together at home, alone, no parents, no siblings, no friends. She's dead close to her family, so she went home a week before to have an early Christmas with them. That was the same weekend we had our staff party at

140

college. Clau and I shared a taxi back, one thing led to another . . .

Fran got back on the Tuesday night. I'd spent all that time trying to work out how I felt. I mean I wouldn't have done that with Clau if I truly loved Fran, would I?

When she got back, she walked through the front door and I wanted to tell her what had happened. I'd never done something like that before. I mean, I'd never cheated before, that wasn't me. I didn't do things like that. I just wanted to get it off my chest, out in the open. But I kept thinking, how's she going to take it that I'd done that with someone she thought was her friend? The worst thing was, she felt bad cos I'd been alone all that time – it was the longest we'd been apart. And she kept trying to apologise. She'd even bought me an early Christmas present to make up for it. A games console, imagine how that felt. That first night I left it. And the second night. But the third night . . .

She was sat where you are, I was sat here, I just looked over, stared at her for ages. She was all curled up reading a Jane Austen book and I said: 'I don't love you any more.' I still can't believe I said it like that.

She just carried on reading.

'Did you hear me?' I said, 'I don't love you any more.'

She looked up from her book, her face was set like stone. 'I heard you,' she said. 'I was just wondering what you expected me to say.'

'I don't know. I just thought you should know.'

'Do you mean you don't fancy me, or you don't love me?' she asked. I shrugged.

'Don't you dare shrug at me, Melvin Rivers. Don't you dare sit there, tell me to fuck off and then shrug at me.'

I stared at my feet for ages, then I said, 'I still fancy you. I'd still have sex with you, but I don't love you.'

'So it's not my body, it's me.'

'I suppose,' I said.

'Is there someone else?' she asked.

What do I say to that? Maybe it was someone else, maybe it wasn't. I just knew I wouldn't have been with Clau if I loved or respected Fran.

'No. Not really.'

'WHAT DO YOU MEAN "NOT REALLY"?' she screamed at me. She even threw the book at me, luckily it missed, cos it was a hardback.

'I mean, I have an idea of the person I love in my head and it's not you.'

'YOU WAITED UNTIL WE'VE BEEN MARRIED FOR FOUR YEARS TO DECIDE I'M NOT THE PERSON YOU LOVE IN YOUR HEAD?'

'NO! YES! I DON'T KNOW. I ONLY KNOW I DON'T LOVE YOU ANY MORE. I CAN'T HELP IT.'

I thought she was going to throw something else at me, but she fell apart. I'll never forget how she sat there sobbing, how it felt to hear her cry and sob. I wanted to go to her but I couldn't move.

'So what are you saying?' she asked. Tears were pouring down her face at this point.

'I don't want to be with you any more.' Yes, I actually said that. She went upstairs and I sat here for ages because I couldn't move. I think I was in shock, more than anything. I'd never been such a bastard in my life. I mean, there I was, breaking her heart, ruining her life and I was so cold. So cold. I was just . . . cold. Eventually, I went up to her and she was lying on the bed. She kept saying between tears, 'Why? Why? What did I do wrong?'

You're probably thinking I couldn't get much worse, but I could, I did. I started comforting her, cuddling her, then kissing her and then . . . then . . . I ended up making love to her. All the time I was resenting her, wishing she was Clau. Fran just cried the whole way through and then afterwards she said, 'What did I do wrong?'

142

We talked for ages, and all I could say was, 'You're just not what I want.' Anyway, when I fell asleep a few hours later, she got up, packed a bag and left. It was three days before Christmas. I went out on the day before Christmas Eve to the pub, I couldn't stand the silence in the house. That was the one thing I hadn't really been prepared for. The silence. It was awful. When I came back she'd cleared out her stuff. All her office, her clothes, make-up, books, CDs. I figured she must've had help. All she left was a cheque for the bills and half the mortgage for a month, her keys and a phone number where to direct all her business enquiries. I haven't seen or spoken to her since.

Christmas was hell. I couldn't work out how to tell my family, or anyone else. How do you tell the world you've failed at a marriage to the most wonderful woman on earth? How could I tell everyone that for the past year or so we'd hardly spoken? Or that the longest conversation we'd had in twelve months was the night she left me. Clau rang but I couldn't speak to her of all people. I spent the whole of New Year's Eve and New Year's Day on dope, beer and whisky. I thought I was going to die on 2nd January. Part of me wanted to die on 2nd January.

If I could go back in time, I wouldn't have been so cold. I would've been . . . Oh I don't know, I can't go back in time, I'm officially separated from my wife and I haven't spoken to her cos I haven't got a clue what to say to her. Neither of us has started divorce proceedings and I'm sure she'd call me if she had anything to say to me. So, the official reason we've split up is that I'm a total bastard and she was blindsided by that, just before Christmas . . .

Had I, Ceri D'Altroy, been a person without a predisposition to saying what I thought, I would've said, 'You're not a total bastard.' As things lay, I was, and he sounded like a total bastard. Not a fraction of a bastard, or a bit of a bastard, a *total* bastard. However, it did take two to wreck a marriage. In Mel and Fran's case, even though I'd only heard one side of the

143

story, it did indeed seem that they'd both neglected their marriage. And, of course, there was Mel's 'thingy' with Claudine.

'Don't worry, you don't have to say I'm not a bastard, I know I was. I still get pole-axed when I think about what I did.'

'I wasn't going to say you weren't one.'

Thankfully, he laughed instead of fitting me up for a patio foundation. 'So anyway, Clau hates me. She thinks I was perving over that student.'

'Did she say that?'

'No, she didn't have to. All she said was, "You look like you're having a good time, don't let me interrupt you" and then she and her four harridans of witchville went prancing off.'

'She doesn't hate you.'

'She's just jealous, right? Cos that will make all the difference.'

'Look, Mel, we all bandy about the word "hate" as if it's as whimsical as air, but it's a very strong emotion. I can't see her feeling that in an instant and then it staying with her till she dies.'

'You reckon,' Mel replied.

Touchy-feely reasoning wasn't going to work. I changed tactics. 'You do know that student fancies you, don't you?' I said.

Mel sighed. 'Oh she's just an ego boost.' He registered my raised eyebrows. 'Yes, I know, I'm a bastard. But my wife's left me and the woman I love is with somebody else, I need an ego boost.'

'Ever thought of a career writing country and western lyrics?' I said before I could stop myself.

Mel laughed.

'You knew what you were doing when you let her drape herself all over you. You should be grateful she wasn't trying harder to kiss you when Claudine walked in.'

'Suppose.'

That feeling, my curse, brewed itself in my heart. The need to make things better. And the more those big hazel eyes simpered at me, the stronger the feeling got. I clamped my teeth together, trying to stop myself from saying something, anything to make him feel better, to make this situation all right. The last time I did that, I'd ended up with Whashisface Tosspot. But, even as I wrestled with myself, I knew I was fighting a losing battle. I might as well have tried to stop watching television for a year or two.

'Claudine doesn't hate you. She's just jealous and,' *Lord forgive me for what I'm about to do, but he needs it, you can see by the look on his face he needs it,* 'being jealous is a good sign. She was probably taken aback at the strength of her reaction to,' *God, I promise I'll make it to church sometime soon if you don't let this blow up in my face,* 'seeing you with another woman. Even if she is a student.'

He threw himself forwards in his seat. 'You really think so?'

I nodded, unable as I was to say 'yes' to the nonsense I'd put out there. It was probably true, but also not as uncomplicated, what with Claudine still being with her fella and all.

'You think I should tell her the student meant nothing?'

'No, Mel, I think you should make sure the student knows it meant nothing. That there was no "it" in the first place, before it gets blown out of proportion and it gets back to the college that you're knocking off a student. Ignore the Claudine thing. It'll be all right. You've been mates for years, it'll blow over.' *And anyway, have you forgotten she's with someone else?*

Mel slid out of the seat, slid onto the floor, still managing to keep his tea upright. 'I did love my wife, you know,' he said. 'I didn't stop as quickly as I made out to her. I was so busy making her leave, I guess I never really thought about how

145

much I was hurting her. I thought about getting rid of her, stopping myself being unfaithful to her, but I never thought about how much I was hurting her. Can you believe that?'

Er, yes I could, actually.

chapter fourteen

Lost

Jake wasn't wrong about how far it was from here to up there, aka, my bedroom. The relevance of *Star Trek*'s space time continuum wasn't lost on me at moments like this. I'd got the space, but did I have the time (or energy) to get up there? (It regularly occurred to me that the reason I was still single had something to do with my ability to drop *Star Trek* into normal conversations.)

Mel had ordered me a taxi at three, it'd arrived at four-thirty. Saturday night-morning was clubbing till all hours night, so taxi firms, naturally, concentrated on getting them home first. People like me who wanted to go a couple of miles down the road had to wait till the large fares were dealt with.

I'd gone to say to the taxi driver that I should charge him a waiting fee in the same way he'd charge me one if I kept him waiting for an hour and a half but, uncharacteristically, my mouth didn't work. Possibly tiredness. Or, possibly, because he was a big white geezer with a shaved head, a gold tooth and a grunt for 'hello'.

After I'd paid him plus tip (I was a veritable coward in the face of such scariness) I found myself at the bottom of the stairs looking up at them, realising how never-ending they were. In fact, they reminded me of that scene in *Poltergeist* where the corridor seemed to lengthen each time the mother tried to run down it. By the time I hit the second set of stairs I'd be climbing a stairway to heaven. Or thereabouts.

Luckily, I hadn't taken my duvet upstairs from earlier. *Jake and Ed won't mind if I kip down on the sofa, just this once, will they?* I asked Narcissus, who was still silently checking out his reflection over the fireplace. Unsurprisingly, he didn't answer.

I peeled off my leather trousers – never as good an idea at four forty-five in the morning as they were at ten last night – and sighed as air hit my legs and flesh gave way to gravity. I was never so grateful as that moment when the trousers were pulled away and my flesh could return to its natural place on my body. I yanked the gold top off, but left on my bra and knickers. If I kicked off the covers by accident I didn't want Jake or Ed to come wandering in to find me sprawled naked on the sofa. And, in my universe, it'd be the weekend their parents decide to visit.

Birds had started to chirp and cheep and generally create a 'we're awake, why aren't you' row outside, and the sun was obviously going to be putting in an appearance quite soon.

I wrapped the duvet around me like a cocoon so my skin wouldn't become stuck to the leather of the sofa, snuggled down, lay on my side facing away from the window. There was a time when the reason I was coming home at this hour was because I'd been out having sex. When I'd got into a taxi at four-thirty in the morning with dull throbs left by another person tingling across my skin. I'd need to have a shower before slipping between the sheets, wondering how long I should wait before I called them.

I most certainly wouldn't have spent the night in the company of a good-looking man and not even considered jumping his bones. Cos even on the many (MANY) occasions when I discovered a bloke wanted me for my ear not my body, there was a time limit. Chucking out time at the pub, usually. Possibly midnight if he was very, very lucky. No bloke had exceeded the two in the morning mark before. Not if sex wasn't ever going to be on the agenda.

But Mel, with his suicidal tendencies, had made me stay. It hadn't even occurred to me to leave. In fact, if he hadn't started to fall asleep at three o'clock and hadn't been completely spark out at four-fifteen I would've spent the night with him. Listening. *Only listening.*

I'd got worse. Moving up here had made me worse, not better. I hadn't 'started over'. The Commandments were so underused I'd forgotten how they went – much like the real Commandments.

I hadn't started over at all. I'd become so embroiled in people's lives it didn't even enter my mind that I had a life. In fact, did I have a life? What was I feeling before the party? I can't even remember. I can't actually remember what I was feeling or thinking about before Mel. I pulled a cushion over my head. I'd lost myself in other people's lives.

Click, went the front door, as someone closed it quietly. I peeked out from under my cushion as a form slunk past the living room and went towards the kitchen. That looked like Jake.

Except it didn't. It looked like a depressed version of Jake, his head hung low, his body moving listlessly. He could be coming down after a major drugs binge or, I took a moment, yup, no mistaking it. The air in his wake sparkled with sex. And it *certainly* wasn't from me.

I threw back the covers, got up, picked up my duvet and wrapped it around myself in the manner of a movie starlet after she's had sex and is off to the kitchen. (Those beanpole actresses made it look so easy, wrapping heavy bedding around yourself AND walking. It wasn't. At all.)

Jake sat on a stool by the breakfast bar, staring out the back window even though the blinds were closed. He hadn't turned on the light and the kitchen was in semi-darkness.

'Where've you been, you dirty stop-out?' I whispered. Whispering seemed to fit the mood.

'Getting screwed in every way possible,' Jake replied.

easter holidays

chapter fifteen

Just Good Friends

First day of the Easter holidays. First day of my first official holiday as a lecturer. *God knows what I'm going to do with it.*

Saturday was officially the first day of my holidays, but after the whole Mel/Jake thing on Friday night/Saturday morning, the whole of Saturday spent in front of the TV with Jake and Ed, recovering, and most of Sunday spent in front of the telly with Jake and Ed, I hadn't really felt like I was on holiday.

I snuck down under the covers. And besides, this was the first weekday in ages that I got to sleep in. Weekday after weekday of lying in would follow. Kids' TV and eating chocolate. There was no bad here, at all.

I rolled over and listened to the silence in the house. It was pure silence. Jake and Ed had both gone home to see their parents last night. Both had been concerned that I might be scared being on my own in the house. 'Not me,' I'd said bravely. The scary clown from *It* hadn't entered my mind until Jake had hit the M1. He'd left last. He'd dropped Ed down at Leeds station in town, Ed had a very long journey down to Cornwall so wouldn't reach there until sometime today.

Jake had then come back and had something to eat before getting himself ready for the drive back to Scotland. Involuntarily, my body sighed as I thought of Jake . . .

After I'd gone into the kitchen, Jake had filled me in on the details of his love life.

Jake was a good-looking lad, nice personality, had the capacity to be a bastard but only if really pushed. I did often wonder if he was too sensitive. Cared too much about other people, took them at their word even though he didn't trust anyone. He thought too much about others. (That was probably the pot calling the kettle black but I had no choice in it. I had the wants of others thrust upon me, Jake was just too considerate.) If he saw something he thought someone would like, he'd most likely buy it for them. They'd be surprised, pleased, but rarely did he get it back in kind. As in, very, very, very few people did the same for him. Few people thought that much beyond their own world. The way Jake was so giving was odd considering he was an only child, some might say. However, it's likely that was part of Jake's motivation – he wanted to give too much to be loved too much. He probably thought he had to buy presents for his friends to make them play with him. As an adult, he thought he had to be extra nice all the time to make his friends love him.

Jake did realise that the buying of presents and niceness was a fragile basis for a friendship. That he could never be sure if they liked him for him or his niceness. If he showed them his nasty side would they still be there for him? A couple of times I'd been tempted to sit Jake down and tell him to scrub that 'trample all over me' sign off his forehead. I mean, take the whole 'you don't need a reference to move into my lovely home' episode with me. I could've been anyone from that chick in *Single White Female* to Michael Keaton in *Pacific Heights*; I could have been on the run from a mental hospital. But Jake took me at my word when I said I was normal. Jake was too nice. Which was why he'd been screwed over in his love life.

Basically, the story went like this: Jake had known this guy, now renamed The Git, for years. They'd been good mates, had a laugh, but The Git had a long-term boyfriend. A year or so ago, they'd got drunk together, one thing led to another and Jake and The Git ended up in bed. Jake, not having any confidence in his attractiveness knew that The Git wouldn't leave his fella, so they just got on with being mates. But, they were constantly flirting and one day, when they were both sober, they'd ended up in bed again. It'd happened regularly after that; every month or so, Jake and The Git shagged.

That night, at the party, Jake had gone to find The Git, not to find drugs, they'd gone home to The Git's place, had sex, ended up having a long chat. Jake had basically gone vocal with his feelings, told this guy how he felt. Not a great big, I love you, more a 'I've felt a lot for you for several years and I'd like to know how you feel. Cos we can't be sleeping together every month and let it carry on like this indefinitely. I just want to know if there's some hope for us, you know, somewhere down the track. I'm not expecting you to leave your fella, I just want to know how you feel.'

And The Git had told him to f-off, but in a lot more words. It'd sounded so cruel, so unnecessary, I felt like I'd been slapped. *And I wasn't there.*

'Go on, say it,' Jake said tiredly when he finished his hideous tale.

I'd made tea and we'd gone outside onto the patio to watch the sun come up. I was sat in my underwear, hidden and

155

warmed by the duvet; Jake was curled up in his chair with my long black coat draped over him.

'Say what?' I asked.

'What everyone else says: "You should just forget about him now. Put him right out of your mind and move on." Go on, say it, you might as well, everyone else has.'

'In case you hadn't noticed, I'm not like everyone else,' I said, a little offended that Jake would think that of me. 'And anyway Jake, I'd never say that. Not to you, not to anyone.'

'Really? Why not?' Jake asked, eyeing me suspiciously.

'People only say "move on, get over him" because it's a nicer way of saying, "I'm sick to death of hearing about this, just shut up will you."'

Jake double-took. Clearly a 'thought into head, out of mouth' moment. But it was true, I simply should've dressed it up a bit nicer. 'It's true. I'm sorry to put it like that, but it's true. People get to the point where they're so frustrated at listening to a tale, they shut off from it. And how do they stop you from wittering on about it? Tell you to move on. I'd never say that to you.'

'Why not?'

'Because if you knew how to move on, you'd have done it already.' I pulled my knees up onto the chair so I could double-up the duvet. Watching the sun say hello was very nice but also very cold on a late March morning. 'I know it's not a simple case of forgetting him. If it were that simple, half the books and films and songs out there wouldn't have been written. Actually, half the books, films and songs out there shouldn't have been written . . . but that's beside the point. In the grand scheme of things, getting over someone isn't easy. And you shouldn't harass yourself or let anyone else harass you about it. If you want to hurt over this guy, go right ahead. They're your emotions. It's your life.'

'What do you think I should do?' he asked.

'That's the whole point, isn't it Jake? It doesn't matter what I think, or what anyone else thinks. What matters is you do what comes from the heart.'

'I did, and look where it got me. I told him how I felt in a light way, nothing heavy, not making any demands and he told me to fuck off. I just don't think I deserved to be treated like that. I mean if like he said, he knew all those years how I felt, then why sleep with me? You know he said he slept with me out of friendship. Like I couldn't have handled a rejection. Rejection's bad, but this is worse. I mean, why wait until now to tell me to get lost?'

'Because, sweetheart, it was a lot easier to ignore it. And, of course, it didn't do his ego any harm.' Ouch. Another head to mouth moment that got away from me.

Through the pale blue light of sunrise, Jake stared at me, surprise smeared all over his face.

'Yeah, well, it's true.' I looked down at the pattern embroidered on my duvet. 'All that noble, "I slept with you out of friendship" stuff is nonsense. Once is pity. Twice is being too nice. Once a month is enjoying it. The attention and the sex. Mate, if I had someone as good-looking, lively and good-hearted as you following me round, I'd be flattered. I wouldn't want to get rid of you, I'd be sending out mixed signals left, right and centre. I'd probably end up sleeping with you. It's human nature.'

'Maybe,' Jake said quietly.

'I'll let you in on a little secret that I've gleaned from all my years as a listener of tales and as a rejected woman. You can flatter almost anyone into bed. There's only a small, small,' I raised my finger and thumb and showed Jake how small, 'minuscule number of people who are immune to flattery and they're the ones who don't like sex very much. Because the way to anyone's libido is through their ego. I mean, think of the people you've slept with solely because they were extra nice to you or made you feel special or kept on about how great you were. Everyone has their ego trigger and almost everyone can be flattered into bed once you find it. If you hang around this guy long enough, you'll get him into bed again for sure. Even though you've had this chat and he's said all this stuff.'

'You think?' Jake said a bit too keenly. Considering how badly he'd been treated not an hour ago.

'Yup. He's done it once, he'll do it again. It's just a question of how long you're going to put your life on hold till it happens again.'

Jake stared off into the distance, he seemed happier. Which wasn't the point. It so wasn't the point. He shouldn't have been fixated on the fact he could shag The Git again if he wanted to.

'Ask yourself Jake, is just another shag good enough for you? Because, mate, now that he's treated you like that and finds out he can still get away with it, a shag and ill-treatment is all you're likely to get.'

I lay back in bed, listening again to the silence. To my breathing. My life force going in and out. I looked down at my chest, moving up and down. I held my breath, then let it out. I could've gone home too. Returned to London for a few days or the complete break. But London was my *bête noire* now. Somewhere I'd rather not go to unless it was to see specific people. Because it wasn't my home. My bank statement with all my mortgage payments and loan payments and insurance payments may say that London was my home, but in my heart, home was where my body was. Not where my accent was from.

I jumped when the phone rang. The house was that silent, that still. I rolled over in bed and picked it up. 'Hello.'

'Right, D'Altroy, get out of bed and get your arse round here.'

'How do you know I'm in bed?'

'You're always in bed.'

'True. And why, exactly should I extract myself from it at only midday on a Monday when I've got *Oprah* starting in an hour and a half?'

'Fred's gone away with his football mates; the girls are off in Spain, so we're going drinking, and you're staying over afterwards,' Jess said.

'What now?'

'The very second you get here.'

'But . . .'

'But what?'

'But nothing, I suppose.'

'OK, get a bus round here and we'll start in the Grey Horse, work our way down Town Street.'

'Are you sure you want to do this?' I asked.

'What do you mean?'

'You're not as young as y—'

'Brrrrrrr,' the dialling tone replied.

We'd been sat in the Hog's Head, the fourth pub down Town Street, for less than an hour when the barman came over with a clear drink in a clear glass on a silver tray.

'Excuse me love, sorry to interrupt, but someone asked for this drink to be sent over to you,' he said. He was blushing profusely.

'Ahh, it's from you, isn't it?' Jess laughed.

'No, love. It's him over there, by the fruit machine.' Jess and I went to look. 'Don't look,' the barman hissed. 'He asked me not to tell you who it's from straight away.'

'Did someone really send her a drink?' Jess asked, looking at me and on the point of laughter. Cheeky mare. Obviously didn't realise that my beauty inspired such acts from men.

'No, love, it's for you.'

chapter sixteen

Pulling

'We're in a pub in Horsforth, not a bar in bloody LA,' Jess said, looking around the bar. A tall, tanned man grinned at her and raised his glass to her.

'You've pulled,' I hissed at Jess. He wore a shiny suit, the kind that no man looked good in – not even my beloved Angel would look good in that.

'He probably meant it for you.' Jess slid the drink over to me.

'You wish,' I replied. 'Oh God, he's coming over.'

'Hide!' Jess shrieked quietly. For a women of her age, she moved with lightning speed, but she wasn't quick enough for me. I grabbed her arm, held her in the booth. 'You're going nowhere, lady,' I whispered, then: 'Smile for the nice gentleman.'

'How you ladies doing?' the man said in the fakest American accent I'd ever heard. His eyes sparkled in Jess's direction.

Neither of us spoke. Shock, I think. It's not every day you're confronted with a man who sends over drinks, wears light-reactive suits and talks with a fake accent. 'Fine,' I finally said. I was, after all, far more used to this than Jess.

I kicked Jess. 'Ow!' she said. 'Ow, I'm fine.'

'Do you mind if I join you?' he asked Jess.

Jess's head swung round to look at me. *Rescue me* was written in her eyes.

Not on your life, I said back. I'm sure there was something I needed to get her back for. 'If you'll excuse me, I'll just be off to the *bathroom*,' I managed with a straight face, slid out of the booth and went prancing off to the toilets.

I took my time returning from the loo. Jess, who I was sure never fully appreciated what it was like to be constantly approached by weirdos, needed time. To learn. As I reached them, her eyes swung up to look at me.

'I was just telling our guest here that we're off to meet our husbands for dinner, aren't we?' she beseeched. She was two seconds away from throwing herself on her knees at my feet and begging me to get her out of there.

'Yeah,' I replied, trying to keep a straight face. 'I just noticed in the *john*, that we'd be late, if we didn't leave now.'

Jess grabbed her bag.

'We could finish our drinks though, if you want,' I said.

'No, no, you know how my other half gets when we're late.' Jess shot out of the booth.

'At least let me have your phone number?' the man begged.

I felt a little sorry for him then. He wasn't just some weirdo, although he was a weirdo – nobody persisted with that fake accent unless they were a little strange – he genuinely liked Jess. I could sense that. He thought she was beautiful, he liked the way she laughed and had watched her for a while before sending over the drink. *That* was why he'd sent over the drink. He liked the way she pushed me away when she really laughed. The way her hair flowed down her back, the way her eyes were intense when she was listening.

'Oi,' Jess said, shaking me, 'come back to earth, we're leaving.'

162

'Sorry?' I said, struggling to focus on her.

'You checked out of reality then. We're going to be late.'

'Yeah, right,' I said. For a second, I hadn't been myself. Now that was weird, that was an out of body experience. The way I expected drugs to feel. How I felt then was the reason I didn't take drugs – I always wanted to be in control of who I was.

'Have I seen you around The Met?' The guy was very good-looking. Shaved head, brown skin, very dark eyes framed by long black eyelashes. And he was, of course, talking to Jessica Breakfield. A woman who was clearly old enough to be his mother. Not that I was bitter or jealous or anything.

'Maybe,' Jess replied, cautiously.

The guy took this as a green light and sat opposite her at our table. 'You're in the psychology department, aren't you?' he said keenly.

'Have you been stalking me?' Jess asked.

'No, I've just seen you around college and always wanted to come talk to you but never had the courage and here you are in my local.'

'You want to talk to me about psychology? I only do that Monday to Friday between nine and six.'

'Not particularly. I just want to talk to you.'

I was whistling silently, checking my nails, running my tongue around my teeth because it made no difference if I was there or not.

'Can I get you a drink?' the guy asked.

'Erm, Ceri, do you want a drink?' Jess asked.

The guy looked at me, surprised. He really hadn't noticed I was there, all he saw was Jess. 'I'll have a double vodka and coke,' I said. If you're going to ignore me, you're going to pay for the pleasure.

'I'll have the same,' Jess said.

'Two double vodka and cokes,' he said and toddled off.

I turned to say something to Jess and found another man had appeared. He was crouching down beside her, grinning, talking to her. *God, it's going to be one of those nights.*

I glanced around the pub, drinking in the atmosphere. I liked the Black Bull. It had an old worldliness about it. Twee with its flowery curtains and matching flowery seats and flowery carpets. All worn with constant use. The bar, which was down the steps from where we were sat, was a big square overcrowded with its drinks and hanging glasses and peanut packets. At this time of a Monday evening, the pub was quite empty. A few people stood in groups, others stood alone.

Unexpectedly I was confronted by a pair of eyes. Eyes that were staring straight into mine.

I tore my eyes away, but too late. Too late. The damage was already done, the eye contact already made. And, from the corner of my eye I saw he was coming my way. Maybe if I just kept my eyes down and looked like I didn't want company he'd just walk on by. Y'know out through the wall and window behind me.

'Hi,' a voice said beside me.

I looked up from my drink and found myself looking into deep, dark eyes.

'Hi,' I replied.

'Do you mind if I join you?'

A lot of words telling him to go away came out of the great big mouth in my head, but they didn't come out of my mouth in reality. I glanced over at Jess, with her four men chatting away to her. 'If you want,' I said.

'You looked so lonely sat here on your own.'

'Me and the Lone Ranger, we've got a lot in common. Except I can't ride horses. And, of course, I don't do the mask thing.'

164

He laughed. 'I know a lot about loneliness,' he said.

'Why, are you the real Lone Ranger?' I asked facetiously.

'In a way, I suppose.' His tone was so serious I wondered for a moment if he was the Lone Ranger reincarnated. If the original one was dead, not that I knew. 'I was just stood over there, watching you and thought, She looks like a woman who knows a thing or two about loneliness.'

This was true.

'It hurts, doesn't it? Being alone and lonely and not really knowing when it's going to end.'

'I suppose.'

'I did find a way out of it, though, in the end.'

'Really? How?'

'I turned to God.'

So this is it, is it? Jess gets three, no, four good-looking men clambering over each other to get her attention while I get some kind of soldier of God, who goes out to pubs to recruit his victims.

'I found a group of people who showed me the true way forward. They became my family. My salvation. The ones who I turned to in my hour of need.'

And, I'm sure they don't ask you to give them lots of money, try to distance you from your family and brainwash you into doing whatever they decide The Bible *says you should do.*

'Do you believe in God?' he asked.

'I was brought up a Catholic.' Y'see, at this point, most people would be lying or saying get lost. Not me. Heaven forbid that of me.

'And do you still go to church?'

Lie. Just lie. 'Not as often as I should.'

'Maybe you should give our group a try. We meet once a week down in Headingley. Maybe I can give you the address?'

'Yeah, why not,' I said.

165

He pulled a card out of his jacket pocket, started writing on the back.

'My name's Brad. Can I look forward to seeing you there?'

'Maybe,' I said. 'Possibly.'

He grinned. Far too wide for someone who'd only secured a possible maybe out of me. Maybe because he'd got that far in his spiel. I'll bet few people gave him that long. Certainly not in a pub.

'Anyway, Brad, it's been nice talking to you, but I think I should rescue my friend over there.'

Brad and I both looked over at Jess, who currently had four men around her. Each talking, trying to get her attention.

'She might not need that much rescuing,' Brad replied as Jess and her admirers laughed, quite heartily. 'Why don't we talk some more about loneliness.'

'Yeah, sure, why not?'

'It were you,' Jess said, gesticulating at me with her half-smoked cigarette gripped between her forefinger and middle finger. 'It were. That's the only explanation for it. I was fine until you got here. No, actually, I wasn't fine, I was perfectly happy. And, suddenly, we go out for a few drinks and I'm being chatted up left, right and centre.'

'But—' I began.

'No.'

'But—'

'NO!' She punctuated this with her cigarette.

Jess had spent the rest of the night fending off the advances of the four men; I sat sipping my drinks supplied by her admirers, talking to Brad The God Botherer about loneliness. Jess got to have her ego flattered by young good-looking men desperate for her to choose them; I got to hear all about his salvation. From being a lonely boy to a lonely man who

166

thought he was homosexual but was saved from all that by the group.

Then, to add insult to injury, ten hours later, Jess had reassessed the situation and decided it was all my fault. *MY* fault. *MY* fault that I had to drag her out of the pub after last orders and pour her into a taxi while she was wailing, 'Let's go to their party. I'm sure it'll be fun.' And *MY* fault I'd also had to hold her hair while she threw up in the gutter outside her house. How, exactly, it was my fault I wasn't sure. I hadn't sent the men to come talk to her. I hadn't forced alcohol down her neck. I'd been the one trying to go home at nine o'clock, only to be told no by a certain Dr Breakfield.

'How—' I began.

'No,' Jess said firmly, her finger silencing me. 'It were you. I'm old and happily married. I don't need you dragging me out and letting me drink too much, making men fancy me. You are a bad influence, Ceri D'Altroy.'

Jess drew long on her cigarette, expertly flicked ash into the ashtray. 'You know, Ceri, you're my best friend and all that, I love you and all that, but God, I'm not going out drinking with you again.'

'Fine by me, Dr Breakfield,' I said, lying back on the floor. 'But just remember, it was your idea to go out in the first place. And there's another two weeks left of the Easter holidays.'

summer term

chapter seventeen

Collision

I always leave it too long.

Always. Right to the point where I have to run the last bit while trying to cross my legs and think of deserts and dried earth and other things desiccated. In this spirit, I hit the door of the staff loos on the top floor with the speed and force of the London to Leeds Intercity Express at full speed, thereby causing somebody who was trying to leave the toilets to reel back. Luckily, she wasn't knocked over, but her bag flew out of her hands, its contents exploding over the white tiled floor. We both stopped, startled still, for a second.

'Ohhhhh, I'm sooooo sorry,' I said, coming alive and going to her. She was the colour of new-fallen snow, her body trembling as she held onto the basin nearest the door. Her grip on the basin anchored her as she said, still shaken: 'It's all right.'

Clearly it wasn't. I'd never seen someone the colour of new-fallen snow. So white, so pale she was almost luminescent. 'I'm so, so sorry,' I repeated. 'Are you OK?'

'I'm fine.'

My need to pee wasn't gone, simply postponed. It pressed

on my bladder, wanting to be let out. 'Here, let me help,' I said.

I bobbed down, gathering her belongings: battered diary, three blue pens, one red pen, black leather purse, four 2p coins, bulging make-up bag, No7 mascara, toothbrush, black mobile, Clear Blue pregnancy test. The usual stuff you found in a woman's handbag. Apart from the pregnancy test, obviously. Or maybe it was just me. Maybe I was behind the times and every sexually-active woman carried pregnancy tests as well as condoms.

As I retrieved each item, I placed it on the side of the basin. She hadn't moved, she still stood with both her hands behind her as she clung to the basin for dear life. 'Um, is there anything else I can do? Can I get you a drink of water or something?' I asked. The word 'water' instantly shrank my bladder and doubled its contents. I tried not to do a 'gotta pee' jig as I stood beside her, but I probably swayed a little.

'I'm fine. Really.' She turned to face me. 'I'm fine. You go.'

'Sure?' I replied, not too keenly I hoped the second the word was out of my mouth.

She bent stiffly and picked up her bag. 'Absolutely. I'm fine.'

'OK.'

I ran to the nearest stall, almost ripped off my jeans. I probably even let out a sigh as I relieved myself.

When I finally left the stall she was still there. She'd put most of her belongings back in her bag, but was staring at the pregnancy test as though it'd threatened to kick her head in if she so much as moved. *Now what do I do? Ask her if she's OK again and embroil myself in someone's drama? Or walk away, leave her to it? Not in my nature, obviously.* But, I was already in the Mel and Claudine drama. It'd been more than two weeks since I listened to Mel's tale after the party. And then there was Jake's drama. (He was walking around putting a brave face on things. He'd even declared to Ed and me, 'The Git is dead to me. We do not mention him in this house, we do not think about him in this house. He is gone from my life.' I don't know if Ed was convinced. Because I was. Not.)

Could I take any more? *Should* I take any more? *Walk away*, one part of me said. *Just dry your hands and back away from that upset woman.* Another part of me argued: *Can't just leave her here. She needs a friendly shoulder, someone who cares.* Sickness speared my stomach unexpectedly, almost kicking the lunch out of me. The sickness pangs of someone who was so scared, lonely and damaged they could hardly breathe, gripped me. I reached out to the sink for support. This was the sickness of someone who was just about keeping things together. Every part of them was on the verge of cracking.

I'd only come in here to wee, I wasn't meant to be feeling any of this.

As it was, fate took matters out of my hands because the mystery woman suddenly burst into tears. Silent sobs, with plump tears that rained down onto the pregnancy test box, her face crumpled in pain, her whole body quivered. She held onto the basin with both hands, her blonde hair swinging back and forth as she cried and cried and cried her heart out.

Without a second thought, I went to her, put my arms around her and gently pulled her into a close hug.

'I don't know what I'm going to do,' she sobbed.

Trudy stopped crying after a couple of minutes. Her nose still ran and she trembled in a way that meant she was just about controlling the tears. She'd managed to tell me her name as I steered her into a cubicle.

She took the wad of loo roll I offered her.

'I'm a bit upset,' she offered in return for the loo roll. She dabbed at her wet eyes. 'Just a bit upset.'

I was 'just a bit upset' when an *Angel* episode finished. *This ain't 'a bit' upset, baby.* I didn't say that, obviously. I leant back against the wall of the disabled cubicle, watched her sit hunched over on the loo.

'Do you want to talk about it?' I said. 'I mean, you can if you want. I'm a good listener. I've actually got an honorary degree in listening from the International University Of Auralogy.'

She said nothing.

That was meant to make her at least smile.

'You don't have to if you don't want to, of course. We can stand and sit here in silence for as long as you want. I haven't got any more lectures today.'

Trudy ran a hand through her bobbed hair. 'There's nothing to talk about. I'm getting what I deserve.' Then she ran her sleeve under her snotted nose, forgetting the loo roll in her hand.

'What's that then?'

Her eyes flashed with venom at something. 'You reap as you sow, isn't that what they teach you in school? You reap as you sow. You get what you deserve.'

I ransacked my memory but I couldn't find the exact point in time when that phrase entered my repertoire. Or when I started using it, but I doubt it came from school. 'I went to a convent school, but I don't remember hearing that from there. I do know the phrase.' *It's entered my mind a few times with the types of things I hear.*

'Well it's what I'm living now.' Trudy paused, balled the tissue up in her fist a bit tighter. She looked me up and down as though I was wearing a nun's habit and I was about to start

174

lecturing her on the Good Book. 'I suppose you disapprove of me, you being a Catholic and me having this,' she raised the pregnancy kit packet, 'but no wedding ring on show.'

'I'm not exactly a virgin . . . um, I'm in no way a virgin and I'm not married either, so let she who is without sin and all that.'

Trudy's face turned. She suddenly became a vicious, poison-spitting demon. Her blue eyes narrowed to slits and her features became so contorted, they looked like they could actually reach out and punch me. 'Do you sleep around? Do you sometimes wake up beside someone and not know his or her name? Do you hate yourself after every single time but can't stop yourself doing it anyway? Do you have to use one of these,' she lifted the box again, this time like a trophy, 'and not know who the father might be?'

That would be no – to every single question. 'Um . . .'

'Didn't think so! So you can drop the "I'm down with your pain, sister" bit because you have no clue how I feel.'

Not exactly true. I had some clue how she felt. And I was only trying to help. I meant no harm. I was offering her an ear in a time of need. There was also, of course, that saying, something about hell and its lovely path constructed with good intentions.

'In fact, why the fuck am I in here with you? Who the fuck are you? Just piss off, will you! PISS OFF!!'

I stood my ground. Not because I knew she didn't mean it; not because I wanted to reason with her. I was too shocked by her change in mood to do much else. Not the humour, so much as the suddenness of it; the severity. She'd gone from upset to brutal in 0.21 seconds. Naturally, I'd been told to 'get lost' before. But never so forcefully – not by someone who didn't know me a lot better, anyway.

'DIDN'T YOU HEAR ME?' Trudy bawled. 'PISS OFF!'

I attempted a smile, to show her there were no hard feelings. There really were no hard feelings, on my part anyway. I was only doing what came naturally, and it wasn't me who was crying in the work loos. All right, that's not true. There were some hard feelings. Outrage pumped in my chest as I fumbled to slide back the lock and exited.

Outside, a woman with wet hands stood staring at the disabled loo. She double took as I came scurrying out, then she jumped as Trudy slammed and locked the loo door behind me.

I stood, frozen in time, immobilised by embarrassment. No one was meant to hear me being ordered to leave a cubicle. Ever. In the probability of life, the grand scheme of things, no one should hear you being ordered to leave anywhere, let alone a staff loo cubicle. The woman stared at me. I stared at the woman.

In a moment that Dali would've been proud of, I reached out, pulled a couple of blue tissues from the wall dispenser and handed them to her. Still staring me straight in the eye, she accepted the towels, said thank you and proceeded to dry her hands.

I wandered away, my work here was done.

chapter eighteen

Don't Listen

The thing with Trudy bothered me for days. No matter how hard I tried to forget it, it niggled at me. Not just in my quiet moments when I had nothing else to occupy my mind, even in my manic moments, like running for the bus; trying to find the right green olives in the supermarket; teaching. Even when I was sat in the library, reading journals, concentrating really hard, I was besieged by her.

It'd been a week, as well. A week when I should have been able to get her out of my head. And this wasn't a week to be trifled with. Seven short days in the future I had a meeting with my research supervisor. The professor who would assess how well I was doing, if my non-lecturing work was up to scratch, or if I was on a wild goose chase. And, ultimately, if I'd have to go back to London to pick up my life where I left off.

All the same, Trudy invaded my thoughts. It wasn't simply the 'piss off' thing that replayed itself and replayed itself in my mind – that naturally smarted my pride – but, two Twix, one Crunchie and a packet of Doritos later, I was calm enough to see the funny side of it.

What kept drawing me back to Trudy, what made her a persistent ghost in my mind was the way she'd cried. How in an instant she'd fallen to pieces in the arms of a stranger. What she'd said about herself upset me too. What she did. How hard it must be for her to know what she was doing wasn't making her happy, but to keep doing it. To keep on keeping on, even when it was making her so unhappy she hated herself. She might've thrown it in my face, but I really was down with her pain. It hurt me as well. I'd experienced what she'd experienced as she wiped snot off her face with her sleeve; as she gripped the basin. I'd literally been tangled up in her aura of misery as sure as if I'd been her. Trudy was alone. And terrified. I'd felt that through her and it'd almost knocked me off my feet.

That was nothing new.

Feeling through others, others feeling through me was nothing new. My version of that thing called empathy went beyond simple understanding. It was the actual feeling. The actual emotion. Like the time with Ed when I understood how he felt about Robyn. Like the night when I felt Mel was suicidal. Like the moment I understood how that dodgy man in the bar felt about Jess. And now this thing with Trudy. I understood how these people really felt because I felt it too. Their emotions jerked through me just as they jerked through them. Their emotions crushed or consumed or energised me as sure as they did to them. I felt others in a cloying cloud that seemed to descend then transport me to the midst of their souls, the very core of their hearts.

Before, these experiences were periodic, the occasional sensation. Like getting into a lift and suddenly being overpowered by morning sickness. Someone in there was pregnant and there was no chance whatsoever it was me. This person was keeping it a secret because she didn't know what to do yet, and how I knew it, I didn't know. I simply felt it.

Another time, I was sat on the tube, reading, when the page was splashed with a fat teardrop. I reached up, touched my cheek, I was crying. A flood of sadness followed. I hadn't been sad two seconds earlier, the book wasn't sad but I was overwhelmed by unhappiness. I wiped the tears before anyone saw, but the sadness and teariness only left me when the man next to me got up and left. Just like that, one minute my emotions were swimming in a sea of despair, the next, when the man next to me got off the tube train, I was fine.

Yet another time, I'd been stood in a bank queue and I couldn't stop myself laughing. Waves of joy kept coming and coming until I found myself covering my mouth to stop the giggles. Soon I was laughing so much I had to leave. Outside, I had no clue as to what had been so funny.

But those things only happened when I was tired. When my mind was relaxed and weary and finding it difficult to keep a grip on reality. It was like a seventh sense. Not quite being psychic. Just having a super-enhanced perception. Extra Extra Sensory Perception for feelings, I guess.

Except that was stupid, wasn't it? What I felt was probably based on understanding people. And if there was one thing I had a lot of, it was understanding. Understanding how they got themselves into certain situations and how they felt about them afterwards. How people just kept going over and over, trying to sort things out but couldn't because they couldn't get any perspective on them.

Like with Trudy. She was crying because she was scared and alone. And she had to do that test alone.

She's probably done it now, I reasoned. *She's done it now, got the result, decided what she's going to do. And she's done it without me holding her hand or sharing her pain. Just like a few million other people around the globe manage to do every second of the day.*

I sighed, sat back in the library chair, rubbed my eyes before I put on my glasses. I'd been in the library most of the day and my eyes were exhausted. The best cure: the blue-framed glasses I'd had a tantrum about being prescribed. (The woman in the opticians had stared at me in disbelief as I turned down every frame in the shop because, 'I look like my dad in them'. I proceeded to try to talk her into finding that I didn't need them after all. You know, couldn't the diagnosis have been wrong? Anyone would've thought that I needed to have them welded to my face, not that I needed them to see things more than ten feet away. That was why we never mentioned them, not even if I was wearing them.)

I closed my eyes. Trudy. Her face, her crying face, appeared behind my eyes. That was how my mind worked. I didn't focus on her snarling, 'Who the hell are you, PISS OFF' face, the heartbreaking one plagued me.

She bugged me, harassed me, upset me because I couldn't, with a word or deed, make it all all right for her. If anything, I'd made things worse: Trudy wouldn't have said all those things about herself if I hadn't hugged her. Now she was walking around, knowing that someone else in the world knew how she felt about herself. Usually, too, saying things out loud made it all the more real, all the more horrific. I'd prompted her to go vocal with her traumas.

A chill crawled across my skin, tingling my scalp, someone was watching me. My eyes flew open. Across the wide, light wood table on which were spread the spoils of my hours in the library, stood a lanky man. His close-cropped blond hair made his ears stick out, he wore baggy charcoal suit trousers, a white shirt with the top button open. He looked familiar. But then, most people looked familiar to me especially when there were so many faces in the college. This man, though, grinned at me as if he knew me, his green eyes excited as he yanked out a chair and deposited himself on it.

'I've done it, Ceri,' he said.

I physically jumped out of my seat at his voice. 'Jesus Christ, Ed! I didn't recognise you.' I *still* didn't recognise him.

'Huh?' Ed replied.

I waved vaguely at his head, the white shirt.

'Oh,' Ed ran a hand over his head, 'that.' He brushed off my shock with a blasé wave.

'That?! Ed, you're a different man. You're a man.'

'Shhhhh,' a couple of people replied. This was a proper library, even though it was in a college. People actually came here to work and they expected silence with it. When I was a student, the library was an extension of the common room. Here, these merchants of no fun wanted to study.

I leant forwards too. 'Done what exactly?' I whispered just as loudly.

'I took your advice.'

My blood froze, my bowels turned to water, my hands grabbed the table for support. Ed had just uttered four words I NEVER wanted to hear.

I may dish out advice, I may think of myself as a cross between Oprah, a therapist, and Gynan from *Star Trek: Next Generation* but, Jeez, I never wanted anyone to *take* my advice. To listen to me, yes, but not to hear me so well they do what I say. For all the 'faint heart', 'life half lived', 'life's too long' speeches I gave, I never wanted people to screw up their lives by following them. They'd only partly worked for me, and *I* believed them. I'd hashed together my theories and insights from a lifetime's telly-watching and a couple of months of self-help book reading. How could anyone do what I said from just being told about it? By me, too. Who was I in the grand scheme of things?

'Which advice was that then?' I asked cautiously, knowing it wasn't that he start ironing his clothes inside out to stop them getting a sheen to them.

'Faint heart never won fair lady. I asked her out. I. Me. Ed. I. Asked. Robyn. Out. Me. I asked her out!'

'You never!'

'I did.'

'Shhhhh!' From around the library.

Moving like a woman possessed, I grabbed papers and pens, my glasses case, books that were mine, picked up my bag. 'Come on.'

We stood outside the library in the long, wide corridor with light wood parquet floors and beige walls. It was late afternoon, most students were either heading for late lectures, heading for home or were heading for the canteen. Everyone had somewhere to head to, except me and Ed. Ed, technically, shouldn't be here anyway, what with his educational institute being way down in town.

Not caring about the mess I made, I dropped the bundle in my arms and leant against the noticeboard outside the library. Ed leant facing me.

'So . . . so,' I prompted, with a frantic 'come on' gesture.

'I went up to her when she was in the union. That's our union, the union at The Met.'

Yes Ed, I get the idea.

'She was with all her mates. She's so popular . . .'

Usually I'd go sit on my own cos I don't like going up to her when there's loads of people but this time, I went over, asked if she wanted a drink, dead cool like. She was a bit taken aback. But she smiled at me with her beautiful lips, her eyes still looked surprised, like, but she said, 'I'll have a vodka and tonic.' I mean, I'm never that forward, not in front of her mates. I always wait

182

until we're alone to talk to her. I'm just too shy and she's just so beautiful.

My palms were all sweaty and my heart was beating dead fast as I spoke to her, Ceri. You would've been so proud of me, I kept thinking, 'A life lived in fear'. I bought the drink, took it back and then asked if I could have a quiet word with her.

'Sure,' she said. I think she was impressed with my change in image. She kept looking at me as though she was seeing me for the first time and she couldn't stop herself smiling.

We went to the other side of the bar and I looked her in the eye. Right in the eye. And I said: 'I was wondering if I could take you out to dinner next week, Robyn.'

Just like that. No stuttering, no ums, no ahhs. I just asked her.

And she said: 'Sure, why not. When?'

I said: 'Wednesday?' Cos you know, Wednesday's the night most people have free isn't it? I wouldn't presume she'd be free Friday or Saturday.

And she said: 'Give me a call over the weekend and I'll come round to yours first. My flatmates will give us a hard time if we meet at my place.' Then she asked the barman for a pen and look . . .

Ed raised his hand. Across the back of his right hand, in curly-girly writing was a phone number.

'Bloody. Hell.' I couldn't think of anything else to say. I was stunned he'd done it. Even more stunned that she'd said yes.

'I know!' Ed replied.

I looked at him again: eyes sparkly, face flushed and excited.

'*Bloody hell!*' I repeated.

'I KNOW!' Ed grabbed me into a bear hug. 'And it's all thanks to you.' He rocked me as he squeezed the life's breath out of me. 'Thank you, thank you, thank you.'

Ed's happiness was infectious. The Mount Fuji of grins spread across my face as he smothered me with his joy.

183

From the corner of my eye I spotted a cloud. A dark storm cloud on the horizon of happiness Ed and I were hugging on. I shifted slightly in Ed's arms to face it head on.

It was him. The man from the pub a few weeks ago; from the party the other week.

Staring Man. Standing there – glaring at me.

'Who's he?' I asked Mel.

It was late in the day. I'd got into a routine of doing research during the day and prepping (oh yes, I was a proper lecturer now, I even used lecturer terms) in the early evenings. That way, students wouldn't catch me in the library because they were either in lectures, the pub or their beds during the day; and they wouldn't wantonly drop by my office in the evenings because they generally thought I was away home. I'd sent Ed off earlier with promises to listen to the entire retelling of the 'I. Asked. Robyn. Out. Me. Ed' tale again when I got home.

I dropped by the Senior Common Room to have some time away from essays and my computer and found that I wasn't alone in how I planned my working day: there were quite a few other lecturers in there too. About fifteen of us, dotted around the SCR, either eating dinner or prepping or marking, or doing what Mel and I were doing, sat side by side taking a break.

When I asked my question of Mel, Staring Man had walked into the SCR. His body, which had looked like an artistic stroke on a page, moved very easily, elegantly almost, as he'd crossed the expanse. He went to make himself a cup of something in the kitchenette area.

'That's Bosley,' Mel replied.

'Bosley?' I asked. 'What kind of a name is Bosley?'

'Bosley, as in *Charlie's Angels*,' Mel said, speaking slowly, as though I was thick for not immediately getting it.

'Right,' I said. 'Course . . . Why do you call him that?'

'It's not just me, everyone calls him that. The thing about Bosley is, he's got an army of women friends and that's all they are, friends. He's always surrounded by good-looking women, whenever we bump into him he's got some gorgeous woman at his side and nothing ever happens between them. You know, like Bosley in *Charlie's Angels*, sexy women, no sex. And our Bosley is always rescuing these gorgeous women from some drama or another.'

'Really?' I asked, trying not to sound too interested.

'Yep. A couple of weeks ago, me, Bosley, Craig, and another guy got together at my place to play cards. Bosley arrived last. He'd literally walked in and sat down when his mobile rang. One of his friends was stuck in Sheffield, she was pissed and had lost her coach ticket home. She was crying and saying she didn't have enough cash to buy another one. So, Bosley gets up, goes and drives over to get her. He went all the way over to Sheffield and back, just cos she's his friend.'

'And he wasn't trying to get into her knickers?' I asked, as casually as possible.

Mel leapt forwards in his seat, twisted to look at me. His eyes were alight with the suspicion of my question having a double meaning. It did, but not how Mel thought. I wanted to find out what sort of man he was. If he was driving miles out of true friendship or if he was doing it because he ultimately wanted to get a shag out of it. Either way you looked at it, it was a nice thing to do, but the motivation behind it would have a bearing on why he was glaring at me. Was he stalker material or just someone who had an unfortunate stare that I got in the way of? Obviously, trying to get into her knickers was stalker potential; not trying to get into her knickers was unfortunate stare.

Mel, who had no idea what went on in my head, thought I was asking because . . . it was obvious from the grin on his face what he thought.

'No,' Mel said, 'he wasn't trying to get into her knickers.' His eyes twinkled even more. 'Why? Are you interested?'

'No,' I said. *Not in the way you mean.*

Mel's grin spread, infecting more of his face. 'You are! Ceri loves Bosley. Ceri loves Bosley!' he started chanting under his breath.

'Shhh,' I whispered and pulled him back down beside me. 'Stop it. I do not. I just spotted him at that party the other week and was wondering what he was doing here if he's not a Met boy.'

'He lectures in the Media department – that should interest you, seeing as you used to be a journalist. And he was at that party because he shares a place with a couple of Met people,' Mel said, still grinning, 'just like you. And, he's from London, just like you. You two have got so much in common. You're meant to be together.'

'Don't start, Mel,' I said.

'I could put a good word in for you if you like,' Mel said, behind his grin.

'Stop it. I'm not even remotely interested.'

'Now, are you sure? He's a mate. I'll just mention you were asking about him. It's no trouble.'

'Don't you dare,' I hissed, then pinched Mel's leg. He yelped, loudly. A few people in the room looked up at us. 'You are such a big girl's blouse,' I whispered. 'I didn't even pinch you that hard and you're practically screaming the place down.' Staring Man, who was leaning against the kitchenette counter, was doing what he did best: staring. He glowered at us from over his coffee cup. I shifted uneasily in my seat and looked away.

From the corner of my eye I spotted Mel waving at Staring Man. I looked up in time to catch SM's reaction: he nodded a slight hello back, then looked away. Looked away in a manner that suggested he was studiously avoiding looking at us again.

'I think Bosley fancies you,' Mel whispered, leaning in close to my ear. 'He looks well jealous. I've never seen him look that pissed off, ever.'

'Yes, he does look jealous,' I agreed. 'And you've just told me that he's always surrounded by gorgeous women but nothing goes on.' I turned to look at Mel. 'Ever thought that he might fancy *you*?'

chapter nineteen

Sex, *please*

I sat on the edge of the bath, smoothing handfuls of conditioner into my hair.

I loved conditioning my hair. Knowing that with every stroke I was making it shiny and soft. I got a real sense of joy from squidging it into my hair and running my fingers down from the roots to the tips, feeling my hair soften under hand.

The simple things in life pleased me. I'd discovered this the longer I lived this life in Leeds. Seeing Jess once, maybe twice a week; and not so much as a sniff of male action. Well, not if you didn't count Ed and Jake. Both of whom I didn't count. Since that weekend back in London thing, the three of us had become very close. It was like having two more brothers, except now one of my brothers was white, with shorn blond hair, and hailed from Cornwall; and my other brother was white too, with rusty hair, an eyebrow piercing and a faint Scottish accent. Was it any wonder I found true happiness in conditioner? And *Angel*.

I slowly pulled a comb through my hair, thinking about what had happened in my life since I'd touched down in Leeds. In ten weeks.

Ed and his date, which was, what – Sunday, Monday – in four days.

Claudine and Mel. Mel and Claudine. She wanted to pretend nothing had happened between them. Mel kept saying he was in love with her, conveniently ignoring his wreck of a marriage. And between them nothing was being sorted.

Gwen. I'd become her new best mate. The dinner invite hadn't materialised, but she'd started sitting next me on days that weren't Wednesdays – she even came to my shared office to find me and sat around until I made her coffee. Then I had to make conversation. She talked to me like we had anything in common. She was younger than Jess, but she was most definitely madder than Jess. Always it was with the demon year group. She could never forget them. Or ignore them. When I tried to change the subject, it worked for a few minutes. She was like a crying child you tried to distract with a toy – it'd work for a while, but their attention would come back to why they were crying in the first place. With Gwen it always came back to that first year group. I'd started to keep score of how often she mentioned them in a neutral conversation. Her personal best was twenty-five in one Wednesday.

For my sanity and because I could see how much it bothered her, I went to the demon year group, as a group and in tutorials, and suggested they attempt mediation, to explain to her what was wrong. 'Don't just sit there and say, "I don't gerrit". Explain what your problems are in a practical way that she can sort out.' My idea had fallen on deaf ears and consequently they fell on my ears via Gwen.

Trudy. The mystery crying woman. I wondered if she existed. I hadn't seen her. Not in the SCR, not in the canteen, not even in the corridors. The whole thing was so surreal. Possibly a reminder from on high that I shouldn't be involving myself in other people's lives?

I tossed the comb into the bath, which was lined with islands of shampoo foam, and went back to running my hands through my hair, feeling the conditioner squidge and slip through my fingers.

Saturday night and I was sat here alone, rethinking my life. Ed was out with his mates, Jake was out with other mates. I suspected he was sneaking off to see The Git, but hadn't said owt. This was a sad state of affairs. I was young, vibrant and nearly thirty and I was getting my pleasure from conditioner and the prospect of watching David Boreanaz be a 250-year-old vampire. And, let's not forget, said vampire couldn't have sex because one moment of true happiness would result in him losing his soul and turning bad again.

Speaking of which, when *was* the last time I'd had sex? Or even a snog. Or even the hint of a snog. Two months ago? Nope, I've been here two months and I've certainly not had sex here. Two months before that? Nope, that was Christmas and no action there. Six months. Hadn't had sex or the sniff of sex in six months. Time really does fly when you're not getting laid.

The weird thing was, for someone who loved it as much as me, I hadn't really noticed. Not till I got here and ninety-five per cent of the people I encountered seemed to be motivated by sex. They all seemed to be at it or trying to be at it or had been at it but were pretending they hadn't been at it.

They all served to remind me I wasn't at it. And, for the foreseeable future, I wouldn't be at it. I hadn't even spotted a man I fancied. And that was rare. I could talk myself into liking the most unfanciable of men. Whashisface Tosspot, who I lived with for a year, being the prime example. Not only was he the individual put on earth to make me believe in God, by proving the devil did exist, he wasn't even good-looking as a compensator. All he had was . . . nope, nothing, can't think of one thing that he had going for him. Actually, no, he got married nine months after I moved out. That proved that he wouldn't bother me again. Ah, see, there *is* good in everyone.

Part of the not finding anyone else to even fancy, I suppose, was because my last 'relationship' with Mr Perfect Penis (PP) had petered out to an open ending, before Christmas. (He'd earned himself that moniker because it was the most perfect specimen of male manhood I'd ever seen. Not that I'd seen that many in my life, it was just huge and belonged to someone who knew how to use it. Despite its size he hadn't used it like a battering ram.)

I'd met Mr PP through work friends and I'd been instantly drawn to him. He was so overtly sexual, but didn't realise it. His dark hair speckled with grey, his dark eyes, his mouth, his body, were all rather unremarkable – on anyone else. On him, that combination turned my head. Unusually for me, I decided there and then that I was going to have him, that night. I spent the whole night talking to him and generally trying to wow him with my sparkling personality. I hadn't bothered with make-up that day, not even lippie, so had to resort to Plan B: my sparkling personality.

We'd laughed and joked all evening, then I'd invited myself round to his house for coffee. Even then he didn't get it. Didn't realise I fancied him. He'd been the perfect gentleman and made me coffee, got me biscuits and offered to order me a taxi home if I was tired. 'So you don't fancy me then?' I'd eventually said when I realised I was going to get sent home without so much as a lascivious look.

'Well, yeah,' he said, shyly. 'But, I didn't think you'd be,' he looked down at his coffee, 'well, I didn't like to assume . . .'

'And there was me thinking I was being so obvious.' My eyes held his dark eyes. 'Any more obvious and I would've been wearing my knickers on my head.'

191

We both burst out laughing, until the laughter slowly petered out. Our eyes met over his coffee cup and we leapt on each other. The cup became a casualty of passion.

During the night as we cuddled up and laughed in bed, we laughed like we'd been taking drugs, except we hadn't. Odd things were he-lare-re-us! Like how he'd once got locked out wearing only a towel and it'd taken him ages to wake up his flatmate. Not at all funny unless you were there, but we'd laughed and laughed about it for ages. Going through lots of different 'what if' scenarios, like 'what if' his flatmate had taken a sleeping pill and hadn't woken up for ages? 'What if' he'd had to walk down to the end of the road to the phone box and reverse the charges? Like I said, he-lare-re-us. I'd been snuggled into his chest and his arms were around me when he'd said suddenly, 'I want you to know I don't usually do this kind of thing. Don't usually meet someone and then go straight to bed with them.'

'Er, me either,' I replied. I had no problem with going straight to bed with someone. In general, people spent far too much time judging others on trivial things like how soon they slept together. All that mattered was that I was OK with it. At that point of my life, though, I didn't just leap in to bed with just anyone, more out of a lack of opportunity than anything else.

We'd walked to work the next day, both shell-shocked that we'd had amazing sex – six, *six* times in one night – when we'd met five hours earlier. You don't usually expect quality and quantity when you hardly knew someone, but we'd lucked out.

Mr PP and I saw each other a couple of times a week for a couple of months, but he had a lot of emotional baggage and I'd decided not to help him carry it. Whashisface Tosspot had helped me see the folly of trying to help a man with his luggage. He was never grateful afterwards – he just found someone else to share his luggage-free life with. Under Mr PP's workload, his connection to his ex and my new-found ability to not put my life on hold while I waited for him to sort himself out, it'd ended with neither of us ringing or emailing each other.

Before, I would've put it in the lap of fate. *If it's meant to be, it'll be*, I'd think and say, while checking phone, mobile, email several times a minute. With Mr PP, I'd decided that I gave it my best shot, I offered him the best minutes of my shagging life – and if he was too busy or caught up with his ex to get in touch, then there was nothing I could do. That was the thing about giving my best – I could walk away, conscience clear, memory clear. No way I could rework things, rewish things, cling to something that was well past its shag by date. I only wish I'd learnt that sooner. It could've saved me a ton of heartache and tissues and humiliating phone calls when I was pissed and lonely.

Through the stillness of the house, I heard my mobile ringing in my bedroom and dashed for it. I picked up the phone gingerly between my forefinger and thumb, not wanting to get conditioner on the plastic cover, pressed a button to answer it.

'Hi, Ceri, it's Claudine.'

I'd given her my mobile number in case she wanted to go out sometime. Which she didn't because she'd been avoiding me since the last time we went out. She had most likely woken up the morning after we went out and been horrified by what she'd spontaneously told me.

'Hi,' I husked back. I was still a bit out of breath from the epic dash up the stairs from the bathroom. So much for my gym membership.

'What you doing tonight?' she asked. She had an edge to

193

her voice. Not upset. Not angry. Hard to put my finger on the exact emotion, but distressed was nearest.

'Erm, washing my hair,' I replied. She was going to think I was the most exciting woman on earth. Pavlov, hair-washing on a Saturday night. If only she knew I'd been planning on updating the work I'd done on my research study later.

'Oh,' Claudine replied. 'So you won't be, erm, wanting some company then?'

'Is everything all right?' I replied.

'Of course. Course. I was just, erm, ringing on the off-chance that you were . . . no. No, it's not all right. It's all wrong,' her voice wavered, teetering by the tips of her vocal cords before falling into an abyss of tears.

Ah. Not really in the position to be receiving visitors. Especially not ones so gorgeous they gave me – secure and comfortable with my looks and body as I was – bouts of self-doubt. Just walking beside tall, willowy, elegant Claudine made me want to walk on tiptoes to extend my five foot four frame.

Bad Ceri, bad, bad, bad. Can't believe you're thinking twice about letting her come around because you've got slicked down hair and no contraptions holding you up and in. Especially when you can make yourself presentable before she gets here. And besides, she's not coming to look at you, just talk to you. Stop being so bloody vain.

'Do you want to come over? I can't go out cos I've got wet hair and stuff, but come here. I've got some nibbles and the boys are out.'

'Are you sure?' she asked cautiously.

'Course.'

'OK. Thank you. I'll be there soon.'

'Erm, how soon?' I was doing mental maths on how long it'd take her to arrive and how much time I'd have to put on a bra and change out of my tatty Judge Dredd T-shirt and Mr PP's paint-splattered jogging bottoms.

'Um, about two seconds. I'm outside.'

Few people who I haven't had sex with have seen me braless. Jess has cos I've spent so many nights at her house over the years. Jake and Ed have but only during my bedroom to bathroom stumble if they're up. Claudine had just become the latest person to see me *sans* mammarial support. Not that she showed any signs of noticing or caring. In fact, she didn't seem to notice how unlike me I looked. Unless, of course, I always looked dishevelled and underdressed and everyone expected it.

I'd braced myself for her to come stumbling in, tears in eyes, body quivering, ready to collapse into sobs. Instead, she'd arrived with four bottles of wine in her arms, 'I didn't know which colour of wine you liked so I bought two of each,' she explained, leaning forwards to offer me the bottles. I took two, led the way into the kitchen. Claudine stood by the worktop near the back door and from her voluminous coat pockets she produced eight cans of beer. 'I thought you might prefer beer, so I bought that too.'

While I busied myself with glasses and a packet of tortillas and dips I'd been saving for later, Claudine returned to the living room, to do what she was doing now. Pacing. She stalked backwards and forwards in front of the fireplace with its fake coal fire nestling in its black belly; her reflection catching in the *Metamorphosis of Narcissus* every time she passed him. She was intent on walking a groove into Ed's cream fake fur rug. Occasionally she'd stop, sit herself in the sofa under the window, cram a handful of tortilla chips into her mouth, gulp down red wine, then clench her fists as she ground her teeth.

I said nothing. Not one word during all this. I wanted her

to start her way. Even saying something as innocuous as 'What have you been up to' could tip her into a dialogue about her weekend instead of her getting to the point.

'Kevin and I had a row,' she explained after I'd drunk a can of beer, very slowly. She held up her hands, like she was showing me the size of a fish she'd caught. 'A huge,' she widened the gap between her hands, '*huge*, row.'

She picked up her wine glass, knocked back its contents, pushed her hand into her black hair, causing the top to stand on end. 'About Mel.'

'Oh' my face said. My mouth didn't ask any of the questions that were fighting to get out, most prominent being: 'Did he guess about you and Mel?'

Claudine sighed. Then sighed again, threw herself back into the sofa. 'It's all such a mess,' she rubbed the make-up off her eyes as she seesawed across them with her fingertips. 'And it's all my fault. I just want two men at once, and I . . . Kevin said some horrible things. He was right though.'

'What happened?' I asked.

She sagged in her seat. 'Earlier, Mel rang, asked if I wanted to come for a drink up in town. Kevin and I were only watching telly and I thought, why not. I asked Kevin if he wanted to come and he lost it. I mean, he totally and utterly flipped out. He grabbed the phone off me, told Mel we weren't going anywhere – except with a lot of swear words – and hung up.'

Shit. I filled her glass of wine to the top, she needed it. 'Oh God,' Claudine began again . . .

He started ranting on that Mel was always around. That we couldn't get through one day without Mel's name being mentioned or him calling up.

   'Our weekends are fucking precious, Claudine, we don't spend any

time together during the week and now HE's imposing on the only time we get together.'

'He's my best friend,' I replied.

'I'm your boyfriend. You see more of him than you do of me.'

'No I don't,' I said.

'You spend morning, noon and night with him, Monday to Friday. And tonight, the one fucking night we get to be alone together, you want to go out with him. ALWAYS HIM.'

So I said, 'He's my best friend.' Lame, I know, but I couldn't think of owt else to say.

'Why do you have to have a man as a best friend?' Kevin asked. 'Are you fucking him?'

I must've gone pale cos my whole body went cold. But I screamed back: 'You bastard.'

'You are, aren't you?' That's why he's always around, why you light up when he's around. You're fucking him.'

'I am not!'

'Well, you never let me near you nowadays.'

'That's not true.'

'When was the last time we made love, Claudine?'

'A few days ago, I don't know, I don't keep score,' I said innocently.

'Try three months. And even then I could tell you weren't into it.'

I nearly fell over, Ceri. I mean, I didn't know it was three months. Three months? That's impossible, we couldn't not have had sex in three months. 'THAT'S A LIE!' I said.

'Is it? All I know is, you're not getting your kicks at home, so you must be getting them somewhere. And my money's on your precious Mel.'

'What are you saying?'

'I'm saying you and Mel are at it every chance you get.' He started pointing at me. We were both on our feet at this point. 'And the pair of you are laughing at me behind my back.'

'You bastard!'

197

'Whore!'

I slapped him. He pushed me. And I fell back onto the sofa. He looked so mad, so crazed at that point but also really hurt, then he stormed off upstairs.

I just sat there shaking. After a few minutes I grabbed my coat and keys and left. He heard me shut the door I guess cos he opened the bedroom window, leant out and started screaming: 'GO ON, GO OFF TO YOUR FRIEND. GIVE HIM ONE FOR ME!' all the way down the street until I turned the corner.

And I ended up here.

'Why didn't you go round to Mel's?' I asked.

'Kevin would love that,' she replied. 'Me going round to Mel's now.'

'You're not so angry you'd go round to Mel's and shag him to spite Kevin?'

'*No!*' Claudine seemed aghast at the idea. I examined her face, her widened eyes, her turned down mouth. She *was* aghast at the idea. 'Of course not.'

'Never even crossed your mind, huh?'

Claudine's forehead folded up like finely-corrugated iron as she frowned, then shook her head. 'No.'

'I would,' I stated, after a few draws on my beer can. 'I'd have brought a bumper pack of condoms and would've tied him to the bed and rogered him senseless. If I was as angry as you were when you first arrived, Mel would be getting the shag of his life right about now, but that's just me.'

'I wouldn't do that,' Claudine stated simply.

No, unfortunately, you wouldn't. 'Might as well get hung for a cow as a mouse,' I said.

'Eh?' Claudine said. That look of 'you're a nutter' was back.

'I mean, if you're accused of something, why not do it to make it worthwhile getting accused.'

'It was only an argument with Kevin.'

I nodded. 'But I thought you said Kevin was nothing compared to Mel? This was your chance; what you've been waiting for. If not to leave, then to start an affair. It was what you needed to press play.'

Claudine was back to downing wine. 'I only slept with Mel that one time because I was very drunk and the thing between us had reached fever pitch.'

Should I mention that she'd told me, while looking me in the eye, that she'd *almost* slept with him? No. No one likes a reminder of their lies and half-truths. 'Like I said, Claudine, I know very little about very little.'

She didn't hear me. She ploughed on: 'It was Christmas, we were all in a festive mood, Mel and I got a taxi home together like we'd done a hundred times before. We sat so close in the taxi, his leg pressed against mine. As we turned into his road he kissed me on the cheek. Then we looked at each other and we kind of leapt at each other, started kissing properly. Kevin was away, I didn't want to go home to an empty house . . .'

'Is he a good shag?' I asked. 'I always get the impression that Mel would be quite adept at it.'

Claudine smiled like the cat who got the cream – several times. 'He was . . .' big salacious pause, 'what was that word you used? Adept? He was *adept*.'

I grinned back, while my heart sank like a tank in quicksand. Claudine's answer to that red herring of a question presented me with many, many problems. I didn't give two figs what Mel was like in bed, it wasn't as though I'd ever find out, was it? I just . . . let's put it this way: say I was in her situation and I'd had the biggest row ever with my boyfriend. If my boyfriend called me a whore, accused me of shagging around, I would've stormed around to the cause of the row's house, with booze and condoms, got myself good and drunk, attempted to shag said man, realised I couldn't do it, burst into tears and passed out, with the strong likelihood of choking on my own vomit. Failing that, I would've at least gone round to a good friend's house and repeated the scenario, minus the condoms and hopefully without the attempted shag bit.

I certainly wouldn't be sat in the house of some bird I'd met a few times. And if this person I didn't know very well had asked about the love of my life's sexual prowess I would've thought and said, 'Mind your own business, you nosy mare.' I certainly wouldn't *tell* her. I'd automatically think she fancied him. I didn't know her well enough not to assume that. Which led me to deduce one thing . . . From the depths of the corridor, the theme of *I Dream Of Jeannie* started. Claudine's mobile.

'That'll be Kevin. Ringing to check I'm all right.'

Kevin? Yeah, right! It's Mel. He's rung back cos he rang you at home and Kev's given him a mouthful then hung up on him, so he's ringing to check you're OK. Kevin won't be calling. He thinks you're mid-coitus with Mel.

Claudine stumbled blindly around my living room, searching for her coat and mobile like a heat-seeking missile looking for an iceberg. She finally found it, in the corridor where I'd hung it. 'It's Mel,' she said, after checking the mobile's screen.

'Is it?'

Claudine nodded, drunk and miserable. 'Shall I answer it?'

How the hell should I know? 'Do you want to talk to him?'

'I want to talk to Kevin,' she wailed.

That's the Kevin who isn't a patch on Mel, right? That Kevin?

The mobile stopped playing *I Dream Of Jeannie*.

Claudine stumbled drunkenly back to the sofa. She was, it had to be acknowledged, a lot drunker than me. And I was on the verge of closing my eyes and sleeping where I was. Why had I let her drag me into this piss-up session? I was so easily influenced. Offer me alcohol and I rarely said no. This wasn't my trauma but I was drinking like it was.

I Dream Of Jeannie started again. Mel, again.

Claudine snatched up the phone, looked at the screen, visibly sagged. 'Mel.' She spat his name out as though it was phlegm.

'He probably won't stop calling until he knows you're OK,' I offered, kindly. This was nice speak for: PLEASE STOP THAT PLINKING MUSIC HACKSAWING INTO MY BRAIN. NOW!

She answered the phone and spoke at length to Mel. It sounded like:

'Fnugh.' (Fine.)

'Hml, know.' (I know, I know how you feel.)

'Dwnan know.' (Don't know.)

'Fnugh. Fnugh.' (Yes, I'm fine, stop asking.)

The only thing I really understood was: 'Ceri' which probably meant she was telling him she was with me.

From the way she pursed her lips like a sulking school girl unfairly separated from her favourite toy, it was clear she wanted Kevin to be on the other end of the phone.

I poured Claudine into a taxi right after that phone call because she was on the verge of tears. I knew, even if she didn't, she'd get a lot further in making up with Kevin if he saw her shed a few tears. She didn't look like a habitual crier and Kevin, after their row, would probably appreciate it. There was no point her crying on my shoulder, I was already on her side.

I collected glasses and bottles and cans by the light of the television. I threw away what was left of the dips, then got down on my hands and knees to rid the carpet of tortilla bits and dip drizzles. Jake was fanatical about certain things such as food bits on his cream carpet, but the bathroom could go uncleaned for months and he wouldn't care. (Not that it did go uncleaned for months, *I* couldn't stand it.)

Wearing my hair-washing clothes, I got into bed, switched on the TV, turned down the sound and lay in the flickering light, thinking. Not just about Claudine and Mel. More the wider implications of Mel and Claudine.

The fact your life can change in the blink of an eye; the misunderstanding of a phrase; the kissing of someone you shouldn't. The pain of wanting something you simply can't have.

Wanting something so much that you make yourself and everyone around you miserable because you can't have it. It was madness, but we all did it. There was this film I saw once that encapsulated that madness quite neatly. It was a shite film, but I remember one of the main characters saying something like, 'Why do people love those who are not in love with them? Is that not madness? Does a man go to the airport to pick up his brother when he has no brother?' It *was* madness, but we all still did it. Even when I could see the hopelessness, when I knew there was no chance whatsoever of getting what I wanted, I craved things, made myself sick over things. Even when I knew, no matter what I did, I couldn't have that thing (Drew Tucker, case in point). Mel and Claudine were doing it now. Deep down they both knew what they wanted, it was simply easier to ignore it. Pretend it wasn't happening, wasn't staring them right in the face. Part of that was self-flagellation. Punishing themselves for what they did that one night. Fair enough, they did a bad, bad thing. Feeling guilty was part of the cheating package. What I wanted to know was, why was I being dragged in to share in the punishment? I mean, I hadn't had sex in six months.

202

chapter twenty

The Morning After(ish)

'Have you seen Claudine? Is she all right?'

Mel, complete with chaos, had flung himself into the seat opposite me in the canteen. I'd only nipped down there for a break from library duties. I was not having a good day. Gwen's demon group had been excruciatingly fractious, most of them hadn't done the set reading, the rest didn't understand the reading and thought, for some reason, I would understand it better than they did. Admittedly, I was being paid to understand it better than they did, but I was only human. I had a life – of sorts. I hadn't meant to get ridiculously drunk on Saturday and spend Sunday recovering and then staying up later, reading and planning.

It'd hit me as I had to re-read something for the sixtieth time, while drying and tonging my hair, that I wasn't as young as I used to be. The days when I could pull an all-nighter and still function the next day were gone. I'd wanted to tell the group that. Instead, I stood in front of them, trawling my brain for any dregs of my psychology degree that would help me get on with this so I could get to the library and read up some more for my meeting with my research supervisor tomorrow. Eventually, we'd all admitted defeat, I sent them off to do the reading and come back next time with valid questions instead of their favoured refrain of 'I don't gerrit'. I'd scuttled off to the library for some eleventh-hour reading. Trying to work out what the supervisor may ask me about. What she'd think was wishy-washy in the stuff I'd sent to her.

I'd staved off hunger pangs until two-thirty so anyone who was likely to want to communicate with me would be off doing something better. Ha.

'I last saw her at about three Sunday morning, and she was fine then. Drunk, but fine.'

'She's not in today. I'm really worried about her.'

'Have you spoken to her?' I replied.

'No. Her mobile was switched off all of yesterday. I called the house once and HE said he'd kick my head in if I showed my face around there. I'm really worried. I think he might hurt her.'

'How do you mean, hurt her?'

'You know, get physical.'

And you didn't think to go round there, try to rescue her? What a man.

I mentally slapped myself for thinking such a nasty thought. I was tired and wound up, my life could unravel tomorrow. The supervisor could put an end to my heart's desire. But that didn't give me an excuse to be nasty. Even if it was just mentally nasty.

'Has he ever hit her before?' I asked.

'No.'

'And has she ever said she's scared of him?'

'No, but he sounded so angry.'

'I'd be angry if I was him. And if the person I saw as the root of all my problems kept calling, I'd probably threaten violence too. Just threaten it, mind.'

Mel's silence said, '*I'm not convinced.*'

'They've got a lot to sort out,' I added.

'It's just not like her to miss a lecture. Something must have happened.'

'Must it?' I snapped.

'Yeah!' Mel said desperately. 'You don't know her like I do. This just isn't like her.'

I didn't growl, I didn't sigh. I counted to five, threw down my fork. 'Why can't it be something good that happened? You know, they took themselves off somewhere where they could be alone without the phone constantly ringing and people dropping around so they can talk.'

Mel shook his head. 'No. No, I don't think so.'

I sighed. Couldn't help myself. I didn't have the time or energy for this. 'Two things I've learnt about these things, Mel, if something bad had happened, you'd have heard about it by now – bad news always travels faster than good news. And,' I softened my voice, made an effort to sound sympathetic, 'because you're part of the problem, you probably can't be part of the solution right now.'

Mel's big hazel eyes watered up. I knew that look well. It plucked on my heart strings. 'You're right of course.'

Usually. Usually those eyes played my heart strings like a harp. Today they aggravated every nerve in my body. I tutted. 'No, I'm not. You said it yourself, you know Claudine and Kevin better than I ever will, so only you know what the problem is.' Mel's face brightened a little.

'Look, Mel, I'm sorry, but I have to go. I've got a really important meeting in the morning and I haven't done even half of what I'm supposed to do.' I got up, taking my half wolfed down food with me. 'I'm sure it'll be OK. Bye.'

I almost got to the library. Almost. All right, I got outside the canteen, my heart strings playing such a loud instrumental of 'Endless Love' that I couldn't hear anything else. Not the people leaving the canteen, not the students in corridors, not anything. I stopped, took a deep breath, turned around and went back to Mel. He'd looked so dejected, so genuinely worried . . . I'd obviously learnt nothing from the whole Trudy episode. And it wasn't like this meeting tomorrow was my first proper assessment or anything. My future in Leeds didn't rest upon the outcome of this meeting tomorrow, did it?

'All right,' I said, sitting back on the orange plastic chair.

Mel glanced up, his face brightening as he saw me. Rarely are people so pleased to see me.

'This is what we're going to do,' I said. 'I'll call Claudine and make up something about her leaving something at my place on Saturday if Kevin answers. And then, if there's no answer, we can go around, check it's all OK.' *Although if it isn't, I don't know what we'll do.*

'Really?' Mel said. 'You'll do that?'

I hate myself sometimes. I am weak. I allow myself to be swayed to the will of others too easily. Saturday night, case in point. This moment, another case in point. 'Really. But first, tell me what you're so worried about.'

And he did.

'You're too nice for your own good, you,' Jess said to me later.

'So you wouldn't have gone back?' I replied.

'Oh yes, course I would, but if I'd told you that story, you'd have said, "You're too nice for your own good, you", so I'm saying it back to you. It's what friends are for.'

'I suppose.'

'But it was all right in the end? With Claudine?'

'Oh, yeah, it was fine. They'd gone away, like I said, to sort things out.'

'I bet Mel was pleased.'

'I wouldn't say pleased. More like, relieved, plus . . .'

'Plus?'

'Plus a whole rainbow of emotions I wasn't sure one person could feel in about three seconds, but, anyway, love, I'm going to try to get some reading done before this meeting tomorrow.'

'Try to do some reading?'

'Yes.'

'Ceri, do or do not, there is no try.'

'Yeah, all right, Yoda. I'd better go.'

'All right, good luck. Call me tomorrow to let me know how it went, bye.'

'Bye.'

chapter twenty-one

Advertising

I'd practically stripped my left thumb of its top layer of nail by the time Craig arrived in my corner of the Senior Common Room.

Craig, who was researching his PhD and teaching in the sociology department, gave me the impression that he'd been waylaid on the road to something bigger and better. I also suspected he'd be studying for his PhD for nigh on for ever for that same reason. He was a man with far too many things on his mind. He'd be talking to you one minute, his dark brown eyes watching intently behind his thin framed glasses, then he'd 'sit back'. Not physically, mentally. Mentally, he'd take a back seat to the conversation, his mind calculating something of extreme importance.

'There you are, Ceri,' he said, dropping his regulation paper pile on the table where I sat. 'I've been halfway round the college looking for you.'

'And you didn't think to look in here?'

He thought about it for a second, shook his head. 'No.'

'I've been here since,' I looked to the large white clock on the wall above the far door, 'eight-thirty. My office partner had tutorials from 8a.m.'

'Oh,' Craig said.

'You didn't try my office either, did you?' I said.

Craig's brown eyes stared at me as he shook his head.

If I wasn't so nervous about my assessment, I would've laughed. As it was, I was so nervous I'd worn a skirt. I'd even flirted with the idea of wearing a blouse, I'd gone as far as taking it out of the wardrobe but I didn't actually put it on. I stuck to my favourite long-sleeved red top that was slightly bobbly, but fit me perfectly.

When Craig had come bursting in, I'd been contemplating another herbal tea. The last six hadn't calmed me down. Maybe lucky number seven would do it. I wasn't used to these kind of nerves. It felt like my first day on the job all over again. Only worse. With this, there was no blagging, she'd had a chance to read what I'd done so far. I had a whole lot of reading stored in my brain cells. But still, I felt I should be doing something more. Something. Anything. I was of the busy generation. I couldn't do one thing at a time. I was often writing and watching television; reading and listening to the radio. It also felt unnatural to be prepared and finished in time; I was usually working right up to the wire. Some of my best work had been done two hours before a deadline.

'Anyway Craig, what was so important you looked practically nowhere for me?' I asked.

'Oh, oh your research supervisor called. She's got food-poisoning, she can't make your appointment.'

'What?' My chest loosened, my stomach tightened. 'WHAT?' I slapped my hands onto my cheeks. 'Why didn't she call me?'

'She called you at home, your flatmate said you'd left; she tried your mobile, it was off; so she called here and I told the secretary that I'd find you.'

I flopped forwards on to the table, all my muscles unclenching.

'I've been terrified the whole weekend for nothing. Nothing.' I could've enjoyed getting drunk on Saturday night. Not been so brusque with Mel yesterday.

'At least you've done the work,' Craig offered.

I met his philosophical gaze with one as hard as flint. 'Don't get all positive on me Craig, I'm not in the right frame of mind. My nerves are shot. I've been dreaming about this meeting. It's so important.' I got up, went to the white jug kettle on the kitchenette sideboard, flicked it on. I raised a cup to Craig, he shook his head.

'It's like getting all dressed up but with nowhere to go.' I folded my arms, leant back against the counter top, lightly butting my bum against it. I pointed at my dark denim skirt. 'Literally.'

Craig checked his watch, sat down. He obviously had time to spend with me. 'What's your research about anyway? I know you said before that you're not doing a PhD, you're just doing research but I never got around to asking what it's about.'

He hadn't 'sat back' yet – this was a good sign, I still had someone to talk to. To unload on. And after the way I'd worked myself up into a frenzy, there was rather a lot that wanted to be unloaded. Poor Jake and Ed had been tiptoeing around me all Monday night – even offering me herbal tea and cheesecake had been tantamount to offering me an 'outside' (i.e., calling Angel a big girl's blouse, and asking me to step outside for a fight to the death). Neither of them, rather cleverly, said, 'You've got nothing to worry about.' I would've battered them if they did.

Craig was actively listening right then. He probably realised, though, I'd be unloading whether he was listening or taking a jaunt through his mind.

I poured hot water onto the tea bag. The scent of peppermint wafted up in the steam leaving the cup. 'I'm writing a paper on subliminal advertising,' I explained. It was, of course, more than that. More than just a case of 'subliminal advertising'. It was more to do with perception and communication and the way our conscious and subconscious minds worked independently and dependently. How we found out things without being directly told; how we told people things without actually saying them. On the most basic level, it was about how we perceived things without realising we'd perceived them.

Take for instance the case of someone calling you a few minutes after you've thought about them. You think, that's strange, I must be psychic. However, it might not be psychic ability at all. It could actually be that at an earlier date you'd said you hardly went out on Wednesdays. Maybe you'd mentioned that telly was much better on a Wednesday night, or that you preferred going out on a Thursday rather than a Wednesday night. So, that person you're talking to unintentionally, subliminally, has it in their head that Wednesday is the best day to call you. You, without realising it, always think of that person on a Wednesday because you've started on some level to associate them with you not going out on that night of the week. Also, subliminally, you've told them that the best day to call you is a Wednesday. So, when they call, it's not cos you're psychic or have super-enhanced women's intuition, you have subliminally communicated when to call you.

And that was my study. On subliminal perception, on the ways people subliminally advertise things.

This information had a strange effect on Craig. A light bulb seemed to go off in him and he physically sat forwards in the chair. 'Yeah, course. It's quite obvious if you think about it.'

I frowned, put down the kettle, stirred the tea. 'What do you mean it's obvious?'

'Well, that's what you do, isn't it? You subliminally advertise sex.'

The spoon slipped from my fingers. Huh? How had he come to that conclusion? Wasn't I the one who hadn't had sex in over six months, and who had accepted the most exciting my life was going to get was through trying a new hair conditioner? And had Craig actually looked at me? Apart from today, which was a glitch in the otherwise normal wardrobe, I had an asexual way of dressing. I wore combats and jeans. Long-sleeved tops. All right, so I wore big hoop earrings and I occasionally slicked on lipstick, but I in no way advertised sex, subliminally or otherwise. Pamela Anderson had nothing on me breast-wise, but there were hoards of men who would swear on the continued longevity of their penises that the last thing that came to mind when they looked at me was sex.

'I don't,' I stated with a frown.

'You do,' Craig replied. 'You make me want to have sex every time I see you.'

The spoon, which I'd picked up, slipped from my fingers onto the side again. 'What?'

'You make me want to have sex every time I see you.'

I stared at him. 'It's true,' Craig shrugged.

'Craig, have you seen me? I'm hardly *Baywatch* material. Apart from these babies,' I said, pointing at my chest, 'I'd probably be turned down for *Readers' Wives*.'

Craig shrugged again. 'I don't know what it is about you. You don't show flesh, except for that little bit of curved abdomen where your tops never quite reach the top of your trousers. And your bum's not exactly pert, but it's juicy and round. And your breasts, always encased in jersey tops, but . . . I don't know, I really don't. Maybe it's the way your hair's so black and the way it touches the nape of your neck, or the way you smile and show all your teeth . . . to be honest, Ceri, I

212

don't know what it is, but I can guarantee that after I've seen you, I'll have sex with my ex-girlfriend. Most of the time I can hardly bring myself to talk to her, but I've been with her almost every day since you started. We even have a laugh together.'

'Bollocks.'

'It's true. I don't know why, but it's true. I mean, before, I hated her. Really hated her. I'd go out of my way to avoid her or anywhere she might be, but I swear to God, since you started working here, I can't keep away from her.'

I picked up the teaspoon, ran it under the tap. I dipped it back into the cup of brown liquid, an oily film had formed and when I withdrew it, clumps of the film stayed on the spoon.

Without thinking, I poured milk into my tea. Stirred. I put the cup to the lips, the strong scent of peppermint stopped me drinking. I looked into the cup, it looked horrible, it would've tasted worse.

'Anyway Ceri, got to go, but good luck with the research.'

'Mmm?' I replied, looking up. Craig was halfway out the door with his papers in his arms.

'See ya,' he called.

'Oh, yeah, see ya.'

'Well, it's obvious, isn't it?' Drew said to me on the phone. 'He fancies you.'

'No he doesn't,' I said. Drew now knew the conversation with Craig word for word and I'd waited with baited breath for his opinion. He came next in the list of people to consult when I had a dilemma. Jess, with her several trillion degrees came first, she was the smartest person I knew.

Drew, who went under the moniker of 'my other best friend' only seemed to be contactable via phone nowadays even though we worked in the same city – in fact, I saw him more when I lived in London.

'Only a man who fancies you notices all that about you,' Drew added.

I sighed. 'Will you stop. He doesn't fancy me. It was only when I told him about my research that he brought it up. I mean, I'd told him I was single before, he never leapt on that. It was only the subliminal bit that got him to say that. He was obviously speaking as he thought, not flirting.'

'Oh.'

'Anyway, it'd be a pretty bad way to flirt with me, wouldn't it, saying he was still knocking off his ex-girlfriend?'

'True.'

'And he's not the first person to say it to me. Someone else said the same thing but not in the same way. And *they* certainly didn't fancy me.' That's what had freaked me out about what Craig said, it reminded me of Jess saying that I made men fancy her. I made people do things and that couldn't be right. I had to get a third opinion. Hence the calling of Drew at his management consultancy conference, which I'd never do unless it was a real emergency. Which this was, in a way. 'Do you want to have sex after you see me?'

Drew thought about it for a few seconds. 'No. Can't say I do. Sex doesn't even enter my mind.'

Big foamy waves of relief washed over me. I wasn't a freak. I didn't send people scurrying off to satisfy their lusts elsewhere. Then I was completely affronted. The Git. After flirting with me for all those years, after cuddling up to me and having pornographic conversations with me, sex didn't even *enter* his mind. He really was an affection tease, wasn't he? Or, horror of horrors, had I always been so sexually uninteresting to him that he could flirt with me by rote? That thought made me shudder.

'Tell you something, though, I did always pull with you around,' Drew's voice said thoughtfully.

214

'What?'

'Yeah, thinking about it now, whenever we went clubbing, I'd always pull. Always. It was weird. It never happened when I went out without you.'

'WHAT?!'

'It's true, you were like my lucky charm. I couldn't get a girl to look twice at me when I went clubbing without you, but with you, I was like the most popular man on earth.'

'So how did you pull Tara then?'

'That was a fluke. And she didn't go for me for my looks, it was my personality that attracted her.'

'I didn't realise just how bad her taste was.'

'Funny. Anyway, are you sure this guy wasn't coming on to you?' Drew asked.

'No. I mean, yes, I'm sure he wasn't coming on to me. At least I think he wasn't.'

'So you admit the possibility?'

I thought about it. It was a possibility that Craig was coming on to me. So slim a possibility it didn't even qualify as a poss. 'It is possible. Less possible than, say, me marrying Angel, but a possibility.'

'You're a freak, you know that?' Drew replied.

'And that's why you love me, right?' I said.

I could hear him smile down the phone. 'Absolutely.'

'But what does it mean?' I said, flopping back into the office chair.

'Don't know,' Drew replied, the line rustled as he switched his mobile from one ear to the other. 'Maybe you just appeared in one of his dreams – of the moist variety.'

I sighed. 'It didn't sound like that.'

'Or maybe it's an X-file. Y'know, one of those mysteries we'll never work out, like how you, an almost thirty-year-old woman, could still believe you're going to marry Angel.'

'You know, sod you Drew, time will prove me right on that. And when it does, you're going to be a bridesmaid – and wear a dress.'

Drew laughed.

'Oh, you laugh, but you will.'

Drew laughed some more. 'Anyway gorgeous, gotta get back to it. Talk to you soon?'

'Yeah, talk to you soon.'

'And don't worry about what that bloke said. He probably just has a very poor flirting style. You know, trying to get you into bed by being clever. He wouldn't be the first, that's for sure.'

'Yeah, you're probably right,' I said. A voice at the back of my head said, *He's not right, you know he's not right.*

chapter twenty-two

Good Enough

The day of Ed's Big Date dawned and I was nervous.

Actually I was shitting myself, for want of a better expression. This was Ed. This was his one big chance to impress the gorgeous Robyn. And I'd been the one who'd pushed him into doing the deed.

Oh God, what if this all turned nasty? What if she was a nightmare and she made his date hell? Who would he blame? Who would he have every right to blame? Me, of course. *Then* what would I do? Find him another woman to lust after? Yeah, right. Most people needed love in their life. And if not love, then someone or something to lust after. Robyn was Ed's *raison d'être*. The reason he got out of bed most mornings. The reason he'd hacked off his hair and retired his lumberjack shirt. And I'd practically held a gun to his head and forced him to ask her out. I wouldn't be surprised if he turned that very same gun on me and blew my brains out.

He'd have every right. I would, if he took away my *raison d'être*. My purpose, the one thing that kept me believing in love and happy endings. There were times, during those barren weeks, months and years where all you had to keep you going was seeing that one person, that perfect computer, those exquisite shoes – that one thing that made the rest of the bad times that plagued your existence worthwhile.

Case in point: my obsession with *Angel*.

I was enough of a psychologist to know that it'd gotten out of hand, that I'd started to believe he and I were meant to be together for ever because I hadn't seen a man or a computer or a pair of shoes that gave me the same kick. Nothing got my undivided attention like him. Nothing made my heart beat faster, or my stomach tingle or my face smile like he did. Consistently.

But, finding out that your perfect shoes would, over time, amputate your little toes; that the computer would give you incurable RSI; or that person you loved was actually sent to this earth to make you suffer a lifetime's worth of indignity (or, after one shag would lose their soul, then hunt down and kill all your friends, oh, wait, no that's Angel) was information you could live without. And you usually only found out the downside of your dream when you got the thing you wanted, in other words: be careful what you wish for, it may come true. In Ed's case, going on a date with Robyn.

I went to work on that Wednesday morning as usual, but I left after my last lecture. Didn't hang around in the library or work in my office or go anywhere near the Senior Common Room to get my weekly dose of Gwen. I came straight home and spent the entire bus journey offering up a prayer that Robyn would like the posh restaurant he'd planned to take her to. That she'd laugh at his jokes. She'd appreciated the sacrifice he'd made with his hair. That she wouldn't lurch with disgust if he tried to kiss her. That she would see past anything that could possibly put her off and realise what a genuinely decent guy Ed was. He and Jake had gone out of their way to make me the third wheel on their

Stanmore Vale tricycle. They didn't have to, they just did because the pair of them were good people. *Please God, let her realise that.*

Ed was in his room when I got home. I didn't disturb him, didn't want to add to any anxiety he might have with anxieties of my own. I pottered around the kitchen, attempting to cook but getting distracted by thoughts of Ed coming home after his date a broken man with nothing left to live for. Every self-help book I'd read and started to read had mentioned something about visualisation — visualising the result you wanted from a situation, seeing it in your head helped it to come true. Would it work for other people? Who cared? I settled myself on the sofa nearest the window.

OK. Ed and Robyn. Had to visualise something great. The perfect date.

I didn't know what she looked like, Ed's description — 'an angel on earth' — hadn't been particularly helpful, so in my mind's eye she became Halle Berry, a gorgeous woman, no mistaking.

Right, visualise Robyn/Halle and Ed sitting in Teppanyaki, that Japanese restaurant in town, he tells her a joke. And she . . . she tuts and carries on eating. No. No. She . . . tuts and carries on eating. OK, change scenario.

Ed says he'll see her home. She smiles, agrees, says most blokes just put her on the bus. They get to her front door, which bears a remarkable resemblance to our front door. Once there, Ed says he had a great time, can he see her again? She smiles and says yes. Ed asks if he can kiss her, she replies: 'Euck, no!'

Noooo, that was going so well.

I opened my eyes. *Ah, sod it. If she upsets him, I'll just do away with her and visualise my way through the perfect murder.*

*

219

I answered the door to Robyn at seven-thirty.

And double-took at her. Halle Berry had nothing on her. She was so stunning, *I* had faint stirrings in my loins. Her hair was plaited to waist length (when I had plaited extensions, they never looked that perfect) and framed her slender face with its wide nose. She had dark brown eyes, full lips and styled eyebrows. And her skin, flawless. It could've been make-up, but I was sure it was natural beauty. And probably not drinking, not smoking and doing the gym thing. Her and Ed would make a great couple: her, all slender limbs and poise; him, tall and, when he stood up straight, he looked quite manly. At least she'd made an effort, I thought with relief. Having said that, she didn't seem the kind of woman who'd leave the house without making an effort. She certainly wouldn't do a Ceri D'Altroy and leave the house to get a newspaper and bottle of water with her uncombed hair squashed under a scarf, wearing crumpled clothes, an uncleansed face and unbrushed teeth.

'Come in,' I said, stepping aside to let her in.

She stepped in, headed straight for the living room, like she'd been invited to do so. She certainly knew how to own a place by doing something as innocuous as walking in to it. Probably something she learnt in acting class. She was an artist, *darlink*.

'Would you like a drink or something while you're waiting?' I asked, with a smile. 'Ed shouldn't be too long.' I was on my best behaviour, didn't want to do anything to ruin Ed's chances.

'No,' she said. 'I'd rather we got going.'

'Oh, Ed won't be much longer.'

She moved her face as if to say, *He'd better not be*, then sat on the left-hand sofa, instantly brightening it up.

'Music?' I said, moving to the stereo.

'Do you have any acid jazz?'

What, that music that makes me think of bad and lengthy eleva-tor music? 'Er, no. I'm sure I can find a radio station that plays it though.'

'Don't bother.'

Right. 'What about telly? *Corrie*'s started.' I had one hand ready to hit the 'on' button.

'I don't watch *Coronation Street*. I went for an audition once and I didn't get it. It upsets me to watch it.'

H'OK. I withdrew my finger. I stood by the television, with this incredible urge to twiddle my fingers and hum out of tune. Minutes passed. More minutes passed. I knew Ed would've heard the doorbell. Even he wouldn't be stupid enough to keep her waiting. Not if he wanted the date to start off well.

Robyn's dark eyes flickered over me, giving me the distinct impression it was my fault Ed wasn't in front of her.

'I'll just go see what's keeping him,' I said to her.

She hinted at a thin smile of gratitude with her lipsticked lips, then decided not to bother.

Ohhhh, does she not like me. She's not the first woman not to like me. I doubted she'd be the last. Just like I didn't partic-ularly like girly girls; girly girls didn't particularly like ungirly girls. Which was cool. As long as we both stuck to our respec-tive areas of expertise – her: hair, make-up, boys: me, science fiction, psychology and using my brain.

I pegged it up the stairs, turned the corner, sped to Ed's door and tapped on it.

'Ed?' I whispered loudly through the door. The living room door was still open, I didn't want her to hear.

No answer.

I tapped again.

'*Ed!* Ed, Ed, what you doing? She's getting really wound up down there.'

Nothing in reply. I knew he was in there, I could hear him walking around. Pacing, whispering.

'Ed. What are you doing in there?'

Nothing. Pacing, whispering. I tapped the door again, louder. 'Ed, open this bloody door,' I hissed. 'What are you doing?'

The door unlocked, his head appeared in the fraction he opened it. 'I'm stuffed, Ceri.'

His blue shirt collar stood on end on one side, horizontal on the other side. His tie was tied over it, his face flushed, his eyes wide and desperate.

'What do you mean, stuffed?'

He was breathing hard, a possessed man who still had the devil at his heels.

'She's going to leave if you're not careful,' I said.

His terrified eyes searched mine. 'I'm stuffed, Ceri, I'm stuffed.'

'Stop saying that! You're not. Tell me what you mean.'

Ed jerked the door open. 'I mean, this.' He pointed to his lap. I followed his pointing finger.

Outlined in his trousers, loose as they were, was a long, thick shape. The material of his loose trousers was taut around it emphasising it. You couldn't miss it. I tore my eyes away, thinking, *Who'd have guessed that skinny Ed was so big?*

He grabbed my wrist, pulled me into the room, shut the door behind him. 'I can't get rid of it,' he said.

'What?'

'I can't get rid of,' he pointed southward again, '*IT!*'

He paced the length of his room. 'I've tried everything I know. I've tried playing with it, orgasms, ignoring it, cold showers, flicking the top of it . . . nothing works. I can't get rid of it.'

'Not even flicking the top of it?'

He shook his head.

'How hard did you flick?'

'Hard! Fucking hard! It hurt. It bruised, but it wouldn't die. I can't go on a date like this. She'll think I'm a sleaze. And I can't even change cos these are the biggest trousers I've got apart from my jogging bottoms.'

He was indeed, stuffed.

'And, and, I swear, it's got bigger. It was never, well, you know.'

'Eh?' I said, trying hard not to stare at it.

'I'm not saying I was small or owt, but it was never that big.'

From my side of the room, I raised my hand, held it up in that area so Ed's lower half would be hidden and I wouldn't be tempted to gawp at it.

'How long have you been like this?'

'All day. I was pleased at first, I kind of hoped I'd be up to the challenge. I mean, I'm nothing. I'm not as good-looking or funny or famous as her other fellas. I don't know, I just . . .'

'Hoped, prayed, wished you could be better in one way,' I cut in. 'Just one way, you want to outshine the competition. You can't change your looks, you can't change your bank balance and it'll take her a while to get to know your true personality. But in one way, just one way you want to stand out. Be superior, be worthy.

'This is, this was, your one chance with someone you've wanted, yearned for, for months. This person is number one. You never thought this day would come and now it has come, you're terrified that you won't live up to the challenge. That now your dream's come true, it's all going to go wrong because of you. Not cos she's a cow, but because of you. You not being good enough.'

I suppose you could say I had some vague idea of how Ed felt. That deep yearning, that not good enough feeling, that wondering 'when will it be my turn to get the big prize?' Self-help

223

book, smelf-help book, when you never got the boy – or girl – you didn't feel good about yourself. Your positivity was eroded, you seized on every little sniff of romance as THE NEXT BIG THING.

'That's all very well, but what the hell am I going to do?' Ed wailed.

I shifted my hand a fraction, peeked at what should have been his very big pride. The first – and last – time I saw a male member nearly as big had been attached to Mr Perfect Penis and I'd initially been disturbed by its size. When I got to know it, it'd been all right. But I'd been overcome with lust for him from the instant I saw him. It remained to be seen if Robyn even liked Ed; if he went out on a date like that, she'd think he was disgusting. She'd leave before he even got to the restaurant, let alone offered to pay for dinner.

'There's only one thing you can do, mate,' I said.

chapter twenty-three

The Love CV

'You told him to what?' Jess said, when I told her the sketchiest details of Ed's predicament.

We were back in the Black Bull. So much for her not drinking with me again. Although, technically, she wasn't drinking with me again in that respect. We were about to go shopping in Morrison's, Horsforth, so we'd done our usual and gone for a fortifying drink down the road beforehand. We used to go shopping every Wednesday night when I lived up in Cookridge years ago. After *Star Trek: Next Generation*, she'd drive round, pick me up, we'd shop then go back to our lives. We'd slipped back into that routine, but this time on Tuesday, after *Star Trek: Voyager*.

'Well, it was either that or cancel the date. And, short of maiming himself and being rushed to casualty – which I'm not sure would've convinced her anyway – he couldn't cancel. Not if he wanted another date with her. It'd taken the poor lad months to work up the courage to ask her out in the first place. Which, I suspect, was why he was in that state.'

'But still . . .'

'What would you have got him to do, Dr Breakfield?'

Jess shrugged. 'Cover it up.'

'I kid you not, it was huge. Not being funny, right, but I've only ever seen one penis that large and, to be honest, it wasn't as big as Ed's was and I was a little scared of that one. Every other part of Ed's trousers were baggy on him, but it was like a huge pole, straining there. I can't get the image of it out of my mind. And I don't want to think like that about Ed. Not ever. Anyway, if I'd told him to cover it up, he'd have had to hide behind a large *AA Road Map* for the rest of his life.'

'Did your plan work?'

I shrugged. 'I don't know.' I sipped from my pint of beer Jess had bought me. 'But I haven't seen him since that night. Neither has Jake.'

Jess stopped. She'd leant forwards to scrunch out her cigarette in the ashtray but stopped and looked at me. 'You're joking! Tell me you're joking.'

I shook my head. 'Jake said that he got a message on his mobile from Ed and it was just hysterical laughter.'

'NO!'

'Oh yes. And that's not all. When Jake called him back, Ed just mumbled "bliss" and hung up.'

Jess put out her cigarette and shook her head incredulously. She turned to me, shook her head some more. 'Let me get this straight. You advise someone to tell a woman he's got the hots for her so desperately that he's perma-erect and it *works*? She actually buys it?'

I pushed the ashtray closer to her. 'There was more to it than that,' I replied. 'I told him to tell her the truth. To explain how much he liked her, why he liked her, because it was more than her looks. The guy genuinely adores her. So he told her. Not the "I adore you" bit. More the *reasons* he likes her, for example, he remembers exactly what she was wearing when they first met, he listens when she speaks, he gets excited every time she even looks at him. He often wants to tell her something because he knows she'll appreciate it. So he told her. And he also told her how inadequate he feels compared to her other boyfriends. How he was terrified that he'd screw up on this date and he'd not get another chance. And how his perceived inadequacies had worked like Viagra. I'm assuming it worked.

'With an ego the size of hers, I'd have been more surprised if it hadn't worked.'

Jess nodded slowly, her face deep in thought. She leant forwards and took a cigarette from the packet that lay between us, her arm slung across her stomach.

'Don't take this the wrong way, Ceri, but it occurs to me that you live everyone else's life with the volume turned right up, but your own life is pretty barren.'

'Barren?' I said.

'Don't get that pet lip with me, Ceresis D'Altroy.' Now she was using my full name. What was she going to do next, slash my throat with a broken bottle? 'I said not to take it the wrong way.'

'What way is there to take it?'

'What I mean is, you can do almost anything with someone else's love life but yours, well, you think you're going to end up with Angel.'

'I can't help it if all the men I meet turn out to be freaks.'

'What about Vincent? He sounded nice enough.'

'Yes, and he could only have sex if *Inspector Morse* was playing in the background. He couldn't even get it up if it wasn't on.'

Jess's face double-took into true disgust.

'I don't tell you everything, you see. I do try to protect you from the horrors of my love life.'

'What about, erm, what was his name, Luke?'

227

'Forgot to mention his girlfriend was eight months pregnant.'

'Adam?'

'His ex-wife cheated on him so all women, particularly his girlfriends, are devil's spawn. Of course, then there was the time some guy smiled at me and he almost beat him up'

'Paul? I met Paul, he was lovely.'

'Yes, when I saw him, he was lovely. But he kept disappearing for weeks after we'd seen each other. When I called it a day, he started sending me pornographic emails telling me how much he wanted to F star star K me.'

'What about the, erm, television producer?'

'Was getting married and I was his last fling. I found out when I opened the local paper and there he was with his bride.'

'The graphic designer?' Jess's voice was waning.

'Some bloke pushed him in the street, so he went out the next day with a knife in his jacket in the hope he'd see the bloke again and stab him.'

'The other graphic designer?'

Jess braced herself to hear about this one.

'Erm, let's see, his best male friend turned up one night, to join us in bed. And he was really "upset" when I said no, got dressed and left.'

'The guy working on his novel?'

'He stopped calling me after three dates. You can go through the whole list of men and at the end of it, you'll find they all have one thing in common: they are all freaks. I don't do it on purpose. I don't go out looking for them. But they seem to have this ability to track me down. Hunt me out of the crowd, as it were, like I'm a wounded animal.'

'Doesn't that worry you?'

'Yeah! These are the thoughts that keep me awake at night.

228

I'm convinced I'm going to spend the rest of my life alone or dating freaks. I don't know what it is, but I can pick a nutter at thirty paces. And I'm scared I'm going to keep doing that for the rest of my life. The closest I've got to a relationship was with N— Whashisface Tosspot, and look how that turned out.' (It turned out with me sneaking around for months buying a flat without telling him so he couldn't stop me with his line in emotional blackmail (aka Jedi Mind Trick/Work Of The Devil). He was a man about it, though: when I told him I was moving and started packing, he didn't say anything. At all. Or try to stop me. It had nothing to do with my brothers being with me, I'm sure.)

'What about that thing with you and Drew?' Jessica asked, looking in her cigarette packet and finding it empty. She tossed it back on the table.

'Drew has a girlfriend, remember?'

'Yes, I remember. But he was always so keen on you, why weren't you interested?'

I almost choked on my beer. 'Me, not interested? I think you'll find it was the other way around.'

'No,' Jess said, thoughtfully, 'the way he used to look at you . . . I remember in lectures I'd always catch him staring at you. Even when you'd both finished college, I remember at parties he'd be all over you. Or would look so jealous if he saw you talking to another man. It was . . . I reckon you were his reserve option.'

'His what?' I said, eyeing my best friend. I didn't like the way this conversation was going. Actually, I didn't like this conversation at all. I didn't need to be reminded that my love life was, as she said, 'barren'.

'I think he thought of you as the woman he'd end up with if something better didn't come along.'

My head creaked round to face Jess full on. 'Excuse me!

Who are you? Because I'm sure my best friend isn't allowed to say such things to me.'

'God, Ceresis, you're being really touchy today.'

She was doing it again – calling me by my bloody full name.

'Touchy?' I stated. 'You've just said that I wasn't important enough for Drew to fall in love with unless he had no other options. And you've just called me Ceresis twice. Why wouldn't I be touchy?'

'No sweetie—'

'Don't you "sweetie" me, Dr Jessica Breakfield,' I cut in.

'So you'd prefer Ceresis?' she replied.

I gritted my teeth and bared them at her.

'OK, *sweetie*, what I'm saying is, there's something about you. Makes men think that they can be   I don't know. Whashisface Tosspot did it, he sucked the vitality out of you so he could get a personality. By the time you and he ended, he was a different person. He didn't speak in that ridiculous way and he actually had conversational skills. He'd even stopped tucking his jumpers into his jeans, if what you told me was true. As a result, he ended up getting married less than a year after you got away from him. Drew used you as some kind of surrogate girlfriend, always coming back to you when things were going wrong, his safety net for not getting disheartened when another one of his relationships went pear-shaped. He kept coming back to you until he met his current girl-friend . . . there's something about you.'

A chill went through me and what Drew said to me the other day came to mind. '*You were like my lucky charm. I could-n't get a girl to look twice at me when I went dubbing without you, but with you, I was like the most popular man on earth*,' his voice said in my head.

'Loads of women get treated badly by men,' I said to Jess, trying to dislodge that thought from my head. This was all going down the 'you make me do things' route. A particular route I wasn't keen to venture down right now. Or ever again, for that matter.

Jess nodded. 'True. But you're different. Have you ever been in love, Ceri?'

I didn't have to think about that question. Not at all. Have I ever been in lust – absolutely (Mr PP, prime example); have I ever been in deep like – yup (man I usually called 'Love Of My Life', who left me for someone else); have I ever been in stupidity – damn right (Whashisface Tosspot, take a bow). But love? It was odd when I thought about it. When I really thought about it. I was, the coming summer, about to start the fourth decade of my life and yet, I hadn't experienced romantic love. I hadn't said it to someone and meant 'I love you and I'm in love with you'. Well, no one who wasn't Angel, Arnold Schwarzenegger, etc. I'd never looked at someone in front of me and thought, 'I love you. I can't live without you' and knew he felt the same way.

I'd been through the whole spectrum of emotions in my life, anger, lust, hate, rage, joy, happiness, indifference, anticipation, but I'd constantly skipped over the segment where romantic love lay. Jess was right, my heart was barren. It'd never been toiled over and planted and weeded and watered by someone else. It'd never been loved, like other people's hearts had been loved. If I told people that I'd never been out with anyone, they'd immediately bring up the man I lived with. Not knowing, not understanding that I'd *shared* a flat with him. I had my own bedroom. That everyone around us, particularly his family and his friends, thought I was his flatmate – and the woman he sometimes shagged – and because of that, I was never invited to weddings or christenings or family parties. And people who thought I'd lived with someone never knew that the one time he ever said 'I love you', he'd immediately taken it back by

231

adding, 'You do realise I mean I love you as I love all my other friends, don't you?' If I told people I hadn't been out with anyone, they didn't realise I meant, I hadn't ever been with anyone long enough for the L word to come up.

So, no, I didn't need to think about whether I'd been in love before.

'Not with anyone who's loved me back,' I replied to Jess. 'None of my relationships last long enough for me to fall in love and have them fall in love with me.'

'That's really shit, Ceri,' Jess said. Her voice sounded how I often felt when it came to the subject of my love life, defeated. Others may whine about their troubles with men, but I'll bet every one of them had some good relationship years to show for it. They'd experienced that mythical state known as 'In Love'. I had . . . Whashisface Tosspot. And if there was ever a man you didn't need on your love CV, it was him. For him to be the best you can do, well I wouldn't employ me as a partner if he was the best reference I had.

'I know,' I said to Jess, agreeing with her my love life was indeed shit.

'But at least we've got chocolate and beer,' she said, her voice rallying suddenly Trying to drag us out of the bog that was my love life.

'True,' I agreed.

'So, let's get going to Morrison's and not leave until we get some of that.'

'God, Jess, you're going to be fifty,' I said, wondrously.

It was one of those moments where I said what was on my mind. I'd looked over Jess, tall, slender, waves and waves of auburn hair and hardly a wrinkle in sight – despite those propagated theories on smoking and skin. She looked about thirty-two, thirty-three at the most, not closer to fifty. Fifty.

My best mate was going to be fifty when I hadn't even cleared my thirties. Which was why I said it.

Jess froze as she put mushrooms in a plastic bag. 'Thanks a lot Ceri,' she said incredulously.

'I didn't mean it like that,' I said.

'Oh, and how *did* you mean it?'

'That you don't look that old.'

Jess's eyes widened.

'No, no, no, no, that came out wrong, too.'

'Hmmm,' Jess replied, twisting her face to show how unimpressed she was.

'It was a compliment,' I floundered. 'Honest.'

'Hmmm,' Jess replied.

'I suppose I'll go get the peppers,' I said, waving around the plastic bag in my hand. I turned on my heels and headed towards the capsicum section of Morrison's.

'You're going be fifty too one day,' Jess said as I walked away.

'I know,' I said. 'I wasn't saying you would and I wouldn't.'

'If you're lucky,' she hissed.

Jess, who was generally laid-back about most things was probably cross with me now. I really hadn't meant it like that. Even though she'd not an hour ago told me my life was barren, reminded me I'd never been in love and called me Ceresis (*twice*), I hadn't meant to upset her. To curry favour, I wandered past the peppers and round to the next aisle, I'd get her a frozen pizza, then jazz it up with vegetables and make fresh garlic bread. *Then* she'd forgive me. The route to Jess's forgiveness centre was, like mine, through her stomach.

I turned the corner, to the next aisle. And there he was. About to lean in to grab a frozen pizza. My heart skipped a beat.

Staring Man.

Instinctively I jumped back out of sight. My heart galloping in my chest. I pegged it back to the produce aisle.

'Jess, Jess,' I hissed loudly.

'What?' she replied, still in a strop.

I beckoned rapidly to her. 'Quick, quick, come here.'

She glowered at me for a second.

'*QUICK!*' I hurried.

She came wandering over. I grabbed her arm, dragged her to the corner. I stuck my head around the corner; she did the same.

'There he is,' I said.

'Who?' she asked, even though he was the only one down that aisle.

I pointed. 'Him!'

'Who is he?'

I shrugged. 'I don't know, but he hates me.'

'Why?'

'I don't know.'

'You must have done something.'

'I haven't! I've never even spoken to the man, but every time I see him at college or in the street or in the pub, he just stares at me.'

'Really?'

'Yeah.'

'And you've never spoken to him?'

'Nope. I just turn around and there he is,' I opened my eyes wide, 'glaring at me. I don't know why.'

As if he had a radar for people staring at him, SM looked up.

Jess and I both jumped back, clinging to each other. We got ridiculously silly and ran back to the trolley, both of us shaking and giggling.

'But why is he always staring at me?' I asked, when we were sure that he hadn't clocked us and stopped giggling.

'Hmmm,' Jess said, thoughtfully. 'I don't know. You're this striking woman with this presence wherever she goes, and two of the biggest, natural breasts known to man, I haven't got a clue why he stares at you.'

'Even when you're being nice you're a sarcastic cow.'

'Something to do with being nearly fifty, I think.'

'I didn't mean it like that.'

'Yeah, yeah.'

'Can we get back to the matter in hand? Staring Man. It's really disturbing.'

'I've told you before, disturbing things happen when you're around.'

'But why does he stare at me? Those big eyes staring at me from this blank face. It gives me the willies.'

'Ceri, sweetheart, I'm sure that's all he wants to give you.'

My eyes almost leapt out of my head. 'JESSICA BREAK-FIELD! I can't believe you just said that.'

Jess shrugged. 'It's true. Him, man. You, woman. He wants to, what's that phrase you youngsters use? Oh yes, roger you senseless.'

My eyes widened and my mouth fell open. 'Filthy mind.' I took over the trolley-pushing duties. 'Filthy mind.'

I pushed the trolley down the aisle, towards the long line of narrow checkouts. 'Filthy, filthy mind.'

Jess lit a cigarette against the strong breeze in the car park, then stood smoking it by Fred's car, while I pushed the trolley back and went to retrieve my pound coin. I was still reeling from her filthiness. My best friend wasn't meant to say things like that. That was one of the advantages of having a best mate who was older than you, they didn't say such things. Having thought that, Jess and I were of a similar mind, and I did have a tendency to let my imagination run free when it came to sex.

235

Especially, when it came to Angel . . . I stood patiently behind someone as they struggled to retrieve their pound coin from the trolley contraption while I contemplated Angel. I often wondered what it'd be like if *he* gave me the willies. Well, I knew, from the detail and the vividness of my imagination what it'd be like. Fantastic. One of those nights you'd never forget. Even when you were eighty-nine you'd drag it up from your memory and hold it up to scrutiny. And every time, you'd get those chills and tingles down below. Oh yes, one night with Angel would be like one night in heaven. A bad pun, but so tru—

'This thing's broken,' the man in front of me said. My knees involuntarily weakened at his voice. It was deep and warm, like sinking into a hot bath after a hard day, like snuggling down in front of a real fire when it's snowing outside. His voice made all my body tingle with pleasure. (I really was rather sexually frustrated, wasn't I? I was getting excited over a voice!)

I looked up at the source of the voice. He looked back at me. We both started at who we were looking at. Staring Man.

I ripped my eyes away, my face and body suddenly aflame. This was the closest we'd ever been. And after what Jess had said about him wanting to give me the willies, my body started to burn with embarrassment. My knees had gone weak when I heard his voice. Him, the man who obviously disliked me. Waves of red-hot mortification crashed down on me all over again.

'This thing's broken,' he repeated. His voice still had the same effect on my knees, even though I knew it was him.

'Oh,' was all I could think to say as I looked back at him. I suppose I'd never thought he had a voice. He seemed to glare at me more than anything else, so I knew he had eyes and a face. But not a voice. I'd also now worked out that he had a thing about Mel. It was abundantly clear. He'd been giving me evils because he fancied Mel. He'd seen me leave the party with Mel, so was pissed off about it. Then, he'd seen me hugging Ed, jumped to the conclusion that I was doing the dirty on his Mel. I'd be the same if, say, I thought Fred was doing the dirty on Jess. Then in the SCR, he'd seen me acting all normal with Mel and probably thought I was some two-faced slut who was going to break his precious Mel's heart.

'I suppose we should go find someone to report it to,' he said.

'But that would mean queuing and talking to someone who will invariably decide that my need for my pound back gives them licence to patronise me,' I observed, even though I was still rather overcome by this ill-meeting. All we needed was a spot of moonlight and I'd be well within my rights to start quoting Shakespeare.

'True,' he replied.

'Do you have a hairpin or a nail file? I've got a mean trick to get pound coins out of these contraptions, no probs. It's a South Londoner thing.'

'Really?' His eyes doubled in awe. He was impressed.

'No,' I replied. I'd not have said it if I thought he'd be *that* impressed. 'I just say things like that,' I explained. 'I can't help myself.'

'Oh, right. Kind of like Lieutenant Barclay?'

My heart stopped. 'You reference *Star Trek*,' I breathed. My heart started beating again, but I was suddenly breathless with admiration and awe. It was always a genuine shock and moment of true kinship when I met someone who wasn't me or Jess, who could drop *Star Trek* into a normal conversation. If he didn't hate me and fancy Mel, I'd be seeing him in soft focus, hearing romantic harp music and melting in his arms, right about now.

'You know my references to *Star Trek*.' He sounded equally

surprised and impressed. We let a moment of silence pass between us as we formed a bond of mutual admiration.

'Are you *DS9* or *Voyager*?' he asked.

'I'm *Next Gen*. But *Voyager*'s second.'

Anyone listening to us would think we were talking in code, unless they watched *Star Trek*. *Star Trek: Next Generation* (my favourite); *Star Trek: Voyager* (my second favourite); *Star Trek: Deep Space Nine* (I'd grown to love it over time); and then of course there was the original series, but not necessarily the best.

SM raised his eyebrows. 'I'm a bit torn. *Voyager*'s good, but then, so's *Next Gen*. I think, though, I prefer *DS9*.'

'Most men do cos a lot of it was war games and politics. I had a bit of a *DS9* marathon once and really got into it. I can't help liking old Avery Brooks either.'

'What, Mr Hawk himself?' SM teased. 'You like all that wearing shades at night stuff?'

'You did *not* watch *Spenser: For Hire*,' I said, aghast. *God, maybe I dismissed those harp players and the soft-focus visuals too quickly.*

'I did too!' SM replied, not one hint of embarrassment. 'I've even got a few episodes on tape.'

'Me too!' I replied. 'But despite Hawk being in *DS9* I, er, can't give up my love for a spot of Will Riker and Jean-Luc. And Worf.'

SM's face broke into a huge grin, softening his chiselled features. He was really quite attractive – but that was probably a lot to do with us having such a big thing in common. Television. 'I like a bit of Worf myself, but I was glad he and Deanna didn't get together in the end. I can't abide Deanna Troi.'

'Me either!' I laughed.

'Have you seen *Enterprise* yet?'

I shook my head. 'Nope.'

'Me neither,' SM replied.

'Can't say I'm that keen on the idea, but I'm sure it'll insinuate itself into my affections like all the others did.'

'True,' he said.

We let another moment of *Star Trek*-induced admiration pass in silence.

'So, how long have you known Mel?' I asked, groping for the only other subject we had in common, hoping to bond there, too.

SM looked down at the trolley he had his hand on, started fiddling with the lump of metal that held on tight to his pound coin. *I'm right, he does have a thing about Mel. And this is my chance to show him Mel and I are just mates. That I'm not trying to muscle in on his territory.*

'Not long. Well, since I started at All Souls, about two years ago. He's a good bloke is our Mel.'

Our Mel. 'Yeah, I really like him, h—'

'Oi, D'Altroy, what are you doing?' Jess's voice cut in. I jumped slightly, then turned around. She was leaning out of the driver's window of her car, looking rather impatient. By standing there, trying to ingratiate myself with what was, essentially, The Enemy, I was lengthening the time between cigarettes for her.

'Hey,' SM said, 'how about I give you a pound and you give me a pound then it'll seem as though we've got our pounds back from the trolleys.'

'Good plan,' I said. I rummaged into my jeans pocket and handed over a pound coin.

'Got change for a fiver?' he said, holding out a five pound note.

I looked at him, unimpressed.

'Only joking,' he said, with a smile, then took a pound coin out of his jeans pocket and gave it to me.

'See you around,' I said, then scuttled around the metallic blue Mondeo and got in.

'Yeah,' he said. Staring Man started off across the car park towards, I presumed, his car.

'So,' Jess said as she pulled out the car park onto the road, 'hates you, does he?'

'Thanks to you, missus, he still does. I was just about to tell him that Mel and I were just friends, so he knew I wasn't trying to get off with his man, and you came along tooting your horn and shouting your mouth off.'

'I did not toot my horn. Besides, I think the only horn going on around here came from him – and it wasn't for Mel.'

'JESSICA BREAKFIELD!' I screamed. 'WHAT HAS GOT INTO YOU?'

'Nothing for a while, actually.'

'OH MY GOD!' I screeched, then clamped my hands over my ears, 'DON'T YOU DARE SAY ANOTHER WORD UNTIL WE GET TO MY HOUSE.'

chapter twenty-four

Bruiser

'What the blinking hell happened to you?' Craig said as I wandered into the Senior Common Room.

Being Craig, he said this so loudly, most people in the SCR looked up, double-took at me.

After taking a deep breath, I replied: 'I walked into a door.'

How did that sound? Exactly. Had someone said that to me, I would've looked the same way as Craig and most of the people in the common room who were openly paying attention were looking at me then: *Yeah, right. Who were you fighting with, why were you fighting and do they look worse or better than you?*

Some of the faces around the room went back to conversations they were having, the notes they were reading, the coffee they were drinking. Some of the faces carried on openly staring at me. I didn't blame them, I'd got it on the bus into work, I'd got it in the street, I'd got it wandering through the corridors, I'd got it in my lecture first thing this morning. Anyone would think people hadn't seen a woman with a huge, great bruise on her face before.

Craig frowned very hard at me and my reply.

'I did,' I said. I carried my paper pile and my body, then

slumped into the seat I always sat in. The tan leatherette seat would soon have a groove in the shape of my butt, I sat there so often. I noticed people who were sat there when I came in, moved. I probably unintentionally glowered at them for being anywhere near my seat. I liked that seat. It gave you a good view of most of the room, the dining/kitchenette area and both doors.

Gwen was sat next to my favourite seat, but I didn't care. If it was a toss up between the seat and her, or any other seat and not her, I'd take my seat. It was a fair pay-off.

Craig, the man I supposedly subliminally incited to have sex, followed me from his area of the SCR, sat himself down on the table opposite me.

'What happened, babe?' he asked. First time he'd ever called me babe. I recognised his softened tone, his brotherly expression. They were subliminally saying, 'Tell me who it was and I'll go get them for you.'

I did look a fright, though. Even I had to admit it. I'd worn my glasses – the cursed glasses – to take the edge off the vicious bruise that currently resided on my left cheek. I'd been surprised by its severity – and I'd been there when I'd been bashed in the face. What with my skin being such a dark brown, I thought it wouldn't be so bad. But this bruise was darker than my skin, tinged with black and purple and yellow. I'd baulked at myself in the mirror. Spent a lot of time trying to find angles to stand from that didn't make it look so bad. I did indeed look as though I'd been on the wrong end of a prize-fighter's rage.

Gwen was staring at me too with maternal concern. Nice though it was that they all cared, their concern was misplaced. I'd got double the amount of affection and care and attention from Jake. Again, trying to coax out of me what really happened.

'Do you really want to know what happened?' I asked Craig, tiredly.

Craig nodded.

'And do you promise you'll believe me, no matter how obscure the story?'

Craig nodded again. His whole face was frowning with concern.

'I walked into a door. Or, rather, a door swung into me. I was coming out of a sweet shop down in Headingley and someone coming in at high speed smacked me in the face with the door. It was all rather embarrassing cos I stumbled backwards, reached out to steady myself and pulled down a free-standing rack of greetings cards with me. I don't know if you can imagine it, me, lying on the floor, under a rack of cards, writhing in agony on a Saturday lunch time, but it is truly my idea of hell. And then, to add insult to injury, literally, I woke up Sunday with a mind-splitting headache and this huge bruise on my face.'

'Really?' Craig said.

'Yes, Craig.'

'Sure?'

'Positive, Craig.'

Craig still eyed me suspiciously.

I sighed. 'Thank you for your concern though, it's really touching.'

'OK, but if you need to talk . . .'

'I'll come find you. Thanks.'

With one last suspicious look, Craig got to his feet and went back to his life. I'd be telling this story for ages. I wondered who'd be the first to bring up the fact that where there's blame, there's a claim. I knew exactly who I'd be suing.

I was going to get stuff photocopied. In reprographics.

Since that encounter with Deirdre Barlow Glasses woman

I'd done what other people did and camped out in the photo-copying room and did it myself. Anything to avoid a row. Today, I didn't have the energy or time. I needed far more doing than normal and to be honest, why should I stand there breathing in fumes and getting Repetitive Strain Injury from pushing buttons when she and the rest of her 'gang' were paid to do it?

This time, I'd got Sally to get me the forms in advance and I'd filled them all in. All I had to do was take down my load, explain what needed to be done and to put them on 'Urgent', which meant I could get them done in forty-eight hours. 'Emergency', which would cost the department more, would be done in twenty-four hours. Deirdre Barlow Glasses hadn't explained that to me, had she?

Standing outside, I read REPROGRAPHICS (they'd changed the colour of the sign from orange to yellow because that was the kind of krazy with a 'k' type of people they were), took a deep breath and pushed open the swing doors. I even managed to put a smile on my face. Try not to annoy the people who can screw you over, was one of my many mottos. *Great.* The woman on duty behind the counter was, of course, Deirdre Barlow Glasses.

'Hi,' I said. 'Could I get these done on urgent?' I had my sweetest voice at work as I showed her my bundles, each with clearly marked instructions on Post-Its.

Her face remained like stone. Without moving any other part of her body, her arm reached out and retrieved a stack of forms from their envelopes on the wall beside her and slid them across at me.

'I've already filled in the forms,' I said, still smiling. I dumped the books on the counter, plucked off the forms and handed them to her.

She looked at them as though I was offering her a turd.

'They're the wrong forms for an urgent request. You'll have to fill these in. And make sure you've got the right budget code.'

Deep breath. Stay calm. She can screw you over. 'OK,' I said, took the forms. 'Can I borrow your pen?'

'We don't lend out pens. We have this problem with getting them back. Or not, as is usually the case.'

'Good thing I always carry one, then, isn't it?' I replied and pulled one from my pocket. 'Wouldn't want me walking off with your million-dollar pen.' That bit I said in my head.

I heard the swing doors open behind me and moved to one side to let the person coming in take their chances with the photocopying bitch from hell.

'Hi,' the male voice said. 'I've come for my stuff.'

My knees weakened at the voice.

'Ticket?' the woman demanded.

'Here we go,' he replied. 'I brought it in three days ago.' My knees did that melting thing again. I glanced up to see who it belonged to.

The man glanced sideways at me. Again, we both started at who we were looking at. Staring Man. I should've known by the effect he had on my knees.

I ripped my eyes away, my face and body suddenly aflame. I put the pen back to the sheet, but my hand was shaking. I couldn't even write properly because I knew, KNEW he was staring at me now. I could feel his eyes on the side of my face. I lowered my head even more, twisted my neck slightly so all he could see was the back of my head. I could still feel it though: I could feel his gaze, steady and unwavering, burning holes into the back of my black hair.

'We haven't finished your photocopying,' Deirdre Barlow Glasses said. 'You'll have to come back.'

'What?' Staring Man said.

'You'll have to come back later.'

'Don't talk to me in that tone of voice,' he said. 'I'm not the one in the wrong here. I asked for urgent repro and I've not got it. Would you like to accompany me to my lecture and explain to my students why I haven't got the material ready?'

Go Staring Man, go Staring Man.

She said nothing. Maybe she'd shaken her head.

'No, thought not. So don't give me attitude, lady. Just so you know, I'm not paying full price for this job and I'm going to be reporting you to my head of department.'

'While you're at it why don't you report me to God too?'

My head shot up. Cheeky cow. Not only was she rude to me, she actually had the audacity to nick my sarky retorts. Deirdre Barlow Glasses had gone, disappeared into the depth of the repro world and Staring Man was glaring at me. Actually, he was glaring at the part of my face which currently housed a massive bruise. I thought we'd sorted out all that stuff between us the week before last, but no. I hadn't got around to telling him that I wasn't interested in Mel. And, as it turned out, ten days was a long time between Staring Man and me.

'Er, look, I was, erm, hoping to run into you,' Staring Man began, then winced, looked down and started blushing furiously. 'I mean, I was hoping to see you.'

'Oh,' I replied. My heart was going ten to the dozen. Things had gone distinctly downhill between us since those halcyon days of the supermarket car park – because that person who'd been coming into the newsagent's at high speed and who'd helped the door connect with my face had, in fact, been Staring Man.

When I'd opened my eyes, dazed and confused as I was, I'd looked up and through the hail of greeting cards, there he was, doing what he did best, staring at me. Although, to be fair, shock and horror were carved into his features.

I'd let him and a couple of other people help me up but I'd legged it before anyone could say anything, including 'sorry'. Like I'd said to Craig, moments like that were my idea of hell. It'd been so busy in there, I couldn't bear to stay. I'd just pushed my way through the crowd of voyeurs and walked away as quickly as possible, clutching my face. I'd had to lie down for most of the afternoon when I got home because I felt so dizzy and sick every time I moved.

'I'm really sorry about, erm, your face,' Staring Man said. 'Is it painful?'

I shook my head. 'Not really. I mean, not any more.'

'I'm really sorry,' he repeated. 'You left far too quickly on Saturday for me to apologise properly.'

'It wasn't your fault, I wasn't looking where I was going.'

'Aww, you can't be blaming the victim. I was worried that you might have had concussion or something. Is there anything I can do?'

'Breathe?' I said, then cringed. *How the hell did that get out of my mouth? How did it get into my head in the first place? I can understand 'battered to death with a teaspoon', I can understand 'carpet that doesn't show up blood stains', but, 'breathe'?*

'Sorry?' he asked.

'Umm, you asked if there was anything you could do and, well, it's obvious that you can breathe.' *So, just as obviously I had to say it.*

Surprisingly, SM laughed. He had a laugh that matched his voice. Rich, deep. More tingles of pleasure flickered through my body. 'Another Lieutenant Barclay moment,' he said as though he understood. 'But, I must say, you're right there, I can breathe. What I meant was is there anything I can do—'

Deirdre Barlow Glasses chose that moment to reappear. 'If

you come back in half an hour, we'll have your stuff for you,' she told SM. It didn't seem to bother her that she'd just interrupted our conversation.

SM turned his glare on her. 'I'd say thank you, but I've nowt to thank you for, have I?' he said. 'See you around,' he said to me, then left. He'd obviously been put back into a bad mood by Deirdre Barlow Glasses. I watched the swing doors flump together behind him.

'Hi,' I said to the woman behind the counter. 'Filled in the right forms this time.'

Had she not:

a) nicked my sarky retort

b) interrupted my attempts to re-bond with SM

c) been a miserable old whore

I would have offered her a sympathetic smile – I knew what it was like to be on the receiving end of a Staring Man glare.

'Forty-eight hours,' she said. 'And don't forget your slip, you won't be able to get your photocopying without it. We will charge your department, though.'

'Thanks,' I replied. 'You have a nice day now.' *If you know how.*

'Ceri, hi,' a voice called from down the corridor as I was heading towards my office later that afternoon.

I stopped, looked around. I should have known by the squeak. Gwen. She came bounding towards me.

'I wanted to talk to you about the other day,' she said.

'Why? What did I do?' I asked, trying not to act shifty. Deirdre Barlow Glasses had reported me. The cow. She was probably in church now, reporting me to God, too.

'Nothing, nothing,' Gwen squeaked.

'So why do you want to talk to me?' I asked, eyeing her suspiciously.

'Maybe it's best we have a word in private,' Gwen said.

The cow. The miserable old cow had *reported me*. I was so going to be chucking a lighted flame in there at some point. All that paper and chemicals would go up in an instant. 'Are you sure I haven't done something wrong?'

Gwen rested a reassuring hand on my forearm. 'Of course not.'

Now she was plain scaring me.

'How about we go to my office. I think it's empty,' I said to Gwen.

'Perfect,' Gwen replied.

Gwen sat on the green tweed, armchair-type thing beside my office door, then patted the seat beside her. She'd piled her hair up into a bun today, she had on her usual flowery uniform, but her face was all maternal concern and sympathy again.

Something bad has happened, I realised as I sank into the seat beside her. *She hasn't even got a cigarette out.*

'Ceri, I know I am your line manager but I think we've made a connection. We've become friends, haven't we?'

Have we? I thought. She wasn't like my other boss who thought we were friends because she told me too much about herself. But we still weren't friends. Not by a long stretch of the imagination. But, I nodded.

'Good,' she smiled, 'I'm glad you feel we're close. Which is why I wanted to talk to you about your face.'

'My what?' I said.

'The bruise on your face.'

I raised my hand to my cheek. It'd gone down quite a lot in the past three days, and it'd stopped hurting so I'd forgotten about it, I didn't go in for looking in mirrors that much.

'What about it?'

Gwen looked down at her hands. 'I know it's very hard to admit what has really happened, especially to people you don't know very well, but I want you to feel you can come and talk to me. About anything.'

I don't get you, I thought.

'I mean, when one of my friends was being physically abused by her husband, it was virtually impossible for her to talk about. She had bruises all over and an excuse to match each one. I don't want you to feel you have to suffer in silence like that. I understand. I mean, last year, I was attacked.'

My eyes widened in horror.

'In the street. It was hideous and very, very frightening. They only took my mobile phone, but I had bruises and scratch marks all over my face. I found it very, very difficult to talk about it. So, you see, I understand what you're going through. You can talk to me. Any time.'

'Gwen, thank you. But I really was smacked in the face by a door.'

She bunched up her lips in an 'are you sure?' fashion. Jake was still on that kick as well (Ed would've been too had he not spent ninety-nine per cent of his time Missing In Action with Robyn). The only person who believed me was Jess, who knew I was prone to daydreaming and that accidents generally followed. My daydreaming was the reason why I'd never learnt to drive.

'Thank you, though, for your concern. It's good to know I can turn to you if I need to. But in this instance I don't need to. I should've been paying attention to where I was going. But thank you. I'm touched you care.'

Gwen left, having made me promise to talk to her if I needed to. I had considered for a fleeting moment telling her what was on my mind. It was a moment so fleeting it was gone before it entered my head. After she was gone, I moved to my side of the desk, collapsed onto it, rested my forehead on the cool work surface.

God, this obsession with Angel had to stop. It'd gotten so bad I was actually seeing him everywhere. And I mean, everywhere. It was he who gave me the stupid bruise in the first place. Couldn't very well tell Jake, Ed, Craig or Gwen that, could I?

I'd thought I spotted him, David Boreanaz/Angel on the front of a magazine and double-took as I reached for the newsagent's door. Next thing I knew there was a blinding pain in my face and I was groping for support as I went flying backwards. Then, I was lying on the floor and it was raining greetings cards.

Just earlier, with Staring Man, I'd actually thought he looked like Angel. Except Staring Man had the most amazing eyes and I'd never seen David Boreanaz's eyes in real life. SM's eyes were a bronze colour. Shame he used them to glare at me. Shame, actually, he fancied Mel. But, at least now we'd made some sort of contact (pun not intended but very painfully true). And now he felt guilty about the door-face thing, it would hopefully be the end to those glares.

If SM didn't fancy Mel, though, he could have been my Angel replacement. The one I lusted after until Angel/David Boreanaz came up to me in the street, asked me for directions, looked deep into my dark eyes and realised there was no other woman on the earth for hi—

Oh my God, I need therapy. I thumped my head on the table. I need to get a grip. And then keep that grip on reality. I was never going to have sex again if I carried on like this. And that *would* kill me.

chapter twenty-five

Confessions

'I'm going to tell Kevin everything.'

Claudine was stood in my shared office doorway and she said this like she was asking if I fancied sneaking into her office for a crafty joint. There was a hint of the naughty, but total casualness about it. My pen hovered over the marking of a below par essay while I looked at her.

'I'm going to tell him about me and Mel. That I slept with him and that we've snogged twice since. But it's all over.'

Are you mad?! He'll kill you, bury you and build a patio over the spot before the 'we snogged twice' bit is out of your mouth. 'That's, er . . .' I hazarded, didn't know what to say except 'stupid' so stopped.

'Do you want to come in?' I asked instead.

Claudine stepped into my office, shutting the door behind her. She sat on one of the armchair-type things by the door, placed her bag and pile of papers on the armchair-type seat next to the ceiling-high bookshelves.

'I'm definitely going to tell him,' Claudine said, in a 'don't try to talk me out of it' fashion. She clasped her hands in her lap, and leant forwards over her knees. I was surprised anew that Claudine didn't smoke; she was the type of woman I always expected to smoke. I watched her from my position across the desk; her agitated manner made me want to smoke.

'I decided last night,' she paused, 'and this morning, but that's not important. The important thing is, I'm going to tell him.'

Claudine's tone had the conviction of someone who, if they talked long enough, would convince you they were doing the right thing. They knew they'd never convince themselves, so they didn't even try.

'I didn't realise it was over between you and Kevin,' I said neutrally.

Her eyes doubled in size. 'It's not. Why would you say it was?'

'Because you're going to confess to him. I just assumed . . . I suppose I shouldn't assume.'

'Assume what?' Claudine said quickly.

'Well, if you're willing to do something that's going to end your relationship, I assumed you'd reached the end of the road.'

Claudine gave me a wider-eyed demented look. 'What I have reached is the end of my tether. I can't deal with it any more. I can't go home, look at Kevin, talk to Kevin, sleep beside Kevin . . . all the time, carrying this secret with me. It's driving me insane. And every time we have sex, I'm so wary that I'll say "Mel", I can't relax. It's doing my head in. I can't bear it any longer.'

I nodded, as though in understanding but the last thing I was feeling was understanding. 'What are you going to do when Kevin breaks down and starts sobbing his heart out?' I asked.

'He won't cry,' Claudine said, aghast.

'What will he do?'

Claudine shrugged. 'I don't know. He'll get angry I suppose.'

'You suppose? You mean, you're going to cause him all that pain and you haven't thought about how he'll react?' *What, are you some kind of sadist?*

'He'll be angry, of course, but when he calms down . . .'

'Calms down? Claudine, he's not going to calm down. He'll probably not forgive you. Ever. *EVER*.

'The calming down and talking things through are for films and story books; the anger and shouting and smashing things and never wanting to see you again, that's reality. That's what you've got to accept will probably happen if you confess all.'

Claudine stared at me with her mouth and eyes agog. I'd never been stern with her before. I wasn't being stern now. Not really. I just wasn't condoning her decision, as she'd expected me to. Claudine's eyes watered up.

My tone had been a bit sharp, though. I shouldn't have gone from nice Ceri to cross Ceri in one go. It was bound to jar her. However, she was talking nonsense. I sighed internally, looked down at my desktop to get myself calm and make my voice nicer, less harsh. 'Claudine, tell Kevin if you want, but don't forget he has a heart too. Don't break his just to make yours lighter.'

'But our relationship is based on a lie,' she wailed. Next would come the wringing of the hands. Swiftly followed by gnashing of teeth and rending of clothes.

'No it's not,' I reasoned. 'Your relationship is based on all the things that brought you two together all those years ago. Your relationship is based on all the things you've done and worked towards together in the past however many years. Your relationship isn't based on a drunken shag that happened six months ago. It may very well influence and affect your relationship, but it's not the basis of it. If it *were* based on that shag . . . well, I don't know.'

'What about Mel?'

254

Rat-a-tat-tat. The office door opened before I had a chance to say 'come in'. Mel stuck his head around the door. 'Hi Ceri, I w—'

His face lit up and clouded over at once when he saw who was in the office with me. Claudine's face did exactly the same thing.

World War Three was about to kick off in my office.

'I'll come back later when you're not so busy,' Mel said, focused on Claudine.

'Are you following me?' Claudine snarled at my visitor. 'On top of everything, are you following me too?'

'You're off your head, you,' Mel said.

'Look who's talking,' Claudine said.

'What the hell is your problem?'

'Everything to do with you.'

The volume of their voices was rising. I got up, went to the door, to shut it.

'Listen babe, it was you who stuck your tongue down my throat last time.'

'Yeah, and it was you who stuck his dick in m—'

Whoah! Not for sensitive ears. I shut the door on my way out. I paced the corridor for a while. Then I checked the clock at the far end of the wide corridor. Eight o'clock. The canteen was shut. I had nowhere to go, except, possibly the bar. Much as I enjoyed the odd drink or eleven, I couldn't face going in there alone; sitting alone. If it were a proper pub I wouldn't feel so worried, I'd have something to read too, but in college, students would see me all alone – I'd be one step away from being the lecturer with a tweed jacket and pipe, emanating pathetic aloneness.

I turned, started my slow walk back up the corridor. Maybe I *should* go to the bar. Get myself a pack of cigarettes. With Mel and Claudine, I was tempted to take up a life-threatening habit.

In fact, between those two, what Craig and Jess said, Ed disappearing to be with Robyn, Gwen, Jake wearing the aura of a man wronged, and Staring Man, I was quite tempted to take up heroin. Have an out of body experience that would remove me from this world I'd moved in to. London was crazy, Leeds was certifiably insane.

Time ticked on, I wore a groove into the corridor carpet, voices rose and fell from my office. But there were no smashing sounds or blood-curdling screams of anguish and death. I couldn't even go home because my bag, coat, iBook and the essays I needed to finish marking tonight were still in my office.

An hour later, I jumped back as the door was wrenched open and Claudine came stalking out, throwing: 'If you fucking come near me again I'll kill you,' over her shoulder. She completely blanked me as she marched down the corridor, heading for the stairs to the next floor and her office.

Mel's head popped around the door. 'SLUT!' he screamed after her.

Thankfully, no one else was around at that hour, so only I jumped at its suddenness and severity.

Claudine did the smoothest 180-degree turn I'd ever seen, came stalking back up the hallway, growing about a foot with each step. By the time she reached us, she was twenty foot tall.

Her face had narrowed into a knot of anger. So scary and hideous did she look at that moment that I leapt out of her path and flattened myself against the wall as she stormed past. I don't know if Mel saw it coming, but I felt it, heard it, winced at it when her fist connected with his face.

She didn't even stop, she spun on her heels in another smooth 180-degree turn and stalked away again.

'That's going to be a right shiner,' I said to Mel, who was holding his cold beer bottle against his cheek.

He took the bottle away and nearly pulled a sarcastic smile, hindered by the pain in his face. 'Thanks, Ceri, you're a great help. I always like it when people point out the bloody obvious.'

I tried not to laugh. 'How long have you known Claudine, again?'

'Nearly eleven years.'

'And even though you know her so well, you didn't think calling her a slut would end up with her smacking you one?'

'I wasn't thinking, that's the point. I wanted to hurt her; get the last word in.'

'Well you did that. "Ow!" wasn't it?'

Mel glowered at me. I probably shouldn't be taking the piss. I'd no doubt added to Claudine's foul mood by vetoing her plans to unburden her conscience.

'Why were you two rowing anyway? You were, are, mates,' I said, feeling a tad responsible. What I'd said had been in Kevin and Claudine's best interests. And Mel's. He would've been in for a sound beating if Claudine had blabbed. (Never understood what was sound about a beating. Surely it should be unsound? That was the whole point.)

Mel returned his bottle to his face, right after he rolled his eyes. 'Who knows. I don't.'

'So you spent an hour in my office listening to Claudine shouting, and said nothing?'

'Yes.'

I planted my tongue in my cheek and raised an eyebrow at him.

'Well, a little. No. She shouted, I shouted, we both shouted.'

'Why?'

'Ever since that weekend, you know the lost weekend, she's been off with me and, I suppose, I've been off with her.'

Don't ask why, don't ask why. Don't get any more involved. Not your problem. NOT YOUR PROBLEM. 'Why?'

'You know Ceri, I'm really pissed off. I mean, it's all right for her, she's got someone, she can just bugger off for the weekend and be happy with him and I'm alone.' Mel slammed his bottle onto the table. 'It's not fair. I care so much for her and I know she loves me. You don't make love to someone like she did if you don't love them. (At that moment I couldn't believe Mel was thirty. You don't make love to someone like she did if you don't love them, indeed. Where did he get that sort of idea from? Reading too many love stories, and watching too many Hollywood movies, I'll bet. I was more than a little partial to them, myself. But even I didn't believe what he'd just said.) So why is she still with him? Why?'

'I don't know,' I sighed. *Except I do know, and you, buddy, don't want to hear it.*

Mel sighed slightly, looked away across the bar. I looked him over again. The man who Jake and Ed used to try to set me up with. He was good-looking. Fresh-faced but experienced. Long lashes around hazel eyes, sexily-curly hair, distinguished but friendly features.

Mel caught me checking him out and his eyes held mine. Lust shivered through me. Things were bad – I was starting to have impure thoughts about Mel.

'You're actually quite vaguely attractive, aren't you?' Mel said.

Talk about your damning with faint praise. 'Thanks Mel, that's probably one of the most insulting things anyone's ever said to me.'

'I didn't mean owt by it, I only just noticed. You're all right looking. And I had this sudden urge to kiss you. I was thinking about Claudine and I get that urge every time I think about her.'

I leapt on that like a woman who hadn't eaten in days offered a slice of hot buttered toast. It reminded me of what Craig had said about me subliminally advertising sex and inciting him to have sex with his ex-girlfriend. 'Really? You think about Claudine and you want to kiss any woman around? So it's not just me?'

Mel thought about my question, even though I wasn't sure he understood it.

'It has been happening a lot lately, I think about Claudine, I get the urge to kiss someone. But I can't say it happened before you arrived on the scene.' Mel sipped his beer, returned it to his face. 'In fact, I can categorically say, a lot of things have changed since you got here. Things between me and Clau were fine until that day you asked us if we were going out together. Our friendship deteriorated right after that.'

Oh.

Mel saw my face fall. 'It's all right. To be honest, I feel better now it's come to a head – smack in the face notwithstanding. Maybe now she'll realise what this is doing to us and leave that idiot.' Mel talked on, explaining why he was glad I'd ruined his life.

chapter twenty-six

Knock Out

'Ceri, we've been waiting for you,' Jake said, practically greeting me on the front door step.

'We? Who? Why?' Suddenly I had visions of an intervention, where all your friends and family wait for you – usually in your living room – to tell you in no uncertain terms that your addiction is destroying you and they love you too much to stand by and watch you do that.

Obviously Jess had blabbed that I watched too much telly. Well, too much *Angel*. I'd slipped from being a recreational user to a full-blown, gotta have it everyday, twice-a-day addict.

'Ed and Robyn are here.' Jake looked rattled. His face was pale, his features were set to permanent frown and even his hair looked shaken. Why? Had he walked in on them at it and been permanently scarred by how truly disgusting sex could be?

I couldn't take any more drama though. Whatever it was, I couldn't handle it. It'd been less than two hours since Mel and Claudine's blow-up, I was still fragile. It'd jolted me to my very core, especially to know that Mel – and probably Claudine – thought I was the cause of that. I incited Craig to sex; I motivated Claudine to violence and I made men fancy

Jess. I didn't want any more drama unless it was on the television.

'What's the matter?' I whispered anxiously.

Jake simply gave me a hard stare, then led the way into the living room.

Ed beamed at me as I approached, although how he managed to get more smile behind that grin was a mystery. Robyn, she of the girly, haughty, "I didn't get a role in *Coronation Street* but I'm not bitter" visage was beaming too. I wasn't sure she knew how to smile.

'Hi,' I said, clocking how close they sat, their fingers entwined.

'Hi, Ceri,' they both said. They'd become Stepford Couple. In the space of, what, three-and-a-bit weeks. This wasn't what I'd been expecting when I'd seen Jake's face. I'd expected Robyn to be holding a gun to Ed's head or something.

'We've been waiting for you,' Ed said.

'So Jake said,' I replied.

'Before you say anything else, babe, I just want to say thank you to Ceri.' This was, rather scarily, from Robyn.

'For?' I replied.

She gave Ed a loving look, the kind of sweet look that diabetics would need an insulin overdose to get under control. 'For making Ed ask me out.'

'I didn't make him do anything,' I snapped. I didn't need this bullshit on top of everything else.

'Yes you did,' Ed said. 'You were the only person who gave me any advice worth listening to. Twice.'

'He's perfect. Thank you.' Robyn again.

'Hmmm,' I mumbled. Would anyone understand if I started upending furniture and screaming, 'IT'S NOTHING TO DO WITH ME! YOU ALL FUCK UP YOUR LIVES ON YOUR OWN! STOP BLAMING ME FOR EVERYTHING!' I glanced at their faces, no they probably wouldn't understand at all.

'Anyway, what we wanted to tell the two of you is, we're moving in together,' Ed said.

My heart double-flipped. Oh. My. God. It'd been under four weeks. I tried to keep an impassive face, but now I could see why Jake was so shaken.

'When?' I managed from my shocked mouth. I really did think I was unshockable.

'As soon as possible. Robyn would ideally move in here cos it's bigger than the place she shares, but if Jake says no, we'll move in to her place.'

'Oh.'

'And, this bit we haven't told anyone, not even Jake, but, I'm going to give up college, get a job and next year we're going to get married.'

'Give up college?' Jake managed.

I did not speak. I was lying spread-eagle on the carpet, KO'd by the news.

'This is all your fault,' Jake said to me in the kitchen.

Ed and Robyn had skipped off upstairs to their little love nest and Jake had asked me into the kitchen for a quick chat. He might as well have ripped off his shirt and offered me an outside for the friendliness he'd put into the request for a talk in the kitchen.

He'd practically dragged me to beside the back door, shoved me roughly against the sink worktop, and then stood over me like he was going to resurrect the bruise that had just started to fade on my face with his fist. Jake was really quite big and scary when it came down to it.

'How? How is this my fault?' I said.

'You made him ask out that gold-digging hussy. And now look.'

'Gold-digging?'

262

'Ed's minted.'

'What?'

'He's a millionaire's son. She's no doubt found that out and now he's going to give up college.'

'Millionaire's son? Don't talk soft. If he's minted, why does he live here?'

'He doesn't have to. Ed could buy this whole street of houses if he wanted. But he doesn't want, he just wants a normal life. And he's not going to get that if he gives up college.'

I ran my hand through my hair. What the hell is going on? Ed, a millionaire's son. Ed and Robyn moving in together. Claudine punching Mel. Had the world gone mad?

'Ed's life was going fine until you encouraged him to ask her out,' Jake said.

'He wanted to,' I said lamely. 'I couldn't have made him if he didn't want to. I mean, I didn't hold a gun to his head.'

'Ed looks up to you. You've got this, presence . . . he said that after that first day you moved in here. When he talks to you, he feels like anything's possible, even if it's the most stupid thing on earth. I've been telling him to either ask that, that,' Jake lowered his voice, '*woman* (I never knew anyone could get that much venom into a two-syllable word) out or forget her. All his friends have been telling him that for ages. One word from you, and he's cut his hair, wearing smart clothes and asking her out.'

'I didn't tell him to cut his hair,' I said, lamely.

'Whatever. Just sort it out.'

'What?'

'Sort it out. Stop him from doing this.'

'How?'

'I don't know. Just sort it out. Stop him. It's your fault he's about to chuck his life away, so it's down to you to sort it out.'

I just looked at Jake.

He jabbed his finger viciously at me. 'I mean it. Sort it out Ceri. If Ed ruins his life because of this, I'll never forgive you. And I doubt Ed will either.'

Jake went slamming out of the house and there was me thinking he'd be devastated if I left. 'I was the only one who didn't tell you to get over The Git,' I almost called after him. 'I listened, I let you own your feelings.'

His trail of bad vibes still hadn't dispersed when Ed came trotting down the stairs minutes later. And I hadn't moved from my semi-cowering stance by the back door. Three shocks in less than three hours was more than I could take.

'Has Jake gone out?' Ed asked, heading for the kettle.

I nodded. Ed bounced as he walked, a jolly little spring to his step. He was happy. Any idiot could look at him, listen to him and know that. Ed was in the happiness zone. It might not last, but was that any reason for me to do as I was told, nay, ordered and tell him he was moving too fast.

'We're going to get a takeaway, want some?' Ed asked as he plugged the kettle back in. 'Pizza. I can tell Robyn wants a Chinese but she said to get pizza cos you and Jake might want some. And if we get garlic bread and stuff it'll make a right old feast.'

What are you doing Ed? And is it anything to do with me? Have you too become a victim of whatever it is I'm supposed to do to people? Or is it a coincidence?

'So, do you?'

'Um, um, no. I'm not that hungry.'

'Oh come on, you know you want it,' Ed coaxed. 'What's that expression you use, I'm sure you could choke some down.'

'Go on then, you've twisted my arm. I never could say no to a good feeding.'

Ed grinned. Went to leave, stopped, came back. Kissed my cheek. I put my hand to my cheek, his kiss had been as light as a feather. 'I wouldn't be feeling like this if it wasn't for you, thank you.' Then he bounded out of the room.

chapter twenty-seven

The Question

I have no life.

It's official. I have no life, I am merely living vicariously through other people.

Take, for example, Mel and Claudine's drama. They were actively avoiding each other. Even in the Senior Common Room, when one entered, the other one left. They'd got an official face on it, of course. A 'hi' face that told the world that they're both so busy they haven't got time for each other. While everyone we worked with believed that, I knew the real story.

I, for example, happened to know that they'd once been more than friends. And I also knew that the lamppost Mel walked into that caused his bruise happened to be five foot eight, with black hair and a surprisingly strong right-hook for her slender frame. She was also very angry at the time. (I noticed no one sat him down and asked him if he was being abused. They all believed his heinous lie without a second thought.)

The most unsettling thing about the Mel and Claudine story was, though, I didn't just know their story. I *was* their story. I was part of their drama and I experienced their emotions. What they felt, I felt. It was my seventh sense magnified.

I was Mel, in love with someone who wouldn't leave her partner for me. Clinging to the hope that one day she'd wake up and see sense. I was Claudine, convinced that I could be in love with two men at once and almost breaking my heart to try to reconcile that. I was both people, knowing how I felt, suspecting how the other felt, not really knowing what I should do.

But the seventh sense didn't end there. Not by a long shot.

I was also Ed. Rushing into something because she really was The One. I had no fear, no doubt, no indecision. All I knew was, when I left her place to return to mine, I felt as though I'd left my arm behind and needed to go back and collect it. And, within seconds of shutting my front door, she was calling me, begging me to come back because there was an Ed-shaped hole in her life. I'd never known anything so easy, passionate, comforting, so right.

I was Gwen. Suddenly dissatisfied with everything. It wasn't just the demon year group any more. Every year group wound me up. Every lecture rankled me. I smoked more and more, trying to push down this feeling of powerlessness; this knowledge that I'd chosen this path and I was going to be doing this hideous thing called lecturing for the rest of my days.

I was Jake, scowling now about what Ed was doing with his life. Scared that he was doing the wrong thing. Worried my best mate was about to do something monumentally stupid, something he couldn't go back on. And under it, really scowling about the twat who was meant to be my friend but used me for sex then treated me like dirt when I told him how I felt. I was also jealous. How come Ed got it right and I got it so wrong? Robyn was a stuck-up tart, The Git was meant to be my friend, but Ed was happy, I'd been used.

I was Craig, in desperate need of a reality check on my feelings about the ex I can't stop sleeping with. She winds me up, she's a bit of a psycho, but nowadays she's the one person I want to spend all my time with. I can't possibly love her, could I?

And then, of course, there were the students. Constantly trailing to the door of my shared office, pouring their hearts out. Not that I was their tutor. Just, it seemed, available. *Did I have such an eventful life as a student?* I'd often wonder as another student poured out a plot more complicated than anything I saw on *Sunset Beach*. There was something very disconcerting and disturbing about standing in front of a group of people and knowing who'd shagged who, who'd screwed over who, who really hated who. The students spent so much time pouring their hearts out in my office that whenever there was a knock on the door these days Sally picked up her papers and cup and left because she knew the people wouldn't be visiting her.

My brain, my heart, my time were crammed with people's passions, loves, hopes, hates, sorrows, emotions. I had to keep track, remember who had told me what, who hadn't told me what. What was told only after swearing me to secrecy, what I was supposed to pass on, but discreetly.

I wasn't simply listening to problems and stories and lives, I was living them. At least, that's how it felt. I felt it all. Not empathy. Actual feelings. The actual emotions. I ached when they ached; I vacillated when they vacillated; I loved when they loved. I'd had this before, only not as consistently like now.

Before, like with Ed, like with Trudy, like with Mel, like with the man who fancied Jess, it was periodic, the occasional sensation. Now, it'd got worse. Intensified, concentrated. Never-ending. When someone cried, I genuinely experienced those ripples of distress and teetered on the brink of tears myself. If someone told me of their joy, I felt my heart leap and do an excited jig. Like, I suppose, some men get sympathetic labour pains, I got sympathetic life experiences.

I felt all their joys, all their fears, all their upsets, as though I was doing the living myself.

And it was sucking the real life out of me. Even the unmitigated highs and joys of other people's happiness didn't make up for it. It wasn't my happiness. I may as well have described my perfect birthday present, down to the Bagpuss wrapping paper, then watch someone else unwrap it without so much as a glance at the paper, then smile, say it's lovely, then put it aside and never pick it up again. You were happy they had it, but you, sure as eggs is eggs and chocolate is chocolate, wanted it yourself. It was *meant* for you. *Built* for you. You deserved it, just as much as the person who had it. You'd appreciate it more, too.

All this emotion by proxy meant I hardly knew what I felt any more. *If* I felt any more. What did I have to feel about? Everyone else had the life, not me. I experienced the emotion, but I didn't get closure. Didn't get the end result when others got their problems sorted or they went back to the thing that made them ecstatic. I ran the race, but never finished and got my medal. I was constantly jumping from one race to another, running every race just as hard, but never finishing. The roads to hell, perhaps?

And it showed no sign of abating. I literally had no life. My only time alone were those moments I fell asleep and those moments when I woke up. In between, my mind was in constant motion. My mind was sampling everyone's life, snatching titbits here and there until it was a constant soundtrack to my waking hours. Snatches and excerpts of other people's experiences playing on loop in my head.

One night, at the end of May, I found myself outside Jess's house. She was marking very important final year experimental reports, but let me in anyway.

I lay with my head on the kitchen table, crumbs from the sandwich she'd eaten earlier grinding into my right cheek.

'Jess, you've got to help me,' I said, staring forlornly at the side of the tea cup she'd placed in front of me.

'I don't know why everyone comes to tell me everything – good, bad or indifferent – or why I can't say no, but I really think I'm going mad. What is it about me? Why me?'

Three days later, she had the answer.

chapter twenty-eight

The Answer

'I think I've worked it out,' Jessica said, stretching out on her sofa. 'Finally.'

I sat on the floor, the soles of my feet touching, my knees splayed out.

'I'm all ears,' I said.

'Actually,' Jessica said, 'you're all heart.'

'Hey! All right, I might not be the kindest person on earth all the time, but I do try. So less of the sarcasm.'

Jessica drew on her cigarette, exhaled, waved the cigarette smoke away from my direction. 'No, no, I really mean it. Literally, you're all heart. Basically, we can talk philosophically, or we can talk biologically, or we can talk physics, but the end result is the same.'

'What the blinking flip are you on about?' I replied.

Jessica smiled. 'Remember how Craig said you advertised sex? He was right. Remember how I said you made men fancy me? I was right. And, remember how poor Ed got himself into that state before his date and he said he thought he'd got "bigger", well he probably didn't realise that you had something to do with it, too. And you know how everyone has been blaming you for all the changes in their lives? They're right too. Basically, Ceri, you're Cupid.'

chapter twenty-nine

Stupid, Cupid

'Pay attention, this is complicated.

'In chemistry and biology, there's the law of osmosis. I don't know if you remember it from school, but basically, say there are two substances that are separated by a semi-permeable membrane, you know, like a barrier that has tiny, tiny holes in it. If the molecules of the two substances are small enough, and there's a very concentrated amount of the substance on one side and a slightly less concentrated amount of the substance on the other side, the side with less will attempt to move into the concentrated area through the holes in the barrier. You understand? Less will move into more.'

I nodded, not knowing where this was leading.

'It's the same with you, Ceri, but in reverse. You have so much love and affection and sexuality locked up inside yourself, it's started to leak out. In the form of pheromones. As we both know from all that work you did on subliminal perception, there's evidence to suggest that love and sexual attraction are governed by those tiny hormones called pheromones. With you, and the abundance I suspect there is of love and sexuality inside of you, it's leaving the concentrated area that is you and dispersing into the outside world which has less. It's osmosis in reverse. More is moving into less. You see, you've never really used that love and sexuality and affection inside you, so it's being secreted out of your body as pheromones. Out where it's needed.

'Think about it, people think that negative emotions if internalised for too long can cause illness, well with you it's love, a positive emotion. So love's not going to cause illness, so it's going outside to where it's needed. And because you've never really used all that love and affection and sexuality, it's been building up in your body and your body needs to let it out. The only way it knows how to release that pressure is to leak it through your pores. And, as you know, skin is a semi-permeable barrier.

'Everyone knows that women's periods synchronise themselves once they live together for a time and the reason they do that is because of pheromones. What I didn't know until I read your original degree thesis on subliminal perception was that when women live long-term with men, it's been found that their periods become more regular – again as a result of pheromones.

'Now, the main reason I think that what's happening to you is mostly down to pheromones is Ed. Remember his predicament with his penis? I'll wager you were extremely nervous for him, very worried that he wouldn't be good enough for that date. You were probably sending out so many conflicting pheromones and vibes that his body subliminally picked up on it and he ended up in that state. Physically, his body wanted to be good enough and that was the only way it knew how to do it.'

Jess paused. 'Are you following me so far?'

'Yeah, sure, why not,' I replied flatly.

She lit herself another cigarette, slowly breathed life into it.

'All right, now, let's link all this to what we know about

273

Cupid philosophically. The Romans, who had Cupid as their god of love, needed a way to explain the often irrational ways that people behaved once they fell in love, the seemingly bolt-from-the-blue, narcotic state people experienced love as – hence they drew Cupid as having a bow and arrow. To get that "wham" thing across. Your love, affection and sexuality – released as pheromones – are hitting people like a bolt from the blue. That's what Craig meant about you subliminally advertising sex. Your pheromones are, subliminally, like your bow and arrow, they encourage people to have sex.'

Jess paused. Smoked in silence.

'Sticking with philosophy, I have to say, the way you behave is like the original philosophical incarnation of Cupid. The thing is, Cupid, the original Cupid, was a life messer-upper. He may well have been the god of love, but he's only seen as all-good since the Christianisation of the Roman and Greek religions. The Christians couldn't leave the god of love as a naughty entity who went around making people do things they wouldn't normally do – so they fixed the stories and myths so that people falling in love with the wrong people were just cute little mistakes. Not huge great problems.

'But the original incarnation of Cupid was quite disruptive. That's what's so true about you saying that you keep messing up people's lives—'

'No, *I* didn't say that, it was everyone else who said that,' I cut in.

'OK,' Jess conceded, 'everyone else says that you mess up their lives, that since you've arrived things have gone wrong. Or, at least, have been disrupted. Disruptive, that's what you are. You can't help it. You turn up somewhere and lives are transformed. Wherever you go, people are experiencing that bolt from the blue, they are facing up to things, admitting their feelings, following their heart's desire. And, it must be said, you do have this knack of making people open their hearts. You've always been like that.

'Take me, for example. I keep in touch with my ex-students, but you're the only one who has changed my life and made me a friend, influenced me. Made men fancy me. And that's why, I reckon, you have very few lasting friendships. It's as though once you've disrupted someone's life long enough for them to make the necessary changes you move on. You don't even realise you're doing it. You're like the Littlest Hobo, but with people's hearts and minds.

'I reckon it's only come to a head now because you're following your heart's desire. And, I suppose, you're releasing lots of happiness hormones out there. Showing everyone what's possible when you do what your heart really wants you to do. But following your heart's desire isn't easy. In fact, it's hell, the most disruptive thing you can do to your life. The reason why people keep coming to you, keep blaming you is because you're modern-day Cupid. And you leave The Cupid Effect wherever you go.'

I let Jess's words settle like dust around us. Let them soak into the atmosphere until the air was saturated with the nonsense she'd just come up with.

'You're insane,' I said. 'I thought I was mad, but you want locking up.'

Jess just smiled, lit herself another cigarette. 'Sweetheart, your track record alone proves you're Cupid. Look at the men in your life, I couldn't believe half the things you told me the other week. And I'm sure there've been more of them. Ones that you've kept from me, but, after all that, with not even one decent relationship, without ever having experienced real love, you still believe in love. You're still *capable* of love. You must be Cupid. Because only Cupid would take all that nonsense and still be the loving, caring soul you are. Most people give up over less, but not you. And you still have room in your life for everyone else's dilemmas and problems.

'Apart from everything I've just told you, probably the most damning thing of all is your name.'

I said nothing, waited for her to explain.

'When you shorten your name to Ceri, you're actually shortening it to a name that comes from the Welsh word meaning "love". I don't know where your parents got it from but your full name, Ceresis, comes from a very obscure and ancient Latin phrase which literally translated means "Heart's Desire". You're actually called Heart's Desire. How more modern a Cupid do you get than that?'

I turned from her to look outside at the trees, the sky, the world. Everything beyond the window was normal, the same, all right. Everything had changed and flipped and upended in here. I turned back to Jess.

'D'you really believe that?' I asked.

'Absolutely,' she said.

I nodded in reply. Nodded because I couldn't speak.

Then burst into tears.

chapter thirty

Reluctancy

'I don't want to be Cupid,' I gulped between sobs. 'I just want to be me. Ceri. Ceresis, at a push. Not "heart's desire" or disruptive. I just want a normal life.'

Jess rubbed my back, hugged me and let me sob while variations on the 'I don't want to be Cupid' theme spilt from my mouth. Eventually, she left me crying my heart out, went to the kitchen and came back bearing tea mugs. I'd heard her rummaging around the kitchen drawers, probably looking for chocolate or anything with chocolate in it. Like that would help. My reality had been smashed to pieces and she was giving me tea and looking for something with forty per cent cocoa solids in it.

Jess handed me a blue mug with a big smiley sun on the side. Tea. Real tea, very, very strong and very milky. If I drank real tea, I drank it so strong it could tarmac roads. I suppose this was a real emergency. I was still shaking from my epic cry and Jess held onto the cup a fraction longer so I wouldn't drop it.

'It's only a theory, love,' Jess said, freeing another white stick from its packet. 'It's not the gospel. What do I know about biology and chemistry and physics and philosophy?' She put a flame to the cigarette, breathed life into it. 'All right, I know about philosophy because I teach the philosophy of psychology, and I know a bit about biology and pheromones, but what do I know about the rest of it? I mean, come on, what do I really know?'

She was only the cleverest person I knew. Which was why I'd turned to her in the first place. 'But you believe it, don't you?' I asked her, sniffling back the sobs.

Jess took two long drags on her cigarette, exhaled them just as lengthily. Then she sighed even more lengthily. 'Wish I'd never opened my mouth now,' she said.

'Just tell me the truth, you've never lied to me before, so tell me the truth now. You believe I'm some kind of modern-day Cupid, don't you? And I leave, what was it you called it, The Cupid Effect, wherever I go. You believe that, don't you?' I'd banished the whiny, crying sound from my voice by then, which was good cos it was starting to piss even me off. 'Don't you?'

Jess reluctantly looked at me, her eyes searching my face for some kind of semblance of sanity, or ability to deal with her revelations. She sighed again, obviously finding no such sign of sanity. Not surprising since I felt so on the edge I might lose my grip and fall deep into the pit of insanity. 'Yes sweetie.'

I sagged in my seat, took a sip of the tea. Jess had put sugar in the tea. Good for shock, I guess. I wanted to cry again. This couldn't really be happening. And if it could be happening, then why did it have to be happening to me?

'I don't want to be Cupid,' I said again.

'It's not that bad, is it?' Jess said, stretching out on the sofa. 'Being responsible for people finding their heart's desire, for people falling in love, and for people having sex. That's nice. That's good. Most people depart the earth with-

278

out ever committing one act of public servitude; you get to do loads.'

True. But . . .

'What about me?' I hit my chest. 'I want my heart's desire and love and . . . and sex! What about me? When do I get all that?'

I sounded selfish. Possibly, maybe, because I was feeling incredibly selfish. Charity begins at home, and so do expectations of love and affection. Jess pulled a slight, 'hard luck' face. Not a full one, not even a quarter one, just a fraction, a hint of a grim smile, eyes slightly sad.

When do I get all that? Never, clearly.

'And anyway, why do I have to be Cupid? How come I don't get to be Venus or Aphrodite?'

Jess looked guiltily into her tea, smoking as though her life depended on it.

'Really, I want to know.'

'Because,' Jess began, 'because . . . people fell in love with Venus and worshipped her . . .'

'But no one noticed the little fat git with wings. He just went about disrupting stuff and being unnoticed.'

'Yooouuuuu, could put it like that.'

I felt my bottom lip go again.

'Put it like this, at least you'll never be short of a wedding invite or two.'

'Does this mean I'm going to be disrupting lives and not getting proper love for the rest of my life?'

'To be honest, Ceri, I don't know. I don't have all the answers. I spent a lot of time on the Internet and in books pulling together what I have told you. The original Cupid did find love, but he loved her from afar for years and then he lost her. It could be different for you. Like I said, I don't know. But

279

it's been like this for at least ten years, I suspect it'll be like that for ages. I think, sweetheart, you've got into a bit of a self-fulfilling prophecy situation, no matter how hard you try, you do it anyway.'

'I don't mean to.'

'I know, that's the irony. You don't mean to, but you can't help it. It's your nature. I mean, didn't people used to call you Auntie Ceri when you were in college? I seem to remember you always being surrounded by people who had problems. You could walk into any room anywhere and within five minutes you'll be talking to the person in the room with the biggest problem or biggest dilemma. You don't mean to do it, you just do it. Something in you draws out that kind of honesty. And it encourages people to, for better or worse, follow their heart. That's who you are, it's what being modern-day Cupid is all about.'

'Yeah, yeah, I get the idea.'

'Look, somebody's got to do it. I'm sure there's been someone like you for ages. Hey, you could be like Buffy, you know, into every generation, a Cupid is born. She will be the disruptive one.'

I glared at Jess. 'Oh yes, ha, ha, let's all laugh at the funny Ceri who's going to be alone for the rest of her life, shall we. Ha ha. Excuse me while I hold my sides to stop them from splitting at how amusing all this is.'

She hung her head. 'All right, what I was going to say was, somebody's got to do it, my only bit of advice is to go with it.'

'Yeah, course you'd say "go with it". It's all right for you, Mrs Married With Gorgeous Children, I'm the one who gets to, well, not. I'm the one looking at the next forty or fifty years of my life alone. Course you're going to sit there and suggest "going with it".' I put down the tea on the floor by the armchair. I had to get out of there before I started laying into Jess for only telling me what I didn't want to hear. I got up, grabbed my bag and my jacket. 'I need to go for a walk, think things through.'

'All right, love.'

I spun around, my whole body aflame with anger. 'Don't. Call. Me. That.'

chapter thirty-one
Cursed

So, this is it, is it?

This is my talent. My purpose in life. I am here to make other people fall in love, have sex, find their heart's desire. But not me. I don't get any of it.

I sat in Burley Park, on a bench in the middle of the park. The grey concrete path wound around me. The emerald blanket of grass rose and fell in tiny hills and odd-shaped mounds.

I was hunched over, my shoulders tense, my hands pushed deep into my suede jacket pockets. Another few minutes and the jacket would be ruined beyond repair. It wasn't raining, it was pouring. The main reason for me being hunched up. As if that was some protection from the weather. It was merely a physical reflex, though, the rest of me didn't care if I drowned in rain.

I'd sat there for about forever since I'd left Jess's house. Water drizzled down my face, down my neck and inside my clothes, while frizzing my hair.

This is my life, is it? My talent, my gift, my search for the holy grail. My huge, throbbing, pus-filled curse.

This so wasn't fair. I know I'd said this to Jess, but now it screamed in my brain: WHAT ABOUT ME?! When do I get that love and sex and settledness?

It wasn't as though my life was purely focused on finding a man. It wasn't. Part of me expected love. Not a man, but love, companionship, someone to pull around me like a person-shaped duvet at night. Someone to share and share alike with. Love in its purest sense.

It wasn't like I was asking to win a few trillion pounds on the lottery, was it? Or to walk along the Pacific Ocean floor. Or win a gold medal. I just wanted love. I'd waited patiently for years for that. What I got, what I was rewarded with was everyone else's life.

I was modern-day Cupid.

Jess was right, of course. That's what was so awful about it. As soon as she said it, the scales fell from my eyes, the barbed wire screens lifted from my brain.

The world suddenly stopped being like those old-fashioned photos I'd seen of the world – all black and white; mono-chrome. As all of Jess's words hit home, I stopped seeing the world as three-dimensional. Everything became colour. The world had more substance, it was multidimensional. I couldn't simply see things any more, I experienced them with all my senses. Everything had its own frequency that it reverberated on, and now I knew my *raison d'être* I was attuned to these frequencies. Every frequency. Life became more than a three-dimensional experience, it became a multidimensional experience. It was so hard to explain when the only way I had to explain it were words and they and their meanings were firmly lodged in the reality of three dimensions.

I was plugged into the world, for real. And I didn't like it. Not one bit. A little knowledge is a dangerous thing. Whoever coined that term wasn't wrong. Now I knew this, I couldn't unknow it. I couldn't deny it.

Right now, I was so unconfused. This was how it felt when I first put on my accursed glasses. I'd turned to the optician and said, very loudly, 'Oh my God, I can't believe how much I couldn't see before.' And they gave me headaches for ages after I started wearing them because, I guess, my brain was seeing more than it had in a while; too much information was entering my head. I could see far too clearly. And, hey, now I could live too clearly. I had no more confusion. No more veils and fuzziness. No more drifting aimlessly wherever life was going to take me. That was why I felt others' emotions. Why I'd start crying for no reason; why I felt morning sickness when I'd never been pregnant; why I felt everyone else's confusion, hurt, hate, humiliation, joy, love, lust, ecstasy. Because I was cursed to. I was modern-day Cupid.

I'd always felt a tad different to everyone else. It wasn't the feeling that I was unique, tortured, misunderstood; not that no one understood me, it was that I understood everyone else. I knew too much about how everyone else could find what their heart was sickening for; fix their relationship; speak their mind; follow their dream; get a life, etc., etc., etc., even though I had relatively no experience of most of those things myself, I could talk and advise on them as though I'd been there, done that – several times.

I remember when all this started. The first event when I put my big mouth and need to interfere and need to help to proper use.

I'd gone on a walking holiday in the Lake District with a couple of friends. Post O-levels, pre-results, almost my birthday. I was sixteen and the three of us had our reasons for going: mine, to get away from my parents; Kathleen, to do what she wanted; Marian, to walk.

We spent most evenings and lunchtimes in the central lodge, me not drinking, just eating. I'd been dragged out walking a couple of times and it'd tripled my appetite. But, wherever we were, walking, eating, sitting, there also seemed to be this desperately unhappy couple nearby. I say desperately unhappy couple, but it was her who was miserable, under constant fire as she was from her husband. He constantly called her stupid, ugly, fat, pathetic, etc., etc. . . . in a voice that reverberated around the lodge or rang out through the hills. He never seemed to stop criticising her clothes, her walking abilities, the way she ate, the way she breathed at one point.

Everyone focused on their food when he started taking potshots at her in the central lodge. Everyone listened to his abuse; feeling embarrassed for her, feeling embarrassed for themselves but no one wanting to get involved. I wasn't embarrassed, I never felt embarrassment, all I experienced was rage. Deep rage and shame. Every word, every insult went through me as though directed at me. Meant for me. My rage, indignation and humiliation built up, day after day until day four.

By then, I'd forgotten that the rage I felt was irrational considering I'd never had a boyfriend in my life, I'd never experienced this type of constant abuse and, for all I knew, he was right. Maybe he did look at her and feel physically sick because of her body. Or her face. Or the way she breathed.

On that day, I felt how she felt. Not felt for her, felt through her. It was as if she was projecting her emotions straight into my brain and heart and I could feel her hurt, her humiliation. She also loved this man, that was apparent, she had a bond with him. All of this was being broadcast straight into me. I found it harder and harder to push food into my mouth because of what he was saying and the effect it was having on me. The pain, the anger, the resignation.

'Look at you, how am I supposed to even want to touch you when you sit there with that look on your face and all that blubber melting onto your seat and the way you eat, the way you drink. You've got . . .' his staccato voice shot across the room, ricocheting off the embarrassed silence.

Before I knew what was happening, I was on my feet, my friends had faces of horror, Marian went to grab me but it was too late, I'd spun to face the couple. 'Who the hell do you think you are?' I shouted at him.

The pair of them stopped, stared at me in abject shock.

'I asked you a question,' I shouted, 'who do you think you are to sit there talking to anyone, let alone your wife, like that?'

Like the bully he was, rather than say anything to someone who challenged him, he simply sat there and stared at me.

'I mean, we have to sit here, night after night and listen to you abusing someone constantly, and for what? For killing someone? For mutilating someone? No, for her size. For the way she eats. For the expression on her face. How dare you. How *dare* you.

'I mean, you can dish it out, but can you take it?'

He stared at me. No hint whatsoever of pummelling my face into silence. 'I asked you, you can dish it out, but can you take it? Hmmm?'

Miraculously, he just shook his head at me.

'No, thought not. Well, let me tell you, Mr Loud And Rude, you're not Mel Gibson yourself. In fact, you make David Hasselhoff look rather appealing. And, even though your looks aren't all that, you don't even have a nice personality to compensate for it. So, do the world and us a favour and SHUT UP.'

I turned to the woman. 'And you, have you no self-respect? I mean, I can understand that you put up with this in your own home, because at least then you can ignore him, or put rat poison in his food or drop the odd cup of tea in his lap, but in public? How dare you sit there and let him abuse you in

286

front of everybody. I know, I know, you love him, but there's one person you should love more and that's yourself and . . . and, the fact you can sit there and let him abuse you night after night means you need, you need . . . I don't know, you need to think about how much you mean to yourself.'

The silence after my storm frightened me. It was pure silence. Everyone in the room was probably holding their breath cos not even the sound of respiration could be heard.

Then the room suddenly erupted into applause. Everyone around me was clapping and congratulating me for doing what no one else would. I came down from the head rush that had pushed me into action, giddy, unsteady on my feet. And, mortified. Who did I think I was? I was worse than him, at least he knew the person he was insulting, I'd never met them before.

I turned on my heels and marched out of there, shame burning in my ears and on my face. Ironically, I went for a long walk around the lake not far from the hostel.

I was shaking for most of that walk, I still couldn't understand what I'd just done and why. I sat by the edge of the lake, staring into it.

'Hello,' a voice said, some time later.

I turned around. It was the woman. She looked older close up, her blond hair streaked with white, her face lined and her eyes puffy and reddened, probably from crying. She stared at me, I stared at her. She sat down and we sat in silence for a while.

'He wasn't always like that,' she said eventually. Sadness and frustration were like a shroud around her. A shroud that encompassed me.

'Well that's all right then,' I snapped. 'He wasn't always like that so that gives him a good excuse to behave like that now.' This really wasn't me talking.

'It's not like that,' she said.

I gave her a hard look. Shrugged. 'Why do you care what I think, anyway? I'm just some sixteen-year-old, what do I know about life, right?'

'I . . .' she began. Stopped. 'You stood up for me and I feel I owe you an explanation.'

'I also insulted you, or have·you conveniently forgotten that?' Why couldn't I shut up? I'd been known to go without speaking for days and now I had a cross between verbal diarrhoea and abusive Tourette's Syndrome.

'Yes, but you were trying to help me.'

'Two wrongs don't make a right. Or make it all right.'

This seemed to go over her head. 'It was like you were reading my mind back in the lodge. Like everything I was thinking was coming out of your mouth. Even down to the David Hasselhoff thing.'

I *knew* that wasn't me speaking, I quite fancied David Hasselhoff in *Knight Rider* at that point, not that I'd *ever* tell anyone that.

'*But, you're going to stay with him and carry on letting him treat you like that, aren't you?*'

Her face contracted in pain.

I sighed. 'I just said that out loud, didn't I?' I said.

She nodded.

'Sorry,' I mumbled, then stared out across the lake, everything seemed green up here. Green and wet. Haze hung over the lake, moisture oozed out of the air. You could feel the wetness in the atmosphere as you inhaled and exhaled. Except I couldn't because her emotions were choking the life out of me, making it hard to even breathe. I didn't want to be around her much longer, but I couldn't get up and walk away. I'd started this.

'How long have you been married?' I asked.

'Fifteen years,' she said in a small, small voice. She married him a year after I'd been born. I'd barely have been walking when she said 'I do' to him.

Her expression was taut across her face, each facial muscle tensed while she tried to control herself, then she crumpled, giving in to tears.

Now look what you've done. 'I'm really sorry,' I said. 'I didn't mean to upset you.'

'It's not you,' she said through her tears. She wiped her sleeve across her eyes; I would've offered her a tissue but decided she probably didn't want the dried-up snot rag that had been squatting in my jacket pocket since last winter.

'You just . . . when I thought about marriage it wasn't meant to be like this. You don't think it'll turn out like this. And I don't know how to get out. I just don't know.'

I put my arm around her shoulder, it was expected, and who had started her blubbing? *Moi*. She leant in to me and started sobbing for real. I thought I'd seen crying before, but I hadn't. She wailed and talked and explained her predicament. All the while talking like she expected me to have some answers. I had no answers, I was sixteen for heaven's sake. I hadn't kissed a boy, much less gone out with one, got married and worked out how to leave him if he started to destroy my soul.

We sat at the lakeside for a long time. And then she got up, dried her eyes, dried her nose and wandered off into the mist that had settled over the path leading to the lodge. I sat waiting, counting seconds, waiting until she got far enough away so that I could get up and run back to the lodge. It was creepy out there and I'd seen a horror film or two in my time. In fact, by the time I went speed walking back to the dormitory we were staying in, I'd convinced myself a monster lived at the bottom of the lake and Jason from *Friday the 13th* or *Halloween* or whatever was lurking in the bushes with his carving knife and hockey mask. But that was a hyperactive imagination for you.

I never saw her again. The woman. I never knew her name, I just knew her ailment. And, while she constantly came to mind, while I hoped it'd been all right in the end and that she worked out how to pack a bag and walk away for ever, I never did find out what happened.

Things had continued from there. Since that holiday, my life had never been uncomplicated or uncoupled from the intimate lives of others.

I shut the front door a little too loudly as I dripped and squelched into the house. The anger in the slam brought Jake to the living room door.

His eyes doubled in size when he saw me.

'Cezza! Look at the state of you! Are you all right?' He came to me, obviously ready to offer comfort.

'I'm fine,' I snapped. 'Perfectly fine, thank you very much.'

I hadn't forgotten his role in my current predicament. I didn't want his help or affection or a hug. Especially not when I knew how cross he was with me about Ed. I trailed a wet patch up to my bedroom.

I cried as I took off my sodden clothes. Not as big a cry as I did at Jess's place. More a constant cry. For one who didn't cry very often, I was certainly making up for it. I trembled and cried during the whole disrobing and showering and putting on my pyjamas process.

It was like I'd just been chucked by my first love, my big love and my dream love at the same time. Except, this was worse. More painful. This wasn't merely the loss of love, the loss of *grand amour*, this was the loss of the *idea* of love. This was accepting that it'd never happen to me, that I would shuffle off this mortal coil without ever knowing what really being in love feels like. Without knowing I could be myself, my nasty self, my nice self, my manic self, my depressive self, my hopeful self, my totally fucking loony shouldn't someone lock me up self with someone and still find they loved me. Still find they were there in the morning.

Getting to the end of my life and finding it'd never happened would be one thing; knowing at this stage of the game it'd never happen just made me want to take my ball home and never play again.

What was the point? I'd never win. Not when I had this Cupid thing oozing out of my skin.

I remember reading this quote once that went something like: 'A poor person who is unhappy is in a better position than a rich person who is unhappy. Because the poor person has hope. He thinks money would help.' Much like myself. I thought love will help.

After two days in bed, feeling soooo sorry for myself I couldn't even bear to put on *Angel* because the pain of knowing he'd never love me was too great, I realised something. All I had to do was break the curse. If I wasn't so loving, so caring, so open to callers twenty-four/seven, how the hell could I be Cupid?

All I had to do was not be Cupid.

So simple, it was scary.

All I really had to do was be cold. Be a cow. Start secreting negative hormones like the rest of the population.

How hard could that be?

chapter thirty-two

No Life Contact

Claudine knocked on my office door the very next day. I knew it was her because she'd rung my mobile earlier and left a message asking if I was coming to college. I hadn't called her back. And when she knocked and turned the handle, I froze. Sat very still and held my breath in case she put her ear to the door, listening for signs of life.

The door was locked. I'd come in to surf the Net on my time and college money and prepare for the next day's lecture and tutorials. I had the time to talk to Claudine, but not the inclination.

My time was my own now. It'd do no good to start off on the wrong foot by talking to Claudine. Even though I wanted someone else to run all this Cupid Effect stuff by, I didn't want to be in a position where I might have to listen to any more of their traumas. That was part of the problem, wasn't it? I felt it, I dealt it.

She knocked again for luck, in case I'd fallen asleep and hadn't heard her the first time. This was unnatural, not jumping up and running to the door to open it. Not being ready to listen and offer advice, but I'd get over it. I'd have to. I was doing this for the good of my health and for the good of my love life. It was for their own good, too. I wouldn't always be around, would I? I might go back to London in February when my contract came to an end – who would they whinge at then? Who would they blame their mess on? They had to stand on their own two feet. Accept that what ailed them was of their own doing. I didn't ask them to shag their friends or to hate their students or to give up college.

Yeah, Ceri, say it a few more times and you'll believe it.

Claudine wandered off and I ignored the urge to leap up and sprint after her, check she was all right. I turned to my computer screen, got back to reading movie scripts.

'Hi, Ceri,' Claudine called down the corridor later that week as I left the office.

I'd been doing the locking-the-door thing whenever I was alone in the office, I didn't go to the common room or to the library, not the library in college, anyway. I hid in a variety of pubs within walking distance of the college. Sometimes I'd go to the main university library, careful not to run into Jake or Ed. If I went to a pub down in Horsforth, I made sure it was different to the one I'd been to the day before – I wanted to ensure that if someone saw me somewhere one day, they wouldn't be able to 'accidentally' find me there the next day.

It was like being on the run, I felt like a modern-day David Banner at the end of each episode of the *Incredible Hulk*, slinging his bag on his shoulder and wandering off to another town where no one had heard of the Hulk. I also felt like the original *Fugitive*, with one eye over his shoulder on the police and one eye in front, searching for the one-armed man who'd offed his wife. I was constantly moving, constantly aware that

I might be spotted by someone who knew me and wanted to talk to me.

At home, so as to avoid Jake and Ed, I hid in my room until they'd gone to sleep then made dinner. I called my family so they wouldn't call me and if one of the lads came knocking, I pretended to be asleep or naked.

It was a lonely experience, I spent a lot of time in my head or with my nose in a book or itching to be doing something that involved other people – but I'd get over it. I had to. This was an extension, I suppose, of the no eye contact thing. This was no life contact.

I didn't realise, though, how much I lived for human contact. I thrived on it. Not the 'please sort out my life' part that seemed to plague my very existence. My new life did nothing to help the loneliness I felt hounded by. Duh. It just accentuated it. The irony of it being, I was avoiding eye contact in the life sense; I was being alone now so I wouldn't be alone for ever. The desired ends would simply have to justify the means.

'Haven't seen you around much,' Claudine continued, although clearly, *clearly* I was getting ready to chew half my body off to get away from her. 'I've called you loads. And emailed you.'

I shifted weight from one foot to the other. 'I know,' I said, stifling the urge to explain and/or apologise for not being her personal, unpaid therapist, while swiftly asking her what the problem was. And, if I needed any more reminding, she, like most people, wouldn't give a monkey's left eyebrow what ailed me.

'Are you OK?' she asked.

'Yup, fine,' I replied.

She looked at me, I looked at her. Silence came to us like a soft falling of snow. Claudine was wondering how big-mouth

Ceri had mutated into duo-syllabic woman; I was wondering how I was going to keep it up.

'Have you been avoiding me?' she asked.

'Course not.' *I've been avoiding everyone, you're nothing special in that respect. It's nothing personal.*

Claudine's elfin-cut hair had grown. She seemed older, taller. That was because she was skinnier. Probably not eating properly because of the *ménage à trois* she was embroiled in. A truthful word or two from me could end it. I could say what she needed to hear. It wasn't my place, not now – it never had been. I ached for her though. My heart reached out to her. I wanted to make her safe. I wanted her to eat properly, to sleep properly, to live properly, and if I could help her do that, then . . . but what if she gets to a place like this again and I'm not around? She'll totally fall apart, won't she?

'Claudine, I can't talk right now, I've got to dash,' I forced myself to say. 'Bye.'

'Is it cos I punched Mel?' she said, stepping into my path.

'Sorry?'

'Are you pissed off with me because I punched Mel?'

'Course not,' I replied.

She didn't look convinced.

'Claudine, you can punch whoever you want. Apart from me. If you punch me, I'll kung fu your ass. But I don't mind who you punch.'

'I've missed our chats. Are you sure I haven't done something to upset you?'

I nodded. 'I've been very, very busy. Loads of research to do.'

'If you're sure . . .'

I nodded. 'I'll see ya, bye.' Guilt pounded in my head as I walked away.

★

From Mel, I got: 'Is it because I said you were quite vaguely attractive?'

'Nope, I'm busy.'

From Ed: 'Is it cos Robyn might be moving in?'

'Nope, I'm busy.'

From Jake: 'Is it cos I had a go at you about Ed?'

'Nope, I'm busy.'

From Gwen: 'Oh, Ceri, I'm glad I caught you. Demon year group have pushed me too far this time and I'm goi—'

'You wanna be talking to an exorcist, mate.' Of course, I didn't say that. I just remembered a phone call to my parents I had to return, told her I'd be right back and went off home.

It made me pause and think, though, that they all – apart from Gwen – thought that they had offended me with their small acts. I suppose, if I was in their position, I'd rack my brains for some explanation as to why someone who was available twenty-four/seven had suddenly shut up shop. But, I'd started so I'd finish. It was a lot more difficult than I expected. As hard as breathing without two functioning lungs, as hard as thinking without a brain. Totally unnatural.

chapter thirty-three

Slip Up

'Hi, it's Ceri, isn't it?'

I kept my head down as I nodded. I so did not want to talk to this person. Of all the people on earth, I did not want to talk to him. I'd spotted him across the bar in Leeds City Centre that I was doing my marking in and hadn't got my stuff together fast enough to make a run for it.

That'll learn me to get everything out on the table. Just have what you need out, the rest of the stuff should be piled up, ready to be hoisted into my arms, so I could peg it at a moment's notice. (Some Fugitive/Incredible Hulk type person I was. I couldn't even get out of a pub in under thirty seconds. Imagine if I really had the police and a reporter after me, I'd be done for.)

'Do you mind if I join you?' he asked, sitting down anyway.

He, who? He whose name was not to be mentioned in our house. He who slept with the fishes (and every other form of aquatic life for all I knew). He who was named Terry at birth but had been renamed The Git by me. Him, Jake's man. Or not, as the case was. I'd seen pictures of him. I'd even been introduced to him once long ago at a party Jake, Ed and I went to. Now he was sitting opposite me as I said, 'I'm a bit busy right now.' Even though it'd been a week and a bit into my no life contact, I still hadn't managed the art of being out-right rude, but I didn't look at him as I told him I wasn't free to chat.

'Right,' he replied and sat there anyway. 'You're Jake's flat-mate, aren't you?'

'We live in a house,' I replied. I could probably get a bit more frost into my voice, but not much.

The Git laughed.

'Jake talks about you all the time. You and Ed, you're like his family. I guess it comes from him being an only child. You and Ed are like his brother and sister.'

'Really,' I said. Yup, I could crowbar more frost into my voice and there it was – icicles were hanging off that one word.

The Git leant forwards over the table, obscuring my papers with his elbows. The world revolved around him, clearly. I sat back, focused on his bare elbows. I couldn't look him in the face without scowling.

'I'm glad we've met up,' he said.

'No, we didn't meet up, you came over and disturbed me,' I said. 'I'm in the middle of marking.'

'OK, I'm glad I've seen you, then. I'm really worried about Jake.'

I raised my eyes to him then. Oh no! Jake. My heart sprinted, my breath came in short bursts. I'd been shutting him and everyone else out. Had something hideous happened while I was doing that? 'Why, what's happened?'

'I rang him the other day, he sounded really down. I asked him if he was OK and he said he was at college and he'd call me back. And he hasn't. That's just not like him. He always calls me back when he says he will.'

'Do you always call him back when you say you will?' I asked.

He frowned, thought about it. 'No.'

Well then, my face said. I looked back down at the work I was marking, raised my pen.

'No,' he put his hand between my pen and paper, 'but I'm busy. And then I forget. It's not like I do it on purpose. I'm just busy.'

'And Jake isn't?' I asked.

'But Jake's just always been there. For him to not call me back something must've happened. I'm really worried.'

I slammed the pen down, raised my eyes again to him. 'Do you know, Terry, I try not to judge people. Mainly, because of the "let she who is without sin cast the first stone" thing and also because I hate it when people judge me but, BUT, I really think you're the most odious type of person. You're an arrogant, self-serving little prig and I can't even bring myself to think that you're a nice person who does bad things because you're not, are you?' I paused. 'You treat Jake like dirt then you're surprised when he cuts you out of his life. In fact, you have the *audacity* to be hurt.'

'You know nothing about it,' he retorted.

'No, I don't, so why did you come sit over here? Why? Because you want me to do your dirty work for you, so you just wandered over here and decided to charm me so I'd get Jake to talk to you.

'Mate, and I use that word because that's how I speak, not because you are in any way a friend of mine, I've only heard Jake's side of the story, but the fact you've come worming around me just proves what a git you are.

'Jake opened his heart to you. He asked you to tell him how you felt, he wasn't asking you to leave your boyfriend or for you to say you loved him. All he wanted was for you to tell him if you had any feelings for him because you've spent seven years sending him mixed messages, not to mention having sex with him. All he wanted was for you to say something like "I don't think of you in that way" or "I love you like a mate" so he could let go and move on. He did not expect you to sit there and say "I do not love you. I've always known how you felt and I kind of hoped if I ignored it you'd go away. And, by the way, everyone you know has known how you felt and – while they've all been laughing at you – they've tried to convince me to go out with you but y'know, I couldn't face it. Because you know what, you're funny, and gorgeous and clever, but you're missing that certain something that makes you lovable. And, you know all those times I've shagged you, well, it was out of friendship, not cos I've felt anything, despite all those mixed messages I've been sending and how I've reacted in the past when you've gone out with other people. Oh, yes, there was also that night when I told you that if you loved someone, then you should tell them how you feel but when you tell me I just piss on your emotions." So, buddy, do not sit there and tell me I know nothing.

'You've known Jake for so long, you know how sensitive he is, you know how hard it is for him to open up and admit how he feels and you still, *still*, couldn't even afford him the luxury of being patronisingly nice. Anyone who could do that to a friend is a freak.

'Now, please go away and if you can manage it in your egocentric world, stay away from Jake until you find a way to treat him with some respect.'

The Git stared at me and my newly-vented spleen. He'd probably never been told about himself before. Everyone tiptoed around him because he was so gorgeous and did a good impression of being a nice bloke. Everyone around him thought he was a good bloke, a nice lad, really great. The only people who saw the real side of him were the ones who, like Jake, loved him and wanted to be with him. They were

300

the ones who got screwed over because they were stupid enough to fall completely for the nice-guy act. And, well, people like me had to pick up the pieces. Really pick up the pieces. Everyone else just got sick of hearing about it and started to tell the ones like Jake to just put him behind them. To 'get over it'. While I, *I* felt it. I had to feel for Jake and pick up the pieces and want to cry and feel his pain and understand and fret about it. I was the one who got to understand how even when Jake said it was OK he was just putting a brave face on it because he was so humiliated that all his friends knew and had tried to talk The Git into going for it. And all his friends probably sat there discussing it and pitying and wishing he could get a grip. I was the one who knew he was so humiliated because if The Git hadn't said anything, he'd never have been any wiser and in some cases ignorance was bliss; what you didn't know really couldn't upset you.

I glanced up, The Git was still there. 'No, really, I mean it. FUCK! OFF!'

A few people in the pub looked around as he, still wearing that wounded face, got up and walked away. He even left his drink on the table, left a short glass with orange juice and melting ice cubes to dribble condensation on the table as he left the pub.

I watched his back leave the pub. Then it smacked me in the face. Hard. So hard I had to drop my head into my hands.

I've done it again. I've only gone and done it again. I've gotten involved. I've broken my silence. I've behaved like BLOODY, TWATTING Cupid again.

Oh well, just this one thing couldn't hurt. Could it?

chapter thirty-four

Down and Down

'Hi, Ceri, it's Viv. Remember me? I used to be your old boss. Actually, I was your boss and your friend. I know I didn't come to your leaving do, and I know I didn't speak to you during your last month working for me, but we were friends, weren't we?

'Anyway, I was just ringing to see how you are. And to get your advice on something. My husband's sister is going to work abroad and she asked me to go with her. I was wondering what you thought I should do? I mean, you gave up everything to go chase a dream in Leeds and I was wondering if I should too? Anyway, give me a call or email me, I need to hear from you. Bye.'

After the incident with Jake's man, I became hot property. My life became the epitome of 'treat 'em mean, keep 'em keen'. My mobile rang off the hook with people calling me 'for a chat', i.e., to tell me their latest problems. I was literally getting calls back to back.

The people from Leeds realised I'd taken my ball home so didn't bother me as much. It was everyone I'd known in London, everyone from my past stepping into the breach. 'Just ringing to say hi, see how you are'; 'haven't spoken in ages, just wanted to catch up', i.e., I want to tell you my problems, I want advice, I want to share my latest love news with you.

The woman who was living in my flat and whose boyfriend had moved in, rang to tell me they were getting married. Having lived together for, what, four months, they couldn't imagine being apart. They were getting married in December – six months' time – and would I possibly consider
a) being a bridesmaid
b) letting them stay in the flat when I moved back to London

A few days later she rang again to ask me if I'd consider selling my flat to them. They'd pay almost double its worth cos they'd really fallen in love there and wanted to stay. I was still going 'huh?' when my paranoid ex-boss Viv called to ask about her love life.

A day later, Whashisface Tosspot rang out of the blue. I hadn't spoken to him in almost three years, and let's not forget that I didn't say his name out loud so he wouldn't ever call me. But I'd answered my mobile not recognising the number and it was him. He'd simply wanted advice on why his marriage was going wrong. Was it because he'd only known her nine months when they said, 'I do' or was it because I'd cursed his marriage? What should he do?

My first ever boyfriend called to tell me he was getting married, finally, to the woman he left me for ELEVEN years ago. Oh, by the way, his best mate was getting married in Skipton at the end of the month and he'd been told to invite me. On and on, people who I didn't even know had my number were calling me, or emailing me. Or finding me via the college website and dropping me a line. I took to turning off my mobile for hours and hours – only to find my messages backed up to the answermachine's capacity; I only spoke to my family on my home phone and I started to develop a phobia to email.

It was as though something was trying to tell me: 'You think you had it bad before? Well, this is what it could really be like. Count yourself lucky it's not everyone beating a path to your door, all right?' After ten days of this, I conceded. Gave in to it.

I lay in bed one Tuesday night and accepted my fate. Accepted my fate may have been overstating the case. It was more a case of resigning myself to it for the moment, until I could find some kind of get-out clause.

'All right, God, The Universe, Karma, Whoever You are who has placed this upon my head, You win,' I said out loud. 'I will go back to being what I was before. I'm not necessarily saying I believe I'm Cupid, modern-day or otherwise, I'm just saying if it's my purpose in life to fuck up friendships; incite people to have sex with their exes; make young boys get married too young and make older women unhappy with everything, then I'll do it. I've learnt me lesson. No shirking my responsibilities.'

I closed my eyes and tried to sleep.

'Oh, PS, I'm not saying I'll go about my duties happily, though, all right? Just as long as that's clear.'

chapter thirty-five

'I'm Back, Baby'

I made my reappearance in the canteen the next day. I'd not mustered up the energy to face a Gwen session, so hid out in my office until lunchtime. Screwing up her life, making her unhappy would just have to wait. It was one-fifteen by the time I got to the canteen. I got food, a charming-looking Caesar salad with a side order of chips. (The chips served to remind me that I hadn't been to the gym. At all.)

I took a couple of steps away from the cashier and immediately found myself not only up Shit Creek without a paddle, but also without a boat. On one side of the canteen, in the blue corner was Mel, hunched over a magazine he so wasn't reading; in the red corner sat Claudine, doing the same with a book. It'd got that bad they couldn't even sit together. Both looked up when I left the safety of the company of the cashier and, even without my glasses I saw each of their faces light up.

Mel waved and beckoned me over; Claudine grinned and pulled out the chair beside her. A surge of rage overcame me. I loved neither of them best; I wasn't sure I liked *people* at that point.

How dare they? How dare they use me as a tool in their stupid row. And, God forgive me, it was stupid.

I walked between the two warring factions, found the middle ground (a table equidistant to both tables) and placed my tray on it but I didn't sit. I went to Mel, because I'd met him first, 'Come join me,' I ordered. It was a pleasant order, but an order nonetheless.

Mel was overjoyed at being invited to join me at the big table. Who knew eating with me would be so exciting – many men before him would've paid good money not to eat with me. He got up, picked up his tray and magazine, minced over to where my tray was. The campness came from trying, through his walk, to stick his tongue out to Claudine. *Na, na, Ceri loves me more.*

While Mel minced, I sauntered over to Claudine. 'Come join me,' same tone, same order.

'No thanks,' she replied, glaring at Mel.

'It's not an invite,' I explained, 'it's an order.'

Claudine's eyebrows shot up. *You are ordering ME?* those eyebrows said.

'Claudine, you have burdened me with the very minutiae of your love life, the least you owe me is joining me when "invited" (I made the dreaded air quotes) to.

'And you, Melvin Rivers, can sit your butt back down,' I said, very loudly, so it carried and everyone who was dotted around the middle ground and Claudine's corner, heard. Humiliation wasn't out of the question. This Cupid thing had some perks and being outrageous, saying anything, was one of them. The Universe, Fate, God, Karma, Whatever, expected it of me.

'Well?' I said to Claudine.

She sighed, screwed up her face, then reluctantly got up, gathered her tray and book. 'Don't expect me to talk to him,' she warned in a low voice.

They sat as far away from each other as possible, but were

still technically sat opposite me. *Had I really done this? Had my Cupid curse really prised these two close people apart?*

In that moment, I felt a flash of power. It passed as quickly as it came, overtaken by annoyance at these two people who, literally, should have known better. Because not even me and my big mouth and my pheromones and other 'qualities' could've torn apart their friendship if they weren't so bloody pathetic. They should know better, they knew they should know better, but insisted on playing games. And, not very good games, either. My six-year-old niece could play mind games better than these two. If I thought for one minute either of them was genuinely attempting to hurt the other one, I wouldn't be so annoyed. Annoyed and frustrated. It was clear, if you thought about it. And, hey Mel, hey Claudine, I'm sure you've done nothing else but think about it. You both know what is ticking away in your hearts and minds, neither of you wants to face it, though. You'd much rather live in discomfort than face the truth.

'OK,' I smiled. 'Dearly beloved, I have brought you together today, because I think you both need to be told what's going on in your minds.'

I paused, struggling to get warmness back into my voice.

'Claudine, news flash, you do not have to be "in love" to "make love". It's all right to have sex with a man and find that afterwards, you don't want to run away with him. Admittedly, your boyfriend might not see it that way, but you did what you did. You can't unsleep with Mel. Pretending it didn't happen won't change things either.

'I'm telling you, categorically, you're not in love with Mel. You may love Mel, but you're not in love with him – I know it's not what you want to hear, but it's the truth. And he certainly doesn't compare to Kevin. If he did, you'd have left Kevin, life or no life. Well, you'd have at least done it more than once.

'So, bloody stop trying to convince yourself that sex equals love. You might be an old romantic, you might *want* to be in love with Mel, because, well, you've known him for years and he's lovely and he's a good friend and he's a great shag, but you don't. Just because all the elements are there, doesn't mean it'll work. You know I'm right, it's already in your mind. Which is why, when I asked you that night at my house why you didn't go round to Mel's and shag him senseless, you were horrified. You wouldn't do that to Kevin, not twice.'

Claudine opened her mouth to speak.

'Shut up. I'm talking.

'Before I realised what I wanted to do with my life was wreck it by coming up here, I read this quote. It went: "Ours is a world where people don't know what they want and are willing to go through hell to get it." That's you, except you do *know* what you want, can't accept that, so are willing to put yourself through all types of hell to get what you think you should want.

'My advice, the last bit of advice you get for free is this: tell Mel you're not in love with him. Once you say it out loud and the sky doesn't come crashing in, you might actually believe it.

'Then, go home, talk to Kevin. Sit him down in a room, look him straight in the eye and talk to him. At the root of all of this is the fact that, despite how beautiful you are, how lovely a person you are, you have low self-esteem. Mel made you feel good, he gave you the attention you craved from Kevin. You needed Mel to tell you you're beautiful and worthy. You probably felt indebted to him for giving you that ego boost when you needed it most. That doesn't mean you have to talk yourself into being in love with him. Tell Kevin you need his attention and his time, roger him senseless, and then start building the next stage of your life together.'

I twisted a fraction in my seat. 'Mel. You are a commitment-phobe. There is nothing wrong with it, some of my best friends are commitment-phobes, you just shouldn't have got married when you did.

'You felt the fear, you did it anyway and you screwed over three perfectly great people in the process.' I raised my fingers.

'Number one: your wife. She never stood a chance because you thought you wanted a mythical person who was gorgeous, fertile, funny, fun, etc., etc., when all you really wanted was a friend. Which, she wasn't. That was her one fatal flaw.

'Number two: Claudine. She was your get-out clause – not just with your wife. I'll bet you've compared every woman you've met to her. And, I'll bet my flat, my savings and my lunch that none of them matched up. They were all in a different league, none of them good enough. When you were looking for a way out of your marriage, Claudine became the reason. Not the fact Fran wasn't the type of woman you wanted in the first place. If you loved Claudine like that, you'd have done something about it. Don't give me that, "you have no idea how it is to love someone from afar" look. I do, I've done it far longer and far more intensely than you could ever do, and you know what? It's bollocks. If you truly love someone, *truly*, you would do something about it. Anything to get them to love you. I learnt that the hard way. You wouldn't wait until you want a reason to get out of your marriage to engineer a one-night stand. To basically do something you felt was so unforgivable that you'd be forced to end your marriage. If you love someone, really love them, you would, at least, have done the whole, sit them down the night before you get married thing and tell them how you feel.

309

'Much as you love Claudine, she has always been Ms Convenience. And now you're free, she's Ms I Should Want Her. Mel, if you really love her, really want her, then get down on one knee and propose right now. And find out what she says. But you won't cos you're not in love with Claudine, no matter how much you love her.

'The third person you've screwed over is you. You have spent so much time avoiding yourself and your fear of being tied down, you ruined your marriage, almost ruined your friendship with Claudine, got smacked in the face. You're allowed to be friends with a woman without wanting to shag her. You *need* to be friends with women without shagging them. It's a radical, scary concept, but as Mark Twain said, "Courage is the mastery of fear – not the absence of it." Be brave. Accept what happened before Christmas for what it was – a way to get out of your marriage, a drunken fumble, then be friends with Claudine again, instead of a reminder that you had sex. Despite what you've been led to believe, sex isn't the be all and end all, it's just sex. If it was more with Claudine, you would've done it more than once.

'And, once you're friends with Claudine again, try getting on the phone and apologising to your wife. The fact you hardly spoke to her for the last however many months of your marriage should tell you something, namely, you'd both for-gotten what it was like to be together as two people rather than as "a couple". Which is the root of your commitment-phobic nightmare – the reason you want a friend, not a wife. You've always thought that once you get settled, fun goes out the window but that doesn't happen with friends. It doesn't have to happen with couples, but you don't know that yet. In time, I reckon you'll sort out your head, you'll get some per-spective on the whole thing and will be able to have a settled relationship and not run away from it, but for now, apologise to Fran. It's not her fault you wanted to live in a fun house twenty-four/seven.'

I paused, sagged in my seat, spent. I never thought I'd get tired of hearing myself speak; I'd never thought I'd get tired of talking.

'Now, one final thing. Something aimed at the two of you. In all of this, you seem to have forgotten something very important: you two are friends. Beyond the sex, the marriage break-ups and the face-punching you two are real friends. Nothing should stand in the way of that. So many people are crying out for someone they can trust, for that kind of friendship. You've got it – stop fucking about with it.'

I dropped the leaf of lettuce I'd used as a pointer and got up, picking up my tray as I stood. I didn't hang about to see what they did next. I didn't need to. All those two really needed was someone to say what they didn't want to hear. Voice their inner turmoil.

I took my tray up to my office – my office buddy Sally wasn't in on Wednesdays – and I sat at her desk so I could stare out the window as I ate.

Knock! Knock! came two minutes later. I was never going to have lunch, was I?

'Yes?' I called, twisting in my chair to look at the door. I had a crisp piece of iceberg lettuce poised to go into my mouth. I lowered it when Gwen's head popped around the door.

'Hi, Gwen,' I said, steeling myself for a rant. She had over a month's worth to deliver. 'Come in.'

'Just a quick word,' she said, fixing me with her blue eyes. 'There'll be a memo coming around later, but I wanted to tell you in person first.'

'Oh?' I said. The funding to the department's been cut – I was out on my ear.

'What's the problem?'

311

'No problem,' she said. 'I've resigned.'

She didn't even look serious, much less sound serious. 'Got to go. Bye.'

Oh my giddy aunt, uncle, nieces, nephews and unlikely to be born grandchildren.

chapter thirty-six

The Real Gwen

This was something I never thought would happen. Gwen and I sitting in the Fox & Hound, having a drink together. I'd bolted after her to check she was serious. She confirmed she was. Before I knew what I was doing I was saying we should go for a drink round the corner and down the road.

She'd leapt at the offer like a thirsty woman in a desert. I'd forgotten that I was the nearest thing she'd got in college to a best mate. Or a mate.

'What's going on?' I asked her.

I'd got myself a beer and her a brandy. I remember her saying once she liked brandy.

She lit up a cigarette, I held my breath.

'I've resigned,' she squealed. Then she covered her solar plexus with her hand. 'That feels good and scary to say at the same time.'

'Why?'

She shrugged. 'I felt like it.'

'Have you got another job?' This was like pulling teeth.

'No.'

'And you're going in a month?'

'Yes. They want me to do the summer, supervise the exams and whatnot. But I'm going in a month.'

'You've got interviews lined up?'

'No.'

It's all right. Don't panic. She's got a husband, he'll take care of her if she falls on hard times. And you've probably got nothing to do with her screwing up her life by leaving the only paid position she's qualified to do.

'When you wrote to me about a position in the psychology department, did you have other things lined up?'

WHAT THE HELL HAVE I GOT TO DO WITH IT?

'No.'

'But you still took a chance on giving up your life. What if we'd written back saying "no vacancies"? What would you have done?'

'No, you see, I hadn't resigned from my job in London when I wrote to you.'

'Emotionally you had.'

'What?'

'Ceri, you don't really believe we'd have given you an interview on your qualifications and experience if we thought you were committed to your job in London, do you?'

It's not my fault, it's not my fault, la la, it's not my fault.

'The reason I gave you that first interview was because of the passion in your letter. Everyone who read it said your enthusiasm and passion and *joie de vivre* came through in it. That's very, very rare. Almost extinct these days. You put everything into that letter and you couldn't have done that if you were happy with your job.'

'I was still doing it though. Still getting paid. Still paying the mortgage, etc.'

'You had emotionally left. I emotionally left my position here ages ago. And now, I'm physically leaving too.'

'What does your husband say about all this?'

Gwen moved her gaze from me, to the other side of the bar.

'I wonder what it's going to be like, waking up on the day after I finally leave and know that this is the first day of the rest of my life.'

Clearly, transparently, screamingly obviously she didn't want to talk about what her husband said about her decision. When has that ever stopped me wading in mouth first?

'What does your husband think about your decision to quit?'

She replied first with the filthiest look known to woman-kind. Part of me expected her to jump up onto the rickety table and sing: 'Hey you! Don't rain on my parade!'

Once my face was smeared with her filthy look, she said: 'He's fine with it. Whatever makes me happy makes him happy.'

When I first saw *Cat On A Hot Tin Roof*, I'd never heard the word mendacity before. Immediately after I saw it I heard mendacity everywhere. And now, I was sitting beside a woman whose very name could be mendacity, she reeked of it so. At the very least her husband didn't approve; at the most, he didn't know. Actually, at the most, he didn't exist.

'I still haven't been around for dinner yet,' I said. 'I'm free most nights for the next couple of weeks, how about we fix a date?'

'Vernon is away,' Gwen said, faster than a speeding bullet. 'Business.'

'For two weeks?'

Gwen sighed the sigh of an annoyed creature. 'Why are we talking about Vernon? It's me who has resigned.'

'You haven't resigned in a vacuum, there are other people who'd be affected, namely your nearest and dearest.'

'Keep talking, Ceri, you've just about disinvited yourself to my leaving do.'

Well slap my face and call me Cupid, Gwen had a nasty

streak. She wasn't simply demented and unable to be happy, she had viciousness behind them there squeaky vocal cords.

'I suppose I'm just being selfish. If you leave, who'll – *[suffocate me with smoke/bend my ear by whining alone/make me grateful for my deep voice]* – encourage me? Who'll – *[remind me to avoid pastel flowers/show me how not to teach/make me avoid the common room]* – be my champion in the psychology department?'

Gwen looked away, lit a cigarette, I wondered if she was fighting to put that nastiness back in its box, or if she was formulating a clever way to tell me to fornicate off.

'You'll survive,' she said. *Ah, so we were still being nasty.*

'I guess I'll have to.'

'You haven't done that badly so far. I'll have to do your assessment before I leave, and you haven't done too badly.'

There it was again – praise so faint it was damning. First Mel, now Gwen.

'You're very popular with the students,' she went on. 'Although, that's not always a good thing. You're there to assist their learning, not befriend or entertain them. Students need someone to look up to, to respect, they can't do that if they think of you as nothing more than a buddy.'

'Yeah, you're probably right.'

Gwen looked at me.

'No, really, you're right. I'm a big interfering nerd, but I can't help it. I just have this gift for being too nice. You know, when people vent on me, I don't have the gumption to ignore them, or tell them I'm not interested, I just sit there and listen. If some student looks bored, I try to make things more interesting.' I slid down in my seat. 'I wake up every morning saying to myself: "If someone tries to embroil me in their life today, I'm not getting involved. I'm not allowed. Just don't listen; just don't care. Let them go about their screwed up lives without you." And then, someone will sit down beside me, start to unload, and rather than go glassy-eyed and tune out so they don't do it again; rather than get up and walk away, I listen. I care. But you're right, I'll try so much harder next time to be short, uninterested and to be the unfriendly lecturer that everyone respects. Thanks for that reminder.'

Yes, I actually said that. Out loud. She was leaving, I could. Also, I was thinking, *What's the worst that could happen if I said what I thought?* She could glass me was the worst. Seeing as I couldn't imagine that vividly enough, I went ahead and spoke my mind. Jess would've been proud of me. Jess would've glassed me. But that was my best friend for you.

Moreover, I wasn't sat in the Fox & Hound, passively smoking and drinking on an empty stomach for my benefit.

'I, I didn't mean to upset you,' Gwen said, suddenly sounding much more squeaky again.

'You haven't. I'm crap. I needed to be told, didn't I? Cast ye not pearls before swine and all that. I might've gone on through life, being nice to people for the sake of it.'

Gwen now looked suitably shamefaced. I felt no guilt. Why the hell should I?

'I'll get this next round in,' Gwen squeaked, then scuttled off to the bar. Some people just don't know when you're trying to help them.

chapter thirty-seven
Saving Ed

Claudine and Mel had been relatively easy to sort out. All they needed was a verbal head banging together. If that hadn't worked, I would've gone in for a bit of literal head banging.

Gwen, on the other hand, was a work in progress. Later, obviously, I'd been visited by the guilt demons for being so sarcastic when she obviously wasn't happy. It was true, no one resigned into a vacuum. And no one upped and resigned because they'd emotionally left. You might want to, you might dream of it, but anyway, blah, blah, work in progress. Another chapter, another time. I'd sort her out later.

It was Ed that I didn't want to encounter.

Robyn was about to move in. Jake had given his consent, all the while glaring at me. Later, when Ed had bounced off to his room to start making space for his new love, Jake had glared at me while offering me a cup of tea.

I'd left it a couple of days after that to broach the subject. In fact, four days. In fact, four days that seemed to be more a week. I was that much of a coward. I didn't want to burst his bubble. It was all right for Jake, he wasn't being asked to go life-destroying.

Ed's hair had grown a bit, taking the harshness off his face.

His face was so flushed with joy, his body was back to being clothed in his usual type of attire, the jeans, the heavy metal T-shirt, the lumberjack shirt but this time they all looked cleaned and ironed. You thought you knew someone, but that bendy kid with the blank stare was richer than I'd ever imagined anyone could be. The son of a tinned foods manufacturer, so he was. The irony of that being Ed constantly looked like he needed a good feeding. How the hell would I approach this, anyway? 'Ed, that good-looking woman you're so enamoured with, well, Jake thinks she's after your cash, and well, he might have a point . . .' I mean . . .

Anyway, a week later, I climbed the stairs like a woman approaching the gallows. I wanted him to be happy. Even if for a little while. It was the reminders of those small pearls of happiness we needed to cling to in those times when you were so lonely and hurting you thought it'd never end. Ed might not get this happiness again.

I knocked, turned the doorhandle. 'Ed, you got a minute?' I asked.

'Course,' Ed grinned, pausing in folding up his clothes. 'Come in.'

He indicated to a small clear space on his bed. 'Sit yourself down.'

I sat on his pillow, pulled my bare feet up, moved a little to get my bum into a comfortable position. His room was almost as large as mine. He'd even squeezed a small sofa in the corner, it was like a studio. Nice carpet, pale blue walls, high ceilings. Oh for God's sake Ceri, it's not as if you've never been in here before.

'Hi,' I said. Always the best way to start a difficult conversation.

'What's the matter, Cezza?' Ed said, sitting on top of a pile of clothes. Seeing as he'd seemed to wear the same set of clothes until of late, he had rather a lot of clothes.

319

'Ed,' I began. 'I know you're totally . . .' *What's the word, infatuated, in love with, brainwashed?* '. . . with Robyn, but I wonder if it's all moving a bit too fast.' That didn't sound too bad, did it?

'Yeah, it is. But I'm happy Ceri.'

Fair enough. I'll be going then.

'I know Jake thinks that,' Ed said. 'He's made no secret of it, but I thought you'd understand.'

'Ed, you're getting married next year. You won't have known her but a year before you make a lifetime commitment. I do understand, but it doesn't stop me worrying.'

'I love her.'

'But why do *you* have to give up college? Why not her?'

Ed got up, went to the window, perched himself on the wide window ledge. 'Jake told you, didn't he?'

'Told me what?'

'I told him to not tell a soul, but he told you how much money my family has. And he thinks Robyn couldn't possibly love me for me being me, it has to be for my money. Well, my family's money. I'm not worthy, I'm not good-looking enough, I'm not funny or witty or clever enough, it has to be my family's money. Is that what you think too?'

'It's crossed my mind, but no, I don't think that. Even if your family were as poor as church mice, I'd still want to know why you have to give up college and her not. You're in this fifty-fifty. Why do you get to make the big sacrifice?'

'Really?'

'Yes, really. I don't think for one minute you're the sort of person who would live off his family money. You'd get bored. You need to be working, Edwardo, you're that kind of lad, so why give up your chosen path?'

Ed stared at the ground, then looked up at me. 'Ceri, I hate college. The only other person I told that to is Robyn. I mean,

I really hate college. I was only doing a PhD cos I couldn't think of anything else to do. I finished college, and it made sense to carry on. And now, I've got a reason to give it up.'

'But Robyn shouldn't be your reason.'

'She isn't. I said I've got a reason, I didn't say Robyn was that reason. She loves college, she's staying till the end of the year.'

'And your reason is . . .?'

'Only Robyn knows. And me, of course.'

'Of course.'

'Robyn and I have this plan. It was my idea, a vague idea, and then I told her and she helped refine it.'

Ed moved off the window sill, went to his desk drawer, pulled it open, pulled out a folder, bulging with papers. He handed me the folder. On the front was scrawled *Ed & Robyn's Top Secret Project*.

I opened the orange folder, flicked through. There was page after page of what looked like a business plan. Letters from banks, info on business loans, specs on office space. 'What is this apart from your Secret Project?' I was too stunned by how much was done to take any info in.

'We're going into business. But not like that. The only part of my college life I like is the teaching part. And I love literature and plays and Robyn's an actress. She knows lots of actors who'll be willing to give up their time for a while. So, well, we're going to set up a touring company. We travel to schools, teach them about putting on plays, how all the boring stuff they read was meant to be done. It'll help get children interested in literature.'

Vague idea indeed.

'We won't make big profits. We'll just charge a fee to cover costs and to allow us to live. Any profits will go back into the business at first. I mean, it's top secret now, but when Robyn finishes college we'll get to it. We've almost got the funding sorted and . . .'

I could warm myself by the fire that burnt in Ed's eyes; I could lift my heart with the passion that fuelled his words. This really was the real deal for Ed.

'And you're going to do all this with Robyn?'

'I told you before it wasn't just a wank thing with Robyn. It's not just a sex thing with her now that I've got her. It's an every thing. Cezza, I don't know if we're all supposed to be with one person all our life; I don't know if we've got soul mates, but I do know Robyn is the only person I want to work towards something with. I'm on this road, she's on it with me. "A life lived in fear is a life half lived." That's what you said.' (I knew that would come back to haunt me at some point.) 'Now that's what I'm seeing through. I might very well hate Robyn after a few years; our business might fall flat on its face, but it might not. And at least I'll know. I'm young enough to start again if it all goes horribly wrong.'

And what do you say to that? Go back on everything I've ever done myself?

'I'll leave you to it, then.' I stood.

'Thanks, Ceri,' Ed said.

'For?'

'Speaking your mind instead of just being nasty to Robyn. I really do love her.'

'Good for you, sweetie.'

'Oh, and I haven't told Robyn about my family's money. The only person I've told was Jake and now you.'

'Don't worry, I shan't tell another soul. Not even Jess.'

'Thanks.'

No, sweetheart, thank you. For reminding me why I gave up my life down south in the first place. Wasn't it, life's too long not to go for it?

*

'Mission accomplished,' I said to Jake, when he came back from college later.

'You talked to Ed?' he said, relieved and terrified in one go.

'I did.'

'And he's going to slow down. Not leave college?'

'Jake, he's happy. He's really happy. Leave him to it. If it does go horribly wrong, you'll be the first one he comes to. Unless, of course, you're going to turn your back on him.'

'Course I wouldn't. But Ceri, you do realise that you can't ever leave us now, cos if it does go horribly wrong, you're going to be picking up the pieces too.'

'Yeah, you might have a point there.'

Jake's face came over all mysterious as he said, 'Oh, I got a letter from Terry today. He kind of guessed I wasn't speaking to him or opening his emails, so he wrote to me.'

'And what did it say?'

'Quite a lot. He apologised for what he said that time. He said that he was really ashamed of how much he hurt me. That it didn't occur to him how hard it was for me to say all that and how his panic that I was making demands on him made him say all those awful things. He also explained that he'd flirted with me because he likes me, but thinks we'd make a nightmare couple, which is fair enough really. I just wanted to be treated with a bit of respect. For him to know that because he didn't love me he had no right to ill-treat me or be rude to me, you know?'

I nodded.

'Anyways, the letter went on and on, apologising, not trying to excuse himself and he ended by saying could I ring him and meet him for a drink so he could say all these things face to face.'

'Are you going?'

'I've been.'

'And?'

323

'And he's nipped down the road to get some milk.'

'Does that mean he's getting another chance?'

'Yes. And you know what, it doesn't matter what you think, or anyone else thinks, it's my life. My emotions. I can give the bastard a second chance if I want to.'

'My work is done, here,' I replied, then leant across the sofa to grab the remote control.

There was a short rap at the front door.

'I just wonder who the woman in the pub who called him an arrogant, self-serving little prig, could've been,' Jake said as he went to answer the door. 'You wouldn't know anything about that would you, Cezza?'

'Why would I?' I replied, innocently.

'Why indeed.'

chapter thirty-eight

Love is in the Air

'Champagne, champagne,' Claudine waved two bottles about as she sang her way into the centre of the Senior Common Room. 'I've got champagne. It's even cold,' she said. 'Someone get the plastic cups.'

The Senior Common Room was unusually full. It was nearly the end of term and almost everyone came to college every day because they had things to finish before the summer. All except Gwen, she'd started coming to college less and less. She had that, 'what are they going to do, sack me?' attitude. Whether she had another job seemed to be contentious. Whenever I asked her, she gave me an enigmatic smile Mona Lisa would've been envious of and said she had something sorted out.

Craig furnished the champagne bearer with small white plastic cups. Mel appeared to help Claudine open the bottles.

'What are we celebrating?' Craig asked.

'Oh, just the newest addition to my jewellery collection.' Claudine held out her left hand – flashing her engagement ring. 'Actually, I didn't have a jewellery collection until yesterday,' she confessed.

Everyone crowded around, even the men oohed and

awwwed at the gold ring with three sapphires glinting on her hand.

'We're going to get married just before Christmas. It'll be a small service, but we'll have a big party, which I hope all of you will come to.'

The crowd murmured yes as plastic cups with champagne were handed out.

Claudine, looking radiant, grinned from ear to ear. Her skin was back to being vibrant, her cropped black hair was glossy again.

She'd put on enough weight to make her look healthy as well. 'Three weeks ago I was plotting to be single, albeit unintentionally, and last night I got engaged. Who knew things could change so suddenly. Isn't life funny?' Claudine said. 'Cheers.'

'Cheers,' the room replied. People broke off into little groups, started chatting amongst themselves. Most of the women stayed where they were to admire Claudine's ring. I stayed in my seat, I'd look at the ring later. I was happy for her. She deserved this happiness with Kevin, but then, so did I. Not with Kevin, obviously. But with someone. And I wasn't likely to get it, was I?

Moments like this made me feel sorry for myself, again; dragged me back to my 'what about me?' lamentations. Really though, what about me? When would I get a ring on my finger or even a declaration of love? Or have those bouts of loneliness abated?

I stared forlornly into my plastic cup of light, bubbly liquid.

Never, was the short reply.

'Life *is* funny,' Mel said, flopping beside me. 'I called my wife.'

I looked at Mel. It was because of things like this, people like this that I'd be alone for ever. *Come on, you do care*, a voice inside said. *Pretend all you like that you don't want to know, but you do. You're a nosy cow and you're going to spend the rest of your life doing it. Yer might as well enjoy it.* 'Oh?' I said.

'I told her everything. Everything. She wasn't happy. In fact, she abused me quite a lot. She used language that would make a sailor blush. And she hung up a few times. But, I apologised, for everything and . . . we're having lunch on Saturday. Ostensibly to talk about our divorce. After the abuse, though, we had a laugh for the first time ever. A laugh, like I do with Clau. We could become mates after all.'

I nudged him. 'I knew you could do it.'

'Yeah, just needed that kick up the arse. Clau told me that she and Kevin had a really good chat. She told him that she thought she was heading towards something with me and that she wanted them to sort themselves out before it happened. He took it really well, apparently. So, they've managed to move on and, *voilà*, one engagement later.'

'And you're all right with that?'

'Yep. I am, actually. I thought it'd devastate me, but when she told me, I was so overwhelmed with happiness for her, I realised you were right. I wasn't in love with her. I was in love with the idea of her. Like you said, she needed attention. I needed to talk to Fran.'

I lowered my head onto Mel's shoulder, looked at Claudine being the centre of attention. 'You and me, kidder, we're not so different. We should stick together,' I said to him. Mel tucked a lock of my hair behind my ear. Jake and Ed would have a fit if they saw us. So would Staring Man.

'Can I get a bit of champagne, please,' Trudy asked Craig. I'd begun to think that she didn't exist. I hadn't seen her at all since the loos.

'You're looking unusually chipper these days, Trudy,' Craig said as he filled her plastic cup. 'Anything we should know?'

An audience of expectant faces held their breaths and awaited her response. I stared into my plastic cup and started counting bubbles. I wondered if any of them had actually been on the receiving end of one of her outbursts.

'The reason I look so "chipper" these days, you cheeky *get*, is that somebody inadvertently gave me a reality check. Made me face a lot of things I'd been hiding from.'

That was open.

'And,' Trudy ploughed on. 'I might as well tell you all now, I'm going to have a baby.'

Another collective sigh went around the room. This was celebration city today. As everyone crowded around her with questions about due dates and names, I chanced a look at her. Just to see what she looked like when she wasn't shaken up, crying or screaming abuse. Our eyes met, and, before I looked away, her face relaxed into the most beautiful smile, then she mouthed: 'Thank you.'

After time had passed, and people had left the SCR to finish finishing off for the end of term, I caught Craig watching me with my head still on Mel's shoulder, us talking about nothing much. His face showed he was thinking hard, like he did when he 'sat back' in a conversation. Then, he said, very loudly: 'Has anyone noticed the vibe that's been going on around here since Ceri started?'

I stuck two fingers up at him. It was an automatic gesture though. I didn't actually care what he said. I'd be more surprised if he'd said: '*Have you noticed how nothing has changed since Ceri started?*'

'We were all stuck in this rut of normality before, and then Ceri turns up and Claudine's engaged, Gwen's resigned and Trudy's up the duff. And I, well, I am back with my ex-girlfriend. And, all right, most of you have heard me say she was a psycho but once I got to know her, she really wasn't that bad. Or mad.'

'I thought you went out with her for two years,' one of the women admiring Claudine's ring said.

'Exactly. I only started to bother with her when Ceri started. And once I bothered, I found out there was goodness inside her. She's really sweet. I like this vibe around here, though,' Craig said. 'It's like, anything's possible now.'

'I know what you mean,' Claudine said. 'It's like, the sky's the limit.'

'Yeah,' Mel added. 'It's like everything is good underneath even if it's bad on the surface. There are lots of good vibrations.' He sang: 'Good vibrations are all around us.'

'That's, love is all around us, duh brain,' Claudine said.

Craig's mouth dropped open as he swung round to gawp at me . . .

summer holidays

chapter thirty-nine

The Cupid Effect

Why I had to meet Gwen here, I didn't know. I wasn't a big fan of airports at the best of times. Mostly because you had to travel halfway across town to get to them. It'd taken me ages to get to Leeds Bradford airport by public transport. I'd tried to get Jess to drive me there and she'd told me where to go.

I wandered across the concourse, feeling lost and cross. *Meet me in the main bit*, Gwen had said. I'd not realised there was so much to the main bit. And there was every danger of me making eye contact with someone, seeing as I was looking for her. I was hot and bothered. I should be at home, in bed. I was going to London in two days, I needed all the sleep I could to handle sleeping on my parents' sofa for a while. The offer on my flat had been tempting, but I hadn't accepted it. I'd not known what I was going to do next February when my contract was up so I wasn't going to be selling owt until I decided.

Gwen had made sure I'd travel practically across the world to see her by saying she had my copy of my assessment with her and she'd give it to me if I met her. Crafty old woman.

'Ceri!' a voice squeaked across the concourse. I looked around. No one who looked even vaguely like Gwen stood among the crowd. She waved. I double-took. A woman with long black hair stood where Gwen should have been. She wore a black vest, a denim overshirt and, whoa, shorts! Gwen was wearing shorts. I looked behind me to check this woman wasn't waving at someone else. No one behind me. Which meant, shorts woman was Gwen.

We sat on a bench, her rucksack on the seat between us, Gwen leant on the rucksack as she talked. She'd handed me a white envelope with my name on the front the moment we sat down.

'It's your assessment,' she said. 'Don't open it yet. Wait till I'm gone, then you can't tell me off.'

'So this is your new job?' I asked, prodding the rucksack.

'The Ancient Traveller? Yes.'

'Hey, less of the traveller bit, you, you're only going on holiday,' I joked.

Gwen laughed. 'No, I'm going away for at least a year. And if I come back, I'll be moving to London or Dublin. Or maybe even Paris. But not Leeds. Definitely not Leeds.'

'Don't tell me, you've emotionally left Leeds.'

'By Jove, I think you've finally got it.'

She was all right, Gwen, when she wasn't being her usual self. And she so wasn't looking her usual self. Shorts. I glanced at her shorts and then her legs. Double-took. Her podgy pins were a patchwork of scars. Some circular, others deep and long. The skin on her legs, which had obviously not seen the light of day in years, were bluish white, making the disfigurements more prominent. *That's* why she wore thick tights no matter what the weather.

My heart raced all of a sudden, sickness washed through my stomach. I wanted to tear my eyes away from her legs, wounded as they were.

Ouch, there it was again. An aching for someone. For

334

Gwen. This really hurt though. My legs began to throb with the agony she'd endured. With whatever it was that caused her scars. I suddenly knew what it felt like to not be able to wear skirts or shorts. How much self-disgust went into bathing every day and seeing your skin marked like that. The non-physical pain of knowing that if you went out without tights everyone would stare at you in horror and fascination. No one would skip over your legs, see it and accept it. There'd be pity or disgust, never indifference. I inhaled deeply. This was part of Gwen's problem. She never felt normal. She couldn't be. I felt that now. I understood that now. Probably why she latched onto me. I didn't know anything about her, so that made me an ideal friend.

'It's going to take getting used to,' Gwen said, raising and straightening her legs, 'showing off my legs. I haven't worn shorts in . . . years. Not since I got married. Actually, about a year after I got married.'

More pain shot through my legs, but this time the pain carried on travelling up to my heart, as everything finally, finally fell into place.

That day in my office when Gwen thought I'd been beaten up flashed through my mind. *'When one of my friends was being physically abused by her husband, it was virtually impossible for her to talk about. She had bruises all over and an excuse to match each one. I don't want you to feel you have to suffer in silence like that. I understand.'* At that time, she saw me in her. She thought I was suffering like she was and had tried to reach out to me. Tried to save me. I might've guessed if I hadn't been so consumed by the Angel/huge bruise on my face thing. Not that I would've been able to do anything. Except, possibly, not be so down on her when she resigned. Not given in to irritation when she 'whinged'. I'd kind of guessed there was something behind her odd behaviour, her inability to be happy or to relax. But I hadn't cared enough to pursue it. Her problems weren't 'sexy', literally, like Mel and Claudine's. How could I do that? I thought I was open to all callers at all hours, but no.

Gwen looked from her legs to my face. 'But it's all right now,' she added, obviously seeing my concern. 'I finally did it. That's why I quit, that's why I'm here.'

'Finally did what?' I asked.

'This is my escape, Ceri, from all the things that held me back.'

'Your husband's not going with you?' I asked cautiously. I just wanted to double-check I'd decoded the speak about her legs correctly.

'Vernon's gone on a business trip for a few days. I think he'll be surprised when he comes back to find me gone and our joint savings account and our investment account and the accounts he had in my name a few thousand pounds lighter. In fact, he'll only have £10 left in each of them.'

'Where are you going?' I asked.

'On the third flight out of here. Three's my lucky number, so I'm going to get on the third plane. Which means, I need to be going.'

She stood, hoisted her rucksack onto her back. She was truly transformed. Her black hair flowed down her back, instead of being pulled back into a bun, or straightened to hang around her face like slabs of dead meat. Her body was comfortable. Not slender, not tall, comfortable. At ease. Relaxed. She moved with elegance and ease. As though some-one had finally given her permission to enjoy moving in her body. WHAM-BAM! It hit me. No cigarette. That's why she looked different. No cigarette. No look as though gagging for a cigarette. She looked about ten years younger with this com-fortable persona.

'I've told the college to offer you a permanent position.

They might not, but I've told them. Your research supervisor is very impressed with what you've done so far, she thinks it's PhD material, so you could stay, do a PhD. You'd have to work on getting yourself funding and getting the title right, but you could do it. Although you might not want to stay, but I think you should.'

'I might, I haven't decided what I want to do yet. February is a long time away.'

'I know. But with all the changes in the department, this is probably the time to decide if you want to stay or not.'

'Thanks, I'll think about it.'

'You do that.'

'OK, bye.'

'Bye.' Gwen turned and went to walk away, then she suddenly spun on her trainered feet. 'All this is thanks to you, Ceri. That's why I wanted to see you before I went.'

'No,' I raised my hands, 'do not put any of this on me. Good or bad, do not put it on me.'

'Have it your way. But when you breeze into a place, so openly following your heart by leaving your comfortable life, going back to living like a student and being happy with what you're doing and who you are, please don't be surprised if people copy you. Especially people like me who thought they were stuck as they were for ever.

'When you show people it's possible to live their dreams, don't be surprised if they,' she took my hands, squeezed them, 'thank you.'

Didn't I say not to put it on me?

'I'll email you from wherever I end up,' Gwen called over her shoulder as she headed off towards the bank of check-in desks.

'OK,' I replied, then spun away before I saw which desk she was heading for. It was Gwen's big adventure. I didn't want to impose on it by knowing which place the third flight out of there went to.

To be honest, I had always thought of Gwen as a bit of a cow. A deranged cow who didn't know what made students tick. I thought she was one of those people who would love teaching if it wasn't for the students.

When, really, I had no right to judge her. I had no idea what went on in her life beyond the faculty. Her dress sense shouldn't have mattered. I thought I'd left all that vacuous nonsense in London. Not that I thought I was into it. I used to put down people who found dress sense and labels and looks important. But I noticed when Gwen didn't 'fit in'. I noticed the thick black tights, I scorned her because of her thick black tights. Never knowing that they hid the horrors of her life.

I walked around people, heading out of the airport. The pains in my legs had gone now I wasn't near Gwen. As I moved, I felt something odd about my face. I reached up to check what was wrong, found my fingers resting on my teeth.

All right, despite everything, this kind of thing did make me happy. I did find myself enjoying it. Other people's joy was heartening. The Cupid Effect meant I'd be alone, without long-term sex and love for the rest of my natural life but, sometimes, other people needed it more than me.

epilogue

Just In Case You
Were Wondering . . .

'All right, that's it,' I mumble, slap my hands on the table. 'I'm sorting this out once and for all.'

Jess reaches out to me, but no, nothing is going to stop me. Jess and I had dropped in to college so I could get some stuff done, we could have some cheap lunch and then we'd head off to Otley for the day. But, as I sat eating with my best mate, I'd glanced up to see *him* again. Staring at me.

'Leave it, Ceri,' Jess says.

'No, he can't go around glaring at people and expect them to put up with it.'

Jess makes one more futile grab for me as I pass her. I storm around tables and chairs and the odd diner and head for his table.

'Excuse me,' I say, standing opposite Staring Man at his table.

He glares up at me, his bronze eyes fixed on my face.

'Why do you keep glaring at me?' I demand. 'What have I done to you?'

He frowns slightly, but manages to keep the glare going.

I fold my arms, rest my weight on one leg and continue in

my sternest, non-shouting voice. 'I've hardly spoken to you, but in the past six months you've done nothing but give me evils, why?'

'I haven't,' he replies, and his rich voice weakens my knees as usual.

I pull out a chair and sit down. 'You have.'

'I, er . . .'

'You. Have.'

'I admit I've been staring at you. But not giving you evils.'

'All right, the jury's still out on if you were giving me evils or simply staring, but why? Have I got some sort of growth on my face that only you can see? Do I remind you of someone? Do you hate black people? What?'

Staring Man blushes, searches my face for a moment, blushes some more. 'Well, I like you, don't I?'

'Eh?'

'I think you're beautiful and I'm too shy to just come over and start talking to you, so I stare at you instead.'

'Ah.'

'Besides, I thought you had a thing going with Mel. You left that party together and you were together quite often. Even in the supermarket car park when I thought we'd made a connection over *Star Trek*, you brought up Mel. But I still had hope cos I know Mel hates *Star Trek*. Then, like a moment from my worst nightmare, I hit you in the face with that door and, after that, well . . . it became academic if you were with Mel or not; no matter how charming or funny you try to be, no matter how much you bond over *Star Trek*, no woman's going to go out with you once you've knocked her halfway across a shop floor. So I gave up and went back to staring at you. I didn't mean owt by it. I just like you. A lot.'

'Oh.'

He smiles, and again, the grin softens his chiselled features.

He runs a hand through his short, spiked-up black hair. He's about my age, maybe a fraction older, but his face looks like he's lived, like he'd have a story or two to tell. And he likes me.

I relax into the chair, I can't help but smile back. He's very attractive. When I first saw him in the pub, he reminded me of an artistic stroke on a page, didn't he?

'I really didn't mean to glare at you,' he says.

'Hmmm,' I reply with a raised eyebrow.

'How about I apologise by buying you a drink in a public place, lots of people around so you know I'm not some mad staring stalker. Oh, and without any doors to hit you with.'

'It *was* six months of glaring. Really hard glares.'

He laughs. 'How about dinner then? Dinner in a public place, I'm afraid, though, there might be doors involved in a restaurant.'

'I'm willing to risk it if you are,' I laugh and steal a chip from his plate. 'I'll be in college tomorrow afternoon, you can call me to arrange it. We could go down to Town Street or New Roadside.'

'Tomorrow?' he asks.

'Unless you're busy.'

'No, no I'm not. Tomorrow would be great. Fantastic, even.'

'Tomorrow it is then.'

Staring Man grins, really wide. So wide, I have to look away. I haven't had this in a while, someone who thinks I'm beautiful and looks so pleased at the thought of having dinner with me. I'd actually forgotten how it felt to have someone fancy me, not just want to unload onto me. I'm not feeling anything problem-like from him – no need to share; no ulterior motive. He's just looking forward to dinner with me. Wow.

'Your friend's trying to get your attention,' he says, indicating behind me.

'Friend?' I glance over my shoulder. Jess is staring at us, open-mouthed. She thought I was coming over to start a fight, which I was, and now we're grinning at each other and I'm stealing his chips. She's going to faint when I tell her about dinner. Oh, Jess, Otley.

I get up, 'I've got a prior engagement, I'd better be going,' I say. Then I remember. 'Oh, my name's Ceri. Ceri D'Altroy, I'm finally in the college phone book. What's your name? I can't keep calling you Staring Man. Which I only called you in my head and to my friend, over there. But not to anyone . . .' *Ceri, shut up. Now. NOW!* 'Anyway, what's your name?'

He rolls his eyes and sighs silently. 'I've got a bloody stupid name. Blame it on my parents. They wanted a girl, so when they got me, they kept the name but didn't even consider that it'd humiliate me for the rest of my life.'

Ah ha! Someone else who understands the torture of being callously named. Ceresis, indeed. 'Go on . . .'

'It's all rather embarrassing, really. That's why everyone at college calls me Bosley.'

'It can't be that bad,' I say.

'You'd be surprised.'

I frown. 'Oh come on, just tell me what your name is.'

His bronze eyes meet mine as he says: 'Angel.'